A word from the Author.

The idea of this war story was originally planned to be a nonfictional, unauthorized memoir - historically referenced, explicated accurate true tale that Jack Churchill is perhaps best deserving. It was intended to be served in its fullest and most autobiographical form. In many ways, it is still very much incorporated into the final product, albeit with a dash more flamboyancy for flavouring.

I delved deep into the historic abyss of significant and trivial detail alike, researching anything and everything remotely related to Jack Churchill primarily during the Second World War. During this process, I had a spellbinding epiphany that would drastically divert the direction of my manuscript. I flexed my artistic licence and remodelled the adjective, fact-based documentation, striving to still deliver the details amongst the type of entertainment that would now be categorized as fictional action/adventure. What better way is there nowadays for being informative than through the artform of storytelling? The revelation came whilst exhuming those buried accounts, hearing those firsthand versions and unsung war stories documented in soldier diaries, video documentaries, and recorded cassettes made by the families in their elder's twilight years. I peeled back layers of history, uncovering for me what I believed to be the quintessence of the man himself, especially the eccentric archetype. He was built different ... why not tell his tale differently? It became evident that Mad Jack Churchill was anything but as colourless as the black and whites depicted him to be in old photographs, not that that was ever thought to be the case. Consequently so, I supposed him to be deserving of something more stimulating and amusing than another run-of-the-mill nonfiction publication. He was more than just history, he was legend. After all, what is believable about a commando charging onto a beach during the Second World War with a sword and longbow? Any form of chronicle would be deemed doubtful by any audience and branded *fabricated and untrue ... so I took it that step further from the beginning and just ran with it.*

Thus, my intention became to make this book (and any subsequent books) just as action-packed, saucy, and humorous as they were hard-hitting, historically accurate, and to pay heartfelt respects to what transpired all those years ago. I aspired to tick all the boxes, pull out all the stops, and leave no stone unturned whilst retelling the true story.

As a result, born out of a playful and fictitious gambit, the final draft of the novel based on this man's extraordinary life shaped up as more of an action-packed and extravagant fictional biography rather than a stale history lesson. An entertaining bedtime story instead of a monotonous research article. And why not have fun with it? If you are a staid history buff, allow for the mere prologue of this novel to act as your assessment of what is to come and how to receive it. If your nose turns at this notice, don't bother turning any more pages ... because yes, I allowed myself to have a blast telling this story, as I believe Mad Jack himself would. Not as a form of gloat, but for the entertaining factor that one could not doubt coursed through his veins along with pure heroism.

Although a work of fiction, <u>The Unstoppable Warpath of the Unkillable Jack Churchill</u> is built on a solid foundation of true historical fact, down to names, quotes, dates, and locations. This has been done intentionally to recreate as accurate a retelling as possible and to help respectfully keep the memories alive of those long since gone from this world. A vast amount of research went into the development of the setting for the saga. Irrespective to the improvisation in this fictitious retelling, pages drenched with additional palates of detail constructed by the author's overactive imagination, Churchill's story was born from a thorough understanding of the legend through the method of true accounts dated and written by those closest to him at the time.

KING QUEEN JACK WAR

THE UNSTOPPABLE WARPATH OF THE UNKILLABLE JACK CHURCHILL

Volume V of the fictional biography

BENJAMIN BLACKIE

Page/Turner

King, Queen, Jack, War:
The Unstoppable Warpath of the Unkillable Jack Churchill

Typeset: 20, 18, 12, 11 pt Baskerville Old Face
11.5 pt Rainydays by *bruag*
11.5 pt Arial Narrow
10 pt Times New Roman

FIC014050

1. Historical - Fiction. 2. World War, 1939-1945 - Fiction.

I. Title.

A823.3

ISBN: 978-1-7638082-3-2

Published by Kindle Direct Publishing
2025

So here it is - a glass raised to the man.

This literature, however fictitious as it may harmlessly digress, is a celebration of a gentleman born from the stuff legends are made of.

A fête of his fate, a bit of fun, action, romance, and war - in its dubitable inexplicitness - lays a sincerity paralleled with the eccentric essence of Mad Jack Churchill. I hope this is conveyed entertainingly and with all due respect.

You have now been cautioned of the fictitious recounting that threatens to entertain as well as enlighten. Enjoy.

O.K., go.

PROLOGUE
The Enemy of my Enemy is my Feind

The wide-open estate grounds were once affiliated to the former cotton mill known as *the Glenn Mill* in *Oldham*, and had been repurposed by the British Army in 1939 for the establishment of a prisoner of war (POW) encampment. As it stood today, encircled by analogous rows of eight-foot-tall, barbed wire fences and *cheval de frise* barricades, patrolled around the clock by riflemen guard, the pitch was now the home to nearly two thousand Axis prisoners of war from Nazi Germany.

Now that the climate was changing in England, the detainees would typically be tasked to perform manual labour, predominantly in agriculture, set to purpose in the nearby lands under armed escort. The treatment of the prisoners, though strict, was commonly of the most humane pretence—better than anything reportedly experienced in the opposition's camps across the English Channel.

While still in an early development stage, the British government had introduced a specialized program instilling a type of 're-education' for the prisoners. This camp had initiated this program. The curriculum was intended to demonstrate to the German POWs the true evils of the Nazi regime whilst advocating the advantages of democracy.

Although the prison camp predominantly housed those with the rank of *sergeant* or lower, due to the tide of war, exponentially more enemy combatants holding higher positions were residing within these ranks due to the overpopulation of POWs being captured abroad—and only after thorough due process and interrogation at *the Cage* in *London*. Due to an alternative structuring of hierarchy, this occurrence coincided with the fact that the German militaries were so vast in comparison to the rest of the world, they retained more members of higher-ranking positions.

Once the incarcerated officers were ringed dry by the *Prisoner of War Interrogation Section (PWIS)* of the *Intelligence Corps,* what was left of the boche ended up in either army-occupied *Grizedale Hall* located in *Cumbria* (designated quite inventively *'Camp 1'*), or in this camp, the repurposed Glenn Mill (almost equally unimaginative in its designation: *'Camp 2'*).

In these internment camps, enemy prisoners were free to wait out the remainder of the war in a state of tranquil harmony. Encaged brutes, however, they were free of service and out of circulation. What they would eventually become was up to them and, ultimately, the ways of the war ...

Beneath an overcast morning sky, through which the glistening sun failed to pierce the lurking silver veil, the pre-lunch period saw the impoverished prisoner populace of Camp 2 on a recess in the enclosure. Huddled in murky woollen greatcoats atop of their tattered grey uniforms, the POWs were allowed to roam the muddy clearing between the established barracks and the fences to the south-west facing *Constantine Street* and the flat marshland beyond overlooking the forestation before the *River Medlock.* The prisoners could converse freely, share cigarettes, and mingle under the watchful eyes of patrolling riflemen and static guard towers.

Riding a thundering American-made olive-drab Harley-Davidson WLA motorcycle, a green beret-clad man with a striking sterling stare and a pencil-thin moustache, dressed in a khaki military suit, cruised along *Wellyhole Street,* rounding the bend onto Constantine, where a guardhouse and boom-gate checkpoint restricted further passage.

An armed guard with large gloves gave clearance to the soldier on the loud motorcycle, waving the coasting rider through after observing his recognizable credentials. Just the soldier's rank and insignia were enough for clearance to at least access the car park of the Camp 2 admin office.

Beside various other civilian and military vehicles alike, the rider glided his rumbling Harley-Davidson into a vacant space, parking. The bike was the new 42WLA model, one of many that had reached England at the start of the week as a part of the lend lease program from the *United States of America.*

Once the throttling engine disengaged in a controlled dispel, a pressed trouser leg deployed the well-oiled, springy kickstand, and a well-polished boot touched the gravel of the carpark ground. A view of the hemmed pantleg then rose onto the rider, who was dressed in a pressed, tailored, military battledress baring the insignia of the British Army; furthermore, a red emblem sewn onto his patch indicated that this soldier was no ordinary *G.I. Joe.* He was from *Commando,* within the *1st Special Service Brigade.*

Of medium height, five-foot-nine, and what he proclaimed as *trifle solid,* the bike rider bore the rank of *major,* with a freshly pinned *Military Cross and Bar* commendation across his breast from a very successful recent operation in the North.

Bearing unconventional tendencies for certain, the soldier was armed at the hip with what must have been a ceremonial sabre of sorts, although he was only dressed in a standard issue outfit. Upon a second glance, the sword piece was a Scottish *Claybeg*—the single-handed cousin of the *Claymore*—complete with a customized brass knuckleduster handle with eyelets for the fingers. The hilt design purposely bore resemblance to the American M1918 trench dagger and had clearly been a commissioned job by a skilled and unorthodox blacksmith armourer.

Ensuing the inspection of all aspects of his battledress, his insignias, and his peculiar armament, attention finally raised onto the recognition of the man's face ...

In the event of any uncertainty towards the identity of this eccentric English gentleman, it was none other than *Mad Jack Churchill.*

Dismounting the Harley, Churchill removed a pair of leather riding gloves and tucked them into a straddled satchel on the side of the motorcycle. With his fingertips, he pressed out his freshly detailed moustache and straightened the green beret upon his blonde-haired dome. As always, he was neatly groomed, freshly shaven, and photogenic as fuck.

The aging lateral scar indentation across his left cheek was only outshined by a new one above his right eyebrow. It was a freshly healed pink colour and only recently seeing the light of day from beneath a bandage.

Jack grabbed at the circular mirror affixed to the handlebar, angling it thusly so that he could inspect his good looks with an inverted brow and pursed lips, ensuring they were on-point. They were.

Breaking his picturesque entrance, motion ahead caught Churchill's attention as a young, attractive dark-haired lass, dressed in a frilly yellow and white polka dot dress, noisily struggled to retrieve a cardboard crate from the backseat of her parked silver Austin four door. She would have worked at the repurposed mill, likely a desk hand or a secretary to the administration side under contract for the military, just like the rest of the non-military personnel at the joint.

She murmured in strife as some of the pile slid from a collapsing side, threating to wind up in the muck on the ground—however, Churchill was fast to the rescue, sliding in behind her petite frame to assist. He contained the falling manila folders from the collapsing crate and then insisted on taking the whole thing from her clumsy mittens. She had on freshly applied red lipstick and recently curled pomps through her hair which gave it much vitality in the daylight.

He said as he aided, taking the load. "Here. Allow me, ma'am."

"Oh, th-thank you ..."

The lady backpedalled in a shuffle, allowing not only for him to take over and save her, but also to breathlessly observe the soldierly handsomeness of her saviour, becoming immediately wooed by his masculine form, scent of his aftershave, and good looks. The soldier's stare had the lustre of a precious stone as it observed her speechless demeanour whilst she forged a hesitant, nervous smile. The depth within his piercing blue eyes just about made her weak at the knees.

She remembered to breathe after a moment.

"Are you ... alright?" Jack asked finally.

"Y-yes," the lass beamed tensely. "Eh, thank you, mister ...?"

"Jack," Churchill announced, placing the saved box onto the roof of her car. He fixed the corner and tucked the grips properly so that it would not fall apart again so easily.

"*Jack*," she recited whilst attempting to mask her sudden onset of besottedness. Able to read the emblems on his uniform, she further incited his title. "A *Major?*" she gathered correctly. Appearing rather informed, this confirmed that she must have worked for or at least with the military side of the mill/prison.

"That is correct, ma'am. Need a hand taking these in?" Churchill offered—an ulterior motive for gaining him access was well hidden by the proposal by a Good Samaritan. Truth was, he did not have an appointment at the prison today—nor an official agenda at all, in fact.

"No, that's fine, thank you, sir."

Closing her car door and collecting her crate from the roof, Jack watched her leave with a courteous simper. She headed towards the front doors of the office harnessing an appreciative smile of her own, which lingered. There was an armed guard just inside who prepared to hold open the entryway for her arrival, acting as a doorman.

"Say, ma'am," Churchill turned on the charm, teetering on the edge of smittenness with this lovely vixen—like he always did, forever the gentlemanly womanizer in his mind's eye. Well versed in throwing his Achilles' heel, Jack stayed the dutiful course of his questioning, trying hard not to fall victim to her natural charm and take in the colour of her eyes the way that he always characteristically did.

"Yes?" she stopped and turned.

"Say, if someone wanted to visit an inmate to heckle a few obscenities and potentially, respectfully, offer them the *V* ... how could one go about doing so? Excuse the French."

Facing Jack, the lady squinted slightly—hopefully due to the light penetrating through the clouds, and not because of an indirect insult to those incarcerated. She shrugged, seemingly not so impressed by Major Churchill as she was five seconds ago after his suggestion of a pejorative nature. Her facial expression had now fallen flat from her smile. "It's a fence, dummy. Wait for them to be out in the yard and shout through that, like every other passer-by does," she tipped her pretty head, indicating the stretching fence line that ran along Constantine Street.

Through there, Churchill caught a glimpse of the open clearing.

There was a lot of activity and assemblage going on across the field. The countless prisoners were exiting the numerous barracks, treading through holed shoes and musty socks onto the cold dirt of the wide open and the chill of the fresh air.

Upon returning his view to her, the sun lit up the irises of her eyes.

Churchill became momentarily hypnotized by her natural beauty as the warm light from the morning sun briefly shone through the clouds, causing her green eyes to glow like jade gemstones.

Battling the weakness tickling the rear of his knees, Jack flexed his winning smile. "Of course."

The lady returned the beam, hung up on their strange yet pleasant morning encounter.

"*Miss Blagbrough?*" the guard, who was awkwardly still holding open the door, questioned from afar. "*Are you coming in, ma'am?*"

She gestured affirmatively and then returned her face to Churchill, replying to him courteously. "Have a nice day, Major."

"Call me Jack. Same to you, Miss Blagbrough."

"*Mabel,*" she informed.

Churchill acknowledged her given name and tipped his beret, watching the callipygian lady leave, because, *of course he did.* Once she wriggled her union attire-wrapped posterior up the three plank steps and through the door, Churchill caught her throwing a final gleam over her shoulder to him, distracted whilst engaging in conversation with her colleague in the foyer.

The door closed over and Churchill silently smirked.

Confidently, this happily married man gratified himself as he strolled away.

With his hands behind his back, Jack scouted along the outer fence line. His dawdle hinted an underlining swagger, as if a pipe march was forever sounding in his ears. After several paces, he paused, scanning aslant through the translucent wire gauzes and into the crowd of motley dressed German POWs. The horde of gathering captured souls paid him no mind across the flat distance.

A patrolling guard in a brimmed brodie helmet carrying a bayonet-fitted Lee-Enfield rifle skyward against his shoulder wandered by between the wire fences, dutifully carrying out his rotation, and he eyed Churchill's presence outside the camp boundary. They acknowledged one another.

"*Sir,*" the young guard remarked through the fence. It was not his place to question, but most of the time when someone from the military, whether it be army, intelligence, or otherwise, sought a prisoner they usually went through the available channels and made an appointment. It was much easier that way, therefore they could set a private room up indoors. He looked up and down Churchill's attire, namely at the sheathed sword at his hip. The brass-handled weapon was incredibly out of place.

Churchill greeted the passing guard with a brisk nod, breaking away from his inspection of the faraway prisoners for just a moment. Before long, his sterling stare returned and scanned out into the flock of inmates, searching like an aficionado.

Reaching a midpoint in his march, he squinted to focus ...

Many of the inmates had similar European traits such as the man which he searched. A man who had, until very recently, haunted his psyche.

Speaking of haunting—

From out of seemingly nowhere, a man in a fashionable and outdated military suit emerged from behind Churchill, approaching the same fence grid at a sudden speed which caused him to shudder.

He was an older gent, with rugged ash grey features and a matching grey moustache above his upper lip. It was patchy due to a duelling scar that carved a slit through the facial hair and was one of approximately four permanent serration grooves on the man's weathered face—evidence of being a true badass and once a force to be reckoned with.

Endowed with a broad barrel chest, this man was tall, about six-foot-five, kitted in the attire of the obsolete 1930s service dress of *the Queens Own Cameron Highlanders*, complete with a kilt patterned in the earthly regimental colours of the *Cameron of Erracht*. With an aslant pom-pom bonnet upon his dome, this was an attire of which he would be forever entombed.

He was Lieutenant-Colonel Sloan MacLeòid: Deceased.

Friendly ghost haunt, imaginary friend, and wise wanker of endless war-bound wisdom, tethered for eternity to one Jack Churchill. Can't have Mad Jack without the mad.

"*Mornin' Jackie,*" his scratchy Scottish voice asserted with grumbling brogue. "*What er yoo doin' owt 'ere, eh?*"

"Sir," Churchill casually acknowledged his lifelong friend and mentor. The angel—and sometimes devil—on his shoulder of conscience. "Just visiting an old friend."

MacLeòid grumbled with an underlining dissatisfaction. "*I think yoo mean old* Feind."

Churchill remained silent in his contrition.

He had conviction to his cause, and even though that consolation was opposed to what his erudite apparition advised, it was enough to allow him ample sleep at night. He had made his bed by keeping his nemesis alive, and he was content sleeping in it.

"*Yoo should'a killed dat twat!*"

"No," Churchill countered. "Like I told you before, internment for a soldier such as *Friedrich Feind* is a fate worse than death. Killing him would have been a mercy. Men like him desire a glorious death in combat. I am not about to grant my enemy his wish."

"*Speek ov tha Devil ... an' he shall appeer, laddie ...*"

The callout by the haunt severed the topic of conversation, and Churchill followed MacLeòid's abruptness, trailing his gaze through the wire fences and into the crowd of imprisoned fellows, singling out one figure in particular who had ceased motion in the flowing despondent horde as they dispersed throughout the open clearing.

Across the distance, the man was staring them down.

Staring Jack down.

Even from this range, close to three-hundred feet in distance, Friedrich Feind's dark features were exclusively distinguishable. The indentations on his duelling-scarred face caught shadows from the angle of the morning light, making the positive identification easier. The crooked nose which he bore was a new feature; one he had collected in his last encounter with Churchill.

"*He's lookin' straight et yoo ...*" MacLeòid stated rhetorically.

"Well, he sure as hell isn't looking at *you,*" Churchill responded, throwing his argumentative invisible friend a sideways glance. Unsurprisingly, MacLeòid had already vanished.

Churchill found his focus, facing forwards and onto Feind.

The former *Hauptsturmführer* within the prison camp looked well—not mentally, of that he cared little—but in regards to his physical health. It had been two months since his capture in *Vågsøy.* That had been sixty days of uncleanliness, borderline malnourishment, not to mention dire isolation, and rotting interment. That sort of thing typically sunk a free-spirited man's eyeballs into his ever-more predominant skull as it slowly drained him of life.

Feind recognized the onlooker beyond the fence line as his archenemy, simultaneously as Churchill identified him. A strange, tense aura existed like an invisible haze. A fog of war, clearing. Like magnetism, they were drawn to each other—the same way they had always been, like on the tarmac in Oslo all those years ago, and more recently again on the war-torn streets of South Vågsøy, when their paths had once again crossed and their grudge-match settled. It seemed that in this life, they were destined for combat with one another. Like a transcribed romancing of war, their encounters were fated and inevitable just as long as thou shall both live.

Disinclined at first, Feind eventually started to approach the fence across the grassy clearing, casting multiple peeks across his greatcoat shouldered flanks. He could see the customary respondents at present; British guards in the towers and patrolling at the fence lines. As per usual, when a wanderer would stray from the pack, all ogles were on target as he strolled towards the inner perimeter. He was well within the constraints of the camp, so there were no risks of him being shot by a sentry, but the heat of the attention by the men with rifles was at a higher intensity to those in the main yard.

"Hullo, *Fiend,*" Churchill announced once he became within vocal range, closing in his strides. The mispronunciation of his surname was, as always, intentional bait to gain a heated response. A deliberate cheap shot that never got old.

Hands in his tattered overcoat pockets, Feind held an askew brow halting a few paces away from the fence line, looking askance at Jack.

"Vhat do you vant, English-man."

"Thought I'd come say *hi* now that you're all settled in," Churchill expanded with a dash of well-deserved egotistical condescension in his tone. He had not perceived just how awkward this conversation was going to be. "So, eh ... how's jail life, then?"

"Iz lovely."

Churchill raised his chin to nod. It was an obvious mistruth.

"How's the schnoz?" Churchill then questioned. Ever since he had delivered that fateful flying punch into Feind's face during their last fight—the final blow—Feind's nose had never looked the same, and probably never would. Jack had broken it proper, and it had never been set right by the doctors ...

Another war wound to decorate the boche's already scarred face.

Feind's sustained deadpan gaze was his only response; the same brown eyes located above a well and truly enlarged roman nose shape. The thing was a crooked gonzo.

In his stance, Churchill disengaged, gesturing that he was about to leave. Although his visit did not have a true purpose, he tried not to make his passing statement sound too much like the winner's boast he subconsciously intended to deliver. "Right, well, I've got a war to fight. I guess I better let you get back to ... whatever it is you lot do in there ..."

"You zhould have killed me, English-man."

Delivered in a solemn tone, the words hooked Jack. And it was in this moment of passive aggression that Churchill suddenly found his assertive footing. This wasn't an awkward stance anymore. It had stemmed into belligerence—familiar territory. In some circumstances, certain parties are more comfortable in war, in conflict. Mad Jack Churchill was one such person.

"Nah," in a downbeat manner, Jack scrunched his nose and happily disagreed. "I think *this* suits you better than death."

And he wasn't referring to an ever-lingering discomposure.

Feind was a soldier—like Churchill. Both men had followed orders their entire lives; orders to kill, to evict, to dislodge other men; civilians and soldiers alike. Whole families. Spirits of those acts would echo in eternity, haunting their hosts eternally and forever. Bad dreams. Nightmares. Conscious thoughts in the background of everyday life. Death would silence such spectres, hence *the easy way out* for somebody who indulged in many of the latter of those duties.

"Likewize."

The comeback by Feind was out of place, but there was something in his delivery that attracted the undercurrent of Churchill's attentiveness. Conceivably, the threat declaration wasn't just something lost in translation by the foreigner. There appeared to be meaning in his intimidating tone.

Processing it for an extra second, Jack's brow inverted. "Pardon?"

"I vas zurprised at your zwordsmanship in Vågsøy ... your zkills are much zharper now, ja?" Feind asked askew of their prior topic. It felt like a topical misdirection aimed at him, but Churchill found solace in the fact that he was standing on the free side of the fence, so he pulled on the obvious string of bait.

"I've picked up a thing or two since Oslo."

"*A zing or two?*" Feind playfully repeated, followed by his posture altering with an exuding confidence. He lowered his eye level to the dirt, shaking his head. "Tsk, tsk, tsk."

Rooted behind the fence, Churchill's piercing stare focused upon this foe, not losing sight of his target for a second. There was a climax due of this contention, and he was going to get a clear shot at whatever it was at any second.

There was no way that Feind knew the truth of where he had advanced his sword fighting skills ... From whom he had gained them ...

Nobody knew. Not even history.

Jack had obtained them during his short stint in Switzerland in 1939, whilst recruited into one of *Orde Wingate's* off-books black-budget Auxiliary-ops units known by very few. Obtaining that knowledge in any way, shape, or form was an impossibility, and Churchill was confident of that fact. Yet, life is not without its idiosyncrasies ...

Feind ceased his staring into the mud and made exact eye contact with Churchill through the two layers of wire fences.

"It vould be a zhame if your zuperiors found out that you vere trained by a *Nazi* ..." he finally delivered. The sentence came as a punchline harder than the one Jack had issued Feind when he had flunged off the turret of that tank in South Vågsøy.

Churchill scoffed. "Pardon?"

His response and tone were incriminating.

Churchill's face dropped flat.

Was this true ...?

How was this true ...?

We knew the war. We knew the era ... but we don't know Jack.

"You don't know what you're talking about," Churchill responded in a deflective tone, albeit too late to be convincing to someone so sure they knew the truth. If this had been poker, he had just shown his hand. On an all-too-obvious back foot, he engaged a passive-aggressive defensive conversational mechanism. "It appears *cabin fever* has set in mighty early for you at the Glenn Mill, old boy."

"No *cabin fever*, English-man," Feind responded in kind, somehow educated enough in typhus history and the reference to isolation and madness. "Merely, I am playing zee cardz I have been dealt."

There was something in Feind's defiant body language that gave Churchill certainty that he knew a hidden truth; that he had, actually, been trained in the art of swordsmanship by a German man within the Nazi Party— but that was a classified story for another day ...

... perhaps a day soon.

Confidence reinvigorated Churchill, and his tone altered in his response. "This is England. In this kingdom, I am a decorated war hero. Nobody would ever believe the nonsense from a caged-up, roughed-up, bashed-nosed bellend Hun, such as yourself," Jack asserted, trying not to make it seem he were mentally grasping at straws. And if Feind was to pique any interests with his claim to fame, he likely would have already done so when the interrogators had him, not now he was in a POW camp.

Even in Britain's current state of affairs, where paranoia is high and inquests are frequent, nobody would care what songs he had to sing now; it was too late. His band was shit with out-of-time percussion.

"Zey vill after I prove it."

Adopting a deflective stance, Mad Jack issued his winning smile before eyeing him deadpan. "There's nothing to be proven."

"Jah, jah. After all, it'z not like you left a paper trail linking you to your enemy; zending mail to Deutschland, mail to a regiztered *Nazi* Deutsche, tsk, tsk."

Churchill's tense frown and smirk withered away.

Mail to Germany ...

... then it clicked.

"Oi! You said you didn't get my letter, you cheeky git!" Jack suddenly called, half-joking in his exclamation due to the fact he still did not feel threatened by Feind's threats of political warfare.

Feind's face remained mostly expressionless. "Natürlich! Of courze I got your letter, doof English-man. And _why_ zee _fuck_ would I ever vant to have *tea und bickies* with you?!"

"I was just being gentlemanly. Extending an olive branch."

Feind appeared scorned by the gesture.

"Fuck your *olive branch*," he spat out the side. "Leck mich am Arschloch, du Missgeburt."

Churchill squinted at the German, unable to interpret a single word— but whatever it was, Feind's tone of delivery made it sound unpleasant.

Trying to hide the realization that Feind could possibly have a real go at discrediting him with this truth-laden tale, Churchill justified his reasoning for reaching out a year ago. It was after his motorcycle accident, prior to his marriage, seeing the world through rose-coloured glasses—a temporary lapse in judgement. Not to mention he was still having feverish hallucinations following the infection from a bullet wound sustained in his shoulder during the Dunkirk Evacuation.

He explained. "Listen, I was in a transitional stage back then ..."

Another circulating patrolling guard appeared close on their flank, so close, that Churchill suddenly opted to keep the volume of their topic of conversation down and to a minimum.

Suspicion was extreme right now in England. Word of *spies for Germany* were a dime a dozen during this heightened state of paranoia, and people everywhere were encouraged to phone in any suspicious behaviour to the authorities for thorough investigation. Right now, he felt like he was beaming hot due to this bellend's efforts. He nearly had to loosen his necktie.

"This was a mistake," Churchill suddenly said unto himself prior to glancing about the confines of the prison camp, strangely feeling like the walls were closing in. "I shouldn't have come ..."

"*Oi!*" the guard suddenly raised his voice, strutting near and catching his rifle diagonally for extra staunch. It was a different patrolling guard than before. This one was a gaunt Cockney-sounding fellow who reminded him greatly of a pair of characters he used to serve with in the Second Manchester Regiment a few years ago. "What's tha bloody meanin' ov this, eh?"

"Good morning," Churchill responded as the guard came near. When he spoke in a casual tone, Feind took the opportunity to consider scurrying away.

"You can't be doin' this, sir; chattin' wif tha prisoners!" the guard exclaimed, referring to Churchill on the outside speaking with a prisoner on the inside. He cast Feind a quick glance, too, shoving his rifle his way to halt him. "Oi, you, stay there a minnit, eh?!"

Feind halted, raising his hands outwards in a nonthreatening manner.

While the guard was suspicious of the interaction between the two, he paid note of Churchill's rank and insignia on his uniform.

"I assure you, there is nothing going on here, my lad. Just passing by and thought I'd share a word with old mate, here," Jack said absolvingly.

"Oh ... righto, then. You're a *Major?!*"

After witnessing Churchill's uniform insignia and the rank registered with it, the guard took a moment to reflect. He exchanged a look between both Churchill and the prisoner on opposite sides of the fencing.

Churchill bobbed his head.

"Wif all due respect, sir, cut it out, eh? It can't happen, yeah?" the guard continued. "It's against tha rules. I'm allowed to shoot 'im, now, y'know ..."

Churchill glanced at Feind right as his brow flourished concerningly.

The guard looked to him and back again. "But I won' ..."

"Can you?" Churchill asked—half serious. His excitement at the prospect was legitimate.

The guard flicked the prisoner a gander, briefly considering the proposition. Although, technically, it was authorized to an extent, it wasn't well worth the paperwork associated with such an incident. Not to mention how it would then implement a British Army major. There would be a lot of explaining to do.

"Please?" Jack asked in the short hiatus of discord.

"Nein," Feind pleaded, retreating an extra step.

The guard smiled his crooked teeth, looking between the two, eventually on the British officer. "Nah. He's awlright. S'long as ya say nothin's goin' on, eh?"

"Of course not," Churchill excused with due respectfulness. The man had a job to keep, and he was doing it well not differentiating the chain of command.

"Cheerio, den. You got'a go into tha main office 'roun there and make an appointment ta speak to tha prisoners, eh?"

"Yes, of course. I'll organize it right away."

"And *you!*" he turned to face Feind, who was frozen stiff. " *You* need ta stay tha fuck away from tha fences, yeh? Unless you wanna get shot, ya stupid Gerry."

Nodding in understanding, Feind started to back away—

"Oi! Not yet! Stay put!"

Confused, Feind halted once again.

The gronkish guard flipped his view back around to Churchill.

At this stage, he wasn't sure him acting so askance was due to his perception of the situation. To put it bluntly, he seemed quite the ignoramus, one worthy of valid questioning as to whom would trust him with a firearm.

"An'... is that a bloody broadsword?" the guard questioned, taking note of Mad Jack's attire and mad armament.

"A *claybeg,* yes," he corrected.

"A claybeg?!"

"Indeed. It is the shorter, single-handed version of the claymore."

"Tha fucken handle on that fing, though, eh?!" the guard's head twisted as he marvelled. "If ya don't mind me askin', sir, why not a handgun for a sidearm? Dun' that thing pull your dacks down all day?"

"Eh," Churchill rationally repelled. Irrepressibly overwrought, he almost forgot to drop his most prized motto. *"Any officer who goes into action without his sword is improperly dressed,"* he finally verbalized, still managing to maintain eye contact with Feind through the fences.

The guard absorbed the explanation. It made him stand up straight.

Likely reasoning above his comprehension, that explanation was justification enough. He took one last glance over at the prisoner and then back again at Churchill.

"Right'o. Well ... have a good day, sir."

"And to you."

"And *you!*" the guard again jousted his Lee-Enfield at Feind through the wire. "Off ya go! Goo'n! Get!"

Feind reversed a few steps, half expecting to cop a bullet in the back for some reason by this loose cannon of a sentry guard.

Unmoving, Churchill watched as the rifleman moved away on his patrol after breaking up their conversation at the fences. After a few dozen paces, they saw the guard turn his head, checking if they were still there. Churchill started to turn and take paces away, and it was enough of a sign of good faith that it did not attract the guard for a second half-witted tongue lashing.

Feind stated in his natural dialect: "Ich fühle mich genug besucht..."

Churchill looked confused, and he watched as Feind started to back up, eventually turning away and strolling back towards the recess pit of gathering German prisoners.

"Auf Wiedersehen, English-man!"

"Wait! *Feind!*" Churchill hissed, raising his voice to a dangerous level. His thirst for knowledge on this information was making him desperate enough to risk bringing down a world of political hurt if he got busted breaking the rules here. "Who did you talk to?! What did you tell them?!"

Feind heard him.

At first, his resolve did not falter.

"*Who did you tell?!*" Churchill cried louder, strafing him on the outside of the fence as he faded farther into the distance. This lack of catharsis was going to eat him up inside.

Feind smirked and shook his head, making Churchill suffer by not knowing what was coming next for him around the bend of the connecting line.

He mouthed his next—parting—sentence over his shoulder, ranging across the distance as he faded, becoming absorbed by the crowds of POWs:

"*You. Zhould. Have. Killed. Me ...*"

Behind the wire fence and in a huff, the confused and concerned Jack Churchill nearly walked into somebody standing like a statue: the idle figure caused him to pause dead in his tracks.

It was MacLeòid.

"*Oi!*" Churchill mouthed instinctively, stepping around the entity as though the figment of his imagination actually existed in his path. His gaze remained focused on Feind as the prisoner withdrew further into the crowd of inmates within the Glenn Mill POW camp, gone from sight.

He cussed, defeated. "Bollocks."

MacLeòid viewed Churchill, soon sidling beside his pace in order to deliver one last line of wisdom for today's council.

"*Yep ... yoo should'a killed dat twat.*"

For the first time, perhaps *ever,* Churchill could not agree *more* with his Highlander haunt.

KING, QUEEN, JACK, WAR

The Unstoppable Warpath of the Unkillable Jack Churchill

' Weapons and war cannot be pure. '
– Orde Wingate

A silent barb of electric lightning twinkled ecstatically in the rainy night sky above Germany, illuminating the barbed wire fences surrounding the grounds of the *Sachsenhausen Concentration Camp.*

The soft pitter-patter of the rainfall outside the prison barracks would have been somewhat soothing if it wasn't so damn loud upon the crookedly layered sheet metal tin roofing. Leaks within were plentiful.

Captive American journalist *Felix Hardy* rested on his uncomfortable wireframed bed bunk, ignoring the noise of the storm. Head on his rugged hessian sack which housed a muddy shoe to act as a headrest, his hands levitated before his maw and drew in close, for his dirty spectacles often betrayed aid to his poor eyesight, especially in the low-light conditions of the barracks at night.

Scratching transcripts within his frayed and torn notepad with his broken stub of what remained of a wooden lead pencil, he made adjustments to his existing notes. Over the past few days, the captive *Lieutenant-Colonel* Jack Churchill had been the astute raconteur of his life's story to the talented biographer and fellow inmate, who was also the chief editor and author of the *Battlefront Gazette* newspaper. Right now, they were located in one of the many over-crowded ligneous prisoner barracks inside of the POW camp located deep behind enemy lines in *Oranienburg.*

The Sachsenhausen was designed a little differently to most generalized camps, as it was primarily reserved for the highest of value felons to the fascists such as prestigious or political prisoners of war known formally as 'prominenten'.

The wooden-framed chain wire beds were piled so close together, most were only accessible from the ends. The barracks they occupied inside the Sachsenhausen-Oranienburg was home for prisoners from all walks of war, and not just captured soldiers and downed pilots. Residing within were civilian teachers, poets, artists, and numerous other men of various vocal and social political statuses who the Germans deemed too important to execute for fear of loss of intelligence at a later date of inquiry.

The prisoners were all packed tight in the barracks at night. Bodies stirred in attempted slumber, snoring, shifting on the wire supports beneath the double-folded blanket mattresses of their uncomfortable beds, though most people slept paralytically numb; so depressed they were in a phantasm stuck reminiscing the better days of the freedom they had taken for granted. Some of the men preferred the mucky floorboards to the wooden slats, often broken, and lined with nothing but rags and an old boot for a pillow.

If it were not for the storm, the place would have been ghastly silent at night. Unbeknownst to them, the bad weather was a virtue, for it hid the ever-present sounds of weeping men throughout the aligned bunk beds.

This place was absolute hell, but oddly the men found a bizarre day-to-day coziness to their predicament at the Sachsenhausen. There was an acceptance that this was their lives now and a strange sense of safety was instilled since they were away from the danger of the frontlines of war.

Most recently in his recording of Mad Jack's biography, he had gone into detail about *Operation Archery* and capture of his archenemy Friedrich Feind—a life spared that he should have taken.

Hardy focused on his notes. There was something he had written in the closing of this most recent volume, and he felt it didn't gel right. He scratched it out ...

'Germany soon after reinforced their Norwegian Atlantic line with the supplementary deployment of over thirty-thousand additional troops. Back in their motherland, conceivably, Hitler now had concerns that Norway may be the zone of destiny in this war ...
... then again, ~~maybe he just didn't know Jack.~~*'*

Surely to anybody reading this—optimistically, if they ever got out of here and this manuscript saw the light of day or even made the publisher—any prospective readers content in picking up this dribble and giving it a gander would already 'know Jack'. History would know him—at least, know the bullet points of his life and triumphs. This statement was an irrelevant allure, proposing some long-winded attempt at overdramatization and subverting expectations.

Of course, we all knew Jack. Why wouldn't we?

Hardy's attention veered, talking just loud enough to be heard over the looming thunderstorm and precipitative raindrops as they pitter-pattered on the barracks rooftop. "So, Jack ... what's next on the *warpath* for the *unkillable* Jack Churchill ....?"

The hoarse voice of the grumpy Churchill admitted a firm one-word declaration for his long-time acquaintance and recent biographer. "Sleep."

He barely heard him.

Hardy was on the bottom level across from Jack, beneath an apparent heavy sleeper. The two of them occupied the last rows against the back wall of the prison barracks, resulting in a slight degree of privacy from the other prisoners of war crammed into the shed like stale sardines.

The forfeiting tone broke the writer's scratching pencil strokes dead in their tracks. Through his cracked and cloudy spectacles, Hardy's big brown eyes focused on Churchill's conceding poise as he laid on his bunk. He was energetically hoping for another gracious chapter dictation of the man's life of which he could ascribe to paper, creating another chronicle as well as passing the time in incarceration.

Hardy's *All-American* jawline tensed as he pouted his lips in disappointment, laying to rest his scribing pencil. He responded glumly to Churchill's closing. "Huh? Did you just say *sleep?*"

"Yes, *sleep.* We've been going at it non-stop for days, lad. About time to give it a rest, eh?"

In the instance of hearing Churchill's voice deliver that disappointing blow, Hardy ceased jotting in his notes and sat up in his bunk, causing the wireframe to release a thousand uneasy creaks and torquing wire squeaks that were audible amidst the plinking pitter-patter.

Unshaven and battle-scarred, this present-day 1944 edition of Jack Churchill differed a lot from the one Hardy depicted in his recent works, retelling his soldierly life. Indentations of scarring were prominent across his pale left cheek and tired brows. Dry blood and grime from uncleaned wounds littered his weathered and unshaven face.

Hardy held a glance at the vision. He was alit as an embossed silhouette by the occasional sporadic lightning flashes shining in through their only window, half covered by a series of hanging clothing, freshly aired and stained brown from sweat and mud. With shrilling creaks, this aged envisaging of a bearded Churchill twisted around in the shadows of night to face him in the gloom.

Although exhausted, he appeared restless.

His want of sleep was fair enough, and Hardy had already conceded.

They could always pick up again tomorrow out in the yard and after some kip. Wide awake and repositioned in a much more secluded sitting, he wanted to continue with this yarn. However, lacking Churchill's interpretation and deliberation, Hardy did not lack his own knowledge of what happened after the events of the fabled Operation Archery, where their saga had last ended ...

Personally, Hardy had suffered from a life-threatening pneumonia of the lung following the raid, which saw him hospitalized at *St. Bartholomew's* in London for almost a month—thankfully—on the army's dime. He was put on a trial wonder drug that thankfully worked.

Something obscure caught Hardy's attention in the barracks ...

His view craned towards a close dripping sound, discerning that the soft surface of which the leak from above dripped was in fact a man's flesh. The dark skin belonged to a fellow POW named *Bayume Mohamed Husen,* a man from *Tanganyika.* Husen kept a cryptic backstory from the other prisoners, and little was known about him, other than that he was the only black man in the entire camp. An unfortunate reality, one which the many dark-humoured Brits within isolation, bound by the strangeness of POW comradery, joked that it was as if the Germans had overlooked his execution. If Husen's situational disadvantage was not ironically humorous in itself, the fact was that his broken African-German English translations were often comical.

Seemingly unbothered by the brook of rainfall piss-streaming on his sleeping head, the peculiarity drew the journalist's keen eye. The simple fact that Husen wasn't moving from the water wasn't a good sign.

"Oh God ..." Hardy discerned, drawing attention. "I think Bayume might be dead ..."

From the low single of his wire double-storey bunkbed, the older, bruised and battered, tired and fatigued, malnourished version of Jack Churchill bore a mildly concerned gleam. "Oi. Bayume. You alive, mate?"

There was no response.

Churchill searched about his bunk, collecting a packet of linen-finished playing cards and tossed it, impacting it against the back of the man's legs and gaining a sudden rise from the sleeper.

"*Oi, wot tha fook?!*" the raspy accented voice of Husen erupted, suddenly wide awake. He flipped over, disturbed from his deep slumber and exhibiting a thunderous grimace upon his dark—and wet—features. Reactively, he found the box of cards and pegged them back at Churchill's bunk. The cardboard package tore mid-air, spraying cards across the vicinity.

"*Conts, Imma tryin' ta fookin' sleep ov' 'ere, aye?!*"

Churchill huffed quietly, annoyed at himself whilst inspecting the indoor rainfall of suited playing cards. This was now the second night in a row they had upset poor Bayume, causing him to tilt with reasonable frustration. With the upmost earnestness, Churchill expressed regret, raising his voice slightly over the volume of the shower on the barracks roof. "Apologies, old chap. Was just looking out for you. You were getting rained-on!"

Hardy also owned up and apologized. "Yes, sorry, Bayume."

"*Sorreh noothin'!*" Husen reacted with his deep accent, hissing at him also and pointing a firm finger his way. He was tired of his barrack mates' constant story time slabber as well as their other antics to help pass the time whilst imprisoned. "*Youse doo'et again'n I'll spit on ya dicks, ya understan' me?!*"

Hardy pursed his lips firm to stop himself from laughing at this newest misuse of intimidation by the African. Last night, it was the threat of beating somebody off with his bare hands, tonight it was spitting on another man's genitals. It was either a physical threat against one's penis or an accidental homosexual act—something Husen mis-used and mis-threatened quite regularly, resulting in hilarity.

In contrast, unlike last night, Churchill didn't respond with a witticism. He simply rested back down, attempting to collect the many stray playing cards and returning them to the fold prior to returning to slumber himself.

Hardy got comfortable again and re-examined his notes in the near darkness. He conceded that any future volumes in The Unstoppable Warpath of the Unkillable Jack Churchill would have to wait until tomorr—

"War wounds ..." Churchill's gravelly voice alluded, finding the mental energy to further his reflexion whilst he gathered the cards littering his bed. Since he was sleepless, may as well continue.

Hardy's attention piqued, though he opted not to pry too hard for fear of scaring off the opportunity. He merely raised his chin, spying an open rhetorical window longing for salivating question, but he refrained.

Seemingly on a tangent, Churchill resumed, continuing the retelling of his biography in a low voice so that only they could hear. "It was a period between battles. Concerning ghosts and war wounds left untreated. You see, they can fester. They can haunt."

"*Ghosts?*"

Numbed by the very thought of an embarkation on this next journey, Churchill's head finally bobbled, examining one specific play card which had landed situated on his pillow, somehow ending up beneath where his head was: an *Ace of Spades*. "When they come back from the dead, I've found it's always with a fiery vengeance."

"Didn't think you believe in ghosts ..."

Churchill didn't respond to that.

As the rain fell soothingly, he adjusted himself for comfort.

"The ghost of which I refer is *Ernst-Günther Baade*."

While lying in silence, Hardy's pencil nub etching away, taking notes, Churchill involuntarily rubbed his left cheek after speaking that man's name. He felt the scar indentation upon it and traced it with his fingertips—a significant relevance approaching. The ante substantially upped.

Hardy perched himself more upright. He wasn't expecting this information to come to light. Until now, he hadn't heard Churchill speak Baade's name without the upmost contempt. Of irritation. Of unending loathing—even more than that of his personal archenemy, Feind. This man was somebody he had, in the past, claimed was 'not human'.

Speechless and stalled in unvaried suspense, Hardy licked his pencil tip. He was ready to climb down this rabbit hole. "O.K., Jack. Go."

A ♦   A ♦

War Wounds

'Following Commando's victorious return home to England, Jack, again came into considerable publicity which he was not unenthusiastic to flaunt. He and the others deemed 'celebrities' of Commando were hailed as heroes by all the local press, and as a result, the morale of the United Kingdom had never soared so high following this very successful delivery: one black eye, to one Adolf Hitler. The British war effort was as feisty as ever, and that vivacity was largely due to the success of the raid on the Norwegian islands of Vagsøy and Maløy codenamed Operation Archery. Due to my stint in a London hospital following the raid events, suffering from severe pneumonia, I was unfortunately unable to cover an article on him as passionately as I had for the lustrous 'Dunkirk Jack!' issue, however the spotlight still found him. An anecdotal flavouring was to the gash Jack sustained on his forehead at the end of the raid—a 'war wound' as it were shined-on to the press, but in reality, it was from a bottle of Moselle that accidentally broke during the post-action carousing. Problem was, the wound had healed too quickly on the return voyage—must have been the salt in the sea air. By the time Mad Jack was England-bound, it had already dried and partially faded. Jack said: 'I had to touch it up from time to time with Rosamund's lipstick to keep the wounded hero story going'.

'Once the dust had settled, Jack and the Merry Men of No.3 Commando resumed life back within their comfort zone in Largs. After a brief R&R at the hailed 'Commando Castle', they resumed their notoriously punishing training at the Hollywood Hotel grounds, preparing for the next war ...'

1942, February
Hollywood Hotel (Commando Base)
Largs, Scotland

A vortex of positive change blew amidst a political gale at Whitehall, propelling the paddlewheel of the British war machine and building steam at an exponential rate of acceleration. Now that it was awoken, arisen, and autonomous, the momentum could not be arrested.

The gents of the prominent No.3 Commando had a base in the small town of *Largs, Ayrshire,* located along Scotland's west coast and the *Firth of Clyde.* The tranquil area was once trending for tourists from *Glasgow,* not that many travelled during these trying times of imminent war and rationing.

On the Largs base, the administrative arrangements for Commando were crude to say the least, with the main offices housed in a repurposed local ice-cream parlour called *Nardini's,* while the troops established workable headquarters in converted offices at a gasworks, a coal yard, and at a cigarette kiosk on the main. Sure, the Largs set-up was functional ... but it was also a proper eye sore.

One of the focal particularities of Commando regulation was that the troops did not necessarily live in army barracks, such as they had in their preceding divisions at *Inveraray.* Instead, they had the option to seek their own private housing, that each soldier found for himself locally and paid for from their daily service allowance. By default, accommodation was available at the repurposed *Hollywood Hotel,* which the Royal Navy had requisitioned during the pre-war expansion of His Majesty's militaries. The grounds were huge and there were plenty of lodgings for the troops by the base fields that they used for exercise.

Naturally, seaside resorts at *Hastings, Weymouth,* and *Paignton* became favoured choices of residences by Commanding Officers considering they had plentiful supplies of local bed-and-breakfasts and guesthouses.

This positive arrangement encouraged the initiatives of civilian living and spared the men the usual cleaning and maintenance duties of an a-typical army barracks. Commando strived to break the mould with regulation like they did warfare tactics and training.

Beneath dreary, rolling clouds that whispered precarious promises of rainfall before dusk, Major Jack Churchill stood beneath an awning shelter, overwatching the active training fields currently crawling with troops in sludge-slicken khaki unforms.

Clad in his green beret upon his straw dome, a weatherproof olive smock over his service dress, Churchill oversaw *Captain Peter Young's* section. They drilled on a gruelling obstacle course, lathered in mud.

If he hadn't already been before, Young was now a Commando veteran. Although exceptionally still a baby-faced lad, Young had long since shed his prior moniker of *Young Young*—a nickname up until Operation Archery the soldier had carried since his hazing days.

At present, the muddy men were currently constructing low formations amongst the dug-out trenches, presently lacquered with muck from all the damp weather. Thankfully the snow season had passed, but the climate still remained perpetually soggy.

Within his thirty-man section, laden with full gear, webbing, helmets, unloaded rifles and packs, Churchill recognized a few familiar faces, such as the permanent cauliflower ears of *Lieutenant Bruce Giles*, younger brother of the legendary *Johnny Fredrick Giles (JFG)* who had been killed in action recently in Vågsøy. In his brother's footsteps, Bruce had recently taken the mantel of becoming a prominent boxer—albeit in the lightweight division, due to his size—even training under none other than local legends *Lofty King* and *Bill Chitty*. Bruce had taken time off from regular service after the loss of his brother, who had been buried along with a few others at sea on their return voyage, paid the grandest of respects by the Royal Navy. He had escorted his personal effects back to their hometown of *Clifton* and spent time with family before recently resuming his commando calling.

Corporal Ernest 'Knocker' White was also amongst Young's section of training troopers. As always, for as long as Churchill had known the man, dating back to their shared time serving during *the Phoney War* era in France in the *Second Manchester Regiment*, Knocker White was chomping down on a gob full of chewing gum. Forever in his maw, whether they were balls-deep behind enemy lines, under fire, or receiving a commendation, you could bet your bottom dollar that within that man's mouth was some gum. This was conceivably why he had such a defined jawline, as though it had been chiselled by *Gian Lorenzo Bernini* himself—at jest, undoubtedly intact with the signature micro penis behind that clover leaf.

Churchill's observational survey from the sidelines of the course also made out *Sergeants Joe Mills* and the one-eyed, eyepatch-wearing red-headed Scottish pirate *George 'MacWilly' MacWilliam* amidst the crowd. MacWilly was carrying *'Louise'*: his beloved Mk. II Lewis light machine gun, which had a pan discular-shaped magazine mounted upon the top of the

WAR WOUNDS | 13

receiver, and a thick tubular cooling shroud that extended 27 inches at 4.5 bore. T'were an odd weapon of choice, like his last, when MacWilly had been seen wielding the heavy and unconventional Vickers machine gun—also named after a woman: 'Vicky'—back in their days in the Second Chesters. A funny contrast, the Phoney War period seemed like mere Halcyon days compared to the battles of late.

It seemed Captain Young had them about to drive a formation push from the trench line and into the obstacle course—hopefully, the way they had established as textbook SOP. This was a preexisting manoeuvre columnized differently in attempt at advancing more troops, farther, more quickly, as well as improving navigational control for those following the team leaders. It was fortunate that Churchill had decided to observe the training fields at this minute. He was about to see this new drawing board tactic in action.

From afar, Churchill heard the order rendered by the leading Young, whose voice not only carried the torch of leadership, but also inspired the others. He led from the front, much alike his predecessor presently watching them from the sidelines. His voice pitched across the field, enabling his men to mount the lip of the trench, rifles at arm. A combined force in formation, the troopers followed their various team leaders into an all-out charge towards the forward obstacle course as the thunder from the pending stormfront boomed in the closing distance.

Churchill's sterling stare intensified as he watched.

The troop action wielded volume; their battle cries were audible in a deepening bass from across the field and beneath the growling rumble, yet somehow something about the tactic left a bad taste in Churchill's mouth—and no, it wasn't the stale arrowroots served with questionable lard he had with his tea moments ago in the office. Watching Young's instruction of the men was like pulling teeth. It was not that he was *wrong* per se, just *different* to the way Mad Jack would have driven the charge.

The old Jack would have been roaring from the bleacher ...

Hurling and heckling like a rabid coach at a rugby game ...

Jumping on the spot, shouting alterations ...

... however, Churchill simply let it slide.

He couldn't always be there with them; his Merry Men of old.

A combination of promotions and propositions reminded him of that impermanence. It was time to let them grow on their own, fight on their own. Go to war ... without him.

With a dissatisfied gleam over his expression as the raindrops started to patter the surrounding grounds, he evoked impermanence. Churchill revolved around and headed back towards the establishment of the hotel where there was adequate shelter.

Churchill made it back to the Hollywood Hotel as the downpour became constant. His chosen water-resistant smock over his attire kept his top half dry.

Once under the cover of a breezeway outside of a lower-level conference hall, Churchill slipped the gaberdine off his person and hung it on the same hook he had found it. There were a series of trestle tables set up just by the door, arranged for the gear of the men out in the field when they returned.

"Jack," the familiar voice of *Lieutenant-Colonel John Durnford-Slater* acknowledged from offside and beneath the same wall-less breezeway. Attired in a brown officer's battledress uniform not dissimilar to Churchill's, including the iconic green beret worn aslant, Durnford-Slater appeared. His words were spoken from beneath his well-maintained lampshade moustache. The thing may have been as brown as his hair of head, but sadly also twice as thick. It seemed that old mate had started to severely thin over the course of this past winter; balding from the stress of carrying the entire No.3 Commando division on his shoulders for a year and two whole wildly successful raids—Archery, one of which, had proved to be a huge success. For his part, Durnford-Slater received the Distinguished Service Order and a recommendation written by *Brigadier J.C. Haydon,* a high-ranking commander in the Royal Navy and a part of the command ships involved in the raid. Haydon credited Durnford-Slater's *'personal courage, complete coolness, and quick grasp of the situation'* with inspiring the confidence of the men and ensuring all objectives were achieved. The published mention further described how, when the attack was in danger of stalling, after the leading troops *'lost five out of six officers, and nearly forty percent of their effective strength'* he took personal command to restore the situation under heavy fire.

"Been looking for you."

Churchill replied, removing and shaking his beret of droplets. He had to really speak up now, due to the rainfall past the awning as well as pouring on the roof above their heads. "Well, you found me."

"Indeed," Durnford-Slater took some strides closer. He watched as Churchill combed his hair with his fingertips and moulded his beret back upon his head, planting it firmly.

Durnford-Slater glanced about the wet Hollywood Hotel grounds, spying the troops in the distance. Still training in the shower, their shouts and ruckus were barely audible now that the rainfall had increased thusly.

"What are you doing out here?" Durnford-Slater judged playfully. "Watching the lads trot about in the weather are duties beneath a *major,* wouldn't you say?"

Churchill pursed his lips, nodding along. "Perhaps I miss the mud?"

Before he even had to come up with a whim or ploy to further explain his obsessive desire to oversee even the most minute of operational tasks, Durnford-Slater smoothed the edges.

"Eh," he confided, sidling more closely to Churchill and sharing his overwatch through the downpour and the troops beneath it. He was not blind to the generational parallel and was aware of the sentimentality. "Truth be told, twelve months ago, I stood where you are; observing the lads. I was right where you are, and *you* were out *there;* Young now in your shoes."

"How times change."

"Even now, I fight the need and want to play in the foxholes with my men, dwelling on the past."

" *'Study the past if you would define the future',*" Churchill quoted with quaint relevance.

Again, unknowledgeable in such literary quotations, Durnford-Slater peered across his shoulder to his cohort. "Who's that? *Shakespeare?*"

Churchill chortled. "He wishes. *Confucius.*"

With a glower, and a smirk that tickled the corner of his mouth, Durnford-Slater delivered his own unparalleled witticism. "Didn't he also say something like *'Man who walk through airport turnstile sideways going to Bangkok'?*"

Churchill laughed modestly.

He'd heard that one before, but it was rare someone as sensible as John Durnford-Slater displayed his sense of humour, so he indulged him for it.

Digression aside, Durnford-Slater returned to the topic at hand as well as aligning his prior intent. "Excuse any impudence, Jack, but I feel as though you've been avoiding me the past few weeks?"

Churchill quickly felt trapped.

Truth be told, he had been.

Since the closing of the operation and the submerging of Archery's aftermath, and the wild whirlwind blowing word of their success for miles, Churchill had been eyeing off the Commanding Officer position for the new *No.2 Commando.*

The original No.2 Commando, which had been in leagues with No.3 Commando during Operation Archery, had since become redesignated as the *11th Special Air Service Battalion,* commanded by none other than *Lieutenant-Colonel Robert 'Lucky' Laycock,* fresh from his ventures in the *Rommel Raid* also known as *Operation Flipper.* Flipper had failed with significant casualties, including *Geoffrey Keyes;* the ex-*Combined Operations Headquarters (COHQ)* director *Admiral Roger Keyes'* son. The loss had struck a chord at Whitehall, some taking it as a personal loss.

All unit structuring within the original No.2 had been maintained from Commando and migrated into the newer Special Air Service abbreviated as *SAS.* Subsequently, in the stretch of just a few weeks, the new, albeit 'second'

No.2 Commando had been registered to replace the old and would be recruiting from scratch any day now with the goal of becoming as formidable a force.

Jack Churchill was contemplating applying for the leadership role to run the entire battalion-sized unit of the 2nd No.2 Commando—history would agree, confusing unit designations were what the British Army did best.

Unfortunately, Churchill's acceptance of the No.2 role would mean migrating from No.3 Commando; the unit he had helped hand-raise beside Durnford-Slater since its rebirth in the early days at the Inveraray *Combined Training Centre (CTC)*, during the *LayForce/Commando* feud.

The eighteen months of brotherly bonds felt like a lifetime to let go of and, understandably, Churchill was reluctant to break the news of his potential departure to his mentor and commanding officer, hence his distancing of late. The two shared neighbouring lodgings within the *Kelburn Castle* in Largs *(Commando Castle)*, and yet he hadn't spoken a word to his colleague in over a week. The fact that Durnford-Slater found his adversity obvious should not have come as a surprise by now ...

While No.3 resided in Largs, this second No.2 would require him vacating and residing somewhere closer to the new *Special Training Centre* (STC) established in *Paignton, Devon*—the opposite side of England.

"I, eh ..." Churchill's eyes widened as his brain searched for a viable excuse for Durnford-Slater's on-the-spot query. "I'm not sure if I know what you mean, sir?"

Predicting this apprehensiveness and softening the blow, Durnford-Slater levelled with his friend. "Jack, I'm not daft ... I know about your expression of interest with the new No.2."

Churchill's held gaze defocused.

It suddenly occurred to him how stupid this insistent repentance he had about leaving No.3 was. It shouldn't matter if he wanted to advance in the army. Jack knew he was due for a promotion following the events of Archery, it was just somewhere in the pipeline. The progression of military rank was the byproduct of outstanding conduct on the battlefield, and he had received such merits hitherto his warpath. Jack had been awarded a Military Cross and Bar—no small token of appreciation by any standards.

With a promotion, Jack would hold the title rank of lieutenant-colonel, matching the position of his current superior officer. Grasping the commanding officer's role for No.2 would then be as easy as taking a treat from a toddler. The meat and potatoes already existed in the way of a preexisting positive reputation with those at Whitehall—and not just because of the stick-and-string/sword-wielding eccentricities that got him thrust into the spotlight in the first place. From even before Vågsøy and Måløy, his list of accolades outshone many others, and he came highly recommended.

A weight lifted, he let out a sigh in lieu of the reveal.

With the news off his chest, Churchill turned to face Durnford-Slater, only he had not the words. "Sorry, John."

Durnford-Slater scrunched his brow and scoffed. "*Sorry?* Blood-y-hell, Jack, if anyone deserves to be put in charge of a unit, it's you. You've earned it."

Absorbing the uplifting compliment like a ray of sunshine in the storm, Churchill's piercing blue stare elevated, finding Durnford-Slater's firm gaze. He often looked up to this man, finding motivation in his strengths, especially in the early days when he was getting Commando off the ground. Durnford-Slater had administratively fought tooth and nail against Laycock's desire to graft No.3 Commando into his LayForce, and Jack attested to his perseverance on that bureaucratic front. Likewise, he had also learned a lot about diplomacy and political perseverance from him.

In many ways, the two had grown far together in such a short time.

Typically, Churchill was none too shy of modesty, and this time he accepted Durnford-Slater's recognition with a genuine bow, full knowing that the deep-seated respect was mutual. "Sir."

Durnford-Slater took a few steps nearer the clove of the awning, watching the rain fall from the gloomy underside of the clouds. Out in the open, Captain Young started to bring his men in from the field, calling it quits for today's exercise. Across the closing distance, they were inbound, about to use this area to divest and disarm. They had maybe a minute before they would be swarmed by the presence of Young's drenched men, and so Durnford-Slater quickly planted a lasting tease upon Churchill's ears:

"Shame you're not a *lieutenant-colonel.* Bearing a title of such would have gotten you well and truly across the line at Whitehall."

"Yes, well ..." in a tone befitting a contrast, Churchill combined a sarcastic shrug. He knew darn well that promotion was on its way somewhere. Formality had gotten the better of that bath star beneath the crown he already had on his insignia of major.

Durnford-Slater pivoted and faced Churchill.

In his palm he held a small box resembling a cufflink case.

Churchill's expression fell flat ...

They were no cufflinks.

He knew exactly what that was!

It took a lot to catch this confident soldier off-guard. Jack Churchill was forever a marshalled type, but Durnford-Slater had just managed to surprise him, shaking that unbridled composure.

The case housed his stripes ...

His express promotion, effective immediately!

Evidence of Churchill's surprise was captured by Captain Young's drenched men of the Troop as they closed in, coming in hot from the windblown shower outside. Their excused presence was unspoken by their higher ups, as technically they were the ones not where they were supposed to be.

"Congratulations *Lieutenant-Colonel* Jack Churchill," Lieutenant-Colonel Durnford-Slater stated aloud as the men encircled the undercover area like a wet audience.

They all caught wind of the promotion, applauding their major-turned-lieutenant-colonel as Churchill accepted the wooden case into his hands. Inside were his new ribbons, which would be sewn onto his shoulders, and pins for his shirt collar tabs.

Permitted a slight leniency in their demeanour given the moment, the men carried on and applauded boisterously. There was clapping, whistling, hooting, and joyous smiles all around.

Time stood still in that moment for Jack Churchill.

Ceremonial reprieve wasn't typically enough to paralyse Mad Jack—perhaps it was this surprise gifting by his superior that had done the trick. He snapped out of his momentary lapse, noting his onlookers as the portion of No.3 men praised his acceptance of the promotion whilst stripping their gear onto the situated trestle tables.

Durnford-Slater had timed this formality well.

"And one other!" he added raising his hand above the celebrative tone, presenting from his pocket yet another small brown box. It was another award intended for another trooper present.

"Corporal White, where are you? Step forward!" Durnford-Slater announced above the crowd of rowdy, cheerful commandos.

He lagged, but eventually the hesitant regimental officer stepped forth from the gathering of muddy men to accept his merit. Due to the tide of war, ceremonies such as this were all they ever received for commendations—they were lucky to have it and not just receive it in the mail.

Durnford-Slater had no hesitation in taking the soldier's squalid paw in a gentlemanly handshake, then firmly planting the carton in his grasp—

"*W-w-wait!*" the urgency in the voice of furrowed eyebrowed Hank Peace cut through the applause, conveniently intervening with a dry towel to first clean Knocker White's filthy hand before he could make physical contact with either his CO or his commendation.

"Congratulations, trooper! Thank you again for your outstanding leadership and courage during the raid on Vågsøy Island," Durnford-Slater praised while Knocker White, pale as a ghost and with the sparkling stare of a stunned mullet, gazed upon the box. His eyes widened as he opened the lid containing a *Distinguished Conduct Medal.* The surprise was shocking enough to momentarily stop his jaw from chewing.

This was an exceptional occurrence considering Ernest White was not an army officer—he was a mere petty officer. The rarity of this stature of receiving an order such as this was undeniably the rationale behind its deferment during the initial assembly where the other typical commando officers present for the raid had received their medals, ribbons, and distinctions. It was well earned, given White's performance during Operation Archery.

With a beam, Durnford-Slater turned away, and the men of the section enveloped around the shy Knocker White, soaking him with raucous commendation, drenching him the same way the rain from the storm soaked his clothes through to the knickers.

As if he had something to say, Durnford-Slater snagged beside Churchill, shoulder to shoulder. He hovered there for a moment until Jack cast him a sideways glance to prompt his lingering oration.

He addressed him straightforwardly. It seemed more than a passing salutation for Churchill. Jack detected something weightier in his tone, an unspoken validation towards his course of pursuit.

"*Lieutenant-Colonel.*"

Churchill flinched a smirk beneath his pencil moustache, forcefully drawing a regulation flat expression of which to return the salute along with the slightest of respectful head tilts.

He responded in kind. "*Lieutenant-Colonel.*"

'Neither one of them knew it here, but this would be one of the last times these two commandos would exist to perform in jest. One of the last times they would exchange wordless communication through their adapted passive undertones. The last time they would share a command. Perchance, deep down, they did know, and this was a comfortable yet pleasant farewell, a placeholder, so that they would not have to acknowledge the long goodbye. Imaginably, it was that unshakable melancholy that coincided with the shadow of the day. The undercurrent of undeniable anguish that underlined every word they transcribed. A persistent despondency. The perpetual dejection. Perhaps that was why, no matter how they ended it, their conversation culminated in what felt like an exodus. With Archery, their professional relationship had run its course, and it was now time to go their separate ways. The universe already knew it ahead of time. These two men were just behind the curve.'

'Whatever the case, they had finally caught up.'

1942, February
Combined Operations Headquarters
Whitehall, London

Stepping outdoors of the Combined Operations Headquarters building in Whitehall, the formally attired Lieutenant-Colonel Jack Churchill passed beneath the *Admiralty Arch*, draping him in shadow on an otherwise fair day in London.

The Admiralty Arch was the landmark building that provided pedestrian access between *Trafalgar Square* to the north-east, and a strip colloquially known as *the Mall*, which extended to the south-west. This main thoroughfare strip in London is recognized as the centre of the Government of the United Kingdom, lined with numerous departments and ministries, including the *Ministry of Defence, Horse Guards*, the *Cabinet Office*, and the COHQ was rather centralized in London. And right now, Mad Jack was standing amongst it during a busy business day.

Whilst he was taking it all in, a male voice cut through the pedestrian crowds from his blind flank, gaining Churchill's stray attention in the flowing passage of attired men (and women) in a flock of civilian and military suits, mounted fedoras, and carrying briefcases or stacks of manilla folders. "*Jack!?*"

Churchill paused his persistent strides and swooped his beret-donned head. He almost didn't recognize the gent at first, it had been so long:

Lieutenant-Colonel Augustus Charles Newman.

Beneath his aslant dark officer's beret, Newman bore an honest face.

He possessed a weary, droopy set of eyes, and a long, narrow nose.

Newman was dressed in his army green suit not unlike Churchill's, albeit with a lot of differing insignia pertaining to *the Essex Regiment.* He was a fresh addition into the *Special Service Brigade* family, which contained units like Commando—specifically the new No.2, of which, due to his history of expert judgement, he was rumoured to be tasked with overseeing the recruiting process.

Inclusive of that recruiting: the battalion commanding officer, themself.

The very role Churchill was in contention for!

This meeting could not have been more meant-to-be ...

"Colonel, sir!" Churchill responded kindly, gesturing prominently with a handshake rather than a tacky salute since they were of equal rank.

"You can call me *Charlie*," Newman stated as he accepted Jack's hand firmly. *Charlie*, his preferred name, rather than *Augustus*. "We're both colonels, after all."

"Fine-o-fine, sir," Churchill admitted, unequivocally retaining the formality for the foreseeable future. After all, Newman was in charge of hiring for the leadership role. It was great that they were already acquaintances; friends, but not *too* friendly. Titular formality was a healthy buffer, Jack thought.

"What brings you to Whitehall, Mad Jack?"

Churchill conversed casually. "I was dropping in another letter of recommendation to *Commodore Mountbatten*. You'll find it with his secretary in house."

"Another one?"

Jack gestured a confident bow.

Newman formed a sly smirk and offered Churchill some wisdom in a low-key tone. "Jack, you know that you've all but got the role, right ...? Why bother coming all the way *here*, and handing in *more* credentials—in person, mind you, rather than by post—like any other normal human being ... it's not the eighteen hundreds anymore, we *have* got this thing called Royal Mail, you know ...?"

Coyly, Churchill continued unphased. "Well, sir, to quote *Bonaparte*, *'if you want a thing done right, do it yourself'.*"

"*Napoleon* Bonaparte?"

"Yes, sir."

"Jack, I'm inclined to rescind the promotion if you go on quoting a bloody Frenchman."

"Apologies," Churchill responded, hoping Newman was joking. The bloke had such an expressionless face, it was hard to tell. It consistently drooped, as though somebody had just run over his dog.

"I'll rescind it on the double if you are an apologizer," Newman recommended. They may have both been lieutenant-colonels, but Newman was ten years his senior. That was a decade more experience in the service and in life, which Churchill respected. Therefore, his advice consul held merit, not that Churchill really needed the pep talk. "And for the second time: call me *Charlie* for Christsake."

"Yes, sir. Charlie."

Newman finished walking with Churchill a few paces through the busy Whitehall centre, and he stopped to face him in the crowd of flowing business suit pedestrians going about their day like schools of flowing fish.

"You can relax, Jack. You are a leftenant-colonel and an accomplished commando. You have experience under your belt, which your accolades reflect with sparkling asterisks. You've kept your friends close, and you've got them in all the right places ..." Newman further counselled.

Hearing it helped reaffirm Churchill's confidence. He took his hand one last time in parting ...

"Let nature take its course."

The two British officers became distracted by a slight commotion.

It was a group of civilians venturing nearby a posse of uniformed American soldiers. Since late January, the Yanks had been flowing into England via Northern Ireland, ahead of the American involvement in Second World War. The insignia of the troops read that they were from the *34th Infantry Division*, also known as the *'Red Bull'* division.

Since the events of *Pearl Harbor*, the Americans were suddenly onboard to take on the Nazis. Thus far, their only participation in the effort had been in an extremely mild defence against the Japanese dive-bombers who were already embarked upon kamikaze runs on surface targets. They had very little to be macho about ...

"Christsake," Newman remarked at their shrieking—basically posing for autographs as though they were rockstars. "They're overfed, overpaid, overdressed ... and now they're over *here*."

Churchill sulked. "*Americans.* Bunch of bellends, sir—" he corrected himself quickly and before Newman caught wind of the slur, "—*Charlie.*"

Taking absence, Newman eyed him. "Godspeed, Mad Jack."

"And to you, sir—*Charlie.*"

Once Newman had shook his hand sternly and then walked away, Churchill lingered for a moment, taking in the sight of the men in American army uniforms. They had rocked up to this war two years too late, acting as though they were here to settle the score ...

Actual bunch of wankers.

He shook his head displeasingly, and marched on.

Although Jack had somewhere to be, the sight of an establishment caught his eye before he hit the road; a pub which sold alcohol.

He had one more stop before his next foray ...

At such an early hour, the entry was a small surprise.

Churchill quickly sought the barkeep within, firm in his questioning.

"Excuse me, barman. You wouldn't happen to sell dessert liqueur, would you? I require a bottle as a gift for an old Feind."

1942, February
Glenn Mill (Camp 2)
Oldham, Lancashire

A uniformed sentry with a leather-holstered Webley revolver raised a salute to the brim of his brodie helmet as Lieutenant-Colonel Churchill rounded the hall from the reception in the main building. Unlike his previous visit, he was a registered visitor today at the prison camp, escorted by a short clerical man in a short sleeve shirt and a short tie; a man even short of hair and balding on top, bearing a thin combover greased slick across in a vain attempt to hide the inevitable shine of old age.

"*Colonel, sir!*"

Jack returned the salutation. "As you were, guardsman."

The troop audibly responded with vigour, whipping his arm down.

This building interior was originally the administration and logistics office for the old Glenn Mill prior to the army's requisition of the land, converting it to a POW camp. Now, it was a reception desk followed by a doored-off security checkpoint leading to the prison camp. These connecting halls lead to the bowels of a smooth-running prisoner processing plant and housing, the maintaining of a well-oiled ecosystem of segregation and ... *equilibrium.*

It was all about balance at this camp. The prisoners held within these high-exterior walls were both isolated in confinement and set upon a resolute path of rehabilitation. The conduct within Camp 2, though as strict as necessary for a plantation harbouring a conditioned enemy, was certainly more altruistic than those situated with the opposition. The equilibrium component was an experimental program implemented by the British government inculcating re-education to the submissive war prisoners, intended to demonstrate the true wickedness of the Nazi regime, all the while promoting the numerous advantages of a democratic system, altering their state of mind to a change for the better. Of course, they were always viewed as wolves in sheep's clothing amongst the flock steered by the shepherd waving the Union Jack.

Today, Jack Churchill was here to visit one of those wolves.

And this time he had an appointment!

After passing another saluting sentry in the hall, Churchill's escort directed him through an open single door. They stepped nearer an entryway, and the two made way for a female as she exited a room across the hall carrying a ream of paperclipped paperwork against her blouse.

Her green eyes marked Churchill and immediately recognized him, beaming a smile of her pearly whites from between her bright red lipstick. The two remembered each other from a previous passing encounter.

"Hello Mabel," hand on the doorknob and momentarily stalling their passage, the announcement by his office escort rung a much thankful bell in Churchill's memory of her name in the nick of time. She had appeared more than just a pretty face in a coffee-coloured satin blouse and dark circle skirt, but now he had a name for the face.

"Miss Mabel Blagbrough," Churchill recalled as she enclosed the short distance before the two men in the tight hall. "How do you do, ma'am?"

"Well, thank you, eh?" she was momentarily amiss as her emerald eyeline scanned across his military suit, spying his many stitched emblems. What threw her off was the last time she had seen this handsome chap, he had not borne the rank of lieutenant-colonel. The freshly embroidered chevrons appeared new on his threads, which was what sparked her total recall. "Major Jack."

Before Churchill needed or had to make the correction, Mabel's gaze climbed and read his new rank representations.

Her tone was as equally as colloquially playful as the first time she had pronounced his name. Perhaps it was just her natural tone of voice. She was rather cute and petite for a pronounced lady.

"Oh. *Lieutenant-Colonel* Jack, now, I see?"

Churchill's winning smile formed as he gestured her accuracy.

She denoted that the promotion was fresh. "Congratulations."

"Gratitude, my dear," he bobbed his beret-clad dome along with the pleasantries. The appreciation was followed by a slight hiatus in their conversation, though, it was not awkward. Mabel's footwork slowly continued her journey, orbiting beyond them by but not surrendering eye contact for a time.

She finally remarked through her teeth. "Okay, bye, then."

"Have a nice day, ma'am."

This was a dangerous level of flirtatiousness.

Mabel held her gaze until she vanished around the corner.

In the echo of that moment, Churchill pondered this unto himself.

This was hardly the first time a member of the opposite sex had paid him this sort of attention since his marriage to *Rosamund*—to whom he was happily wed—therefore not his first time repulsing the attraction as such, only ... it wasn't as much a deflection as it was a self-comprehension by the man that *that* was as close as any relations were ever allowed to come forever more. It was a reality he found himself still coming to terms with.

Self-assurance aside, Mabel had a certain aura around her; an angelic glow, so to speak. It was undeniable and attractive, even to those bound. Unacknowledgeable.

Jack tipped his head to the short office bloke who was escorting him.

"Who *is* that?" he inquired beholding a level of fixation.

The greasy combover holding the doorknob seemed just as engrossed on the fleeting sight of Miss Blagbrough as Mabel had been on the striking Lieutenant-Colonel Jack Churchill.

His answer accommodated a shake of his balding dome. "*That there* is the one and only Miss Mabel. She's ... she's everything; secretary hand, office admin, caretaker."

Jack sloped his stare. "*Caretaker?*"

"Yes, sadly," Baldy nodded with an unempathetic chuckle. "We've caught her on more than one occasion tossing packets of cigarettes and teacakes she bakes over the fences. Contraband."

"Oh, dear. You mean ... to the prisoners?!"

"Yes," he sneered again, distasteful of her atrocities. "Nobody at the Mill deserves her ..."

Churchill silently chortled, pushing the air from his nostrils. His initial thoughts were *why on earth would anyone want to do such a thing for the enemy?* ... but then again, if the tables were turned, he could see how that may be beneficial to the supposed rehabilitation of the POWs. These spoils could have just made that light at the end of the tunnel a little bit brighter for those encaged belligerents.

"She's been an employee at the Glenn Mill since before the army takeover," he continued, leaning further into the door of which he had long since twisted the grip. "I tell ya what, though," he declared with such valiant sincerity, "if I wasn't already married, I'd be workin' hard towards slippin' a ring on that gal's pretty lil' finger."

Churchill's judgemental stare followed his balding head inside.

Luckily Baldy was in front, so he didn't see Jack's checked expression as he nearly unsuccessfully failed to subvert his leer. It was clearly laughing *at* him, not *with*. With *any* and *all* due respect, she was well out of this bloke's league, but it was cute that he thought that in some universe, he would have had a chance with the likes of such a specimen.

Once inside, he whipped his beady eyes back around to Churchill, allowing him entry into the small and dark interview room. The lights blinked on, barely wakeful and remaining dim for a stretch. Jack was fast to flatten his expression. He saved face by raising his own left hand, examining his own gold wedding band.

"I feel you, lad," he concurred convincingly.

Baldy missed Mad Jack's aimed lampoon, instead agreeing with Churchill's response to his assertion of forlornness and fidelity. He nodded, respectively patting the army colonel on the sleeve as Churchill passed him in a dawdle further inside. It was an ominous bare room with a collapsible table and two skinny timber chairs. It felt a lot like an interrogation room and likely had been used as such. The British PWIS of the Intelligence Corps, a special branch of *MI19,* may have been all about the firm implementation of change through re-education on the outside ... but on the inside, they were just as firm with their bare-knuckled fists with any Tom, Dick, and Dummkopf they captured. Many withholding prisoners probably found this out the hard way in rooms such as this a long time before their submission for re-education.

"Your prisoner will be in shortly if you'd like to take a seat, sir," his escort said departingly, and Churchill cast him an appreciative sign on his exit.

The door closed, leaving Jack alone in the dimly lit room.

He planted the weighty wooden case that he had been carting from London on the table. The contents of the crate had been checked and cleared by security.

It became suddenly relevant to point out that for the first time in a long time, Churchill was unarmed. Upon visiting the prison camp, for the safety of the inmates and the safety of everybody in the building, visitors were regulated to remove any weaponry. This included sidearms, knives, and in the case of Mad Jack, his custom claybeg.

It had been rather humorous trying to pass the 38-inch sword through the reception window that commonly received pistols, pens, and knives.

Inside Jack's carton, there was nothing more than a token of appreciation on behalf of the British Army for a particular POW who had been more than forthcoming with accurate intelligence, proving valuable for future reconnaissance and operations. It had been vetted by prison security.

Churchill wouldn't have believed it if the information from the said inmate had not been evaluated by his own brother, Thomas Churchill, who worked out of various intelligence sectors. Combining the unfounded information from this POW with aerial photographic evidence that had been offered by the captive proved to be valuable insight for the army. What he had said had genuinely borne fruit.

He caught sight of his own mirror image in the ink-black reflectiveness of the one-way mirror lining the inner wall. From up close, the half-silvered glass staining made the mirror look like some sort of portal into another world; a shadow world. There seemed to be nothing beyond it but darkness, which was what Churchill expected considering this was not an informative visit. The PWIS had gotten all that they could out of this prisoner, and this was a registered informal visit. There would be nobody watching within the enclosed room ...

Jack stepped closer and laid his eyes upon his own reflection in the mirror. He examined his striking pose in his military suit and beret, taking the time to adjust his sleeves so that they slackened proportionately. He then adjusted his collar and tie while he was alone—

"*Jackie.*"

Startled, *Churchill flinched!*

The room he was in was empty, as he could see from the reflection, but the voice was from right beside him.

Inhaling a rescue breath, he glanced to his side before closing his lids and recovering. It was none other than Lieutenant-Colonel Sloan MacLeòid, his friendly ghost haunt.

In the low tone of his Scottish intonation, MacLeòid was apologetic that he had startled his lifelong friend. "*Sorry, laddie. Aye, didn't meen ta scaer yoo ...*"

Ignoring him momentarily, Churchill finished straightening his tie.

"Of course *you* don't have a reflection," he finally uttered, taking a jab at his friendly ghost's probable malevolence. If it were the words of *Bram Stoker* or *H.P. Lovecraft* or the like, MacLeòid would be giving off a sulphuric odour, leaving a corroding residue of his haunting presence.

"*E'm glad yoo've come to yoor senses ...*"

Churchill frowned at his reflection, turning to face his kilt-clad Scottish friend as he circled the desk in the middle of the room, brushing his mitten across the wooden crate on the tabletop.

"*Please tell meh there be a shank under the bottle, en yoo're plannin' ta fillet tha Frankfurt when he shows?*"

Halting his action, Jack wrinkled his forehead. "Pardon?"

MacLeòid blinked, confused as to how Churchill was planning on killing his adversary in that case. He had been stripped of all ideal weaponry. Then, it came to the ghost. "*Aye, I get et. Yoo're gonna use yoor bare-farken-hands ta do tha deed! I like et, Jackie. Make et look like an accident or sum'thin', eh?*"

Churchill followed his pacing patrol around the table and revolved, again facing him. "No."

"*Nay?*"

Jack was hesitant to continue this conversation with MacLeòid—with himself. Abruptly, reluctancy overcame his urge to converse. The one-way mirror behind him suddenly became extremely obvious. Anybody could have been watching these eccentric one-sided theatrics and been asking *what the fuck?*

Before MacLeòid had a chance to reiterate his wishes for blood, the door on the opposite side of the room exteriorly clicked unlocked, and opened inwards.

Churchill became fully straight, hands linking across his belt buckle.

He watched with a puffed chest as an unrestricted Friedrich Feind was cautiously escorted inside by an armed guard. Beyond the open door was the frolicking noise of a functioning prison yard, complete with crowds of men talking with European accents and the sound of heavy iron bars on doors sliding closed, jailcell keys rattling.

Feind's dark features and brown eyes found Churchill occupying the room. The guard behind his person moved him into position, overbearing his reluctance. The two locked stares for a full ten seconds before the guard rounded his posture, indicating for him to take a seat and to prepare to be handcuffed to the railing mounted horizontally across the table.

As instructed, Feind complied, continuously gawking Churchill.

Now that the weather was changing in England, the prisoners were typically issued work yard clothing. They were given tools and put out to work, primarily in agriculture and maintaining livestock. Their cultivation support would help stock the cupboards of the British people, as well as fuel the various food chains necessary to feed the war machine of Great Britain and her allies. Given the state of his soil-coated attire, Feind had obviously been instructed to participate and had been plucked out of such duties today in order to meet his appointment with a British Army representative: it was a surprise that it was *Jack Churchill.*

"Secured, sir," the guard complied once the prisoner was anchored to the desk with shackles.

"That'll be all, thank you, guardsman," Churchill responded, returning a mechanized salute which saw the guard off in regimented silence.

Once he left, an uncomfortable silence continued with them both sharing the same room. Feind simply ogled his nemesis—and although the expression *nemesis* was true, Churchill didn't see it that way any longer. Not if Feind was willing to move past it.

To his knowledge—and surprise—Feind had turned over a new leaf since his internment. All his communicated information handed over to the British Intelligence had checked out, and was legitimately invaluable; enemy positions, names, ranks, and so on. This was the same intelligence which had been vetted by his brother.

Unmistakeably, this did not mean that he was prepared to extend (another) olive branch to the fiend from any past transgressions. If anything, for obvious reasons, Churchill found his willingness to surrender valuable intelligence against his nation fascinatingly noteworthy. And, truth be told, he was personally interested to know why nothing had amounted of his admonition about revealing an element of Churchill's own secret past to prominent inquisitors—the stuff he had *supposedly* known and the songs he had *supposedly* sung.

It must have been an empty threat to say the least.

After a solid stare-off, Feind's gaze sought the collars of Churchill's attire, noticing his increase in rank. The promotion seemed not to surprise him. He breathed singly with his German accent, somewhat sincere. "Congratulationz, *Colonel.*"

The overwatching MacLeòid huffed and glared to the side of Jack's face. "*Pffft ... what er farken disrespectful dickhead ...*"

Mad Jack ignored the haunt and after a moment, he seemingly disappeared, retracting back into the ether.

"Yes, cheers," Churchill finally replied with a sense of casualness, dragging out the hollow timber chair on the tilted floor and planting himself opposite Feind across the table, now at an equal level. "And thank you for your forthcomingness with our intelligence community. I am here to formally commend you for your cooperation—verbally, of course. However, I do bring an offer of appreciation ..."

Feind's chin raised.

Albeit legitimate, he wasn't buying Churchill's compliment.

His eyes fixated beyond the token and onto Churchill's, reading him like an open book. It took him all of three seconds to scent an underlining agenda present, hidden beneath the British soldier's portrayed pleasantries and conducted formalities.

An extended moment of silence followed.

"Vhy are you really here, English-man ...?"

Churchill reached over and gathered the box, nudging it an extra inch across the surface of the table to Feind who simply glanced unenthused. The liquid contents encased in a glass bottle within the wooden carton were obvious by the weight of the force in the shove.

Feind's flat eye level raised from the crate and back onto Churchill.

He was uninterested in the gift and was more interested in uncovering the hidden agenda he detected in the undercurrent of their discourse.

After another prolonged moment of wordlessness within the echoic four walls, Churchill lifted a palm at the gift, gesturing that it was the sole reasoning for his being here.

Again, Feind disregarded interest in the exhibit.

He tipped his head, allowing for the dim light of the room to colour the contours outlining the deep duelling-scars of his face. Now that shaving was not permitted, the patchiness of the marks on his jawline were even more evident as bald incisions where the hair would no longer grow through scar tissue.

Jack proposed finally. "*That.*"

Feind remained unconvinced, instead deciding to break the ice for the Englishman. "Nein. You vant to know vhy you are ztill vithout any die rüge, eh? Vithout any reprimand ..." he insinuated accurately. Even Churchill did not want to admit his intrigue in Feind's cause. "You are ... curiouz."

Churchill held his well-tamed, well-groomed poker face well, holding his firm sterling eyeline upon Feind. His visage lacked any articulation that could be interpreted by the German.

"There won't be a *reprimand* because I am undeserving of such, and my up-tops know it," Churchill finally admitted in truthful conclusion to this threat. He moved his hands to gesture the tabs of his uniform—the fresh ones newly sewed on. "Case in point."

Feind's deadpan seemed equally as expressionless.

Either one of them could have held a royal flush at this juncture.

Perhaps it was how little he truly knew the man to gauge his mannerisms or maybe it was a cultural thing, but Feind's movements seemed somewhat animalistic; the way he tilted his face in his stare, studying him, practically pricking his ears, piquing attention. Perchance it was some intimidation tactic taught at Führer school that either went completely over Jack's head or beneath his radar. Whatever the case, he didn't let it coerce him in any way.

"Your accusations were a good attempt at defamation, though, I'm sure," Churchill followed up. He genuinely admired Feind's gallant bid at striving to knock him down a few pegs in the eyes of the magistrates of the British Army. It was the only avenue the desperate Hun had left to trek in order to take a swing at his enemy. Churchill arched forwards and over the table, under the light. "The truth is ... I am curious to know *how* you even know about *Switzerland* in the first place?"

His stare intensified on Feind's, trying his hardest to read him, to harvest the faintest clue, however the soldier's tells were dimmer than the edges of braille.

This circumstance was a strange one. Typically, when he had to read this fellow, it had been across the tip of a sword point, not across a tabletop.

Churchill calmly asked again. "How?"

Feind's gawp finally blinked.

"I do not need to anzwer any ov your queztionz," the German etched with his cuffed fingers along the desktop. They still went nowhere near the package Jack had brought him. "Your people cleared me."

Churchill waited a full five seconds before loudly slapping the table and springing up. Standing, he revolved and tucked in the chair, tending to the door in an unexpected expression of leave that even surprised Feind.

"*Guard!*" Churchill barked before returning his attention to Feind with a departing tone. "I guess that'll be all then, old chap. I thought I'd drop in since I was in London and say hullo. I'll be changing units soon ... heading even farther south, so, eh ..."

The door behind Feind opened and the guard attended, about to dutifully escort the prisoner back to the general prison population.

"... I guess this is good*bye* and good ... *luck,* I suppose?" Churchill frowned with a forced confusion. He was done with Friedrich Feind and all that came along with his existence, such as some of Mad Jack's regrettable history; memories Churchill wished would be expunged. War wounds. Now that the fiend was caught, it was time to move on with his life. This was a whole new chapter of his saga, and one with him not hung up on something that happened years ago.

"Oh, me?" Churchill jestingly answered an unspoken question targeted at provoking Feind into hearing a topical insert of information.

"Du?"

"I'm glad you asked ..."

"I did not azk—"

"Well, I'm off for dinner with my wife ..." Churchill informed, attempting to furthermore victimize and persecute Feind with his free freedom and wealthy wealthiness outside of any incarceration. "You see, It's *Valentine's Day* out here in the free world, lad. I'm off to romance the lady, probably get lucky, you know how it is—oh, you don't?" Jack scoffed contemptuously.

Feind's lips pursed firm.

In the moments that followed, Churchill turned for the door.

The guard called lastly, pointing at the crate as if Jack had forgotten it. Instead of unlocking the handcuffs from the desk, the soldier's hands hovered over the wooden box. The obvious contents were of a bottle of alcohol of some description—whatever it was, it was not accepted within the walls of the camp. The prisoner could not be allowed to possess it. "*Sir, he is not permitted to have this ...?*"

Churchill reacted plainly, holding the doorknob for a spell before reefing it open after his follow-up sentence. "He won't want it anyway."

Both Feind and the guard watched with a confused glower as Churchill vacated the room in a whoosh, leaving open the door and vanishing into the echoic hall.

Out of keen interest, the guard slid open the lid of the crate revealing a silica sand black glass bottle resting in straw packaging. The label of the dark bottle became visible, and before they could even read the title, the captive Feind knew exactly what the contents were ...

He turned up his nose. His nostrils flared.

It was a bottle of Killepitsch.

There was a long story that went along with an offering of this type of liqueur to the man Friedrich Feind, dating back to his days representing Germany in the Olympic Games when, after a dramatic incident, he was shamefully disqualified. Ever since, the token kräuterlikör caused him to recall the incident, and it enraged him.

Jack knew this all too well.

This wasn't a thank you gift from the army ...

... it was a cruel joke intended to kick him while he's down.

Churchill must have predicted this visit would have ended somewhat badly since the beginning if he was planning on leaving Feind with the Killepitsch.

After Churchill exited the room, leaving inmate Feind to be shepherded back into the prison by the guard, from behind the one-way mirror portal, a vigilant and attentive stare studied the wake of the interrogation room in silence. It was an unfamiliar pair of eyes.

After a full analysis, the unfaced, patient observer and his accomplice finally shifted in the shadows of the accompanying room. Ninety percent of the light illuminating their space shined in through the tinted one-way mirror.

Dressed in a woollen tweed suit, the wearer casually placed a fedora upon his neat side-part. He was in his mid-fifties, around six-foot-two, with a rather plump build. A razor-shave type, he was with a toothpick constantly grinding between his teeth, even absent the intake of food. Even now, the wood splinter was pinched firm between his lips. The oral fixation was this particular man's notable nuance.

In the observation quarters attached to the interrogation room, the man in the suit was flanked by a shorter offsider of a differing gender. One might assume she was an assistant of types, given that she was younger, curter, and constantly sporting a folded notepad and pencil—and that she was a *'she'—a member of the opposite sex to a he.* In a man's world and clearly of a formal profession, a lass would almost always be a secretary or, at the very least in rare corporate worlds, a *subordinate.* That being said, this was a brave new era of women in the shared workforce.

She was a shoulder-length brunette with minimal makeup, dressed in a grey herringbone wool utility skirt suit designed by the new *Incorporated Society of London Fashion Designers (IncSoc)*, a membership organization founded with the ideals to promote British fashion and the textile industry, consequently creating a luxury couture to sell abroad for continued support of the British war effort. Thus, she suddenly seemed less of a *secretary* and more of a charged *businesswoman*—a scarcity, indeed. A lethal scarcity.

Perchance she was even an investigative partner by the primary, sourced during these rationed times.

In the shade of the silent room, after donning his stylish fedora, the suited man twisted to address his colleague over his shoulder.

Wiggling the toothpick between his teeth following the observation, he finally instructed tunefully a phrase she was used to hearing on the daily:

"Write that down, eh?"

She did.

As the attentive clerical business-*gal* did so, scratching away in the background the details of which they had just captured regarding their person of interest for what could only have been an active inquiry, his focus lowered back down onto a manila folder that lay open in his grasp.

It was a confidential uniform dossier, complete with paperclipped photograph of the target:

Jack Churchill.

1942, February
The Clipper
Dumbarton, Scotland

Churchill made Scotland right on dusk.

He had left London before the majority of the Saturday traffic, departing Oldham at approximately 1400-hours, where he took the northerly route via *Burnley* rather than *Preston* and *Lancaster*, through *Kendal, Carlisle,* through to Glasgow, finally reaching Dumbarton a little after 1800-hours.

His borrowed military-issue green Harley-Davidson 42WLA motorcycle coasted into the quiet small town off the main strip known as *Glasgow Road,* sending thundering reverberations against the solid sandstone buildings situated on either side of *Hill Street.* He did a lot more than what the speed limit permitted.

Clad in a straight khaki military suit and green beret, the pensive sunset rider upon the Harley felt he was a regular of the local populace, and this arrival felt more like a homecoming than a visit.

Tall gas-powered street sconce lanterns of the municipality coincidentally illuminated as he entered town, almost as if he were traversing landing lights or limelights at a theatre.

The streets were busy with foot traffic—even busier than the typical Saturday night life. There were countless couples out celebrating Valentine's Day, making the most of the occasion during these war times and warming the cool night with activity.

Passing down the city street, Churchill watched the partners pair.

He found the sight relatable: a squad of young lads, likely from the old Inveraray base (Jack's old stomping grounds). Dressed in their khaki greens; boots polished, hair greased, and foreheads oily from the stress and social pressures of finding young, attractive last-minute companions for the universal night of love. Out on the prowl, they were hunting to find equally as desperate lasses. The yin to that yang were the clusters of female parties also out and about. Full flocks of done-up ladettes, roving as members of the opposite sex, just as thirsty, raring, and shameless.

The desperation and vulnerability this year was amusing.

Forming his winning smile as he spied the various groups out on the town, in search of alcoholic beverages, loud music, and good times in the form of a tryst, Jack almost drove his motorcycle into a wall on several occasions after rubbernecking at the figures of some of the good sorts as he cruised past. Was he was just getting old? The fashions seemed to be getting more and more risqué and revealing as the years went on. Outfits for ladies were lower cut, showing a distracting amount of leg. Dress cuts were smaller, showing more shoulder and skin of the neckline. Tighter, too, leaving little to the imagination. Then there was the hair and makeup. Some of these broads were like walking primped pin-ups the way they were dolled up and dazzling.

Churchill finally coasted his bike into a parking spot outside where he was due to meet his beloved for a romantic dinner: a local dine-in known as *The Clipper.* This was a successful seafood restaurant located directly across the street from the *St. Augustine's Scottish Episcopal Church*—the hallowed grounds where he and Rosamund Denny had tied the knot. The restaurant held much more sentimental value than just its location; it was also one of the first places Jack had taken Rosamund on a date back when he had been stationed at the Combined Training Centre in Inveraray, located along the remote shores of the *Loch Fyne* on the outskirts of Dumbarton.

With his wife soon to be linked on his arm, they were bound for a romantic night out on the town, full of fine foods and rich desserts, reminiscences, laughs, and an eventual promise of intimacy once back to their cozy two-bedroom cottage. Their lodging wasn't much, but it was home. Something quaint, hospitable, affordable on a soldier's wage during a time of rationing, and located just around the corner from Rosamund's hospital where she shifted as a nurse. They had eventual plans to move into a larger residence in the direction of Jack's hometown of *Deddington.* This was conditional to Churchill's service status and, of course, the projection of the world war.

Churchill had a lot on his mind the entire way from London, replaying in his mind over and over his conversation with his captive archenemy Feind at Camp 2. Although nothing had come of the vengeful POW's half-empty threat about exposing some of his closeted grey past to the authorities, Jack could not help but still be hung up on the fact that he knew about it at all.

Now that he was more sure than ever that Feind knew nothing more about Switzerland than the fact of its existence in history, it was deducible that it may have also been the extent of its pursuit by anybody at the PWIS. Henceforth why he hadn't heard of or from anybody at Whitehall who might be investigating any of the allegations.

Upon coming to this conclusion, relief should have flooded him with dopamine. However, something was lingering amidst the levels of his intuition, informing him that this was yet to be over ... but right now, it was time to switch that all off.

Running fashionably late, Churchill parked and dismounted. He straightened his suit and tugged down his sleeves whilst he hurried, rounding the darkness of the poorly lit carpark, entering the warm glow of the streetlamp-lit exterior at the front of the busy establishment ...

What he laid his eyes upon took his breath away.

... and with it, all his haunting troubles.

Rosamund Churchill.

His wife was waiting for him out front.

Time slowed in that moment for him.

December through to February were generally the coldest months in Scotland, however, this year had not followed the typical temperature tropes. The weather was warmer later at night, and this evening's fashion reflected that with the cut of skirts a lot shorter than usual, less of the optional stockings, and jackets worn over colourful sleeveless cocktail dresses. Rosamund's vibrant attire was no different. She had picked up something new for tonight, a type of figure-flattering surplice bodice dark velvet cocktail dress, with coordinating elbow-length gloves. The skirt was full length and wavy, which caused the material to slink intricately beneath the lights.

The perfect lighting of the setting sunlight's cast shadow and the warm glow of a streetlamp lit Ros up like a beacon for Jack in that dress.

She turned heads in all the right ways.

She had her dark hair in fresh, wavy curls ...

Her lips applied in ruby red ...

Winged eyeliner done just the way Jack liked it upon her pale features, how it best extenuated her big, sky-blue eyes ...

Rosamund called for him like a siren.

He was a ship at sea prior to this moment, and she stood out like a lighthouse in the night. A true north upon his confused compass. A course corrected.

Excited upon seeing him, she waved from afar, smile beaming as she stood before the busy restaurant. There was a bowtie-wearing door greeter and wait staff by the entrance, directing customers to their booked seats. She simmered down her demeanour for his arrival, acting coy with a relative callback:

"You made it, soldier?"

"Yes, ma'am," Churchill replied with an exultant grin held firm below his pencil-thin moustache as he then swiftly came in sharply to scoop her in an excited embrace, collecting her petite physique beneath his arms and hoisting her high, causing a scene for onlookers. Always the show-off, Jack was lucky to have found such a type of lass who was not easily embarrassed in public.

He placed her down after a smooch and took a step aback, holding out her hands to the sides.

Taking the sight of her in and causing her to blush further, he exhaled a compliment. His smile beamed. "Wow."

Once their affectionate salutations were finished, Jack led a blushing Rosamund inside the lit establishment and they were seated by pleasant wait staff. Reminiscent of their first date at The Clipper, he ordered her a Cuban Daiquiri and himself a whiskey neat. They were both eager to order the house crab, which they remembered from their previous visit to have been quite exquisite for the price, and it was. During a heavily rationed era regarding food menus, prepared seafood of such high calibre was a rarity—and not cheap.

For dessert, Rosamund enjoyed a slice of dark mud cake with cream and berries which she shared with her husband. As always, Churchill did not order dessert himself but rather enjoyed an espresso.

The whole night, Jack hid well his heavily bogged down mindset.

Although she could probably tell, this wasn't the time or place to speak his mind, nor was his wife the person to speak this problem to, especially regarding the questionable secrecy of some of the context. And so, Churchill hid his mental dilemma, flogging the obviousness off as him being tired from the trip from London, which was perfectly viable.

For what he lacked in mental capability over dinner, Jack well and truly made up for with post-dining affection, which he alluded to once he gained his second wind from the caffeine in his coffee. Rather than get tired, he got horny. He would joke to himself: *was a man ever actually not horny?*

On the way there, Rosamund had gained a lift from a taxi to Glasgow Road where she had met Jack. On the way back, for the first time in a long time, they shared a ride upon the motorcycle, which Ros always found surprisingly thrilling though only in short doses.

By the time the two lovebirds reached their cottage home in Dumbarton, the heat of passion was on. The two sensually locked lips from the moment they dismounted the bike, barely able to get through the front door without crashing against it and rolling against walls, shedding elements of clothing whilst tenderly caressing each other's bodies. Rosamund's handbag was tossed inside, her heels were flicked off her feet in their small foyer, and the door was slammed shut for privacy. Jack's own shoes were kicked off, his day bag dropped, and the door keys rattled as they were cast across a side table doily, collapsing a small picture frame.

Their only interruption was that born of their household love, *Toto*, their moggy, who was starved not only for attention, but for dinner of his own. This was a love more for Ros than it were to Jack—especially now since the feline was about to interrupt their passion.

Toto meowed loudly when he became nudged by their trundling stance, and Rosamund immediately saw to him, collecting him from the ground for an apology by way of a pat and a cuddle.

Churchill took the instance to properly lock the door and use the facilities to refresh, whilst Rosamund caught a breath from their romantic passion and grabbed a can of ration pet food from under the sink.

The mild interruption of married life need not matter.

He watched her for a moment; her figure-flattering surplice bodice dress slipping revealingly from her shoulder, her hair coming undone, whilst she bent over in a well-hiked shirt in order to perform the mundane task at hand.

Jack's head tilted, taking in the view.

It was the most resplendent and sexy thing he had ever laid eyes on.

She caught his lingering stare and beamed. "What?"

"I'm going to go slip into something more comfortable," he denoted half-humorously, casting Ros a glimmer of his raised brow, as if the connotations weren't obvious enough.

She faced him, still a little tipsy and unbalanced.

With a playful smile she giggled. "I'll see you upstairs. Hopefully you don't put on too much?"

Churchill took to the stairs, still stripping off his layers and setting his suit jacket neatly upon the railing on the second storey. Once up, he unbuttoned his cufflinks whilst flipping the light for the small bathroom.

He stepped in and closed the door, fully untucking his khaki shirt and lifting the seat before draining the main vein. Over his shoulder, he observed his reflection in the mirror positioned above the sink. His hair was a mess from the ride and from being pinned beneath his beret—and probably from Ros running her fingers through it just now. It was a particular turn-on of hers.

Whilst maintaining his golden stream with one hand, Jack brushed his hair with the other. In a moment he would tidy himself and wash his armpits and nether region—

Abruptly, *he jumped! Startled!*

Right in that moment, causing his stream to coat the seat from the severity of his tense muscled flinch, Churchill caught a glimpse of the figure of a tall man from behind the shower curtain in the background of the bathroom. The curtain was thrust aside, presenting the forever well-dressed MacLeòid in his glengarry cap with pom-pom.

"*Sorry, laddie ...*" the Highland haunt apologized from the bathtub.

"Bloody Hell," Churchill muttered, his heart beating a mile a minute. He recovered his urination accuracy, maintaining his flow. When he responded, Jack hissed in a whisper to protect the surreptitiousness of his invisible friend and their ongoing secluded conversations. "Why? Every time? It's always when I'm taking a slash?!"

"*Aye noe, sorry.*"

Jack focused, finished, and flushed.

He grabbed some tissue from the roll and cleaned his spill before washing his hands. Over his shoulder in the mirror's reflection, MacLeòid finished dismounting the bathtub and stepped down behind him on the laid bathmat over tiles. It was mighty tight in that bathroom right now, even causing Churchill to lean back when he positioned himself at his side.

"Do you mind?" he asked abruptly after unbuttoning his shirt and peeling it off. He grabbed a towel and balled it, about to dampen it to cleanse areas of his skin for freshness.

"*Oh*," the Scottish ghost was made aware of his overstepping intrusion, and he took a big pace back. "*Where's tha missus?*" he asked, making obvious small talk.

"She's downstairs, feeding the pussy," Jack responded irately. "What do you want?" Churchill followed up as he cleaned his armpits and sternum. Then he dropped his dacks and would do the same for his genitals, much to MacLeòid's noticeable discomposure.

MacLeòid had to remember why he was here. "*I thought that maybe yoo'd wanna talk 'bout yoor dilemma?*"

"*Right now?!*" Jack hissed with his cock and balls in his hand, cleansing them thusly. He waved the wet towel in MacLeòid's face, which the ghost stuck his nose up at in disgust. Needless to say, that over the years, he had interrupted Jack doing a lot worse. "Sir, I'm a bit ... *busy!*"

Churchill gestured to not only his well-groomed and now cleaned stahlhelm of funk, but that this *cockblocking Casper* would soon be also interrupting him getting down and dirty with his wife at any minute. She was probably already waiting in the next room.

"*Aye, but I could sense dere be somethin' on yoor mind, laddie ...*" he watched on for a moment, becoming distracted by an unavoidable observation. "*Wha? Since when do yoo shave ye bollocks, mah boy?*"

"It's called *manscaping*," Churchill defended.

"*Man-scaping, eh?*"

"Like *landscaping*, only, it's your twig and two berries."

"*Aye.*"

After the brief digression, MacLeòid's expression loosened and his attention sought Jack's in the reflection of the bathroom mirror, where he straightened his pom-pom bonnet and fixed his grey eyebrow hairs.

"*Soe, den ... wat 'bout Feind?*"

Although he was busy and his mind mostly on other things, Churchill's ears pricked at the aforementioned circumstance—at the name, mostly. It was true that his considerations had not drifted far from that topic.

MacLeòid implored caringly. "*C'mon, laddie. Talk ta meh?*"

Churchill's maintenance ability slowed and then stopped all together.

His eyeline climbed, facing his friend in the reflection of the bathroom wall mirror. "Well ... it's just *that*, isn't it," he began to explain his preoccupied mind, keeping a low tone. "Feind gave them a lot of useful information recently, and that intelligence all checked out. It was all confirmed by our boys at Whitehall, even Tom ..."

MacLeòid nodded attentively, listening.

"*Und whats wrong wif dat?*" MacLeòid probed. "*Man's er cornered rat, Jackie. He probably thenks et's gonna git 'im special privileges er somethin'. Und awl his supposed info on yoo, 'bout the trainin', 'bout Switzerland, et obviously didn't check owt. Et wasn't credible.*"

"No, I know," Jack dropped his leg back down after tending to his gooch region. He was completely naked in front of this fellow, and fine with it. It was humorous.

"*Yoo're a big fish noe, Jackie. Yoo needn't worry.*"

Churchill justified his concerns. "At your highest moment ... that's when the Devil comes for you."

"*But et'll take moar than some strung-out Hun talkin' shite to convict yoo ta da masses. Especially dem lads high up en ol' Whitehall. Dey may be political sharks en suits but et doesn't meen dey're gonna hunt at tha first sign ov hearing dat dere's blood en tha water.*"

"But that's just it ..." Jack allured. "What if he just hasn't talked to them about it yet ..."

"*Mebee no wun cares?*"

Jack frowned, contemplating Feind's potential methods. "He's playing the credibility card ... he's drip-fed the brass intel; built himself up to be a reliable source."

"*Ya fink he's ratted on his own brethren ta knock ya down a peg? I'd be flattered, laddie.*"

"Well, that's the thing. Obviously, you save the punchline for the end ... where it does the most damage ... a fatal blow ..." Churchill's attention dwindled for a moment whilst he theoreticized further.

MacLeòid's focus froze. His stare lingered.

"I mean, think about it, he wasn't trustworthy before. Now he is, because he's given them names, ranks, locations, operational histories ... the whole nine yards ..."

"*He's er Nazi, laddie. Trus'me, he schtill ain't trustworthy now.*"

"*Touché.* But now that all his other intelligence has been well received, this ace up his sleeve is an ace in the hole he needs to get in the spotlight—"

"*Yoo fink he'll come up aces?*"

Churchill torqued his neck. "Like he said, I think he'll play the hand he's been dealt—"

"*Jack?*" Rosamund's voice called through the door from the bedroom. It had been a while since he had withdrawn into the washroom. She was rightfully suspicious of the longevity of his absence—he wasn't exactly lacking, but there wasn't *that* much dick to clean.

"Be right out, dear!" Churchill replied before facing MacLeòid and noticing the expression on his face. He was starting to pick up what Jack was putting down, and his claim was feasible. Feind wasn't a dumb git. He knew how delicately to pull on the political threads.

Churchill returned his attention one last time to his invisible pal, leaving him with one last *what if* that was crippling him mentally. "I think nothing has come of his threats because he hasn't fully issued them yet. And *that* is what's haunting me ... even more than you, *sir.*"

MacLeòid seemed almost offended. *"I'll hav'ta trie harder, den, eh?"*

"Now, if you'd excuse me ..." Churchill excused as he shuffled before MacLeòid in the tight bathroom space between the sink, the wall, and the bathtub, and he reached out for the door. "It's *my turn* to feed the pussy."

Admiring that innuendo, Colonel MacLeòid formed a big, cheeky grin that broke the mould of the mood Jack often put him in.

He let him pass with a deserved pat on the back.

"Aye, laddie."

Buck naked, Churchill dragged open the slide door, revealing a darkened bedroom of which the bathroom acted as a makeshift en suite. The light from the washroom illuminated his profile like an *Auguste Edouart* piece.

In the dimly lit room, the warm glow from a nightstand lamp set the mood. Rosamund was relaxed on the bed, sprawled on the doona cover, still clothed in her dark velvet cocktail dress, now loosened. It had become much more revealingly disorganized, exposing her bare legs, where she had stripped herself of her stockings whilst awaiting her man. The shoulder straps to her dress had fallen down her arms, showing the skin of her chest and barely able to support the fluid bust of her contained cleavage.

"You made it, soldier?" she said playfully, letting her hair down.

Confident with his athletic physique, Churchill paused for a moment before her, putting on a show whilst fully exposed. He was a silhouette of a sculpted contemporary gladiator against the bright bathroom light in all his full-frontal glory—and it was all for her. Fluids flowing and blood pumping, Jack tried not to instantly chub-up, but the sight of her along with the promise of warm tenderness to come was all that now played on his mind, and the excitement of sex was inflating his desire by the inch.

Rosamund clearly liked what she saw, wriggling impatiently within her pose on the bed with a grin and veering eyeline, ready to receive her man in every which way she could. Her eyes wandered up and down—mostly down— and she instinctively—lustfully—licked her lips, longing for him to come closer.

Libido surging more so now than ever, that licentiousness cracked in the comfort of their relationship. Rosamund's contagious smile preserved upon her happy face, and she was positively brimming with exhilaration and carnal excitement.

"Always, ma'am." Churchill finally flicked off the light behind him and casually stepped forth into the seclusion and comfort of their bedroom, where Ros revealed one more surprise for her husband as he came close. She hiked the skirt of the dress further and separated her legs for him, showing how she had already removed more than just the stockings in his absence.

She maintained her cheeky and playful beam while Jack arrived standing over her with a member he could no longer tame with thoughts of grandmas and baseball. He swooned in close above her, and although he was appreciative of her sensual offering, he preferred to kiss her tenderly on the lips for now, merely tantalizing her with his caressing touch down below.

Lips locked and eyes closed, her tiny hands grappled with him gently, working with fluid motion as the heaviness of their breathing began to increase due to his precious contact on her—in her. The arrangement of her two hands strangely reminded him of a neutral grip of a golf club, a technique he mastered recently on the greens near *Ardteatle* last year when he had gone with some of the base lads—a strange thought to have at such a time, but since it was his nine-iron meat club being wielded for tee-off, he was okay with it.

Out of sight down below, his fingers indubiously knew their way around her region. They, at first, traced the smoothness of her inner thigh, teasingly climbing upwards and gravitating the tender padding outlying her most pleasurable palace.

The two sunk further backward onto the soft doona of the bed, engaged in the deep comfort of an affable embrace.

Rosamund's fingers ran feverishly through his blonde hair as they kissed with a steamy passion. Before long, Jack's wet lips abruptly broke free from their French embrace upon hers, only to now eventuate southerly, engorging her with his tongue, her legs spreading further open for him. Still partially clothed, she was now relaxed and leaking exquisitely from her undone top whilst on her back.

It had been a long while since she had experienced his touch.

Waves of heated pleasure overcame her very quickly.

Her cheeks warmed to a shade of roses and her heartrate intensified, causing her to throe uncontrollably. Before long, Jack resurfaced over her to kiss passionately some more.

Meanwhile, with little guidance, he easily found his way inside her.

They connected passionately at the lips as well as the hips, conjoining in a familiar gyrating rhythm. A cadence formed between the two that carried on into the night as love was made.

1942, February
Kelburn Castle
Largs, Scotland

As scheduled, Churchill returned to his lodgings at the Kelburn Castle ahead of what would be a busy Monday morning. He desired to be present for mail call this week, as it was highly likely he would be receiving his official letter of authority confirming his appointment as Commanding Officer for No.2 Commando. The post usually arrived at 0800-hours, and for somebody who was up from dawn, it couldn't come quick enough.

Racing the sunrise, Jack awoke before the birds.

By eight a.m., he had already completed his morning run, had his eggs, toast, and coffee, and had subsequently decided to sharpen his archery skills out the back of the castle grounds. This was near the same location where the unfortunate explosive mishap had occurred last September; as tasked by the Lord of the grounds, a goal of Commando in his absence had been to eliminate the pesky, unkillable tree stump by *unconventional* means ...

So, they got day drunk and bombed the bastard thing!

This was intended to happen without harming a nearby plantation of saplings, where the estate grounds had a collection of unusual and special trees and gardens; an exotic plant collection that was of high horticultural value. Needless to say, the tactical removal did not go to plan when an overuse of TNT had resulted in numerous instances of structural damage to the castle as well as turning those prize-winning flowers into very expensive mulch.

In the distance from the castle and into the luscious surrounding greenery, the noticeable colour rings of white, black, blue, red, and yellow circles painted upon a perpendicular-placed canvas were visible. The sun was out this morning, illuminating the greenery through the thick canopies above, belonging to the many trees of the grove.

These canvases were situated archery targets which Jack had positioned prior to assuming a firing position. He now prepared to strike an archer's pose; standing side-on and steadying his breathing with his trusty takedown longbow by his side and in his left hand.

He had been equipped with this bow ever since his original longbow was destroyed during the final hours of the Dunkirk Evacuation in 1940. This piece, also made of yew, was slightly more modern as far as medieval weaponry was concerned, and more compact. The stick-and-string contraption was assembled from two halves, screwed together in the middle handle piece. Once compiled, the assembled unit was just as sturdy as any archer's armament.

This morning, Churchill was attired in his uniform; a khaki brown battledress, complete with his green beret worn aslant, and his trusty brown leather cylindrical arrow quiver strapped firm across his chest for shoulder-access to his feather-tailed ammunition. The embossing of *'MD-1, 1939'* was present at the rim of the custom magnetically-bookended quiver and housed his bodkin-tipped arrows.

After a moment, Churchill commenced this archery exercise.

His sterling stare focused on the target, over sixty metres away ...

His right hand raised out by his head, and he drew the feathery end of an arrow from his shoulder quiver, quickly laying the weightless projectile across the fistmele distance above his bow handle. Nocking the bowstring, he then raised the bow outstretched whilst, with the other hand, craning the one-hundred-pound strain of the longbow yield in what was referred to as an anchor point.

He held aim.

He fired.

The loosed arrow whistled through the air, jousted with precision, where it struck the target board with an impactful *thwump!*

Low outer ring ...

Not great, not terrible.

Lowering his stance and exhaling, Churchill frowned whilst he focused on the distant target. It wasn't his best work—but far from being his worst.

It was funny how even the slightest ounce of stress lingering on an athlete's mind can sway results. Forcing the underlining stress of the situation to the back of his mind, Churchill drew another arrow and fired, striking a bullseye in the dead centre.

He exhaled with his winning smile.

That was more like it.

At an archer's pace, Churchill primed another arrow from his shoulder quiver and took aim, drawing the bowstring to the creaking anchor point where he rested his breathing and closed one eye, taking aim once ...

"*Bet ya ten shillings he can't do that again ...*" the voice of an old friend said from his six, making him smirk. Churchill's mouth curled whilst he tensed his draw, remaining focused. He knew precisely who the owner of that remark was, and he was keen to attend to their presence as soon as it took those odds.

Sch-TOFF!

The arrow currently in the bullseye split down the middle as the new bodkin-tipped arrow asserted itself through the middle, carving the wood in two strips and spitting splinters.

The presence of others in the castle gardens became apparent to Churchill, flanking him on either side and bringing with them an ample amount of peer pressure to his target practice.

Veteran Commando *Lieutenant Arthur Komrower* was the man who had waged the bet, and who now held a blank stare upon his mug. "Bullshit," he stated aloud, dumfounded that Churchill had just done that Robin Hood-bollocks so willy-nilly.

The other commandos in the crowd in tow with him chuckled at his misfortune at doubting Mad Jack's archery abilities. He, of all people, should have probably known better.

Returned to Commando Castle only recently from his extended medical visits, Komrower was wrapped in long leg and long sleeve grey sweats rather than uniform. Although the healing of his war wounds had made great progress, it would be a while longer before he was training with the lads in the field again. Fresh salmon pink scarring on Komrower's neck and face was visible following the horrific burns he had sustained during their last big commando raid, when a friendly phosphorus shelling had been dropped too close to their shoreline of the Vågsøy Island landings. Severe burns ran the whole way down his side and leg, impacting his mobility. He had been on the mend since the 1st of February, and still required a cane to walk steadily as seen now beneath his weight.

He had finally been let out of treatment and was scheduled to return to No.3 for active duty within the next few weeks. His appearance back on campus was premature, but he probably missed his brothers and was always welcome on base.

A testament to this commando's heroism was that even after he had received his burn injuries, Komrower had still fought the fight that fateful morning, albeit at a hobble. The entire raid, he remained near the frontline, including being present during the final push at the heavily fortified *Ulvesund Hotel:* the enemy's last remaining stronghold and the final domino to fall during Operation Archery.

In Komrower's company, which all originated from the castle, were a few others of Mad Jack's regular Merry Men of No.3 Commando. A few of them were carrying mugs of steaming joe from breakfast.

Lowering his bow, Churchill approached Komrower and the others as they converged on his training session on the castle greens beneath a sunlit morning. They were all mostly dressed in their gear ahead of today's training at the Largs base.

With him was Young, MacWilly, and Knocker White—the latter of which was carrying a closed letter from mail call.

"That'll be ten shillings," Churchill said cockily.

The surrounding men hazed him, though Komrower shook his head. "We didn't shake on it!"

Churchill cracked a smile and took his hand in firm embrace—albeit one that was still respectfully gentle due to his injuries.

Drawing no immediate attention to the fact White was carrying his future, Churchill refrained with all his might. Rather, he responded to his visiting friend who he had not seen for a while, and in typical satirical fashion.

"It's good to see you, Arty," and he nodded to the others. "Lads."

"You, too, Jack," Komrower replied genuinely.

After the gleeful reception, Churchill's gaze honed in on the mail, and Knocker White stepped forwards with the envelope, presenting it forth like a dutiful ring bearer. These few Merry Men were amongst the closest to Mad Jack, and they were all up to date on what the letter inside the packet contained ...

They were both saddened by the forthcoming news of their commanding officer's transfer into another unit as well as proud of his promotion. It was the natural order of things when soldiers excelled, they progressed throughout the hierarchy. This often meant leaving bonds behind—as well as forming firm new acquaintances. It was a constant cycle of comradery.

Churchill tore open the sealed letter marked *'strictly confidential'*, quick to unfold the paper.

Right as Jack's steel stare grazed across the ink typing rows, one of the words in the opening paragraph distracted his immediate attention, snagging his brain's momentum upon reading the rest of the words compiling the body of the text—it said: *'unfortunately'*. Without him even reading another word, it already set the disappointing tone for the unveiling, following quickly by an overwhelming sense of confusion.

They all watched Churchill's delayed facial reaction ...

They saw his eyebrows flinch, then slowly form a frown ...

They observed his expression unfold in the complete opposite way to what they had been expecting given the *sure thing* of this contained preferment.

Young was nearly as confused as Churchill was with this reversal of expectations. "Well, what the heck does it say ...?"

Churchill didn't respond.

He didn't read it either. Couldn't.

Instead, he just fell flat.

"Jack?" Komrower questioned beneath a quizzical glower, stepping around by his side and examining the open document full of typed print. Jack allowed him to possess it, and to address the others on his behalf as he appeared to be absent words.

Both MacWilly and Knocker White exchanged a glance.

They knew Jack Churchill pretty well after all these years of service and they had rarely seen him disappointed or upset, but this was definitely a combination of both of those emotions.

He didn't get the battalion.

In his native Scottish brogue, Sergeant MacWilliam murmured a consolation to his pal. "Good thing we didn't bring that bottle of brekkie champers ..."

Their view fell onto Churchill as his eyeline traced off into the distance.

His pupils defocused, falling deep in thought as a wave of melancholy befell them all like the shadow of an arriving storm cloud.

Bad news aside, it wasn't entirely the shock of the failed promotion that had stumped Churchill the hardest ... it was the *other* part.

Granted access to the content, Komrower read aloud:

" *'Lieutenant-Colonel John Malcolm Thorpe Fleming Churchill, unfortunately we regret to inform you that your expression of interest and application for a command role for the newly recognized No.2 Commando, 1st Special Service Brigade, British Army, has unfortunately been rejected'* ... blah, blah, blah, yada, yada, yada ... *'due to an active inquiry'* ..." Komrower looked up, puzzled. "A fucking what?"

Young stepped in and confiscated the letter, unsure Komrower was reading it right—surely, he wasn't. "What *active inquiry?*"

Attention shifted from off Komrower and onto Churchill, who now stood idle and with his hand on his hip, the other still holding his longbow, a device as tightly strung as he had just become.

In light of the rejection letter, he only *appeared* to be absent words.

In actuality, he was deeply contemplating his next move regarding his defence of the investigation and where this might all lead.

After an extended moment of consideration, his beret-clad head lifted, focusing upon the canvas board down range—more specifically at the arrows he had just launched into the target, straight and true. They very well may have been the last good shots he would shoot for a while, however there was one particular *human* target he could have probably landed a bullseye if given the chance ...

Beneath his breath, he murmured rhetorically:

"Feind ... what have you started?"

2 ♣   2 ♣

Enemies Closer

Two weeks prior ...

1942, January
Glenn Mill (Camp 2)
Oldham, Lancashire

Up until now, German prisoner of war Friedrich Feind was shown about as much love as any of the other POWs housed at and within the Glenn Mill—so, none.

Under the persuasion of his rough prison guard escorts, he was planted into a chair in the middle of the claustrophobic concrete cell of the stone-cold interrogation room. Pleasantries remaining non-existent, his legs became scootched beneath the tabletop of the masonry-anchored table and his hands shackled via an affixed bar like a horse on a hitching rail. The room was ominously dark, alit only by a singular dull bulb hanging from a cable in the ceiling that swayed slightly after it had become knocked in the kafuffle of movement.

Captured along with the enemy forces of the *Wehrmacht 181st Infantry Division* during the recent Måløy Raid, the *SS Gebirgsjäger* Hauptsturmführer had so far been extraordinarily forthcoming with the divulgence of intelligence. The sharing of such juicy information with various British intelligence communities had caused him to become a well-tapped source by those thirsty for intel within the PWIS. Although upgrades to his enclosure and increases to his portions had been promised with every disclosure of data, the quality of his imprisonment amenities appeared to still be that of any other inmate. Nonetheless, improvements to his incarceration were not his endgame. Unbeknownst to all, an agenda was afoot, and this stage was merely the initial moving part to a much larger and more convoluted culmination.

It wasn't the first time Feind had stared at these four cold walls of the chamber during his stay at Camp 2. He appeared unphased upon his admission to the cell, as well as to the conduct of his handling. He may have been considered a snitch, but he was not naïve. The Brits were using him, and he knew it ... perhaps, even, he was allowing it.

The escorting prison guard made double sure his handcuffs were chained tightly to the welded handlebar in the centre of the table before finally departing, leaving Feind alone in the echoic room. The baggy-eyed German prisoner took a moment to crack his stiff neck and glance upon himself in a rusty two-way mirror that lined one of the adjacent brick walls. There forever lingered a paradoxical presence behind that mercury portal as to who could have been monitoring; observing; recording, but this time, his consideration appeared to be of a harrowing egotistical concern. In the silence, Feind tipped his face in the light, observing his own profile. There were no mirrors in the barracks or around the camp, therefore it was rare to ever take in a reflection of one's appearance anywhere but here ... and he was taken aback at how much he had changed. He barely recognized himself under these torturous circumstances.

His flat face seemed to droop on his silent survey.

A month ago, he had been a bold, fearless soldier within the SS.

Today, he was a shadow of his former self ... and a traitor.

His gaze lost focus as he folded into himself, recalling his own treachery whilst in captivity. He assured himself again that he had a retributive strategy in the works, hence the revealing of certain *selective* confidential information was a necessary expense—albeit his objective was one born of a personal vendetta against a singular man, rather than a nation of men. A major part of his masterplan was betraying his homeland and, for that deceit, he felt an immeasurable guilt for his own countrymen who he had sacrificed by correspondence to achieve that result.

The heavy steel door on the other side of the room opened inwards and another armed guard allowed the entry of two fresh faces undoubtedly belonging within the ranks of the British Intelligence sector.

A solid, towering man stepped in first, removing his brim hat.

He was *glatt rasiert* as it were in Deutsche—a *clean shaven* type. He was dressed in a wool suit that matched his fedora, and upon entry into the room he immediately made stern eye contact with the censured culprit in the centre. He gave a polite nod of respect prior to floating his carried briefcase onto the desk whilst he aligned one of the two seats opposing Feind.

Behind the bureaucratic gent was a bureaucratic lass.

The gender of his cohort surprised Feind. Although the German Militaries were not ostentatiously opposed to placing women in leadership roles throughout the war machine, this component was far less likely to occur in the western world. A known fact for the era.

The female was a shoulder-length brunette with nominal composition applied to accentuate her beauty. A businesswoman type, she was dressed in a dark wool utility skirt suit and carrying a bag case of her own.

"Hallo," Feind welcomed, more perky now that she had entered the room. Prior to her entrance, the likelihood of him playing his typical hard-to-get self for the brass was high. Becoming goosestepped by her presence, this former womanizing playboy Nazi found himself slightly spellbound. He surveyed her up and down as she entered like a fresh piece of meat whilst she stood beside her offsider. She made eye contact with this inmate—a mild hesitation that hinted at a lack of confidence; an apprehension that Feind immediately detected and noted to exploit if need be.

"Good morning, Hauptsturmführer Feind," the man gestured foremost, allowing for his partner to become seated first before drawing out his own chair opposite the captive. They became seated contentedly across from Feind, adjusting the timber chairs on the course concrete floor.

Feind gawked at them both for an elongated moment.

"I uzually deal wiv Herr Lynch," he informed, stating the obviousness that these two bureaucrats supposedly from the intelligence sector weren't his usual MI19 contact from the PWIS.

"We realize that ..." the man said straightforwardly, cutting to the chase. His stare was constantly intense, framed by high arched eyebrows. "My name is *Jethro McNaughton,* and this is *Ms Viviane Garland.* We are constables from a devised section of the *Special Investigation Branch* within the *Criminal Investigation Department.* We understand you recently attempted to lodge potentially incriminating information about an Englishman—a soldier, and a rather high-ranking one at that—by the name of Jack Churchill. And that those claims were rejected by the British Army Intelligence."

Feind's attention progressively piqued.

His firm brow dropped, and he straightened his posture.

"Jah."

McNaughton exchanged a glance with Garland. "Well, we've come to entertain the fact that you may also have information on another man who was present during the same classified events you alluded to in your accusations against Churchill; events occurring in Switzerland in 1939. A man by the name of Orde Wingate."

Feind shook his head, losing interest at the first signs of the presence of someone else's ulterior motive.

He didn't know Wingate. He wanted Churchill.

"Nein. Churchill iz zee English-man you want," he sold confidently. Non-negotiable and stalwart. "He iz guilty of treason."

"Possibly ..." with an unspoken confidence, McNaughton spun his briefcase and popped the latches, retrieving various clumps of investigative materials and evidence. "But I can assure you, my chum is *more* guilty."

Amidst the batches of paper were photographs of this British Army officer known as Orde Wingate. After rifling through the papers, McNaughton offered a black and white photograph to Feind across the tabletop along with identification of the man in question's moniker.

"Wingate goes by the codename *the Otter*. He is a slippery snake, often conducting shady black-ops deals in the grey areas of warfare—amongst other off-books atrocities such as numerous a-typical *war crimes*. I want *him*."

After discerning the seriousness in McNaughton's gaze, Feind lowered his focus on the print and papers. Orde Wingate seemed to be just another tense-jaw looking westerner, with gelled dark hair and an all too unsettling serious stare. In the dinner jacket he was dressed up in in the photograph, he looked like the stereotypical spy-type stylized in infiltration novel works.

Feind denied and shook his head discounting the focal target. "Nein. Churchill is zee one zat you vant. He waz trained by a Nazi named *Ernst-Günther Baade*, und I can prove it."

Mind numb to this German gibberish, McNaughton sunk into his backrest. From his inner breast pocket, he retrieved a cardboard dispenser and gave it a shake, producing a fresh toothpick. He then fixed the piece between his teeth and took a moment to seemingly relish the sensation as though it calmed him.

After an extended moment of silence, Garland threw him a sideways glance. This stalling had derailed their inquest, and it annoyed her, too.

McNaughton finally growled a response, uttering it stern and finite.

"I have no interest in *Churchill*. I want *Wingate*."

Back on track, Garland's stern view slowly returned to Feind from McNaughton. They apparently held an agenda of their own concerning Wingate, and therefore no curiosity in any coinciding vendetta of Feind's regarding Jack Churchill.

Feind squirmed mentally in his seat.

He finally had a fish on his baited hook regarding the Switzerland ordeal of which, to some extent, he had become uniquely privy, and was the fabric holding his agenda with Churchill and an elite German swordsman soldier known as Baade.

After a tense pause, McNaughton abruptly shuffled his seated stance to standing whilst gathering his things. He snatched the picture from Feind's cuffed mittens. "We're done here."

"Nein," Feind pleaded, with an obvious grasp at straws. "*The Otter*," he muttered about himself, seeming to suddenly recall the name amongst his mental allegations regarding Switzerland. "Zee name *iz* familiar, jah."

Although unconvinced, McNaughton slowly sunk back down with his palms on the tabletop. He held a more aggressive glare at Feind, attentively lurching forwards whilst staring deeply into the German's dirty, duelling-scarred mug.

His concentrated look made Feind slightly uneasy.

It was obvious McNaughton was trying to read him, to see how truthful his new claim was. It wouldn't normally work on a man like Feind, unbeknownst to this competitor, this level of perception was practically a well-practised superpower to this investigator. This former *Metropolitan Police* detective had perfected the skill long ago.

McNaughton's firm gaze beamed, bouncing back and forth like laterally shuffling ping-pong, scanning Feind's pupils for microscopic tells.

In those few seconds, he keenly observed his mannerisms, his quirks, his tells. He learned a million truths about the man in but a moment's passing. After a stretch, he huffed and issued simply: "Poppycock."

And with that, McNaughton was followed by Garland. In a noisy shuffle, the two flounced and became upstanding, indicating their intent to vacate. They were done and Feind's time was up.

"No, vait!" Feind besought desperately; nonetheless, the investigators disregarded his plea. They continued on their way out, collecting their briefcases and even reaching the door before something in Feind's blabber hooked them.

"Jack Churchill, he iz a Commando in the British Army! He knowz your man, of thiz I am zure! They zerved together en zee Schweiz! Constable, they know each other, ov zis I am zure!"

"I'm not interested in snake oil, chap," McNaughton gathered, cutting to the chase. "I want the snake!"

"*Dummkopf!*" Feind exclaimed, slamming the table with his cuffed fists whilst he shot up to his hunched, standing pose over the tabletop of which he was shackled. "You muzt play *chess*, not *checkers!*"

There was something sincere in his outburst.

Snagged, McNaughton halted, looking back for a moment ...

There may have been a diamond in the rough in all that garble, and something about it mentally snared his attention somewhat.

"Write that down," he charged, and Garland retrieved a notepad from the top flap pocket of her briefcase and unclipped a pen, adding the phrase to her jotted notes.

In the silent seconds that followed, Feind seemed worked up and nearly depleted.

McNaughton reapproached him in the light of the hanging bulb, staring across the bleak tabletop. Whilst he delivered his retort, he slowly plodded closer to Feind at the table, causing him to slide back onto his chair.

"I was called here today because I was under the impression you had incriminating evidence that I could use as ammunition against my greatest adversary; a man who has eluded me for years ... but that isn't proving quite *so* now, is it?"

"Jack Churchill."

McNaughton shook his head firm. "No."

"Jack Churchill!"

"No! I want *Wingate!*"

"Zen *use* Churchill ... if you get *him*, you get Wingate."

McNaughton breathed the steam from his nostrils. He refrained from becoming too worked up himself—a common issue typically resulting in many exhibits of misconduct in the past.

Thinking that he may have tamed the raging bull, Feind added confidently from his chair: "Chess."

The ex-detective was clued in. He now leaned over Feind on the tabletop, burying him in his shadow from the bulb. There was something in his eyes that underlined a hatred towards his personal nemesis. The question was how far McNaughton was willing to go to bring Wingate down. Feind sensed the level of the investigator's bottled-up desperation—it nearly rivalled his own towards Churchill.

Yet to agree or disagree whilst he processed this information in his mind, McNaughton's stare held on Feind, observing his cocky nature regarding this interrogation which he had swayed into a negotiation.

"It'z about prezzure pointz, Constable," Feind elaborated further and, from beneath McNaughton's heavy stare and flaring nostrils, showing his insight on how to play these types of corruptive games. Lastly, he raised his eyeline from his submissive state beneath the brute's poise, meeting McNaughton's angry gawk. "All you need to do iz find the right one and zqueeze ..."

Like a flash of lightning, McNaughton suddenly lashed out from his calm demeanour and grappled a firm single-handed chokehold around Feind's neck, causing him to eject the chair out from beneath him. Clenching the wincing POW like a vice, McNaughton levitated above the table and became immediately swarmed by the rationale of his colleague as she placed her small hand on his back and wordlessly suppressed him.

He released.

Whilst Feind recovered, hunched over the table and gasping for air, McNaughton and Garland vacated the area, nearing the door. Before they left, he cast him some final advice ...

"If you're lying to me, I will kill you where you stand."

Feind's brow remained inverted.

How could this unethical treatment be allowed?!

He realised that Jethro McNaughton may have been a different breed. A man on fire in the search for his idol, a loose cannon, inscrutable, irreprehensible, and beyond reproach.

Coinciding with the level of his consideration regarding the pseudo cryptic message conveyed by the desperate German, McNaughton let out a long lament through his nose. He then panned his view to his loyal cohort, flattening his suit jacket.

"Write that down, too," he pitched to her, and she did.

Still gasping for air and caressing his throat, Feind watched as Garland opened the notepad, adding the phrase to what must have been the Holy Bible of documented platitudes and wisdoms.

It was then that the devious stare of Friedrich Feind found itself in a new comfort in amongst these new allies. This was certainly forged in the spirit of the old proverb; *the enemy of my enemy is my friend.* Old, but never outdated—and often a calculated causality resulting in success on multiple fields.

The fiend within Feind couldn't help but digress, marvelling at her slender figure once again. This time, it was almost as though he felt privileged enough to do so now that their shady allegiance had been established.

McNaughton leered at Feind. "Churchill, huh?"

His expression hinted at his acceptance of this investigative proposition. It was a roundabout way of getting what he wanted, and feasibly the only way to nail Wingate.

Feind forced a beam, happy to help.

"Alright, *Fiend* ..." decided, Constable McNaughton addressed the prisoner. He did so as he pulled back out the chair in order to re-conduct their business. It was a purposeful mispronunciation of Feind's name in such a way that reminded him of how Churchill would often disrespect him. It didn't sit well, but like Feind had just established, he reminded himself of this necessary evil—*the enemy of my enemy.*

Feind's devilish gaze fixed onto him, prepared to disclose and get this show on the road; a fortuitous and devious endeavour.

"... tell me about this *Baade* character."

Garland stepped around and assisted Feind with his chair, which had tipped. He sat down and slumped, somewhat relaxed.

His plan was working...

He watched Garland return to the opposite side and be seated beside McNaughton. He joshed, "Oh, Fräulein ... Herr Churchill is going to love zeeing you coming for him."

While McNaughton held a deadpan, unamused stare, Garland sat down and interlocked her fingers. This was the first inclination that this entire time, she had been playing Feind with her shyness toward him ... for this time, her eyes were fiery. Behind them was a conduct that rivalled McNaughton's own.

She said bearing a smile before her face dropped scarily flat:

"Oh, darl ... he's not going to see us coming."

Not expecting that sort of talk from the woman, Feind's eyes beaded back onto McNaughton, surprised to see him nonplussed and enjoying the indirect display of discomfort her conviction caused. She was a secret weapon.

"Were you expecting checkers?"

With his own metaphor used against him, Feind smiled nervously.

"Your move, Fiend. How do I get Jack Churchill?"

Feind leaned in, starting his deliberation.

"Mien Herr, zee *pen* is mightier than zee *sword* ..." he deliberated, quickly casting a gleam onto Garland. Growing arrogant in his confidence, he smiled conceitedly. "Go 'head: vrite zat one down."

1942, February
Combined Operations Headquarters
Whitehall, London

At 4:00 in the afternoon, a meeting adjourned within the war room of the COHQ at Whitehall. In a huff, the soundproof double doors that led into the planning office were pushed outwards, and a busy school of big fish vacated in an orderly fashion. The conversing suited military men emerged loudly, dispersing into the small reception area and connecting hall.

Poised parallel with the wall edge of an architectural nook, Jack Churchill waited eagerly in the hall, where he patiently observed their respective congregations. Amongst the group, he recognized a few important officials from within the higher echelon of Commando and the Combined Operations planning sector.

Appropriately attired in his formal khaki suit and green beret, complete with elegant silver buttons and polished shoes—sheathed claybeg sword naturally at his hip—Churchill wasn't hiding from the crowd of familiar faces. Considering the recent unearthing of classified events, those in the know, even if they saw him, would probably avoid a conversation to save face.

"*John,*" Churchill uttered from the sidelines, pulling the sole attention of Lieutenant-Colonel John Durnford-Slater from the conversing busybodies as they flowed from the mass office dismissal. They were each carrying their newest marching orders with heads held high.

Durnford-Slater was walking in league with two other military-suited gentlemen whom Churchill didn't fully recognize. Acknowledging Jack's hail, he excused himself and parted ways, stepping over to meet Churchill in the partial seclusion of the nook. "Jack ...?"

"Hullo, eh, was that about No.2?" with a nod towards the adjourning meeting, Churchill questioned on a tangent whilst maintaining his composure, though Durnford-Slater could read his angsty body language as easily as a stick-up picture book.

Indeed, the meeting *was* about the new No.2 Commando and even touched on their next operational directions, pending the appointing of battalion leadership ... which, excitingly, had also been announced.

Durnford-Slater spoke in a subtle tone after casting a glance back at the others, making sure he wasn't attracting attention with this acknowledgement.

It was understandable that the recently promoted lieutenant-colonel could be a tad irate after being overlooked for the leadership role, of which he had just been made aware. "Jack, listen ... I understand that you are upset—"

"No, I'm not upset! I'm fine! I'm *fine-o-fine,* even!" Churchill raised his voice slightly, making him seem offkey and allowing for Durnford-Slater to see through his veil.

Churchill composed himself following Durnford-Slater's emotive distances with his own, keen to perceive an untold truth. "I just want to know what is going on? I was told I had this promotion *in the bag!*"

"By who?"

"*By Newman!*" Churchill exclaimed profusely and accidently louder than intended. He reeled in his emotion. "And by *you,* sir!"

And he was right. Durnford-Slater could barely look his friend in the eye. He shared his disappointment in them not selecting Churchill. He had become privy to some information that helped him understand why they had elected another man to run No.2 Commando ...

"Care to at least inform me *who* they picked?"

"Newman."

Jack hissed. "*Newman?! He* picked himself?!"

"Well, not exactly—"

"Can he even do that?!"

Durnford-Slater tipped his head at the reality, objectively pondering that legitimacy for himself. "I guess he can. Regardless, it wasn't that simple, Jack. He was elected to command heeding Whitehall's sudden indecisiveness."

"What bloody indecisiveness?!"

"You were scrubbed from the pick, all right? They didn't elaborate, but it was due to some *'active inquiry',* so they put it. Whatever it is, it temporarily prevents you from excelling within the military."

As the words fell upon his bleeding ears, Churchill died a little inside.

It was an investigation into him, into his past. He was distraught and knowledge of the fact crippled him, however he knew he could still come back from this. This was a foreseen nightmare he merely needed to wake from.

"Cast out like a leper ..."

Directionless, Durnford-Slater waggled his beret-clad dome and sighed. "Jack, there have been whispers; allegations being tossed around. Serious ones. They're going to want to speak to you personally. A hearing will catch up with you soon and I suggest you get whatever ducks you need in a row."

"Guilty until proven innocent, then, eh?"

"You know the climate. T'is the season of distrust. Paranoia is in the air. Hence the reason your name had been removed from the selection pallet at the first inkling of a bad scent. Honestly, Jack, that's all I know. They didn't go into much further detail ..."

Jack stooped to a level he wouldn't normally and pried.

Along with these sorts of allegations came rumours and scuttlebutt. He was genuinely wondering how close the hearsay whispers would have been to the truth. "Sir, please. What are they saying about me?"

Durnford-Slater checked over his shoulder and lowered his tone. "They're saying that you were ... well, that you were trained by a *Nazi,* or some nonsense ..."

Churchill's eyes glazed over.

After taking the second to read Churchill's emotive response, which was combined with a questionable lack of immediate rejoinder, Durnford-Slater followed up in a hiss. "Well?! It's not *bloody* true, is it?" The fact that he was now questioning his faith in his friend's own validity was evidently hurtful upon his own soul. He loved and trusted Churchill like a brother. It would kill him if it were even remotely true, and if Mad Jack was anything but an authentic British compatriot and waver of the Union Jack.

"Jack?—"

"Of course, *bloody* not!" Churchill dismissed agitatedly, relieving Durnford-Slater. He then paused and followed it up with a *but* of his own. "Well ... for the most part."

"*Pardon me?*" Durnford-Slater scrunched his face, nearly sucking his lampshade moustache up his nostrils they flared so gapingly.

Churchill shushed him, directing him closer into the nook and away from any eavesdroppers, as the crowd of dismissed officers had somehow pooled by the doors and nearest them.

Within that crowd, a particular head seemed to snap sharply in their direction. It was Colonel Newman. He began to take a few wary steps their way, gravitating, and it caused Churchill to quicken the delivery of his sentiment.

"It's not what it seems or how it sounds. I can explain ..."

"*Colonel Churchill?!*" Newman acknowledged honourably as he wandered nearer, seemingly saving Durnford-Slater from his awkward position between the truth and an allegation—an uncomfortably *firm* allegation.

"Sir!" Churchill responded like a rickety bridge over murky water, lastly extending his hand after a slightly misplaced delay that went noticed. "I believe congratulations are in order."

Newman seemed a little reluctant to accept the gesture, but he did so. "Eh, yes, I believe so. No hard feelings, I hope?"

As though it was nothing, Churchill blew it off. "No, of course not. We can reassess once this whole *active inquiry* nonsense blows over. Because that is precisely what it is."

"You know about your investigation?" Newman interrogated, casting Durnford-Slater an oblique eyeball. Perchance Churchill wasn't meant to know. "Has the committee already contacted you regarding the case review and inquest?"

Churchill facially fidgeted. "Eh, not exactly."

Newman bobbed his head, gauging the reality about how Jack had likely come to know: from his commando comrade, Durnford-Slater—and it was fair enough. It wasn't his place to judge, and he was anything other than a man fair of judgement. As far as he was concerned, until proven guilty, Jack Churchill was innocent of the accusations.

"Well, chin up. I'm sure they don't have a leg to stand on," Newman genuinely proposed, following with an extended hand and parting offer. Before Durnford-Slater's trusting presence, Newman also offered some words of wisdom, of tuition. He held Jack's hand firm as he offered them; an awkwardly long embrace that went unnoticed once Churchill felt the gravity of his words. "Things will happen fast, Jack. You've been a positive public and political emblem for the British war effort for some time now. You've become a *symbol*, but that also makes you a *target;* one susceptible to fitting somebody else's constitutional scapegoat not unlike a well-tailored suit. A lamb to the slaughter, fulfilling someone else's agenda ..."

The entire time Newman held onto Churchill's handshake, he spoke directly to his soul, holding eye contact that exacted the severity of the words he was saying. He didn't know it in the moment, but it was preparing Churchill for the social and political legal battle to come.

Thankfully, Jack was accepting of his advice.

More to the point, Newman proffered further insight. "You're a distinguished soldier, Jack. Battle-hardened, one might describe, but this will be a war unlike you have ever experienced, and on an unfamiliar battlefield. They'll come at you sideways; sidle up beside you and smile before they stab you between the ribs with a stiletto. Be prepared for anything. Trust nobody. Have your own back. You can—and should—trust only in His Majesty's Crown and the court system's due process ... but in this climate, don't expect it to catch you should you fall."

Mouth closed firm beneath his pencil-thin moustache, Churchill physically gulped. This was scary.

In this moment, Newman was like some random old wise wizard, blanketing him in a suffocating veil of wisdom in a time of need. His words were well received.

Once processed, Churchill solemnly nodded. "Understood, sir."

Newman gave a final head bob before parting, also gesturing respectfully at Durnford-Slater, who was clearly privy to Newman's fidelity towards believing in Jack Churchill.

For now, this man was in charge of No.2 Commando—and it seemed he was a man well-fit for the role. This case with Churchill, dragging his title through the mud, may take some time to clear his name. Therefore,

Newman would be at the helm for whatever next mission the Combined Operations had in store for Commando—with or without Mad Jack Churchill, they would be conducted.

Jack called back bravely. "Sir?! Take care of my men, would you?"

Beneath his newly minted green beret, Newman motioned a sincere nod before forming a smile. "You mean *my men?*"

Churchill grinned and returned the respective nod.

In kind, Durnford-Slater shook Churchill's hand and departed to continue his discourse with the other military men. Jack's demeanour was impeding on his brushing of shoulders, but even in his time of peril, Churchill knew when not to overstay his visit. He left.

Once outside of the COHQ building and in the parliament precinct, Churchill strolled aimlessly, stewing deliriously and once again mentally snagged on his predicament. He felt homeless. Unwanted. Untrusted.

He halted in his pace in the setting afternoon sun shadow of the monumental equestrian statue of *Field Marshal Lord Wolseley* landmark, which oversaw the many suited passers-by as they went about their day, passing in numerous directions both in front and behind his idle position on the steps.

Mentally, he had been caught in the net of his own clandestine history, now coming to light. Like the shadow and the sun, there were some things he could not outrun. It was as if through the cracks in his stance, his very progress was coming undone, and the ground was starting to fall beneath his feet. He felt hopeless sitting upon this wall, about to tumble and fall like a certain *Humpty Dumpty.*

"All the king's horses and all the king's men, eh, old boy?"

Jack seemed stuck. Momentarily directionless.

He didn't know what to do. Or where to go.

But one thing was certain ... *he could do with a bloody drink.*

While he went to take a step in the direction of the nearest pub, Churchill caught the stare of a suited man—a tall fellow, masticating on a toothpick between gritted teeth—in the crowd of passing fedoras. What captivated him was the fact that this fellow was, like him, unmoving in the sea of businessmen.

The two locked eyes for an extended moment before Churchill brushed the occurrence off, adjusting the tight brim of his beret upon his forehead and continuing on his path towards quenching a certain thirst; the type that drowned worries ...

In the crowd beneath the Admiralty Arch square, Constable McNaughton's intense stare observed his subject from beneath the brim of his fedora as, in the distance, Colonel Jack Churchill put his hands in his pockets, conveying a haunting depression.

It was like he had acquired his target.

Had him right where he wanted him.

McNaughton craned his neck to his side where stood his sidekick, Constable Garland. She, too, was observing Churchill's body language across the short distance, out in the open.

"Write that down, eh?"

She did so.

Stalking their prey, the two predators vanished into the crowd.

An hour later, Jack Churchill could be found at a popular pub in the business district of London, along the *River Thames,* quickly four scotches in.

He was especially down bad.

Truth be told, his conditions right now mimicked those from Oslo in 1939, just after he had lost the *World Archery Championship* and dishonoured himself in front of everybody that he knew ... only this particular stain would remain *forever.*

He had never been as depressed as that day ... until now. Arguably, he wasn't *quite* there yet ... but he was teetering on the edge of a great and depressive descent. This was an irreparable circumstance, far beyond the point of no return which he crossed in Switzerland.

Tucking his hip-holstered claybeg beneath the bar, he was at the end of the block, having a great old time chatting to his oldest friend who was helping him drink away his problems. They had to shout over the loud live band music and the general atmosphere of the busy establishment. It was happy hour, after all.

It may have seemed like Churchill was ordering a lot of double-parks, but that second glass was for his buddy, Sloan MacLeòid.

"*Like aye alweys said, laddie ...*" MacLeòid hollered over the pub noise and music as he leaned, putting his face into Churchill's as he sat slumped on the bench, wrapping his hands around his crystal. "*Whiskey won't take away yoor pain ... but it's worth er shot, eh?!*"

He tipped one back, as did Churchill with a grin at the whim.

"*Yoo should'a killed dat Hun twiddle, Freddy Feind!*"

"I know it!" Churchill remarked regretfully as he nursed his drink. He made eye contact with the barkeep down the far end, who coincidently seemed to be keeping an eye on this particular patron. "Another round?!"

The barkeep acknowledged, holstering his towel over his shoulder and collecting the favoured bottle of *Macallan* on the way through and popping the cork. "Another for you and your mate—who hasn't shown up yet?" the barman asked sarcastically, though Jack Churchill was too sipped to remember that he appeared to be alone, just drinking for two.

"Cheers," he responded simply, offering the quid from his trouser pocket in a crumbling mess on the bar plane, a little too soused to calculate the maths.

The barman lent in, taking what was owed. As he did, he bestowed some analytical insight. "Sir, you know you're alone, right?"

Churchill adapted. "I am drinking for myself, and ... my friend, who was sadly lost in combat."

After contemplating whether or not to cut him off, the barkeep examined Churchill's sincerity. For a soldier in uniform—and a high-ranking one at that—it was not uncommon for a barman to witness such occurrences. There was a lot of death during war—a lot of loss. Alcohol genuinely helped that ail.

He obliged with a solemn nod, pouring them up.

"*Cheers, laddie,*" MacLeòid rhetorically thanked the barkeeper after he filled both glasses and turned his back shaking his head to mind his business.

Churchill didn't notice, but a few of the patrons were casting a glance to this solo British Army lieutenant-colonel who was getting sloshed at the bar. Granted, it was rather an unbecoming sight to behold.

"*Here's what ya do, Jackie,*" the devil on his shoulder suggested rather diabolically, envisioning the conquest as he suggested it. "*Yoo get chur bow, get chur arrows ... und we drive down ta tha Mill, und yoo snipe dat Hun bastard through tha bars ov dat dere prison fence. Mission accomplished, aye?*"

Churchill listened to the proposed assassination objective.

Although possible, given the range of distance, the bare windage that would exist over that flat expanse shy of the River Medlock, and the accuracy of such a deadly archer making the shot ... there was just no way. And certainly, no honour.

"Nonsense. I'm a soldier," Churchill regarded, bringing his tumbler before his maw. He had made his bed with the decision to incarcerate Feind, and he was planning to sleep in it. "Not a murderer."

"*Bollocks ta dat!*" MacLeòid faced him. "*Yoo're a killer, Jackie!*"

Churchill eyed him. Eyed his drink. "You going to finish that?"

MacLeòid threw the whiskey a glance and then back up at Churchill, who brought his gaze forth and saw himself in the mirror behind the display case at the bar. With MacLeòid nowhere to be seen above an empty bar stool, he was sitting by himself.

The focus of Jack's eyeline scaled back, sighting his beverage.

For a moment, brief as the gusting of gale in July, Churchill pondered his predicament here; wondering if feeding another down the hatch was the correct course of—

"Looks like you're double-parked, soldier!" the voice of an apparent angel spoke on his *other* shoulder, originating from the stool opposite to the one occupied by his Highlander haunt who had now vanished like a fart in said gusting of July gale. The voice was female.

Slightly caught off-guard and rather bewildered, Churchill brought down the tumbler which he was suckling in a hurry, yet to drink all of the golden substance he had intended to sink back. He returned it to a hold before his chest and faced the woman at his left in what was seemingly a trail of double vision.

She was young, early- to mid-twenties, dressed in work life *IncSoc* utility attire, compiled of a suit skirt minus the jacket. Her white blouse was cotton, charitably fitting her figure as by design not to draw attention to her chest. It made it impossible for prying eyes to measure her bust—Jack instinctually tried and failed.

Nevertheless, physical attributes were only one way Jack Churchill checked out members of the opposite sex, and thus he was not too hung up on the inability to assess her shape at this juncture. Orange-red lipstick appearing to be freshly applied, she wore thickly lined spectacles which magnified the golden flecks within her hazel eyes, and that was what next drew him in, nearly hypnotizing him in his inebriated state and helping sober him quick smart and on the double.

He watched as she assertively hovered then sunk her slim-yet-bulbous stern onto the stool at his direct flank, regardless of his welcoming. As she did so, her brunette bangs shaded over her pretty features. She cast them aside with a shake of the head once becoming comfortable, bringing her attention back around to the lone soldier at the bar. His defences down, he noticed her eyes were a juniper green with golden flecks.

Compelling a sight as she was, Jack cast a glance over his side, wondering just where the previous occupant of the adjacent stool had disappeared to before then realizing MacLeòid's habitual act for vanishing due to his posthumous profession.

The beauty asked somewhat promiscuously. "Drinking alone?"

Churchill bantered, raising a palm. "See anyone else here?"

She stared empty a response, remaining wordless.

"No, really ... did you see anyone?" he turned and looked, seemingly buying into his own bit, borderline overdoing it. Politely, she emitted a beam of her pearly whites.

"Sorry?" with a cocked brow, she asked producing a confused smile, for there was clearly nobody there, nor had there been as far as she could tell. "No," she asserted finally.

Churchill bobbed his head, sure of something but allowing for it to blow right on past.

Suddenly askance, she puckered her luscious lips, inadvertently drawing attention to them by Jack's instinctual libido. "Rough day, I'm guessing, eh?"

she then gathered, signalling to the barman to get her a drink to match her new companion's—a whiskey neat.

Almost as if it was ready made for her, the tumbler of volatile nectar was delivered instantly and without a word.

Churchill noticed this convenience, and it sounded alarm bells.

Perhaps, though, she was a regular hussy who haunted this local dive after she clocked out of whatever office workplace of which she clerically attended as a day job.

Hussy or not, this was natural selection. She appeared to be a good sort, and this was a philandering circumstance; a desperate man at the bar, drinking away his sins—speaking with his ghosts. Everyone knew this story—a soldier's story. Jack was no tenderfoot to these types of situations; attractive girl chats with vulnerable man, or vice versa, resulting in multiple alcoholic beverages and flirtatious laughs, an obligatory sob story or two, all eventuating in sex and sensuality in one of the many sleezy upstairs hotel rooms—the same type of cheap accommodation that Jack would be seeing shortly, given that there was no way he would be travelling back to Scotland at this hour and after this many scotches. This inebriation was only amplified by the fact that he had not eaten any supper yet.

Inhibitions were undoubtedly hindered given the level of intoxication, however, Churchill was aware of the connotations that tiny piece of gold band wrapped around his finger on his left hand conveyed; what it encased, along with his heart and his honour. So would she, once she finally noticed it in his drinking hand, raised out before them for the world to see. Worst case, she was the type who would pay it no mind—or even more debauched, see it as a mere obstacle to hurdle before getting onboard for the ride—in which case, Jack would have to declare a more obvious form of denial at a nearing juncture. For he was no disloyal douche nor any longer a village cocksmith. He was a committed commando.

"Say, that's a *really big* sword," she stated after observing the leather-enclosed claybeg at Churchill's disposal. It was impossible not to notice the customized brass handle and eyelets for fingers, forming a knuckleduster. "Looks to be quite a *handful.*"

She shifted around so that his hip flank came between her smooth, stocking-layered long legs, warm to the touch as it lightly grazed. Her skirt had receded on the stool, especially since she had separated her legs a few extra inches in order to reach over and touch the hilt of Jack's sidearm with her hand, reaching above his lap in the most flirtatious of ways. Nonchalant, he cast a glance down at her red nail polished digits as they caressed the brass hilt of his weapon over his crotch, eventually feeling the eyelets of his knuckleduster handle and wrapping a firm yet tender grip—she held it unyielding for a moment, only to release and caress the edges before again gripping the steel, nice and firm. The implication was sexual in nature.

Whilst preforming the provocative movements indicative of a hand job, her eyeline raised and made eye contact with his whilst slowly disengaging and returning her attention to the bar.

Good god, he thought to himself.

She couldn't have projected any additional sexual suggestion if she tried. Next, she would just start jacking it off like a cow's utter, thirsty for milk.

Spellbound, Churchill's throat involuntarily gulped.

Finally raising his jaw from the bar, he tilted his head to face her whilst leaning in, trying his hardest to articulate each word appropriately as not to slur due to his near drunkenness ... but before he could bid a denial of her attention, another subject of inquest became abruptly questioned to Jack by the vixen, and this one set off even more alarm bells.

"Who taught you to swordfight?" she asked, lurching coquettishly.

Churchill's mouth opened, about to respond on impulse, but he halted, suddenly spotting in the background to her the same tall man in a woollen tweed suit. His focus homed in on the target for a full two seconds. Situated in a booth across the pub, the man was seated comfortably with his fedora on the table and a lager in his midst as camouflage. He was staring straight at them, watching this occurrence transpire.

Jack very much sobered now—

"*Sir!*" the barkeep interrupted, planting a frothy beer down on a coaster. "For you."

Suddenly sobered by all these overlapping fateful occurrences, Churchill broke from the hold. Something wasn't right about all of this.

Also, he was drinking scotch, not lager.

It felt like one giant trap, cavalierly ensnaring him.

He stood from the stool, gently disengaging the libidinous lass' fingers from his weapon whilst still holding his original glass, looking down into the new one. There was something written on the coaster beneath it, which he could read as *'Rout. 1B.'*

Although 1B was likely a room number, *rout* was a strange word. In that peculiarity lied the clue of its sender. It was a military term defining a panicked and disorderly retreat, often due to a collapse in morale or leadership. An entendre was afoot, and it appeared to be double.

Casually, Jack prepared his scotch for a final sip whilst inconspicuously retrieving the coaster from beneath it as the broad at his wing questioned his well-being. He pocketed it as evidence to further analyse later.

"Are you okay there, soldier?" oblivious to the note, the lady asked in a low and caring tone as she grazed his sleeved arm with her hand, feigning concern. She puckered her orange-red lips, extenuating their softness once again so that Churchill's eyeline rested upon them, salivating.

Churchill raised the glass up in a toast, indicating to the man across the pub that he knew of his convenient reoccurrence. These suits were evidently planning to passively close in on him, possibly regarding the active inquiry.

The two unacquainted gents made eye contact and Jack skålled the drink, turning to abruptly leave.

"You're leaving?" the woman questioned desperately. Perchance if this was your average bar hussy, she would have handled this rejection differently. This was different. This was a targeted acquisition of his attentiveness. "What about your drink?!" she asked, referring to the lager.

"Send it to your mate over there. He looks thirsty."

"W-what? Where are you going?" in a reach, the woman hollered over the noise.

"Pardon me, miss. I am married," Churchill remarked bluntly.

"When?"

Jack frowned, partially confused. "Almost a year—"

Her face dropped flat, clarifying curtly. "No, darl, *when did I ask?*"

The politeness of his elaborated response fractured, and Churchill held an unsteady stare upon her for an extended moment. He was as confused as he was offended by this siren's song, though now, the glass had shattered; the shards, coming down all around his disordered state.

The jig was up. Time to evacuate.

This siren's song was out of tune.

Across the bar, Jethro McNaughton cradled a warm lager while he sat solo, relaxed in a booth. With a blank expression, he watched Churchill basically call him out with a wordless gesticulation, reject Garland's expressions of interest—and inquiry—towards him, and now disappear into the pub crowd.

Switching off her act, Viviane Garland slipped the bar stool and returned to McNaughton at the booth, scooching a seat opposite him and then sharing his view out over the pub. She wiped the freshly applied orange-red lipstick from her face with a handy napkin, almost disgusted.

"He knew," she reported over the pub noise.

McNaughton slowly concurred, turning his attention towards her.

Apparently, Jack Churchill was a rather crafty individual. He was onto their presence a lot faster than most targets this professional investigator had shadowed in the past. This was both interesting and incriminating towards his character.

Wordlessly, McNaughton calmly brooded at a nod.

"Somebody tipped him off. Want me to *write that down?*" Garland asked in a shout, half serious.

McNaughton cast her a despondent gleam.

He gave her a pass before raising his beer, taking a swig.

"Do you have it ready to go?" she asked.

Taking the sip, McNaughton exhaled with his teeth bared.

He patted the under of his left breast, indicating that he had something concealed within his inner pocket for Jack Churchill—something special.

"You want to just hit him with it now? Get it over with?"

McNaughton brought his attention around, nodding, but with a catch. "Woman, let me finish my beer first. It's been a hell of a bloody week."

The social commotion of the bar faded as Churchill upped the carpeted, beer and vomit-stained stairs and rounded the bend from the ground floor, ascending to the first floor.

He hadn't been to this establishment before, so he only held an approximate idea as to where the hotel rooms would be located and how to access them.

Once around the corner, he saw doors labelled *1D* and *1E.*

Churchill checked over his shoulder before proceeding, making sure that he was not being followed by anyone; either the hot brunette bait from the bar or old mate with the fedora from the booth. He was suspicious that they were from one in the same league, acting against him like some sort of two-pronged attack. To what extent remained unknown.

Once clear, Jack progressed along the carpeted, muffled hall.

He found *1C* and then *1B* ...

Doublechecking the stashed drink coaster from his trouser pocket before knocking, Churchill was surprised to be met by someone clearly expecting him from behind the closed hotel door as it were reefed open before his stance the second his knuckles hit the surface.

"Mad bloody Jack," the half-British, half-Australian accent of a man he had not seen in years welcomed him. Inside were another two souls, both of which he knew—both ghosts from his past.

"*Mad Mike?*" Churchill responded with a smirk erecting from beneath his pencil-thin moustache. He suppressed his happiness in order to deliver a casual one-liner as he always did. "Didn't recognize you without your cock out, old boy."

"G'day, fella!" *Mike Calvert* chuckled a laugh before reaching out and grabbing his long-time friend, retracting him into the room containing two other former—and local—aux-ops soldiers, *Graeme Black* and *Humphrey Ruffell,* closing and locking the door behind them.

It was time for this motley group to set things straight.

Even after the door to the hotel room was shut, the pub noise from the level below caused the floor beneath the carpet to vibrate and the walls to rhythmically reverberate from the bass of the music.

After his old friend sealed them away from the resonance, Churchill stepped into the middle of the carpeted floor in the central space. The hotel room was quaint, comprised of only the bare essentials, such as the bedroom housing a double bed, which was also the hallway to a connecting bathroom with a tiny closet shower, and a small kitchenette with a sink and a counter built into the wall. The walls were a tea-stained wallpaper, peeling at the edges, and the whole place was illuminated via the warm glow from a half dozen low-wattage bulbs situated about the vicinity. Mothballs and sweat were of the odour.

What Jack had stepped into was a strange reunion.

The unexpected rendezvous left him temporarily speechless, alas he countered the discomfort the best way he knew how: with humour.

"Hullo, lads. Smells like cigarettes and semen in here," Jack joshed as he pondered about the sleezy hotel room filled with familiar aux-ops faces which he hadn't seen in ages. Sad thing was, he wasn't wrong. "And I don't see any smoke."

Mad Mike Calvert, who he had met at the door, was once a commander of a detachment of Royal Engineers and held the rank of captain. Complete with a bizarre affiliation with board games, he was a half-Australian, half-British Englishman who, along with Churchill, had embarked into the secret *Auxiliary Operations* back in 1939—the top-secret and classified operations and source of much inquiry and reference of late.

Calvert was of medium build, with short hair and a pair of standouttish ears some might refer to as wing-nuttish. Outside in the hall just now, Jack had referenced the first time he had ever met the crazy—and at the time, naked—half-Aussie pom was when he had bailed him and his best friend *Rex King-Clark* out of a raid on a brothel in northern France during the Phoney War era. Calvert had then recruited Jack into the black-ops or, more accurately, the aux-ops team.

"Grae," Churchill next greeted the uniformed Lieutenant Graeme Black, seated at the kitchenette table on a wooden swan chair. He was a brazen braggadocio man of bawdy humour, with bleach blonde features, including a thick imperial moustache. Black was a familiar face since becoming a regular within the ranks of the old No.2 Commando, assumingly about to be a part of Colonel Laycock's SAS battalion. His uniform insignia was yet to reflect it. Churchill had recently gone to battle alongside Black on Vågsøy Island during Operation Archery.

Black responded with a singular nod.

There was a crystal out before him, housing remnants of spirits.

The two hadn't ever really gotten along in the same sense as any of the other men within Commando, especially the Merry Men of No.3 Commando. Due to the unseen severity of these investigative circumstances, Black had come willingly to support his comrade—likely because, due to the severity of any blowback, his name could also be up in lights. Whether it was socioeconomic standing or on the battlefield, self-preservation was one thing Black excelled at.

Churchill next acknowledged the other man in the room, barely recognizing the chap now that he was all grown up. Although it had only been a couple of years, it appeared that the war had aged him. "Ruffell? That you?"

Wingate exclusively recruited officers for his elite conquests—at least with regards to the Switzerland team. There was, however, at least one exception with Corporal Humphrey Ruffell.

"Sir," Ruffell greeted. He had a few missing front teeth, several prevalent scars on his forehead, and a slit in one of his eyebrows. He was a young non-commissioned officer who, after the aux-ops disbanded, had returned to recesses unknown. At the time of Switzerland, he had been barely nineteen with a shaven head and still embarrassingly wet behind the ears, personally recruited fresh out of basic training by Orde Wingate. After the disbandment he continued to play in Wingate's black-budget sandbox in the Middle Eastern sector. In fact, Churchill, nor any other of the men, had seen or heard from him since Switzerland and figured that he had followed the Otter into the abyss.

"Good to see you're still alive," Churchill remarked with a sincere nod. The kid looked as though he had grown up over the years. He still looked like an angsty teen or man-child, only now his eyes seemed wider and wiser. His skin seemed sun-kissed from all the hours in the Middle Eastern heat.

"Likewise," he responded. Ruffell was a good chap and a loyal soldier which Churchill had always held in high esteem. Hopefully charting the wake of a legitimate sociopath into a warzone for a number of years hadn't corrupted him.

Suddenly causing them all to baulk, the door to their room was abruptly impacted. The aggressive knocks by a balled fist startled them all in this setting.

"Bloody hell, nearly shit me pants ..." Calvert commented as he dashed over light-footedly, spying the peephole for an instant before approving the visitor. He unlocked and opened the door to the amplified pub noise in the hall, shutting it just as quickly behind a man's limped entrance.

A single man in a military suit and green beret slipped inside, quickly eyeing the bed with the desire of collapsing to recover.

It was none other than Lieutenant Arthur Komrower—another familiar face from Commando and one relating to this era of Jack Churchill's past.

"Arty?" Churchill hailed, still bewildered by this entire occurrence.

It felt a little like a surprise party, only, there was no cake.

"Jack," Komrower gasped, a little breathless after his apparent running around out there in the hall. The man must have become an ounce unfit whilst in recovery from his burns, and his pink scarring was breaking a sweat. Running recon downstairs, he had likely been the one who organized to slip Jack the message on the drink coaster, discreetly luring Churchill to this secret meeting in room 1B.

Komrower addressed Calvert, hinting that they had planned this assignation from the start and confirming that Churchill was the last member to the surprise party. He informed the others who were in the know: "I doubled back to be sure they didn't see me."

"Arty, what are you doing here?" the confused Churchill frowned, intercepting Komrower as he entered fully with his cane and a sore limp. The last time he had seen him a few days ago, he was aided by a stick beneath his clipped wing in order to simply stand vertically. "You're supposed to be in hospital! Not dancing around here, skipping about like a fruit."

"I wasn't skipping, I was hobbling," he responded, quickly taking Churchill's handshake in partial embrace as he passed him and sat on the bed beside Ruffell so that he could catch his breath.

Now that they were apparently all present for this impromptu meeting, Churchill glanced about the attendees once more. He was still rather perplexed of the matter, but he sensed the theme.

"Gents ..." he raised his arms out by his sides, holding a shrug. "Anyone care to fill me in on this fiasco?"

"We should be asking you the same question, *Colonel* ..." Calvert teased as he strode through the gathering, finding a 900-mililitre bottle of Johnnie Walker he had brought for the meet residing in the kitchenette. He found a foggy glass in the cupboard and flipped it over, pouring himself a drink from beside Black as well as topping his up. "Because it seems that, all of a sudden, a whole lot of people know about us *Berzerkers* and the details existing from within various *redacted records.* Anyone else want a nip, by the way?"

While that intrigue sunk in with Churchill, Ruffell raised a finger. Komrower was late for the offering, but was also keen for a beverage to accommodate tonight's proceedings.

"Yeah, why not, eh," Komrower said, bouncing up and approaching the small, rickety table. He hung his walking stick on the edge.

Calvert took a quiet hiatus from the discussion topic and found him, Ruffell, and even Churchill glasses including one for himself, which ended up being a mug due to the limited condiments available within the hotel cupboards. He offered one out to Churchill, who was nearly too mentally complicated to compute and accept the offer. Lagging behind the rest, he lastly received the drink, observing them all around the cramped hotel room as they sipped and conversed like this whole thing was normal.

"Condolences, by the way, Jack," Black raised his cup, referencing Churchill's overlooked promotion to lead the new No.2 Commando Battalion. News of his disappointment had clearly consecutively hit the radio waves and the grapevine, and now everybody knew.

The others raised a glass in respect of that notion.

Churchill glanced about them again, still flabbergasted and nursing his fresh drink.

Lips yet to touch the edge of the drink, Mad Jack growled to silence their social forays. He was royally bewildered by all of this. The fact he had been drinking so much beforehand was not helping his comprehension one bit. If there had already been a point established as to why they had all convened here tonight, then he was yet to see it. "Lads, care to fill me in ...?"

"We're here to warn you," Calvert finally answered.

"*Warn me?*"

"Yeah," Black stood and stepped forth, addressing him. "Someone's slowly letting the cat out of the bag about the aux-ops. Strange thing is, that cat's been buried in the dark for so long it was thought dead."

Calvert alluded further. "Details are surfacing. People are being named."

Churchill's brow inverted. "And you think that *someone* is me?"

"No," Calvert denied unequivocally.

They all knew that Jack Churchill was not a traitor.

Black insinuated with as much gravitas as he could concoct in his tone of voice. "There is blood in the water. And the sharks are circling."

"By *sharks* he means *Cuntstable McNaughton*," Calvert elaborated, held up on the point briefly, "and the sheila, whatshername, again?"

"*Garland*," Ruffell informed with his nose in his cup. It was becoming apparent that this lot had already had run-ins with the agents conducting the investigation.

"That's it!" Calvert audibly clicked his fingers, then reflected in digression. "She's a good sort, too, ay, lads? ..."

"Got an attitude on her, though," Komrower input, based on his encounter with the two investigators. "She's a fucking bitch."

"Not wrong," Calvert agreed as they strayed off topic due to the existent sexual prevalence, as men did. The digression was as obnoxious as it was irrelevant to the cause. A show of toxic masculinity that existed within such brutes. "Someone oughta fuck it out of her quick smart. And fellas, I lay my life on the line, as tribute ..."

While the others nasally chuckled, Black scoffed into his scotch. "You'd need a dick for that, Mikey," he said, swiping out and tapping Calvert on the crotch, causing him to flinch and nearly spill the swig of scotch he so confidently took after delivering that derogatory remark.

Remaining stoic through their joking, Churchill quizzed once learning that there was someone of respectable stature actively investigating them. Something had jogged his mind. "They're here ... I think I saw them both tonight ..."

Ruffell gasped, suddenly serious. "*They're here?!*"

Komrower bowed. It was why he had to bail Jack out.

Churchill bobbed his head. "Actually, I'm fairly sure the guy has been following me all day. And the woman; she tried to pick me up at the bar—and *yes,* she is rather attractive."

"Ease up, *Casanova,*" said Black, aware of Mad Jack's mad ways with women. "She was probably trying to get you drunk so you'd spill the beans."

Churchill sneered. "After this week, I didn't need her for that."

"No. She would have been trying to get you alone so that Cuntstable McNaughton could get the drop on you. They would have been playing an angle," Calvert bobbed his head. "That bloke is a cunning fucker. He's no doubt sizing ya up, Jack. He did the same thing to me before he knocked on me door and started pryin', tryin' to paint me in a corner."

Deep in his own thoughts, Churchill pondered pensively.

It all made sense now; the inquisitive girl at the bar asking about his sword, trying to get him to divulge sensitive information while intoxicated, and trying to further his inebriation—attempting to get his shields down. They had likely been following him around prior to witnessing him set into a vulnerable state, opting to capitalize with some well-placed jabs in the ribs in the form of questionnaires. Like Calvert said, they were playing it super smart, searching for weaknesses, for chinks in his armour.

"So, they're the ones probing the aux-ops?"

"They're probing *you,* specifically ..."

"*Probing me,* hmm? Didn't even offer to buy me a drink first. I would have said yes."

"To the *drink* or the *probing?*"

"Perhaps *both,*" Churchill remarked off the cuff as he relaxed enough to finally take a sip of his scotch. He tried his hardest not to appear the way he felt; like the stained and peeling wallpapered walls were closing in on him.

Calvert expanded, putting the pieces together and realigning their conversation. "More to topic; they're investigating how that barmy crank Ernie Baade was invited by Wingate to train you how to use a sword."

The four of them had been found out and interviewed already by the brass. From their line of inquiry, they were able to discern what must have been their main objective—and it wasn't blowing open the aux-ops specifically ... it was just Jack they wanted to bury.

Churchill's eyes rolled with exasperation. "Baade trained us all."

"Granted. But look, I hate to play devil's advocate, but *you're* the one running around with a bloody *broadsword* strapped to ya hip, Jack. It's painted a target on your back."

"It's a *claybeg*," Churchill corrected, placing his fist upon the smooth edges of his holstered brass hilt. It had been his sidearm since the disbandment of the auxiliary-ops, where the group of up until recently nameless and faceless Berzerkers had gifted him the weapon. It was in replacement of his original sword that he had lost during a certain encounter.

"Semantics," Calvert responded and realigned their ever-digressing converse. "Jack, all puns and jests aside, this whole thing is slowly unravelling. It will only be a matter of time before they catch the Otter and he sings all verses of past transgressions. Nowadays, the guy is a glorified war criminal in the eyes of the public sector, and we're all gonna get dragged through the mud of this mess. We'll have a lot to answer for, and I guarantee you; we'll be painted by the same brush."

Komrower pursed his lips. "More than just the *public sector.*"

"So far, they might only be onto Jack, but we're *all* going to be up for a tribunal once this gets out, so we need to get our stories straight. The twat is wanted for a whole bunch of other crazy shit. It's amazing they haven't brought Wingate in earlier."

"They've never brought him in because they can never find him," Black expanded from his new spot loitering between the bed and the window, where he lifted the curtain an inch to spy on the street whilst nursing his beverage. "Every other day he's in the furthest-most reaches or recesses of the world; living life on a razor's edge, fighting a *new* war against a *new* enemy with a *new* special team on a *new* black-budget. Man's like a hermit crab; as soon as someone finds him out, he changes his shell."

"*Shell game,* but with an ever-changing pea," concurred Calvert excitedly, utilizing his board game knowledge for the perfect analogy.

"Unobtainable," Churchill eventually expanded.

"Like a fuckin' fart in the wind, mate," Calvert applied.

Komrower put in his two cents: "He's like a mayfly."

Black corresponded sternly; more exact. "He's a ghost."

"Orde Wingate is in *Ethiopia*," Ruffell informed abruptly, setting it straight and surprising them all. The confession of the news silenced the room. "He's with a group calling themselves *The Gideon Force*."

"*Gideon?*" Calvert mocked at the irony. It was clearly named after the biblical judge who defeated large forces with a tiny band of men. "Prick's always had a poetic way about him, hasn't he?"

"More like an inflated ego."

"Yes, well, they are fucking up anything and everything Italian south of *Kenya* with the aid of the local resistance. They're a motley group of questionable renegades utilizing even more questionable tactics."

Calvert cocked his head at Ruffell's detailed explanation—more so, at his developed pronunciation procurement, articulation, and overall intelligence. Back when they had known him, he was a dummy.

"So, up to old tricks, then, eh?" said Black.

"Y'know, so much about that sounds so bloody familiar ..."

"He get his new lot high on meth, too?" Black interrogated bluntly.

Calvert kept quiet while the others seemed perplexed. Ruffell, too.

Clearly, they didn't know about Wingate's trade secret ...

"What? You lot didn't know?!" Black enlightened demeaningly at the others in the room: Churchill and Komrower, who exchanged equal looks of bewilderment. "Wingate's god complex doesn't end with guerrilla tactics and bloodshed. He was into biochemistry, too. In Switzerland, he had us all hooked on methamphetamine. The prick was spiking the resort water with it."

Komrower scrunched his face. "What?!"

Churchill's stoic stare lingered.

He had always suspected it in later years.

Although it had been experimented with by the Allied Forces, Nazi leaders came up with a miraculous solution for their battle-scorned soldiers with shellshock to cope with the relentless demands of warfare: a drug known as *Pervitin*. This tablet-form methamphetamine-based drug became exemplary for soldier usage, profoundly affecting the performance of the men who consumed it—noted that unfocused consequences such as addiction and negative side effects be damned. It kept soldiers dialled in and focused, able to run on minimal sleep and fight without thought. It harnessed their varying forms of *combat stress reaction* or *battle fatigue* and transformed the diagnosed disorders into fuel for their fight. It turned it into anger for the enemy.

"Yeah, that's right. Didn't you all notice how hyped up we all were, daily, doing stupid shit in the freezing cold? The drugs were to blame for it," Black expanded and took another swig. "I've always been calmer since we stopped *staying hydrated.*"

"Yeah, you're still a dickhead though," said Calvert.

Black shrugged. That was bred in him.

"How do you know where Wingate is, Ruffell?" Komrower queried through the chatter, realigning their initial conversation.

Ruffell had spent the most time with Wingate over the past few years, and he bobbed his head whilst he savoured his scotch, staring into the amber fluid as though it frequently helped drown out a great many voices. Drinking was the soldier's pleasure.

"Because I was there with him, being *questionable.*"

They all understood the hardship of being a part of such harsh special forces. They were often ordered to partake in some pretty horrible actions. Colouring outside of the lines of any government meant they could go against the regulations of the Geneva Convention. Following a man such as Orde Wingate, such an egotistical and eccentric racist, holding political attitudes towards Zionism that were heavily influenced by his Plymouth Brethren religious views and beliefs in particular eschatological dogmas, into such endeavours proved taxing on the core of men whose souls were not immune to the corruption of evil ...

... hence why Ruffell decided to get out.

"I only transferred out end of last year ..." he finalized, unafraid of divulging information to such trusted men, insinuating that *getting out* from a league such as black-ops wasn't as easy as resigning. There was a certain element of fear existent and one feared that having known too much about the dark, they may very well disappear into the black. This was information that they already knew, having been there before—they got lucky at the time, given the brink of war's calling and the abrupt disbandment of the Berzerkers.

"Ethiopia, eh?" Black finally offered, strutting through the small room and between all the perched men. "Jack, just give 'em that sanctimonious prick, eh? Then the heat will be off."

Churchill eyed Black.

Why everything had to be so staunch, so macho with this guy, he'd never know. Everything was always such a dick-measuring contest, just like how his attitude had been during Archery, trying to race him to the finish line for some sort of recognition.

"If only it was that simple," Calvert stated, answering for Churchill.

"Like you said, Grae, Wingate is a ghost," Jack regarded, and elaborated with such artistic flair. "I'm guessing that's the problem with hunting shadows with a Codega. The light shines truth, but it also shines light."

Easily irritable with all things Mad Jack, Black scrunched his face. "What the fuck is a *Codega?* Talk sense for once in your life, not just in riddles formed of fuckin' literarian-grade intellect."

"What I am saying is, even if they know where to look for Wingate, he'll vanish into the shadows and elude their grasp. They'll never catch him, nor do they want to for that matter ..." Churchill expanded, piquing all their interests about the hotel room. "They'll never admit it officially, but he's that blunt instrument the British Army uses when they need to colour outside of the lines of diplomatic warfare. The one that the Government can turn a blind eye while he does their dirty work. He gives them plausible deniability. They'll keep him on the move so that he stays above the reproach of any would-be snowflakes of the public persecution sector here in London. He's a necessary evil."

"You agree with his methods, sir?" Ruffell boldly questioned.

Churchill contemplated his response.

He shook his head with his initial delivery. "No ... but I understand that you can't merge so much black with that much white without creating grey in the middle. Modern-day warfare is too messy; too political. Those lines are too blurry to be neat all of the time. Your smartest bureaucrats know that. The Government knows it. Even the King."

"So, nothing changes, then?" Calvert asked with a gloomy tone. "They just keep on keepin' on? Look the other way and let Wingate commit more borderline war crime activity?"

"We buried bodies out there in the snow ... we're just as accountable for any of this as the Otter," Black contested. "Turns out, the things you bury come back to haunt you."

Calvert justified. "We didn't commit any war crimes. Not really. We smoked some edge-boundary Gerrys and hid the evidence, big deal. Bigger atrocities have happened in the last decade—namely caused by said Gerry. No one gives a fuck about some dead and buried, forgotten Nazis in the snow, mate. We didn't exist and weren't around long enough to commit anything. The Berzerkers were a non-event."

Churchill suddenly recalled a whole lot of the nasty stuff he would be answerable to, along with the other men of the Berzerker unit concerning what they got up to in those winter nights in the *Swiss Pennine Alps*. They were off the reservation and beyond rebuke whilst under the cast shadow of Wingate's wing.

He wasn't proud of it. Rarely thought about it.

He had enough ghosts following him around as it was ...

Forgetting the period ever existed was Churchill's way of expunging it from his mind. It was just a bad dream—a vacation from the monotonousness of the Phoney War period.

Easily gone but never truly forgotten ...

"So, what's the plan?" Churchill finally marched forth in their motley gathering.

"You're usually the one with the plan," Komrower uttered.

Black scoffed, finishing his drink. In his wandering, he had ended up back by the table, helping himself to a refill of scotch. "It will be difficult to find a rock big enough to hide all of us behind. If there are people investigating this thing, they'll eventually find us, question us, and convict us."

"Well, they've already found me and Ruffell."

Churchill looked to Calvert. To Ruffell.

"It's why we met up, decided to warn you. All of you."

Ruffell jerked his head at Churchill. "They've got their sights set on you, sir. They were asking a lot of questions. He knows a lot already—a lot of stuff he shouldn't know. Couldn't know."

"Tell me his name again?" Churchill requested, realigning the crosshairs for this *new* enemy.

"McNaughton," Calvert informed.

Churchill committed his name to memory.

A new enemy.

"And what did you tell them?"

"Nothin'," said Ruffell.

"When questioned, we both denied everything, of course. We had never heard of the *aux-ops* ... of *General Orde Wingate* ... we *didn't know what they were talking about,* if you catch me drift?"

"And we didn't know *you!*" Ruffell furthered, gesturing to Jack.

Churchill respectfully bobbled his head.

Anonymity was a good plan, but a feeble one.

"'*General'* Wingate," Black murmured in disdain. "You know he was never actually an acting *general* until very recently. Guess that was a fib back then, too."

Churchill's nostrils flared.

Amongst all the things he ultimately despised about Orde Wingate, he was aware that during their time spent beneath his thumb, the man was a mere *major.* There was a running joke between him and the brass about referring to him as a *general,* but it was never so.

Calvert stated. "Well, whatever rank he was: we've never heard of him."

"It's a smokescreen," Churchill ascertained, thinking out loud. "If McNaughton is as savage a hunter as you suggest, misdirection will buy us time. Nothing more."

Churchill's dismissive tone regarding their brave deceptions of the British government seemed contemptuous and mildly offensive, and rightfully so. Although they had still done the best thing by denying everything, Calvert and Ruffell appeared a little insulted by Churchill's denigration of their efforts.

Jack eyed them, "Any skilled investigator will obtain the clearance to be able to see that we served together under the same regiment, off the books or otherwise. You both saying that you don't know me may have worked at face value, but it won't hold up next time—and certainly won't hold up in front of a court martial if we're sworn to oath."

"Well, what do you suggest?" Calvert asked, "Because this guy is good. Damn good. And he's fuckin' got a hard-on for *you*, mate."

"He doesn't have it out for Jack, he's got it out for Wingate," Black expounded, sitting comfortably as he deliberated. "I asked around with a few mates I have in intelligence. Apparently, Orde Wingate is Jethro McNaughton's investigative *Holy Grail.* The man's obsessed."

"Why?"

"Don't know. But finding him is his most desirable want and yearn. He's fixated on destroying him on a personal level, aiming to bring him in, no matter the cost. This recent attraction to ol' Mad Jack here is new, but he's like a dog with a bone ... he isn't letting go."

Churchill craned his neck, desiring to know more about this new adversary. "What else did your contacts tell you about McNaughton?"

Black held a small shrug, evoking his findings for anything relevant to the cause. "Experienced. Hardboiled. He used to be a *metro copper,* then a P.I. or something. Didn't sound like he was a family man—married to the job, I'd say. He's determined and very thorough ..."

His mind's eye flowed as Churchill absorbed the intel, letting it paint a picture of this fresh foe—who he visualized in a tweed suit and fedora. Out of everybody present, he understood the drive fuelling an obsession, especially one centred around a specific enemy. He had been in McNaughton's shoes before, regarding the obsession of chasing down an enemy. This was definitely not going to go away.

"Sounds like a proper pole smoker," Komrower remarked humorously, and Churchill eyed him across the room. One of the most valuable lessons a soldier could learn about an opponent was to never assume and to never underestimate their ability. Respect the enemy in order to think like him.

From *The Art of War,* the Sun Tzu quote of *know thy enemy* came straight to mind in Jack's retort, however he went with a less philosophical response, "... *'Walk a mile in his moccasins before you abuse, criticize, and accuse'* ..."

He had thusly accumulated all the eyes in the room ...

... along with a well-deserved wall of static silence.

"... what?" Black finally mockingly barked at Churchill's apparent denigration. Forever the intellect, Jack Churchill's quotes were often heard through an unintentional condescending tone.

"*Judge Softly,*" Churchill deemed—it was also the title of the literature that he quoted. His wandering gaze met those upon him as they judged him for his overconfident arrogance regarding his preferred respect of McNaughton.

Breaking the mood, Calvert heeded with a joshing tone, "... what if the bloke doesn't wear moccasins, though?"

Black chortled at Mad Mike's comedic relief, taking their discussed predicament off on a tangent about men's footwear.

Churchill clarified, paraphrasing the quote. "*Shoes*, then!"

"Any clue on how this has happened, Jack?" Komrower finally asked over the laughter and chatter regarding footwear as it settled. "What sparked all the interest suddenly? Switzerland has been long dead for years ..."

Churchill's face panned around after a moment of deliberation.

"Yes, I believe I know how ..." he admitted, much to their surprise. He directed his question at the officiated commandos in the room: Black and Komrower, giving them a nod. "Do you lads remember that Hun we caught in Vågsøy?"

Komrower snorted. "Which one? We took a hundred of them ..."

"Ninety-eight to be exact," stated Black.

Churchill remarked with an underlining obviousness. "You both damn-well know which one ..."

Both Black and Komrower recall the outstanding one-on-one fight Churchill had with a member of the elite *Alpine Huntsman* that was present during the raid, dipping into their casualties. Churchill had held some sort of personal vendetta against the enemy, taking him in as a POW after winning an epic swordfight.

"His name is Friedrich Feind. We have a rather unpleasant history. Somehow, it appears that he also knew Baade on some personal level. By extension, he's come about learning some incriminating details about Switzerland ..."

The men all sighed in anguish and slumped in distress.

Black hissed callously. "*Us* ... or *you?*"

"*How,* though?!" Calvert questioned, waving a hand. The whole thing was such a huge and uncanny coincidence. "Baade is history! We killed that kraut bloody dead!"

Recalling the events, Black nodded intently.

For all intents and purposes, Ernst-Günther Baade was deceased.

"Small world, I guess?" Churchill exclaimed, rubbing his tired eyes.

"Sounds like you should have killed him when you had the chance in Vågsøy ..." Black muttered in a tenor suggesting that it would have been what he would have done.

Churchill's brow hopped, showing regret. "You're telling me? When he threatened to tell the army about Switzerland, I figured he was talking out his arse, until ..." he huffed, drained. "I should have just killed the bellend in Vågsøy."

"Should'a, could'a, *didn't*," Black sung as he tipped back his cup and stood, banging it down on the table. His body language suggested that he had had enough and was about to leave. "I'll stand by it: the only good kraut is a dead kraut. We should'a all killed Baade when we had the chance, too—the second he walked in the fucking door of that resort!"

Calvert intercepted. "Where are you goin', mate?!"

"Back to base! I'm bored of this shit. Arty—the fuckwit—lied when he said it was something concerning and interesting."

Komrower raised his arms defensively. "I didn't say *interesting*, I said *important*. It's relevant to us all."

"Yeah, well, this is a force of nature now. The brass'll either find out or they won't. There isn't much we can do to stop a whirlwind, gentlemen. Don't let it drive you crazy—or *mad*." He eyed Jack. "Too late?"

"We can get out of the way," suggested Calvert.

"And go where?" Black questioned with a hiss. He added rationally, "We were just followin' orders in Switzerland. We knew what shady shit we were gettin' into when we signed up with the Otter, didn't we ...?"

"Well, that's what we're here to map out," Calvert affirmed. "If we all get on the same page now, *if* or *when* the time comes and we're pulled to the stand, we have a better chance of surviving this thing if it comes to light."

"We must deny it ... all of it ..." Churchill uttered with an affirmative tone. He was technically the highest-ranking officer of them all, therefore, whatever he said, went. Not to mention he was the man accused and had the most to lose. "Until what point the crown declassifies our mission and we legally *need* to speak unredacted truths, we open with fact: we were following orders, and still are by denying the whole circumstance ever existed ..."

The men all nodded in silence. A technicality.

Churchill had a point; if they acknowledged any details about the operation, they could be tried for treason for divulging sensitive information.

"If there is a formal inquiry into the auxiliary-ops and the specifics of what happened during that period, then we'll cross that bridge when we get to it ... but until then, we keep it rigged to blow."

"You know they'll ask," Black declared, and he was right. An official board of inquiry, once set to purpose and there is a notion to declassify, will want to dot every *i* and cross every *t* for the official reports. Nothing will remain sacred. Hands will be shown to be dirty, and blame will have to be put on somebody.

"They can't declassify the operation without Wingate. He has the authority—unless they officially recede it. And he'll die before ever being brought towards a tribunal. Take solace in that fact alone, lads. We legally can't spill the beans, and they legally can't force us without the right consent. We're bound by duty to the crown."

The men around the room let that sink in for a moment.

Churchill was right. Due to formalities, Orde Wingate would indeed need to be brought forward to declassify the top-secret stature of the aux-ops before any member of the public—or prosecution—could be deemed privy to the highly classified information. And that just wouldn't happen. At the worst, they might try to get identified members of the operation to speak about and sign an affidavit, swearing an oath of truth and therefore making that factual in a court martial. If they were all on the same page about denying the mission ever took place, then they were untouchable beyond an unprovable accusation.

Exchanging a look around the dingy hotel room at those presently sharing the same boat, Churchill gestured their nonverbal accord in the way of nod gestures. This included, last but not least, the concurrence of Graeme Black.

"Good," Churchill finally pledged. "Now let's get out of here and back to our respective normalities; try our best to forget about what should already be forgotten."

Komrower elevated what was left in his drink before finishing it.

He said: "May the dead stay buried."

Churchill seconded it, as did Ruffell with a third toast.

"And let's try to avoid these cuntstables, too, eh?" Calvert raised his cup and his voice, following Churchill's lead towards the door. He lingered only to swipe what was left of his Johnnie Walker bottle from the table.

Churchill grabbed the door and cracked it open. The volume of the pub was much louder in the hall. The music from downstairs could be felt through the air.

At a glance up both ends of the vestibule, the coast looked clear.

There was activity, but nothing irregular, so he stepped out into the hall, followed by former Berzerkers; Arthur Komrower, Humphrey Ruffell, Mike Calvert, and finally the ever-unimpressed Graeme Black. The lot of them exchanged parting gestures before dispersing and walking off up either hall—when each avenue abruptly halted.

"Eh ... Jack?" Komrower called his attention, stopped dead in his tracks and pointing his walking stick by the handle like a handgun with a really long barrel. Up the far end of the vestibule was a suspicious looking fellow in a woollen suit, grinding on what appeared to be a toothpick. They hadn't seen him before. It was as if he had hooked around from the corner, planting himself in sight once they had deemed the coast to be clear. He was leaning against the claustrophobic stained wall of the narrow hall.

That was McNaughton.

The lot of them quickly cast a gleam before then glancing towards their six o'clock passage, opting to source another way out of the building, but only to be met by the vixen of the sleuth duo lingering in the shadows of the alternate hall passage.

And that was Garland.

They were shagged.

Analysing their slim options, Churchill opted for retreat.

He hissed. "Fall back!"

The other four wide-eyed men exposed in the hall were stupefied, unknowing of how to deal with this sort of standoff. They weren't exactly engaged in warfare, nor was there an imminent chance of harm or death ... but it was a threat just the same.

With an outstretched arm and open palm, Jack reared them up, maintaining a mild, insouciant demeanour, however there was no denying that this jig was up for them and the time for casual conduct may have already lapsed. They had very few options left, and fight or flight was being engaged in the forefront of all their brains along with a surge of adrenaline.

For Churchill, there may have been no sense in him running from this or even trying to fight his way out of this encounter. McNaughton already knew his name and had him labelled as a person of interest, but the authorities were yet to identify Komrower or Black. They may have been onto Ruffell and Calvert, nevertheless their presence would be better left unidentified here, especially considering they had already been questioned by the investigators, in which instance they both swore to have never known Jack Churchill.

"Retreat! Now!" Churchill reiterated, throwing a glance over his shoulder. He was mindful not to take his eye from McNaughton for anything longer than a couple of seconds, maintaining his focus upon him as though he were a slyly big cat hunting them in the jungle. The lot of them returned through the doorway.

"What are we going to do, *run away?*" Black jousted as he led the column of them back through, pirouetting on the carpet within the same musty hotel room. They were now cornered in 1B. "It's our own Government, they already know who we are!"

"No, Jack's right!" Calvert exclaimed distressingly, heading across the bed and towards the outer windows where there would undoubtedly be a fire escape platform or a ladder leading down to the street. This was hardly his first unorthodox escape out of a seedy hotel room. "They don't know who you two are! We may have already been made, but we can't get seen having a fuckin' party together after we've just sworn we'd never known a *Mad Jack Churchill!* That in of itself is a crime!"

"Oh, fuck's sake!" Black finally agreed, assisting him with the stuck window. The two of them fought with the heavy, dusty curtain, thrashing it about whilst they tried to jimmy the slider latch.

Meanwhile, through the open door and out in the hall, Churchill boldly set to meet his new adversaries head-on. Holding apart the closing walls, he remained unprovoked and motiveless as they each began to cautiously approach on either side of his position.

Churchill twisted to spy Garland over his shoulder—

"*Jack Churchill!*" McNaughton called through gritted teeth, closing distance at a leisurely pace. Over the resounding bass of the downstairs music, his stern voice rebounded from either side of the narrow passageway, recalling Churchill's attention.

His view abandoned the green-eyed, gold-speckled vixen as she silently enclosed on his position like a stalking feline, and Jack's sterling stare intensified upon the constable as he enclosed. For the first time, their eyes properly locked.

"I was wondering if we could have a word with you?"

Feeling like cornered prey, Churchill turned to be side-on between the two aggressors. He felt his blood pressure rise. Felt his nostrils flare as he took in more oxygen ... *felt the fingers of his nondominant hand insert the eyelets of his holstered claybeg.*

He didn't know how to fight this ...

Churchill glanced back again, discerning Garland's approach from the opposite end. Her hips swayed with her saunter, closing the distance with an unprecedented confidence. Admittedly, she was just as sexy as she had been when she had pretended to hit on him at the bar. Churchill decided to use that callback to segue; to further distract the brass from the boys.

After conducting his examination of her finesse, Churchill whipped his head back around to McNaughton, inflicting whatever damage he could with his charm and winning smile. "Just the one?"

McNaughton was expressionless and seemingly unimpressed.

His marching slowed now that he was close enough to chat ...

The constables must have ascertained Mad Jack as too much of a wildcard to encompass carelessly. Distance would remain their friend until they each felt it safe to enclose proximity to the cornered soldier—after all, he *was* armed and dangerous.

Churchill swapped his look back onto Garland. Within his gaze, she slowed in her gravitational drift towards him, possibly planning to orbit his standing until needed.

"Have we met before? ..." acting brazen and sleazy, Churchill conveyed a sense of intoxication that may or may not have put these two off-guard.

Nonetheless, if they truly were as good detectives as Black's friends in intelligence had conveyed, then they would see right through his ruse. "Say, I got a room for the night ... want to *check it out* with me?" Churchill asked in his most seedy tone. He even followed up the proposal with a bumping of the eyebrows.

"Oh, darl, I'd rather go overseas ... somewhere chilly ... *Switzerland,* perhaps?" Garland playfully probed. She seemed shy on the exterior, but she was gregarious as fuck on the inside. Probably deathly lethal, too.

It was hard not to get at least a little turned on.

"*Switzerland,* eh?" Churchill gassed. "Never been, myself."

Garland mumbled, unconvinced. "Mm-hmm."

Jack levelled out, through with the games. "Well, aren't you a lil' firecracker. You really had me convinced back there at the bar ... thought I was going to get lucky."

"Nah. Just *un*-lucky," she playfully replied to Jack's joust just as the commando colonel realized that she had stopped advancing from her end. She was acting the deadfall to the bulldozer who was enclosing from the opposite side, about to pincer him in the tight hall.

Still consciously guarding the doorway, Churchill's beret-clad dome turned to face McNaughton. He remained unmoving, now close enough to size up with great detail.

Dressed in his woollen tweed suit with matching fedora, McNaughton was tall and of a plump, solid build. He may have been athletic in his youth, possibly even served prior to joining the police force from which he was recruited into whatever internal investigative squad he was now a part of for His Majesty's armed forces. He was a razor shave type, probably cut by a favoured local barber—a trusted one who also plucked the many greys he was now unable to avoid once he hit his half-century. He wore a constantly serious stare, framed by high arched brows.

"Well, then ... what do you lot want to talk about?"

"Funny, you didn't even ask who I was ...?!" he tipped his head. "Been expecting a visit from the authorities have you, Colonel?"

"Yes, you got me. I did jaywalk on the way over here."

"Jaywalking is not illegal in the UK."

Jack bowed. "Touché."

"Nothing else hiding in the closet?"

Churchill appeared to think long and hard, still playing for time, "just some coat hangers and mothballs. Some might say I live life expecting the unexpected, *mister,* eh?"

With gasbagging starting to sound a lot like shit talk, McNaughton was beginning to catch on to the fact that he was merely attempting to buy time for his friends' escape.

Eyes sidewards, Churchill casually angled his view back into 1B.

The boys were still inside, still trying to get the window open that led out of the hotel. They were running out of time.

Jack's stare flustered, but he held his poker face well.

"It's *constable*. But, then again, you already knew that didn't you?"

Jack shrugged, half-heartedly.

"Who you got hiding in there, eh?" McNaughton asked noninvasively as he trotted a step nearer. He maintained distance slightly as not to provoke a physical altercation, playing his cards close to the chest.

Churchill awkwardly chuckled, confusing McNaughton. "My lad, hopefully in a minute ... *nobody.*"

McNaughton frowned ...

... then realized this was a charade.

"*Get in there!*" he hollered, lunging forwards and at Churchill as though he was a linebacker at the end zone.

Rather than fight his advance, Churchill quickly reached out and grabbed the door handle, reefing it shut with all the force he could muster. With a deafening *slam* the wood frame of the doorway sealed shut and locked tight as all hotel rooms do.

The door closed right as both McNaughton and Garland loomed over either one of Churchill's shoulders; neither one of them obtaining a good look inside or being able to prevent it from closing. They grabbed at Churchill's khaki sleeves and pushed on the door, however his grip remained firmly fixed on the handle. They were too late.

"No!" Garland cursed, futilely banging on the closed surface with her palm while Churchill firmly pinched the brass doorknob with both hands so that it could not be twisted. McNaughton made short work of his effort, forcefully removing them and shoving him away in order for Garland to attempt twisting it open with a rattle, but it was locked.

"Whoops," Churchill remarked, acting dumb and patting down his jacket pockets. "Don't suppose one of you guys have the key?"

"That's cute," McNaughton said at Churchill in the hall whilst he masticated his wooden splinter. Then to Garland: "Go downstairs and find staff. Get us a master key—"

From inside, they heard the muffled sound of glass breaking.

The window!

They mustn't have been able to get it open, so, out of desperation, they had broken it for their exodus into the night.

Like a trigger, the two investigators kicked into action, ramping up a gear. After Garland grappled with the door some more, McNaughton passed his grasp of Churchill onto her, positioning himself to be able to attempt kicking it in with a heavy foot.

"*Move aside, please!*"

He was a big fellow. Rock-solid. He would likely get it first try.

"People only run if they have something to hide!"

Although they were still playing hard to get at this juncture, Churchill couldn't allow for this capture to occur. At the last second, he snatched his arm free from Garland's grasp, next shoving himself into a clumsy shoulder tackle to off-guard McNaughton in the thin, echoic hallway. Garland let out a squawk as he defied her clutches, staggering her slightly as the two men engaged in a cocked-up scrum, where she was unable to intervene. Over the loud jazz music booming downstairs, she was also mostly unable to call for help.

McNaughton managed to hold his own against Churchill, recovering his balance and reasserting his footing at a brace.

The two grunted and scoffed like animals.

Before long, the two scufflers were hunched, leaning into one another whilst they grappled tensely onto each other's arms and shoulders, roughing up their respective suit jackets. Barging side to side like ships in turbulent seas, they dented the shitty thin plaster walls with their forceful shoves. The tense wrestling was highlighted by both men locking eyes whilst grimacing, baring their teeth. It was a drastic escalation in hostility, and either party had their own reserves of bottled-up aggression to unload at this interval.

Two provoked titans ...

It was time to take some of the stress out.

During their tight brace between the walls of the hall, McNaughton ramped up his drive, mustering strength and forcefully shoving Churchill backward and into the side of the hallway. This action dislodged several hanging picture frames of the Thames and Big Ben that broke loudly. They also knocked off a mounted sconce, causing the detached electrical light to hang loosely and flicker and strobe.

With an almighty *thud,* Jack's back damaged the plasterboard.

He retaliated by doing the same thing with a sudden burst of force, pressing off the flat, twisting, and shoving McNaughton by the shoulders into the opposite side, where the two embraced in a violent hold that tore clothing and turned flesh red from tension. They wiggled in clamped holds before finally breaking free of one another's white-knuckled clasps.

Their scuffle turned into an all-out brawl as across the degree of short distance, Churchill pushed off and slogged McNaughton across the face with a tight right hook.

The commando launched a punch into the constable's head, tilting him abruptly and ramping this whole bout up a notch now that their extremities were on the table for use as weapons.

Jack reared up an ounce, observing his work.

Losing his fedora hat from the swing, McNaughton had bitten through his toothpick, expelling the remaining twig with a spit from his tongue tip. Flushed in the face, the man was absolutely fuming, making it obvious that he had been secretly hoping for fisticuffs all along. After springing on the spot for an instant, hinting at some sort of boxing ability, he moved at Churchill, taking him by surprise with his sprightly spirit.

Once in close, he parried a multitude of the commando's defensive and counteroffensive attacks in order to drive multiple jabs of his own into his dimple chin, nose, and even his stomach, coming in from the low centre.

Stunned, Garland observed from the rear.

Although she held concern for her offsider, she also clearly knew the competency of his ability, and had complete confidence in McNaughton coming out on top.

Stunned by the skill of this old codger, Churchill took the hits, losing the green beret off his dome in a momentarily symbolic gesture. He straightened up and recovered fast, even returning a few punches before the two of them were locked into another rigid grapple, further tearing their suits and popping a few buttons. With a dozen grunts, they flung each other against the tight halls of the hotel hallway like a pair of supercharged bumper karts, cutting sick.

Blood eventually trickled from each of their noses as they scuttled, eventuating in Jethro McNaughton dipping low and driving his solid fists into Jack Churchill's kidneys whilst he had him anchored over in a fold, winding him repeatedly.

Striking him again and again, the blows deflated Churchill.

Each punch hit him so hard that his feet lifted from the floor.

He'd be pissing blood tomorrow.

Now that the commando was slightly weakened, McNaughton pushed him away and squatted in lower, spear-tackling into Churchill with such momentum and power that it actually collected his whole body weight with the manoeuvre. Carting his mass, McNaughton thrust him *into* the locked 1B door as though he were a battering ram.

McNaughton anchored at the last minute, detaching his payload and launching Churchill—who sailed, flailing.

In a loud *crash!* the wooden door broke off its hinges by the force of his throw combined with the fall of Jack's dead weight.

Churchill toppled inside the room with a thunderous *thud!* landing on the door on the floor like a toboggan, coated in a cloud of powder which caused him to cough his lungs out. Seemingly yielded, he was unable to get up from the severe hits to his organs.

Straightening his suit, the bloody-nosed McNaughton stepped into the dusty room after Churchill, scanning it quickly with a hunter's stare. The room was vacant. Cold night air gushed in past the swaying curtains from the broken window that lined the far wall: undoubtedly the other occupants' escape route. Whoever they were, they were now long gone, thus McNaughton saw no need to further pursue.

"Now you're in even deeper shit," McNaughton gauged between catching breaths through his leaking nostrils, circling back and over Churchill on the floor and into the light of the doorway. He retrieved a small cardboard box full of toothpicks from his inner breast pocket and gave it a shake. "Y'know, it's a felony to assault an officer of the law."

"I didn't know you were," defended Churchill with an involuntarily closed eye, wincing from the pain in a held squint.

"What?!"

"You never showed me any identification, you brawny bellend ..."

McNaughton leaned in his pose and growled, frustrated that he could not press any further charges against Churchill due to that technicality.

Equally as breathless as he was victorious, McNaughton puckered his blood-covered lips as he bent over to collect his fedora from the floor in the hall, puffing it out. He spat a golly of gore onto the debris-filled carpet in the hallway, which was beginning to fill with concerned patrons from within the neighbouring rooms of the hotel inspecting the tussle. At the same time, he collected Jack's fallen beret and flung it his way.

"Pick your shit up."

Churchill involuntarily received the attire, stowing it partially in his grimacing poise along the floor.

"The warrant ...?" McNaughton rumbled at his stunned sidekick, and Garland presented an envelope which he in turn snatched before tossing it insensibly onto Churchill's incapacitated collapse. "The name's Constable Jethro McNaughton of the Special Investigation Branch, Criminal Investigation Department. *That there* is an official letter of attendance at the GCM, Colonel. You're due in front of the *Judge Advocate General* in five days ..."

The summons letter landed on Churchill's debris-covered body. Still catching his breath, the wounded commando barely acknowledged it whilst squirming on his side, clutching at the sides of his battered abdomen.

That had been their purpose tonight: serving a warrant letter to Churchill to appear at a General Court Martial before the Judge Advocate General (JAG). But instead, it had turned into an infantile slugfest and bout of blood.

"What's the charge?" Churchill grumbled, preventing him from leaving now that the letter had been served.

McNaughton took a carefree second to finally insert a fresh splinter between his teeth. The sensation seemed to calm him down from his high, relaxing his breath. He answered, finally. "Treason."

Churchill felt for the envelope.

He could barely hold onto it, he was in so much pain.

"You stupid twit," still reeling in obvious hurt and breathlessness, McNaughton cursed over Churchill. Messily, he wiped the blood from his nose, observing the amount of crimson stain on his finger. During his departure, he decided to level with the accused. "Truth be told, I don't give a shit about you, Colonel!"

Judging by his tone, he was being candid.

Churchill slowed his exhales and listened well, lurching up from the splintery wreckage of the door.

"I want *Wingate* ... that's all!"

"Why me, then?"

McNaughton tried again to exit, but Churchill's questioning brought him back. "Because he's a fucking phantom! Impossible game to corner in the preserve. If it means convicting *you* of treason on his behalf for working with the enemy or conspiring against the King, then so be it. Putting you behind bars will bring him to the surface."

"Wingate doesn't care about me!"

"Contraire, Colonel. Once your name is up in lights, like regular clockwork, he'll show at Whitehall to try and cover his tracks of your black-ops bollocks ... and that's where I'll be, lying in wait to clap his cheeks."

McNaughton audibly clapped his facial cheek twice.

Churchill pointed at him with a sense of humorous irony. "I don't think that means what you think it does, my lad."

McNaughton was oblivious to the term's sexual meaning, but a spankings' a spanking, nevertheless.

"So, what happens to me, then?"

McNaughton stated in that same forthcoming tone, levelling with Mad Jack again with a scary sincerity in his voice. "You're a military man, Colonel ... surely you have heard of the expression *collateral damage?* You can rot in a POW camp with your treasonous friends for all I care, as long as I get my man."

From the floor, Churchill eyeballed him sternly.

This gent had a lot of pent-up hatred towards Wingate, and it seemed to be spilling over. It was on a whole other level compared to what he had previously expected. For all his emotional rage, McNaughton still approached it in the right way and without lashing out too far.

He took a calm breath. "See you in court."

Before the investigators could take two steps to vacate the hall, Churchill's voice called back their attentions to the 1B doorway. His own ineffectuality overwhelmed him as he lay in a crumpled wreck, barely able to find his feet in his concussed, intoxicated, and defeated state. There was little Jack could do to fight his own people, especially considering he was halfway culpable of McNaughton's impending accusations.

He was no war criminal ... but Churchill would eventually be held as accountable as Wingate for the indiscretions of the Berzerkers.

"Oi, what'd Wingate do to you, anyhow?!" Churchill barked as he leant in the doorway, sensing an underlining vendetta fuelling this man's personal war. His trounced tenor was that of a rotten child, furious at the repercussions of his own revealed wrongdoings. He would pour those frustrations on whatever topic he could, and McNaughton happened to be in the firing line. "Did he shag your missus or something?!"

Churchill taunted him as best he could on the spot as he found his feet, exploding out into the narrow hall of the hotel to hold his best composure. His eyes and voice chased after them.

The exodus of both McNaughton and Garland dwindled, though his attention returned one last time onto Churchill, as did hers. However, upon witnessing the pathetic sorrow of the mildly inebriated and now extremely concussed commando's posture as Churchill slumped into a mess after sliding against the wall, there was an encapsulation of triumph. There was no need for a witty come back. They had defeated this troop.

Gritting his toothpick, McNaughton left one last parting wisdom:

"'May you be in heaven a full half-hour before the Devil knows you're dead'."

The use of the traditional Irish blessing caught Churchill, causing him to involuntarily hold his breath. After what felt like a full five seconds, he remembered to breathe. The phrase essentially wished someone a quick passing into the ether, implying that sinful souls may be accepted into Heaven so swiftly that even the Devil wouldn't have realized they are absent from Hell.

Jack had heard it before, but not for a long time and only in passing.

Never had the saying been relevant to him, per se.

It was probably the coldest thing anybody could have said to him in that moment. It indirectly implied that Churchill was the sinful one and, upstairs or down, he could die for all McNaughton cared. He had his endgame agenda, and nothing would stop him from achieving it—not even the collateral damage dealt along the way.

With professionalism and withstanding integrity, McNaughton straightened his suit before he plodded along, nursing his head wounds under the escort of his partner.

In the wake of their departure, Churchill felt the walls he had so valiantly kept propped open finally crush him. He slid down against the parallel claustrophobic adjacencies, boxed in. Suffocating.

Managing to take a deep breath, he finally exhaled all the fear of dread and worry that had been bottled up within his chest for weeks. That part of the race was finally over and, for what it was worth, he was sort of relieved. Even in the guilt that had come to light, at least he had direction. It was soon to be all out from the shadows and into the harsh light of day.

No more running. It was now time to face this head-on.

Collecting himself, Churchill dabbed the blood at his nostril with his knuckle. His dressage suit was chaotic; untucked, stained, and torn, buttons pulled from his collar ... it was very unlike him.

Jack Churchill was a disaster.

Seated slouched against a wall, amongst the collapse of the splinters and dust ruins of the hotel room door, his stare lingered, fixated on an entire other mess that lay ahead of his warpath ...

Was this the beginning of the end?

Rolling thunder boomed in the skies above 1944 Germany.

In the middle of an endless night, the constant rainfall drowned out all peripheral audio containing their storytelling exchange—good thing, because the details were becoming especially spicy, and starting to come full-circle with regards to Churchill's short-lived, ultra-top-secret aux-ops career. In a previous chapter, they had circumnavigated the event without any incriminating detail during the initial retelling of the soldier's life; though, it was about to become relevant to the present portion of this warpath timeline ...

"So, what happened next ...?" Hardy asked with a concentrated frown as he leant across his bunk bed with a folded leg, fixated at his bunkmate and storyteller, Mad Jack. The events of this perpetual chronicle were starting to subvert his expectations as he knew of the history. If Churchill was trialled for treason, then how could he fight in the upcoming Italy Campaign by July of 1943? This allusion to incarceration didn't make sense historically, and Hardy was salivating to learn how the dots joined.

This true story was obviously not over.

At present, the weathered future version of Jack Churchill sat propped up on his bunk bed, resting against a splintery ligneous bedpost.

Pencil moustache no longer visible amongst his sprouted facial hair and lengthening beard, Churchill's mouth spoke the words as follows. "A court-martial happened. A war on a battlefront, for which I was most unprepared and inexperienced."

"They put you on trial?"

He gestured with an indecorous nod. It was but another displeasing moment from his life's story that Churchill was not too happy to divulge but was about to out of its necessity to this content. "An official inquest led to that, yes. It was a long and gruelling process that wore me thin. Honestly—it exerted me more than any battlefield."

Constructing his question so it did not appear to be out of jealousy, Hardy leaned in. "Well, did you tell *them* ...?"

Jack eyed him across the gloomy barracks.

"I mean, you would have had to have sworn an oath, right? Sworn on the King! Did you tell them about the secretive 'black-ops' stuff ...?"

The story was again teetering on the edge of the sensitive information that not even *he* was privy to acquiring in the past chapters of Jack Churchill's biography. Around the time that Churchill had been drafted by Wingate via Calvert, plucked straight out of the Second Manchester Regiment during his service in France, 1939. A chapter known as Dice. Until now in their documenting, Churchill had considered it irrelevant to the story to deem un-redaction. However, it would seem the details of what happened during those guarded winter months in Switzerland were about to become very, very relevant.

"*Aux-ops*," Churchill corrected the terminology to the preferred lingo. "And *no*. Not *technically*, I didn't."

Hardy's lips moved as he exhaled, unable to articulate the words he desired to use to express his exasperation at again failing to learn the finer details of this top-secret, classified black operation.

"I was close to it, though. I had to. My sworn oath to the King, as you put it ..." Churchill expanded further, sending a look over to Hardy who seemed genuinely upset that he was missing out on certain details for his comprehensive Churchill chronicle. These details were known to certain people—albeit a small roomful with some semblance of military clearance—but could not ever be to his *dear readers* of the general public.

Churchill detected his disappointment.

In the lingering silence, he cast Hardy a gleam.

He had truly left him hanging during his Once Upon a War portion of the biography, skipping over the Berzerkers' tale for the sake of secrecy and truly leaving him—and his readers—hanging ... though, it would seem, it was about to become significant.

Accepting that his—their—impending deaths were likely on the horizon, Churchill took a deep breath before arranging his comfort against the rickety wire bed. "Let's go back in time a lil' bit, eh? 1939, December ..."

Hardy's head turned so fast it almost detached.

His tired eyes blinked open, wide awake now.

The knowledge-thirsty American journalist nearly pulled a muscle as he energetically lurched up and rotated around on his bunk, facing Churchill. He immediately found his place in his ratty notepad, readying his pen.

"Wait—*really?!* I mean ... are you sure?"

Forming a smile, Churchill's head bobbled, finalizing his assent. "I will take certain liberties, and self-censor as often as necessary ... some of these boys might still be out in the field ... so, *like it or lump it.*"

Hardy stared confused for a moment ...

"It means: *take it or leave it*," Jack finally translated, clearing up his anglicisms and once again converting his *British English* to *American English*.

"O.K.!" Hardy nodded autonomously, becoming prepared.

He was *very* excited for this bit ...

"Go!"

'Readers, let's go back in time, even more so than the norm. Acting as an interlude to the war in Europe, between Jack's recent return to the Second Manchester Regiment stationed in France along the uneventful Maginot Line, December 1939 ... and the infamous ambush at L'Épinette in May 1940. As the history books would tell, Jack and I would like to steer you away from the progressive median for just a moment, and delve deep into the black abyss ...'

3 ♥   3 ♥

Dice (Part 2)

'In reference to France, Jack said earlier: 'The ladies of the night weren't like the ones in England. They were of a different calibre of sexhibitionism'. Therefore, the French brothel in Lille known as the Anges de l'Enchantement wasn't a brothel, per se ... it was better known as a 'grandee's club'. In late 1939, following their escapades evading local MPs at the ~~brothel~~ gentlemen's establishment, Mad Mike recruited Mad Jack into an area deeper than the authorized covert operation sections of the Secret Intelligence Service (SIS) or the even more clandestine Special Operations Executive (SOE).

'A black-budget venture with plenty of grey motives and white snow, this foreign mission became suitably christened as the 'Auxiliary Operations', and held its advanced training in the Mont de la Gouille mountain range. This location was a pleasant resort area in Switzerland, renowned for its alpine skiing during the season. It was located at the base of some of the highest summits in the Pennine Alps. Like all black-ops units, the outfit maintained full deniability by all sections of the Allied Armies and SIS, SOE, or any other government intelligence office branch.'

'Like any left-field foray entrusted in the hands of Orde Wingate, and wherever complete deniability may have been required by a country's government, it did not exist. Little did this ragtag hustle of Brits, Aussies, Yanks, and other Allied foreigners know, the Aux-Ops unit that would come to be known as the Berzerkers was to be disbanded within five months.'

'Even to this day, five busy, war-torn years later, as I sit here writing this hyperbole retelling of Jack Churchill's life in our shared barracks at the Sachsenhausen, the author still requests to preserve his oath of raised right-hand secrecy regarding revealing details of the surreptitious and fabled 'aux-ops' unit. I have persuaded him to break that pledge for the sake of expanding upon what is an already otherwise overextravagant edition of his biography. Reader beware, I guess?'

1939, December
City Streets
Lille, France

In the black of night, Mike Calvert could handle the borrowed civilian Autovia as though it were a rally car, drifting corners and sliding gears. They outmanoeuvred the cunning searchlights of authority.

"Jack Churchill, Jack Churchill ... I beg your pardon, mate, but by any chance, would you be the one they call *Mad Jack?"* the half-British, half-Australian accentuated whilst manning the helm of their getaway vehicle. Winding backroads, this motley trio were outrunning the enclosing MPs of Lille following the events of a raid on a brothel.

Without a scar yet on his mug, the pre-war Captain Jack Churchill proudly beamed from beneath his clean maroon beret—the signature headpiece of the Second Manchester Regiment, bearing the metal emblem badge—at his positive identification by this new acquaintance.

"The one and only."

And it was with that confirmation that Calvert braced the steering wheel and abruptly jammed his heel into the brake pedal. The Autovia came to an extravagant, screeching halt on a dirt strip several clicks outside of Lille. Now that they had cleared the city limits, there was not a soul to hear them in the night.

Churchill braced against the console.

Captive in the backseat, the unstrapped passenger Rex King-Clark rolled about brutally. He was Jack's best friend and had tagged along for tonight's adventures.

Due to the sudden stop, he bashed into the rear of the passenger's seat. Disorientated, he spied out the windows as the dust cloud trailing them caught up, consuming them now that they were stationary.

Eyes no longer needed on the road, Calvert offered his upmost attention on this eccentric topic of identity correlation.

"*THE Mad Jack?*"

Puzzled, Churchill nodded singularly.

"*HA!*" Calvert hooted overenthusiastically, rolling his eyes into the back of his skull before punching his buzzcut head repeatedly into the headrest. Due to his reaction, Churchill spied a quick gleam at King-Clark in the backseat. "That's bloody hilarious. They call me *Mad Mike.*"

Churchill snickered politely, though still slightly baffled at the previous outlandish overreaction by this possibly unhinged individual. There must have been more to it, and he awaited a real punchline.

"What a ... eh, a lovely coincidence?"

"*Coincidence?*" Mad Mike Calvert questioned with a tone hinting that description to be disenchanting. "No way, mate. What brought us together tonight, Mad Jack, was not a bloomin' coincidence. It was more than that. It was ... *fate!*"

"*Fate?*" Churchill's brow cocked.

Calvert shifted in his seat in order to address him with an absolute straightforwardness to his tone. "Jack, I'm from an unheard of—and certainly not spoken of—freshly established task force. We're currently charged with recruiting like-minded men from His Majesty's armies for higher than *top-secret* projects. They'd be a team of *shadows* running behind the borders and frontlines with operations into enemy occupied Europe ..." he elaborated, piquing interest, "... and I remember *your name* from the shortlist of blokes who I was to start rounding up from tomorrow. Mad Jack, you've obviously come highly recommended to us and to our unit's oversight which, although secretive, is completely official as far as recruitment is concerned. You would be effectively *on-loan* to us if you elect to join. All the while, your position among the Second Manchester Regiment shall remain, reserved in case you were to reconsider at any time."

An extended moment of silence enveloped the interior of the Autovia. It was Churchill's time for consideration.

Calvert's serpent tongue slithered. "To put this plainly, your status right now as a captain in the British Army is still somewhat *ordinary.* I ask you, Mad Jack ... how would you like to roll the dice and go *extraordinary?*"

The slight delay of Churchill's response caused Calvert to re-evaluate his candidacy for a brief moment; evident in how it caused him to cast a look of uncertainty towards the man as he stewed in silence—a silence that Calvert confused with deliberation by Churchill.

As if there was even a question?

Churchill took his time with his response. This was not because he was unsure, but merely because he was enjoying seizing the moment ...

Following his intensive gaze, he concluded his pondering with a seemingly complex riddle. "Mad Mike, I will say to you what the Scotsman with two penises says to his tailor when he queries whether if he parts to the *left* or to the *right* ..."

Mad Mike Calvert eyed him, genuinely intrigued, sensing an underlining joke that accompanied an otherwise sincere response somewhere. "... what's that?"

Churchill nodded with a genuine smile. "Aye."

1939, December
Manchester Regiment Ladysmith Barracks
Greater Manchester, England

The men subsequently mounted a navy ship back across the English Channel, arranging to appear at the Manchester Regiment Ladysmith Barracks in England where Churchill met personally with the chief of staff and the general of the entire *British Expeditionary Force (BEF).*

Churchill would here meet the unit's mysterious oversight ...

Well versed in the exploitation of legal loopholes, the oversight's conduct subjugated an element army's contract of service which allowed a serviceman to venture into a different section of the armed forces at a time of war. This stipulated that the right signatures must be obtained, hence Churchill's formal visit.

Standing in a brightly lit, musty office on the third floor of the barracks office wing, a pressed serge battledress-garbed Churchill stood at attention before the desk of the Chief of Staff.

Present at the barracks located on *Mossley Road, Ashton-under-Lyne,* were *Chief of Staff Henry Pownall,* and the highest-ranking officer of the entire British Expeditionary Force, *General Lord Gort.*

Also among them were two others in civilian dress who, too, were of utmost importance to this signing event ...

The room was silent apart from the scratching of a fountain pen on the thick administrative papers spread out before them. Gort's bushy, overhanging brow and deep-set stare watched Pownall as he signed his name. The document now temporarily excused the British officer in question of his duties as captain in the Second Manchester Regiment. He then took his place at the desk and observed the formality. Gort made his mark, and his focus trailed down the ladder of signatures; Churchill's application, Commander Woolsey's sanction, Pownall's approval, and now, his own endorsement as general of the BEF before finally settling on the two empty place markers for the two other gentlemen in the room. Gort returned the pen to the inkwell and eyed the remaining legal witnesses:

One, Jack had met and knew as his recruiter, Calvert. The other man was an older British gent whom Churchill had only met this morning and who was known to Pownall and Gort by the nickname he had heard one of them call him: *the Otter.*

Churchill perceived the walking pseudonym for a moment wondering how any respectable fellow could end up with such a strange moniker. He had combed dark hair, a clean shaven chiselled chin, and a discernible Roman nose, presumably from an unset breakage. All in all, he looked no different than the millions of other utility suit civilians marching the streets of London or around the Whitehall District, and whilst he currently lacked any military suit or insignia, he had an air of influence about him that boasted cutthroat politics, interwoven societal connections, a prosperous financial status, and a definite military background in which he had certainly taken lives ...

... *dangerous, shadowy, powerful* were a few other descriptive words that sprung to Jack's mind when he looked at this governmental spectre. There was an aura about the Otter that scared even him.

"... there you go," Lord Gort stated, releasing the document regarding Churchill's authorized transfer from the BEF and into the jurisdiction of this discrete shadow operation within His Majesty's Government. He was now, officially, a soldier on-loan, and not acting under property of the British Army or Government.

"Greatly appreciated, Chief, General," Churchill commented with a salute to each, which was formally returned, followed by a handshake. While they observed military formality, Calvert and the other mysterious suited gent in the room finished officiating the document.

Gort made comment with precise memory with regard to Churchill's recent reactivation within the British Army, following a hiatus from service. The general had such a stern atmosphere about him. His hollow glower made Jack feel slightly uneasy. "It feels like only yesterday your name drifted across my desk regarding the *re*-installation in the Second Chesters ... now, you can't wait to get out of the regiment?"

Churchill reclaimed the form from the desk and examined it before closing the file folder. There was a red stamp across the front stating bluntly *Hiatus from Service: Approved.*

"Apologies for that, General," Churchill finally replied. "I heard war calling, but in all earnestness, until the battle breaks out, I feel that I can help the fight elsewhere, sir. Even if it's from the shadows."

"Those shadows are pretty deep, Captain," Pownall remarked with an underlining forewarning. "Be careful they do not swallow you."

"Stop scaring the lad," Gort intervened, his voice more prominent and certainly more positive. "Jack, simply put, I wish that I had more men like you."

"As do most of the women in England, sir." Churchill surprised even himself at the speed with which that witty retort came to his brain and left from his mouth. It left himself wondering if he'd crossed the line of decency in front of his superiors.

The wordless pause was stifling.

However, the general then erupted into laughter, slapping a heavy hand on Churchill's shoulder and leaning on him as if to prevent his collapse.

Gort smiled wholesomely with his tea-stained dentures and extended a hand, shaking Churchill's across the desk. Concluding their business, he then offered the gesture to the mystery gent referred to as the Otter. It was like an official/unofficial hand-off that closed their dealings this morning.

Gort's composure with this man suggested a degree of priorly established camaraderie. This was obviously not the first time the general had signed across men of action to this suited correspondent. "Look after this lad. We'll need him back again soon enough."

"What lad?" the stark Brit's voice boomed in a contrasting tone. Despite speaking at the same volume, his words managed to be louder, conveying a certain captivation. The mysterious codenamed man beamed his crooked, cigarette-stained teeth and held it well—a little too well—slightly unsettling Churchill in the process.

This guy resembled a shark.

A hunter-killer type.

What had he just signed up for ...?

After a second, they all sneered and laughed except for Churchill, who grinned pleasantly along with the men but also couldn't help feeling slightly daunted by the fact he, as far as the British Army was concerned, now no longer existed ...

... he had just signed his life away.

Once dismissed and downstairs of the barracks headquarters, Churchill, Calvert, and the Otter waited at a valet rink, to which their vehicle was hastily returned in the official VIP parking bay outside of the military building.

The three got in. Calvert drove.

Once they exited the gates of the Ladysmith Barracks, Churchill became overcome with a fleeting sense of forlorn for his duties. He had worn the British military uniform on and off since he was a young adult, often boasting of his exploits under the Union Jack ... Now, he was trading it all in for all-black attire and complete and utter secrecy, swapping his iconic maroon beret for a black one with no logo. The change left him with nervous butterflies in his gut.

Heading into the black was both scary and exciting.

Most unmilitaristically, as their vehicle rolled into midday traffic and stopped at a set of traffic lights, Calvert and the Otter unpacked and lit up tobacco sticks in the front, cranking the windows for the waft of smoke. Without a word spoken, they offered one to Churchill, which he declined the habit as always. He hoped that that had not been a loyalty test and that he had just failed.

"Where do we go from here, sir?" Churchill questioned boldly, solely occupying the backseat. "Training?"

The surreptitious Otter eventually replied. "*Training?* You've had your training, Captain Churchill ..."

This anonymous ringleader finally articulated his introduction, turning in the passenger's seat to properly recognize Churchill and hold out a hand in gesture.

"Allow me to properly introduce myself," the Otter said as he offered his attentiveness. "I am *General Orde Wingate.*"

Jesus Christ, Jack thought as his heart stopped ...

Tunnel vision set in ...

He had heard of this character a few times during his career, with Wingate's name often in headlines for controversial reasons.

"General?" Churchill's brow fluttered in surprise. Since rank was the only thing Jack verbally queried about the introduction, Wingate assumed it safe to say that Churchill had heard of his reputation.

Churchill acknowledged with a nod. "Pleasure, sir."

Wingate held a particular flame in his brown-eyed stare as he finally revolved back around from introducing himself to Churchill and shaking his hand. There was something sinister in those dark eyes and it scared Mad Jack.

The man seemed exceptionally out of place for the climate of England. Presumably, it was from spending so much time in the service in sunnier climates abroad, but his flesh had a certain tanned and leathery appeal.

Their blasé temperament lacked any official proceedings regarding formalities and etiquette. Jack Churchill's well-endowed skillset for manners would definitely go to waste with this lot if they shared Wingate's unsettling temperament. This unit reminded him of a privateer's tale: conscripted pirates.

The whole theme was very *grey,* and very *off the reservation.*

He recapped something Calvert had mentioned on the boat ride from France: *'there's white* (the army), *black* (black-ops) *and then there is grey in the middle—*that's where we will be operating'. He now fully understood this.

Knights who lacked all proper conduct.

Soldiers without a uniform.

Churchill mostly recalled Wingate from a few hearsays and ghost stories in the past. Stories he had primarily heard from closest friend King-Clark, who had worked in a unit constructed by Wingate last year, which surrounded the controversial and heavily Whitehall-dismissed *Special Night Squads (SNS)* in Palestine.

To his partial knowledge, before it was quickly disbanded, the SNS was an early attempt at British black-ops. It was a befitting squadron until they were held responsible for getting up to some nasty scuttles behind enemy lines in the black of night while nobody was watching. After it was placed under Wingate's direct command, the operations became more frequent and more ruthless, with some horror stories even reaching them at the front. The local Arabs even complained to the British about the unit's brutality and harsh disciplinary practices. Members from within the field squads criticized Wingate's methods, stating that during the raids on Bedouin encampments, they would behave with extreme viciousness and open fire without mercy. More than once, he had lined rioters up in a row and shot them in cold blood—technically unsanctioned executions. Furthermore, there were allegations against him of civilian abuse, murder, even rape. When put to trial, Wingate did not try to justify himself, simply stating that *'weapons and war cannot be pure'.*

These guys were not privateers ... they were straight-up pirates.

In the backseat of their commute out of London, Jack had hoped they had not heard his gulp after Wingate turned around, displaying that Roman schnoz and his permanently impassive stare.

"Training?" Calvert added with a chortle as he drove, shedding light on the obscurity, probably feeling as his recruiter that he owed Churchill as much. He kept his eyes on the road and craned his chin to speak over his shoulder. "Nah, mate, you've already had your training, it's why we picked ya. You rolled the dice and got double sixes ..."

Churchill played along with this game enthusiast, assuming that he was some sort of piece on a board, considering the analogy. "What did I land on?"

" War," Calvert faced forwards. "Go straight to *war.* Do not pass *go.* Do not collect *two hundred dollars."*

The metaphors always came back to Calvert's apparent obsession with board games, but Churchill felt it was an insight into the mindset of his newest allies. How they felt towards their lives and their role in the war, that it was all a game to them.

Be that as it may, Churchill nodded approvingly.

His usual humorous side was still somewhat dampened by all the looming secrecy of his new assignment. He was a ship drifting into uncharted territory—potentially hostile.

When entering the dark abyss, an overwhelming sense of anxiousness was natural. Both Wingate and Calvert seemed to respect that, if they detected it at all. Churchill had the car ride to reflect upon the sentimentality of his feelings before it would be time to staunch that stiff upper lip. It would soon be his turn to roll the dice and move himself along the board ...

... luckily for Jack Churchill, he never loses.

"War?" he invited, projecting a sense of fearlessness and courageousness that he believed these two hard-asses might expect to hear. "I didn't think there was a war to fight yet?"

Churchill's statement bore fruit.

In 1939, war had officially been declared, but there was technically no *warfare* as of yet—at least as far as Great Britain's Army was concerned along the supposed frontline. Jack knew this first-hand.

Wingate eyed Churchill in the reflection of the driver's mirror with that deathly stare of his.

"There's always a war. You just need to know where to find it ..." his unblinking eyeline hovered for longer than it needed to before it finally declined in yaw, now watching out of the windshield.

"... and what if you can't find one?"

Wingate rocked about in the passenger's seat, watching the world go by out the window. He answered a little too casually for comfort:

"Then we start one."

1939, December
Winterthur Resort, Mont de la Gouille
Swiss Pennine Alps, Switzerland

Preparation for the unit was not to be in dreary England.

Instead, touring by discreet civilian passage prior to assembly, the individual additions to Wingate's unit exported into the winter wonderland of Switzerland.

Upon the outbreak of war in September, like all European countries, Switzerland had immediately mobilized their armies, preparing for an invasion by Nazi Germany. Military defences were fully organized and able to fortify positions throughout the country within days, and their borders locked up tightly. Thoroughly detailed invasion plans were drawn up by the German military command to attempt taking the landlocked country, nevertheless, they were discarded due to a combination of military deterrence, economic concessions to Germany, and good fortune regarding the urgency of Switzerland's incursion in comparison to France or Italy. Due to the terrain, a costly alpine war was strategically impractical for them.

As a result, Germany did not attack.

Attempts by Switzerland's minute Nazi party to affect an *Anschluss (connection/joining)* with Germany failed miserably, fundamentally due to Switzerland's strong sense of national identity and long tradition of direct democracy and civil liberties. The Swiss press vigorously disparaged the Third Reich, often infuriating its leadership in Deutschland. In turn, Berlin denounced Switzerland as a medieval remnant and its people renegade Germans, and so on as the distaste towards one another reached the boundaries of hostilities.

Through diplomacy and supposed good luck, Switzerland managed to maintain its neutrality to the war. Assisting in Hitler's disinterest in invasion, the possibility that Switzerland remained neutral could be beneficial as a haven for Nazi spoils (such as gold) and criminal exports seeking exoneration from persecution by the Allies.

His plane flew into the *Aéroport de Sion,* where a befitting Mad Jack dressed entirely in civilian attire was ushered to a funded vehicle by a personalized valet.

They rode in a pearl white *1933 Panhard et Levassor.*

The drive was long, bringing his arrival time into the afternoon. After winding a lush and visceral backroad across some of the slickest slopes along the highest summit in the *Swiss Pennine Alps*, the awe-stricken Churchill's private taxi pulled up near the valet rink of a double-storey log ski resort located in the *Mont de la Gouille Mountain Range:* a popular tourist destination and resort area on the junction of Switzerland and Italy, famous for its alpine skiing. The holiday establishment was named the *Winterthur Resort* after some famous Swiss botanist who was from Winterthur.

A true sign of the times, the commencement of war had seen tourism at an all-time low. The establishment appeared to be empty.

The temperature this time of year typically put the Mont de la Gouille Mountain Range somewhere between 10-degrees and minus 10-degrees, depending on the day. Needless to say, when Churchill climbed out of the cab, he was blasted with an icy reception much colder than anything he could recall experiencing in his life. Dressed in his civilian clothing, his luggage had packed no uniforms or paraphernalia presenting insignia, as requested by Wingate. Churchill, nor any others invited to this underground meet, were permitted to be represented by any sort of identifying dressage. As a result, he dressed up for the occasion in typical Mad Jack elegance ... and thusly, a blisteringly gust of cold air blew straight up his Scottish kilt sending his nuts on a full-scale retreat into his pelvis.

From the trunk, the driver collected his passenger's luggage—one of which was a strange suede soft case, approximately six-feet long, which had required him to open the pass-through mechanism of the folding back seat in order to fit it.

Bracing the icy current caressing his genitals, Churchill wordlessly tipped the driver before collecting his two bags of luggage and hastily upping the half dozen creaky ligneous stairs before the large front foyer of the establishment. He didn't have much time to take in the view or read the signage before working the heavy wooden door.

In a heave, he shoved open the wind-blown entrance to the resort, shuffling inside. Once the burdensome door closed behind him, and the whistling pitch of the breeze outside muted into a tranquil indoor serenity, he caught a breath. He entered a luxurious heated foyer that was welcoming as a flash of warmth both in the sense of temperature and colour. The entire open area was wood and brass, and seemed quite prestigious, complete with a dangling crystal chandelier that sparkled and glistened, as well as many hanging tapestries and ornaments with golden frames and polished pomp. Even at his feet, the carpet was an aged velvet red with trim.

Even though it was only the late afternoon, the foyer of the resort was empty. Although the centre isles and passageways were illuminated adequately by sources of natural light, diffraction created much gloom in the shadows, especially in the corner spaces of each nook and alcove.

The echoic, grand lobby seemed to be only occupied by a single attendee at the front desk; an elderly male concierge, assumably, due to the red blazer and name badge. The friendly seeming fellow glanced upon Jack's noisy, windblown entrance.

After removing his tangled scarf from around his neck and straightening his military unit tag-free black beret upon his dome, Churchill carted his two bags, progressing towards the reception desk.

The scent inside was thick with the fume odour of an indoor fireplace, emanating from the radiating heat source of a nearby connecting lounge room/public common space on the left of the foyer. Raging with contained heat and glowing a balmy orange, an enormous indoor stone mantel fireplace against the far back wall reached to the ceiling between two gorgeous windowpanes that offered a view of snowy forestation outside. It was quite picturesque.

The guest shared space felt homely and appeared cozy ...

... it was also occupied by a few men, going about their business.

With a subtle glance as he sauntered along the carpeted entrance, Churchill made out the presence of several other apparent lodge guests in the connecting lounge and side bar. The lodgers within the common space were all men, dressed in combinations of sportswear, sweatpants, loosely buttoned-up shirts with undone cardigans. Beanies, gloves, even thick woollen socks. Some smoked pipes, others, cigarettes. Almost all of them had an alcoholic drink.

Other than the relaxing beverage, one other thing they seemed to all have in common was their regulation shaves and haircuts, with fellow trifle-builds, heights, and sprightly age. They may have been disguised as civilians, however one thing a soldier preferred to remain in was the type of heavy booted footwear. If the other attributes weren't enough to give their profession away, an astute stare such as Churchill's made for that specific detail.

They were soldiers—nay, *mercenaries.* As he now technically was.

There was approximately a dozen of them, maybe more.

At least he was in the right place.

In turn, Churchill's presence caught their eye. They traced his posture, studied his every move. Tracking his pace, they adjudicated his every portion in an exchange as he did theirs in the vibe of an animal kingdom, sizing each other up. It mimicked the wild: predators and prey, and Churchill was yet to know where he would fit in this food chain.

On a whole other level, he saw the devil in their sets of eyes; sunken, war-straddled stares lingering beneath scarred eyebrows, patchy facial hair, and rugged scorns that unforgivingly belied their young ages, forever trapping them behind the yawns of old men sough after a sip of turpentine to drown the spirits.

Through their underlining malice and ugliness, Churchill was but only a reflection, for he, too, fit their exact profile ... and was even checking-in for the exact same reason.

They were all here looking for the same thing ...

A fight.

This was a clinic, and they were all addicts ... addicts for war.

Whilst he drew nearer to reception, Churchill panned his gaze away from the men in the lounge and onto the concierge. Although he knew them to be not a threat, rather potential allies, he still held his ground with the stare-off until he reached the desk.

He wouldn't be considered below them in the food chain, at least.

As he approached the concierge, the single attendee in the blazer averted his eyes. He was an older chap, potentially even the proprietor or at least sole vender of the resort. Calmly, he rose and drifted away rudely ...

"Eh, hul—Hullo?" Churchill asked as the old man vanished from sight through a curtain-covered doorway. The chap was old, but surely not senile.

In a huff, Churchill set down his bags and hitched an arm, elbow resting on the counter where there resided a shiny silver bell set. Although he was tempted to tap it for assistance, something told him that it would not recall the attendee.

After a few quiet seconds, he gazed out to his side, eyeing the quiet grouping of men in the lounge area right as their culminated focus finally fell from off him, back to their various newspapers, books, wristwatches, cradled alcoholic beverages, or even just out of one of the many frosted-over windows where they observed the snowfall outdoors. They minded their own businesses as if Churchill's was none of theirs.

With his sterling stare squinting to capture detail, Churchill tried to spot anyone he knew—which, in total, there could be only *one* other than their mysterious group leader, and that was Mike Calvert. He couldn't see either man in this small crowd.

Growing impatient, Churchill tapped the service bellend—

"Glad you could make it, Mister Churchill," the British voice of Orde Wingate announced from offside, taking him by surprise. He must have emerged from the dark connecting hall near an elevator and wide staircase access for the hotel's upper floors.

He noted the use of his pronoun rather than his rank. It seemed purposeful.

"General, sir. Greetings."

"You can holster the military decorum here, Jack. Relax."

"Yes, sir," Churchill remarked, embracing the super-eccentric man with a handshake of which he was fast to remove the glove from his right hand prior. He immediately noticed as Wingate's arm extended out his sleeve that he was curiously wearing multiple wristwatches, approximately three on each arm, perhaps more hidden under the sleeves. The man wore the jewellery as routinely as a lass would bangles. What the actual fuck?

A form of pleasantry, Churchill disregarded Wingate's peculiar peripherals, but not before he intercepted his own slice of dyslogistic pie. While the two men greeted with a firm shake, Wingate's signature carnivorous stare gave Churchill's attire the once over—especially the tartan kilt wrapping his lower half.

Jack had packed two kilts for this winter venture, both of a heavier type of tartan. The warmer thread counts were roughly *K/4 R32 K32 Y/4* and were fabricated for the temperatures of Switzerland. His selection for his arrival into the mix was the *Shepherds' plaid*, also known as *Border drab*. This 'Border tartan' kilt was comprised of olive drab and beige in check design.

"Please ...... call me Orde," the host retorted after a pause, forming what would soon become thought of by Jack as Wingate's *Cheshire cat grin*. It was unsettling, for he always did so in a downward lurching gaze.

Churchill acknowledged, but preserved an ingrained etiquette.

"Yes, sir."

Wingate's view finished taking in Churchill's clothes before making comment with regards following the extensive examination. "Well ...... I'll be buggered. Please excuse my flabbergastedness. Seeing you dressed like this; this *kilt*, this *get-up* ...... you remind me of an old acquaintance ..."

To add to the growing social discomfort, Churchill was fast realizing that Wingate seemed to pause a lot within his sentences. This constant lingering .... combined with his .... habitual prolonged gawking .... was a concoction for labelling him an awkward social anomaly. By default, Jack was starting to think all the rumours about the Otter to be factual, namely the one that labelled him a proper weird cunt.

"Must be a handsome devil, then," a little late to the comeback, Churchill commented with a little reinforcement by his winning grin. He found himself immediately grasping at resolve, forcing himself to calm. He didn't know what it was in the air, but the presence of Orde Wingate made him uncomfortable. Knowledge of his prior conducts could have been the reason; flooding memories of the horror stories, or maybe it was just that predatory glower of his. It elevated his heartrate, and he felt like he needed a drink.

"Ha-ha," after a pause whilst he processed the quip, Wingate finally laughed out loud. Naturally, the weirdo had an awkward laugh. It exploded out of nowhere, as if he was slow on the uptake of the joke but it retracted twice as fast, returning his face to a flat and resting expression. "I wouldn't know. Unlike him, I don't have eyes for that sort of thing ..."

Although Churchill maintained a polite grin, he wasn't sure to take offence or not to the homophobic remark because of the relation to wearing a kilt. "He is ... queer?"

"Who?" Wingate's expression felled, in questioning.

Jack's eyes flicked sideways. "Your acquaintance."

Did this guy have memory loss?

Was he on something?

Or was this just Orde Wingate whacko?

Still processing, Wingate recoiled an inch.

This topic had become knotty but could be saved. Churchill was not exclusively homophobic. There was nothing wrong with a man being light in his loafers for it affected him nil, nonetheless, he was unsure on Wingate's opinion on the touchy topic of sexuality. The Otter may have been a notorious eccentric racist; however, they were talking about someone he knew personally, and it may have insulted his host.

"Eh, he's, eh, let's say a little ...... camp."

"*Camp?*" Churchill raised a brow, keen and able to save the situation from gracelessness and discomfiture. He questioned sarcastically, indicating broken ice with a gleam. "But how can that be? I thought you said he wore a kilt? The Scots are red-blooded. They knew nothing but hardihood, gallantry, and toxic masculinity."

Wingate straightened out. "I meant, you remind me of him, not only due to your ensemble, but ...... for your traits, also, Mad Jack. He, too, charges into modern-era battle with a bloody big sword."

"Sounds like he has great taste in attire and armament. We'd get along famously, I'm sure."

Wingate still held his social lark as they chatted. "Oh ...... we'll see."

Unknowing how to react, Churchill just stared.

He held onto his smile, but it was fading fast, submerging in this gauche ocean of which he still felt vastly adrift.

"It's a ...... *complicated* acquaintanceship. Explanations later, perhaps over a beverage?" Wingate delegated an offer Churchill could never refuse.

Churchill tipped his mounted bonnet. Although he had gotten away scot-free just now with potentially offending his new boss, impressed within him along with the constant need to uphold etiquette, Churchill was stubborn with his humour boundaries and the need to press them. It helped to establish any constraints for later in their company. "Alcohol? You know the way to a man's heart, Orde. Are you sure that *you're* not a lil' bit queer?"

Wingate chuckled hysterically at the sense of comedy. It was great to know that he and Jack could both take 'em as well as belt 'em out. He eyed Churchill's dressage once again and baited for more teasing humour. "I am not the one in a skirt."

It wasn't funny but Churchill laughed, taking it on the chin.

"Aren't you cold in that thing?" Wingate conversed further as he escorted Churchill into the lounge connected to the foyer. They left his things at the unmanned concierge desk.

"Not at all," Churchill deflected. "Sorry I am a tad late. The airport was snowed in. Delays all-round, I'm afraid."

"Perfectly fine," after a pause, Wingate questioned aloud with a wave gesture. "Did you ...... meet the mob, yet?"

While Wingate persuaded Churchill along, shepherding him into the connecting room which had a sunken carpeted floor connected by a dropped step, Jack had time to make another assessment of the Otter; his long pauses during communication, his strange stare, his wooden movements ... perchance the man had just simply copped too many shockwaves from exploding hand grenades during his illustrious career as a blunt instrument?

Maybe a bit of shrapnel to the cranium, even?

He started to force an understanding of the fellow. There had to be a reason for his weirdness. Nobody this peculiar progresses to the rank of general. Politics weren't a well-versed topic of Mad Jack's, nor was pretending to understand them. Perhaps he had a lot of friends in high places?

Churchill followed his gaze beyond into the shared lounge and carpeted games room where now ... the area was strangely vacant.

"Eh, yes, I, eh ... hold on, there was a bunch of people here a minute ago—" Churchill was startled. The realization of their absence ended his sentence prematurely. After glancing around the warm lounge area, unable to see a single one of the men he had seen just mere seconds ago, he turned back around to face his escort, Wingate ... only to catch a glimpse of nearly all ten men now standing within his precise proximity. They were arranged and posed photogenically, like a class photo.

Churchill had not heard them move at all.

He hid his surprise and shock well.

"G'day, Jack!" now present with the group was Mad Mike Calvert.

He stepped forth from the group of at-ease postured civilian-clothed men. Wolves in sheep's clothing, none of them sported any form of military uniform—as requested—but all of them looked soldierly.

One of them had a pistol—seemingly an M1911—bulging in his back pocket. The machismo did not end there, for another was using an army bayonet to clean dirt out from beneath his fingernails. These supposed civvies were sporadically armed.

Suddenly, Calvert stepped forth with an introductory tone.

As one of the more established members of Wingate's circus, he did well to act as a moderator, showing Jack the ropes as well as introducing the gents as they became relevant.

"Jack Churchill ... meet *The Berzerkers.*"

Churchill greeted along with a nod. "Hullo, lads."

The gesticulation seemed to not be immediately reciprocated.

The men were all expressionless and robotic, as if they didn't speak the English language or something. There were maybe two slight nods of the head in his direction, implying greeting, along with silence and maybe a sniffle.

They appeared to not take kindly to fresh meat.

"Now, just to be clear, that's Berzerker with a *Z* ... but Orde will soon get to that. Oi, say *hi,* ya rude pack'a wet dogs!" Calvert remarked vociferously when he released Churchill's handshake, standing alongside him to face the other members.

They remained silent.

It was as awkward as it was ominous. The tension was undeniable.

"Don't worry. You're like a new pup to the wolfpack, but they'll soon open up and take you in as one of their own, I just know it," Calvert comforted Churchill. "This is just how this lot say *hello* to new people. It doesn't happen very often."

Jack's head tipped. "If this is *hello,* I'd hate to see *goodbye.*"

"*Nice skirt!*" one of them said like a heckle, followed by another.

He was a Brit, naturally.

"*You a poofter or somethin'?*" an Estuary English accent commented rudely.

"It's a kilt. And no, whoever said that," Churchill frowned whilst giving the explanation to someone whose lineage suggested they should probably know better (if educated).

"*Did you bring fuckin' skis?*" another one of the Berzerkers spoke, a Welshman this time, coming off quite discourteous with his tone. His boot coarsely tapped Jack's suede bag laid at the foot of the concierge desk.

Churchill stood tall, eyeing the question giver. There seemed to be a severe lack of respect and decorum among this group. He realized that they would be slightly immoral having been stripped of their military décor, but he didn't think he would be stepping into a juvenile frat. It was like he was a substitute teacher showing up for class in severe need of disciplinary advice.

Feasibly it was their way of a haze, and thus Churchill did not allow for himself to be offended—or intimidated, for that matter.

What the Welsh questioner was referring to was the second bag of luggage in Churchill's possession at the base of reception. It was a long, six-foot case housing some form of specialty equipment. Concealed within was his longbow and basket-hilted claybeg sword: his weapons of choice.

Churchill responded proudly and with modesty, not stooping to their level. He retained his polite protocol. "Eh, why, no. Though, had I known this get-together would be located at a ski resort, I would have packed a pair."

"*So, what is it then?*"

"They are my tools of trade, lad. My weapons of choice—"

Record skip.

Abruptly cutting him off, a man suddenly shouted over him.

"*BERZERKER!!!*"

Unexpectedly and from completely out of nowhere, one of the men—a short and stocky buzzcut kid, approximately twenty years old or less—ripped off his beanie and bellowed at the summit of his lungs, lunging from the assembled crowd with a scarily rich bawl.

It was a *battle-cry* catching Churchill by surprise, like a bombshell had gone off. He tensed as the young skinhead, whose movements were mostly restricted by his coat, upped, sprinted, and tackled into his lower half.

An apparent argy-bargy out of nowhere, the two toppled over one of the lounges and onto the carpeted area of the common space lounge room.

Churchill was fast to counter, however.

Utilizing his long-acquired combat training, he revolved with the attacker in his grapple, managing to fling him clear after following through with a reverse shoulder-roll, using the almost bald grunt's own momentum against him. The throw exposed his bare, hairy legs from his hiked kilt, flashing every onlooker with his bare pale ass in a flash.

The assault was primitive and unprovoked—conceivably some sort of humiliation for the new guy. Regardless, Churchill took mild offence and reacted thusly. This was extremely random and odd, but instinctually, Churchill balled both fists as he became upstanding, ready to fight.

Fast to regain his footing at a bent stance, Churchill beheld a wide-eyed gaze. Adrenaline fuelled his immediate defence towards anybody else who may attack him.

Men laughed. The tension simmered down.

"*Oi! Oi! Ya crazy prat!*" Wingate called at a sneer, intervening late in the puerile façade. Through his Cheshire cat grin, he aimed at Churchill a low-key "Sorry, Jack!" And to the random bald kid: "Enough, ya daft git! He doesn't know what you're on about yet! He's been here for two bloody seconds!"

Unbeknownst to Churchill at this point, the very foundation tactic this special breed of combat fighters was taught was to shout the term *berzerker!* as they viciously attacked in a fashion such as thus. Following their standoffish introduction, this was but a playful example and unofficial initiation into the unit for a stupefied and unsuspecting Mad Jack.

A few of the surrounding men audibly chuckled, relentless in their oppressive mirth watching the strange actions of the skinhead who instantly snapped out of his attack, facing Churchill dead on.

The two met at an equal stance in the lounge room, and Churchill started to sprout a look of concern towards the other men of the unit. His guard would now be permanently up with this lot.

Disengaged, the buzzcut stepped in close, this time with his guard down and his palms open in a welcoming gesture, showing respect. He bore the attitude of a cocky little shit.

"Jus' 'avin' a laff, aye," he stated with a Welsh accent and ear-to-ear grin—which revealed that he already had two missing teeth, likely from crash-tackling random strangers and bashing his head into solid objects.

Jack eyeballed the man. There was something not right about this kid on an almost attention-deficit level. As well as the few missing fangs, he also had several scars on his shaved forehead and a slit in one of his eyebrows.

Eventually, he overcame his hesitation to accept the humble handshake, and he stepped in—the gesture becoming a partial shoulder hug by the buzzcutted kid, which Jack had no choice but to accept in embrace.

"Respect, lad, aye. You took that hit like a champ, bruv."

Churchill called his attention back before he walked too far away.

"Oi. What's your name, young man?"

The kid stood tall. "*Humphrey Ruffell.*"

Jack jested as he stepped back up into the foyer, examining the lounge room with the fireplace along with Wingate and Calvert. "Ruffell, eh? I'll get you back for that one day."

Ruffell cracked his edentulous smile in acknowledgement, and Churchill did the same with a manner of mutual respect signifying that the first steps to a brotherly bond had been born.

The others guffawed, patting Ruffell on the back as they rejoined their immature and unfledged ranks, retiring into the warm lounge and bar area to share more laughs and more drinks. Churchill hadn't realized it yet, but partaking within the Berzerkers comprised much more socializing with alcoholic beverages than the Second Manchester Regiment or the British Army, in general. It appeared to be a favoured pastime of Wingate's, and therefore bestowed upon the men with absolute imprudence.

They may have worked hard ... but they partied harder.

"Eh, Mister Wingate, sir?" the elderly concierge appeared at the desk, calling over their enigmatic leader. Wingate wordlessly excused himself and tended to the worker in the background, likely having a discussion about something to do with their extended stay at the Mont de la Gouille Winterthur Resort.

"Surprise, *Mad Jack!*" with a sarcastic tone pronouncing his nickname, a blonde fellow—the same one with an obvious handgun stuffed in his back pocket like a wallet—stated amongst the mirth as they all departed back to the lounge after the show. It was the familiar face of Graeme Black, albeit a younger incarnation.

Freshly recruited from the *South Lancashire Regiment,* he was a tad more juvenile, still with his sun-bleached hair, but minus the full-blown imperial moustache that he would grow out. No surprise, he was a douchebag before joining Commando.

This was apparently all in what these men considered good spirits.

It resembled grade school when the teachers weren't around—only, this time, Jack Churchill felt as though he was the one about to lose his lunch quid.

"Welcome to the _special_ Special Z Unit, lad!" another man carrying a crystal tumbler clanking with ice cubes blubbered, followed by the whispered snake hiss of *'Berzerkerrrr'* by a few other fellows as they dispersed to return to their social activities in the lounge, of which they had apparent control over. They appeared to be the only guests in the entire hotel at this present moment in time—an orchestrated arrangement.

Churchill leered uneasily as the rest passed. Some shook his hand and grunted a form of salutation; others simply tossed him a raised chin of respect. All-in-all, it appeared that Wingate had approximately two dozen elite beings for this team: the Berzerkers.

"Welcome," the biggest gent loitered to speak. He spoke with an American accent and stood at least six-foot-ten, with broad shoulders and the meatiest of meatheads Churchill had ever recalled laying his eyes the girth around. He cranked at the lower back in order to eye him as he passed, forcefully shaking his mitten. He was intimidating but seemed friendly enough.

"Cheers," Churchill responded as the ogre passed, and he quickly gravitated towards the familiar Mike Calvert as if to make comment about the man's size, but shelved it for later. It *did* go without saying.

"With all due respect, brother," another one of the team commented in an Edinburgh accent as he grabbed Churchill's shoulder. He was of fair height, with his light hair in a simple French-style braid, sides cut shorter than a buzz cut. His Scottish accent was familiar to Churchill, being from Edinburgh rather than Glasgow (like his recurring friend) the intonation was more refined and of clearer pronunciation. "Es far es initiations goe, yoo just passed wif flourisheng colours, laddie. Mus' be tha Scot in ya, eh?"

After a slight hesitance, he responded with a potential overshare, deciding that he had nothing to hide from these sorts. "My great grandfather was Scottish ... He went mad and drunk himself to death ..."

The bulky mohawked Scot chuckled and nodded, accepting.

"Wha'er'wey ta goe, eh?"

In constructive agreeance, Churchill tipped his head. "Died the way he lived."

"Aye!" the Scotsman remarked in parting, following the rest of the hustle venturing into the carpeted common room that was about to be full of a dozen rowdy Englishmen.

"That thing isn't regulation," Churchill remarked about his hairstyle.

"Not a lot of what ya see 'ere is, mate."

That understood, Churchill bobbled his head whilst painting even more of a detailed picture in his mind regarding the dress and appearance regulations of Z Unit ... *there were none.*

"His name's *Scotty,*" Calvert pointed, presenting Churchill with a crash course in identifications. "And *those blokes over there* are *Joe, Arty,* and *Bort.*"

Most of the men namedropped by Calvert—*Scotty Wellings, Joseph Batey, Arthur Komrower, and Matthew 'Bort' Botfield*—regarded their identifications with an acknowledgement to Churchill, which Mad Jack reciprocated, greeting simply. He was able to relate their relevant nicknames for the most part.

"Bort as in *abort?*"

"Nah, Bort as in Bortfield, with an *R,*" Calvert quickly attempted an explanation regarding the amusingly convoluted backstory of the black-haired, blue-eyed, steely stared fellow with prominent cheek bones. "But his name's actually *Botfield.*"

"Oh?"

"Yeah. He joined 'bout midway through Palestine, only, there was another recruit there at the same time named *Matthew Bortfield,* exceptionally similar to *Matthew Botfield.* Confusing, eh?"

"Indubiously."

"Yeah. Well. Took us about a week to realise they were two different blokes," Calvert cackled at the hindsight tale of duplicated identity. "We noticed it a few times and assumed that either admin had made a manifest misprint or we'd miscounted during rollcall. One of 'em always said 'here', so we were like *fuck it,* and moved on. Anyhow, one of 'em dropped out soon after, but we just kept calling Botfield *Bortfield* for the laughs and then that eventually got abbreviated to just Bort."

"Fair enough," brow raised, Churchill dipped his head, moving on to the next quick question he had regarding these new faces. He nodded at the bearded Batey. "That mane surely isn't regulation, either?"

"Nope," Calvert said simply regarding Batey's shaved head and short boxed beard. He had a few indentations scarred through his scalp, of which his pallor complexion suggested a Nordic background.

Not much else in the way of formal introductions were exchanged in the moment, but the pretty boy in the middle was Komrower, and this was he and Churchill's first interaction. They would become friends and later, like Black, commandos. The chiselled jaw and dimpled cheeks of Arty Komrower were yet to become scarred as they would later during Operation Archery.

Calvert furthered, naming a few of the other men present, "The rude cunts in the corner are *Grae* and his mates *Brad* and *Mick*."

Black, *Bradley Rushworth*, and *Michael Dredge* barely gave Churchill an acknowledgement. This wasn't due to their supposed antisocial behaviour, per se, but rather because they were all apparently several drinks in and were at present hovering over the *Kimberley* phonograph cabinet in the corner of the room. A former Donkey Walloper from the *Royal Horse Artillery*, Rushworth appeared to have a silver tooth at the front, bore a shaved head, and heavy five o'clock shadow. Dredge was a Londoner from the *Royal Fusiliers*, and was clean shaven, tall and thin, with short brown hair, and a compulsion to chuckle loudly whilst excessively enjoying the unhealthy but often comical mockery of others, perhaps even a borderline katagelasticist. Each man cradled a tumbler of whiskey neat, smoked a cigarette, and were engaged in a good time.

Churchill eyed past them and surveyed the hi-tech unit right as somebody within their rowdy trio dropped the brass tonearm, touching the needle to the record. It created a scratch before tuning sound and playing music.

The unit possessed the popular *Pfanstiehl* needles that thrived for quality and longevity. Rather than the horn-style speaker that was typical of any gramophone or record player, the oak wood cabinet housed a speaker, as well as utilized two connected Thoren-branded speakers set up nearby, connected by copper wire. The music set-up was quite prestigious and would have been expensive, possibly even qualifying as high fidelity-grade.

"Is that a gramophone?" Churchill commented, observing the system from across the room. A few of the men huddled around it, cradling beverages whilst they selected something to play and set the mood whilst another few of them tended the bar or lounged around.

A man appeared from behind Calvert, sidling alongside Churchill along the rim of the room. He was of an olive complexion, wiry short hair that was receding, and spoke with an Israeli accent. "Yes, but this one is American made. The Yanks call them *phonographs*, isn't that right, Habibi?"

The large Yank Jack had just met earlier replied with a raised glass and playfully puckered lips, blowing Dayan a kiss.

With a grin, the Israeli turned to face Churchill and introduce himself. He extended a handshake. "Moshe Dayan."

The gesture was accepted. "Jack Churchill."

"*Baruch aba,* Jack."

Calvert interjected as Dayan moved away to join the others socially.

"Moshe and Orde go way back. He's come and gone in our antics since early Palestine. Does admin-grade shit, mostly, rarely trains with us. Processes a lot of the intelligence that comes in from various sources, as well as maintains many relationships with Orde's mates in the Middle East. He's on gap from being a command instructor for the *Haganah* leader's courses at *Yavniel.*"

"*Haganah?*" Churchill frowned, unfamiliar.

"*Israel Defence Force.*"

"Of course."

Churchill acquired more intel for himself. "What about the giant American? What's his story?"

"That's *Jerold Lee Douglas.* We call him *Gentle Jerry.*"

"*Gentle?*" Churchill cocked a brow. "I thought we were black-ops? Wouldn't *gentle* be the opposite of the desired prerequisite for such a pernicious profession?"

Calvert just smiled and held it.

Before long, Churchill finally detected a hidden contempt, and Calvert finally conceded. "Jack," he started. It then became evident that he was cradling a scotch and that it was nowhere near his first for the afternoon. "I'm way too drunk for you to be speaking such big words, yeah?"

Churchill pursed his lips and nodded. "Off day, eh?"

"*Off day?*" Calvert stated. "What's an *on day?*"

Churchill stood confused by the formality and duties of this *Special Z Unit*—of which, until just now, he had no clue the official name of. It appeared they had no military decorum whatsoever.

"Nice work with that, by the way. These guys are mostly fuckwits, but don't stress on it. It's a necessary gene for our particular breed. This unit operates in a marginally different way to anything you're used to in the Second Manchester Regiment. Most of these guys have almost gotten kicked out of the service for their eccentric behaviours."

Churchill absorbed, still mildly perplexed.

His momentary pause called for some exposition by their lurking fearless leader as he returned from his discussions of formalities with the resort staff.

"They've been selected because of their traits," Wingate added before towing their conversation away, leaving everybody to get settled for the night. It was rare he hung out and socialized with the other recruits. Of a night, he would often retire to his own quarters within the resort and not emerge until the following day. "We're all a little *mad* around here; each in our own way—just like you, Mad Jack. Consider it the principal prerequisite."

Churchill held an extended glance.

After panning about with his carnivorous stare, Wingate laughed with a theatrical state. "Worry not! Embrace it! You'll need it to keep your sanity in what comes next ..."

Churchill watched Wingate fade away as he upped the metal-framed spiral staircase that led to the upper floors of the resort, where most of the hotel rooms were located. "Mike. Show him to his room."

"Yes, sir." Calvert responded, stepping over and helping Churchill collect his luggage bags from the floor.

Another mercenary from the Berzerkers walked past, tapping Churchill's six-foot-long bag with his combat boot as he attempted to collect its handles. "Hi," the last man in the foyer greeted almost wordlessly with a quick handshake on his way into the lounge room. He was English, short, gaunt, with pale skin and a thin handlebar moustache that was a little lopsided. "What's your gear, then, eh? You said before that it was your *weapon of choice?*"

"A *longbow* and my *basket-hilted claybeg*," Churchill addressed him properly, standing proud and with the effects now by his side.

"A fuckin' what?"

"A sword."

"A *bow and arrow* and a *sword,* eh?" the moustached merc commented before joining the others in the lounge. He, as well, had a couple of teeth missing—an apparent recurring trait of these Berzerker members. It was beginning to unsettle Churchill, as he prided himself on his winning smile and feared for its loss. "You'll likely enjoy the way we operate then. ECQC, especially is our gig, lad!"

"Bala, *Jack*. Jack, *Bala*," Calvert made the quick introduction on the fly as Peshawar-born *Bala Bredin* also joined all the others, leaving just Churchill and Calvert on the edge of the foyer overseeing the gathering as the sound of the music caused them to raise their voices.

Bredin said before stepping into the lounge room to join the social happening, "Welcome to the team, Mad Jack."

"Cheers," he said, and then to Calvert: "*ECQC?*"

"It's what the cool kids call *Enhanced Close-Quarter Combat*. We specialize in the advanced hand-to-hand stuff—up close and personal with a range of splendid toys ... You'll see tomorrow. Calvert added with a nod. "Bala's our QM."

"You lads have your own quartermaster?"

"Too right. Wingate's got connections everywhere, including within the Ministry of Defence. He organizes to get us a lot of fancy gadgets and weapons, and Bala usually knows what they are and how to use them ... or he works it out—most times without disaster—and then teaches all of us. At the very least, think of him as our test dummy."

"And is Bala his real name?" Churchill inquired about the man he had just met.

"Nickname," Calvert frowned and eyed the ceiling. "Actually, I don't even know his real name. Leftenant Bala Bredin is all I've ever got when I met the bloke two years ago, though I did hear he was nicknamed during the RMC after a racehorse owned by *the Aga Khan*. Served with the guy for a stint in the SNS, you'd think I'd know his pedigree, ha."

Churchill had many more questions. Too many.

He was getting too tired from his day's travelling to absorb any more information and was now salivating for socialization with this lot over a beverage once he was shown his room.

Calvert called the lift. "There're a few others 'round somewhere. I'll find n' introduce you to them tomorrow—if they haven't bitched it and RTU'd already."

"How bloody many of you lot are there?"

"A few. Numbers rise and fall, faces come and go ... people leave, drop out, y'know ..." Calvert admitted. It was another insight into their lack of formality. "Don't expect to remember everybody's name."

Jack bobbed his head. "So, *Z Unit* ... how'd that come about?"

The mechanical elevator arrived loudly, cranking away.

The chains needed some fresh oil, as did the manual gate.

Calvert explained as they stepped in stride towards the arriving elevator within the lobby of the resort. "Wingate mostly recruits officers, but some exceptions are made. The way Orde explained it to me when I started is in an *A, B, C* all the way to *X, Y,* and *Z* kind of way. If *A, B,* and *C* are sectors of regular army, artillery, horse guards, you know like cadet school through to light infantry grunts, NCOs, eventually officers, up the other end *X* would be about special ops on that spectrum, *Y* would be classified ops, maybe spies and double agents ... well, we're the *Z*. We're the aux-ops. Completely off the reservation, we don't even fuckin' exist, mate. Not officially. Not even to *King George* or even *President Roosevelt,* himself. We're the polar opposite end of the scale of existence and any form of service statuses."

Churchill nodded, understanding, but still his clouded thoughts were heavy with a hundred complex questions. This was all so interesting; he just couldn't turn it off. "How does the unit get funding, then?"

Eyes back up at the analogue level-indicator for the arriving elevator, Calvert smirked cleverly in regard to the question, involving a smart answer to come. He was glad Churchill was intelligent enough to ask it.

"The Government, technically. But Orde is partnered with a whole bunch of gnarly shite. He's more on-the-record financier is some well-renowned war documentarist and, well ... its war time baby. Business is good."

"We're not documenting anything, though, are we?"

"Fuck no, mate. There's not a camera for miles," Calvert remarked as the elevator dinged, about to open. "Ultimately, it's the perfect way for the allied war effort to pump funds into this project but also keep it completely off the radar and out of any Whitehall ledger. If anything goes wrong, they've got complete deniability."

Churchill jested a great big nod.

What a brilliant idea someone had at the War Office.

They stepped into the lift with all the luggage. All rooms at the Mont de la Gouille Winterthur Resort were seemingly on level two.

Calvert conversed further. "Important things to know about the Alps is to keep your socks dry and feet warm and stay hydrated. Drink like a fish, thank me for it later. Apparently, somethin' 'bout the cold air 'n high altitude dehydrates ya faster than usual? Don't worry, I'm sure you'll hear all about it from Orde."

"Sure."

"Meet back down here for supper at nineteen-hundred-hours."

"Where?"

"Just in the lounge and bar. The kitchen is next to it."

"A place this big has no mess hall? No dining room?"

"It has a banqueting hall, yeah, but ... it's being used as our *war room*," Calvert answered, sliding across the wire gate and pressing a button on the panel. The elevator that the resort had was controlled by electronic components, complete with fancy backlighting. Business would have been good here before the war. It was funnily ironic how tourism had died because of it, but under these unique circumstances, the war was keeping it in business since Wingate's black budget had seemingly bought out the whole hotel.

The lift hummed as it operated, gyrating softly while ascending them to the next level. Whilst it performed its sole task, Churchill asked, "What about other guests?" This should not have been necessary after Calvert had just explained the secrecy of the aux-ops; everything they did should be done confidentially and could not be seen by a member of the public.

"Didn't Orde tell ya? He's booked this entire joint just for us!"

Churchill remarked under his breath, back on topic. "Oh, well, if that was check-in, I can't wait for this evening's entertainment ..."

Calvert escorted Churchill from the lift and along the left hallway passage. This resort level was much quieter away from the lobby and the connected lounge where the social conversing and music presently emanated from, however, there appeared to be a mezzanine with a balcony at the far end of this passage lined by a railing. Beyond that railing was a bird's eye view of the fancy lounge area. The area was architecturally abstract and open and, as a result, the noise, warmth, and light still travelled up somewhat.

These rug-lined wooden halls were dark and shadowy, illuminated by electric-powered sconce lights every ten metres. The warm glow did very little to light the passage and acted more as a limelight for guests at night. Light from the connecting balcony shone a glow that laterally illuminated the passage, casting a resonation of light enough for them to see.

"This is you: number eight," commented Calvert as the door opened before them, unveiling an empty room. "Benny's old room."

Churchill's brow tilted after Calvert went silent.

"What happened to him?"

"You ... you don't wanna know ..."

Following the ominous disclosure, Churchill gulp—

Calvert slapped him on the shoulder, catching him off-guard. "Just fuckin' with ya. He's fine. Benny got recalled back to England for *reasons.* Came down with a case of *littlebitchitus,* they say."

Incredulous, Churchill didn't question that condition.

Instead, he stepped inside his lamp-lit quarters, carting his luggage. The place felt homely and had been kept relatively tidy by the previous occupant considering there was no room service to clean it. The drawers were closed, the bed was made—not uncommon to have been shared by a fellow serviceman—and the small kitchenette appeared tidy. The bathroom, too.

"Nah, look, Benny was alright. Kept to himself. Bit of a whiner, complaining about everything. Drank a lot, too. Maybe too much."

Churchill's brow cocked. "There such a thing?"

"Fuckin' hope not!" he chuckled madly.

Calvert went to leave him, seeing him off for a moment.

He pulled the door over. "Settle in. I'll see you soon."

In the centre of the floor beside the bed, Churchill revolved and gave him a nod. If he had been a bellhop, he'd have even extended him a tip.

Grateful for the tour, Churchill simply offered him the gesture of acknowledgement before stepping over to close the door softly, veiling himself in a comforting silence for what seemed like the first time in a day of tiring travel, aquatinting, and exposition.

Jack hoisted his bag onto the bed. It was a double, seemed soft.

He unzipped his luggage, though something on the nearby dresser drawer mantle caught his attention, and he wandered over, observing himself in the slanted vanity mirror.

Rested upon a doily was a half-full bottle of single malt *Bushmills* along with some clean-looking crystal tumblers and a decorative decanter. There was a folded-over piece of paper resting against the bottle, creating an A-frame. It read simply:

Good luck.

There was nothing on the inside of the note.

It acted as more of a gift note; a caveat ...

Jack touched it, reading it prior to casting it aside in favour of pouring himself a drink. He uncorked the bottle and gave it a sniff before upturning a glass and free pouring a nip—

Movement behind him in the mirror's reflection caught his attention.

Before he c—

Tschh!

Like a strike of indoor lightning, the glass on the dresser exploded with a shattering shrill, causing Churchill to flinch and pinch his eyes closed, becoming sprayed with whiskey. The action was as though a whip cracker had snapped his lash with a surgeon's accuracy.

The movement he had noticed in the darkened quadrant of the hotel room was a man. Cloaked in blackness and absent any identifying features, the dark figure in a balaclava stepped forward into the lamp light. In both arms, he was holding a smoking pistol that remained aimed at his head ...

He had Mad Jack dead to rights.

Calmly ... Churchill placed the bottle of Bushmills back on the dresser, brushing off his palms of glass fragments and whiskey droplets from the eruption beside his person.

Tension rose steadily as the gun remained pointed at his head.

This faceless gunman had him in a compromising position, unarmed and vulnerable. Jack Churchill could have been a dead man here.

In the fleeting seconds, Churchill surveyed the weapon by its barrel. The piece was long and more extended than a usual handgun, which suggested use of a sound suppressing device known as a silencer—a futuristic gadget that quietened gunshots, and very likely to have been the type of gizmo Orde Wingate's men could have easily acquired. Upon a further glance of the sleek frame, it appeared to be an American *High Standard*. The model had an elongated, thin barrel, likely chambered in a low calibre for the functional silencer, likely rimfire .22LR.

A voice from the hall:

"*That'll do, Danny Boy.*"

Unexpected as to what would happen next, the faceless gunman suddenly lowered his weapon and audibly safetied it with a sharp metallic snap before striding to vacate. The one known as Danny Boy wordlessly complied and vanished into the resonating volume of the hall. Dutifully robotic by nature, Wingate's masked assassin-esque asset remained in proximity, spying on the situation through the cut holes in his ski mask.

In his absence, the tread of Orde Wingate hooked in, leaning on the doorframe and observing his newest addition as he stood naked; as good as dead.

Churchill's chin raised.

Nobody said a word for a full five seconds.

"Jack ..." Wingate finally spoke in his eccentric, protracted fashion. There was something new about his demeanour, about his tone of voice. He seemed serious. "I don't take ...... passengers."

Confused by all of this and covered in whiskey fumes, Churchill eyed him precariously after taking a quick glimpse down at his stinging hand, expecting to see blood. There was none. He was somewhat shaken by the scare; by the gunshot and the show of an assassin's weapon pointed his way, nevertheless, he remained composed. This may merely be yet another trial.

"This another test?" he asked.

Wingate remained suspensefully silent.

"If it was, how do you think you went?"

Churchill examined his stance, emitting a chortle. "Not *overly* well."

Wingate pushed off from leaning on the doorframe and entered the room, addressing Churchill with his dark eyes. "You were caught off-guard ...... unarmed ...... and unaware. There are no training wheels out here, Mister Churchill. No second tries. I have zero tolerance for dead men ...... am I understood? You must be prepared for anything."

Although already vertical, Churchill stood up straighter. "Yes, sir."

"Truth is, this was not a test ...... this was rollcall."

Emerging from behind Wingate, passing in front of the ski mask-clad one known as *Danny Boy*, Moshe Dayan swooped in, tending to a certain admittance ritual for those entering the Special Z Unit Berzerkers.

"Your I.D. discs, please, Jack?"

With mild hesitation, Churchill removed his fibre identification service tags from beneath the layers around his neck. The labels were a standard for servicemen and were inscribed with Churchill's blood group, service number, initials and surname, and even his religion.

Lifted over his head, he wound the lanyard before placing it into Dayan's open palms. "Thought you were just the admin."

"I am, chaber, I am. This is a mere formality."

Like everybody presently staying at the resort, the dog-tags were collected by Wingate's associate and added to the pile hidden safe within the led-lined *Ratner* safe behind the concierge desk.

For all intents and purposes after check-in ...

... he no longer existed.

None of them did.

"We're *well-oiled killing machines* ..." Dayan made mention before leaving. The renowned phrase seemed to follow Orde Wingate's ventures across history. "Ulam, machines do not possess names. Just omets; grease, gumption, et cetera, et cetera."

Dayan left, leaving Churchill and Wingate alone—Wingate, still cast literally and figuratively in this new light for Jack to see.

"Tomorrow ...... meet me here," he said, placing a folded card upon the short entryway table by the door which housed a key bowl. "We can see what you're made of, Mad Jack ..."

A few more seconds of silence followed, which Churchill watched wordlessly, unexpected of anything that could happen next.

Wingate left the room, but not before offering one last mention of advice. "Stay hydrated."

Well-Oiled Killing Machines

1939, December
Proving grounds near the Mont de la Gouille Winterthur Resort
Swiss Pennine Alps, Switzerland

They wasted no time in beginning Churchill's extracurricular training.

Outside, the brisk morning air of the snow-blanketed wilderness surrounding the resort was as refreshing as it was frigid. In the Switzerland outdoors existed a natural ease, relaxing and oxygenating, while at the same time, suffocating and tetchy—the soldier's curse; an incessant need to remain on guard and aware of the environment, which, in this dense nature, was a vast encompassment.

This endlessness of nature was as daunting as it was beautiful.

Icy glints and frost-kissed branches were at every fissure of daylight.

Beneath the skeletal canopies were cold shadow and snow piles.

Senses were innately altered.

Located a short distance into the winter woodlands contiguous of what could be categorized as the resort grounds, one could no longer see familiar landmarks—even the monumental Alps, unless they sought a clearing large enough to establish a vector. There were zero traces of any structures, of roads, of mountains. Everything recognizable had been swilled up in the density of the snow-covered vegetation.

In these parts, any man's daring intrepidness would waver to instinctive impulses, needing to work harder due to an unexpected realization of a clear and latent vulnerability. Out in this bliss, one had no way of knowing if they were truly alone. They could have very well have been walking into a threat or form of hostile territory.

Pupils contracted due to the blinding whites but then dilated to maximize visibility beneath the cold shades of shrouding canopies.

Ears remained pricked at any noise that the smothered surroundings hadn't dulled down.

Heartrate increased, flooding muscles with blood, should it happen to hasten to action.

Existing in this climate was exhausting.

Strung yew longbow down by his side, quiver of arrows slung and strapped over his shoulder, the woollen beanie-clad Jack Churchill arrived at the coordinates north of the resort where Orde Wingate had instructed him to be the night before, and at the inferred hour.

He stood idle for a moment, glancing about.

With every exhale he emitted a visible cloud of warmth.

The terrain of Mont de la Gouille was encompassed by such pure nature, it exhausted Churchill, requiring him to search the cantina from his parka pocket and consume an extended swig.

The water source tasted cleaner than usual. Churchill had thought this when tasting the ice-cold stream from the resort tap before his slumber the previous night and again this morning. There was an odd salinity to the water, perhaps delivered from an older sort of reservoir tank or piping. The type of snow-filtering attached to the resort may have caused it—he had noticed the filtration unit mounted on ground level on the rear of the building in the morning light. This concept was hardly mind-bending, as Churchill had visited a lot of different countries during his life and, nearly each time, the local waters had tasted different to those of England. Conceivably it was due to the lack of pollution in the air that had developed his expectations of taste.

Churchill took another drink.

From his six, a Scottish brogue grumbled. "*I doon like him, laddie.*"

In the absence of company, the Angry Scotsman had been summoned, appearing from the nether.

Unperplexed by the appearance of his Highland haunt, Churchill barely tipped his ear in order to listen good before taking another drink from the canteen.

MacLeòid expanded. "*He guvs me tha heebie-jeebies.*"

Jack frowned. "Who? *Orde?*"

"*Nah, tha otha codger som'ere out 'ere en tha blisterin' cold! Yeah, yoor nu uncle Otter-man. Somethin' 'bout him's a bit owl, doon yoo say?*"

Churchill waggled his head a little after he mused. "We're all a little mad, aren't we? I'm out here, in this *blistering cold,* carting a stick and string, chatting to a man who I saw die ten years ago and has been visiting me daily ever since."

"*Touché, aye guess.*"

"Nah, he's fine-o-fine, sir. A little *off,* sure. But fine."

"*He's got noe knoewn rank, noe knoewn uniform ... noe noetable experience, noe knoewn allegiance,*" MacLeòid went on, trudging in the snow around Churchill's standstill. "*I doon like 'im!*"

"You don't have to like him to trust him."

"An' yoo trust 'im?" MacLeòid responded. As always, the dead man was dressed in his dressage uniform, now holding his ungloved hands over his triceps for extra warmth to his chest, as if he could feel the winter cold.

Jack eyed him. "I didn't like you and I trusted you."

MacLeòid reeled. *"Bollocks! Ye farken loved me, laddie! This chap, though ... He seems like tha type ov melt who walks all tha way over ... all tha bloody way ... an' comes an' pees en tha urinal reight beside yoo, even though tha restroom es completely empty, an' he could pee elsewhere ..."*

Churchill elevated a brow.

It was one hell of a description befitting a man.

He silently eyed his friend during his longwinded analogy.

"... but he doesn't! Yknoe what aye meen, Jackie ...?!"

Churchill knew better than to fuel that nonsense with a reply or acknowledgement, but on some strange level today, with these strange circumstances involving this strange fellow, he actually understood his eccentric apparition's wisdom.

"You know what, I ... I actually do," Churchill scoffed a chortle, surprised at his effortless comprehension. He eyed MacLeòid's stature, shivering in the chill, and asked him whilst nobody was within eavesdrop range of this madness. "What, you cold or something?"

"Freezin' me farkin' furry nuts owf," MacLeòid exclaimed quite matter-of-factly, as if the feeling of the low temperature were at that second more important than the topic of conversation.

Churchill shook his head. The response was quite obvious, but then again, MacLeòid was supposed to be dead, so sympathy was naturally lacking in that regard.

Upon reaching hydration, it was then that Churchill realized that he was in the specified vicinity ...

With a brief inspection of his surroundings, he discerned that some of the tree trunks within the forestation were marked with a glaring red *X* marked in paint or chalk.

"I think we're in the right place," he whispered (to himself).

In his Glaswegian tone, MacLeòid sidled up and whispered with haste seeing that this exercise may have been about to begin. *"Take errythin' he sez wif er grain ov salt, Jackie ... Yoo don't need him or what he has ta owfer from some piddlie textbook, laddie. Tha guy es er coupl'a sandwiches short ov a picknick, ef yoo git me?"*

Wordlessly disengaging from this chinwag, Churchill nodded at the advice as he focused upwards while MacLeòid continued to further his moot point.

"He only has one oar en tha water ... es a coupl'a bottle's short ov a six-pack ... a—"

Jack cut him off with a hiss. "Yes, I get the idioms, thank you."

The gesture wasn't fully out of agreement with the nutty Scot spirit, but more out of politeness of receiving the recommendation.

Now that MacLeòid had vanished, Churchill was able to conduct an expanded inspection of the immediate area; an arena of which he had stumbled into.

The astray archer took a moment, revolving about on the spot.

There were more Xs. Three—four, even.

They were targets!

As Jack's focus homed in, he assumed this place had been set up as some sort of assembled course. A comprehensive challenge in the form of environmental target practice—knowing the Otter, potentially with a twist ...

Rather than immediately call out for his instructor, Churchill recalled several things Wingate had advised him of the previous night: things about *no training wheels, zero tolerance to dead men*, and *being prepared for anything*.

Churchill's gloved hand raised towards the cylindrical quiver mounted over his right shoulder, rifling for the feathers of a singular arrow. With a quiet timber rattle, he drew the bodkin-tipped projectile, nocking it to the bowstring of his longbow.

From here on in ... he would progress rigidly and cautious, bearing an archer's pose whilst he trudged in the snow, beholding the eyes of a hunter.

Silence remained for an extended moment. The only sounds were that of the cold morning breeze whistling through the seasonally anorexic sticks and trees, and snowflakes brushing through scruff foliage.

Prepared for anything, Churchill had expected this type of contest might have been the case. When Wingate had given him the directions and time of which to meet here, he had followed it up with a lasting quote:

'We can find out what you're made of.'

It sounded like a challenge and rightfully so given the mantra of the madman; thus, Jack had come prepared with an already strung longbow, and his original basket-hilted claybeg mounted over his bulky parka, accessible upon his hip. He had done it up an extra notch tighter in case Wingate felt it prudent to make him literally jump through hoops.

After a few light-footed steps in the crunchy sleet, scanning about the vicinity like prey sauntering into the jaws of death, about to willingly spring a trap, Churchill called to no avail. "Sir?!"

Fog floated, drifting aimlessly in brisk breezes, dampening sound.

He started to thaw as it warmed, and he felt his heartrate rise.

Trying a different approach, one bearing enticement, he taunted:

"Come on, Orde. I haven't got all day?!"

Wind gusted.

Birds tweeted, frolicked in the wild—

Suddenly, an unorganic sound filled the air: the skirling pitch of a signal whistle, that took Churchill reeling back to his days at *Royal Military College* basic training in *Sandhurst.* The sound resonated in the echoic wilderness, and it shook Churchill into a reactive state to which he was fast on the draw.

It was a familiar state of pitch: two short blows ...

In the army, that meant commencement.

Sch-TOFF ...

Acting fast, a bodkin-tipped war arrow was sent downrange, deeply penetrating an obvious target X painted upon one of the trunks with a meaty *chock!*

The next tree beyond that came into focus ...

Three seconds later, also hit with an arrow.

Chock!

Churchill gave the loosenings an energetic amount of force. Arrow tips penetrated around an inch and a half into the trunks with a healthy tremor, quivering of transient force.

Twirling on the spot of this assumed home plate, Churchill nocked another arrow and located another target as he made it. The last tree of a half-dozen marked with a red cross was hit dead centre. No misses.

Maintaining rear footing whilst he encircled the field, Churchill drew another arrow and reached anchor point, scanning in a 360-degree radius for another target when—

Three short blown whistles. Conclusion.

With a huff, Jack collapsed his draw.

His focus drew to a rugged-up figure as he stepped into view with a crunch of crushed snow. He had been present the whole time, secretly spectating.

Wrapped in layers, scarf, gloves, and a beanie, Orde Wingate removed a steel signal whistle from his lips. After trudging closer in the icy slush, he pivoted to examine the accuracy of Churchill's archery shots more meticulously than he had from his hidden position.

The archer responsible for these impromptu shots had been approximately thirty to fifty feet away, lowering his six-foot conifer yew longbow in disengagement. Even firing the unit in the cold with gloved hands, he still mastered accuracy and precision. It was no simple feat—so therefore, was not enough to impress.

"Fine shooting ...... Mister Churchill," Wingate commented, waving the metal pea whistle like a sports coach. "Not bad ...... Not bad at all ..."

Churchill didn't seem to exude much at the show of gratitude, feasibly as it seemed like false praise. This accomplishment was not that fascinating, even he distinguished that. The targets were of a simple scope, range, and dispersed in an ideal, predictable array. He could have done this wearing a blindfold, though he didn't state that wittily out of fear of Wingate actually making him do it.

"Ah, modesty ..." Wingate trudged nearer by two steps, still remaining far enough away for them to need to speak-up. "Your ...... self-effacement ...... knows no bounds, Jack. I respect that."

Having barely broken a sweat, Churchill assumed that maybe his modest demeanour could be seen as a weakness or a hesitation towards excelling in their advanced training schemes. He decided to shine them on. "That was a warm-up or something, right? Why don't you give me something harder?"

Wingate smiled like the Cheshire cat. "You wish to go straight to the final lesson?"

"Fine-o-fine," confidently—perhaps overly—Churchill stalwartly slept in his made bed. "When shall we begin, sir?"

Smile simmering down, Wingate waved a hand, not revealing any of which he had in store to test the skills of his newest operative. "When you collect your ammunition, Mister Churchill."

Plodding through the snow, Churchill walked over and plucked one of the closer arrows back out from a tree. He stowed it in his over-shoulder quiver before trekking over and collecting another, keeping a keen eye on the stationary Wingate as he stood idlily, hands in his pockets, observing his mundane progression.

Churchill collected another arrow. "Okay. What next ... Orde?"

He was gone.

Without hanging much on it, Churchill sighed and stowed the arrow over his shoulder and into the gaping mouth of the quiver, preparing to step on uneven ground towards the next nearest target tree—

Twish ...

A weighty, circular object fell like a dropped pinecone, swallowed by the snow at his feet, disappearing from sight as Churchill's view craned in sloped pitch to inspect it.

Jack stood languid, staring down at the carved crevasse just in time to observe a suspicious plume of thin smoke rise from the cavity hole made by the sunken object ...

It was a hand grenade!

Grunting awkwardly, Churchill mustered the strength to move quickly in all of his layers, tossing himself into a dive as far enough away as he could make with the one step as he ran out of time—

Bo-OOF!

In a flash of white light and a thunderous fracture, the shockwave from the depth-dampened explosive yield flung him over like wind in a sail, and Churchill contorted into a horizontal tumble, becoming buried and coated in white powdery snow.

Blankets of ice shook from the branches of the crowding tree canopies above, causing it to shift and slide, piling over everything below in a layer of cold. Nearby foliage was impacted by the force of gushing air, becoming blown clear of settled snowflakes.

Due to the lack of harsh shrapnel damage—and the fact that it made no sense for Orde Wingate to want to kill him—Jack discerned quickly that the thrown device was likely a blank grenade, like the ones they use during basic training. However, they were still packed with gunpowder and exploded loudly, and could be quite dangerous if observed up close, hence his now ringing ears and bruised organs.

Head up from the frost, the winded Churchill mustered the strength to quickly hoist to his feet, becoming alert and vigilant.

Shaking the slush from his body, he quickly clambered up and moved through the knee-deep snow with his head on a swivel, focusing hard with a squinting stare through the disorientation of blurred eyes and ringing ears he was currently experiencing.

Following what sounded like an axe blade lopping into wood, he immediately noticed a fraction of peripheral movement close by.

Via an attached rope and pulley system in the above tree branches, a severed piece of weighty lumber swung vertically into view like a pendulum, travelling before a veil of sprinkling snowflakes. The entire midsection of the lumber was marked in the same red chalk, and hence Churchill identified it in that split-second as the next, moving target.

Quickly, Churchill drew an arrow from his quiver, nocked, and he drew the bowstring of his snow-slicken longbow whilst he traced the mark, gauging its speed and momentum.

He loosed with an elastic whipping sound.

The arrow skimmed off the back end of the log, chipping the bark and even causing it to twirl. The sent feather tailed projectile disappeared into the whiteout backdrop, likely lost forever.

Dropping to a knee, Churchill harnessed another arrow against his line, anchored, and fired, getting the log centre-mass on the backswing. The arrow impaled the trunk bark, causing the momentum to alter slightly, jiggling on the line.

He heard another chop from his flank—a different side all together, and from a different location to where Wingate could have disappeared to after his loitering. This meant that in this whole show, he had grips out here pulling strings behind the curtains; greasing the wheels and pushing these log swings like a theatrical composition.

Twisting forty-five degrees, Churchill marked another vertical log lurching up high as it dropped from a tie line, tilting with the gravity and gaining speed in its weighty swing, leaving a ghost of white particles in its roving wake.

Still on a knee, Jack drew an arrow and tracked the trajectory, about to fire his arrow at the target as it passed the centre of gravity of its lowest point, however, he decided to make up for the miss on the initial target.

Upping the ante, *he aimed higher ...*

Closing an eye for precision at this thin target, Jack raised an inch and loosed his arrow specifically at the attached line tied to the log, severing the rope with a snap of dust and fibres.

The heavy log dropped to the ground in a cloud of snow and chalky mist, acting as the coda to this orchestral chaos.

In the aftermath of the onslaught of action, posing tall and confident after that excessive takedown and show-off, Churchill drew another arrow and sent it into the dropped log with a profound sounding *CHOCK!*

"*That it, eh?!*" his blood up and still catching a breath from this sudden conquest, Mad Jack observed for any bystanders who may have been aiding Wingate's training seminar this morning. This orchestra was clearly not performing alone.

Empowered by overcoming those unexpected trials and tests of dexterity, he was beginning to recognize in himself that he excelled better when under the stress and tension of combat. He taunted: "*That all you lot have for me?!*"

With barely a sound, another anchor tether became severed by use of a bladed instrument, sending another suspended tree log swinging towards earth.

This time, *it was heading straight for Jack.*

Carting two-thousand pounds, the lumber closed in swiftly.

Whooooosh ...

Churchill's eyes grew wide.

Like a charging bull, the horizontal tree log speared towards him, carted by an admirably complicated crane system that had been engineered to both hold the weight of the heavy lumber, but also transport it on a dynamic parallel arch, swooning in low against the ground and at its target: *Jack Churchill.*

His sterling stare sparking, Churchill's eyes became as big as the span of the lopped log upon realizing his new predicament.

Reacting quickly, he launched himself onto a forward shoulder roll, avoiding the deadly path of the incoming battering ram that threatened to cave in his ribcage had it contacted his person.

Revolving out of the powdery snow in his roll, Mad Jack raised his gloved hand to grab an arrow which he could plant in a patch of the marked sides of the log target, only ... *he had none left.*

His gloved hand waved through the air above the quiver.

Considering that he should have still had a half-dozen bodkin-tipped war arrows stowed and at the ready, Churchill became confused. His head snapped in a turn, spying the gaping slot absent ammunition to use with his longbow.

He instantly noticed that strewn across the snow from his tactical evasion was a cluster of timber arrows, accidently jettisoned from his quiver during his shoulder roll. No thanks to gravity, the faggot of twigs was piled messily like the kindling of a campfire.

With a set of sparkling wide eyes, he spied the return charge of the swinging battering ram, predicting he had mere seconds to arm himself appropriately and act before it would revert in its backswing, and his arrow ammunition rested in the direct path of danger ...

Thinking resourcefully, Churchill stood tall—his gloved hand reaching into the metal basket hilt of his hip-mounted sword with the goal of unsheathing his other medieval weapon and putting it to use. He would meet the log on its return voyage, slicing the ropes harnessing the timber, therefore winning against the opponent in a roundabout way.

Entering this new danger zone, he casually stepped into the line of passage. He feared no consequence, as he would have his trusty silver sidearm at the ready and about to protect him.

Once enveloping a firm hold of his ceremonial claybeg, Jack tugged.

And tugged.

And tugged.

He looked down, confused as to why his sword would not retract from his leather sheath. It was like the weapon was glued into the scabbard.

Whimpering with astonishment, he glanced down and to his hip.

Discarding his longbow at a toss, he tried with both hands, shaking the neck of the scabbard profusely, fretting that time was running out ...

... the log closed in.

Displaying a desperate sulk, Churchill took one last look at the stump as it hurtled in to claim his life, swinging on its ropes with a taut creak and groan and whoosh of air.

At the very last minute, Jack braced, spinning himself to soften the blow—an act that very well may have saved him from multiple broken bones and a concussion.

The unstoppable log impacted against Churchill, acting as a medieval battering ram and launching him like a cannon ball into a cloud of snow where he exploded in a puff, becoming partially buried.

Air having been removed from his lungs like a vacuum, Churchill inhaled intensely. Embracing his core, he lurched upwards with a grimace, searching himself for any breakages—thankfully, there appeared to be none, however, his arm felt jarred, and his neck hurt. He would likely be feeling that in the morning. He suffered as though he had just been hit by an automobile.

"It was the ice," a voice advised as a figure stood over him. It was Wingate. "The frost. Sometimes it makes steel stick to bindings."

Spluttering, Churchill ceased his wincing and glanced up.

He seemed moderately defeated.

Not bothering to try and unsheathe the sword again, Churchill simply processed that information while he opened and closed his hand, restoring feeling. He would not forget the lesson. Logically, it was either the blade becoming iced and friction refraining the unholstering, or if the scabbard was made out of some type of contracting material, it may have shrunk around the type of steel the sword was made from. Perhaps both had contributed to the mishap.

Still catching his breath, Jack removed his now dented canteen from his pocket. Not only was it indented, but the neck and spout of the bottle had become fractured during the impact and was now leaking the water contents.

Incentivizing him to get up, Wingate offered his personal canteen of water. He asked, though, it was more of a request. "Drink?"

Ultimately, Churchill begrudgingly accepted Wingate's offer, as well as his other one of assistance in climbing to his feet in the snow. Winded, it took him an extra moment to recover vertically.

'Orde Wingate would not be the only one to train the men of the Berzerkers of Special Z Unit, though he did seem to offer the most comprehensive—albeit left-field—wisdom. Through their combined, shared insight, these recruited Berzerker's would each be compelled to bring something to the table of tactics. Shared skillsets, combat traits, acquired tactical understanding, a pool of their combined experiences of warfare knowledge.

'Before the end of the first week, the Z unit Berzerkers introduced Jack to their mastered form of advanced hand-to-hand combat, the integral part of Wingate's enhanced close-quarter combat regime, referred to as 'berzerker'. This attack would consist of the men screaming at the peak of their lungs, so loud that it would disorientate and intimidate any prospective enemy, 'BERZERKER!!!' as they struck, not unlike the Japanese Banzai attack. This would instil the enemy with fear and catch them off-guard, therefore adding extra seconds to their reaction time. By then, the Berzerkers would be in close with bladed *weapons, knives, or other close-quarter ordnance, eliminating soldiers before they even had a chance to spot or call out a target.'*

Once upon a subsequent morning, the temperature was paradoxically warm.

The crisp, cold air had been softened by the light of a sunny morning, one which caused the ice to twinkle and sparkle as the motley group of rugged-up mercenaries trudged outside in the snow, reaching an isolated location not too far from the resort grounds. It was in a partial clearing, illuminated by morning sensation. It was a flatter expanse than most other predominantly sloped wilderness areas Wingate often scoped for his training arenas.

Unbuttoning and removing his overcoat like the others preparing for physical activities, Jack Churchill still stood as verdantly to the crowd of qualified Berzerker members.

Each mercenary had with them a freshly topped-up canteen of resort tank water and was chugging it down hard by the time they reached the zoned area for practice. Having always been filled at the Winterthur Resort establishment, they were always rich with the bitter-tasting reservoir, however Jack subconsciously confessed that after nearly a week drinking from this source, he could barely taste the sullenness anymore. As with the altitude, he had acclimatized.

Ceremoniously, they issued Churchill with a M1918 mark I trench dagger. This was an American trench knife designed by officers of the American Expeditionary Force (AEF) for use in the previous world war.

The brass-handled American service knife had a six-point-seven-inch dagger-shaped double-bladed tip, and was still extremely popular within the armed services, typically no longer favoured due to the weight of the knuckleduster grooved handle designed for bludgeoning; for punching.

Jack eyeballed the melee weapon. He had seen one of these knife models before, but not for a great many years—the first thing that sprung to his head in reminiscence was in 1930, Burma, seeing it stabbed inwards on a diagonal, penetrating the moist, green bark of a slanting pagoda tree lining the river in *Phyu;* a memorable training exercise. A lesson referred to as *Excalibur,* and taught by his very Highlander haunt, Colonel Sloan MacLeòid.

The M1918 had been inherited as the preferred weapon of choice by the Berzerkers, specifically chosen as it were optimal for their style of energetic, brutal, and violent close-quarter, hand-to-hand combat. Some of the mercenaries even armed themselves with two pieces; one for each clenched fist, tucked in at either hip like a pair of saddle bags or cowboy six-shooters.

"You guys train live with these?"

"Of course."

"We're not sissies, mate," Rushworth said, silver tooth prevalent.

The use of the word *sissy* caught Churchill's consideration, for it was typically something he was used to hearing MacLeòid say.

"No wonder you lot are all missing so many pegs, eh?!" Churchill regarded as he stood in his scarf beside Mad Mike Calvert, cradling the issued weighty trench knife.

Giggling because he was aware of the numerous mishaps sustained whilst they had trained with the bladed trench knives in the past, Calvert couldn't agree more with Mad Jack's call as they watched the more fledgling members of the Berzerkers unit 'warm-up' to train.

They stripped down their layers and engaged in full-fledged fury, running at one another like crazed silverback gorillas, fighting for dominance, tossing each other head-over-turkey. It was a display unlike Churchill had ever seen before—outside the leagues of a football game—all the interlocking and tumbling, wrestling, flinging, squeezing ... *and all the while each time screaming at the top of their lungs the unit's battle-cry: "BERZERKER!!!"*

In an unarmed exercise, five or six per side, the men clashed like charging stampedes of a souped-up rugby scrum, hyped up on the sugar from candy. They were fuelled by something ...

An undying devotion to the cause to one's country, or ...

... perhaps the patriotism just ran in the water.

'Although the archer Jack Churchill's talents lay elsewhere—predominantly in the ranged division—he retained the behaviours and flairs he observed in the men of the unit as they exercised in their Neanderthalic fighting style. The Berzerkers would focus on a technique that carved in close to their enemy's whereabouts, typically subsequent an ambush, where they would rush them, gaining short distances as quickly as possible. They even strategized ways to accurately dodge supposed enemy shots through expertly calculated predictions, manoeuvres, exacted agility, and by other magical means—not in a science-fiction fairytale sense, that was. There were extremely calculated methods to Wingate's madness. He taught them that men—exclusively, the various multinational trained soldierly forces whom they would oppose—have a relatively precedental and predictive pattern when *it came to aiming guns at targets. Cause and effect and firearm ballistics suggested that recoil always tipped upwards and aims always swayed to the right. Typically, an adversary's rifle only had one good shot before they needed to cycle their bolt-action levers. Once the Berzerkers learned how to duck or roll under shot-lines or enact an agile rugby-style change of direction speed, dodging as triggers were pulled latter to sighting an aiming pose, enemy gunfire became plausibly frivolous to avoid, even easy to predict the motions of potential enemy shooters—and that was even if they had a chance to react in the first place. In such small numbers, covertness and cunning could easily overpower an entire regiment if enacted with precision, purpose, and deliberation. This was theoreticized but also tried and practised.'*

"Death ...... is merely a state of mind ..."

While the monotonal voice of Wingate lectured, the crowd of men—predominantly the 'newcomers' of the unit—intensely listened, observed, and attuned.

The group of layered men stood out in the snowy woods in weather not too dissimilar to days prior. The ice glistened beneath the morning sun as the leafless canopies above started to thaw.

Members present such as Calvert, Black, Dredge, Scotty, and Bredin, who had been with Wingate in Switzerland for a longer period, not to mention some who had even served with him prior to the Special Z Unit, seemed to have heard his mantra before. It was already instilled in them.

"So, I just wanna get this straight, eh?" Batey spoke up, stroking his beard nervously. He was standing beside Churchill and one of the other newer gents, Arthur Komrower. His query was aimed directly at Wingate, who had just finished his lesson speel.

"*Good,*" Komrower remarked confidently to the man beside him in a whisper. "*I wasn't the only one confused.*"

Batey underscored. "You want us to run *towards* the gunmen?"

Attention appealed to Wingate who observed along with a few others from the sideline of this sprinter's track. Adjacent to them were three unarmed candidates (Churchill, Komrower, and Batey) opposed by three reluctant shooters (Rushworth, Bort, and Gentle Jerry) standing thirty yards away, possessing *Greener General Purpose* kitchen door guns (single shot shotguns, typically chambered for smaller gauges like .410, for hunters and youth shooters).

The weapons were presumably loaded.

Wingate responded as a reiteration to his previous direction.

"I want you to ...... *attack* the gunmen."

"So, you want us to *get shot?*" Batey questioned, hesitant to assume any form of sprinter's pitch in order to race the aim of these targeting shooters. Batter up on the home plate, and they were the pitching balls.

"Death is a state of mind," Wingate repeated just as cryptically, though, this time, he permitted elaboration. "Do you know what a *juggernaut* is, Joe? It is a large ...... unstoppable force ...... that crushes everything in its path."

The sceptical Batey appeared unconvinced and Komrower looked conflicted. Churchill stood between them, suspiciously quiet in his own reservations. There had to be a catch. Had to be a way to win.

Although unorthodox was in the description of what they signed up for—along with other words such as ambiguous, hazardous, questionable—their training thus far, although dangerous and irrational, had been lessons, nonetheless. In their forging to become elite and extreme, all training so far had led them somewhere ...

... all this lesson seemed to point them towards was certain death.

Wingate continued, "What about, then, a *berserker?*"

"You mean us? What we call ourselves?"

Batey seemed confused. A tad agitated. Frustrated, even. Irrespective of this in his flustered state, he disposed himself via portrayal of his ever-sarcastic sense of humour. "You lot should have become known as *well-oiled dying machines*. Eh? The only thing you're killing is yourself."

Churchill piped up, flexing an intellectual ability that may help save his compatriot Berzerker out of a hot spot. "By definition, a *berserker* is a fearsome, fearless warrior who fights in a trance-like fury, possessed by war ..." with the spotlight now on him, even Wingate's right-hand men, Mad Mike Calvert and mister et cetera himself, Moshe Dayan, raised their chins, impressed by Churchill's spot-check knowledge. "Originating in *Old Norse* literature, *a berserker* is depicted as having bear-like strength and the wildness of a beast in battle, sometimes even biting their shields out of pure, uncontainable rage. They are said to be unkillable."

Taking no offence to his show being stolen, Wingate proposed his point through Churchill's extension. "Precisely. One entity is *unstoppable* ...... the other, *unkillable*."

While Churchill began to detect a method lurking beneath the madness, Batey piped up again, still unconvinced. Logic was too sound. "If I run at that cunt with the gun, and he shoots me, I die. There is no mere *state of mind* about it ..."

Wingate grew tired of his conjecture, and gestured to the three gunmen whilst Batey said his piece. "You lot, there ...... someone shoot him."

Of the three holding shotguns, Rushworth seemed the most eager to blindly follow their eccentric ringleader's instructions. Without any reluctance, he cocked the hammer claw with his thumb and raised his farm gun down range, about to yank the trigger without hesitation ...

The bearded Batey's eyes grew wide as the three unarmed men glanced down the firing line. Rushworth's flank men exchanged a quick glance whilst watching the spectacle. Perchance even they were an ounce uneasy about this event unfolding.

"Don't worry," Jack murmured with confidence to the man at his side. His tone suggested a doubt anybody was about to die. "Surely, it's not loaded."

"Eh, I'm pretty sure I saw them load them ..." Komrower said whilst taking a half step back, moving away from the target: Batey, while Churchill confidently assisted him in standing his ground.

Churchill barked, strong-minded. "Then they're blanks—"

Before anybody could object or even brace, the deafening loud shotgun gusted grey smoke like a sudden violent cough. Equally as violently as the sudden gunshot, an impact struck Joe Batey across the chest, throwing him over into the snow in a cloud of white powder.

"*Jesus Christ!*" Komrower shouted while flinching, hobbling away from the chaos of a man being shot dead before his eyes.

Churchill glanced to his flank—it was now absent the human being who had been occupying the space. He had heard the individual pellets impact and pierce Batey's body, collecting him in a gush of force.

Now sunken in the snow and motionless, he laid a charred corpse.

His fatigues appeared torn, and parts of pink flesh from his chest were visible through the resonating smoke.

"*Are you mad?!*" Churchill exclaimed through the dissipating echo of the gunshot in the wilderness, waving a hand over the floored Berzerker. Through all this apocryphal training, he drew the line at senseless murder.

He was shocked to see that the string of men at Wingate's audience stand were unphased. In fact, some appeared to find it humorous, especially Dredge, who was cackling boisterously at the display of harm. His laughter caused a few of the others to hoot and applaud, but this was only because they knew the grand scheme of what was happening ...

They had been through this already.

Wingate held a deadpan.

His unnerving brown stare lined Churchill. "We're all mad, Jack."

It was then an agonised murmur sounded from the snow, and Komrower was fast to react, hopping past Churchill and tending to Batey as he came to. He assisted him in sitting up, wiping some of the residue from his wound site.

Churchill's eyes were still wide with confusion.

"Fuck. That stings."

"Rock salt!" Calvert remarked in a shout, and Bala Bredin tossed a brass shell to Churchill who instinctively caught it, inspecting the specially made ammunition. The shells were loaded with salt.

Although he was starting to see the picture, Churchill remained unimpressed. "What ... were you planning on hunting some mashed potato out here or something?"

Vehemently, Black shouted. "No, just little bitches who don't wanna do what they're told—"

Apparently possessing more patience than most, Wingate silenced him with a hand across his chest, indicating he had a soft spot for Mad Jack Churchill.

"This is preposterous," Churchill disagreed. His tone may have sounded argumentative, though, his critiquing of Wingate's tutoring was grounded in sound logic. "We would never find ourselves in a situation such as this ..."

"A gunfight may find you anywhere."

"Tactics. Strategy. You plan your attack; you take the enemy by surprise. Not to mention we would have ranged weapons, too!"

"Yeah, right," Black berated. His growing dislike towards this eccentric, avid archer, sword-wielding show pony was starting to show. "Your stick 'n string would work in taking *one* of these blokes out ... but what about the other shooters? You gonna challenge 'em to a swordfight?"

Wingate analogized, stepping down from their sideline and appealing to Churchill's supposed condemnation. "Swords aren't constructed with premeditation. Forged in a fiery heat ...... they are *relentlessly* ...... beaten into shape with a hammer and anvil, then cooled to achieve the desired Rockwell ...... That strength is not found in strategy, Mister Churchill. Not really. In a most carnal way, swords do not fear death. They embrace it. Endure it. Fuck it. They face it ...... head on."

Jack gesturally conceded to this lesson for now. "And what of the *state of mind* part about death. That sounds like a neat trick."

"Being shot doesn't mean death," in an oversimplification, Wingate alluded and Churchill's brow raised. He was overcome by a wave of confusion; his logical, conditioned mind trying to understand Wingate's rationality.

"So, what you're saying is, that you're going to teach us how to *not* die when we get shot?"

Wingate's saunter finished, now up close to Churchill.

He spoke with a low tone. "No, Jack. When we're done here ...... I'd have taught you how to not get shot in the first place."

A lingering, deafening silence followed as Wingate walked away as if he had just dropped the mic, leaving a confused Churchill in his wake. As the new guy, he probably shouldn't have challenged his methods further, however, there was a new and inexplicable defiance running through Jack's veins here; in this place. His blood pressure had risen, and his pride was uncontainable.

This whole thing was an Occam's razor-shaped headache waiting to happen. Churchill huffed like a bull out his nostrils. "Pardon me, sir, ... I've never been shot, myself ... though, I can imagine that *anatomies* and *analogies* each respond very differently to a bullet."

"What happens if I shoot you in the head right now?"

Wingate hinted to the armament at his side. A pistol was holstered within a clasped-up green leather holster. The *Theuermann* dropping pattern alluded to its modernization, suggesting it housed a contemporary type of automatic sidearm, prospectively a Browning Hi-Power. Those guns utilized double-stacked magazines and were thus a smaller calibre, such as 9mm.

"I die."

"Why?"

Churchill flexed his analytical intellect. "Anatomically speaking? You fire a cartridge through my skull. Depending on the calibre, you either put a nine-millimetre hole between my eyes and the lawless lead bounces between the confines of my well-calcified cranium making Swiss cheese out of my cerebrum, or it's a forty-five and you blow the back of my brain out of my skull like a purged constipation after a morning espresso. Either way, my motor function ceases instantly and, therefore so do I."

"Yes, but *why,* Jack?!" Wingate stressed, wanting more than science.

Churchill halted, confounded by his overall conscientiousness.

Discombobulated on how to further explain his point to such an intellectual soldier, Wingate appeared flustered, searching for examples. "Swords. You ...... fight with a claybeg, yes? What is the quickest way to kill a man with a blade."

Not speaking from experience, Churchill remarked matter-of-factly.

"I suppose you lop his head off?"

"Correct. Severance ...... from the neck. Did you know that a man's sentience ...... can survive for a while after decapitation."

Frozen by attentiveness, Churchill absorbed this medieval detail, to which he was aware but not fully educated. It made sense that a partially derailed maniac such as Orde Wingate would have been and this only added to the autonomous auric unease that was constantly trailing the fellow like the waft of a protein fart.

He spoke as though he were an expert in the matter. "Erroneous to most fictional portrayals of beheadings, the human head remains conscious for up to twenty seconds after decapitation. This was proven ...... when an anatomical researcher, condemned to the guillotine in the seventeenth century, told his loyal assistant to ...... observe his execution; to ...... study it. Upon his death by decapitation, this devoted *scientist-deemed-heretic* planned to blink every second for as long as he could after the blade guillotined him at the neck ...... he was counting ...... The assistant counted twenty blinks after severance. So, in all inaccuracies regarding decapitation implying instant death, however briefly ...... the head does remain alive."

It might have been intellectual fatigue, but Churchill conceded.

"Hence, *death is merely a state of mind?*"

Wingate snapped his fingers. "Precisely."

He formed and held his Cheshire cat grin.

Within the transpiring seconds, the three candidates watched Wingate's expression fade to flat, and he sauntered back to the perimeter of their training exercise, joining the ranks of those established members of the Special Z Unit. Komrower whispered beneath his breath whilst he helped hoist Batey from the snow:

"This git's going to get us lot killed."

Although in that moment Churchill agreed, he couldn't help but state the obvious whilst he trudged after their mad as a march hare leader as he regrouped with the established members—therein lay the logic.

"Well ... *they* aren't dead yet."

They must have been doing something right.

'God-only-knew from whence Wingate funded the group's special gear and guns. Not to mention organizing and financing the visitor ventures from all over the world—not only to teach them how to use the unique weaponry, but how to master it. Along with deep pockets, the Otter also had a long reach. During early 1940, he had members from non-aligned militaries tour the Winterthur Resort in the Mont de la Gouille Mountain Range to skill share. The members of Z Unit had checked their morals at the door. This was an agreed-upon prerequisite. Although extremely questionable, tolerance levels became tested as their skill attributes did.

'In February, they received a visit from a Finnish fellow nicknamed Marokon kauhu (The Terror of Morocco). Aarne Juutilainen was his name. He was an expert strategist and mastermind in all things guerilla warfare. By invitation of Wingate, Juutilainen holidayed in Switzerland from his command along the Kolla Front under Major General Woldemar Hägglund. He brought with him a youngblood, rising star Simo Häyhä, AKA 'The White Death'. Häyhä said very little, however he trained the men in something different to their typical melee training, this time in ranged warfare. Häyhä was said to have had over two-hundred sniper kills to his name—an astonishing number, even to these wayward Berzerkers. The men were in awe. Apparently, it was something to aspire towards ...

'The following fortnight, a tanned Italian Egyptian, whom Wingate had met one year during his many off-book tours abroad, arrived. He showed the men how to better use blunt and pointed instruments to inflict grievous bodily harm, specifically where in the anatomy to inflict the more irreparable damage to the human body. He shared some differing styles of hand-to-hand combat, favouring a type of Cinquedea blade dagger—these were like fighting with knives shaped like big equilateral triangles, though he made it work ...

'Next visitor was an oriental man from some part of Asia who required an interpreter. Through a shady acquaintance of Wingate's, he was organized to teach the men a form of weaponless kung-fu (or kicking and flailing, or some other form of self-defence that Jack can't quite remember, nor did he absorb well). A few of them picked it up, managing to retain enough to get a nod of approval from the Asian. Due to the Berzerkers' heavy recreational drinking, they all flunked the physical trials for this lesson, somehow getting overly excited and apparently offending their Oriental visitors by bursting out into uncontrollable laughter during their subsequent sparring session. Thus, the visitor departed in a huff with their payment after just two days ...

'Other than tactical aggression and devastatingly lethal hand-to-hand deliberation, an equally vital element to the Berzerker training was stealth. To be a ghost. This was necessary so that the men could get in close to enemy patrols, beneath their vectors, and along their frontlines before exploding into deadly and precise hand-to-hand killing, truly exercising their Berzerker combat styles. To advise certain stealth tactics to the men, such as how best to conduct espionage, infiltration, sabotage, and reconnaissance was a middle-aged English-born French operative known only to the unit as Seahorse. During the previous war, he had enlisted in the US Army and served on the Western Front as a dispatch rider, seeing much action in the Polish-Soviet War of 1919 to 1920. He fought alongside the Poles until capture by the Soviet forces, where he avoided execution by escaping, killing Soviet guards with his bare hands in the process. In the years since, Seahorse had engineered his body to become a weapon, mastering several different types of hand-to-hand combat techniques. In a conversation with the men after his seminar on combat, the Frenchmen mentioned with great compassion that upon the outbreak of war, he attempted to join the British Army but was unfortunately turned down due to numbers. He then attempted to join the French Foreign Legion, but they were unaccepting of Britons. After consigning his car at the service of the British Air Attaché in France, he became granted permission to join the RAF in September, which was where he had met a contact of Wingate's en passant.

Wingate mentioned to Jack that he was putting out his feelers to another associate from east of the front, especially for _him_. This transnational mystery man was a certified master in the art of swordsmanship and HEMA (historical European martial arts), and Wingate felt Jack could learn greatly from his shared practices considering his opted bladed sidearm. Detail of his visitation would remain in limbo for a while ...

From within their own numbers, team members shared their own skills—albeit eccentric and elaborate. One man knew advanced survival techniques in the wild, another knew how to use blow darts utilizing poisoned tip ammunition that had a lethal (or nonlethal) range of up to thirty feet. They were practically soundless, too. Another unit member taught them how to throw knives true and balanced, and Mike Calvert educated them about explosives.

Jack attempted to bring to the Special Z Unit the art of archery, which they would have benefited heavily from in the way of stealth combat, as arrows were a completely silent way to eliminate enemies at varying ranges. However, medieval bow competence became fast outweighed by the use of new, state of the art, modern-day compact crossbows that Wingate had managed to obtain through friends within the SOE. Two types dominated: the 'Lil' Joe' pistol crossbow and 'Big Joe 5' shoulder-fired recurve crossbow arrived along with some more high-tech gadgets purchased by the Otter's shadowy government and military contacts, some of which were inside of the Ministry of Defence 1 (MD-1): the main armorer for the entire British Military, casually labelled 'the Toyshop'. These crossbow weapons shot smaller arrows known as bolts. They fired at higher velocity with minimum effort, and were therefore preferred to Jack's longbow, as it required far less skill, strength, and experience training. Jack disliked the modern contraption merely because it required far too much time and effort to reload per shot and seemed rather clumsy overall.

'In late February, another shipment of funded tech arrived from the MD-1 for the Berzerkers to utilize, and Jack couldn't even believe some of it actually existed ...'

1940, February
Winterthur Resort, Mont de la Gouille
Swiss Pennine Alps, Switzerland

Night vision.
　　The Otter had acquired magical scopes known as *'infra-red'*.
　　Located in the resort kitchen, the rather large and sterile space which had become the unit's armoury and munitions storage depot, Churchill lingered upstanding along with a few other interested individuals. Today was mail call for the men. Their regular service addresses were forwarded through various secure networks before finding them in Switzerland.

Focally, they were each present to investigate the monthly arrival of new gear from the Ministry of Defence 'Toyshop', wanting to be present during the unboxing of these new and exciting contraptions.

Wingate entered behind the amassed group crammed into the kitchen, his arrival quickly saw him escorted to the front, where he observed his quartermaster Bala Bredin crack open the crates. What he unveiled was a pair of portable sets designed by popular Berlin-based General Electricity Company and producer of electrical equipment *Allgemeine Elektrizitäts-Gesellschaft (AEG)*.

The device was codenamed: '*Vampir*'.

Insulated in packing hay, Bredin excavated the goods.

They were portable, powered by battery backpack, and the connected torch sight could be mounted upon most modern weaponry. The wired packsack the wearer had to carry may have been cumbersome, but it enabled the scope user to literally see in the dark—*and it wasn't a gimmick!* Churchill and the other men got to witness the tech in use first-hand, reporting it was almost as if seeing during daylight hours, albeit during a severe red sunset.

"Cutting-edge machinery," Bredin summarized after perusing the instruction manual and analysing the equipment.

"Looks like a bloody strobe light connected to a Number Eighteen Wireless Set," Black commented after recognizing the resemblance to the high-frequency portable man-pack radio transceiver employed by the British Army. It looked both heavy and clunky.

The balaclava-clad Danny Boy peeked in over his shoulder, watching from the recesses of the kitchen. He appeared to be expecting something with the mail today ...

"The device shines an active infra-red searchlight on a subject—like a conventional *tungsten* light source, y'know, '*black light*'—through a filter permitting only infra-red light ..." Bredin spoke almost directly to Wingate. "Now, what's most interesting is that that's a spectrum *invisible* to the naked eye ..."

Wingate comprehended, somewhat knowledgeable about the theory of the technology after attending via invitation a prototype unveiling the previous year. His unnamed source who had obviously supplied him—and the Berzerkers—with the gear in order to test in the field had also updated him on the tech via a nutshell format.

"Da fuck does *black light* mean? Isn't that a metaphor?" Mike Calvert questioned sardonically, overhearing the chatter in the kitchen from a connecting room. It was generally always a fuss when a new delivery arrived via truck at the Mont de la Gouille Winterthur Resort. It meant new toys.

"I think you mean *oxymoron*," said Churchill.

"You're an oxy*moron*," responded Calvert.

Bredin continued, "In combination with an image converter—that's something that accepts the upper infra-red spectrum of illuminated images—whatever is focused on in the dark by the black light becomes visible through the enhanced scope, as clear as day. It should appear like an overly contrast-saturated black and white image to the user."

Churchill avidly listened. "Like having a handheld torch at night, but one only the eye of the beholder can see."

"Precisely."

"Ingenious."

"Expensive!" Black interjected—rightfully so.

The great many advances in machinery supplied by the MD-1 via whatever interceptive foreign accomplice, considering its German origin, empowered the Special Z Unit Berzerkers, making them feel invincible. And with such an advantage on the battlefield ... how could they not be.

As Black divvyed up the various coloured and shaped envelopes of mail from the men's loved ones back home, Danny Boy lurched in and collected a parcel addressed to him. The aggression of his snatch caught the attention of some of the surrounding men, and they watched him retract whilst ripping into the package, displaying a matching set of clear handle strips for a handgun.

"Hey, swell sweetheart grips, Danny Boy," said Gentle Jerry, whose height caused him to oversee the Berzerker's new possession. They appeared to be shaped for the popular M1911 service pistol, though seemed a little elongated, made to fit the strange .22LR High Standard gun that he favoured. The clear grips were made possible by use of forged acrylic, either *Plexiglass* or *Lucite*, which had been invented sometime over the past few years. They were becoming popular for troops to carry in the armed forces since the grip was clear, and they could place a loved one's photograph safe under the acrylic. Typically, the picture would be a girlfriend or wife, hence the term 'sweetheart grip'. However, children, parents, siblings, or other family members also made appearances. Some soldiers would even use a pin-up girl torn out from a dirty magazine.

Dredge scrunched up his nose.

"Danny Boy ain' got any sweethearts!"

The stocky mohawk-welding Scotty piped up rather humorously.

"Oi, let 'im be! He'll chuck a picture of 'is mum in there, eh?!"

Danny Boy did not retaliate. Rather, he navigated through the many standing bodies in the small kitchen, butting shoulders like a bullied pinball before disappearing without a trace, likely to install his new pistol grips in solitude.

Although it was in jest, the funny thing was that Danny Boy did indeed place photographs of his mother beneath his pistol grips. This humanized the robot for a lot of the Berzerkers, who correspondingly felt regret for tormenting him. As they progressively found out, the man was unhinged. They were shaking a bottle that could pop off at any minute.

From one of the other smaller cartons included in the delivery, Bredin found another piece of obscure paraphernalia. This time, it was something he did not recognize; a cylindrical piece of hollowed leather, bound in a tailored diagonal strapping harness seemingly arranged to go across one's torso. "What the fuck's this thing?"

Churchill recognised it. "That's an arrow quiver."

Wingate mentioned surely. "That's *your* new quiver, Jack."

The kitchen/armoury fell silent as they watched Wingate place down the night vision scope into the open crate of hay and assess this new accessory of Mad Jack Churchill, acquiring it from Bredin to quickly inspect before handing it over to its rightful owner.

With a willing pair of open hands, Churchill received it.

The holstering device was modernistic, customized in brown leather and embossed with the designation via the coat of arms from the armourer: 'MD-1, 1939'. This new container contained an industrial magnet ingeniously sewn into the lining of the toe pad. The metal used in the heads of the bodkin-tipped ammunition, when stored, would attract in the magnetic force, and refrain from falling out from the quiver if he was ever perched on an angle—a practical advancement observed by Orde Wingate during one of Churchill's earlier training sessions. The custom quiver seemed as though it could house approximately two-dozen bodkin-tipped war arrows.

Churchill breathed in the smell of freshly stretched and oiled leather. The stitchwork was seamless and the dexterity of the build was impressive. "It's beautiful."

"Practical, too," Wingate stated, showing him the underside where there was an imprinted symbol signifying that there was a magnet in use. With the knowledge that his bodkin tips were metal, Churchill's practical mind filled in the rest. It was rather ingenious, and one might go as far as to call it thoughtful as a gift if it weren't for the obviously tactical rationale applied by Wingate.

Jack genuinely looked forward to wearing the addition to his attire, likely indefinitely. "Sir," he said graciously, "thank you."

'A portion of their upcoming tour would ostensibly take place in snowy conditions, and the quickest and most silent way of transportation around the slopes was by off-piste skiing.'

Shortly after the unboxing of the newest Toyshop delivery, which included Churchill's new quiver, attention befell upon Mike Calvert. He and a few other layered Berzerker men appeared to be preparing to endeavour on a ski outing.

"Want to stretch your snow legs, Jack?" Calvert asked him.

Seemingly, this was the grand activity they were all preparing for in the main foyer. They had with them sets of alpine skis and poles, as well as elbow and knee guards, and helmets.

"You ski?"

Churchill had skied only once before in his life, in the *Meall A'Bhuiridh Massif* in *Glen Coe, Scotland.* The 'Hill of the bellowing'.

With absolution, Churchill responded. "Of course."

"No, I mean, *can you ski?"* Calvert interrogated. "This ain't no holiday resort ..."

A little confused, Churchill scanned around.

"Oh. I thought that it was ..."

Cracking a smile, Calvert's head bobbed. "Well, it is ... but what I mean is, the type of skiing we do is proper piste off."

Churchill's brow tweaked. He assumed the half-Aussie was utilizing yet another wordplay, this time of the term *off-piste* used in reference to a type of rogue skiing done over areas of snow that have not been especially prepared for skiers. Like bush-bashing, but at-speed. It was extremely dangerous and wild in many circumstances. "You mean, *off-piste?"*

Calvert barely nodded, electing to continue his conversation. "We go at a hundred k's an hour, mate, weaving between trees like *Snakes and Ladders* on fuckin' dropped fuckin' acid, you get me? You touch a branch doing the speeds we do, and you will shatter like a game of fuckin' *52-Pickup.* These boys, we may be technically the king's men, but we don't bother putting *Humpty Dumpty* back together again if you get me, Mad Jack?"

Churchill dotted his expression and then added keenly.

"I *get you,* Mad Mike."

"Well?"

Jack tossed him a gleam and a smile. "Let's break a leg."

1940, March
Proving grounds near the Mont de la Gouille Winterthur Resort
Swiss Pennine Alps, Switzerland

Chock!

   Chock! Chock!

The arrows fired from a single bowman were done rapidly—surely too rapidly for there to be one archer?

Approximately five seconds, total, all targets bullseyed.

The combination of speed and accuracy had become mastered by this expert toxophilite, for he was no longer an *athlete* training to play by the traditional *1440 Round* rules in a competitive sport; with targets 30 metres (fore) and 70 (hind), and with 120 seconds to loose six accurate arrows ...

Now, he was a tried *killer* preparing to eliminate enemy soldiers. The distances would vary, and the speed of his loosing shots was now just as crucial as accuracy. He had *mastered* and *exceeded* archery.

His eagle-eye blues were zeroed with the intensity of a hunter killer.

Disengaging from the kill, they defocused on the distance.

Tensing his fist from the taut hold he had been mastering, Jack Churchill lowered his longbow. Standing in the showy winter wilderness, he cast a gleam to the watchful Orde Wingate, who had only just removed the signalling whistle from his lips having just initiated the assessment. He did so with a raised left brow, failing to hide his amazement at the result. Sometimes it was hard to tell with Wingate's expressionless resting gaze, but this time, the flowing undercurrent of surprise was evident.

Churchill had been practising in order to show this new technique off to the Berzerker ringleader, proving that archery was better from the bow than the fancy recurve crossbows they had imported from the SOE, training vigorously for use in the field, and it was because he had now possessed a secret weapon ...

This new archery method he had mastered was not modern. Rather, it was quite old. Five-thousand-years old, in fact. Long since forgotten in this day of projectiles and firearms.

The method allowed a skilled longbowman to hold several arrows in his shooting hand, pinched between the fingers causing a fist to look like a porcupine. From that establishment, the archer was able to nock and release one arrow at a time with each pull of the drawstring. The old theory testament was that an expert archer could effectively rapid-fire up to three arrows using this technique when positioning the arrow butts correctly between the fingers in the anchoring hand in a specific way.

So far, while Churchill would admit that this process was indeed faster in burst-fire chains than the typical speed-shooting technique of acquiring a new arrow from his quiver with fast, smooth motions between each shot, he could master maybe three at a time before needing to collect more. Typically, three subsequent arrows would do the trick when the archer was so accurate, he practically only needed the one initial shot.

"Marvellous, Jack. Just marvellous," Wingate said simply, wobbling his head with astonishment. This could potentially be a useful tool for a forward reconnaissance or enemy frontline infiltration unit.

Churchill cracked his winning smile between breaths from the exercise. He raised his right hand, taking the time to open and close his fist and extend his fingers thus. Holding multiple arrows between his knuckles whilst straining firm to draw the string was painful, nonetheless, he was starting to feel the girth of his grasp grow with practice.

He was becoming the most superior archer to date ...

While Wingate offered his praise, Churchill leant in and collected his canteen from his possessions in the snow. He was always thirsty in the mountains. Like Calvert had said: a combination of the altitude and temperature—then again, it was feasible that working this bloody hard to become the world's finest soldier worked up a sweat.

Jack tipped the canteen back, emptying it until its final drop under Orde Wingate's watchful eye whilst he finished applauding from gracing the routine.

"Pretty bloody good, eh?" Churchill overweeningly commended himself. His overconfidence of late had become almost overbearing—but it was what was required to keep his head above water with this lot of big-headed chads.

"No more self-effacing, I see?"

"Do you respect boastfulness?"

Wingate halted in his trudges, pocketing his mittened hands.

The fact he stood so far back set off alarm bells for Churchill's tactical awareness. He had grown to know the guy over the past two months; know his training strategies. There was likely an extension on this test designed to target his sentience, and Jack was ready for it ...

... was ready for anything, like Wingate wanted.

"Do you remember what it was I said ...... the night you joined us?"

Acting coquettish, Churchill toasted his canteen. "Stay hydrated?"

He then tipped it, showing that it was empty.

With a Cheshire cat grin, Wingate said not a word.

Letting the canteen drop to the snow at his buried boots, Churchill readied himself. "As long as your masked chum doesn't pop out behind me with his lil pop gun, we're fine-o-fine ..." he regarded wittingly, and then provocatively, "It mightn't end well for him, is all."

To whom he was referring to was Wingate's apparent factotum in a ski mask named Danny Boy. The close-mouthed odd-sort seemed to be a cloistered shut-in compared to the rest of the extroverted Berzerkers and was very much a loyal myrmidon.

Wingate's held grin fell flat. "How did you know ...?"

Silence.

Then suddenly, Churchill's attention pulled to the right of Wingate's perch, spotting a ski-mask wearing man reel out from behind a tree trunk wielding what appeared to be a twelve-pound warship cannon at the hip. Upon a further glance, the two-handed piece appeared to be a heavily modified Vickers machine gun, or at least possessed the exterior barrel of one, specifically the thick cylindrical water-cooled tubular front, painted white. The cylindrical drum was the barrel, and the eight-inch mouth appeared smoothbore.

Before Churchill could identify the threat further, the barrel puffed smoke with a bass-filled *PHOOF!* that chugged a rather large projectile his way—more precisely, above him, due to the angle of which it was craned lowly by the user.

His sterling stare intensified as the slow-moving projectile that had been fired extended into a canopy, unfolding above his position, carried at the corners by four weighted anchors.

The aerodynamic material was made of yarn strands.

It was a net.

The canvas-coloured ensnarement mesh dropped over him like a parachute, about to consume his position and confine him.

This would surely mean failure.

However, Mad Jack was ready ...

Upon realizing that he had not the time to draw and loose an arrow, nor that he had a specific target at which to shoot, he instead considered using his longbow as a bow staff like a stick dancer, though, he figured that would prove too clumsy and potentially troublesome in freeing himself from the trap.

For this occasion, he had the perfect tool.

Jack recoiled into himself, ducking his head and bulging his right shoulder to willingly accept ensnarement by the launched net. Such was required in order to *slice it in half with his sword!*

Churchill's right hand hooked in low at his left side, inserting his grip into the silver basket-hilted claybeg, latching firmly.

The net dropped around him like a blanket, capturing him.

Right after the swooping collapse, Churchill engaged in a burst of energy, drawing the sword from his sheath as well as slicing through the netting in one fell swoop, the icy blade not sticking to the leather this time, due to strategically applied lubricant—a suggestion by the unit's knowledgeable quartermaster.

The deflated webbing of the mesh net slit open like a hessian sack, and Churchill stood protruding and prepared, posing with his silver ceremonial sword like a medieval murderer.

Flourishing the blade at his hand, Churchill stepped around in the snow, scanning about for another test Wingate may have set about for him ... there were none.

Instead, the Otter applauded.

"Was that a test?" Churchill joked.

"Do you think you passed?"

With cocky response whilst he flaunted his banished sword in the air with a *whoo-whoosh* prior to sheathing it away like a quickdraw gunslinger. "Flourishingly."

He had seen that Jack had emptied his bottle ... and *was Johnny on the Spot* with a replacement, fresh from his backpack. He had apparently loaded an extra for his mentee, offering it wisely along with the full canteen and his tea-stained smile. "Must stay hydrated."

'History alleges that, prior to Jack's amalgamation into the unit and during their intense specialized training sessions in Switzerland, a flagless, faceless rogue unit would venture out at night and into enemy territory, thirsting for a fight. During this era, there were numerous enemy patrols across the countryside that lined the borders. It was conceivable that a small pack of wolves wouldn't have to search far to find a sentry or two to maim and silently slaughter.

'Whether they conducted these hunts with or without the deniable endorsement or knowledge of their bizarre CO, Orde Wingate, remains to be known. Unauthorized endeavours transpired in the shadows, and the bodies of enemy combatants were buried in the snow of the Swiss Pennine Alps ...'

1940, March
Winterthur Resort, Mont de la Gouille
Swiss Pennine Alps, Switzerland

The second-storey log Winterthur Resort was gloomy near midnight.

Outside, illuminated by moonlight, the cold, blizzard-esque winds were visible as it carried granule snowflakes, passing between the trees and branches like the squall of the sea. The draft from the breezes created a relaxing whistle.

Indoors, coming upstairs from the warm common room lounge area, where the men had been conversing after dinner for the night and housed a perpetually stoked open fireplace, the air was marginally colder in their respective lodgings.

Tonight had been a prosperous night for Churchill.

The mildly intoxicated men had given Mad Mike Calvert's cards a workout, playing a few games of *poker*, one game of *canasta*, and even a round of *bridge*. However, when they had dumbed it down to *blackjack*, Jack had really profited. It seemed this lot only ever wanted to *hit*, never *staying*. They lived very dangerously—a reflection of their current status as hot-headed, risk-taking Berzerkers—whereas Churchill maintained the ability to think rationally. Staying where the others busted resulted in him emptying their wallets.

Head sunk deep in his duck down pillow, Churchill listened to the pitch in the exterior air. It may have been relaxing to some, but on this night, it aided only in his lack of slumber.

His platinum peepers remained wide open in his dark room.

Lying in bed for over an hour now, he had been unable to drift off to sleep. This had not been the first time he had suffered from severe restlessness of a night. He possessed an uncommon ability to promptly fall asleep like flicking a switch. It was a bodily skill Churchill had honed during his service in Burma, as sleep was pivotal for peak performance. In spite of that, during much of his stint in Switzerland, it failed him greatly.

A sigh of frustration informed him of a dry and parched mouth, and Churchill craned up and searched for the tall glass of crystal-clear water on his nightstand. He scooped it up, downing the liquid in a guzzle, like it was about to evaporate. Placing the empty glass back down on the stand, it bumped into two other empty tall glasses from nights prior.

It occurred to him—again—that he had never drunk so much water in his life, even in warmer climates like Burma.

In the deathly silence of the night, an unusual creaking noise caught his attention from the exterior of the log building. It was followed by a muffled bump heard through thick cabin walls. The sound was from outside, on ground level, within proximity of his room window located on the second floor.

Due to his wired and awakened state, Churchill's head tipped, listening intently for more sound. Dressed in his warm flannel pyjamas, Jack flipped the covers and soft-footedly approached the curtain. He carefully flayed back the drape with his fingers and slanted his view askew, which gave him a good point of view of the hill and slope to the south-east. The entire snowcapped forestation was illuminated by the full moon high in the clear sky above, causing it to glow in a blue hue.

The wind had died down, though white powdery dust still gusted about, gently caressing tree saplings and swaying tree branches.

At first, he spied nothing ...

No motion, whatsoever ...

... but then, a shadow cast by the lunation's glow provided evidence of movement, and it caught his keen eye.

There was someone outside! At this hour?!

Like a stalking feline, his head twitched in order to track more motion and, after a patient moment, he noticed bouncing silhouettes on the shady pale texture of the ground. The dim motion was a profile against the sparking white ice between the trees, and what he saw was most definitely no animal. It was a human being.

Eyes blurred in profound consideration, he pondered to himself, humouring his curiosity. There was plenty of firewood already in the storage reserve, but even so, everybody had gone to bed by this hour. Whoever was out there was conducting indecorous action.

After a further few seconds of pondering, his inquisitiveness became too much to bear, and an investigative sensation overpowered his desire to climb back into the warm and comfortable double bed in his room.

Hoisting his luggage suitcase onto his bed, Churchill hastily unzipped the bag he lived out of, quickly changing into his skin-tight black thermals, his ski pants, and lastly his button-up hooded jacket. He grabbed his gloves, his beanie, and his unstrung bow and brand-new quiver of wooden war arrows.

As if the motion was an extension to his physical body, as Churchill took a step towards the door, he lugged his leg over his longbow stick and purposely anchored a loop around it with his appendage. Bracing the poundage, he then used his arm to bow the nock and loop the eyelet of his rawhide string tautly. Although both the stick and string audibly tensed, he strained very little performing this task. With his very next step, he strode forth and reached the door.

Quiet as a mouse, he twisted the knob with his fingertips and dragged it open. An unfortunate creek emanated, though hopefully nobody in the neighbouring rooms heard it.

The spooky halls of the resort were eerily quiet at night. All that remained on in the way of luminance were the dim sconces that lined the timber hallway, filling the void with a limelight-type horizontal warmth that glowed in intervals and caused a lot of recessing shadows.

Once downstairs and into the dark and inert lobby, the sock-wearing Churchill silently slipped into the common area, carrying his boots and bow. The big mantle fireplace had died out downstairs, and it was now cold as a result. Since nobody was up at this hour, the entire building was empty and echoic. In fact, the loudest thing he heard right now was the sound of his own heart pounding inside his head.

Whomever had been moving about outside had been doing so purposely and trying to be as discreet as possible.

Not wanting to lose his mark, Churchill hastened quietly to the rear glass doors of the resort and pushed one open just enough to rotate outside.

The air was freezing beyond the rear entrance. The windchill assaulted his cheeks and eyes as he quickly placed down his bulky snow boots on the portion of deck wood beside a mat, slotting all ten piggies of his two sock-clad feet into each gaping hole.

Barely lacing them up, he dropped to a low stance, scanning the dark tree line in the distance with his bow at the ready. This was precisely where he had sighted the movement less than two minutes ago.

... he waited.

... he watched.

... *he saw more movement in the flailing distance.*

Through the trees, about fifty yards to the south-east, far.

In a strafe, Churchill hopped over the railing of the deck, free falling almost three whole metres before engaging in a shoulder roll in the snow—this time, unlike *many* other times before, a recent upgrade to the Jack Churchill attire prevented the arrows from spilling from his shoulder quiver. The powerful yet lightweight magnet sewn within the reservoir of the leather housing was capable of pinning his cluster of arrowheads, holding them upside down. In the past, executing such a stunt without the aid of the new metal-attracting retainer had resulted in something much resembling fumbling an open box of matchsticks.

Powdered with snow and ice, Churchill upped from the roll and put his strongest foot out in front of him, off the mark like a competing athlete running for gold. Sprinting in a quick dash across a moonlit open terrain, he then advanced low beneath canopy shadows like a predator stalking prey, leading into the dark and ominous forest, where he tracked the exacted movement like a deadly round of shadow games. After catching a more detailed glimpse of some of the unknown's progress, as well as identifying fresh tracks in the snow, he was sure that whomever it was he was pursuing in the middle of the night was definitely both *human* and *armed...*

He advanced, utilizing his preexisting army orientation tracking ability as well as his newfound hunting skills, gaining ground on his game in order to gain an advantageous position, soon becoming positioned tactically aslope the deduced target on a gradient.

Resting in position, Churchill drew an arrow and nocked the drawstring. Once a clear line of sight was revealed, he yanked firm on the drawn bowstring, ready to loose an arrow at this hounded quarry ...

"*Oi!*" he boomed in a harsh whisper from behind his longbow sights and charged draw. Hot air was visible in his breath in the beaming moonlight. In the silence of the forest at midnight, his voice was echoic and expansive, and carried further than it had to. It would have shaken the exposed individual to his core ...

... had he not known of Churchill's presence.

This was a trap. And Jack had just sprung it.

The masked target down below froze and complied—too willingly.

They raised their mittens and halted on the spot.

"State your business around these parts!" Churchill questioned the man within his drawn sights. From here, he could effortlessly put an arrow through either one of the eye sockets of his ski mask.

Cl-cl-click.

The hammer of a firearm cocked behind Jack's ear ...

Churchill's eyes grew wide from behind his drawn longbow.

He felt the cold steel of a gun barrel being shoved into the back of his neck by a blindsiding assailant in the darkness. It was at that moment that he realized just how far in the deep end he was this night.

Should 'a stayed in bed.

"Well, well, well. Mad Jack ..." a familiar voice stated from behind the weapon—spoken with a familiar half-Australian accent.

"... Mike?" perplexed, Churchill stated before even turning. He slowly disengaged the draw on his bow, reluctantly removing the arrow from the notch in the line, and completely surrendering. He turned to see that there was a crowd behind him—fronted by Calvert. A couple other Berzerkers of the Special Z Unit loomed, all armed, posing out from behind Mad Mike like an album cover. This renegade unit was comprised of almost a dozen men, all dressed dark, warm, and deadly.

"The *fuck* are you doing out here, mate?" Calvert questioned in the cold, tilting his pistol into the sky in order to safely collapse the hammer. "Ya tryin' to get ya'self shot?"

"Could ask you lot the same thing ...?" Churchill replied, glancing back down the slope and to the singular man he had caught out in the open, now recognizing him as being Corporal Humphrey Ruffell, dressed all in black. He pulled his balaclava mask up over his face, wearing it like a beanie and grinning his toothless beam whilst upping the slope to rejoin the group.

Present in the assembly behind Calvert, also drawing back their ski masks were Dredge, Black, Scotty, Komrower, and Gentle Jerry. The one figure who kept his balaclava covering his face was the intimidating killer-type known only as Danny Boy—in fact, Churchill and many of the other men within Berzerker were yet to see his whole face, even socially. Each of the men were dressed in dark fatigues, beanies, gloves, and wrapped in lightly kitted webbing, supporting an assortment of gear, such as arbitrary armaments, guns, crossbows and—naturally—the Berzerker weapon-of-choice, the M1918 trench knife. At least one of the brass-handled combat daggers were tucked into each belt.

Held at their moonlit mercy, Churchill noted that their fearless leader, Orde Wingate, was not present amongst this motley mutiny.

Ruffell climbed the snowy slope in a series of hiked trudging treads that promised to ache his quads come morning, regrouping after playing bait for this trap spring.

Breaking the menacing silence, Dredge inserted debatably with his Estuary English tone. "Oi, *we* caught *you,* you daft git. Remember?"

Jack's wide-eyed stare sought him. "Yes, but I could have taken you all out. I knew you were behind me. You were all next ... starting with *you.*"

Calvert snorted smugly, though the situation was still far from calm and relieved. Churchill's presence was clearly an unwanted one against their existing hidden agenda, though it seemed to be a best-case scenario.

"Mike, we should call it quits for the night," Black trudged forth and stated to Calvert. He carried strapped before him a customized Lanchester submachine gun, painted black and fitted with one of the unit's trench knives at the forefront via a canvas strapping. This meant that the brass knuckleduster eyelets of the hilt acted as an extra grip on the automatic weapon. The blade was now a bayonet on the submachine gun for prospective close-quarter encounters.

He released the shoulder-tight cradle of the blackened weapon in his possession, casually approaching their stand-off atop the slope and scanning the dark horizons in their wake. The others remained hidden around the vicinity, partially in formation whilst they guarded the perimeter.

Brushing past Black's vocalized proposition, Calvert's nostrils flared whilst he questioned Churchill. "How'd you catch us? How'd you know where we were?"

"Colonel Mustard with the candlestick in the Common Room ..." Churchill stated decoratively, feeding Calvert's board game addiction by referencing a popular murder mystery game. It was a good connection considering their lodgings at the wooden resort.

Black huffed over Churchill, utterly despising the humour he often emitted. He did not like anyone, but him especially.

"No, really?" Calvert enquired.

"I heard you leaving."

"Impossible," stated Black. "We were as quiet as mice."

Churchill ogled him. "With elephant hooves, maybe?"

"Did you tell the Otter?" one of the others asked directly.

Churchill eyed him, then Calvert: their apparent tacit and silent leader of this knave black ops team within a black ops team. Churchill could tell that Mad Mike was surveying him with an incredibly specific gleam. He was reading his every glimmer, gaining a reading on whether or not he was truthful with his next response ... luckily for Churchill, he was honest.

Steadfast, Churchill responded. "No one knows."

There was a sigh of relief amongst the men, and Churchill caught further wind of the prohibited nature of their illicit exploits. It was probably because what they were doing, if caught by an authoritarian, could be perceived as heinously as an act of war and incite an invasion by Nazi Germany into the neutral zone of Switzerland. They could get a lot of innocent people killed if one of their forays into occupied territory were discovered. They weren't just playing with fire ... they were taunting an inferno.

"Mike," Black implored, sidling close. "We need to head back to the resort. We can't take this numpty out with us ..."

"Nah. We can trust him," Calvert advised the men, of which it appeared that only Graeme Black disapproved. "He's all right. Aren't ya, Jack?"

Black cursed, taking a stride aft in anger.

Churchill remained expressionless and stoic.

"Depends. Just what is it you lads are doing out here, eh?"

"We're gettin' our fix ..." Calvert stated as the boys began to disperse, moving out towards whatever their clandestine objective was; somewhere out in the middle of the wilderness of nowhere.

Churchill stood idle and quizzical. "*Fix?*"

Calvert elaborated. "We hunt and kill krauts at night ..."

Taken aback, although suppressing his reaction well, Churchill glanced around at the others, specifically, at their armaments. Their weapons were sharp and lethal, predominantly gear for silent killing.

"Enemy patrols move out north from the *Aosta Valley* at night ..." Black furthered, fighting his yearning to persist blunted towards Churchill. The Aosta Valley was the mountainous autonomous region in north-western Italy, located below Switzerland, and a geographical stone's throw from their off-books base of operations in the Swiss Pennine Alps. The outskirts were accessible by slope routes. Switzerland may have been neutral; nevertheless, Italy was littered with the foot soldiers of Hitler's Third Reich.

"Dey march erlong tha boarder ..." Scotty expanded. Each of these men seemed to be on the same page regarding the mission brief. Conceivably, this was not their first rodeo.

"... and then some of them, *POOF!* ... never-fuckin'-return," added Dredge with an ounce of looney theatrics that caught Churchill's attentive, wordless ponder at their questionable motives.

"They used to refer to the SNS as *well-oiled killing machines* ... we're not dissimilar ..."

Churchill's gaze returned to Calvert as he supplementarily illustrated.

"We kill 'em ... and then we bury 'em. Fuckin' fascist cunts never know what hit 'em."

Black threatened. "Just like we'll bury *you* if you breathe a word of this to the Otter, or Dayan, or any of the other fuddy-duddies in the unit."

Michael Dredge concurred, eyes hounding Churchill. "Yeah."

Churchill's sterling stare twinkled as it searched Dredge's own eyeline, and he saw the seriousness in his gaze, however Jack remained unfazed by the attempted bullying. The seriousness of his hazing became intensified by the fact that, this time, Calvert did not offer any defensiveness regarding the topic.

And he thought Orde Wingate was the crazy one.

Mike Calvert was a canine off the leash!

They should have probably invited the Otter along. Judging by his level of craziness and lunacy, Wingate would have been down for a bout of *midnight murder in the woods.*

"Fine-o-fine," Churchill began his long and expounded retort, even taking a step to be face-to-face with these disgruntled soldiers, full engaging them mano a mano. They each held intense eye-contact for an extended moment before Churchill's head pivoted to address the others who surrounded the vicinity. "With all due respect, lads ... I do know a little something about sneaking out of the house after bedtime, making sure not to wake your sleeping *Uncle Otter.*"

The men perched silently. They recognized Churchill's entendre.

"Just ask Mike, here."

Forming a mischievous grin, Calvert nodded past Churchill's shoulder to Dredge and Black. Mad Jack and Mad Mike had, after all, met on a black-label night out in Lille's red-light district. Together, they had evaded the military police during a raid.

They had a legacy of truancy.

"Well, *Mad Jack,*" the boardgame fiend Mad Mike questioned, referencing blackjack. "Are you *hitting* or *staying?*"

Churchill calmly continued pleading his case, "Albeit, my prior nights out on the town after hours didn't dance on the topic of whatever international diplomacy there is in-place right now between the Swiss and the Huns ..." with a sense of profoundness, he returned closer to Calvert. "... but let's just say, if you'll have me, I, myself, am *too* in need for a fix of war. Hit."

5 ♠   5 ♠

King, Queen, Jack, War

1942, February
Westminster Conference Grand Hall
Whitehall, London

The preliminary hearing of one Lieutenant-Colonel John Malcolm Thorpe Fleming Churchill was to be held at 0900-hours the subsequent Monday to the issuing of his court orders and would be treated as a *secret trial*. Due to the sensitive and classified information to be potentially disclosed during the hearing, this implied no public apportioning or admission by any unauthorized Kingsman or non-classified military personnel and excluded citation capture via stenographer (transcriptionist).

The courthouse selected for the proceedings was one favoured by military courts of the United Kingdom located in the hectic hive hub for all things government and military, Whitehall.

From Scotland, Churchill arrived in London the night prior, acquiring a room at a local inn.

Upon arriving at the Westminster Conference Grand Hall the following overcast morning, he was surprised to be greeted by so many familiar military and political figures for a would-be 'secret trial'.

Dressed formally and donning his green beret stylishly aslant, the scar-faced cheek of Mad Jack Churchill upped the stairs outside the front of the court building which were wet following a solid night's soaking of drizzle. The limestone structure was another of several buildings established during the Tudor period of architecture, such as the overuse of Palladian windows. Churchill navigated through a herd of crisscrossing morning busybodies in a combination of civilian suits and military battledresses, finally arriving before the familiar faces of Lieutenant-Colonel Robert *Lucky* Laycock and Lieutenant-Colonel John Durnford-Slater. Both these high-ranking army men and Commando associates had been summoned for the tribunal, as prospective character references for the accused.

Like Churchill, both men were dressed in matching service dress military suits, complete with green berets mounted upon their heads and red No.3 Commando unit insignia on their arm patches. They were each well decorated, as displayed by their many chevrons and sewn patches.

"Colonels," Churchill greeted as he contacted the two men, expecting the announced salutation to be a humorous set-up for an easy riposte considering all three men now shared the same rank following his recent promotion. Instead, Churchill's unsolicited arrival was rather rudely intercepted by two military police by the hall entrance. They approached him with an abrupt acceleration, acting to isolate the defendant by order of the prosecution ...

The gravity of the situation suddenly felt heavier.

"*Colonel Churchill!*"

"*Colonel, sir!*" white-gloved uniformed guards hailed, cutting him off three steps before Durnford-Slater and Laycock, and before they had a chance to return any acknowledgement.

"*Sir, you are to come with us immediately and without resistance.*"

This may have been a secret trial, but their execution of their orders turned a few heads of the busy bee passers-by as they seized Churchill on the elegant front steps.

"What is the meaning of this?" Churchill scowled and his mood of pleasantries faded. He maintained an allure of his winning smile towards his army associates; his commando comrades; his military mates ...

... unbeknownst to Jack, they were soon to be situated on the bench as *lay members*, seated by the Judge Advocate General.

They weren't here to support him ...

They were a part of the god damned bench!

Laycock attempted to reassure Churchill. "It's regulation, Colonel."

"We're not allowed to speak before the hearing ..." Durnford-Slater informed stridently, raising his voice out of the growing concern he could read on Churchill's face as the two royal MPs effectively scooped him up from beneath the arms of his dress suit, escorting him at haste into the side door of the courthouse.

Laycock placated Durnford-Slater with a supportive touch on the shoulder. It was also an insistent restraint, keeping his respected colleague from overstepping due to his subjective interest in whom the trial concerned. Durnford-Slater and Churchill had been through a lot together this past year and had grown close. They were very well-respected colleagues—brothers, even. It was understandable why the man let that fretful tone of voice slip and felt sincere sorrow for his friend being hung out to dry. Allocated a seat at the platform today for his unbiased opinion of the man, Lucky Laycock shook his head with disgust at this slice of wicked unlawfulness. They were dragging a hero through the mud.

Before entering, Churchill, *the defendant,* passed two other familiar faces in the crowd: Jethro McNaughton and his good-lookin' offsider, the green and gold-eyed vixen, Viviane Garland.

They were the two prejudiced constables from the Special Investigation Branch. They had each come dressed officially and stood proud with conviction, poised amongst a posse of legal lawyers in shark suits: *the prosecution.*

His latest enemies.

Beneath a puckered brow, Churchill eyed them all in passing, marking them for contest. In that same elongated moment, whilst ushered under guard within the chambers for the commencement of the tribunal, Jack's sterling stare sought the confident glare of McNaughton.

Their stares fought a thousand arguments.

Churchill seemed obdurate and vengeful in his drifting gawk.

McNaughton was secure in his conviction and thus remained self-assured and firm in his judiciousness.

The fight was on.

The military court process itself was a meticulous legal leviathan.

A warzone in its own right, it was a type of battlefield just like any other, only one in which Mad Jack Churchill had zero fighting experience.

Most offences by members of the military against service law were dealt with by their commanding or executive officers through what was known as a disciplinary hearing; typically held somewhere locationally minute, such as in a barracks headquarters conference room. It was always on the record, but typically low-key. Regulations stated that a CO may deal with an offence by way of a summary hearing if the offence is minor, and the accused is of or below the rank of lieutenant-colonel in the Army or Royal Marines—which put Churchill shit out of luck as of a week ago, due to his promotion. Offences that could be dealt with internally included *being absent without leave (AWOL), insubordination, ill-treating subordinates, malingering, conduct prejudicial to good order,* as well as various other offences against civilian law, such as *assault, theft, careless driving, sexual assault,* or *criminal damage.* Offences which could *not* be dealt with summarily included but were not limited to *assisting the enemy, misconduct on operations, mutiny,* and *desertion* ... which, again, put Jack shit out of luck, for his allegations touched across more than one of those topics.

Before long, Churchill's constricted caboose became directed indoors and through the building, finding the courtroom, where he was parked behind an uncomplimentary trestle table disguised beneath a fancy tablecloth. Once situated behind a pair of tucked chairs by his expressionless guards, he took a serene sigh, retaining his composure, even in the face of this legal jeopardy.

The two white-gloved guards delivered him to his destination, remaining impassive and dutiful. *"Sir, any knives or weapons upon your person?"*

Churchill's wandering gaze found the guard.

Given the severity of the proceedings, he had opted not to mount his claybeg upon his hip today. This was a mistake for numerous reasons—biggest of all, he had broken his own golden rule. He was improperly dressed.

Unable to think of a worthy witticism, Churchill merely shook his head and allowed them to vacate, leaving him alone.

Soon, the cold air inside the vacant courtroom combined with the harrowing silence caused him to feel increasingly incommodious, damaging his usual unbreakable calm to some measurable extent.

A windowless room located deep within the echoic bowels of the law building, what walls that weren't lined with wooden gallery booths were bare, trimmed with square architraves, and lined with a few ornate tapestries and framed art hanging sporadically.

The ceiling was twenty feet high, wizened with detailed decorative aesthetics, in keeping with the same classical architectural architraves.

Located at the very front of the room, running in defilade to his position like a target down a firing range, was a long table upon a raised floor like a stunted stage. The table was clothed in a golden-trim royal silk skirting that reached the floor. The desktop was arranged with office stationery, upturned glasses, and jugs of fresh water positioned every two seats.

The room was so soundproofed that within those moments of silence, Churchill could hear his own pulse pumping within his ears. All of a sudden, this whole shenanigan had crept up a gear in urgency and gravitas. He started to obtain a better understanding of the severity of his situation, as even his own heartrate became made aware of the magnitude of this official summoning.

In the silence, his stern eyeline fell completely onto the neatly coated table before him. Memoirs regarding an outdated tradition recalled the ceremonial accuracy for a commissioned offer present at a court martial to draw and lay down his sabre upon the table before the commencement of the due process. The gesture was a symbol of their rank and reputation being put in abeyance. Upon the conclusion of the trial, the tip of the sword would be turned towards the accused if they had been found guilty by a court of law.

It was a silly and old practice, however as a chivalrous man and a heartly traditionalist, had Jack brought his trusty claybeg sidearm, he would have made an effort in upholding this tradition before these wig-wearing magistrates. Alas, today was a rare circumstance where this warfighter found himself uncharacteristically unarmed.

Before more meditative pondering could befall his heavy brooding, a door opened at the posterior of the courtroom. Within these echoic chambers, the sound caused him almost to flinch in that moment of mental, off-guarded weakness, and Churchill watched as a convoy crowd of military dressed men and authorized people in civilian suits entered, storming the room with their bureaucratic presence. Being a secret trial, they must have directly been related to the state of affairs or at least have been attorneys with some form of clearance. There were approximately six in total, not including McNaughton and Garland who entered last and remained standing against the back wall beside a uniformed MP.

A busybody balding man with a thin combover lacquered with pomade swiftly entered, sidling beside Churchill. Panting a little, he placed down his briefcase on the tabletop, standing before the tucked chair neighbouring his own. Next, he offered an open hand to his apparent client.

"Hello, I'm *Lionel Spencer.* I've been appointed by the court system to legally represent you," he informed as a matter of fact.

"Eh, hullo ..." Churchill responded hesitantly, taking his handshake as a formal gesture, barely acceptant of any offers. "I wasn't aware I would be needing any legal representation for a preliminary hearing?"

"A *preliminary hearing* to a *secret trial,*" Spencer responded, twisting and opening his briefcase to retrieve a file containing a single sheet of paper and a document. "I'm afraid they can nail you to a cross as soon as the bull gets out the gate on these ones. From what I understand, this hearing is too *top-secret* for even my ears to hear it ..."

Churchill's focus drifted to the lawyer's hands as he retrieved relevant paperwork. He glanced within the void of the open case, catching a glimpse of several '*how to*' style textbooks. This guy was a formality packrat here to collect a cheque, nothing more. A ritual pawn piece hired by the army to appear diplomatically fair, reasonable, and supportive, and provide a sense of fairness to each offender. He was a government flunky whose only duty of presence was to make defendants feel defended in the prearranged court of law.

Jack's eyes rolled from off him and to the front of the room where the elongated bar table was situated parallel to theirs, awaiting the judge and lay members to appear and become seated, beginning today's ~~execution~~ hearing.

"I'm merely here to make sure you know what you're agreeing to if any *deals* are made; *plea bargains* as we say in the 'biz. Don't worry about the jargon."

Churchill's brow cocked hearing the man's tone.

"Eh, I'll be waiving my right for an attorney, *don't worry,*" he responded in just as condescending a tone towards the lawman as he had just received.

"Oh, you'll likely think differently once I show them our letter from the King ..."

"*Letter from the King?*" Jack dared ask.

"An ace in the hole, my friend. You'll be glad I stuck around."

Spencer possessed a smug look on his mug, facing forwards and waiting patiently for the court to commence. He held the white paper in his mitts.

"You'll see."

Rather than react, Churchill's eyeline meandered, cruising about the courtroom. He had little to no patience for these sorts of formalities and legal jargon bollocks, poppycock, hogwash, gimcrackery, or any other informal definition that British culture can convey for this legal courtroom bullshit. It was perchance at the roots of his overall frustration towards this inquiry, regardless of the pressure and tension housed by the accused. These types took this sort of business so seriously, as though they were fighting a good fight—clearly, none of them had been to war.

As Jack huffed and puffed internally, he browsed over his shoulder at the apparent audience privy to knowledge of the existence of the aux-ops. He identified Colonel Sloan MacLeòid within the crowd. The Angry Scotsman was dressed in his formal attire with military kilt, as always, and took up an isolated seat in the bleachers of the chairs, very out of the way.

He nodded at Churchill once he noticed his presence.

Jack discreetly bowed back before facing forwards just in time for the front side door to the courtroom to open inwards. Another soldier dressed similar to an MP, a *bailiff*, entered the room first with a buoyant stride and spring in his step. Close-shaven and smooth, the official fellow held open the door with his gloved hands for a row of dignitary personages and bigwigs who followed suit.

"*All rise*," he declared authoritatively.

At the rear of the room, those who were seated, elevated.

Stars of the show: the low glowers of the notables remained forward as they toured through, aligning behind the chairs positioned behind the longer bar table opposite Churchill's docked position in the middle.

There were two double tables established supporting eight lay members and a central figure, likely the judge.

The majority of the men Churchill couldn't identify, although he could guess that there would be a member from each sector of the British Military. He obviously recognized Durnford-Slater and Laycock, as well as Chief of Staff Henry Pownall. Since Churchill had seen him a few years ago, Pownall had risen to the rank of *Vice Chief of the Imperial General Staff at the War Office* and was now on the cusp of assuming the title *Commander-in-Chief of the British Far East Command*. The sole fact they had pulled him into this preliminary hearing was cause enough to sense the scale.

The MP guard then closed the door behind a final entrant of their grand entrance, confining them for the session, and all lowkey chatter and whispers from the rear of the room evaporated into an eerie silence.

"*The honorary Judge MacGeagh presiding.*"

Sir Henry Davies Foster MacGeagh was the appointed Judge Advocate General of the Armed Forces. He wore an official court gown as he entered the courtroom, finding a seat directly in the middle of the bar. MacGeagh was a tall, older gent, with a portly build and circular reading spectacles resting on the tip of his nose, forcing him to tilt his head downwards in order to focus farther than four feet. He wore a white magistrate's wig.

"*Be seated.*"

All those present promptly pulled out their chairs and formally sat.

Appearing uncomfortable, Churchill scanned the room once again, becoming one of the last to be seated amongst the noisy commotion of tucking chairs against metal table legs hidden behind overhanging tablecloths.

"Good morning, ladies and gentlemen," Judge MacGeagh greeted officially with a rapid glance about the room whilst breezing across his assorted papers and organizing the proceedings. Through his circular spectacles, his peepers scanned the case detail, where he noted contemptuously an obligatory stonewall. "Eh, yes," he remarked, "another *Article 23* that doesn't exist, I see. Let's get on with it, then ..."

This must have been a tiring era for black-ops controversies hitting the courts in a secret trial fashion.

Regardless, he proceeded. "We're calling the case of the *Criminal Investigation Department* on behalf of the *British War Office* versus *Lieutenant-Colonel John Malcolm Thorpe Fleming Churchill*," he perused up with a throwaway remark. "That's a mouthful."

Churchill murmured. Only Spencer heard it.

"*That's what all the ladies say.*"

MacGeagh continued. "Are the representatives ready?"

Over his lenses, he cast a focusing eye to his right flank where some men in suits on the bench, effectively *the prosecution*, cast the judge a head bob, prepared for court.

"Ready, your honour," Spencer replied with a discernible nod.

"Very well," MacGeagh conveyed, moving their tribunal forwards. "Colonel Churchill, the prosecution alleges you of committing *high treason* and *conspiracy of conducting disloyalty to the Crown.* How do you plea?"

"Not guilty, your honour," Spencer appealed.

"Hang on. Hold your horses," Churchill faced his appointed attorney and then verbalized attentively enough to gain the attention of all those at the judge's bench. He audibly stood, flattening the front of his battledress. "Sir, for starters, I opted to not be represented legally by your *Mister Spencer,* here."

"Colonel Churchill, when speaking to his majesty, the Judge Advocate General, you are required to address him formally as *your honour,*" the bailiff announced from the bench edge with his hands tense behind his back. He acted as a sort of mediator for the session; a bureaucratic bouncer.

Churchill looked to the bailiff and bowed respectfully.

"Apologies, *your honour,*" Jack corrected, addressing MacGeagh directly and delicately smoothing over any tarnished progress. He gestured sincerely, implying no disrespect.

"Understood, Colonel," MacGeagh allowed, respecting that this may have been Jack Churchill's first time in court. "You are aware that such dismissal of legal aid could end disastrously in your circumstances? Unless you graduated law school somewhere between *the Second Manchester Regiment* and *No.3 Commando?*"

Churchill chortled. "Regrettably not, sir."

"Eh, yes. Well then, I advise that you leave the courtroom articulation to your legal representative at least for today, then, hmm?"

"Perhaps my legal representative will allow me to speak and step in only when he needs to?" Churchill affirmed with a sly lean inclined to Spencer who remained wordless should it implicate him later. He shrugged, facing the judge's table and lay members. This normally doesn't happen.

Unwanted, Spencer pursed his lips, riding a chair.

"Very well, Colonel. The court recognizes that you waive your rights for an attorney. So, do I have it that you wish to change your plea from *not guilty?*" Judge MacGeagh questioned, favouring a possible easy settlement of verdict.

Churchill heard the question and shook his head airily. "Not at all, sir. I'd merely like to better understand two things: first, how the prosecution prompts to allege such claims based on top-secret intel; information classified by the Crown worn by His Majesty? And second, who in fact is *the prosecution?*" Churchill formally probed, making waves. "Because, and this could be my *uneducated articulation,* but it seems the defendant is all alone at the bar, with no physical prosecutor?"

MacGeagh seemed unamused by Churchill's display of courtroom lionheartedness. His stare was directed down at the papers during most of his wordy bout, only raising to view him after the fact. "Colonel, this is a court martial. We *are* the prosecution."

Jack's view shifted, glancing about the room and onto McNaughton within the crowd for longer than a split-second before facing forwards in the silence. "Your honour, am I to understand that you are therefore the judge, jury, and executioner of my case? Because, if so, referring to me as a *defendant* may be somewhat superfluous for there is nothing to actually *defend.*"

This argument caught MacGeagh off-guard, and the judge removed his glasses in order to better look upon him with his own eyes. Due to his prior temperament, those present within the courtroom half expected him to grab his gavel and tap the table, holding Churchill in contempt. Before any such action could be asserted, a man to MacGeagh's side dressed in a civilian suit raised his hand, gaining the attention of the tribunal. Without a word spoken, the judge then let him take the spotlight.

"I guess then, I am the prosecution, Colonel," the man informed before identifying himself to those present. "*Deputy Chief William Barney* of the Special Investigation Branch."

This man was McNaughton's boss.

"Sir," Churchill acknowledged respectfully. "Very well. Then the defendant would like to pose one final question to the prosecution: what evidence?"

"*What evidence?*" Barney asked formally, half expecting some sort of an objection from the JAG. "There is no evidence, Colonel. The court wishes to gain a formal admittance from you of any treasonous acts; a confession."

"You're officially requesting that I commit *high treason* in order to prove that I didn't commit *high treason?*" Churchill asked formally, though purposefully confusedly. "That request, in and of itself, must be a crime, is it not?"

"Colonel, I wasn't born yesterday, and neither was Deputy Chief Barney," MacGeagh formally addressed Churchill, cutting the shit. "We're here with authority under the jurisdiction of *His Majesty King George VI;* King of the United Kingdom and the Dominions of the British Commonwealth. Believe me when I say we're hereby *officially authorized* to derestrict your retained intel, and you are sworn by an oath to answer all questions to us both fully and truthfully."

"How do you propose I lodge my counterstatement when no direct allegations have been made?"

Barney leant across the table, taking back the spotlight from Judge MacGeagh. In that moment, MacGeagh's growing frustration towards Churchill's stubbornness finally became evident. "The prosecution hereby requests the official declassification of the operations deemed 'auxiliary operations' during December 1939 to April 1940 in the neutral zone of Switzerland. The defendant will be found guilty by association of those details."

Churchill's brain ticked over. "Okay. So, you've just re-worded my previous question?—"

"Objection, your honour," Spencer interjected more officially, becoming upstanding besides Churchill. He held up his folder and the bailiff stepped forth to collect it, declaring it into evidence for the case and passing it along to Judge MacGeagh across the room.

Recognizing the papers from earlier, Churchill leant into Spencer during a short hiatus for declarations. He whispered: "Is that thing actually signed by the King?"

"Gosh no. Figure of speech," Spencer informed, eventually leaning in. "I told you to leave the jargon to me."

Churchill nodded, silently comprehending.

Spencer remained upstanding, addressing the bench once they had had adequate time to revise the papers. "The admitted is an excerpt sanctioned from a military contract, signed by the King. It should act as a refresher to the court and to the prosecution. The letter states that top-secret mission particulars cannot be *declassified* without the signing executive of said mission present and obliged. Orde Wingate is still an active high-ranking officer within the British Army, and he is *not* present, your honour. Only *he* has the authority to release the particulars of which the prosecution has requested ... unfortunately, the defendant therefore reluctantly declines to divulge any information regarding the specified dates, for it may incriminate him further."

Judge MacGeagh absorbed Spencer's counterstatement wholly.

After an extended pause, his beady eyes, which grazed through the spectacles mounted upon the bridge of his nose, flicked over and onto Churchill. "Eh, yes. Is that what you were going to say, Colonel?"

Churchill's brow rose, still stunned by Spencer's speech.

"Eh ... yes, your honour. What he said."

During the same atmospheric speechlessness that followed, Spencer leant into Churchill not unlike how Jack had done to him only minutes ago. "Told you so. Sure you don't want me to stick around, Colonel?"

After reading the formal declaration Spencer had retrieved ahead of the proceedings, Judge MacGeagh closed the lid on the folder. Technically, legally, he had solid ground to stand upon.

"Very well," he announced, reaching a red tape stonewall. "We postpone any further hearings until the signing executive for the operation is present."

Spencer nodded in accord. "Which is ... *never.*"

He looked at Churchill and fluttered his brow in a show of overconfidence.

Overhearing Spencer's remark to his client, MacGeagh gleefully conveyed, "To the contrary, Mister Spencer. *Lieutenant-Colonel Wingate* is on his way from Ethiopia as we speak. His flight was merely delayed ..."

And the crowd goes wild.

The news hit Churchill—and Spencer—like a sledgehammer.

Smugness faded.

How the fuck did they find Wingate?! The man was a ghost!

Churchill countered. "Your honour, if I may pose a parting question to the prosecution?"

MacGeagh bowed, allowing such—he would permit such a request from the defendant, but more so humouring Jack Churchill's vain attempt at representing himself in a court of law. He would very likely dig his own grave.

"Is it not in itself a criminal offence for the prosecution to have even obtained the finer details of such classified information in the first place? In a *chicken before the egg* manner of speaking? Established by the British War Office, the first rule about *black-ops* is that you don't talk about *black-ops.*"

MacGeagh death-stared Churchill.

That paradoxical question may have had the JAG stumped.

His small beady eyes hovered above his spectacles, seeing deep into his soul. "Colonel, it is not illegal for a sworn member of the Criminal Investigation Department to *investigate.* In fact, not only is it encouraged, it's in the description of the job. Those particulars will be deemed *classified* until we reconvene in three days. Court adjourned."

The judge collected his gavel and tapped the tabletop. Nearly instantaneously, the people within the courtroom stood, shuffling chairs and dismissing themselves whilst they chattered in gabbles.

It was over.

"Witnesses ..." Spencer stated to his unwilling client during the noise of courtroom dismissal.

Jack's brow raised. "Pardon?"

"*Witnesses!* You always first call the witnesses to give your references of character, it's why we helped sway to have Colonels Durnford-Slater *and* Laycock on the member's board to promote your sense of character to the judge. To positively advocate your honesty."

"To who?"

"*To anyone who'll listen!*"

"My honesty needs *advocating,* now, does it?!" Churchill questioned with an egotistical tenor. "I am a damned Lieutenant-Colonel in the British Army, sir. I have had multiple mentions in dispatches as well as a recent Military Cross and promotion. I'm due for my own battalion, lad. I don't know these people, but by now, they should damn-well know me!"

"*Precisely!*" Spencer audibly buttoned the metallic flaps on his brief case and turned to face his client ahead of their daily discharge. "If they don't know you, they'll know them! You've got to *sell* yourself—*oversell yourself* if you must. Sell your soul as a good soldier; a good man. It will help prove your innocence."

Jack asked quietly. "... who said I was innocent?"

"Sorry?!" Spencer perked, apparently not hearing him properly. "What did you say? Because I sure as hell didn't hear you say what I think you said?"

Discouraged and upset, Churchill shook his head adversely.

Spencer laid a finger on his uniform, levelling with the grunt. "Okay, look, Colonel, I say this with the upmost respect to your rank and to you as a person ... Don't ever *fucking* say that you're anything but innocent ever again. Even if you're not. Got it?"

With an underlining remorse, Churchill dipped his face.

"Now, take care of yourself. I'll see you in three days," Spencer farewelled, tucking in his chair and then buttoning his suit. "Unless, of course, you really want to fire me—in which case, I'll see you in jail, and we can debrief for mere *shits 'n gigs?*"

Churchill looked to him. "Of course not."

"Good! Because I'm getting paid regardless, look," he advised off the cuff and then leaned into Jack to chat softly. "Just trust me on this, okay? Wingate is a nasty piece of work. He's a free bird, constantly in fret of getting his wings clipped. With any luck, he off's himself before we reconvene. And the only thing coming into England from Ethiopia is his cold corpse."

Churchill had to swallow his ideals.

Ostensibly, Wingate had quite the negative reputation through the court system. It appeared that this was not the first time this corrupt character's name and dubious donations to the British war effort had made it to tribunal or judicature.

"This thing won't make it to the Superior Court. Trust in *the King;* in dutiful due diligence, and in a hole-poled justice system that favours loopholes and ambiguities," finalized Spencer. The full stop resounded, Jack visually taking it on board. "See you in three days, Colonel."

Instilling a sense of false confidence, he knocked Churchill on the shoulder before vacating, leaving Mad Jack alone and in deep thought within the centre of the room as all other parties cleared out.

"*The King?*" Churchill invited rhetorically to himself, viewing some of the various tapestries and artworks around the vacating courtroom. Even with all his accolades and accomplishments of late, the battles fought and won, such a profound place such as this caused him to feel small. There were various works displaying numerous high-profile dignitaries and members of royalties: the men which Churchill vowed to serve the ancestors of in loyalty and in war; in his sworn acts. As much within Wingate's Special Z Unit as much as Durnford-Slater's Commando ...

Yet, here he was, standing trial.

It angered him, but he had no one to fight ... *or did he?*

There was no winning smile for Churchill.

No witty remark.

Mad Jack scowled, a serious vendetta now afoot.

1942, February
Glenn Mill (Camp 2)
Oldham, Lancashire

Once the court adjourned, Churchill surmounted a frightening sensation.

The sum of fleeting freedom overcame him, and it was unnerving to say the least. Although directionless, he had not a second to waste. Three days felt like an awfully long time to recess for their case, though percase not in legal timeframes.

Rage brimming, seething simmering, Churchill discerned with a clenched fist down by his side that a targeted visit to his indirect accuser was in order. Conveniently already located in the city and already staring down a northerly trajectory home, Churchill's Harley-Davidson throttled along the motorway from London, headed towards Lancashire. He made the destination by the afternoon, with the plan to press on and reach the Largs base in Ayrshire by the evening.

Parked along the opposite side of the road from the repurposed Glenn Mill internment camp, Churchill dismounted his motorcycle. It was a dreary afternoon, with high precipitation and the threat of rainfall not far off the reservation.

Churchill surveyed the same double-thick tall lining barbed wire fence he had seen on one of his prior exterior visits. Beyond that was the prison camp housing nearly two-thousand German prisoners of war.

The inmates were still on a day jaunt in the campus.

A sea of sorry-seeming troops in mismatched uniforms convened in an open clearing before the closest row of barracks, guarded by towers of riflemen and patrolling troops. They traded cigarettes and conversed somewhat jovially considering their confinement, speaking their native tongue and no doubt illy of their captors.

Clad in his khaki suit and green beret, Churchill wore an imperiously serious frown. The stress caused for his usually immaculate physical demeanour to appear dishevelled—a rare occurrence. His collar was unbuttoned, his cuff lengths extended unevenly from beneath his jacket sleeves and appeared mismatched, and also his necktie was slightly misaligned.

Disillusioned by his current circumstances, and wearing the same scowl since London, Churchill stomped off his bike and approached the exterior wire with a purposeful mindset. He took a harsh moment to study, to survey, *to hunt.* Striding analogously to the outer fence line, Jack's piercing blues longed for one inmate in particular, spying in the distance across the exhibit of replicated internees.

On occasion during his strident search, his purposeful strafing would hitch in his saunter, snagged on a false-positive of identification. Churchill dipped his frown and bobbed his head to see through the crisscrossed wires, unsure of a positive target in a few cases, for many of the boche contained within Camp 2 resembled Friedrich Feind.

And then, he saw him.

Almost immediately, Feind's stare raised above the shoulders of several prisoners in his clique, and he focused afar, noticing the loitering British uniform beyond the yard fence, looking in.

His awareness heightened after his recognition of Jack Churchill.

With his hands in his greatcoat pockets, Feind reluctantly broke away from the group of squalid POWs, strolling unaccompanied towards the outer fences, undoubtedly gaining the attentive eyes of the nearest guard towers.

There were no greetings.

No salutations, whatsoever.

The two just stood, orbiting at a distance.

"Ernst-Günther Baade," Churchill pronounced firmly as Feind's approaching meander halted at what could be seen by guards as a safe distance to the fence line. Due to his grave tone, Churchill's sentence was conveyed more as a statement than a question. In either regard, Feind was left wondering until Churchill finally elaborated. "He was the one who trained you how to swordfight ... he was your mentor ..."

Cards close, Feind did not confirm nor deny.

"He is how you know about Switzerland, isn't it?"

Feind played hard to get. "Pozzibly."

"*Pozzibly* I leap this fence and *choke* it out of you!" Churchill let slip his brimming rage, slapping the outer wire fence with utter indignation. It was a display of anger behind a hollow threat that only caused Feind to smirk.

"Pozzibly I run back into zee barrackz und you get zhot by zee vatchtower?"

"*Pozzibly* I equip my longbow and a high-velocity bodkin-tip war arrow, and I pick you off better than a sniper next time you're allowed out of your sweet barracks for playtime, eh?" Churchill threatened, genuinely assessing the scenario with a can-do attitude. "Zero windage ... minimal obstacles resulting in no significant interference ... less than a hundred-yards out, that's less than three-hundred feet ..." he tilted his neck. "I've made a shot like that before, easy-peasy."

"*Eazy-peazy, lemon-zqueezy?*" Feind jousted, catching the American film reference.

"*Easy-peasy, dead-boche-bellend.*"

Feind tittered at the lame insult.

Humour may have not been the ultimate goal of Churchill's tired mind, but the insult still met its intended inclination.

"You are angry. Good. I merely played zee hand I waz dealt, English-man ..."

Churchill erupted, refocusing their apparent digression. "Why?!" he exclaimed, at his wit's end. "Just, *why?* You may have shagged me over proper with my up-tops, but you've also shagged your own mentor as well. I'll take Baade down with me, y'know? All it will take is a parley letter to the Hun hierarchy from my government to yours, outlining his presence and correlation with us in Switzerland. They'll launch a witch-hunt not unlike the inquest I'm enduring. He'll be complicit in treason and have the choice of a fate met either by the end of a rope or the barrel of a gun. Rather unceremonious, is it not?"

Feind shrugged dismissively. "I do not care."

Taken aback, Churchill stared, perplexed.

For a full three seconds he blinked profusely, re-examining the nature of the response.

"Pardon?" he queried, at a loss. "What kind of pyrrhic victory is that?"

Feind shared in his contemptuous humour and rhetorical question, ending with a genuine rejoinder. "I juzt *hate* you, English-man."

The response hit like the rushing wave of an open floodgate.

Now that the chips were down and the gloves were off, we were finally getting somewhere with Feind's motives. The reasoning behind his left-fielded, long-winded ploy.

His confession continued. "I've *alvayz* hated you ..."

Exhaling audibly, Churchill's successive expression faltered.

He was listening well to Feind, for the first time beginning to recognize the origins of their deep-seated disagreement.

"Ever zince Oslo, you have been zee *bane* of my exiztence."

"*The bane of your existence?!* The absolute *fuck?!*" Churchill retorted, seething with an appalled mystification warming his cheeks. Ever since Oslo, Feind had haunted *his* mind. He was *his* blight, not the other way around, and for him to even consider himself as such only outraged Churchill further. "Let's get one thing straight, you boche bellend, *you* came into *my world* that day in Oslo, alright?! *You* stepped into *my life,* my *house,* and you took a *shit!* Prior to you, everything was fine-o-fine. I had no mortal enemies until *you* were on scene."

"*Likewize!*" Feind declared.

It was difficult to imagine, but for a brief moment, Churchill could envision his recent history through the eyes of Friedrich Feind; a mid-level German nobleman, born from an aristocratic family, and on the upward progression of a pre-war Nazi involvement. Upon visiting his betrothed Swedish princess in Norway for the games in the pre-war world, an English-taunting westerner enters, attempting to steal his missus: a young Jack Churchill, guilty as fuck. After stirring the pot, this exasperating *English-man* then causes a massive scene, successfully shifting the spotlight onto Feind's portrayal of the self-righteous villain and embarrassing him thus. Scepticism would undoubtedly ensue in the eyes of the scarlet, Scarlet Kristina, now that she had seen the light. God only knew what sort of carnage was left in the wake of events at the Oslo airfield, where a sobering Mad Jack confessed his love to this man's betrothed, the confused and albeit naïve demoiselle, before then leaving her forever, circa 1939. He had opened her oppressed eyes. Instilled a spark within her heart that would only continue to ember behind the scenes, unbeknownst to Churchill, that it would eventually ignite and engulf into an inferno, burning their house of cards down like falling ash.

As if he could ever forget her.

As if he would ever fail to remember her; his enduring infatuation with the miscarried Swedish singer baring the epithet of *the Queen of Sweden ...*

Scarlet Kristina.

Her golden blonde hair.

Her plump yet sharp lips, hourglass physique, that generous bust.

Her amazing, serene emerald-green eyes.

She was an absolute goddess, unobtainable by the touch of mortal men ... yet somehow, Feind had succeeded in seizing the enchantment. Had managed to contain the sun, shading Churchill's future in a cold and empty darkness for a while to come—or so he thought. The wounds had healed, but the scars remained forever.

Feind reiterated, showing signs of brimming emotion. "I *hate* you, English-man. You ruined my life that day. Ever zince Oslo, I have hated you enough to vant to kill you."

"What do you mean *I ruined your life?*" Churchill argued with raised arms. "You kicked my arse in Oslo! You defeated me, Feind, not the other way around! You got the girl!" he pressed on his temples, lathering them in order to better comprehend what pained him thusly. "You won that war!"

Feind quietened, revisiting aspects of their convoluted pasts.

Shaking his head in disdain, Churchill added, "I hate the fact that I even *idolized* you for a second back then as the victor!"

"You *idolized* me?" although not the only part Feind took away from Churchill's admission, it caused him to pull on the thread momentarily before moving on. The lingering silence caused the German soldier to readjust his emotional bearings, bringing forth a confession of his own. "Scarlet ... my fräulein ... she left me ..."

Through the wire fencing at the professing German, Churchill's stare softened. His brow flinched, still processing the information. He didn't verbally question the revelation by Feind, but the Hun elaborated regardless.

"... early in the Führer's conquering of Europe ..."

"You mean the Führer's *invasion* of Europe?" Churchill corrected from a western standpoint. From a moral and truthful, historic standpoint. In this unprecedented moment of concession, as disarming as it was to learn that both men shared a lot more in common than they could have ever realized, Jack wasn't about to let this man forget that he was a Nazi.

Feind's gaze ascended as his confessing train of thought momentarily derailed, nevertheless, he corrected his course of deficient sympathy. It was almost as if deep within the man's soul there was a righteousness that recognized the correction of the amendment but was forbidden to acquiesce such. Their disparity evolved on two sides of a spinning coin.

"She defected ..." he declared additionally, still resonating in distraught at the betrayal. Defection wasn't completely unheard of in the early days of the uprising of the Third Reich. Out of fear of incredulity towards the fascist Nazi regime, many families loyal to Germany packed their bags and surreptitiously absconded to the western world, typically the United Kingdom or America if they could bribe that far. Apparently, they were one of such royal families who could afford to flee the fife of the fascist fuckwits.

"Her whole family defected to zee wezt ..." Feind continued, immortally mesmerized by the disloyalty while Churchill listened attentively.

It wasn't unnormal for loyalists to have a change of heart towards Hitler's Germany in light of the full-scale invasion of Europe. Back when the Nazi Party was strictly political, lots of different hands were in lots of different pockets, however, once war erupted and the heat turned up, those who could afford to do so got the heck out of the kitchen. The Sundquist kinfolk were apparently one of these uprooters.

Jack recalled meeting some of Scarlet Kristina's Swedish family during his stint in Oslo in '39, such as *Lord Fredrik Sundquist.* Their family was there as well, in the background. From what he remembered, Sundquist was a strongminded individual, and probably the catalyst for his family's defection, riding the exodus wave through France and across the English Channel in time to evade capture by Nazi Germany, likely spending a great deal of his wealth in accomplishing this emigration. Their ties were quite possibly stronger than most defectors, with his niece's marriage to Feind, a certified Nazi compatriot and bound by wedlock, yet somehow, they must have cut the cord and broke away scot-free.

For a split-second, Churchill could imagine the Lord coming to his senses and getting his entire family uprooted to relocate, outrunning the

German juggernaut prior to the swastika tidal wave tearing throughout Europe; a surge of which he personally rode the cusp out of France at around the same time. The two men could very well have nearly crossed paths during the Dunkirk Evacuation.

Even after all these years, it still hurt Jack's heart to imagine a fretting Scarlet Kristina packing her bags, conceivably against her will, not unlike her marriage, and acting out of the pent-up fear and loathing towards her husband that Jack knew she had deep-down. Despite her matrimonial vow to the nationalistic Feind, she bravely fled a world away from Germany's reach.

In an admission of grief such as Feind's, it was a custom to say something consoling, like 'I'm sorry (that happened)' ... but Churchill wasn't. He was glad she left him and got out, and good on her.

"I had no idea," in that fleeting moment, Churchill still managed to level with his distraught foe. Feind was a strong and stoic character, a man wielding many scars, yet this trauma was too deep to hide—even from his own archenemy.

This was all news to Churchill.

As far as he had ever been concerned, Scarlet married into the Feind family after Oslo, henceforth unifying within the Nazi regime by default and, by that very association, joining the ranks of the Axis. He always envisioned her on the other side of the fence, living large somewhere in the prestigious German motherland, an indoctrinated and ensnared wife waiting for her husband to return home from the war on the western world—the whole world, in fact. He had always envisioned her appearing happy on the outside, but distraught and forever trapped on the inside, bound by her marriage to a madman. Forced to love him, to bed him, even have her hips bear his children ... Living life as a permanent damsel in distress. On a strange angle of progression with his adversary, Churchill felt compelled to err on the side of compassion with his foe. He probed, suppressing his involuntary congenital desire very well, even to himself: "Did she make it out ...?"

Feind solemnly nodded.

"Her and her zizters, jah."

"And Sundquist?"

Feind's discrepant sneer reappeared in the form of an involuntary flinch in the corner of his mouth. He repressed it before replying to Jack. "He did not."

Churchill stared into Feind's soul as he gauged the man's subconscious psychopathic nature, his innate insanity. The vicious side of him which his employment within the barbaric Nazi Germany brought out best, followed by this case in point.

Feind elaborated as he recalled the finer details. "Ve caught him in France vith a bunch of other refugees ... zee old man vaz helping families out of Europe vith hiz Jewish inheritance. Fortunately for him, he had already zent hiz family acrozz zee Channel."

"He refused to tell you where they went, didn't he?" Churchill assumed, presuming that this Nazi cunt probably tortured Sundquist for information; his own father-in-law and, so it seemed, a truly good and selfless man in a time of utter disarray. Churchill gathered, "Scarlet and her sisters made it across into England, but you never found out where, did you? Am I right in assuming that Sundquist perished before giving them up?"

Feind's silence was an unstinting agreeance.

"How did he die?" Jack questioned, mostly unsympathetic as he never truly knew the man, however Feind's devils were in the details of such meticulous divulgence. Like he had already said, he caught up to Lord Sundquist in France. Whether or not he opted to keep him alive would tell a lot about the fundamentals of his profound personality. If there was something relatable within Feind, Churchill could find it and attempt a type of reconciliation ... or if the worse came to the worst, use it as a weapon against him later.

After a pause as the psychotic pondered, Feind's vision hazed over as he recalled the instance of recent history. Probably just another excruciating death amongst the many he inflicted during his campaign across Europe as a homicidal Hauptsturmführer with the murderous Gebirgsjäger Alpine Huntsmen.

His eyes lost focus as he remembered the finer details in Sundquist's death ... *the particulars seemed to stimulate him.*

Feind finally replied to the question about how he died. "Not vell."

Beneath his pencil moustache, Churchill's lips tightened.

This man's sadistic tendencies were well suppressed beneath the surface of a decorated soldier and a heartbroken man ... not unlike the shallow graves of the genocides left in his wake across Eastern Europe, they were barely beneath that surface.

"She made it to England zomevhere ..." the burdened man's brown eyes raised to Churchill. "Außer that, I hit a dead end at every turn, every addrezz ve explored, all abzent ..." Feind's stare reached a thousand yards as he pondered. His pursuit following their excommunication to England probably hit a dead end on purpose. Sundquist had wealth. He had money. He would have spent a fair chunk of it not only on his family reaching the King's land but covering their tracks from the Nazis. This meant no paper trails; new identities, changing their names, heritages, occupations, setting them up with new lives.

"How *unfortunate.*"

"From across zee Rhine, we even employed a local asset; a Bluthund, whose apparent untimely demise obviouzly turned up nothing ..."

A Bluthund (Bloodhound) was obviously some sort of expert tracker and probable assassin employed by and at the disposal of Nazi Germany and, in all likelihood, under the jurisdiction of the *Abwehr* (German military-intelligence service). They were essentially implanted English-speaking spies, much like a sleeper operative. Such was the reason for such heightened paranoia across England of late; rumours of enemy spies becoming outed were a dime a dozen. A lot of them were perceived to have come over in the floods of refugees escaping the invasion, hence why those who had the money and influence to disappear without implementing any British government channels, did so. It eliminated any overbearing scrutiny. One uncrossed t or undotted i resulted in a great many immigrants being processed through encampments: a long and drawn-out experience. Due to the war, the fractured landscape was littered with foreign allegiances and hidden agendas.

That being said, if Nazi Germany had sicked one of their Bloodhounds onto Sundquist's case and he had turned up emptyhanded, it was a good sign. By extension, it meant that Scarlet Kristina had vanished successfully across the pond.

"Maybe somebody threw your dog a T-bone steak," suggested Churchill, off the cuff. Perhaps he had been exposed to too many *Looney Tunes* shorts at the base recently; in where a recurring gag had its star characters easily distract the drawn to the lure dogs' attentions by throwing convenient cuts of meat. They were always T-bone in the animations.

Feind ignored the quip, likely because he did not understand the reference, but more due to the extent of his emotions during their current topic of conversation.

"Doch, one of zee other exilez in Sundquist's group caught later knew zome information; a place zat makez no zense; an eine Vergeblichkeit—how you zay, *foolish errand.*"

"*Fool's errand.*"

"Jah. Ve vorwarded it to our operative before he dizappeared, und he ripozte with only more myztery. T'iz an imaginary place from an imaginary fiction named *zee Never's Edge*," Feind disclosed the fairytale suburb he had traced them to in the United Kingdom ...

... *only thing was, that was not a fake place at all.*

Unbeknownst to him, thanks to his apparent misjudging self-esteem, Feind had been led to believe that Never's Edge was a purposeful miscommunication, cryptic misdirection, or falsification. Maybe even at the very least a grammar correction, lost in translation. Either way, it led Feind to his final dead end ...

Never's Edge did sound fictional—heavenly, even. Feasibly, it carried such spiritual connotations for Feind of her disappearance. It was not outside the realm of possibility that Feind's Bloodhound operative dabbled a little too close to Sundquist's secreted legacy for comfort, and thus he lost his life by way of a protector or security.

Nether Edge, however, was a suburb in _Sheffield_, less than two hours' drive from Lancashire. The Germans evidently missed the anagramic connection where an Englishman who was familiar in local geography knew how to crack the simple code.

Churchill's tensed brow loosened as the realization slid over him like a warm glow. His chin raised.

Scarlet was right here all along!

She had been right here in the United Kingdom!

"I tracked my runavay vife to _Never's Edge_ ... but, by then, zee war broke out, incapzulating my focuz, und crippling any further attempt of me reaching my Scarlet ... the Queen of Sveeden... _my_ Queen..." Feind divulged as an extant pain overcame him, revealing the length of longing for his vanished love. He had pursued Scarlet for the purest reasons of adoration before undoubtedly being forced to let her go and brand her a traitor to Germany.

The focus in Churchill's stare slackened.

He was processing all of this in the forefront of his mind, but moreover, calculating the logistics. Jack knew of a new shortcut that traversed _Hope Valley_ linking Manchester to Sheffield. It could save him some time in a voyage if he was to opt pursuing Scarlet Kristina, himself.

Yes, he was a married man ...

Yes, he loved his wife ...

... but there was an unbreakable crease in the fabric of that matrimony that, still, summoned Churchill to Kristina. At the very least just to see her, to lay his eyes upon thee; _the one that got away._

It was an undeniable primal yearning.

An irrefutable, rapacious fixation.

A wild oat left unsewn. A conquest unaccomplished.

She was an unquenchable, instinctual desire. Pursual of her scent was embedded deep within the codex of men, the closest incarnation of a _Helen of Troy._ Men had fought over her, died for her. This was one decision he couldn't fight himself over, or at least contemplating showing up at her door, entreating into her arms. There was a certain indistinguishable and unforgettable aurora about the nostalgia of their past. And right now, Jack was feeling a little mad.

"Never's Edge, you say?" Churchill asked after an extended pause and moderate contemplation. His tone was slightly condescending towards the heartbroken prisoner's deficient detective skills after he had pieced it together in a heartbeat. "Reckon that's anywhere near _Nether Edge,_ in _Sheffield?_"

Due to the pause and pre-emption of consideration, as well as the perky tone of voice presenting the information, Feind realized a sudden grave error in his confessional truths. The Hauptsturmführer became increasingly conscious of Churchill's awareness of his wife's existence, putting her back on his radar for the first time in three years, only now ... he was in an impossible position to act.

His attention fixated on Churchill through the wire fences.

Feind already knew well what he meant; what he threatened to do ... but he was stuck here. In his stunted mindset, he reverted involuntarily to German, murmuring with vehemence. "Wie meinst du das?"

Uttering no words, Churchill still pondered.

"Vhat do you mean?!"

"Well, you said it, Feind. You played the hand you were dealt," Churchill finally said with an inspired inhale, beginning to walk away now set to a new purpose. But not before he left a parting comment. "However, there is an old English saying: unlucky at cards, lucky at ... something else."

"English-man," Feind managed to articulate, closely approaching the fence barrier. He extended his hands, rattling the cage wire opposite Churchill, causing a scene.

While the attentions of the nearby guard tower loomed, focusing on this prisoner breaching confinement, Feind shouted after Churchill:

"*English-man! Don't you dare zpeak to her! Don't you dare look at her! DON'T YOU DARE TOUCH HER!*"

Churchill turned away, leaving a final taunt:

"Don't worry, I'll tell her you said *hullo.*"

In his absence, an alarm sounded at the prison camp, and guards blew whistles whilst running up on Feind from the inner rink of the barbed wire fence line. Their guns were up, as were their tempers, just about ready to kill the kraut.

Churchill didn't look back.

They could kill him if they needed to for all he cared.

He had a direction to follow.

After being forcefully removed from the perimeter fence, Feind could do nothing but watch Churchill leave on his motorbike along the road, headed for Sheffield.

Baring his teeth, he spat a saliva-filled, sizzling huff.

1942, February
Tintagel House
Nether Edge, Sheffield

The throttle of Churchill's motorcycle rumbled down the small-town streets of Nether Edge right on dusk.

Rolling down the main *Cherry Tree Road,* Churchill was amazed at how Nether Edge had expanded over the years since he had last seen Sheffield. Ten years ago, this ward had a tiny population, now it was apparently diverse enough to merit its own local festivities. To raise morale during these troubled times, some kind of outdoor stage had been erected out front of the landmark known as *Tintagel House.* Crowds were forming on the street like a block party and there were local vendors set up with kiosks and attractions. Blackout regulations were enacted via modifications to the bright lights to reduce their visibility, however they still bloomed in the dusk evening, beaconing across the small-town landscape like a lukewarm lighthouse across a dulling ocean.

The place was alive as though the circus was in town.

The expression needle in a haystack came to mind as Churchill cruised casually along one of the main roads which cut across the district, when finally, he spotted a concrete K1 kiosk out front of a closed for business bank. He promptly pulled in, parked, and dismounted, leaving his headlamp on for a source of illumination as he took to the door of the red telephone box, sealing himself within for a private telephone call.

Churchill collected the telephonic pieces, holding one to his ear and the other to his chin. "Hullo, operator? Hollywood Hotel, Largs, please and thank you."

A female voice on the end: < *"One moment please."* >

Before he had left Lancashire, Churchill had extended his feelers. He had made a call to one of his boys at the Largs base who may have had some connections with the UK Post Office.

The line audibly connected in Jack's ear.

"Hello?" the voice of *Corporal Eric de la Torre* answered, expecting the call back from Churchill. The father of a lass named *Annabel Dean,* de la Torre's on-again off-again significant other, owned a string of post offices leased by the GPO, and therefore may have had access to a names database

of types connected to addresses around the United Kingdom. Two hours ago, Churchill had charged the trustworthy No.3 Commando corporal with the task of finding out not only if such an inquiry was possible, but if there were any new residents of Sheffield by the surname *Sundquist* or *Kristina.*

"Hullo, Corporal?"

"*Colonel Churchill, sir. How were your travels?*"

"About as eventful as one of Durnford-Slater's theory classes on enemy insignias. What did you find out from the missus, my lad?"

"*Nothing fruitful, I'm afraid.*"

Churchill's neck craned at the bad news. Through his silently grimacing teeth he asked. "No luck finding the *database* or no luck finding the *names?*"

"*The names,*" de la Torre informed. "*They don't appear to exist in either the mailing line or key address registrar, unfortunately. Sorry, sir. I wish that I had some better news.*"

Nodding his head sadly, Churchill accepted the apology. He was more so grateful of his soldier's endeavours. "Thank you muchly, Eric. I appreciate your efforts immensely."

"*Yes, sir. Will there be anything else?*"

"No. That will be all."

"*Thank you, sir. de la Torre, out.*"

"Churchill out."

He hung up, stumped, and a little miffed.

After a pause of hiatus upon reaching this dead end, inconsequentially feeling not unlike how Feind would have felt reaching the seemingly paper town of *Never's Edge.*

Churchill stepped out from the booth and took the time to calmly and politely close the door. Now standing in the array of his motorcycle headlamp, he bit his lip in deep thought.

Was this a sign to desist and return from his detour?

The whole ride on the journey from Lancashire he had been dwelling on what it was he would do once he even located Scarlet Kristina in Nether Edge. Butterflies floated in his stomach at the thought of approaching her dwelling and knocking on her door ...

... what would he say?

... what would he do?

... and ultimately, what would his wife think?

Him merely embarking upon this estranged endeavour contained traces of infidelity from an outside perspective, even just by association of the fact, regardless of his intentions; intentions that, truth be told, even he was uncertain of.

This expedition alone in the eyes of Feind, who he had left in his rearview mirror seventy miles ago, was enough of a victory tally. The knowledge of Churchill not only knowing the whereabouts of his wife let alone going to visit her whilst he was trapped behind bars would have been immeasurably torturous for him. For all Feind knew, Churchill was balls-deep in his wife right now, and it was eating him alive as he rotted at Glenn Mill. Churchill took solace in this.

Truth was, the only thing Jack wanted to lay was his eyes; upon her, again. Nothing more.

Ever since he had met Scarlet Kristina, they had ignited some sort of undeniable connection. An imperious potential for passion, a succession of serendipity. Even with Rosamund in the picture, who Churchill loved dearly, there was an element of forgotten closure present, and it could not be ignored by a man strong of head, and even stronger of heart.

Plainly, he failed to save this woman back then ...

... he had to see it through that she had at least saved herself.

Discovering that detail would be another chapter closed in the saga of Churchill's life, and one he could find himself proud of in a time of ever-growing resignation and irrepressible regret at facing his upcoming courtroom firing squad.

Caught deep in the current of contemplation once again, Churchill pulled himself back to the surface for a moment long enough to think rationally. He wasn't due back at the Largs base until after the trial, and for all his wife knew he was still staying in London for work until further notice. He had complete freedom to pursue this divergence further, potentially even staying in Sheffield overnight and picking up the trail again tomorrow with a clear head and fresh pair of eyes.

Anything to distract him from his pending court date in three days.

His eyes started searching for a local watering hole, stepping over to his bike. As he did, he heard something intriguing ...

Singing.

The attraction in the middle of town he had noticed on the way in was some sort of festival or a fete. *Or was it fate?*

Attracted like a swan to a song, Churchill glowered upon hearing an orchestral female voice float through the air, saturating his ears. His lids closed, finding it extremely reminiscent. It wasn't so much that he knew the melody, but the singer ... *and then it clicked.*

His eyes opened.

Jack blinked off the lamp to his Harley-Davidson and took the keys, quickly jogging across the road and joining the march with many other dawdling strangers heading across the park and towards the bright lights of the fete like a flock of moths drawn to a big, bright flame.

Off *Meadow Bank Road,* the low grass field clearing had been transformed into a beaming market fair, alit beautifully by strings of low-dim fairy lights from the park trees and established low-wattage spotlights, as not to call attention to any potential air raids. Even in the face of a potential Blitz, disastrous nights of repeated aerial bombings by Germany, big, bright, and loud fetes at dusk like this one had suddenly become quite celebratory.

Various local vendors maintained stores, sold produce, and staffing at several minor carnival-esque rides generated a playful atmosphere as though *Bozo the Clown* had rolled into town with his circus. Thankfully, there were no actual clowns, as Churchill was secretly not a fan of such.

The occasion for the fete was some sort of fundraising.

A sign near the front read something about split proceeds of the donations funnelling into the development of a local school in Nether Edge. The educational establishment had undoubtedly run out of government funding due to the war—a reoccurring theme of the era.

There was a live band playing on a raised stage, performing in front of the conversing crowd of approximately two hundred people, and growing. The volume of the act was drawing people in ... including the beret-clad out-of-towner Jack Churchill.

Gravitating towards the warm golden glow of the live stage along with the majority of the gathering, flocking from the dusk dimness, Churchill found his place amidst the grass paddock, observing the performance shoulder-to-shoulder with countless jovial locals.

Up on stage right now, a local female vocalist performed.

In the place of *Vera Lynn* covering *'When they Sound the Last All Clear'* was an insatiably gorgeous local bombshell. She seemed somewhat out of place in the small town of Sheffield simpletons.

Glowing up on the podium, she absorbed the stage lights in a glitter sparking Grecian style dress, lighting her lavish curves up like a mirror-glistening disco ball.

She was stupidly attractive in such a dress that complimented her slim figure, encasing what must have at least been a stacked 32DD bust to her chest that got all the salivating boys lowering their eyelines beneath the décolletage.

Golden bouncy hair, luscious red lips, and what appeared to be at least from down in the audience crowd, eyes of glowing hazel hue spliced by a hint of emerald-green.

Hypnotized upon his arrival, Churchill's stare dilated as his face dropped flat.

It was her!

It was Scarlet Kristina.

The Queen.

For the entirety of her concert show, Churchill lurked in the shaded silhouettes of the backend of the flock. Just another face in the crowd.

He was so enthralled by the vision of her, let alone her performance spectacle, that he nearly forgot to join in applause after the concluding act. The clapping of hands in the ocean of glowing, resonating, smiling faces around him snapped him out of his trance, and he joined in to blend in with the locals.

Another local band took the stage, and she was promptly escorted down the flanking steps at the side of the stage, still cheered at and viewed before a hundred attentive eyes—probably mostly a salivating male fan base. Once down, she disappeared behind a curtain backstage where there were a few operators who undoubtedly congratulated her on her visceral performance.

A lone stalker in the crowd, Churchill scoped her stage exit.

Enchanted, his sterling stare pursued from afar as she vanished behind the curtain hangings, disappearing into an abyssal proximity. This girl wasn't the provincial diamond in the rough out here in Nether Edge that the locals probably thought. He knew of her auspicious stardom past in Sweden—a call to fame she was robbed of due to the world war.

Churchill circled the event, uninterested in the next act on stage as the music started again and an energetic master of ceremonies introduced the group, inviting everybody to donate.

A firm voice from his flank announced, clutching at Churchill's attention like a firm nuisance, breaking his concentration. "*Sir, would you care to donate to the cause?*" a thickly moustachioed man in a venue cap effervescently requested, rattling a collection bucket loudly in his face.

Churchill's primary instinct was to dodge him and continue his mission, but the fastest way around this persistent obstacle and therefore putting him back on track was to pay the toll—and donate to a good cause, of course.

None too happy for the wrong reason, Churchill pulled his wallet and collected whatever money he could spare. He unfolded it before the walking moustache to expose an empty crease fold ...

Churchill's face drew flat.

"*Eh,*" he murmured fast as an onlooker paid note, probably thinking *what sort of military-minded man travels to a fete with no money to donate to the war effort?*

He must have spent it all on fuel when he passed through Manchester. Jack instead reached into his trouser pocket, sourcing some clinking change, dropping what must have been about five shillings and a sixpence, lint, and a spare button from off his long-sleeve shirt.

"*Gee, wow ... thanks for your service at least, sir,*" the overconfident fellow regarded with a displeased stare at Churchill before rattling his tin elsewhere.

Churchill ignored him.

His attention returned, facing forwards.

He skirted the edge of the congregation. The blooming lights from the vicinity eventually faded to dark and the noise from the stage lessened the further he hooked around the back of the restricted stage area, locating a series of empty crates, stacked packaging, a makeshift trough for some horses along with stacked haybales, and several parked vehicles on the Tintagel House property that expanded farther yonder and into the mist and shadows of the night. There were busy deck hands and hired help stewed about. Nearly everyone disregarded Churchill's invisible presence as the creeper peeked a corner, laying his eyes back on the star attraction of the night as he located her, and she spoke obliviously with two stagehands.

They exchanged a few words, and the sparkling scarlet hustled on, treading unsteadily on the soft grass with her high heels until she reached a constructed marquee attached to the side of the main building. Judging by what Jack caught a glimpse of within, it was an established wardrobe of sorts for the live shows; probably retaining restricted access as far as venue security went—if there even was any.

This would be it.

He could corner her here, knock on that barely hinged door, and surprise the shit out of her with his presence and charm.

Aways, Churchill removed his green beret, flattening his straw hair and straightening his uniform. For the first time in hours, he adjusted the lengths of his cufflinks, tugged his suit jacket flat across his mid, aligning his dishevelled appearance. He discreetly checked his breath, even pressing out his moustache whiskers before lastly, he paused to reassess his vocabulary for the words best which to say to her.

... eyes down, he removed his wedding ring.

In the moment, he was unsure as to why he felt the need to disarm himself of his betrothal. Much of this he was unsure of, such as his intentions towards Miss Kristina after he engaged her in conversation.

There was a window flap on the tent.

Tearing him from his inner demon battle, Churchill's attention noticed Scarlet inside via a windowpane from his exterior position. She was unaware to her observer in the shadows outside. Having slipped out of her evening dress somewhere unseen, she was now wrapped in a woollen dressing gown of which she tied up the cincture cord around her waist. She must have been looking into an unseen hanging mirror against the inner wall, assessing her appearance.

Jack's absolute focus collapsed upon her.

Like hypnosis, he was entranced.

That was her: *the one that got away,* in every sense of the word. It was hard to believe that she had been right here under his nose for these past few years.

Churchill was engrossed in her self-absorption as her green eyes engaged her own reflection; a look that judgementally studied her own appearance, but then also defocused an ounce in this instance of isolation. It revealed some sort of diffidence, perhaps even insecurity.

Did she like the life she lived?

Did she have regrets? Unbearable apprehensions?

Although his heart involuntarily bled for her apparent self-dejection, Jack felt his heartbeat speed up again as she inadvertently captivated him in a remarkable reverie. Still unaware anybody was nearby the marquee outside, let alone watching her so impiously, she actively reapplied some of her ruby red lipstick and let her hair down from a clip, shaking her golden locks about her neck and shoulders for comfort.

It was in that moment, Jack felt himself stand-down.

In his hands, he arranged his wedding band in order to slide it back onto his fing—

"*Evening,*" a bass-filled male's voice spoke from over his shoulder, catching him off-guard, and causing Churchill to flinch and nearly drop the ring clumsily.

Remembering to breathe after the fright, Jack rotated around in order to view the other man lurking in the darkness behind the stage area. His eyes widened as the tall figure came fully into view:

Fedora, suit, plumb build, and with a toothpick pinched firm and unassisted between his teeth ...

It was Jethro fucking McNaughton.

Even after the realization, Churchill remained stoic and silent.

His head swivelled at the neck as he traced McNaughton's casual trot from the shadows and into a bloom that illuminated portions of his face and tweed suit. He temporarily removed the pick from his teeth and tiffed a splinter clear from his lips.

"You following me or something?" Churchill demanded.

"Or something. *London* to *Lancashire* ... *Lancashire* to *Manchester* ... *Manchester* to *here* ..." McNaughton advised rather intuitively. He had been on his heels this entire day. "I get why you rushed to visit your pal at the Glenn Mill straight after court, but ... what the bloody hell are we doing in *Sheffield,* Colonel?"

"You see, it *sounds* like you're following me."

With a tone of dispute, McNaughton informed his problem as well as the solution. "Yes, well, the court didn't see fit to placing a detail on you, so I thought I'd do the honours."

"They declined to do so because I am a highly decorated officer in the British Army, entrusted by and loyal to the King. I'm not a flight risk."

McNaughton reinserted the twig between his teeth, satisfying his oral fixation. When the walls closed in, they always ran. "We'll see."

A few awkward seconds passed.

"What are you doing back here?"

"Looking for popcorn."

McNaughton jerked his chin over his shoulder. "Kiosk is back that way."

"Some *fresh* popcorn," Churchill iterated, and McNaughton huffed, gesticulating a nod of compliance to the argument, but clearly not buying it. "You know, my head still hurts from where you slapped me."

Churchill death-stared him. "Good."

McNaughton held his ground; ready for the prospective round two.

"Constable, I'll have you know that I am a Commando in the British Army. In self-defence, I could have killed you the other night."

"And what do I look like? A fuckin' *Battersea Boy Scout?* What do you say about being handcuffed to a steering wheel for the next three days?"

"I'll pass, but thank you."

Another few seconds of awkward silence surpassed.

The lead constable nodded casually towards Scarlet Kristina's marquee after a few seconds of silence, indicating his next referral. He had obviously been watching Jack Churchill for longer than the commando realized.

"Beautiful broad in there, eh?" he commented off-key.

He was clearly fishing, so Churchill chose his words carefully.

He shook his head dismissively. "I wouldn't know."

The response was discerned as an obvious subterfuge, had McNaughton obviously just seen the same concert stage show as Churchill. "Either you're lying to me, or you're a fruit."

Churchill chortled.

McNaughton then raised his chin, eyeing Jack's hands. Churchill involuntarily opened them, presenting his ring still in the palm of his hand. Realizing the apparent negative connotations with such a motion, he casually reinserted on his wedding ring back onto his finger.

"It's not what it looks like," Jack stated.

"Oh, cease with the excuses, Colonel. I could have guessed a *Casanova* such as yourself were the philandering type. It's in your nature," McNaughton distinguished from his study of the evidence in addition to the light he already saw Mad Jack in regarding his murderous black-ops secrecy.

"The number of cheating husbands I used to catch out back when I was a P.I., I should have taken you for one a mile away. I must be slipping when it comes to the inconsequentials of crooks. Must have been overshadowed by your treason."

"Piss off. You don't know what you're talking about," Churchill excused as he turned and started to walk away across the grounds, heading in the direction of his parked bike across the field.

McNaughton watched nonchalantly as the accused vacated.

"One day down, two to go, Colonel," his nomadic and authoritative voice chased after Churchill's departure, taking pleasure in the fact that he had just interrupted whatever endeavour he had set out to accomplish this night. "You'll see what I'm talking about in court."

Mid-step, Jack paused and faced the constable.

He seemed a little defeated. Tired, even. Maybe even just disappointed in his government's legal system. This whole thing felt like intentional friendly fire.

After a few seconds of contemplation, he delivered his thought. "That was a nice move with Wingate, bringing him back to the United Kingdom," Jack manipulated the topic in an unexpected change of aversion, shifting gears to take an entirely other avenue: defence through offence. It was a standard negotiating tactic and one that McNaughton no doubt saw right through, starting the diplomatic compromise with a compliment in an attempt to lower his defences. Churchill's poise faced him, hands in trouser pockets. "Now that you've got what *you* want, may I ask why I am even still in your crosshairs?"

McNaughton noticed the fabrication of his ambition, though saw no harm in humouring Churchill's yarn. That, or he wanted to merely play with his food before eating it. "Wingate won't open to confession unless we make him ... we achieve that by pressing *you*. We've got admissible dirt on *you*, Colonel ... not him. Not *yet*. Not until you speak the truth, with every aux-ops detail you divulge hoisting the guillotine higher for his chopping block."

Churchill scoffed, facing the distance for a moment of mental agony.

There seemed to be no version of this juridical process where he made it out of the firing line without taking a fatal bullet.

After a visible sign of exasperation, which McNaughton noted without compunction or sympathy, Churchill raised his arms up by his side only to drop them down heavily.

"We were following orders ... the King's orders ..."

"*The King?*" McNaughton's brow rose, strolling closer to Churchill—and thankfully so, for their discussion was now luring them farther away from Scarlet Kristina's tent so she wouldn't hear and potentially come outside to inspect the commotion, consequently discovering Jack Churchill: a man she hadn't seen in years.

Holding his words, McNaughton took the time to step in close enough to whisper to Churchill.

"Let's look at the deck, here. We've got the *King, Queen, Jack* ... or is it a *Joker?*"

Chin raised as McNaughton effortlessly offended him with his extended vocabulary and suited card game knowledge, distastefully placing Jack as the joker suit, rather than the obvious jack, Churchill wore the brunt of his pitch but endeavoured to hold his ground. "If you take one more step closer, sir, what you'll have on the cards ... is a *war.*"

"A *war,* eh?" McNaughton's brow inverted at the unexpected response. "Well, I know your idea of *war,* Mad Jack. That's right, I know what you blokes did up there in the Alps in the dead of the night. I know about the bodies you buried in the hills ... about the men slain in the snow in the pale of the moon's light. Were you *following orders* then, too?!"

The words—and McNaughton's knowledge of the fact—hit Churchill harder than a battering ram. It stole the air from his lungs. Stole the words from his mouth. The retort from his mind.

Instead, he stood and stared vacantly.

Depleted.

Defeated.

McNaughton barrelled, up in his grills. "Eh? Are these steps close enough? You're in my war now, Colonel. And you're about to become a casualty of it."

Maybe he had pushed Churchill too far, but from an outside perspective, this investigator's strategy here may have been to push him into a revealing outburst; one that may help incriminate Churchill further in a court of law.

However ... he had pushed Churchill *way* too far.

Finally, Jack's gaze returned to focus from a growing thousand-yard stare, and he levelled it at McNaughton.

Calmly, he finally responded. "Well, then. Thanks for the visit ... I guess I'll see you in court, eh?"

Churchill turned and walked away.

Remaining composed after Churchill used his previous catchphrase against him, Jethro McNaughton could do nothing but seethe while he watched the arrogant, smug prick saunter away.

Blowing hot air out both his nostrils like a raging bull, his dagger eyes followed the big-headed, beret-clad ballbag as he vanished from sight, jettisoning this secretive venture and returning to his bike to zoom back to his base in Largs.

It took a lot to catch a man of his stature off-guard ...

... *but this gent had done so.*

Coming suddenly into focus, McNaughton's attention snapped to the left in his blind spot, unexpectedly aware that he was being watched by an unidentified figure barely thirty yards away. A mid-sized person lingered tall behind several stacks of haybales by the hitched horses, staring his way like an emotionless statue draped in gloom.

In the shadows of the poorly lit backstage area, his identifying features weren't clearly illuminated. He wore a stitched flat cap and breathed calmly whilst he silently observed.

McNaughton's tenor audibly admitted his surprise.

"You there! Can I help you?! Are you lost?!" he interrogated, exhuming some of his pent-up frustrations towards Jack Churchill. He turned to face him and strode two unafraid steps in his vector. "Are you looking for something, friend?!"

This unphased onlooker seemed very calm for somebody who had just witnessed and, depending on how long he was observing the exchange between McNaughton and Churchill, had just become privy to a fair chunk of sensitive exposition—though, none of it would have been comprehensible.

His tired eyes struggled to define him, and McNaughton frowned.

If there was one thing he hated more than Churchill at this interval, it was looky-loos such as this lingering local—possibly a meaningless show carney.

"What are you, deaf or something?!"

The man with the flat cap shook his dome. Again, he did not speak.

Wordlessly, he stepped in strafe behind the bales and beside one of the horses. He slowly raised a gloved hand, stroking the hide of the horse whilst it grazed, ostensibly a caretaker for the beasts. It became revealed that he was also dressed in knee-high Wellington boots that were lacquered in mud and sludge.

Toothpick twigging between his teeth, McNaughton's chin waggled as he took in the stranger. A sliver of light from the moon shone across his features, and he noticed the man wore a well-kept short beard that appeared to be covering some evident scarring.

He could have been further the grouch, menacing the stranger by recommending that he mind his own business ... but, so it seemed, he already was.

An ounce of strop in his step, McNaughton marched off in an alternate direction to Churchill, likely back to his own vehicle to return home for the night.

In this second, absent the restricted backstage area, the ominous bearded man, draped in gloom and wearing a flat cap, continued purposelessly stroking the hide of the nearest horse with one of his gloved hands ...

... his other was down behind his back, holding something metallic.

Something that he now re-engaged the safety latch of before discreetly tucking it beneath his jacket layer.

Off-Piste

'At this point during the many off-book antics of the Special Z Unit, any official approval to engage the enemy in an act of war was ... irrelevant. No army or court could contain this black-budget aux-ops, these mercenaries, these shadows. They were ghosts. Deathly trained, lethal, brutal, and ferocious, these bloodthirsty killers were uncontainable. To be set loose and cutting sick, they were fundamentally beyond the reproach of any government. Unleashed and unhinged black devils, roaming free. Like how Wingate thrived, they now survived a clandestine life on the razor's edge, addicts of war. The whole time, unbeknownst to their eccentric ringleader, and right beneath his nose.

'The band of rogue Berzerkers within the Special Z Unit expended the full extent of their anonymity, advanced tactical training, specialized combat skills, as well as utilized their specified equipment and weaponry, to tally up inconspicuous kills against countless Axis patrols in the dead of the night. They engaged in off-radar warfare, burying the evidence in the snowy wilderness of the Swiss Alps.

'In an inadvertent effort to cast stories of 'ghosts in the dead in the night', their actions became rumoured to have haunted the dreams of the enemy along the Italian border. With the Swiss forces mostly mobilized to the northern front, the south was a free-

for-all of passive-aggressive patrolling of the ridgelines by forces venturing out from Austrian bases and traversing the borders to gain unhindered access to Italy. Ghost stories began circulating on Axis fronts that the related deaths of the German patrols being found were possessed snow hounds, reaping the due, dragging them to hell for the sins of their countrymen.

'As Jack previously stated, he refused to elaborate on the specifics of their unauthorized expeditions into enemy territory, however he did mention that the rogue Berzerkers did so on numerous occasions in the months of February and March of 1940, and that although he did not partake as eagerly as the others, he was present for several of the silver-light slaughters. Jack adjudicated negatively on their side that what they did to the unexpecting Germans was cruel and harsh, later justifying the means with that, overall, the krauts deserved everything that came their way ...'

1940, March
Winterthur Resort, Mont de la Gouille
Swiss Pennine Alps, Switzerland

Beneath the clear skies of a brisk morning, a black beret-clad skier took the slopes at the fullest of speeds, slickly weaving left and right with a seamstress's precision, carving in tight between trunks, tree saplings, and other natural obstacles.

Confidence was in abundance as he cut off-piste.

In instances, this death-defying expert skier would sweep past obstacles by mere inches, interlacing with bravura technique, control, and the upmost balance.

Although he wore goggles over his eyes to protect his face from wind-chill, masking much of his identity, other elements portrayed the character to be none other than the scarless faced Mad Jack Churchill, such as his choice of armaments:

Longbow strapped across his chest ...
Quiver of arrows over his shoulder ...
Basket-hilted claybeg sheathed at the hip ...

Churchill skied from the highest point, breaking his previous personal best speed to reach a section of the bottom of a slope, a mile before the resort that he and Wingate had marked as a trial 'kill zone'.

The *skiskyting* (ski shooting) technique combines skiing and shooting, and is deeply embedded in the ancient skiing traditions of *Scandinavia*, where early inhabitants revered the *Ullr:* the Norse god of hunting and skiing.

It was a skill these soldiers would be unlikely to need in a combat situation, but it was satisfactorily mastered nonetheless, with almost all adequate Berzerker members able to execute with dexterity.

Already proficient, Churchill strived to one-up that virtuoso ...

... rather than a rifle, he was going to do it with a bow and arrow.

Entering the kill zone in a whistling, sledding drift, the skiing archer released hold of his bamboo ski poles, allowing for them to dangle from the lanyards on his wrists. Balanced and bent slightly at the knees whilst he glid at a free ski, he acquired his longbow from the loop and drew an arrow from his quiver.

Displaying much finesse and relative ease, expert balance and coordination, Churchill slid in on a smooth glide at kinked knees, tracing the aim of his pointy arrow at a closing target.

The anchored projectile loosed with a whipping sound.

Whilst still skating on the parallel planks, he marked one, two, then three passing tree targets, each denoted via a red *X* before he came to a rigid, controlled halt at the base of a hill located in visible range of the Winterthur Resort, Mont de la Gouille.

Situated rather picturesquely in the winter wonderland, the exterior walls of the log cabin ripened in visibility. A climbing smoke plume climbed into the clouds, signifying warmth within.

After his morning practice session, Churchill dismounted his skis and trotted home.

He entered the warmth within the Winterthur Resort, hanging his peripherals and snow parka alongside the others on the hooks, shelving his clunky boots on the rack. The temperateness inside radiated upon his face, and he stripped the beret from his sweaty dome, becoming veiled in the light of the daylit common space. Today was a Sunday. A day off.

The men were dressed down and relaxed, socializing, swigging—as per usual. Only, at this hour, it was mostly coffee—at least by those who needed it ... those few who were up until the early hours, bedded about the witching hour or later.

They wore a combination of sportswear, baggy sweatpants, loosely buttoned-up shirts with cardigans. Beanies, gloves, even slippers. Some smoked pipes, others cigarettes. Gentle Jerry even had a cigar, wearing a fedora cap low over his forehead whilst lying on the rear three-seater couch, blowing rings.

Music played from the gramophone; *Variations on come Un'agnello* by *Alfred Mirovitch*. A fresh release one of the gents had picked up in a local town on their most recent leave venture. Rushworth, the muso of the group, evaluated that it was a simple yet elegant melodic beauty, praising the work for its clarity and grace. The characteristics of the tune were thick, frequently incorporating the octatonic scale to evoke a melancholy sentiment. It was much more Eastern than they were used to listening to, though Rushworth held some red heritage in his bloodline—it would explain the iron stomach and thirst for the mostly untouched bottles of Medovukha at the bar.

Along with the new music record, they had also picked up some back issues of *Honey* magazines, newspapers, and fresh bottles of wine and various cheeses, the big hit being the brick of French Camembert.

The gents were lounged about, some standing, some sitting.

Some were smoking, all were drinking.

A few of the men seated on the central three-seater were sharing a girlie mag. They had carefully plucked the spread page from the middle, the bearded Batey holding it open like a newspaper so they could all marvel at a gracious pair of titties; a splash-page pin-up named Carol.

Drawn in like a moth to the flame, Scotty hunched over the back of the lounge, a Chesterfield cigarette almost dropping from his lower lip as he took in her baked black-and-white bust. Beside him, Bort was much the same, wearing the cheeky, rose-flushed grin of a twelve-year-old boy, undoubtedly stifling a stiffy beneath a pillow.

From within the connected kitchen which doubled as an armoury, Bala Bredin sat at the island counter assessing some of their new armaments beneath a lamp. Tweaking, repairing, he barely took his eyes from his project in order to gesture greeting at Churchill who nodded a respectful return.

"Lads!" Churchill then announced after a few of them noticed his entrance from outdoors, along with a cold gush of winter air. Of the lot of them, he was the only one on days off initiating some kind of physical activity of his own accord—such as practising his skiskyting. The rest had opted for a glass of white wine or vodka orange juice with breakfast.

More or less ignoring his salutation, the men were audibly hyped up, fighting for a key viewing angle of Carol's generous breasts, on display and primed for a lingering ogle.

After a prolonged moment, Batey noticed another broad on the flyleaf of a subsequent page. It wasn't a stylized photographic page fold, like Carol or Amber before her, for she was clothed and seemed like more of an advert. Nonetheless, the featured lass wasn't a bad sort, either. Instead of a spread, it was a *Q-&-A* article about her prominent musical career in Sweden.

"Oi, get a load of this bird," he stated, folding the page outwards for a better view of her in her showgirl outfit. She had the bust of a king-size bedspread pillow arrangement crammed into a sofa, with cleavage pouring out like an over-proofed bread loaf from an oven tray. "I'd love ta knead those fluffy doughs if ya know what I mean!"

Scotty relinquished his pinched corner of the page featuring Carol now that his eyes focused upon the small article on a female artiste titled *Scarlet* in glittery cursive font. Aloud, he read the headline of the editorial as he oversaw it, promoting her promising musical career, articulating with emphasis: "*The Queen of SVeden ...?*"

... From the connecting room whilst he leant his skis on a railing mount, Churchill's ears pricked ...

... His attention honed-in so quickly that his conscious state blurred and dizzied, as if he had just skålled a bottle of booze ...

He hadn't heard—or consciously thought—of that title or of that woman in months—not that that hadn't stopped her from haunting the odd dream during slumber. She still resonated red raw on his brain, impairing him, like healing wounds on the back of his eyelids ... she possibly always would, scarring like any hurt.

What a coincidence?!

Surely, there was no way they were talking about Scarlet Kristina.

Wordlessly, he stridently moved within the current social activities, entering the warmth of the lounge with his ears pricked and attention carving like a scalpel. Impulsively, he gravitated towards the play-acting men with the porno magazine possessing a very relative article.

Brain intoxicated by the everlasting longing she had imprinted onto his soul, he became compelled to get a better look, involuntarily looming and caught in the undertow of her represented presence ...

"Lemme see?!" keen for a perve, Komrower commented from an adjacent single-seat sofa. He effortlessly lounged off the arm whilst cradling his champers like God reaching in *Michelangelo's* fresco *'The Creation of Adam'.*

Batey offered him a mere glimpse of the gorgeous goddess as Scotty leaned further into him, prying with fingers like an open claw, attempting to delicately snag the flailing page as though it were a winning lottery ticket.

On the periphery of their horseplay, drinking hot beverages and playing with suited cards, Mike Calvert, Humphrey Ruffell, and the one known as Danny Boy sat distantly on the cane bergère multi-seater lounge that ran along the interior brick wall separating the common room from the resort lobby. Generally, it took a lot for the latter to engage in social activities. In contrast, this morning, he wore his musky ski mask up around his forehead, occasionally engaging with the others where he could, wordlessly observing the social instance like a mute spectator from his seat on the edge of the lounge beside the polished wooden step-up into the lobby.

If Hell had frozen over, he may have even decided to wash the musty balaclava he constantly wore. From sweat and facial oils, the thing smelt like almonds and old cheese.

Upon this rare reveal, seeing his face and his scars, the boys had not made a big deal of Danny Boy's conspicuous facial features. He looked as though he had been through a lot for such a young age, with several indentations around his jaw and chin, one in particular ranging out from his mouth. Let's say in his case 'a map of the world on his face' was an understatement.

In this moment, his pale stare locked onto the article ...

Onto the woman in the photograph ...

Never had this taciturn seen such beauty.

He was mesmerized. Spellbound.

Scarlet Kristina __did__ have that effect on men.

Upon laying his impartial eye, the Queen of Sweden had just stolen his heart. His distinctly scarred face fell even further flat than was thought possible, and his sunken eyeline became locked on target: an assassin on mark. The image may have been achromatic, but the level of detail of her features burned into Danny Boy's retinas forever ...

Instant. Infatuation.

The quiet man's head tilted, catching a better gleam of the photograph in the magazine as the page sagged. Hypnotized, he mindlessly upped to his feet from his seat on the stair, leaving behind his steaming coffee and hand of cards, advancing towards the fellas on the lounge seaters whilst they playfought and grappled like hooligans.

"Pardon, lads ..." Churchill raised his voice over their boyish racket. He was very likely the most desperate to obtain a copy of this article, considering his past of estrangement with the woman, however he was not about to engage in their boyish shenanigans to obtain it. That would be one sport he would be too competitive to compete in, given the stakes. "Did you just say *Scarlet* as in *Scarlet Kristina* ...?"

Tearing the pages from Komrower's perverted glance, Batey pulled the magazine in close, eyeballing the article to scan—distracted once again by her naturally prevalent cleavage. "Doesn't seem ta have her surname on 'ere ..." he studied at a frown, glancing up at Churchill and showing him the image. "You know her or somethin'?"

Churchill torqued his head. "You could say that," and suddenly, in a most primal display that was unnatural from Churchill, he extended a hand in yearning. "May I please have a read?"

"Pfft!" the pessimistic voice of Graeme Black scoffed, once again insinuating Jack Churchill of being a mendacious spinner of yarns. "Of course, the great and travelled *Casanova Churchill* personally knows the pin-up Swedish bombshell," he jousted, adding the last bit softly into the mouth of his coffee mug. During their many conversation-sharing sessions, Jack had mentioned that just prior to the war reactivating his diligence, he toured much of Europe and even temporarily worked as a male model. He had considered himself to be well versed in women, his experiences abroad landing him a great many female companions.

He jousted further. "Did you meet her posing for *Cosmopolitan?*"

Still the new guy, Churchill held his tongue as much as he could, but a short and whimsical joust of his own let slip. "Grae, what was it you did before the war, again? Didn't you sell ladies' purses or something?"

Black's face dropped.

Only a few knew the truth about his short—but well-paying—civilian stint prior to the outbreak of war. After moving to London from Canada, where he used to be a reservist for the Canadian Army primary reserve regiment, the *Queen's York Rangers*, Black worked for fashion designer *Norman Hartnell* designing women's handbags.

Gobsmacked, Black turned red as those few who knew giggled.

It was now *he* who bit his tongue, for fear of expansion upon his history.

"Oi, get in line, Jack!" conveniently for Black, Komrower's explosive comment distracted all from the thrown shade. Komrower lurched up from his sofa, spilling a hot drop of his drink and cursing further after it stained his clean sweater.

Churchill gestured his request formally as Scotty once again bowed in a push over the back of the lounge, firm enough to slide the piece of furniture. He reached over determinedly, almost managing to snag the whole magazine from Batey's grasp as though he was plucking a chicken feather.

"Oi, fuck off, cunt!" Batey remarked, fighting back. He was caught off-guard by the tenacity of Scotty's horny heist in almost snatching the magazine. With an audible scrunch of the many pages, he guarded the porno as though the naked females' pictures graphed within were his life source.

With the volume of the playfight escalating, the magazine dropped with a slap to the floor. Appearing from the depths like a pouncing feline, Danny Boy dove forth. He inconspicuously commando-crawled beneath somebody's dangling legs off the lounge in tactful advance, collecting the magazine like a scavenger, specifically searching and tearing the half-page article concerning the Queen of Sweden. Once obtaining it, he recoiled, retracting from sight in the noise like a praetorian having snagged its prey. With his head down and stare entranced in Scarlet's features, he disappeared from sight, zombified in a complete and utter love-stricken trance.

"*Atten-HUT!*"

A commanding tenor in his voice, Moshe Dayan's presence entered the common space from the above mezzanine, leaning on the skeletal metal railing adjacent to a spiralling staircase made out of wrought iron elements. Orde Wingate descended this stairway from above, his comfortable sleepwear footwear tapping lightly on the iron strides with each drop. Naturally, he was dressed bizarrely on this day off. Along with his slippers, he wore wool pants and a balbriggan top beneath a ruby-red silk dressing gown that flowed in the light of the large glass windows that allowed natural light into the huge common space. The eccentric wore at least two wristwatches on each arm, visible beneath the wizard sleeves of his baggy robe, complete with wool gloves. His bed hair remained messy.

Dayan's exclaimed use of military drill may have stunned all those at present in the carpeted lounge room below, however, it was clearly a piss-take, for Wingate purposefully neglected military decorum whilst they were present at Winterthur.

Nobody saluted except for Komrower, who was a regular candidate for such mockery. He cursed, ripping his hand back down from his brow whilst the others scattered about the room chuckled.

Dayan maintained a stern grin on his maw whilst he joined after Wingate in descending the spiral staircase to join the commotion. This appearance seemed somewhat formal; perhaps the brass had news. Whatever the update, it must have been good, for their fearless ringleader wore his famous ear-to-ear Cheshire cat grin.

The men chuckled—mostly at Komrower's expense.

"Just pulling your legs, gents!"

"Yep, good one, *Mister Et Cetera!*" the satirical voice of Dredge heckled in amongst the amusement, celebrating Dayan's successful practical joke.

Holding a coy smile as he revolved the rifling staircase, Wingate finally reached the bottom. Wearing a pair of leather-palmed woollen gloves, Wingate was holding a sealed envelope, fastened with twine. It caught more than a few of the soldierly men's attentions.

"What's this? Everybody on the caffeine this morning!" Dayan added playfully. "Too many late nights out partying?"

Although intended as a spirited and rhetorical remark, a few of the men carried an underlining guilt concerning the comment.

The guilty hounds amid the wolfpack—Calvert, Ruffell, Dredge, Black, Scotty, and Komrower, even the American Gentle Jerry—exchanged impassive stares. Churchill was an addition amongst them, as was the ever-expressionless Danny Boy looming in a connecting doorway, currently entranced by the black and white press article in his grasp. It was in that instant that Jack saw Scarlet; identified the shape of her exquisite eyes, her beautiful face. It was a reprinted picture he had seen of her before promoting her career as a music artist, alas, the resurrection of her name still sent an echo down memory lane, momentarily clouding the forefront of Churchill's

204 | KING, QUEEN, JACK, WAR

mind. She likely would do so forever, and he'd never not die a little bit inside each time he heard her name.

Amongst those chattering and laughing at recent comical circumstances, Wingate wordlessly held the envelope in his gloved hands, demanding a silence to still the atmosphere. After an elongated moment, he stepped out near Churchill in the centre of the lounge room, and the men converged as if it was some kind of reward or commemoration.

"I hold here ...... well, you all know what this is!" Wingate announced with the envelope as though it pertained something they had all been waiting for.

Some of the men who had been present for Wingate's previous operations—even in this Special Z Unit, before Churchill's time—knew what the arrival of that sort of document meant.

"What is it?" relative newcomer, Komrower, had the balls to ask in the attentive silence, unknowing and not the only one. He had been in the Berzerkers a little longer than Churchill, but even he had no idea what that thing was. This was his first time seeing such an envelope.

Good thing Komrower had asked, Churchill thought, because he also had no idea what all the fuss was about, either.

"What I hold here is ......" Wingate cryptically proclaimed. "Fate."

"Orders ..." Calvert confirmed, stepping in close with the others in the spectating group. It was apprehensive news. Granted, it meant that the unit that had been training so extensively, so vigorously for three plus months finally had direction, but it also meant they were properly going to war.

The Otter's right-hand man elaborated eagerly. "This *here* is our first mission partake in the war in Europe."

"Yes!" one of the Berzerkers crowed ecstatically, embracing a few of the nearby soldiers. "Let's kill some fuckin' Nazis!"

"Haven't done that for a while ..." Graeme Black babbled under his breath and Churchill spied him with a dagger-eyed gleam.

"Keen for some killing, are we, Grae?"

It was a jab at something relative, lingering beneath the surface—an incident, of sorts.

In retort, Black observed Jack with an intense glare.

He said nothing in response, though it was clear to those who knew of the nocturnal activities that the two certainly held animosity towards one another.

Churchill slyly held his glance, noticing Black discreetly murmur an encrypted comment to fellow entrusted mercenary, Rushworth, with his silver tooth sparkling with a smile of concurrence. Rushworth wasn't privy to their night-time escapades, but he was complicit in Black's bullying of Churchill just the same. His lack of knowledge regarding the incident of late meant Black's remark had been personal. The two scowled upon Churchill with disrespect.

"Nope," lately retorted Wingate, ceasing their verbal ecstasy, alluding to a concerning detail in the unit's celebratory exchanges with regards to which Axis nation they would be fighting. "It's not the Huns ..."

"The Macaroni, then?" another Berzerker guessed, assuming maybe they would be going up against the Italians, seemingly Germany's newest allies.

Wingate waggled his head.

The only other person who knew who their new adversary would be was Dayan. He made a padlock and key gesticulation upon his American Habibi Gentle Jerry whispering at him, prying for clues as to who.

Ruffell's gummy grin questioned. "Is it the Frogs?"

An amassed askew glance became cast at Ruffell.

Wingate did not need to dismiss that wrong answer.

"Why the fuck would we be fighting the French?" Black leant forwards and queried Ruffell with a solemn grimace.

Dredge gasped a chuckle at the dummy's expense while from beside him, Calvert clipped Ruffell over the ear for offering such an uneducated answer.

The Berzerkers went silent in anticipation, swapping looks and casual converses in wonder. Before anyone could voice another question aloud to guess the target nation, Wingate delivered the intelligence to them prior to the official brief. "It's the Reds!"

The men ... cheered?

It wasn't what they expected.

In that precise moment, the gramophone, currently playing music by a Russian musician, abruptly crescendoed to a finish. The behaviour of the turntable required manual handling, and for the tonearm to be reset. Instead, the unit emitted a phonic hopping sound from the speakers, and Rushworth quickly attended, raising the stylus. It went eerily silent.

They awkwardly concurred in an understood accord. An acceptance.

The Soviet Union weren't an enemy to the West.

British relations with the Soviet Union may have been strained in the past due to factors like *the Russian Revolution*, intervention in the *Russian Civil War*, and ongoing suspicions of communist influence. Although Russia was seen as a potential threat to British interests, Germany's engagement with the Soviet Union fundamentally changed much of the situation. Despite their ideological dichotomy, Britain and the Soviet Union shared the same threat of Nazi Germany, and thus the formation of a new Grand Alliance was upon the horizon and would mark a new era in international relations. While there would undoubtedly be disagreements and mistrust between allies, the shared goal of defeating Nazi Germany would surely take precedence, at least while they were in power. After a prospective global defeat, there would stand only two great nations upon a great territorial divide ...

... perhaps the Special Z Unit were ahead of the adversarial curve.

Churchill stood contently.

He watched as the men of the Berzerker unit processed the news.

Before long, they started commenting, exchanging comments, and generally carrying on as if they had just won some sort of competition.

They were finally going to war ... this time, *officially*.

Or at least as far as Wingate's stature went, *unofficially*.

As the commotion grew, Wingate disappeared back up the spiral staircase. Conceivably back to bed, to brood and process. The reasoning for his absenteeism from their gathering mattered not and never did.

Around the common space, men toasted and cheered, embracing whilst wearing ear-to-ear smiles and exploding with laughter. While the commotion continued, Churchill found himself wondering if this was exactly the right type of war that he wanted. It was a question he had never thought he would be asking himself: if there was even a *right* type of war? It may have taken experiencing war through the eyes of soldiers who didn't authoritatively exist and killed for sport and for fun, rather than for honour for their country and as a duty, to realize it.

Through the volume, Calvert noticed Churchill's reserved composure. He stepped nearer. "You all right, Jack?"

Calvert looked over his shoulder, noticing Churchill's fixation seethed upon Graeme Black's provocation. He lowered his voice, his brow raising upon uncovering a likely truth.

"You're not still sore about the other night, are you?"

Churchill persisted in his stoicism.

Simply, he recoiled and headed for the door.

"I need some fresh air."

Following outside and into the brisk morning air, Mad Mike enticed his disgruntled friend with an imploring tone and a concerned temperament. "Come on, Jack. We should be in there celebrating! We're finally going to get our slice of the war!"

Hands in his parka pockets as he scanned the snowy whites of the surrounding treeline, Churchill scoffed. "Thought we made that fix for ourselves?"

Calvert levelled, no longer guessing twenty-one questions.

"You *are* sore, aren't ya."

"The only thing that's *sore* is my head after depleting so many braincells dealing with that big oaf in there!" Jack deflected, uncharacteristically agitated. He shook his head in disdain. "He makes me want to throw punches into his big melon head. Knock the blonde out of his hair."

What Calvert was discreetly referring to was an incident which had occurred two nights ago during their most recent afterhours outing. The secret pack of raucous Berzerker rogues had once again snuck out for their habitual Hun hunting along the border, the third time now with the more morally minded newcomer included, but the first time they would encounter enemy and action. Churchill's addition was undesired by a few members, namely his biggest fan: Graeme Black.

"Is it Grae ... or was it the mission?"

Stressed, Churchill scrunched his nose. "We're calling them *missions* now?"

"You know what I mean!" Calvert exclaimed, calming his tone when he remembered how off-the-books their 'missions' were on this already off-the-books venture.

Jack shook his head, stating portentously. "They didn't need to die."

The incident, during the relevant cad venture, saw the rogue Berzerkers stumble across the treaded tracks of what they believed to be a four-man German patrol, and they tracked them back to a local housing estate in the most-northern quadrant of the Aosta Valley. This Italian area was loyal to Nazi Germany, and they had set up bases, parading their lands, and guarding the neutral Swiss territory.

Italian families often allowed soldiers to seek refuge from the cold for the night on their properties; in their homes ...

Trailing as an initiate member to this rogue splinter faction, he had witnessed from the outskirts of this hunt what he could classify as an atrocity. Churchill had borne witness to the Berzerkers' merciless measures ...

Their bloods up—like they always seemed to be out here in the Alps— the Berzerkers forcefully infiltrated the lodging at the conclusion of the tracks, gunning for the German patrol, and thusly found and eliminated the fascists within.

This much unfolded without saying, without hesitation, and without question. The moral dilemma Churchill had faced was after the fact, when it came time to weigh justice on the Italian civilians who had harboured the enemy patrol as well as witnessed their slayings. They were comprised of an elderly, immobilized man, crippled due to decades of labour, and his caretaking adult son. Not only had they shown them the upmost generosity, cooking and feeding them, they had also cleaned for them and allowed them use of their facilities in what could only be described as full disclosed hospitality.

Churchill argued that this had possibly still occurred under duress; that the Italians could have been afraid of the Germans, nonetheless, the others did not see it so and they were disputably right. He rationalized that they should be left alone—left alive. Regardless of guilt, they were, after all, noncombatants, and posed no physical threat. Contrary to debate, Black, Dredge, and a few of the other Berzerkers agreed, supposing them a nonphysical threat, however ... they had borne witness to their good works that fateful night in exterminating the Nazis. They could report their observations to other Germans, potentially getting them found out, and then their jig would be up. And like junkies riding the fix, they couldn't have that.

Backing Black's bloodthirst at the time, Calvert had seemed just as hungry for violence that night, and Jack recalled seeing him in a different light for the first time. He wasn't the same half-Brit, half-Aussie, transformational leader he had come to respect ... he was a ruthless killer. A shadow of his previous, sensible self.

Jack excused himself to perimeter duty ... as they killed them all.

Shot them dead ...

Buried their bodies in the hills ...

Burned their cabin to ashes ...

... thus erasing all existence of the incident ever occurring.

The perfect non-event.

Like the char and smoke that had stained his fabric weaves, the circumstances left a bitter aftertaste in the back of Churchill's throat. He was concerned that these knaves within the unit had allowed for the unprecedented power of their lethal anonymity to go to their heads; that they saw themselves above regulation, beyond the rules of engagement, even beyond the humanitarian laws of armed conflict declared by the Geneva Convention.

What was a true enigma, and something Churchill's analytical, judicious intellect snagged on constantly when encountering circumstances such as this—which were, up until now, only minor—was that these were *good men;* rational, logical, honest men. This unit—this *place*—had changed them, had altered their psyches somehow. They had seemingly developed a cognitive illusory superiority, seeing themselves as not only stronger, faster, and better than they mortally were, but also above the principles of the unadorned *rights* and *wrongs.*

Still sore, indeed, the brooding Churchill shook his head sternly, eventually necessitating Calvert's trip out onto the snowy balcony in response to him questioning his disposition and overall moral allegiance.

Just then, the rear door to the resort opened, assaulting them with warmth from the inside in a belch of escaping air. Calvert's attention revolved and he saw Black exiting from the crowd of rejoicing soldiers within the Winterthur. As always, he had browbeat wingmen Dredge and Rushworth in tow.

Dressed snug in parkas and slotted-on snow boots, it appeared they had departed under the guise of wanting to venture outdoors to smoke the potent Toscano cigars they had acquired in town. Made in *Tuscany* and fermented with *Kentucky* tobacco, they were known for their stronger, more bitter aroma. The smoke they exhumed stunk out entire establishments, even staining ceilings.

Once out, it became evident that they were going to be discussing details concerning their extra-extracurricular activities conducted in the dead of the night.

Black halted, permitting Dredge but stonewalling Rushworth, stopping his passage with a firm gleam. He stated simply with a chin-waggle back indoors: "Fuck off."

Rushworth's silver-tooth smile instantly faded as it turned out he wasn't as much *one of the boys* as he thought he was. Wordlessly, he obeyed this denial and returned inside.

Dredge prepared the cigars. The door closed behind them, sealing them off from the rest of the Special Z Unit who remained inside.

"Is this cunt still butt-hurt about the other night?" Black questioned, completely without any resonating sympathy or empathy. There was also an utter disregard for Churchill's emotions on the hot topic, just as there had been towards the Italians two nights ago. "They were fuckin' Nazis, Jack. Get over it."

"You couldn't have known that."

"They were fascist loyalists," Dredge intervened, stressing logic whilst clipping his cigar cap off at the shoulder. He next handed the cigar cutter to Black who did the same, and the two organized a metal lighter in order to start the preheating process whilst they discussed this drama, getting it out in the open air ... thing was, the core was as rotten as the smoke they were about to be inhaling. "The evidence proved that they were guilty by association."

Churchill's face twisted in disgust. "*Guilty by association?!* Do you lot hear yourselves? How conceited you've all become? So, what, we're now *judge, jury*, and *executioners* of foreign relations? This is neutral ground!"

"Technically we were in Italy, so, yeah ..." Dredge smiled smugly.

Churchill arced his arm over their shoulders and in the southern direction. "Mick, we're so close to the border, I could throw my damn shoe and hit Italian soil! Your argument is invalid *and*, it's against the point!" he exhaled through expanded nostrils, breathing fire. He got them back on point. "They could have been oppressed for all we know ..."

Dredge and Black held a sensible chuckle at the slight digression, though they couldn't deny hearing Churchill's argument about them potentially being coerced.

Jack eyed them, growing more infuriated. He was finally fighting back after remaining abnormally quiet on the subject for days. Now probably wasn't the time, but they were the ones pressing on the sore like schoolyard bullies.

"People under duress don't opt to soak the fuckin' feet of krauts!" Black growled from beneath the blonde imperial moustache he was aspiring to grow. His sun-kissed features from the light on the snow made for a grand vivid contrast against his golden hair.

"They could have been scared of saying no."

Dredge dismissed. "I didn't see any guns to their heads ... did you?"

Black shook his head upon inhaling his initial drag from the cig—

He started coughing, spluttering violently.

It broke up the debate.

The cigar was much more potent than he had expected, evident through his squinting eyes and pursed lips. He almost cried, emitting a most disgusted sound from his mouth, preparing to yack.

"What?! What's wrong with it?" Dredge questioned, wide-eyed and concerned. The one in his hand tasted fine, but he was used to them.

"Oh, it tastes fucking filthy!"

Calvert leaned in. "Can I have a puff?"

Black couldn't have offloaded the Toscano cigar faster.

This instance provided a divergence to their present topic.

In a representational gesture, Calvert stepped away from Churchill's side of the balcony and to Black's. He arranged the thick, brown cigar between his thumb and forefinger before taking an inhalation. Like Black, his face instantly changed, spluttering in complete and utter revulsion.

He held it at arm's length. "Oh, fuck, mate, what is that shit?!"

Dredge stole it back, having a quick puff. It tasted fine to him.

"Nothin' wrong with it?!"

Calvert scraped his tongue. "It tastes like I just sucked off a charred Macaroni, mate. To completion."

Dredge chuckled, as did Black, who remarked: "Oi, that's a bit on the nose, innit?"

"The only thing that's on the nose is that fuckin' dank durry, mate!" Calvert exclaimed, still recovering with a disgusted expression as Dredge attempted to give it back to one of them. "Get it away from me."

Getting them back on topic, Churchill emphasized firmly, "Can't you lads read between the lines? The occupation is an invasion, after all! The *gunpoint* part would have been implied by the Germans to the complicit Italians. It almost always is. At the very least, we know they weren't armed combatants!"

"Pfft," Black scoffed, looking about to make sure none of the other Berzerker mercenaries or any of Wingate's visiting fidus achateses didn't suspect the topic of their discreet conversation through any of the nearby frosted windows. Always the haphazard, hot-headed asshole, he argued again with Jack with a logical though misplaced counter: "Nobody is armed until they pick up a gun and try to shoot ya, eh? By then, it's too late."

"Unjustified semantics?! That's your argument?"

"Ah! Forget you, Mad-bloody-Jack! You're a fuckin' sissy!"

"*Pardon?!*" Churchill exclaimed with a stern scowl. His heartrate elevated instantly, at his wit's end and ready to throwdown with this wanker. Presumably it was all the testosterone, but that had been happening a lot whilst amongst this group. He hadn't been called a *sissy* by anyone since Lieutenant-Colonel MacLeòid was alive, slurring insults at him and his Second Chesters in Burma.

Black grimaced, contemptuously. "You fuckin' heard me."

The two squared up out on the snow-covered deck, and Churchill continued along the avenue of rationale, pleading his case. "You're calling me a *sissy* because I don't execute civilians?"

"I'm calling you a *sissy* 'cause you're a lil bitch out here with a bow and arrow playing *Indian* around armed *cowboys!* You're a fuckin' liability!"

Calvert stepped between them, prepared to stop a fight.

"No, go back!" rewound Churchill. "That's what you're implying, right! I don't kill innocent people, so therefore I'm weak."

"Stop putting words in my mouth."

"*C'mon, Jack. Ease up,*" muttered Calvert.

Churchill eyed him. Eyed them both. "I thought we were *soldiers*, not coldblooded *murderers?!*"

"We are coldblooded soldiers, Jack! Wake up! It's what we *do!*"

"No! You've crossed a line! That's what you've *done!—*"

"*Oi!*" Calvert forced himself further between their heated debate, pushing them apart like Moses parting the seas. Through a window inside, he sighted that Moshe Dayan had noticed their intense mood in their isolated space and was now clearly probing it with his stare of intrigue.

Calvert smiled solemnly and jerked his chin as if he was handling whatever dispute was transpiring and that he didn't require any administrative relief. Through the glass, Dayan held his poise a little longer before he nodded, returning to the discussion with the other men inside.

Black disengaged, revolving around and muttering to Dredge, facing their own way over the balcony while Calvert dropped his guarding arms now that this had deescalated.

Churchill called, inviting further discussion. "Mike?"

"Jack."

Churchill exhaled. He was lost for words but since they were on the topic, he clearly desired an explanation for this; this expedition for which he had officially recruited Jack Churchill ... he felt as though it wasn't what he had signed up for. Finally, he whispered his question again, in desperate need of clarification to settle his confused mind. "Are we *soldiers?* ... Or are we *murderers?*"

"I don't have an answer for that, mate. Maybe we're becoming a new breed altogether. Darwinism due to the war, I dunno. Maybe we're a bit of both," Calvert shrugged, truly unsure. His argument was ill-prepared, aimed directly at Churchill in a one-sided settlement. "But let's be frank about the other night, Jack ... how were we supposed to know their allegiance for sure? They could have shot us in the back when we left if we had spared them. Italy is loyal to Germany, this much is fact. At the very least, they would have reported what happened ... we can't have that sort of heat on us."

Churchill huffed while Calvert continued, speaking words he just did not wish to hear. Words of ... *truth* ... of *reality.*

"We just *don't know,* mate. It was a necessary reticence of our existence. By that, I mean, simply ... the dead don't talk."

Churchill intently eyed him. He was sticking to his conviction. "You couldn't have known any of that, any more than you could have known they were devoted loyalists to Germany. There would be stronger evidence to suggest they were under duress—"

"Fuckin' get a load of *Officer O'Brien,* here," mocked Dredge after he and Black ceased their conversation, listening in from across the balcony.

"We're not investigators, Jack. We're triggermen. I know that much, eh? I'd rather be *wrong* than *dead* ... and I know that much as well," responded Calvert diplomatically. His words caused an avalanche of cold silence between the two. "It's *hit* or *stay.*"

At his core, Calvert was an ounce desensitized to war crimes.

Prior to the September declaration, he had served with the Royal Engineers in 1938, where he had witnessed *The Rape of Nanking.* This was the indiscriminate mass murder and widespread rape of Chinese civilians, noncombatants, and surrendered prisoners of war, by the hand of the Imperial Japanese Army in *Shanghai.* This wildfire event not only made him fully appreciate the nature of the threat posed by Japanese imperialism, but the chaos and atrocities human beings were capable of.

Calvert tossed the cigar—because it tasted like a turd log, but also to be symbolic. This was over. He then headed inside, as did Dredge, and eventually Black, who stopped last minute. It was just him and Churchill out on the snowy deck.

"Mad Jack," said Black. His tone altered, more passive than before, attempting to find mutual ground for them both to stand on. It was uncharacteristic of Graeme Black, but then again, perhaps Jack didn't know him well enough to form a rock-solid, concrete opinion. "It's black and white. Witnesses saw us killing in a neutral zone ... they had to go. Plain and simple. Collateral damage."

After his statement was delivered, Black left, too.

Churchill stood idle a moment longer after they left, breathing out the heat through his nose. He seemed to be the moral minority of this batch ... it was either a weakness or a strength ...

He felt a presence behind him.

Lurking like a ghost meant only one thing—it was exactly that.

The manifestation during any other moment of complete solitude pending a great moral dilemma would have undoubtedly conjured a visit from his regular haunt, Sloan MacLeòid. Oddly, Churchill craved to hear some of his twisted wisdom through his Scottish brogue.

He didn't turn to see MacLeòid. Rather, he questioned aimlessly.

"You here to call me a *sissy*, too?"

After a few seconds, there was no response like he expected ...

Finding it strange, Churchill frowned.

After considering that there was certainly somebody looming ominously behind him, he turned sharply with his wits heightened and his fist balled.

There was a man in a dark, unwashed balaclava, standing somewhat casually against the snowy exterior log wall. He had the ski mask rolled up over a scarred maw whilst he enjoyed a warm cigarette between his lips in the coldness of the Mont de la Gouille.

"Danny Boy?" Churchill remarked, standing down an inch.

Luckily, Danny Boy had been privy to the topical information they had been discussing considering his clandestine presence effectively sneaking up on the deck. As one of the rogues of their Berzerker splinter faction, he had been present that night in the Aosta Valley—even enthusiastically partaking in most of the killing, if Jack recalled correctly. The bloke was a bit of a wildcard and likely as mad as a march hare.

Cavalier to the cause, Danny Boy ignored the fact that Churchill had practically just talked to himself. Instead, he spoke his mind. This was the first instance where he had said more than a one-worded response or a mutter, and the presence of a Cornish accent was evident.

"I dun like yer."

Churchill huffed. Nearly smiled. "Impossible. Everybody likes me."

Through the eyeholes of his ski mask, Danny Boy's sunken stare gaped him down for a moment before disengaging, aimlessly glancing out at the forest. With his gloved hand, he flicked the cigarette butt and walked off back around the side of the resort, vanishing just as quickly as he had materialized.

'After all the advanced tactics and training, as well as learning how to ski—a detail Jack was more than happy to gloat about, including how he would show off delivering arrows from his bow accurately as he skied slopes, like how I'd envision coming to play like some sort of arctic Parthian shot—the aux-ops team of the Berzerkers were soon enroute for their first 'official' unofficial mission orders: to help the Finnish Army fight the Soviet Red Army to the north.

'The Special Z Unit men were an unassigned league stripped of ranks, insignia, country, and any method of identification. As dark as this black operation was, itself. Their weapons were customized beyond regulation of the Geneva Convention for lethality. Jack had even come to terms with breaking off the spectacular basket hilt of his shiny claybeg sword, discarding it and its pomp for tactical purposes, as well as practicality ... but an attentive eye could see the parallels to this phase. A metaphor at play, Jack was shedding his morals for the preference of the mission. He was losing a part of himself along with that silver basket hilt.

'Jack made reference to the fact he and the other lads within the Berzerkers used a type of unusual, anodized paint to darken anything that the moonlight may illuminate with its glow and shine, such as the blade of his sword. The entire ceremonial claybeg was now charcoal black ...

... unrecognizable, just like he feared his soul was slowly becoming: black ...'

1940, March
Winterthur Resort, Mont de la Gouille
Swiss Pennine Alps, Switzerland

Receiving their orders from the powers that be upon mount high, the celebrating men of the Special Z Unit had been spoilt with a belated feast. Wingate organized for fresh meats from a deli somewhere in the local *Entremont* district to be couriered to the resort the day before, held on ice in the kitchen ever since. He had organized with the willing concierge of the resort to bring in a respected chef from *Liddes* to work in the kitchen, who had in turn prepared a lovely salt and cracked pepper steak with mushroom sauce, mash potatoes, and even seasoned, steamed vegetables. It was a surefire treat for the mercenaries who most nights fended for themselves in typical army menu conventions, eating canned rations and simple savouries.

Once dinner had been served, the team were further treated by having the enigmatic Otter join them in the recessed common lounge for a chat, a drink, a smoke, and even a hand of cards before the man commenced his habitual ritual of retreating to his upstairs lodgings for the night behind a closed door. The secretive man had an unpleasant early bedtime. A solitary shut-in, he seemed to find greater comfort within his own recluse rather than in the company of others. Conceivably, the most unsettling ratiocination was a fear of attachment to his expendable brothers in arms.

Irrespective of Wingate's favoured pastimes or his questionable association with his men, after their eccentric ringleader had called it quits for the night ... *the kids would come out to ~~play~~ war.*

Hyped and wired, a rugged-up Jack Churchill quietly emerged donning a black beanie upon his head. He was strapped with his brown leather quiver, his sword at his hip, and carrying his longbow.

At the usual midnight meeting time, he crept out the back of the Winterthur ski resort. There, he mutely rendezvoused with the others—Calvert, Black, Dredge, Ruffell, Komrower, Danny Boy, Scotty, and Gentle Jerry—all dressed in stealthy, unmarked attires, including low-wattage headlamps.

The usual suspects for their roguish nighttime activities carted ski gear and poles, as well as their assortment of cunning and unconventional arsenal of weaponry.

It was especially cold this night, with a chill factor well into the minus. Due to valid reasons such as the cold and the fact they had another one of Wingate's foreign visitors stopping by the resort some time tomorrow morning, Jack had a feeling it wouldn't be a late journey tonight, nor would they venture as far across the border. The cold would see to that.

Within the treeline shadows of the moonlit winter wonderland, Black rolled his eyes when noticing Churchill's attendance for the night's expedition behind enemy lines. This was the first time they had gone out since the Aosta Valley incident. Dredge was in accord with the undercurrent loathing. They had likely hoped he would no longer join in on their forays.

Calvert welcomed Churchill, passing him a laterally shaped ski bag.

Inside was a set of ski runners for his feet and poles for his wrists that Calvert and Ruffell had smuggled out for everybody earlier that evening and left in situ of tonight's adventure.

Lungs tight from the cold, Churchill caught a glimpse of Black and Dredge's dual dispositions. In a whisper and with an open mitten, he remarked sarcastically. "Ease up, lads. If your eyes roll any further back in your heads, you might fall off the slopes."

"Did you bring your bow and arrow, *Robin Hood?*" Stating the obvious, Dredge countered wryly in his Estuary English. "Boys, call *Nottin'am.* Tell 'em they can 'ave they *Errol Flynn*-lookin' ponce back!"

"Robin Hood was from *Loxley,* lad," Churchill countered wittily. "You should possibly wear a helmet whenever you do the Berzerker charge training. It appears you've lost a few braincells, and you may be coming down with a case of the dumb."

"*Oi,*" Calvert quietened the rowdy tones as the volume increased. They *were* out afterhours, and this *was* a sly intention. "*Shh!*" he hissed first. And second, "You two can fuck later, but right now, this sexual tension has gotta be stowed, all right?"

Churchill eyed Black and Dredge and vice versa.

They reached a mutual reticence.

"We all here or what?" Komrower queried in a low manner, evidently raring to go. He couldn't tell if it was the anxiety or the cold causing his teeth to chatter.

Barely able to pan his view at the neck, Calvert's scarved peripherals tipped left and right to perform a headcount. "Think so. Masks on."

They all pulled down their balaclavas, masking-up.

"Well, then. Up and at 'em, gents," Komrower then insisted, and they embarked on their newest endeavour into the black of blacks through the whitest of whites.

Off into the abyss of the midnight wilderness, the group trotted to the embankment of the icicle gradient where they took to the off-piste gradients which they would use to traverse the southerly slopes. Utilizing the focused beams of their headlamps to avoid trees, rocks, and certain death whilst moving at speed, they would ski laterally, being sure not to descend too far into the valley.

Their skis carved silently through the scape, traversing the plain some four miles in approximately ten minutes before the nine men reached the divert route to the south-southeast. From there, they ditched their gear in a usual stash place and changed into their hiking boots.

They next trekked on foot along the *Schweiz/Italia* borderline, searching for any evidence of active enemy patrols along a canyon crevasse. Usually, they banked towards the peaks of *Pointe de Barasson,* but tonight they headed towards the region south of the *Grande Tête de By* in the Aosta Valley, geographically entering Italy.

Even with their vast mountain range views, they could see no indication of an enemy presence; no flashlight beams, no glowing campfires. By 0140-hours, the rogue squad still turned up empty-handed, unable to even find the remnants of a recent patrol around the area. This was odd, as the range leading up north to the Grande Tête de By was clear of forestation and visually easily accessible for detachments. It was only logical for patrols to route along this passage, and a vantage point would be advantageous for an outpost. Applying this logic just added to their frustrations of them not finding any enemy to exterminate.

Truth be told, Jack felt weird this night.

He was excited to be sneaking out. Aroused for action, like always.

Maybe it was that certain *something in the water,* adding angst of late, but he honestly desired to get into a fight tonight. He was hankering for something to take his frustrations out against ... perchance he was even angry enough to take the life of somebody deserving, like a no-good Nazi.

After becoming aware of the time, subsequent to a brief discussion on the night's disappointing outcome, Ruffell voiced a suggestion to the others. "We should head back."

"I agree," said Komrower. "If we start now, we should make it back before oh-four-hundred. Still get a couple hours kip in."

The weary wanderers were in an unspoken agreeance.

Beneath the pale moonlight, the adrenaline high of this hunt finally simmered down into a depressive state, hindered further by their own tired eyes as exhaustion started to set in. This venture had been off the back of several others incurring extremely late nights and an overall contribution to sleep debt.

In joint accord, the unit marched in regress, promptly returning to their stockpiled skis and poles and collecting them without incident. After strapping them to their backpack webbing, they took to the rocks, climbing with both hands and weapons dangling. This was the hardest part of their return journey along the landscape of the Mont de la Gouille. The route took them along the cusp of the massif, where they could get high enough to put their skis back on and traverse home down the slopes.

They climbed the mountainside for nearly half an hour before preparing to launch off a slope homeward bound on a north-westerly vector, when the radiance of orange firelight in the gloom hue caught their attention. It was in the near distance, and they were each surprised that they had missed it on the way in.

The resonating glow diffused against a sheer rocky ridgeline to the lower west, and the sensation of the discovery reignited the spark of their war-thirsty desires. They unanimously detoured to check it out.

It was a camp of five soldiers. *Germans.*

They were easily identifiable by the shape of their helmets: the *Stahlhelm.* This Wehrmacht detachment was an external sentry of some kind, possibly a part of a larger patrol. They were camping around a small fire, oblivious to any harm that may have been lurking, preying on their location this far safe and behind their lines.

Upon a short but effective covert reconnoitre by Calvert and Black, the remaining rogue mercenaries stayed at a safe distance in the darkness behind a terrain ensconce, awaiting a gameplan.

"What's the sit-rep?" Churchill asked, squatting low from a higher position than the others on some rocks. Like many of the others, he had rolled his ski mask up over his face, wearing it like a beanie. He was in such a good position that if he raised his chin, his eyeline elevated over the incline and he was able to sight the sentries. They were a stone's throw away, hence their low voices in fear of audio carrying across the echoic valley in the quiet of night.

The nocturnal noiselessness caused their senses to heighten.

"Five Huns ..." Calvert remarked in a whisper, breathing thoroughly from the stress of the silent recon. He revealed a grimace from the hard yakka by peeling his balaclava up and over his face. "But an unknown amount in the tents against the rocky alcove ..."

"They're tents?" Ruffell questioned, peeking for himself.

There were two erected M31 zeltbahn canvas tents against the steep precipice. In the shadow of the moonlight, the patterning camouflaged so fittingly with the terrain, they almost missed it.

"Affirmative," Black corresponded having been present for the reconnaissance. He, too, rolled his ski mask up, finding it easier to communicate without his face covered whilst maintaining their stealth element. He cast a steady look to the other eight Berzerkers' focused expressions. The fact of there being tents meant that there could have been another half-dozen krauts shrouded away. "The ones by the fire could be just the night watch for a larger unit ... we *could* be outnumbered on this one. We need to be smart if we're gonna act."

"Agreed," Calvert nodded.

The others strewn about their nook concurred silently at the option to advance forwards. The only other option here was to back down and return to the resort without incident ... without spilling blood ...

Given the combined thirst for a fight, that wasn't about to happen.

Without further ado, Calvert imposed a plan upon them as their leader. It was the same successful tactic they had used on the last two patrols they had encountered. "We split up. Two teams. One high for top-down cover, one low to drive a jab in the ribs. Adjoined assault."

"Double envelopment," Churchill regarded in agreeance. The strategy was music to his ears as it was potentially foolproof. Not only did they have the upper hand by way of the surprise element, but this multi-directional incursion only further strengthened their assault, making it two-pronged. He torqued his head, fond of the idea. "Fine-o-fine."

Calvert constructed the details of his plan. His stare wandered, searching the best equipped shooters of the group. "Scotty, Ruffell, and Arty. You guys climb up along this rock face. Stay low and silent. Get into an elevated position where you can see the tents below and wait for the ground team to take out the guards."

"The pincer manoeuvre *again?*" Dredge scoffed, appearing jaded.

Black faced him, backing Calvert's logic. "Oi, we don't know what we're up against in the tents. There could be sleeping Gerrys in there with Schmeissers at the ready."

"So, let's blow 'em up!"

"Too loud," Churchill interjected, adding onto Calvert's plan. "Whatever we do, we should do it as quietly as possible. We don't know what type of attention using explosives might bring or who else might be stationed around these parts. Like the Otter always says, you've got to expect the unexpected."

Dredge couldn't argue with that.

Bombs may have been an easy solution, but it was the loudest.

"Not to mention avalanche risk," Calvert furthered, sauntering into the midst of the surrounding men in order to lay out his plan. "Setting off explosives midway down a mountain range probably isn't the smartest choice around. Once in position on the ground, team one quietly drops the sentries and holds at the outer perimeter while team two guards the tents for any subsequent movement. Height will be your advantage. Anybody strolls out to say hello, you mow 'em down."

Black callously suggested. "I say we hose down the tent anyhow. Can't be too careful in a situation like this."

During the democracy manifest, Komrower inserted a proposition on behalf of Calvert, gauging that outcome the reasoning why he didn't suggest it initially. "Too loud, remember?!"

"Ruffell, did you bring your Sten?" Black gestured at Humphrey Ruffell's recent weapon of choice. The brute nodded, snuggling it across his core. The weapon which he referred was a Sten MkIIS submachine gun fitted with a foot-long integrated sound suppressing silencer. The new gun was hot from the latest shipment from the Toyshop. The trade-off to being much quieter was that MkIIS had a lower muzzle velocity than the other variants of the Sten family, due to a ported barrel aimed at reducing velocity to below the speed of sound (1,001ft/s). The length of the compact submachine gun had also grown now that it incorporated an integral suppressor. This addition caused the barrel of the weapon to protrude further by fifteen inches. Although it heated up rapidly when the weapon was fired at a fully automatic rate, it generously reduced the volume from the weapons discharge—it was practically a sizzling whisper. A canvas cover had been placed around the silencer extension for protection from the excessive heat to the operator's supporting hand.

As Black had suggested, the silent weapon could be used to actively *hose down* the tent from the elevated precipice above, laying waste to any enemy numbers that may be lurking inside and be about to respond to the deaths of their sentries.

"Are we not going to be shooting the sentries anyhow?" argued Dredge, who was seemingly still advocating for them going loud with this attack. Perhaps all this silence was hurting his ears, and he wanted to make a racket. "If we're already going to be shooting loud, we may as well just toss a coupl'a grenades in there."

"We don't need to shoot anything loud," Churchill stated, causing heads to turn and face him, prompting an explanation.

"Come again?" Dredge asked with a raised brow.

Jack prepared to elaborate, this time with much more bravado and certainty. He commandeered Calvert's assumed leadership for a moment, even dropping down from the rocks in order to level with his teammates in the short-ranged glow of a handlamp. "Other than Ruffell's special Sten, we don't pull the trigger of any non-suppressed firearms unless *absolutely* necessary. We use our training, lads. This whole time, we haven't been practising at a *rifle range* or at a *skeet shoot*, have we?"

"Suggests the one cunt that didn't bring one, eh?" was Black's sole, sardonic remark. He gestured a nod at the strung longbow in Jack's grasp.

Churchill faced his heckling accuser. "You and I both know that I could drop all of those Huns before they even know what's hit them," he countered boastfully, eager to display his newly acquired speed-shooting technique in the field. "Did you not hear about my deforestations of late?"

"Logs doon shoot back but, do dey ..." Danny Boy interposed from out of nowhere, speaking up in a rare circumstance of discordance. It caused heads to turn, everybody hearing his Cornish accent.

Churchill panned his face at him. "Neither will these ones, trust me."

"No, trus' *me*," furthered Danny Boy in a mumble through his balaclava. He revealed his High Standard pistol—the thing was semiautomatic and substantially silent compared to other guns, thanks to the integrated suppressor resulting in the long cylindrical barrel. It was a rather odd occurrence to have him input anything; either tactically or socially. His confidence had increased in recent weeks, hence his conceited remark: "I'll take all five out."

"With what? That lil *peashooter?!*" Black discouraged, knowledgeable of the small calibre which the weapon fired. It was silent but not deadly. "Best save it for the tin cans, mate."

Through the cut-out eyeholes in Danny Boy's ski mask, he eyed Graeme Black down whilst he reluctantly stabbed his handgun deep into his holster.

"No, Jack's onto something ..." Calvert endorsed Churchill's play. "We've been training in hand-to-hand combat for months. We've had all the schoolings, from all over the world. It's high time we put it to the test. We're Berzerkers ... let's *be berserk.* These wankers aren't going to expect shit, and if it *does* go pear-shaped, Scotty has a Tommy and is going to be up on that hill along with Ruffell, watching our back, right fellas? If it goes south, go loud."

Alongside Ruffell, Scotty bobbed his head. He was armed with the popular American Thompson submachine gun. Loud, but deadly.

"Grae, Jerry, Arty, Danny Boy, and myself will get in up close and do the charge," Calvert designated, cycling the hold of his gear from off his own submachine gun and onto his holstered knuckleduster trench knife. He had two and fitted them accordingly with his fingers through the brass eyelets, blades down in a stabbing motion. He was ready to get down and dirty, leading by example.

"What about me and *Whacky Jacky,* here?" the comical and blasé Michael Dredge questioned. He stepped inwards besides the archer Jack Churchill and his out-of-place strung longbow.

"I packed the crossbows," Calvert nodded at one of the larger packs containing the Big Joe 5 (BJ5). It was a silent ranged projectile launching device; a full-sized shoulder-fired recurve crossbow, and it was currently collapsed neatly with hinged arms bound in a strap. Wingate had ordered for its use from the Toyshop. "Use it in combination with Jack's bow to take out a guard each without a sound. We'll rush the rest with knives."

Disparaged by his designation, Dredge was handed the Joe 5 from the bag. It was folded up and compacted, requiring resetting for use. There was also a lateral carrier of approximately a dozen aluminium bolts which were the ammunition for the modern-era military crossbow.

"Oi, is the little fella in there?" Black questioned, looming over the crossbow bag and willing to give the piece a go up-close. The other crossbow was known as a *Lil' Joe Penetrometer* and was a prototype crossbow pistol with a vertical profile. It fired an even smaller bolt known as a 'toothpick' and was a questionable choice at that, selected for the mere challenge. That being said, if he could get in close enough to point it at a point-blank target, it could actually prove rather useful in this attack.

Calvert nodded. He had packed that one, too.

"Doesn't this fucker still shoot to the left?" Dredge asked about the Big Joe 5, disgruntled at being forced to use the questionable modernized medieval device. The crossbow contraption had proven inaccurate in their last few training runs.

Humoured by their forced armaments while he sat comfy with an American automatic, Scotty encouraged with the upmost witticisms. "So, aim left. Easy-peasy, lemon-squeezy, aye?"

"No, I'm fairly certain Bala fixed that ..." Komrower stated, recalling the quartermaster of their unit working on the device.

Black interjected with a hint of underlining cynicism. "Doesn't matter. Mad-bloody-Jack is here, with his six-foot bow and his twelve-inch cock ..."

"You been spying on me in the shower again, Grae?"

Black switched sights onto him. He had to smirk, as did Jack, who then bowed his head to hide any uncertainty he may have exuded ...

... and to hide a secret silent gulp in his throat.

This was getting real. He talked a big game, but secretly at this stage in his warpath and military career, he hadn't so much as taken a life. Not even with a firearm, let alone his longbow. That may have been all about to change tonight ...

"We'll position ourselves in the tree line to the closest guards and wait for your marks with the arrows. Take out the two standing guards. Once you eliminate them, we'll rush up and take out the remaining three when they get up off their arses," Calvert advised, eyeing his melee supports; Black, Komrower, Jerry, and Danny Boy. They would be like halfbacks rushing the endzone.

Onboard, Churchill nodded. He pointed at Jerry exclusively.

"Don't be gentle, lad."

Gentle Jerry beamed, pulling down his balaclava overtop of his facial features and aligning the eyeholes. "Oh, don't worry," he said muffled, drawing his pair of brass knuckleduster-loaded trench knives with a sinister smile and a wriggle of the fingers. "I won't be."

The men took a short breather while it all set in, eventually moving out on their unsanctioned assignments. While they did, Black intentionally passed Ruffell, issuing him with a parting wisdom whilst he positioned his ski mask to cover his face. "Oi. Once we're engaging the sentries, you light that fuckin' tent up like it's loaded with Huns, you hear? Don't fuckin' wait for us."

Ruffell dipped his head abidingl—

"Oi, I mean it, kid!" Black tugged him back, appearing somewhat overcautious. "Spray that fucker like it's afire and what you're wielding there be a fuckin' firehose. Mag-dump it, reload, rinse, repeat."

"Okay. Got it, sir," Ruffell regarded before climbing the hill with Scotty to gain an advantageous position overlooking the Gerrys with their automatics—of which he was the point man.

"*Grae, come on!*" Calvert hissed as he, Komrower, Jerry, and Danny Boy started down the safe side of the hill slope to flank the enemy position. They would soon be navigating the snow-covered shrubs and shadows like subnivean mice.

Dredge and Churchill remained, preparing their archery weapons.

The point of no return had just passed with their displacements.

Afoot, the game was in play.

The precipice support team:

The combination of the strenuous attention to stealth movement, along with the inclination and then slight declination of the rocky slopes, caused Scotty and Ruffell to each break a sweat in the snow. What wasn't slick with ice was loose landscape, and merely getting into position proved harder than the offensive mission at hand.

The two carted their submachine guns in their arms as they descended the shadowy slopes above the glowing orange fire in the night, moving quietly and disrupting as little geographical dissipation as possible so as not to alert the group of hostiles below the hill. They took their time, moving like sloths. One dropped fumble, one cockup, and it was the game.

They observed the enemy camp from above.

There were two tents positioned before an arranged campfire, with five occupants positioned within vicinity of the fire's outward radiance. There were what appeared to be two snow sleds parked before one of the tents, and seemingly lateral trail marks leading into the forest, likely from where they originated with said sleds.

From their view above, contrasting against the white snow plane, they could see the distant dark profiles of their teammates as they meticulously moved into positions down on the ground, fanning out and encircling the German sentinels with the upmost stealth factor.

Churchill and Dredge stuck to the nightscape shadows of the rocks, filing into the gloom of the sheer terrain, and gaining positions afar from the situation that were also optimal for target zoning, where they found a position placing them approximately one-hundred feet from the hot zone.

Calvert, Black, Komrower, Jerry, and Danny Boy crept through the snow-fallen foliage, situating themselves behind the last lines of concealment before a short clearing and the enemy locale. They were mostly cloaked in the darkness beneath the treetop canopies, shielding them from the harsh moonlight glow.

Every light-footed step they took, they did so at a snail's pace, for the slightest bit of noise could signal the guards. Once gaining optimal positions, they waited.

After the archer's engagements, they would mount their Berzerker charge. They would have between eighty to one-hundred feet to close in an all-out sprint at the remaining enemy, which should leave their odds ratio at 1:2 in their favour. Given that the sentries were oblivious to the surprise attack, and would likely be tired, slow, and unalert, their reduced reaction times following the sudden deaths of two of their kamerads, dropped by a silent arrow each, should make that distance scalable before they effectively bore arms. And even if they were quicker than expected with those Karabiner bolt-actions, then that would be where the advanced evasion and avoidance training would come in while they closed the distance.

They were trained to dodge bullets, after all.

It was a risk ... but about time they put their hours of specialized Berzerker training to good use, testing it in the field, albeit at a small scale.

The ground team:

Calmly, Calvert shuffled a half-foot closer to the enemy-occupied zone, peeking over the top of a noisy bush which he was careful not to touch, as it would be like rattling a bell alarm. He breathed through pursed lips, remaining as mute as possible.

Until now, they had been gradually closing on the enemy, able to smell the smoke from their campfire. Now, he was so close he could feel the heat ... could trace their faces ... read the ranks on their sleeves.

Calvert's eyeline lowered to within his self-profile. His hands were sweaty, so he adjusted the hold on his two knives, mentally collecting himself to stay on course and suppress the imperious shakes. This low sunken in the deep end of impending combat, the anxiety was nearly too much to bear. One had to actively focus on not mentally flailing or shutting down entirely.

To his immediate rear left, behind a thick tree trunk, was the broad-shouldered ogre, Gentle Jerry. Sweat glistened across his cheeks in the cold as he pressed carefully up against it, brandishing his fists and ready for the charge once the signal sounded. In one of his balled fists was a trench knife, ready to deal damage, the other was just pure knuckled fury. His eyes were wide, not with terror, but adrenaline. If he was anything like Mike right now, his heart would be pounding absolutely deafeningly inside of his head. Calvert silently signalled Jerry with a nod, and he returned the notion.

They were in position.

Slowly, Calvert rotated around to inspect those on his right flank.

It took him a second to spot Komrower, who was partially hidden in the shade of the campfire behind other natural blockades, facing forwards and prepared to engage the enemy. He barely made out duo Danny Boy and Black, approaching with his vertical crossbow drawn up by his head, but he couldn't fully see them to signal a nod or thumbs up to synchronize their preparedness. He trusted that these well-oiled killing machines knew their objectives.

Now that they were in position, it all hinged on the instigative incursion by archers Churchill and Dredge ...

The archer team:

On the inner flank, Churchill and Dredge assumed a position against the base of the precipice, cautiously mountaineering a rocky incline nearly three metres from the ground in order to gain a better vantage point of the visually enclosed camp.

The two left their balaclavas rolled up, showing their facial features: Mad Jack's pencil-thin moustache and Dredge's clean shaven character.

Longbow in hand, Churchill drew an arrow from his shoulder quiver.

Hunched at the core and folded low to remain out of view of the enemy targets, he nocked the butt of the deathly projectile on the bowstring, pinching it with his fingertips. From this current stance, he watched Dredge as he took a knee, inching up to the break cover line with his cocked crossbow out of sight, about to reach his firing position.

In the silence of their preparedness, Churchill watched him linger awry; saw an instance of insecurity as it overcame the browbeat soldier's attitude, slightly effecting his physical posture. Weakness was an odd sight to see on such an unshakable man. In the seconds of fleeting anxiousness, Dredge made swift eye contact with Churchill, noticing that he read that mild expression of timidity like an open book.

Rather than hinge on it, Jack furrowed his lips and bowed respectively, eager for him to move past it at his own pace. They may not have been friends, but they were comrades. Berzerker brothers.

It seemed that the two had levelled with one another.

"Jack ... eh," Dredge whispered, either unable to find the right words to express the sudden unset of guilt he had for prior transgressions of disrespect, or quietening himself due to it not being the right time or place for such conduct. He dismissed himself and shook his head. "... don't worry, actually."

In the calm darkness, Jack held his stare.

Once Dredge's eyeline returned from a defocused meander, he simply and silently nodded at Churchill with a genuine delivery, without a word making it all okay.

"Ready?" Churchill changed the subject, putting them back on the course of the mission. These two archers held the signalling gun for this race, and it was up to them to commence the charge with their lethal medieval projectiles.

Dredge cracked his neck and bobbed his head, giving his resting two-handed recurve crossbow a final once over, refamiliarizing himself with the weapon. It was a simple contraption with no safety to disengage. The pike-tip eight-ounce aluminium bolt was set in the groove, with the high-tensile string latched and prepared to disengage at the pull of the trigger, serving like any atypical firearm.

With a spare finger, Dredge raised the rear targeting gauge so that he could aim with more precision and, once confident in his perch on the rock, cast a sideways gleam to Jack. He rekindled his courage. "Are you?"

Forming a grin, Jack looked away and over at the targets by the fire.

He took Dredge's overconfident comeback as an affirmation on his readiness. This was clearly a rhetorical question, as the whole unit knew of Churchill's prior archery experience, including representing Great Britain in the Oslo World Archery Championship.

Churchill tensed as he gripped his longbow, rising into an archer's stance as he pulled his bowstring into anchor point, maintaining a strong hold on the weight of the draw.

Ready to loose an arrow into the aligned target sitting by the camp at any given moment, this silent hunter, cloaked in the gloom of the shadow of the night, grew fully exposed to the enemy. So much so, that the light from their campfire felt warm against his cheeks.

Jack winced in a whisper. "On your mark, my lad ..."

Dredge closed an eye, lining up a mark with his giant slingshot projectile launcher ...

The Germans:

The few members of the Wehrmacht sentry were each layered for the cold in grey heavy wool greatcoats, with silver dimpled buttons that did not reflect the light. This group had painted them olive green, providing extra camouflage. White hooded waterproof shawls covered their greatcoats, providing further insulation and concealment from potential scouts.

Their upper extremities were layered with woollen mittens, scarves, and bulky felt-lined leather winter boots furrowed with wooden soles to keep their feet dry and warm, which caused their boot impressions to resemble horse hooves. They all wore stahlhelm helmets upon their heads, with insulated beanies underneath to protect their ears.

Two of the men were standing vertically and in the possession of rifles either in their grasp or slung on a shoulder strap, and three more men were seated by the small campfire which they had established—likely against regulation, as their positioning along the boundaries was still probably of reserved intelligence considering that, at this stage in history, Italy remained non-belligerent towards Nazi Germany.

If not residing within reach, the bolt-action weapons of the soldiers were at-ease and possibly even unchambered. Those standing had them slung on their leather straps, wrapped around their shoulders, while the trio of comfortable seated men had them leaning off the ground against nearby fixtures, such as a log and a toppled tree trunk.

In the tranquillity of the frosty night, the men chattered in low tones, boiling something in a pot. One of them even said something funny, causing the standing sentries to cackle whilst warming their mittens—

... *ssss—slish!*

A dart barb whistled like an insect, striking one of the standing guards in the jugular notch, situated between both his collarbones and right above his multiple layer's stitches. The impact barely made a noise, other than a puncture of clothing and a fleshy flick.

The crossbow ammunition was so thin, so weightless, and so pointy, it penetrated the close-range soft target. The bolt struck its victim through the lower jugular, puncturing the German's fleshy tissue with considerable ease. Having gotten wedged between the vertebrae in the man's neck and thus stopping the velocity entirely, the foot-long metal barb made it halfway through the man's neck stem, sticking him through like a kebab skewer.

Without as much as a garble sound, the soldier's panicked hands suddenly grabbed at the wound, touching the end of the exteriorly swallowed projectile as red gore started to spurt from the edges of the wound.

His mouth immediately filled with blood as his brethren realized something dangerous had transpired. To them in their perplexed states, they likely considered it a snake bite or a similar act of nature given the circumstances.

Just as he subsided into a heap, they leapt to action, reacting—

... *ssss—CHOCK!*

Following the pitch of another whistle, a larger bodkin-tipped war arrow—this time launched from Churchill's longbow—connected with the other standing sentry, striking him through the breastplate with a wind-striking *thwump!* that sent a deep-toned bass echo resounding audibly across the quiet camp.

The transference of kinetic energy was much heavier for the arrow than the crossbow bolt. The soldier who received the hit involuntarily spun around like being caught in a whirlwind before toppling over on a slant from the brunt of the force. Grimacing with bared teeth, he lost both his unstrapped helmet and his partially unlooped rifle whilst collapsing gracelessly, holding both hands clutched at the protruding stick lodged in his ribs.

In the fuss, the impaled soldier stumbled onto the open campfire, falling into a tumble across the open flames and almost putting the roaring embers out. Absent the licks of flaming combustion, the scene became eerily bleak and hazy. He rolled off the excessive heat quick smart, assessing the fatal damage done to his torso by the arrow with quick, panicked breaths from a deflating lung. A medieval implement had struck him, as well as the others who had witnessed it, with absolute mystification and bewilderment.

Still reacting from the shock and processing the current assault, the remaining three soldiers were fast at attention, searching the perimeter for a point of origin from the silent projectiles. They shrunk down low and stooped behind supposed concealment, quaking in their winter hoofs whilst their hands fumbled to remove their mittens, preparing their cold weaponry for war ...

From out of nowhere:
"BERZERKER!!!"
Multiple English-speaking voices shouted from the darkness surrounding the camp. The conjoined battle cries seemed to originate from a northerly circumference, and not at all from the direction as to where the projectiles had seemingly derived.

The frightened soldiers bore eyes broader than the brims of their stahlhelms. Cradling their Karabiner rifles tight, they shuffled about wide-eyed, aimlessly scanning the many dancing shadows in the darkness when suddenly, they saw the incoming threats ...

... and realized their pending doom.

"BERZERKERRR!!!"
The battle-cry developed into a continuous growling rumble as the rampaging English soldiers charged at full pelt towards the passive German camp. Their blades were borne like the teeth of ravaging wolfpack predators, pouncing upon their terrified prey.

At the summit of the advance, Graeme Black, coasted between their conjoined line of trapsing gallops in order to extend his right arm, presenting the Lil' Joe Penetrometer.

The device looked a lot like an eagle's claw, opening for the clutch.

At what could almost be considered point blank, the vertical profile crossbow pistol noiselessly fired a dart at one of the stunned sentries.

The small, five-inch toothpick bolt slotted one of the three Germans through the face like an iron dart pegged at a dartboard, knocking his head damn near off his shoulders by the transfer of kinetic force.

The soldier's head snapped back when struck, slotted through the soft flesh of the face and impacting against his cheekbone. The impalement sent him craning backwards in a fluster of tossed snow powder, where he struggled to maintain his footing. His lofted rifle twirled in the air for multiple revolutions, discarded by his hands in favour of cupping the severe stinging injury to his face.

The soldier's distressed cry was muffled into his containing hands, but his agony was short-lived. Within two seconds, Danny Boy appeared running analogously to Black, and within his strides he hiked up a fallen log stack that elevated his vantage point at the campsite.

Light from the campfire embers illuminated everything in silhouette, but his aim remained true. Propped up high on the log, Danny Boy engaged a tea and saucer hold of his silenced pistol and engaged targets. This included the soldier Black had just incapacitated, as well as an additional soldier who simultaneously spotted his charge.

T'Ch! T'Ch! ...

The semi-automatic .22LR pistol clapped away in the night, imitating zero muzzle flash from the elongated barrel. The small calibre handgun was recoilless and deadly in the hands of somebody so accurate.

The first double-tap struck the already injured soldier, both bullets hitting him in the sternum, causing him to finally subside, fleetingly deprived of life. His howling ceased almost instantly, becoming an inaudible gurgle before nothing.

A subsequent triplet collected the soldier located at the fallen's immediate flank. The first bullet struck the man's stahlhelm and bounced off in a ricochet spark, however the subsequent deuce collected his forehead above each eyebrow, barely an inch apart, turning him off like a light switch. He buckled at the knees, folding on top of himself like a string puppet, absent skeletal structure.

Before that body even hit the snow, the last remaining soldier became collected in a joint tackle by Mad Mike Calvert and Gentle Jerry (who came in not-so-gently), charging past either of Black's stationary flanks.

Swooping in with the twin stabbing motions of a wild wolverine, Calvert honed in low and grazed the scared soldier with multiple lacerations through his layers as he attempted to parry with his rifle like a bow staff at the last shivering second.

He ultimately shoved the soldier like a brute, creating an ounce of distance. Calvert would have had him with the rebounding strikes if it hadn't been for Jerry's juggernaut strength taking over and assuming the takedown. The unit of the man saw the opportunity to grab the soldier in a bearhug, scooping him under the waist within his tremendous wingspan and transferring his whole weight into a slam.

The bodies collapsed over two parked snow sleds.

In a fit of thrashing snow, Jerry mounted the toppled, crippled kraut, and drove his knuckle-dusted fist into his head with metallic, meaty blows as if he was fluffing a pillow. He followed the assault up with downward stabs from his trench knife blade, finishing the German with a gory pigstick manoeuvre that ensured he would never recover the breath he had just siphoned from his lungs by way of numerous airholes.

It was brutal. It was final.

Like a form of contemporary artistic abstract expressionism, Crimson red slickened the white snow in streaks.

Up on the overwatching ridge, Ruffell's silenced Sten hissed to life, spitting like an icy garden hose, spraying stealthy gunfire through the roof of the pitched tent. He brushed with sideways motions, sweeping back and forth indiscriminately.

In a chattery whisper of pressurized air, the suppressed submachine gun sizzled away like a well-greased rotary bolt, immune to friction.

Sch-sch-sch-sch-sch-sch-sch-sch ...

The gun had a slower rate of fire than most typical models due to the integrated silencer, but the distribution of nine-millimetre calibre bullets was more than enough to decimate the fabric tent canvas below.

Shoulder and tensed chins jolting, Ruffell maintained the recoil of fully automatic fire, swaying his sustained fire up and down and across the tarpaulin cover, shredding it to frays and ravels as the barrage destroyed all that was housed within the tent. There was no evidence to support there being any further manpower lurking within the confines, though, there were some sparks popping from within the housing as well as the occasional sound of bullets striking metal, resulting in spark ignitions and random diagonal ricochet tracers zooming into the night sky.

The Germans had something in there.

While Scotty maintained an overwatch on the ambush with his Thompson trained, Ruffell expelled the entire magazine of his submachine gun within seconds, clicking dry as the side-mounted exterior bolt slammed shut. He energetically ripped the empty stick magazine from the weapon's side-mounted mag well before inserting a fresh one, pinching back the bolt and returning the stock to his shoulder to brace for recoil.

He squeezed the trigger to deliver another payload.

Sch-sch-sch-sch-sch-sch-sch ...

Maintaining fire, he was hellbent on killing everything inside ...

... however, nobody had noticed the leaking, glugging fuel from the perforated metal barrels within the tent until it was too late ...

Fire burst forth from the edges of the tent, spilling like lava, alighting the entire canopy with an intense red-hot glow a silent split-second before the volatile contents within the shelter ignited explosively, blasting loudly like a compressed fireball.

B-Boom!

The pair of eyes through Ruffell and Scotty's ski masks pinched shut when faced with the blinding bright light of the eruption. On the rocks, they ceased all offensive fire and recoiled quickly.

Hot orange fire detonated loudly from what must have been stored fuel drums that were concealed beneath the tent canvas cover, possibly to save it from the harsh overnight ice.

This wasn't an external sentry post for border patrols ...
... they were transporting petrol somewhere.

The cool, gloomy environment was suddenly alit by scorching flame as the drums within the tent popped like fireworks, exploding vertically as well as horizontally. Boisterously. Glistening golden flames splashed against the precipice rocks behind the tent, licking up the cliff face, causing the two situated submachine gunners to retreat further from the heat and blowing smoke.

The fireball wafted outwards, spilling like a rushing flood stream over everything within the immediate vicinity, setting the locale ablaze with steaming hot lava. Everything lit up with a red-hot golden hue.

An invisible scorching heatwave sent out from the blast of the igniting petrol tanks knocked Gentle Jerry on his ass, and as well sent Calvert coiling over into the snow. He quickly revolved around to face the heat, squinting to examine the unexpected fiery scene beyond raised palms which still housed his ionize-painted brass trench knives over his fingers like battle jewellery.

Black and Komrower halted in their charge, blocked by the sheer scorch of the bright explosion that briefly turned night into day. Grinding to a progressive halt and dropping to their knees, they raised their arms to cover their faces from the glow of the belching inferno as it glistened, hungry for oxygen now that it was free from containment and in its final form.

Feeling the heat on their exposed faces, Churchill and Dredge both quailed at the rocks, sharing the same surprised expression as they witnessed the furious fireball light up the night sky as it scaled the vertical stone precipice, even setting alight the underside of a nearby tree canopy. Eventually, the hungry fireball calmed, dissipating back to nothingness, though leaving much of the area singed and sizzling with smoke, aglow with embers. The tents were ablaze, simmering like a volcanic emission.

The Berzerkers should have considered themselves fortunate that the location of their ambush of the sentries was not an additional ten feet closer to the tents, otherwise they would have incinerated like kindling.

Ears of the men ringing deaf, nobody immediately detected an unexpected returning threat ...

A surprise and a jump scare to all, one of the original German soldiers revisited the fray from the casualty list. He was the one who had been incapacitated during the initial onslaught, receiving a medieval war arrow to the chest and taken a tumble over the campfire. Perhaps it was the overload of adrenaline, but he managed to recover during the ensuing chaos after being knocked down and winded. His floored abnegation in the snow was conceivably the reason for his endurance of the explosion shockwave, and thus he had become amongst the first to find their feet.

The bodkin-tipped projectile protruded prominently from his chest as he moved, imitating a trundling toffee apple. Churchill's arrow had conceivably perforated his lung, causing his breathing to be extremely laboured. He hissed and wheezed erratically whilst clambering to reach his flung rifle in the blanketing cold sleet that saturated the ground.

Through the struggle, the spiked soldier managed to obtain his discarded weapon just as his unknown shadow attackers recognized his attempt at retribution, and they acted during the commotion.

Black became the first to attain the German's reprised hostility. Stripping off his ski mask from his face for added focus, he reacted calmly by drawing a handgun from a hip holster and cocking the hammer with his thumb, disengaging the safety. Without hesitation, he delivered two loud shots to the German's upper body causing the soldier to shove into the snow and finally die, resting upright with Churchill's arrow erected like a flagstaff.

After an extended moment, in the aftermath of ambient fire crackling, archers Churchill and Dredge lastly arrived from their rocky position on the outskirts of the surprise attack, carefully examining the pear-shaped hot zone of peril. Everybody was dead except the balaclava-clad Berzerkers.

In the glow of the fiery scene, Churchill assisted a snow-covered Calvert to his feet while Dredge supported Komrower in maintaining the outer perimeter with guns drawn, tracing the darkened treelines surrounding the heated vicinity. Danny Boy galivanted through the smoky scene, tracing the many downed enemy combatants with his handgun. The weapon cracked off more than once as he delivered additional bullets into the many corpses, ensuring their eliminations.

Beneath Churchill's aide, Calvert spluttered through the smoke at the deviant's continued delivery of death. "*That's enough, Danny Boy! Fuckin' idiot!*"

Danny Boy's incessant delivery of carnage ceased, standing up straight and seemingly abiding Calvert's wishes—but not before first unloading what was left in his handgun's magazine until it clicked empty into one of the already dead bodies lying alongside a snow-covered log.

Stepping through a gust of wafting smoke, Graeme Black appeared overtop of the body he had just downed, tracing it with the narrow notch sights of his M1911. The keeled German possessed an ounce of life, and so he fired once more into the body for assurance, making sure he was dead this time. The powerful .45 ACP round from the Colt was like delivering a driver to a tee off, striking him with a cloud of snowy mist.

In an almost tranquil state, Churchill sidled up to Black, surveying the body of the man he had assisted in killing. He had never taken a life ...

... *technically still hadn't.*

Calvert stepped in at their rear, sharing their evaluation. His view panned over the other few deceased Germans, and then eventually towards the brightly burning tents behind them by the precipice. Burn marks from the fireball scorched the grey rock face with charcoal dust.

Positioned above the climbing smoke pillar were Ruffell and Scotty.

During the chaos, Ruffell had been sure to pocket his spent Sten magazine so that nobody would come to find it, minimalizing the evidence of their partaking.

The two gunners appeared to be in the process of voluntarily descending the ridge, aiming to rendezvous with the others down by the obliterated campsite. After a moment of review, the men seemed in accord that the job was done.

"*Let's get outta here!*" Calvert exclaimed through the shrill scene of crackling flames and hissing smoke, partly choking on the haze. Considering they weren't even meant to be here and their goal every time had been conducted under the ruse of absolute silence, this amount of ruckus could only end in their immediate discovery. They had to clear the area and fast— disappear into the night like the very ghosts they were believed to be.

They would soon be long gone, with their tracks covered and the dead buried by the falling snow and ash raining down from the night sky.

1940, March
Winterthur Resort, Mont de la Gouille
Swiss Pennine Alps, Switzerland

On the second weekend of the month, the men of the Z Unit had the Sunday off from their vigorous, unconventional training schedule. They currently had no pending visiting specialists from a foreign nation staying at the resort, nobody showing them a new and exciting way on how to break a man's neck with their thighs or throw a bayonet-fitted rifle like a spear with deadly accuracy up to a hundred feet.

Lounging around the fireplace had become commonplace for these hard-working, arguably hardly working, mercenaries, and right now tea and coffee were the agenda. The men wore combinations of relaxed sweaters, slippers, and baggy clothing, smoking pipes and cigarettes. They took up lounges, reading newspapers and magazines, some stood around the many glass windowpanes, watching as the season of spring saw the winter wonderland of Switzerland start to thaw and renewed life and vigour augmenting the lowland landscapes, enriching it with colour.

Steaming beverage in hand, Rushworth put a record on.

Moshe Dayan stepped down onto the carpeted floor from the lobby, having just used the main stairs of the resort from the upper levels. He was dressed in a loosely buttoned-up tucked-in shirt with an open cardigan.

"What tunes have we this morning, Mister Rushworth?" he asked whilst encircling the three-seater lounge. Scotty had been previously occupying all three seats, lying across them with his arms folded and eyes closed over, relaxed. His mohawk haircut was due for a pamper. He respectfully made room for Dayan to sit, dropping his heavy legs off the edge and scooching upright.

Applying the needle, Rushworth leant on the gramophone case, raising a single brow in order to educate the men on what music was about to bless their ears. He removed the smoke from his lips in order to speak, waving it around in between his pointing fingers like a chain-smoking orchestral conductor. "Some good 'ol *Benny Goodman*."

"*The King of Swing,*" dressed in a plain grey tracksuit, Jack Churchill spoke his trivia of music artists aloud. He was located on an armchair by the fireplace, cradling a scotch neat at nine o'clock in the morning, 'cause when in Rome. He wasn't the only one indulging, as Komrower was nearby standing over the fireplace and absorbing the warm radiance. His crystal of golden nectar rested upon the stone mantlepiece.

Impressed by Churchill's knowledge, Rushworth smirked his way with his silver tooth and nodded. "Famous yank clarinettist from New York."

"*Chicago,*" Churchill corrected. He wasn't sure how he knew that, but he was sure the predominantly New York City-based musician did not originate there, and that it was a misconception.

"Whatever. I really dig his rhythmic swing style compared to other artists like *Louis Armstrong* or *Lady Day*. It stands out, y'know? Stronger clarinet solos backed by a big band format, but also not ignoring intricate arrangements and occasional improvisations. Makes it more raw; less rehearsed. Less safe."

Standing by the kitchen doorway was the bald-but-bearded Batey, unceremoniously arranging his nuts. Listening to Rushworth's spiel before making a single comment, he entered gracelessly and found a seat to enjoy his fresh English breakfast tea. "Fuckin' dweeb."

Carelessly enjoying his music, Rushworth flipped him the V and traced his entrance into the comfy common room.

"Isn't it a little early for swing music?" voiced Graeme Black from his position lining a cushioned window seat where he sat cradling a steaming cuppa joe. Dredge was beside him with his knees folded and slippers up, rotating a dirty magazine in order to inspect some titties.

"Fuck," he remarked, out-of-place, and Black's view casually panned onto him. "Who the fuck glued these pages together?"

There was silence. And then Dredge lobbed the magazine at Black's face, slapping him with the supposedly spunk-christened pages to which he recoiled with the reaction speed of any special forces soldier, deflecting it clear.

The men chuckled. Some more than others. The hysterics were more at Black's sudden reaction to the gambit. Their reaction caused for him to lean over and drive a few punches into Dredge's defending sides; boxing his kidneys and causing him to wince.

Descending from above them all, Bort entered from the skeletal spiral staircase connecting the mezzanine floor. He was wearing a dressing gown tied at the front and soft slippers. "Morning cunts," he muttered with his face down, watching the steps as he dismounted.

"*Morning.*"

"*Morning,*" the men responded pleasantries.

Mike Calvert entered from outside, bringing in more firewood. In a ruckus, he tipped it all in the provided timber baskets by the door prior to stripping off his parka and fully entering the lounge room. When he was in the room last, there weren't this many bodies conscious. "Finally awake, sleeping beauty?"

Bort nodded sluggishly. He had a big one the night prior and was heading straight for the coffee pot situated on the serving tray table beside the entrance to the kitchen. Located alongside, Danny Boy was seated in a single cushioned chair connected to a dining table. With his trusty balaclava rolled up into a beanie, he was hunched over the table where he had unfolded a cloth and was presently field-stripping his special handgun. Multiple sized springs, tubes, and various parts were particularly positioned over a laid-out cloth, and he was scrubbing something with a small brush dipped in oil.

"Whoa, nice bust. You're gonna need a bigger pistol handle for that lady's set o' jugs, Danny Boy," harmlessly commented Bort whilst observing over his shoulder, specifically the girl featured in the sweetheart grips of his piece.

It was the monochrome photograph of Scarlet Kristina.

An element of his new infatuation, he had torn out the photograph from the magazine article he had stolen from the fellas the other day, trimmed it, and placed her behind one of his clear pistol grips.

Because Bort's comment was remarked during a stale silence, most of the men in the common room had heard it, and their ears naturally pricked at the mention of boobs.

As far as they all knew, Danny Boy—the misfit—had photographs of his mother inserted behind the acrylic sweetheart grips on his gun. Considering such, the remark made by Bort would have been extremely inappropriate, and thus, they immediately suspected that the recluse had updated his trinkets.

"Where?!" Batey sprung up as fast as he sat down.

Calvert regarded at a grimace. "Aren't they pictures of his mum?!"

Dredge heckled at a chuckle. "That's his mum, ya slack cunts!"

Batey scanned about the room. "Well, now I definitely wanna have a look, eh?!"

Danny Boy attempted to block Bort's attentive vision of his customized sweetheart grips, turning the receiver of the dismantled pistol over and onto the other side—a side that still featured his mother. Whilst he did, he eyeballed Batey concerning that joust about his mother's breasts. He was probably lucky that his gun was disassembled, for he may have just used it out of retaliation.

Bort pointed. "Nah, look! He's changed one of tha sides to a good-lookin' broad!"

"Oi, be sure you face it the right way next time ya go ta have a wank, eh?!" Dredge heckled further, cackling, and paying Danny Boy out while it appeared safe to do so.

Angsty as a prepubescent teen, Danny Boy dropped the metallic pieces he was currently cleaning into the pile and collected the cloth like a canopy, enveloping the whole lot in order to displace and remove himself from the bullies in the room.

The men moaned and expressed their regret in a flurry of apologetic words, encouraging the oddball to remain and stay. Bort placed a hand on his shoulder, supporting and calming him whilst he apologized, and Danny Boy sunk back down into his chair. He would continue with his cleaning project so long as they left him alone.

"Ignore these fuckheads, Danny Boy," Calvert regarded as he orbited the dining table, shuffling a deck of cards in his midst. He pulled up a seat, implying a deal-in. "Who's up for some blackjack?"

"*Me.*"

"*I'm in.*"

"*Yeah, why not.*"

"King's oath, cunt," Graeme Black uttered enthusiastically by the window, finishing his tea in order to join in on the friendly game.

From his relaxed seat in the armchair, Churchill watched this motley group of larrikins partake in a game of cards. Blackjack was often played at night, when the gamblers were mildly intoxicated, and Jack typically profited. He had mentioned before, this lot of hotheads seemed to only ever *hit* and never *stay*. He understood now that they all lived very dangerous lives ... there was no fun in staying.

"Count me in, too," Churchill added, rising up and sauntering over. He had every intention to join this foray and slap every offer to tempt the bust of 21.

On this bright yet brisk, relaxing morning at the resort ...

Whilst the men loosened, laughed, and drank ...

... Dredge let out a big, calming sigh after taking a sip of his steaming tea, panning his view out the large window that overlooked the north entrance out the front of the resort. This included the long, winding driveway ...

His eyes sprung open. His mouthful nearly sprayed.

Nazis!

Meandering along the drive that eventuated at the Winterthur Resort were two glistening black *Großer Mercedes-Benz 770* cars. The six-seater ultra luxury vehicles both had bright red, white, and black swastika flags mounted on their chassis, flailing in the wind, proudly representing their allegiance to the Axis. The driver and passenger's side doors were also decorated by the cross-esque emblem, with four ninety-degree bent arms upon a red circle outlined in white.

It took a full two seconds to process—and swallow his mouthful of tea, which he nearly choked upon—then Dredge let sound the vocal alarm throughout the quiet double-storey log cabin ski resort at the top of his lungs.

"*Oi, fuck! Germans!*" Dredge bellowed, rearing lowly off the window seat and getting down so that they couldn't see him from outside. With concern upon his brow, he pointed out the tall frosty windows that lined the wall. His tone of voice was apprehensive and panicked. "*It's the Germans! They've fuckin' found us!*"

Upstairs, those who weren't in the common room reached the railing overlooking the common area on the upper storey. This included Ruffell's patchy buzz-cut head, Bala Bredin, and Gentle Jerry.

All that could be heard was conjoined stampeding across the timber and carpeted floors all throughout the building.

The surge of panic swiftly filled the tranquil room of soothed mercenaries in comfy tracksuits and open dressing gowns, and the men quickly collapsed their newspapers and rolled off their cushy sofas. They tossed everything they were doing; thrusting down books, magazines, tossing hands of cards, banging down porcelain cups of tea and glasses of drink with a dozen clinks and chinks.

The off-duty Berzerkers reacted cautiously, and with haste, shooting up and into view of the window, pilling into one another with wide eyes in order to survey the alerted new threat. They quickly approached the frost-coated glass that faced the entrance gaining view of the end of the long drive and valet bay out the front entrance hall ...

Black shoved a few of the men out of his way. Always ready for anything, he casually revealed a loaded handgun from his tracksuit waistline and racked the slide loudly, holding it above all their spying heads. After a moment, he mounted the padded window seat, using the hanging curtain for concealment in order to peer upon the enemy.

Through the frosted glass, they inaudibly observed two vehicles as they became visible between much snow-covered saplings beyond the thick slope foliage. The two cars cruised at a steady pace along the private road, about to pull into the valet rink and park ...

Churchill reconnoitred the cautioned view of the arriving cars.

Something felt off. As though this wasn't a threat.

Whether it was the nature of their crawling speed or their choice of vehicle with the flashy Mercedes-Benzes, proudly representing multiple swastikas for all to hail, they weren't being aggressive. Not in the slightest.

"What do we do?!" Komrower asked in a panic. Unarmed, as they mostly were, he was in a low, guarded stance between two of the comfy lounges.

"We're gon' have ta fight 'em," Scotty's Scottish accent regarded fast and stressed, breathing upon all those huddled. "Quick, let's goe an' git some gats! Set up er defensive position en tha lobby! We can bot'le neck 'em!"

"Agreed!" Calvert regarded, attempting to push them away from view of the cars. "Head to the armoury! Gear-up, fast!"

Those present downstairs—Batey, Rushworth, Bort, Komrower, Scotty, Dredge, and Danny Boy—perceived the edict well, concurring it to be the correct course of action and thus indicating a flock of eager agreement. A war here was far from ideal and possibly meant that this base of operations for Wingate's unit had been compromised, but they had no other choice. The two took a step towards the kitchen, where they met the stupefied Bredin, and where they had catalogued their gear like an armoury. It was chock-full of all sorts of equipment and army paraphernalia they could use to mount an ambush for these unsuspecting Germans.

On the dining table, Danny Boy focused up. His hands were like a magician's performing sleight of hand whilst he reassembled his handgun in fast-forward, inserting springs and pinching components a hold whilst applying mechanisms. The handgun came together quickly, and he topped it off by presenting a fully stacked magazine and inserting it, racking the slide like thus to put one in the chamber. Cupping it tactically out before him, he was ready for a war. He took a moment to roll down his balaclava, aligning the cut-outs with his eyeballs.

"*Wait!*" Dayan uttered over the ramping chaos as the men scampered around him like a flowing current, and it stalled their storm to bear arms for a moment. "We're in Switzerland, neutral ground, et cetera. They can't shoot us, even if they wanted to ... right? As long as we're not hostile."

The way he poised the statement was more like a question.

Extant was an undertone of uncertainty that they didn't expect somebody as diplomatically minded as Moshe Dayan to falter with, and hence they opted to err on the side of defence.

"Well, that's the theory, innit?!" Komrower agreed with hesitation.

"I say: let's attempt democracy!"

"Moshe, they're going to think expressly differently when they see the racks of guns and crates of ammo in the back and put two and two together with what we're doing here!" Calvert delegated, and the men seemed to adhere to his expression of preparedness. "I think we need to get ready for war, lads—"

"*Is that any way to treat a guest ...?*" the overbearing voice of Orde Wingate resounded as he unexpectedly appeared overlooking the common space from the mezzanine handrail. Having just emerged from his room due to all the commotion, he was dressed in a robe over neat flannel pyjamas. Sheepishly, still, their fearless leader moved between the other concerned onlookers gathered at the balcony railing, starting to wind down the descending staircase.

Conceivably something wrong with his brain, but Churchill's first thought judged his outfit, questioning how late it was to be still wearing nightdress attire. Disgraceful.

By the curtains framing the window, still standing up on the window seat and cradling his .45, Black queried. "*Guest?*"

Wingate paused halfway and nodded, addressing the men from above. He appeared quite unphased by the arrival of this German convoy presently pulling into the rink out the front of the hotel. In fact, he was expecting their arrival ...

During the pin-drop eerie silence following Wingate's revelation and disclosure to the group, they could hear the resonance of car engines and the squeak of the brakes as the Mercedes' pulled up directly out the front.

"Granted ...... they are a wee bit early. I told them nine o'clock," Wingate excused on their behalf as he took to the circular metal spiral staircase, descending towards the common room space where he strolled amongst the perplexed mercenaries drifting in a holding pattern. They still had their hackles up, ready for a fight, torn between fighting a fresh war and absolute stunned mullet perplexion.

He wore three different wrist watches up one of his arms, searching them for the time.

"It *is* nine o'clock, sir ..." Komrower informed knowledgably.

Wingate's motion ceased so he could doublecheck on one of his many watch faces. In his constant airy state, he made a gasp of revelation, willy-nilly about the entire situation.

Beholding an inverted frown, Churchill leaned in to question their ringleader. "Eh, all those watches and you still got the time wrong ...?"

Wingate's hawking stare sought him, and then gazed upon all the others, in-taking their defensive stances. "I was thinking more of a *warm* welcome."

"So were we ..." Black mumbled as he finally lowered his weapon, safely collapsing the hammer on his pistol with his spare hand. He stood at ease as Wingate passed right in front of him, approaching the raised lobby and the entrance to the resort. This was the same gateway they had all entered at one point or another.

Over the past month, Wingate had invited some odd and eccentric characters from across the globe into the Mont de la Gouille Winterthur resort—some of questionable allegiance to Great Britain and the United Kingdom, let alone the Allied Forces. And now ... *Huns?* This may have been neutral ground, but this was really challenging the limitations of neutrality.

Before they could linger any further on the topic, they feebly watched as Wingate singularly entered the lobby, unarmed, halting just ahead of their varying stances. Alone, he prepared to receive their new guests with (seemingly) open arms on behalf of the Special Z Unit Berzerkers ...

After a few exchanged looks of uncertainty and discomfort, the mercenaries littered about the connecting space each decided to back their ringleader, this time hesitant to follow his overly hospitable lead ...

The heavy doors of the entrance were pushed open from outside.

A duo of distinguished, armed Wehrmacht soldiers dressed in their grey fatigues with winter coats revolved inwards, holding the doors open with gloved mittens like porters. They each held bolt-action Karabiners slung on either shoulder.

After their entry, two men in officers' caps and grey uniforms entered, carting maschinenpistoles across their chests. They marched their knee-high boots in file into the lobby, escorting another skinny German officer in a leather trench coat and cap and an incomprehensibly circular mouth, which, when pursed, could only be described as rectal-seeming. He held the rank of *leutnant (lieutenant)* and seemed to be from another division than the Wehrmacht soldiers, conceivably from the diplomatic-themed *Nationale Bewegung der Schweiz; the National Movement of Switzerland* (a Nazi umbrella-group formed in Switzerland). This guy was a Swiss countryman but pro-Nazi, therefore was likely to have been very well-received within their ranks—and possibly even made their visit into Switzerland a lot smoother. Well-tanned and manicured, with naturally long lashes, he was a pretty boy to say the least.

This man was armed with a pistol on one hip and a holstered sabre on the other, with a closely shaven glatt rasiert appearance beneath a cap slanted like a ponce, complete with a stylish scarf wrap around his neck.

"Herr Wingate?" the leather-clad officer questioned, saluting.

A gesture of hospitality, Wingate greeted with a pronounced bow.

The German accepted the motion, turning to face the light of the gaping doorway in order to wave in the star of the show ...

He announced vocally:

"I prezent, *Oberstleutnant Ernst-Günther Baade ...*"

From the intense outdoor light, entering into the warmly lit cabin interior, the German oberstleutnant *(lieutenant-colonel)* leisurely upped the five short steps that lined the entryway into the log cabin resort, eventually passing between the two opened doors held by the two armed guards. His entrance was suspenseful to say the least.

He appeared to flow like Moses between the parted seas. There lingered an ensemble of armed uniformed German guards in stahlhelms, remaining by the parked convoy outdoors, lighting up cigarettes to pass the time whilst they stood guard.

From around the corner of the connecting common room, more of the Berzerker gang sidled in behind their fearless ringleader as he welcomed their latest foreign visitor, literally, with *open arms.*

Komrower curiously leaned in as he strode, followed by Calvert at his flanks, like snails with stage fright. They each wore the same unsteady expression as they observed the kits of the armed German soldiers. There was an undying animosity that lingered in their eyelines—one that was reciprocated by the guarded Germans.

Black casually promenaded nearer the edge of the lobby, peering in with a laxed gleam and his pistol folded behind his buttocks—just in case. He seemed to exhibit no fear.

Rushworth, Bort, and Batey stepped up into the lobby, filing in before the front check-in counter and behind Wingate like scared children following their daddy. Moshe Dayan was with them, attempting desperately to remain important and foremost.

Scotty and Dredge peeked in next, rubbernecking like a pair of wide-eyed spectators. And lastly, there was Jack Churchill.

Churchill followed their optimistic stares as he stepped out into the open lobby past a few of the idling others. The light of the open doors illuminated his face, causing him to squint whilst he laid his sterling stare upon the silhouetting figure of notorious Ernst-Günther Baade for the first time ... and he became instantly flabbergasted.

Stylishly, Baade entered:

In a jaunty saunter, one hand was tucked into his belt appendage whilst the other swished at the wrist down by his side, almost as though he was clicking away with jazz snaps:

... Officer's cap aslant upon his dome ...

... Top was a Waffenrock (formal dressage) of a German officer ...

... Bottom was clad in a Scottish kilt ...

Churchill's expression flattened.

His head involuntarily tilted as his eyes sunk in deep focus, taking in every detail of this enigmatic reflection from absolute summit top to abyssal bottom, and back again.

... A certain swagger in his step and winning smile on his face ...

... There was even a holstered sword on his hip ...

This wasn't just a German *man* ...

... this was the German Jack.

Ernst-Günther Baade

1940, March
Winterthur Resort, Mont de la Gouille
Swiss Pennine Alps, Switzerland

"Ernie! Welcome!"

Observing Orde Wingate greet the Nazi visitor with open arms was an unsettling sight to see.

Clothed comically in his pyjamas and dressing gown, the off-books British general and on-books entrepreneur shuffled in his socks and slippers towards the decorated, uniformed German oberstleutnant in a Scottish kilt.

The garment was a medium-weight Bruce tartan, Churchill discerned, engaging with a striking combination of (predominantly) red, with green, yellow, and white crisscross.

Their eccentricities resonated in perfect harmony.

"*My old friend, how are you?!*"

"*Orde! Guten Tag!*" with a smile on his naturally rosy-cheeked and plump pockmarked mug, Ernst-Günther Baade returned Wingate's euphoric openhearted beam with the same degree of ear-to-ear contentment. A sinister characteristic, he held a permanent discerning frown upon his weathered brow, which accompanied an unwaivable resting judgemental stare.

The two men appeared to be old friends, reunited. They had history.

Between the awry onlooking mufti-clad Berzerkers and the armed escort of Wehrmacht soldiers—the sworn enemy to these westerners—each respective party observed their commanding officers embracing like long lost relatives. Warmly, they hugged, patted each other's backs, and smiled for an extended moment of overlapping pleasantries before separating only to kiss one another on each cheek in some form of European greeting gesture. They maintained this genuine warmth for the entirety of the exchange, absolutely smitten with the reconcilement.

Amidst, some of the Berzerkers exchanged sly, sideways glances.
What the fuck was happening right now ...?
Sixty seconds ago, they were expecting a very different welcoming:
One concerning guns blazing.

In unison, they were all *confused*, all *unsettled*, and all *willing* to start lighting these krauts up at the drop of a hat and transform this fancy lumber-land lobby into an open shooting gallery. Turn the walls as red as the swastika armbands these fascists wore with pride. Unfortunately, due to their outlandish and inexplicable imposed mediation, it was an itch out of reach, and they were unable to scratch.

After a moment, the two respective COs disengaged their embrace, allowing for Jack Churchill in the background to gain a slightly better survey of this new acquaintance/*adversary.*

To these men, Baade seemed old. Older than Wingate, at least. Maybe late forties. An abundance of acne-scarring on his face made it hard to guess his exact age, nevertheless the paraphernalia across his uniform discerned a great level of warfare experience through service. He appeared to be a recipient of the *Wehrmacht-Dienstauszeichnung-2;* a second-class long service award and a prestigious military service decoration of Nazi Germany. This merit could only have been issued for satisfactory completion of a long number of years in military service, typically two decades minimum. Undoubtedly, this man had fought and survived *The Great War.*

Upon a sustained observation, Baade had pinned to his collar a *Verwundetenabzeichen:* a celebrative wound badge, tinted black. This was a decoration first promulgated by *German Emperor Wilhelm II,* awarded to soldiers of the German Army who were wounded during the First World War. In fact, Baade had served in the *German Empire* until 1918, the *Weimar Republic* until 1933, and now the reign of *The Third Reich.* Furthermore, the *2nd Class Iron Cross* on Baade's uniform displayed a white metal medal clasp. *The Clasp to the Iron Cross* was only awarded to those who had been conferred with the Iron Cross during the First World War, and who again qualified for the decoration once more during service with Nazi Germany. To state that he was loyal to the cause would be an understatement. This bloke was an archangel of anarchy.

Baade was dressed in a uniform garb not indifferent to the standardized Wehrmacht waffenrock attire, however the insignia and division symbolism was all wrong to fit that army regiment. This early into the Second World War, Churchill didn't have a lot of experience reading the deeper classes within the *Kavallerie-Division,* but if he wasn't mistaken, the symbols indicated that Baade was a part of the *Abteilung 22nd Reiter-Regimental.*

Cavalry.

As in, *German horseback combat soldiers.*

Jack's sharp sterling stare continued to graze across the extremities of the enemy lieutenant-colonel whilst he engrossingly exchanged Wingate's pleasantries. There were exchanges in both English and Deutsche.

The next thing he noticed was the attire clothing his lower extremities: *the kraut had a fucking Scottish kilt on!*

What an absolute pseud, Mad Jack thought with a subtle frown skewing his brow, mildly appalled before he reminded himself of his own usual uncommon fashion choices—he literally had packed two different tartan kilts upstairs in his suitcase, saving their brandishing for the right moment of commemorative dressage. This brief deliberation was rationalized by the fact he was an Englishman, with (albeit distant) Scottish lineage. Nevertheless, it was within their grand tradition to parade the Scots—for a Hun to do so was extraordinarily perplexing and rather outlandish.

It was in that moment that Churchill wondered if Baade's selection of Bruce Clan had been due to the colour; the prevalent red matched the same scarlet as the swastika wrapped around his arm.

Churchill's studying of Baade was not absent a lingering sensation of remembrance, like an echo resounding within his skull. He had heard this guy's name before. Somewhere recently. Somewhere tantalizingly, frustratingly close to the cusp of recall. Perhaps it was just the déjà vu of this circumstance; coming face to face with a Nazi with a sword—*the next was the item of great interest.*

Strapped in a baldric-style sheath harnessed around his shoulder and waistline was an extravagantly decorated *langschwert* (longsword).

Albeit customary for German military men to carry sabres, not unlike the British and other armies of the western world. Outside of ceremony, it may have become an outdated armament for warfare on the battlefield, a blade was still very much the standard issue sidearm in the mind of some might consider akin to the old guard.

This, however, was not a *sabre.*

Far from it.

Baade carried a 55-inch, 5-pound, double-edged, single- or double-handed German Langschwert. It was complete with the uniquely styled inverted cruciform hilt that appeared to form an upside-down *Reichsadler (Imperial Eagle).* The heraldic eagle icon was a prominent piece of Nazi propaganda, typically perched upon the prevalent and pungent swastika. In this case, Baade had the piece customized from the venerated 2nd pattern M1937 Luftwaffe dagger. The acronym *SMF* and word *Solingen* had been stamped into the steel of the hilt like a signature. This represented the forgery of *Solinger Metallwaffenfabrick:* the maker and location of the distinctive creation. Solingen was the biggest blade city in all of Germany, also known as *The City of Blades.*

Evidently, the undying and unwavering belief in his nation's cause was the reasoning for Baade's yearning for a customized sword centrepiece; the cruciform of which making the chevron of Nazi Germany.

This guy couldn't be more of a celebrated fascist pig if he tried.

After this moment of affiliation, the two conjoining associated acquaintances from opposing forces ceased their low talking acclamations, and Wingate took Baade around the shoulder with his arm of a half dozen wristwatches, guiding him towards the crowd of Berzerkers at the rear of the lobby hall ...

It was time for the introductions.

"And *these* ...... are my men," he proudly presented.

They watched as Baade's beady brown eyes bounded from beneath his resting sinister brow, inspecting each of the unspoken and predominantly English-speaking westerners. His naturally sceptical stare seemed to snag upon Churchill, hitching for an extension of time, as if he was drawn to something, entangled in his courageous aura.

"Hallo," Baade remarked politely, giving them a quick once over.

A couple of the men returned the pleasantry; gesturing half-hearted signals, however the cold reception was evident. Even Moshe Dayan—the most diplomatic of the lot—offered barely more than a nodding gesture. A few of the more stubborn chauvinists such as Black, Dredge, and Scotty, maintained an estranged distance from their visiting rival, both verbally as well as spiritually. There was a line present that not even Wingate's crazy ideals and malleable morals could sway them to cross. Like with the other foreign visitors of late, they may play nice while they attempt to teach them a thing or two like glorified substitute teachers ... but the only thing presently running through each of their minds was how badly they want to kill this kraut.

After hearing the German fellow's polite welcome, Batey leant into the ears of his nearest peers, Bort and Rushworth. Although it shouldn't have served as humorous, in barely above a whisper, he remarked rather stalely at the man's kind hello: "What a fucking cunt, this bloke, ay?"

Wingate pointed at Churchill. "Him."

"*Him?* Dis is de vone, jah?" in his best English, Baade asked nicely with an extremely thick German accent. He fixated on Churchill, sizing him up further.

A spotlight cast upon him amongst the other Berzerkers, Churchill felt a prudence prowling within Baade's prolonged, pragmatistic gape. It was slightly intimidating, although he held his ground psychologically, giving Baade back the same scrutinizing stare. This exercise may have very well been Switzerland (neutral), but if he wanted a war, he'd find one today.

Wingate's yearning focus drifted from Jack and back onto his German buddy, speaking straight into his open ear hole whilst he slouched on his shoulder like a devoted lover. He even feigned an accent. "The swordsman."

Unimpressed, his stare lingered. Baade seemed unconvinced.

"He iz, eh ... a *zwordzman?*"

Wingate's view floated back to the currently unarmed Churchill.

"Indeed."

Feeling scrutinized, Churchill maintained a firm posture.

Retained his intellectual innings. His scholarly, stoic stance.

During the extended moment of wordlessness, where normally one man would pose a question or at the very least break eye contact, Churchill's brow barely faltered. His eyes only locked further in with Baade, speaking a thousand tales in those few seconds. Words of dubious moral fibre; of perseverance, patience, and a forced optimism towards the German visitor ... but most of all, an unquashable, deep-seated distain ... after all, this was unnatural, and they both knew it.

The latter was obvious to the perceptive Baade.

In a fitting and relaxed tone, the Otter then questioned his cherry-cheeked chum. "When do you wish to begin his training ...?"

Inhaling through his nostrils, Baade's face raised, eyes remaining on Churchill. He finally peeled them from his prey, done with this stare down. He eyed Wingate, saying simply ...

"Now."

Breaking his uncompromising character a little, Wingate's head tilted at the notion, turned on by this spontaneousness ...

Now ...?!!!

Before he could even question Baade's decision regarding schooling Churchill in the art of combat-level swordsmanship—the primary reason he had invited him to the ski resort—the eccentric German swordsman suddenly brushed Wingate aside with a sweep and reached across to grab the hilt of his stowed longsword. With a forte wrench, he drew the five-foot great sword from its scraping sheath with a teeth-grinding *SSCHHHWINGG!* catching the weight out before him with both hands and striking an unexpected battle stance that petrified all surrounding onlookers, both of foreign and domestic allegiances.

The sudden action caught everybody in the foyer by surprise.

Dredge, Danny Boy, Komrower, and Scotty each backed up a few feet, as did Moshe Dayan, who nearly turned tail entirely. Mike Calvert unfolded his arms and reared a step, frozen in utter shock. A lot of the men became suddenly reminded just how unarmed they were at this second.

Baade lowered his sword tip, pointing it at the accused ...

Slowly reacting, Churchill raised his palms out at Baade's accusation.

He had no means to defend himself in a nominal duel.

The surrounding Berzerkers split apart, practically taking any nearby refuge from whatever was about to ensue. They remained mostly calm due to their ringleader's composure. Although surprised by all this spontaneousness, Wingate beamed like a child, enthralled, and watching on as though he wished he had some popcorn.

He amongst them who came the most prepared—Graeme Black—revealed his hidden handgun at the sight of the aggressing German. Holding his ground, he swiftly extended his arm at the sword-wielding Baade, cocking the hammer with his thumb to show he meant business.

The Wehrmacht guards tensed in their stance as the tension quickly simmered to boiling. They saw the weapon aimed at their kommandant—saw he was about to pull the trig—

"*Halt!*" Wingate bellowed throughout the echoic foyer, ceasing all rising adverse reactions to Baade's offensive gesture. This caused his Special Z Unit men to freeze stiff—all but Jack Churchill. An extension of his halt order was targeted at the Germans of Baade's posse, who respectfully responded and mildly stood down with their respective armaments. Next, Wingate aimed his index finger at Black, who was a hair-stretch away from putting a bullet through Baade's cranial orbit at almost point-blank range. "Holster that sidearm, Leftenant!"

After an intense moment of fighting a very domineering intrusive thought, Black somehow tore away his locked stare from the posed hostile, examining Wingate and abiding his superior's orders. Bearing a menacing grimace, he lowered his weapon's sights, flipping the safety with his thumb. The disengagement went against every moral fibre in his body.

Still without the means to defend himself in a swordfight, Churchill maintained his hands out at either side, showing his submission while he exchanged an intense look with Baade. Other than run away, what could he possibly do in this scenario.

Slightly concerned, Wingate stepped in from offside of Baade's guard, inspecting him with startled eyes. "You mean *now* as in now?!"

The eccentric German clutched his blade at the midsection in a plow *(Pflug)* position, glowering at Churchill and locked-on to target. War at first sight.

Was killing his student a part of Baade's expert training?

"Jah," he spat, dagger eyes on Jack. "En garde, Herr Churchill."

"Hardly a fair fight?!" Churchill countered with a sheepish smile, apprehensive about the seriousness of this stand-off considering his lack of steel arm, however he retained a confident poise—as always.

And thus, Baade taught his first lesson. "No zuch thing az a fair fight, Herr Churchill. A zwordzman muzt be prepared at all timez!" Baade snarled, insinuating his lack of sidearm to be his downfall. "Where iz your zword?!"

Churchill scoffed, slightly overawed by the circumstances.

Naturally backpedalling, he took a step backwards from the raised foyer floorboards and down onto the cushiony carpet of the common room. Baade's stance pursued him, his sword blade encircling his altered trajectory like the needle of a compass.

"Apologies. It appears that I am improperly dressed—"

Anticipating a defective response as such, Baade started to shake his head with disappointment. For the first time since his armistice, he removed sight from Churchill and focused onto the uneasy Wingate, who seemed to be dreading his pejorative unacceptance.

Baade said simply: "Was getan werden muss, muss getan werden ..."

< *"What must be done, must be done."* >

With the same shared disappointment, Wingate threw a dissatisfied glimpse at Churchill. One of the first rules he had stressed to him—to all his men—was to *always* be prepared for war. Mad Jack had failed ...

He had invited Baade to teach a lesson ...

... and a lesson had to be taught.

With no choice but to allow this confrontation to occur, for threat of damaging his delicate, dubious arrangements with the acclaimed German, Wingate corresponded with Baade's mentoring importunity. "Do what you must."

And with that, Baade's view returned onto Mad Jack.

Something in his stare was sadistic. "I guezz your firzt lezzon will be a memorable one, Herr Churchill ... for it will be your lazt."

Raising his sword, Baade took a step forwar—

"Jack! ..."

At that dire moment, the calling voice of Humphrey Ruffell sounded from up above like a siren in the deep. His buzzcut-shaved head hanged over the balcony, setting sail to the forces of gravity a *Hail Mary* for Jack Churchill.

Ruffell's shout caught the attention of everybody—even Baade.

Jack's view pivoted vertically, up at the mezzanine railing located directly above his position just as Ruffell let drop an elongated device from the atmosphere above.

A weighty four-foot lateral device housed within a leather holder dove gracefully in the air, dropping fast. The heavier handled end was enough of a hint for Churchill to guess the designation of sidelong weapon as it descended from the heavens like a gift from *Zeus* to *Perseus*. Fitting, as he was just about to clash with a titan.

Ruffell had retrieved his claybeg from his room upstairs!

Mad Jack's sheathed claybeg free-fell from above, gravitating in an elegant freefalling sail straight into his open grasp below, where he caught the weight and quickly adapted his firm grip of the now basket-less hilt.

In a reefing tear, Churchill separated the sword from the scabbard, resuming the harsh eye contact with Baade, albeit with a newly developed sense of confidence now that he was properly dressed.

Before a proper one-liner could be issued between the titular swashbuckler and his newfound sword-wielding alemán adversary, Baade beamed a grin before launching into a sprightly attack.

Steel clashed.

Surprisingly energetic, Baade held back very little.

During the onslaught of slinging steel, he methodically probed to gauge Churchill's ability, form, and experience wielding his sword whilst he defended in parries, blocks, and counters.

With the acceleration of a flattened pedal, Baade continually pranced against Churchill's guard, causing those who remained close to the action to hastily reel from harm's way so that they did not wind up as collateral damage or get run down.

Immediately on the defensive recoil, Churchill shuffled heels-first with his footwork, focusing on receiving the heavy strokes of Baade's brandished longsword as it swished through the indoor air, cutting with shrill whistles.

The steel of their swords clashed ear-splittingly as the two modern-day soldiers engaged in medieval combat within the interior of the lounge room of the quiet ski resort.

Almost two dozen English and German spectators filed in and encircled the lobby entrance into the lounge room, watching with wide eyes of concern, even adjusting their stances behind their modern-day firearms to allow room for this strange contest. The common space was now a bloodsport arena, and it was time to place bets.

Chink!

Ching!

Tang!

For the most part, Churchill parried Baade's attacks with relative ease. He met each sweep at an acute angle of parry, causing his opponent's razor-sharp blade to skim off his own. With every over-arm swing made by the skilled swordsman, his double-bladed langschwert carved through the air with a piercing *whoosh.*

In his defensive posturing, Churchill reared too far too fast.

In his shuffling backpedal, his buttocks collided with the backside of the heavy cushioned three-seat sofa, causing it to budge firm on the floor. With no room left to retreat or withdraw, and after casting a quick glance at the leather lounge blocking his flow, Churchill instead opted to go *over* the furniture rather than attempt skirting it. It was an extreme manoeuvre during an apparent extreme trial, one of which Baade did not see coming.

Right as Baade heaved outwards to conduct another heavy horizontal shoulder slash, Churchill seized the moment to backbend like an acrobat and trundle overtop of the lounge forming a reverse-shoulder roll. The manoeuvre conveniently avoided the incoming slash of Baade's blade through the air and the steel cut with a sharp shrill. Whilst momentarily inverted, his warm lace-less slippers humorously flew from his feet and flung into the high-open air of the room. One hit the hanging parlour chandelier dangling in the centre of the ceiling, the other vanished with a flopping sound becoming an element of floccinaucinihilipilification.

He somewhat stuck the landing with his socked tootsies—his calves pushing into the knee-high coffee table situated before the lounge seating area with a noisy kerfuffle that upset a half-dozen situated mugs on saucers with spoons. The cutlery engaged severe turbulence, clattering around and spilling cold Earl Grey everywhere, enough to smell a sweet bergamot aroma.

Mad Jack revolved around in time to raise his sword en garde.

What the English show pony expected was something akin to a round of applause for his acrobatic performance. What he got was the scary sight of a German show pony charging at him like an enraged taurus seeing red.

Churchill's eyes grew wide as he witnessed Baade rushing him.

Rather than run predictably straight in his assail, the spritely Hun hocked up his pale hairy knee from beneath his red kilt and hoisted himself onto the topmost summit of a neighbouring single-seater sofa, weighing it into a structural tumble with the goal of utilizing its collapse favourably towards Churchill's new static pose.

Right as Baade's summit peaked, standing ten feet tall, the inclining furniture quickly tilted off balance, resulting in him riding the subsiding piece like a spontaneous boost to further engage Churchill, levelling out like a rollercoaster's descent.

Cushions and doilies fell everywhere, adding to the developing mess in the common room. One particular plump pillow even got caught in a cross-swing, exploding in the air like a duck during hunting season. It may have been lightly snowing outside, but feathers floated like snowflakes about the indoor engagement.

In a burst of speed, Baade dismounted the inclination of the toppling sofa and reengaged Churchill, clashing slick steel sweeps with fluent ferocity.

Chink!

Tang!

Their riled blades crossed and collided some more, and once again Churchill was on the backfoot. Unable to look to see properly where he was shuffling his aimless rearward march, Jack managed to bump into nearly every inanimate object and element of furniture in the room whilst the two duelled, making a grand ol' mess.

To remove any boundaries that may have lurked in each man's subconscious, Baade halted in their contest. In a sudden exhale, he lowered his sword into one hand, standing idle whilst he shook his empty wrist, fixing his cuff.

Panting and breaking a sweat, Churchill held his garde at mid, unsure of what to expect next from this strange swordsman while he caught a breath.

"Satisfied?" Wingate hollered from the sidelines. In this scenario, the controlling Otter appeared to barely have his head above water, and it very much seemed as though he feared an element of Ernst-Günther Baade—not the man, per se, but the killer encaged within. An indication of such trepidation was evident within his shaky undertone as he yearned for this impromptu tournament to urgently end.

Baade cast him a quick eye as he inflated into a more upright pose, slightly disengaging the angle of his sword guard.

Across from him, Churchill seemed to slowly relax, adapting to match his neutralizing body language whilst recovering breaths of his own.

After an extended moment of pause ... Baade nodded, facing Jack.

"I can train him ..." with a nodding head, Baade simply put with confidence. He had apparently decided this over the course of their short-lived swordfight where he tested the extremities of Jack Churchill. "But only after one last tezt ... "

Jack's stare twitched, prepared for more of this war.

"Attack mich an!"

"Pardon?"

"*I zed, attack me!*" Baade barked. "*Do not hold back!*"

"So, you want me to kill you?!" Churchill propounded sternly—very willing to follow through.

Baade didn't respond with words.

His lour straightened. The longsword in his grasp became raised and held in both hands, prepared to defend himself against an attack.

Churchill's agile single-handed grip tightened ...

His stare intensified ...

"He'll probably kill him," Black muttered to Calvert at his side as they watched from the arena grandstands. Calvert's head bobbed in agreeance, supporting their fellow Englishman, whereas a little further along the audience ... Wingate knew better. One particular man in this contest was unkillable, and perhaps it wasn't Jack Churchill.

A smile curled beneath his watchful, beady eyes. "Not likely ..."

Jack attacked with a growl.

The spirited lunge of Churchill's was deflected with ease by Baade, sweeping his blade away like dirt off a shoulder. The overswing struck the stone edging of the fireplace mantlepiece, causing a spark and flint of smoke.

Unphased by the failure, Jack sought the energy to swing again, but not after folding low and performing a wanky twirl in attempt at hiding his manoeuvring. He spun and raised a horizontal swipe not intended to make contact with Baade—he expected him to parry it, which he did—this was so Churchill could regain control of his steel on his dominant side.

Churchill reallocated his footing, feeling a little weightless without any footwear on. He danced in a shuffle to angle himself towards conducting a heave, which Baade predicted and ducked low at a knee with ease. His counter-manoeuvre cockily twirled him around on the spot, shifting the fight so that the fireplace was back behind Churchill. The extreme heat at Jack's back distracted him, causing him to quickly attack again, half-cocked and at a tact unplanned.

Perhaps repetition consistency was key?

Jack dashed in close and with small stabs, utilizing fencing form in order to make an incision against this foe, aspiring to draw first blood for bragging rights.

Chink-ching!

Baade swiped away Churchill's obvious, no-nonsense, and absurdly amateurish *Errol Flynn-ish* like fencing flèche attacks, parrying slight with mere manoeuvres of his bigger blade, holding a low octave stance.

Upon a fast revolution in his multitude of movements, Churchill tried something innovative and threw a spontaneous sidekick into Baade's kidney the next time their blades interweaved higher than centre mass. The hoarier German puffed from the admittedly unexpected hit, wincing and winded. It was true that the kick took him by surprise, but an opponent playing grubby during a duel was not all that unheard of. In fact, if successful, it was sign of adaption—especially on someone as qualified as he.

Their blades fast clashed again with much potency and more confidence than before. This time, it was clear that Churchill was out for blood. There was no holding back—as instructed. He was going to give this Hun what he asked for ...

Chink!

Chink!

Chink!

Baade blocked thrice the same downward strike from Churchill.

The attacks told a predictable story, as all swings originating from the same angles, repeating mirrored, which showed signs of repetition and mental exhaustion by the duellist. This was a common culpability of a mediocre swordsman, and Baade had just seen between the cracks of Churchill's armour; the limitations of his aptitude.

On the next obvious swing, Baade intercepted Churchill's slice at an apportioning angle, permitting a defensive descent of their two falling blades and a reengagement of force. Baade twirled his blade, containing Churchill's claybeg within his motion like a conducted wizardly whirlwind of centripetal force. He waved his blade like a magician did a wand, twirling it like a forceful wrist twister with Churchill's stick in the middle.

The action caused Churchill to wince and weaken at the wrist, losing grip of his sword entirely during the whirlwind manoeuvre.

The spinning action followed through, and Baade caused him to disarm. Jack's sword coiled out of his grasp, flailing into the foreground of their outrageous commotion and leaving him stranded with open arms, unarmed and at the mercy of his aggressor.

In finale, Baade jabbed the tip of his sword harmlessly at his beaten opponent's core, poking him minutely to signify a triumphant win of their contest.

There was a certainty in this indication. Baade had won a thousand swordfights in his life; there was no denying that he was truly an amazing swordfighter—world class, to say the least. The unteachable manoeuvre he had just performed to remove Churchill's weapon from his grasp confirmed that he was so adroit with a blade, that he could have chosen to do that at any point in their fight ...

Churchill acknowledged this.

Baade had been in control the entire time.

Wholly disappointed in himself, Churchill's breathless stare finally lowered, glancing about and to where his weapon—and slippers—had ended up.

The stahlhelm soldiers with the officers' caps and maschinenpistoles and the skinny leutnant with the rectal mouth who had announced Baade's entrance, applauded from within their improvised and motley audience. It was plausible that this was not the first sword show they had seen their kommandant put on.

Of the Berzerkers amid the applause, some joined in and chuckled. Many of them, however, watched the wehrmacht men vacate, still hung-up on their prejudices about their nation's enemy.

Baade absorbed their combined praise, finally lowering his weapon downwards and forming a smile. After holstering his sword in his hanging scabbard, he reached out and offered Churchill a honorary handshake to conclude their competition.

Finding it physically difficult to hide his reluctance, Churchill inched forth, accepting the man's hand and shaking it firm. They locked eyes and swapped half-baked smiles, in that instance reading between the lines of this ritual formality. After all, Jack Churchill used to be an athlete before the war. It was very possible that he was better versed in good sportsmanship than Baade at this juncture, and perchance he might have bought his honesty in acknowledgement and recognition of the victory.

Their hands fell apart.

Baade peered away ... *Churchill's smile receded.*

Extant was unprecedented hatred for the Nazis, sure. But a loathing none like the nature he felt for his own insolvency. This was now the second swordfight in his life he had ever partaken ...

... it was also the second he had lost.

Piercing the rainy calm of the night skies above Oranienburg, an electric flash of lightning flickered dramatically, illuminating the dark grounds of the Sachsenhausen Concentration Camp below like a flashbulb camera blink.

The rainfall outside the prison barracks created a rhythmic resonance that could have been soothing if it were not so loud upon the irregularly layered sheet metal tin roof, which had numerous leaks.

Enclosed by the barbed wire fence perimeter, the many ligneous barracks buildings within the detention estate entombed thousands of inmates, attempting slumber. A furry-faced and weathered Lieutenant-Colonel Jack Churchill and official war correspondent Felix Hardy were amongst them, still passing the time by recounting and recording the unstoppable warpath of Jack Churchill's unkillable life leading unto this moment post-capture.

"You know," Hardy's American accent said, mildly interrupting Churchill's retelling of his secretive past in 1940, "if I hadn't had been there to see you fight Feind in Vågsøy, I would have thought you pretty useless with an edged weapon ..."

Unable to argue that point, Churchill took no insult. Contrary, he found Hardy's stab rather humorous. Across the darkness of the bunks, Jack's ageless sterling stare scanned the writer as he jotted notes in his notepad.

"Looking back, I was still pretty bollocks with a blade ..." he confessed with a wholesome grin of the pleasant youthful recollection, followed by an overshadowing element of abhorrence that caused the beam to become consumed by said shadow. "... then Baade stepped in."

Through his cracked spectacles, Hardy observed Churchill intently as the now-hardened soldier again touched the scar indentation on his right cheek; the relevance of which we may soon hear about.

"So, all I'm hearing is that the reasoning for your indictment was justified for the two constables from the investigation branch. A Nazi *did* train you."

"Remember, it was early 1940, lad. Before the publicity of their horrific atrocities. Before I hated them with the distaste I do now. I wasn't a fan, nevertheless, if I could learn a thing or two from a grand master swordsman—

for free, mind you—what was the worst that could happen. Also, you best learn firm from your master. Natural progression is for the student to exceed the master ..."

After he granted Churchill a moment, Hardy asked for more.

"Granted. What happened next?"

"Baade stayed at the resort ... he taught me things ... helped open my mind to what swordsmanship was really all about—I mean, to a spiritual degree. The man had studied swordsmanship the world over, there was no aspect to the field that he didn't have a relevant platitude, proverb, or sentiment to share. He would often quote works by a German author named *Johannes Lecküchner*. I truthfully had no idea before then, you see, it's not about *swashbuckling* and *foot-stepping*. It's about balance, discipline, control. It's about maintaining the ravaging, ravenous beast inside, whilst also starving it, torturing it, even ..." Jack admitted the admiration as he reverently remembered in-depth details from the Switzerland sessions. "The thing about swordplay is that everybody thinks they can do it until they realize they can't—I found that out the hard way in Oslo," Jack said, forever humbled.

Hardy held off penning the details for a moment. Rather, he sat up straighter, really listening to Churchill's found wisdom concerning mastering the art of swordsmanship.

"One of the first things Baade said to me that really sunk in was the misconstruing of the act of sword-fighting. What men throughout history don't realise when they pick up the instrument, even up until their likely demise whilst wielding the blade against an opponent, is that it's not a simplistic artform. It may seem it, but it's much less a brute game of *checkers* as it is calculated *chess*—and that metaphor really stuck with me. It was not hugely different to how Colonel MacLeòid trained us with *Excalibur* in Burma. Sure, there is physical balancing to consider, your footing and so on, obviously there are necessary things like speed, agility, and of course strength enough to wield the steel ... but all that means sweet Fanny Adams if there is no foundation for you to stand on ..."

Hardy prepared his snub-nosed pencil while he watched Churchill slip back into a deep sense of nostalgic reminiscence, passion, and of a genuine love for the artform.

"... It's about both *physical* and *mental* conditioning. There was a level of awareness to your environment and the cause and effect that one might have to your surroundings that may help harness an advantage; like putting the light of a setting sunset in your opponent's eyes, putting their back into the wind and what have you. *Confidence* and *deception;* that expecting a 'fair fight' was a definite arrogance to get you killed in a duel, however respectful of the customary rubrics your opponent may carry in conviction. Historically, trickery and dirty tactics were not only expected during traditional swordfights, but it was also par for the course. Next was *rhythm of the dance,* or more accurately, the lack of such. Falling into a predictable pattern was a condemnation to the clashing of steel. One too many right steps in a deadly dance of duelling could get one run-through when your opponent comes to predict it. *Intimidation, timing,* and *distance.* Simple enough, eh? That one needs little explanation. But learning when and how to strike, or not strike, at the right time, and being close enough to actually hit your intended target zone is a skill in and of itself. Last lesson was a disciplinary one; *maintaining a mindset of constant caution*—not to be confused with *timidity, hesitance,* or *cowardly,* but rather always having enough good sense to *never* underestimate your blade-wielding opponent."

"That all sounds ... exhausting."

"That's the theory part. You learn all that before even brandishing heavy steel and swinging the blade around your head," Churchill tittered before staying the course of his unravelling regarding the shared sagacity of the infamous Ernst-Günther Baade. Returning to the topic of the man from the wisdom caused Churchill's face to fall flat. "Baade stayed at the resort for only a week—wait, not even. Five days, maybe, if I recall correctly ... whatever it was, his stay was too long."

"Not too long to be able to train you, clearly ... develop you ... help you to hone your skills ..." Hardy justified, but Churchill wouldn't have it. He couldn't see through the fog of Baade's everlasting transgression—a story element of which we were on the verge.

"We trained one-on-one for days," Jack bobbed his head as he recollected, proud and certain of some aspects, but appearing to be nearing the rupture responsible for the rippling effect that would start a tidal wave. The snowball to provoke an avalanche. "By day five, Baade had overstayed his welcome ..."

'Ernst-Günther Baade, for all his unfavoured loyalties and wrongful allegiances with Germany making him forever the enemy, even in neutral collaboration, succeeded in developing Jack Churchill's skills with a sword. After the wild entrance and spontaneous swordfight in the resort lounge, Baade trained Jack outdoors, starting from scratch. He was a wise wielder of the weapon, citing his acquired knowledge from all aspects of both domestic and foreign, modern and ancient swordsmanship practices that he had studied over decades. From the Olympic sport of fencing: the foil, the epee, and the sabre, he had studied The Way of The Sword, or Kendo as it was known in

Japanese. This had involved the use of bamboo swords known as shinai in place of traditional samurai swords known as katanas. He claimed The Art of Swordsmanship by Hans Lecküchner one of his favourites, inspiring Baade to learn the medieval art of Broadsword sword-fighting, including the implementation of maces, bludgeons, pikes, and poleaxes. The man even boasted studying Haidong Gumdo, the Korean art of swordplay, a fighting style derived from the Japanese arts of battoujutsu, iaijutsu, and kenjutsu. Needless to say, he was an absolute god in the practice, and presumably unkillable ...

... and as it turns out, this was a practice that Churchill and the men of Berzerker would soon desire to test ...'

1940, March
Winterthur Resort, Mont de la Gouille
Swiss Pennine Alps, Switzerland

The arrival of spring caused much of the Switzerland snows to start defrosting beneath morning sunrays. The enriching colours of renewed life shifted the winter landscapes they were so used to seeing over the past three months. Ice and snow had been all they had known.

After an early morning sparring session—their last solo session—Jack Churchill and Ernst-Günther Baade returned to the resort, trekking through a connecting valley runoff from the surrounding hills. The transitioning weather saw much of the lowlands visible from the heights of the Mont de la Gouille appearing quite vibrant and searing with reddening tips of auburn and green. The sun was out, bright and balmy. Looking into it provided a new radiance, papercutting one's eyes unlike it had done in this sector of the world before.

Where they were, at altitude, was still brisk and icy. Snow still layered the floor, their boots crunched through it, and icicles still hung beneath tree branches, albeit now visibly dripping in their defrosting state.

From the radiating heat of physical training, Churchill wore one less layer now, with his parka unbuttoned at the clavicles.

After making the mistake of glancing at the sun, he found and put on his circular tinted alpine sunglasses and looked to his right, seeing Baade had done the same with a pair of Meiss-branded ski goggles with celluloid eyepieces. It was an odd style. The world would have seemed very yellow to him.

Dressed in unmarked civilian clothing, as he was during the entirety of his stay, Baade had stopped to take in the view from the Alps.

At a clearing of trees on their track that opened up over the lower valleys, he paused in their trudge in order to take in the vast sight with one of his gloved hands resting upon the holstered hilt of his silver longsword; the customized chevron cruciform positively shimmered in the sunlight.

He commented, flabbergasted. "Wunderschön."

Churchill meandered over, standing beside him with his own basket-hilted sword upon his hip. "This your first time in Switzerland, Ernie?" he asked, also inspecting the breathtaking panoramic view. There seemed to be room to breathe regarding conversations with this imposed mentor of his, now that their time had come to pass—and, admittedly, Churchill was grateful for the lessons. He had learned an immeasurable amount of knowledge.

Baade maintained a smile, appearing almost transfixed.

This was a holiday for him, and so he soaked in the serenity.

"Nein ..." he shook his head. "Juz virzt time zeeing zee zpring."

After an extended moment of admiration of the view, Baade's attention lowered, sighting the wooden walls of the snow-capped Winterthur Resort in their midst. The fireplace was on, sending a grey fume plume into the sky like a smoke signal, bringing them home and to the warmth.

"Let'z fortfahren," Baade stated in partial German, as he often did, indicating progression towards the resort. "Orde wants uz all prezent for hiz inztruction thiz morning."

"More training, eh?" Churchill remarked at the risk of sounding jaded. Whatever instruction Wingate had planned this morning was likely a little different, perhaps a final training session or a show of skills for their visiting Nazi maestro before he set sail. They were due to depart Switzerland by sunrise the following morning.

Baade concurred. "Knowing Orde, zen ja."

Churchill frowned. A strange sensation had overcome him these past few days—a manifestation of a constant transformation he had undergone during his entire time spent becoming a Berzerker within the Special Z Unit. "Ernie," he started, sounding a lot like a parting declaration. Gentlemanly quality was something he wasn't above acknowledging, even to an adversary. "I want to thank you."

Baade's round head turned to face him with his beady brown eyes through his yellow-tinted sunshades. He remained stoic at first, indicating that this overshare by Jack Churchill may have been undesirable, however, his heavily pockmarked skin formed a smile. "You ... wizh to tell me thiz *now*, privately, and not in vront of your friendz, eh?"

If it wasn't for Baade's chuckle following his delivery, Churchill would have preserved that statement as sincere and critical.

His statement carried with it some underlining truth.

There was a healthy disdain between the English and the foreign guests who had attended Wingate's Winterthur Resort. Obviously, this zenith visitor from Nazi Germany was among that derision. There were unspoken rules about affections shown and respects paid. It had to all remain superficial. Truth was, they probably each allowed themselves to like one another because their minutes were now numbered. This was the end.

Although what Baade suggested about confidentiality was true, Jack took mild offence to being outed as one such poseur. "No, I mean it. Thanks for sharing your knowledge."

Baade accepted his sincerity and bowed. "Bitte sehr, Jack. Zwordzmen are becoming a dying breed in thiz modern war ..." he shared insight he had collected over his many years in service, and what he predicted. "Zee world lackz decorum. Lacks ztyle. Warfighting iz changing for zee worzt."

Churchill reeled ...

This guy spoke about war much like he did; over-romanticisms and a charmed, charismatic approach, unlike most modern dutiful soldiers.

"Bezides," he furthered with an ironic snicker, "who am I going to zwordfight on the battlefield if I do not have formidable adverzariez like you, Mad Jack, eh?"

Forming a beam, Churchill huffed out his nostrils.

A strange, paradoxical contrariety existed in this happenstance.

What was stranger was that it comforted men like them.

By the time they arrived at the Winterthur Resort, the atmosphere was more sombre than Churchill had anticipated. He had thought to be walking into another of their ringleader's circus acts, imaginably a flamboyant competition for Wingate to display his show ponies to his guest.

Instead, the environment was unreceptive, almost hostile.

"What's happened?" Churchill asked three of the Berzerker men who were standing by the resort deck, seemingly in exile. They were Bort, Batey, and Rushworth, respectively, each sharing a lighter to smoke some cigarettes.

"I dunno, they booted some of us out," reported Batey, stroking his beard after firming the beanie upon his skin head.

Churchill looked left and out to the open strip behind the resort building. Now that there was marginally less snowfall of a night, the area which appeared to be a leisurely flat surrounded by some natural retaining walls before the gardens stretched into forest had been set up with a trestle table and some chairs, with several arranged duffel bags of gear. Something had been orchestrated and planned to be happening outside, but those plans had been thwarted by something unforeseen, still unseen by Churchill.

Before Churchill could question further, Baade upped the creaky ligneous steps to the exterior deck and immediately opened the door to gain entry inside the resort. Churchill quickly followed, catching the closing door.

Barely stripping off their snow gear, the two sword-sheathed soldiers waded through the kitchen space/Bala's armoury, where Bala Bredin was leaning on a counter with a cautioned look about him. He eyed them wordlessly as they slinked through into the wide-open lounge area, where the atmosphere was bristling.

In a sudden gust, both the warmth of the temperature from the fireplace and the coldness of the staleness in the air hit all respective men indoors.

Wingate was present, as was Moshe Dayan.

The two delegates of the unit were openly discussing some sort of incident with Baade's leutnant: the ambassadorial from the National Movement of Switzerland with the rectal mouth, who was uniformed in his dutiful leather trench coat and cap, pistol on the hip. He had returned, escorted by what seemed like the same few maschinenpistole-carrying Wehrmacht soldiers in their grey uniforms and knee-high boots.

The leutnant seemed overwrought and had been yelling. His glatt rasiert face was red from the strain.

The ponce saw Baade enter and was instantly relieved, stepping in to engage with him in their natural dialect whilst Wingate, Dayan, and Calvert spoke inaudibly, shaking their heads.

Churchill couldn't make head or tail of their conversation; however, he did notice that there was quite an audience within the lounge room and connected lobby. Behind the two Wehrmacht soldiers were another two by the door, that was open, and a German vehicle was parked out front along with a further ensemble of armed soldiers.

Inside of the room were some Berzerkers; Bredin in the kitchen, Komrower, Black, and Dredge occupied the centre lounge, each sitting as though they had gotten in trouble by their principal and there was an issue up for debate. Scotty was on the armrest, armed with the same furrowed brow, narrowed eyes, and pursed lips as all of the other men. Ruffell was leaning on the wall next to Danny Boy, who was seated in the armchair besides the fireplace with his beanie rolled up. Gentle Jerry occupied the other armchair.

"What's going on, lads?" Churchill finally asked.

"*Him!*" the pretentious diminutive voice of the well-spoken, rectal-mouthed leutnant targeted a finger at Mad Jack. "Zat one iz zee archer."

Frowning, Churchill scanned about quickly whilst he stood idle and perplexed, noticing that the Germans had confiscated from his room upstairs his brown leather archery quiver full of bodkin-tipped war arrows, as well as his strung six-foot conifer yew bow.

They were his possessions.

He frowned, furious. "Oi!"

In the same second that things seem to erupt, Baade weighed an anchor on his leutnant's directed finger, pulling down his arm and silencing him in order to exchange several quiet words concerning reprove. There arose an apparent ulterior motive to their visit.

Wingate broke away from Dayan and Calvert, taking several steps towards his understandably upset man. "Jack. Please, remain calm!"

"Pardon?!" Churchill grimaced and jabbed his own finger in their direction, insinuating a misconduct in their favour. "They've gone through my belongings!"

The gunsel-esque leutnant stepped forth and exclaimed in a higher pitch and stronger volume now that Baade was present. His delivery was confident and in a more direct tone compared to any other instance he had opened his mouth, typically hesitant. This time, he spoke with conviction, expressing authority without uncertainty. There was a passionate investigative tale afoot, and Churchill was apparently now a suspect. "You mean to tell uz, that thiz bow, theze arrowz ..." he collected the quiver and longbow from a guard and carted them over for exhibit, "... are not zee zame as zee one I have upztairs?"

Churchill courted. "Sir, that is unknown to me, for I do not go through the possessions of others without their express permission! Well-manners and respectful behaviour that seems to have gone unchecked by yourself and your respective goons!"

Wingate interjected with a slanted gesture, eyeing Baade.

It was apparent that Baade knew little of the circumstances surrounding this event. There had obviously been an ulterior motive present for these Germans' visit to the resort. They were investigating something ...

He held up a finger. "*Die Geister mitten in der Nacht: The ghosts in the dead of the night* ..." he alluded quite portentously. "These men, they appear and vanish. They haunt zee dreams of zoldiers along the Italian and Switzerland boarder. Death by snow hound and zee reaping of zee due, dragging them to Hell for their sins—"

"Pardon me, sir, but what the fuck are you talking about?!" Churchill chuckled in an exhale of exhaustion. He eyed Wingate and the others— Calvert, knew exactly what the leutnant meant. As did Churchill, but the act sold.

The leutnant held a digit vertically, nice and firm. "Ve have proof!"

A Wehrmacht guard emerged with his gun slung over his shoulder.

He carried a crate with his hands, sealing the lid of the contents ...

"A projectile munition left behind at the scene of their most recent atrocity! A war arrow, fired by an archer."

Churchill, Calvert, Black, Dredge, Scotty, Ruffell, Jerry, and Danny Boy, each exchanged sly glances amidst themselves. The sly gesticulation did not go unnoticed by Wingate, Dayan, and anybody else present in the room who was not a part of these special nocturnal activities. The tension was so thick that it could be cut with a butter knife.

Baade cautiously lingered, wanting to see the contents of this procurement for himself. The guard opened the crate. He had not pegged Jack Churchill for the murderous type and, quite frankly, exposure as such may have excited him.

The carton opened.

It was empty.

"*Was zum Teufel ...?!*" the leutnant leant in aggressively, rifling the straw packaging with his hand like a madman. The crate was empty. Even the guard lifted his stahlhelm-strapped chin over the opened lid, inspecting the now empty container.

Confused, Churchill frowned.

He quickly eyed around the room.

They had him dead to rights here—if they matched one of his arrows to those stows in his ammunition, it was a smoking gun. Some sort of suspicious intervention had occurred behind the veil, implying an inadvertent alleviation to his undefendable guilt.

The Berzerker brothers stationed around the place seemed a little disarrayed. More than half the people here were accountable of committing war crimes against conduct of the Geneva Convention; a statute obeyed and respected by the United Kingdom and the British Army. It was an offence punishable by death, and that wasn't speaking for capture and prosecution by the Axis ...

Baade stepped closer to his sheepish leutnant, and they exchanged short, stern words. The leutnant raised his voice and became shooshed by Baade, who yearned to now take control of this situation before it became embarrassing, now the judge to his conduct.

He casually turned to Churchill.

His beady eyes read him, like they had been this entire intervention.

Mad Jack may have been culpable of firing the arrow that killed his countrymen; however, he was certainly not guilty of stealing the evidence. That *had* to have been somebody else; somebody either with much to lose by the exposure ... or, even better, they wanted Churchill to take the fall as a scapegoat for evidence tampering.

This was quite serious ...

As they all dwelled on the gravity of the indictment, Baade literally cut through the nonsense by withdrawing his executioner's blade with a diaphragm-shuddering *SSCHHHWINGG!*

Everyone in the room stood up straight and clenched their buttholes.

Preparing for a defence, Jack's non-dominant hand subtly elevated to encompass his sheathed sword hilt ...

"Zee theft of zee arrow ... iz a cowardly act," Baade deduced, casually assessing the razor edge of his longsword whilst he strut into the centre of the lounge room courtroom. "Zerefore and thuz, I know beyond a zhadow ov a doubt Herr Churchill did not commit thiz crime ov theft."

His stare rested upon Churchill.

With respect, Jack bowed his head.

"Neverzeeless, zee crime outstanding—zee murder ov my countrymen in zee dead ov zee night—iz ztill undetermined and punizhable by zee *law of retaliazion.*"

Jack's stare raised unto Baade ...

An eye for an eye, he was literate to *lex talionis* and believed him more than capable.

Revolving in his pacing, Baade sidled and murmured something to his leutnant's ear, and he reluctantly stepped forth, passing Churchill his confiscated longbow and quiver of arrows. Beneath a heavy brow, Churchill observed the act of custody, hesitant to touch the possessions at the disposal of the Germans as though it were some kind of trap.

"Herr Churchill," announced Baade, acting very much like detective *Hercule Poirot* whilst he worked the room. "Who in this room doez not like you?"

"Nonsense, Ernie. Everybody likes me."

"It vould appear that zombody doez not ... hence zeir attempt at framing you, and thuz getting you *killed* by my hand or the hand of my soldat."

Churchill's view drifted ... floating through the air before finally landing involuntarily upon Graeme Black, standing opposite his discomposed self.

When everybody followed the line and looked towards him, Black felt the walls close in. It suddenly made perfect sense; this guy *hated* Mad Jack Churchill—always had—since the very first moment he had entered the resort. On numerous occasions, he had vocalized and demonstrated this through constant harassment and victimization.

"Fuck you all peepin' at me for?" Black reared up. His hand felt for the handgun tucked into the back of his pants. "I may be a bastard; but it doesn't mean I stole anything from these stupid fuckwits. Only thing I'd be taking from your room at night would be your life. No offence."

Sword in hand, Baade rotated around to analyse Black.

He had never vocalized it, but he had always sensed his disdain towards Nazi Germany the most out of all of Wingate's Special Z Unit. It was very likely that both he and his Wehrmacht kamerads would take great pleasure in eliminating this one in particular—

"No, wait ..." intervened Churchill. He locked eyes with Black, discerning an influx of anxiety as it flushed through his body, turning him redder than a throbbing knob.

... Out of focus to Jack Churchill whilst he reclaimed the spotlight to this theatrical production of whodunit, Danny Boy gradually reached up and tugged down his balaclava ski mask to cover his face. He next silently raised to his feet, subtly vacating the vicinity ...

Successfully creating a hiatus of persecution, Churchill's eyes scanned the toxophilite offering still held out before him. He took a breath whilst he considered something existential, listening intently to the atmosphere in the room for a solid few seconds, before ...

His peripherals noticed movement ...

His investigative mind fathomed, and ...

His lips uttered: "*Where do you think you're going ...?*"

With hands of lightning, he collected his longbow and a singular arrow from the open quiver, nocked, and loosed an arrow out to his side with a sprightful *Sch-TOFF!* that was deafening within these quiet quarters.

The striking arrow caused all to flinch, but none as much as Danny Boy.

Abrupt as a bolt of lightning, the singular arrow punched a hole into the wooden cabin interior wall directly in the discreet balaclava-clad absconder's mouse-scurrying path, causing him to stop dead in his stealthy background exfiltration.

The spotlight of interest fell upon him.

His faceless head glanced around; his eyes telling a tale of culpability.

The guilty.

Calling their bluffs, Danny Boy suddenly sought the urge to run, picking flight over fight. He was almost instantly met by Bala Bredin emerging from the kitchen/armoury, and he was carrying a rather large cannon-like device which had come in from the latest MD-1 shipment.

Witnessing the sixty-millimetre smoothbore barrel mouth of the device, Danny Boy's balaclava eyes decided to indicate surrender. He did not know how to fight that weapon—it could have fried his brain with incendiary phosphite ammunition for all he knew. Slowly, he raised his palms skywards.

"Your move, Danny Boy," breathing calmly through his nose, Bredin remarked, continually issuing the weapon at his face at almost point-blank range. It was enough to make the accused arch backwards an inch. "You like this?" he incited the big weapon. "It's a prototype. Even I don't know what it does."

Wingate appeared overwrought with disappointment.

Rage boiled his blood at this instant.

Standing within proximity of swordsmen Baade and Churchill, he voiced a stern directive to men both foreign and domestic. "Seize that man!" he pointed and watched as the elusive Danny Boy befell enforced restraint by nearby Berzerkers, then offered transference into the custody of approaching Wehrmacht custodians armed with stowed maschinenpistoles. "He's all yours, Ernie. Do what you will with this scum ..." Wingate

addressed Baade, who then ordered his people in German to process the
prisoner and take him away.

This was the last time they saw the man known as Danny Boy.

Wordlessly, the balaclava-clad criminal allowed himself to be ushered
away by the Germans, who escorted him out with a guard grappling
underneath each of his tensely enfolded arms. Through the two holes cut in
his ski mask, his eyes beamed back, involuntarily panning across the Special
Z Unit men left in his wake—explicitly those guilty of the same unspoken-
though-alluded to atrocities as he was. He had always kept to himself, and
none of his actions until now caused any of the men to question his integrity.
The real dog act existed in his attempt at framing Jack Churchill and Graeme
Black for theft of intelligence from their foreign visitors. For this act of
betrayal, he risked the incrimination of his entire unit, including Orde
Wingate.

Frustratingly, there was no clear motive for his actions. Conceivably,
during the intervention of incriminating evidence disposal, he got too greedy,
selfishly allowing for his personal feelings to get in the way. Thus, he
attempted to hang it on his personal enemies within Berzerker.

A unanimous sigh of relief sounded throughout the Winterthur Resort,
and during the restoration of warmth, Wingate approached Churchill along
with Calvert in tow. Black and Dredge were near, along with Komrower,
Ruffell, and Scotty within an intended eavesdrop. There was a vindicative
demeanour about him, one carrying a stern directive and yearn of course
correction. "*The ghosts in the dead of the night,* eh ...?" he questioned
plainly, first eyeing Jack and then scanning about the rest of the men. He had
apparently heard of the same rumour that gave nightmares to the enemy.
"Heard they were ...... dead?!"

Nobody exclusively denied a thing.

Responses inundated the Otter.

"*Yes, sir.*"

"*They are, sir.*"

"Good!" Wingate grumbled, and then tingled their spines and stood the
hair on the backs of their necks. "Because I would hate to have to make
double sure ..."

Churchill queried. "Sir, what's going to happen to Danny Boy?"

Wingate's face turned. His famously unblinking eyeline hovered for
longer than it needed to before wandering to spectate the scene through the
big glass window as the Germans loaded the guilty member into the rear of
the car outside. It seemed as though Baade and his fancily dressed
ambassador from the National Movement of Switzerland were going to
perform their due diligence and take him away for questioning.

"Surely, we cannot let them take away one of our own ...?"

Wingate confronted Churchill and the others. He seemed incredibly frustrated by this show of disloyalty and offered little sympathies. "Danny Boy ceased being *one of our own* the moment he committed a dog act."

Churchill stated boldly, acknowledging the elephant in the room who had apparently gone unnoticed in a trees for the forest sense. "But, eh ... he may tell the Germans about us ... is his capture and probable interrogation not a potential problem risking our exposure?"

"It is, but only as much to us as he is to the Germans present in that motorcade," Wingate cocked his head, adding assuringly with a pat on Churchill's unwavering arm. "Relax, Mad Jack. Do you know how they make Swiss cheese?"

Jack blinked. Although he understood the harrowing example depicting the death of Danny Boy at the hands of many automatic weapons, his intellectual mind tripped up on specifics. "The holes are made by gases during the aging process?"

Wingate eyed him with his empty stare. Offered him his Cheshire cat grin. "He won't make it to Deutschland. Ernie will see to it."

Churchill judged Wingate, then ogled Dayan, and even Calvert.

Danny Boy was about to be erased from existence.

After a solemn silence that reminded all those present of how expendable they truly were during this black operation, Wingate clapped his hands together, refreshing the mood with some optimism. "Well, then. Who's up for a game of cricket in the yard?"

Everyone stood unmoving. Too shocked to react.

There was an underlying degree of trauma existent after this monumental occurrence; both witnessing what was effectively of Danny Boy's end, as well as almost meeting that end themselves, had exposure of their clandestine activities become exhumed.

Wingate's sport suggestion wasn't optional. It was an order.

He led the way.

Although their preference wasn't born of impulse, the men departed from their collective stances and followed suit. Scotty, Gentle Jerry, Dredge, even Komrower were fast to move on from the loss of Danny Boy. Perhaps impermanence was much more commonplace to these other well-oiled killing machines than it was to more ethical, honourable men, such as Churchill.

"*Batter up!*" Gentle Jerry exclaimed joyously whilst they headed towards the back doors, filing through playfully ahead of the others. Calvert looked cockeyed to him with a show of repulsion.

"*It's cricket, not baseball, ya knobhead.*"

"*Isn't it the same thing?*"

"*Ha. Yeah, sure, mate! You can go first, eh?!*"

Calvert snagged in their migration, noticing that Churchill was yet to start gravitating towards the backyard unlike the rest. Their inclination to advance was metamorphic. "You alright, Jack ...?"

Through the glass, Churchill finished watching the Germans close all the doors of the car and begin driving away. This would be the last time anybody saw Danny Boy alive. The compelling influence of communal discompassion was a euphoric experience for Jack Churchill—he couldn't believe what he was seeing and was a part of. Even though he had tried to betray him, it still felt like they were willingly leaving a man behind. To him, it felt unnatural, and he couldn't shake or come to terms with it.

Moshe Dayan peeled himself away issuing an unpleasant gesture at the car through the window, muttering something in Arabic that sounded a lot like *good riddance* and the body language to match. "*Khalas jayid.*"

With nothing to say, Churchill finally looked at Calvert.

Ruffell also remained, feasibly loyal to his mates and awaiting their attendance. Black was standing within the same vicinity, seemingly prepared to try and tolerate another one of Mad Jack Churchill's rants about honour or ethics, just like he had about the Italian family departed in the Aosta Valley.

So, instead, Churchill bowled them a flipper.

"Supercalifragilisticexpialidocious," Jack said (not so) simply.

Those nearby were stupefied.

"Did you just have a stroke?" Calvert uttered, visibly perplexed.

Churchill formed a beam beneath his pencil-thin moustache. His crooked humour may have been the cure right now to get him past this atrocity in scrupulousness. The intellectual in him took over, and he quoted the author. " '*A-muse-ings'*, by *Helen Herman.*"

If King-Clark was here, he would have got a kick out of it.

"Is that some sort of smart-speak or is that the sound she made gooned-up, falling down the fuckin' steps trying to sing *the Boswell Sisters?*" Calvert's brow raised and he smiled.

"What's it mean, Jack?" Ruffell asked. "It's not a real word ..."

Finally sliding away from this hang-up, Churchill playfully pursed his lips. "It's the thing you say when you don't know what to say."

After a second, the three other men began following all the others outdoors for the friendly game of cricket—a fun game organized by Orde Wingate that Churchill would have guessed to be another lame training session.

Black lingered, nodding solemnly at Churchill. "Jack. Thanks."

It then became apparent that in Jack's outing of Danny Boy, he had inadvertently saved Black from an unstoppable persecution. It could have very well been him being taken away by Baade's Nazis and turned into Swiss

Cheese, but Churchill had saved his life by catching a double frame-up by the balaclava-wearing twit.

In accord, Jack returned a genuine gesture.

Following the exciting events of the scheming discovery and subsequent disappearance of the felon, the Special Z Unit Berzerkers engaged in a spontaneous friendly game of snow cricket out the back of the resort grounds—an organized form of recreation intended by Wingate to act as a form of team building fun, and a nice surprise following the months of gruelling, repetitious training. It now acted to lighten the sombre mood, bringing out the competitive side lurking within each of the men: an impulse which was far stronger than any lingering glumness after the exposure and probable persecution of black sheep Danny Boy, who was now, ironically, going to live on a farm.

After some mucking around and chatter, the group retreated inside and to the warmth of the log resort as the cold of night started to settle in for the evening. With the gramophone on and music selected by the artful Brad Rushworth, they drank, gamed, and conversed the late afternoon away until an unexpected impedance recurred: the return of the kilted Ernst-Günther Baade, this time accompanied by the National Movement of Switzerland ambassadorial with the resting rectal mouth pursed tensely. Attires oddly dishevelled, their uniforms were unbuttoned and relaxed, and their demeanours suggested a slight preexisting intoxication from drinks shared during transit.

They had returned informally and to act as arbitrary socialites within this continually strange circumstance. It appeared that they were pursuing their stay at the Winterthur Resort and joining for dinner at the extent of further of hospitality by Orde Wingate. They were delivered by their typical entourage of Wehrmacht soldiers, who had returned to the nearest FOB for the night, likely to the south and across the border, in Italy.

A few of the men hated to admit it, but the time spent with Ernie Baade had been entertaining for the most part. It caused for them to tolerate Baade even further, perhaps even respecting him to a degree.

Prior to all the excitement, Wingate had organized a special feast, celebrating his German friend's last night with them at the resort. He employed two of the kitchen hands back to prepare the traditional all-in-one meal of *Älplermagronen*, also known by the Swiss as *herdsman's macaroni*. The meal consisted of creamy macaroni pasta, potatoes, cheese, onions, milk, and apples. The archetypal version of the meal is made by layering baked potatoes and macaroni with cream and cheese before baking it in the kitchen kiln. This time around, the feast was served with fried onion rings and a thickened stewed apple sauce on top. *Delish.*

It came as a surprise to the men of the Special Z Unit when they hungrily attended supper in the dining room to find that the Nazis were again present, drinking their wine and sharing the table, napkin in lap ...

Naturally, the British mercenaries had to overcome an averseness to join in the festivities. Some even outright refused, feeling this business-turned-personal arrangement just too uncomfortable—and rightfully so. Wordlessly, they took their dinner plates and ate elsewhere.

Some men joined Wingate and his guests at the dining table, however at the risk of offence, they instinctually selected seating at the farthest position at the table from the German company.

Now dressed down in his casual attire for the evening—a pair of brown trousers and a knit pullover vest upon a long-sleeve button up—Churchill became amongst those few who endured supper at the dining table, as did Calvert, Komrower, Ruffell, Batey, and Bort, who occupied one end whilst Wingate, Baade, and his leutnant adjutant remained at the opposite end. The two partitions barely conversed.

Supper was late—forgivable, considering what was on the menu. Having been served tardily, most of the men were already on their third, fourth, or fifth drinks after a day of hard training and so, due to the mild intoxication, inhibitions became compromised. This was flirtatiously dangerous, either bringing walls down for their social boundaries or doubling the fortifications.

Moral aspects became a flouted ambiguity. For the most part, the men retained within the contiguity of their respective cliques, in their conversations at the table during the ensuing dining ... but not for Jack Churchill.

Located towards the far end of the dining table, he indeed indulged Mad Mike Calvert's hilarious tales from the period spent reading for the *Mechanical Engineering Tripos* at *St. John's College* in Cambridge commissioned with the Royal Engineers, all whilst eavesdropping the reticent conversation transpiring at the opposite end. Churchill made sure to not extend his cast looks directly at Baade or Wingate but happened to accidently focus hard through the taint of his scotch to hear in-depth details of their dialogue exchange. They were tipsy, and speaking rather luridly of controversial, explicit topics, baiting Jack's ears to prick.

Although he seemed to smile and participate in their present humorous discourse, Calvert's conversation faded into the foreground as Churchill's sharpened attention homed in with those up the opposite end.

Paraphrased, he intercepted phrases such as:

From Baade:

"... *formulating a zpecial unit of zpecial men ... an intelligence inner circle. Mathematicianz. Chaoticianz. If endorzed, ve vould be reporting directly to zee Führer* ..."

From Wingate:

"... I've been excommunicated before for treacherous indictments. I seem to always get welcomed back with open arms ... It appears having dirt on the right Whitehall officiaries frequently pays off ..."

After hearing that spiel, even in light of Calvert's hilarious punchline which had all the other men up his end of the table red in the face with laughter, foreheads shiny from the spirits and gasping for air between the hilarity, Churchill collected his tumbler with an expressionless face. He hid his interest well, bringing it up to his mouth in time to evade the conjoined amusement and cast a sly sidewards gleam unto Baade and Wingate, spying through the veil of contagious merriment.

These two men were from opposing countries and were basically exchanging business cards right now ...

He felt uncomfortable and disgusted.

A new war was being waged here, and it needed to be fought.

Later that evening, the usual suspects assembled in the common room with their nightly beverages on ice, convening away from the earshot of Wingate, Baade and co., as well as any other member of the Special Z Unit who was not privileged to indulge in the details of their unsanctioned nocturnal activities.

"Can't believe that fuckin' kraut is still here, aye," fresh with a top-up of Carta Blanca on the rocks and with amplified disdain, Black boldly stated as he stepped in. The mostly seated group consisted of Calvert, Ruffell, Scotty, Dredge, Komrower, and Churchill by the short glass cocktail table in the corner of the common room. The surrounding chairs were very low seated. With the soothing backdrop of a record tune, they were currently holding a hand each in a round of blackjack, with Calvert as house dealer.

"Which one?" the half-Aussie questioned whilst shuffling the deck. They did have two of them staying late tonight, multiplying frenemies.

"The Otter's mate!" Black affirmed, frustratedly, missing Calvert's sarcasm. "The cunt who nearly ousted me this morning on account of Danny Dick's bullshit."

They each observed Black as he took a big swig from his white rum and rounded the table, collapsing into an empty space on the couch besides Ruffell. He addressed them more casually whilst allotting his view of them in the dining area which still housed the Germans and their host, Wingate. "It's getting' late, innit? At what time are they getting picked up by the kraut convoy and fuckin' off out of here?"

"They're not. They're staying the night," Calvert confirmed as he swirled his Dewar's blended scotch whisky neat, preparing to knock it back.

"Both of 'em?!" Black frowned, referring to Baade and his leutnant. There was a moment of silence that followed before his subsequent query. "Them two gaylords sharing a fuckin' room or what?"

Calvert nearly choked on his Dewar's.

Leaning on the mantlepiece, cradling his own crystal of amber neat, Churchill's brow rose as he stared out of focus. He had gone with Glentauchers-Glenlivet Black tonight, a dusty bottle he had found in the back of one of the liquor cabinets a few nights prior. He appeared withdrawn, as though there was something dwelling on his mind ...

The sexual orientation of Ernst-Günther Baade was still up for debate. Rumours about the man suggested that he was homosexual, and the campy body language and feminine tendencies heretofore witnessed during his visit to the Pennine Alps all but confirmed this ambiguity. He had no wife, nor mentioned a preference to a sex.

"Ernie is a queer?" Ruffell questioned innocently, naïvely. He appeared to emote a superficial disenchantment by the prospect.

Dredge raised his palms. "What do you think, dopey? The bloke wears a fuckin' skirt for starters?"

Scotty piped up. "Aye, it's a kilt, ya bampy eejit."

Dredge affirmed justly, exchanging one hand from his hand of cards in order to reacquire his beverage. "Well, his adjutant is definitely fruity."

Calvert scoffed. "You mean, *the gunsel?*"

Gunsel had been a title imposed early on—and as a passing throwaway—by Jack Churchill, referring to an outdated slang term similar to a catamite. In his early travels, he had first heard the term gunsel when it was used to describe a young man kept for homosexual purposes—a gay slave.

"That *pretty-boy-look* and that *rectal-as-fuck* looking mouth ..." Dredge shook his head, repulsed. "Have you lot seen the way he constantly puckers his lips ...? You can just tell that cunt sucks cock better than any French broad."

"Why *French?*" Komrower asked intellectually, intrigued.

Dredge held his crystal at his maw, willing to explain some of his unique knowledge of the history of the world. "The French invented the blow job, my friend."

"What?!" Komrower languished with sincerity, eyeing around the group with a genuine concern. "Seriously? I left my unit's tour of France early to join Wingate ..."

While the others chuckled, Dredge raised a brow. "Then, the Otter has robbed you of some good sucky-sucky."

"Wait—are they actually staying in the same room? Together?" Komrower questioned, realigning their brief divergence on fellatio, alluring to a desire for confirmation by Mike Calvert who was in the know. "'cause, their room is across from mine. I don't wanna hear any of that blasphemy. What does one even do in that situation?"

"If the bed's rockin', don't come knockin', eh?" Dredge offered the euphemism for sex.

"*Yuck!*" Komrower shivered.

"Staying in the same fuckin' bed, probably," Black remarked before he took another generous swig, casting a glimpse of secrecy up at the crew in question. "Wouldn't be surprised if Orde joins them, eh? They all seem awfully chummy tonight."

"Wingate ain't no fruit, mate!" Calvert casually challenged with some solemn insight.

"You reckon?"

"There's no-fuckin'-way that he's a queer. Pretty sure he's married."

"*The Otter is married?!*" Dredge mocked, surprised.

"Yeah, supposedly," Calvert disclosed, vaguely. "He courted some sixteen-year-old broad in Egypt, even dumped some other sheila he was with. Bought the cow the second she hit eighteen."

Some of the men scoffed while others chuckled awkwardly.

"Look, regardless, I've served with the man for years but known of him for longer. He's slain quite an explementary amount of woman poon whilst abroad."

"Is that as opposed to *man poon?*" Churchill voiced up from the ring, wondering why there was a specification at all. He had been uncharacteristically unobtrusive. Although likely to being tired from the past few days of extensive one-on-one specialized training, his reticence could have also been attributed to overhearing the unmentionable topics of conversation at this evening's dinner table. He was still processing what he had heard whilst raising his scotch neat to the hole beneath his pencil moustache, absorbing the glow of the crackling flames. The fire reflected in his eye inertly foreshadowing a waged war.

"What say you of these krauts, Jack?" Black asked with a lean, spilling an ounce from the lip of the tumbler as he shook it, showing signs of his level of intoxication. Wobbly on his feet, he raised up and approached him on the carpeted floor. "You've spent the most time with the kilt since he's been here. What's your read?"

Dredge eyed him taking a sip. "Did he try to touch your twiddle?"

The others laughed while Churchill recognized the question for an extended moment, building suspense. He knew they were just joisting, so his brain searched vigorously for a quick whim or a yarn to spin to keep it humorously interesting. "Now that you mention it ... he *did* try to teach me how best to work the hilt of his langschwert. Told me to use both hands. I thought that was a little peculiar ...?"

Confused and concerned, they all listened attentively.

The butt of the joke was there for some but not all until after the punchline.

"When he started showing me how to jack it off, I said *I'm done.*"

The blokes all burst with laughter whilst they nursed their beverages, including Black and Dredge. Jack Churchill's indifference towards Ernst-Günther Baade's sexual preference appeared moderately declared for the record.

Altering the mood to something more tactically specific yet hypothetical, the mohawk-haired Scotty took them on a differing avenue of topical intrigue. "What do ya reckon dat lil pipsqueak o' Baade's has en dat man purse o' his? You no'ice he's always got it on him?" He was referring to the leather man bag leutnant constantly had on his person. The shoulder satchel would be here, now, situated unguarded within whatever room Wingate had chartered him upstairs. "Could be worth er peek if dey're staying tha night, if ya catch ma drift? Could be worth a lot to our folks in army intelligence."

"Wait on ... so we're not going *out* tonight?" Black queried quietly, inferring that they may have still been heading out after midnight to scout for German patrols along the border to eliminate. It would be the first time they had done so after quite so many drinks, but he still seemed keen.

"You mean after the other night?" Calvert glared with a scrunched brow, slouching back with his dealer deck of cards. "After what has just happened 'ere, today, with Danny Boy? Are ya fuckin' kiddin', mate? That sort'a talk stops now, eh?"

As their apparent leader, the Berzerker rogues silently shot him a look while he shook his head. Calvert continued, downing his hand and upping from his pose in order to circle the table.

"Nah, fellas. *The ghosts in the dead of the night* are dead, remember? And I concur. Never again."

Dredge placed a card. "*Hit.*"

"You're on twenty, you cockhead," inferred Ruffell.

"All right, I'll fuckin *stay* then," he remarked, folding his hand and proposing the question to the gang as he did so. "Well, what say you blokes, we run some short-range reconnaissance tonight, instead? Warfare evolved, we can slip into pretty boy's room and sneak a look at what dirty lil secrets he's carting around in that lil' man bag of his."

With a dire implication, Calvert pointed across at him. "Oi."

"Come on, Mike!"

Scotty slouched and opened his palms, fed-up like the rest of the adrenaline junkies. "Aye, come on, laddie. Don't be er soft cock, eh?"

"Oi! No!" Calvert muzzled them both, standing them down. "Fuck no! Fuck that!" he expanded, being sure to keep his voice down so that those in the dining room could not catch wind of their topic. "Can you *imagine* what would happen if we got caught doing any of that shit?!"

Black bobbed his head. "Yeah. They arc up at us like they did today ... then we'd sit 'em down! We'd kill and bury these fuckers out in the snow like we did the last Huns we encountered in the wild."

Scotty chanted, head bobbing. "Fuck oath."

"We should have been planning something like this a week ago!"

Scotty fist-pumped, concurring with a mouthful of drink but pointing at Black in agreement. *Fuck, yes, that!*

Calvert shook his head. "You guys don't understand, you can't just *kill* a man like *Lieutenant-Colonel Ernst-Günther Baade*. I've heard of the guy, alright? Rumour has it, he can't be killed ..."

Black torqued his neck. "Pretty sure a forty-five to the head'll work."

"Not what I meant."

Dredge shrugged, confused whilst all their hackles raised, and interests piqued. "What are you saying, Mike ...? That he's *unkillable* or some such?"

Calvert gestured for him to shush. "What I'm saying is, you can't just do it and not reap some severe repercussions. It's a lot more complicated than you lot can understand, alright."

The men went eerily silent in the wake of the conversation.

"Rumour has it, he sucks man-dick," Dredge tried to return their suddenly ominous conversation mood back to humorous. For the British, it never usually strode too far from comical.

"Think about it, who would you bloody give that intelligence to, anyways?" Calvert questioned rogue trio Black, Dredge, and Scotty in amongst the overflowing mirth. "Really think about it. You take it. Hand it into the brass. The brass is gonna qualify its authenticity; ask you *where* and *how* you got it. We don't technically belong to a nation right now, so it won't even be considered as genuine."

"I'd give it straight to the King, of course ..." Dredge said surely, clapping his hands around his stacked twenty—still waiting on that *hit* to *bust*. "That shit'll trade me a promotion once *this* house of cards come down and we're back in rotation," he added by tossing his cards across the cocktail table and toasting his glass with certainty of his presaging.

Calvert leaned forward, guard up. "What's that supposed to mean?"

"This! It's another Orde Wingate wank-fest, mate," Dredge asserted confidently educated. "This one will burn to the ground just like all the others, and then he'll emerge from the ashes like a bloody cockroach. He'll assume a new role, form another secret group in another faraway land, start this whole shit up again with a new bunch of dickheads."

The phrase of term caught Churchill's attentiveness. He understood the *cockroach* metaphor but pondered if Dredge may have meant *phoenix*.

Given what he had heard at dinner, Dredge was right in his opinion with regards to history repeating itself. It appeared that the Otter was already preparing his next black-label black-ops endeavour—this time apparently joining forces with Baade and operating in potentially darker shadows, too.

"It's all just a matter of time, you'll see. If we're not dead, we'll all be little green army men once again, I assure you. And this whole fuckin' war will be a lot simpler. Point and fuckin' shoot."

"I wouldn't hand it over," Black amused Calvert's prior rhetorical question before taking a drink of his rum. His abstract approach to the hypothetical caught all their attentions. "Say he *has* got intel in that poncy man bag and say he *is* actually a part of the *National Movement blah-blah* ... blast, he would probably have the location of every bloody German outpost in every country bordering with Switzerland. It would be fuckin' *open season* for our midnightly forays, gentlemen. The *ghosts* could ride again and eat fuckin' well in the process ..."

While Black's metaphorical mutter muttered, the ears of the group pricked up as they discovered the confidence within his argument. Their appetites for further nocturnal conquests whetted at the thought of knowing the locations of German patrols between here and the accessible southern border. If they possessed such precise information, they would know exactly where and when to strike to inflict the maximum number of casualties to the enemy. They could drop multiple outposts a night. Heck, at the sake of thinking too big with their surgical strikes ... they could almost liberate the whole country, guarding it like a protective poltergeist!

"Sincerely, I say we ditch all thoughts of tonight's outings in light of this new objective ..." he furthered after a sip of rum. "*Intelligence gathering.*"

Komrower piped up, rather concerned. "I'm confused. Did you lot not learn a thing from what just happened to Danny Boy? The man just got deleted from history!"

Calvert questioned straightforwardly. "Let me get this straight. What you're saying is, in the dead of the night, you wanna break in and steal intelligence from Wingate's boyfriend's gunsel? Steal from our boss' high-ranking *Nazi*-fuckin'-*mate's* potential boy-lover?"

Nazi mate. That was terminology Churchill never thought he would be respectively indulging in his life. Eyes blurred from mild intoxication, his mind was running wild at the eventualities surrounding his current commanding officer's allegiances when his stargaze became abruptly interrupted by reality.

"Oi, Jack!" Ruffell disrupted, hunching forwards over the game of blackjack they were playing simultaneously to casually conspiring war crimes. "It's your turn. You *hitting* or *staying?*"

Churchill awoke from his trance, waking up to the table outstretched before him. He reaffirmed his grip on the cards, and he assessed the hand laid out before him ... there appeared to be an analogy present.

Before he could contemplate further, an interruption occurred.

"Oh, you've got to be fuckin' kidding ..." Black disgruntled across the table, beaming their conjoined attentions towards the dining area right as Wingate drove Baade into the warmth and music of the common space lounge room.

As though someone killed the vibe, the life of the party suddenly fleeted. Some of the boys nearest the sofa lounge upped and vacated the room without context, leaving just those near the cocktail table; the surface coated a bunch of folded hands of cards from what appeared to be a unanimous *bust.*

The unfavoured presence of the Germans was obvious, however it appeared to go unnoticed by the mildly intoxicated kilted oberstleutnant and even more so inebriated host, General Wingate, as they strode into the party like ignorant stars of the show. Baade's adjutant—the gunsel—wasn't present, but couldn't have been far off.

Exchanging discreet looks of discomfort and derision, the remaining occupants of the room had no choice but to ride the stormfront, for jettisoning this late into their casual arrival would be awkwardly obvious, as well as potentially detrimental to a diplomatic relationship being maintained by Wingate and Baade.

"Fuck this, I'm going for a smoke," beneath his breath, Graeme Black regarded with a bitter tone. The remark may have been muttered barely above a whisper, but his action was all too unambiguous. He carelessly tossed his card hand hard onto the table surface, causing a slight disturbance that only acted as a spotlight for his immediate leave of absence.

"I'll come too!" Komrower remarked firmly.

"Arty, you don't smoke?!" Calvert thwarted, confused.

"Do now!"

Barely hiding his discourteousness, Dredge took a deep breath to release a long sigh. "I'm going to turn in." He finished his drink and stood just as they arrived, smiles beaming and likely set on joining in their social festivities. "Gentlemen! Have a good night!" he stated with an overabundance of politeness that exonerated him of any umbrage.

"Oh, so soon?" mildly offended though hiding it well, Wingate remarked gleefully as they arrived. He stepped in close to the area near the glass-top cocktail table along with his guests. Baade had, strangely, linked his arm through Wingate's folded paw like they were on a date. They appeared rather smitten with one another.

The two may have been sinking drinks, but they were nowhere near drunk enough to get away with tipsy shenanigans such as gay gestures or homosexual humour. Their contact did not go unnoticed by those who remained as they marched near, voicing their presence with a blasé attitude. Wingate may have been aiming to trick these men into thinking his German guests belonged. That they were one of *the lads* ...

But the lads weren't having it.

The common room was much quieter now that only Ruffell, Calvert, and Churchill remained. They were arranged awkwardly with their card hands and drinks, having left it too late to escape with any social acceptance.

Churchill sometimes strived to endure social discomposure. He was taught a long time ago that enduring such events makes for stronger and sharper social manners. There was never any harm in testing the water before deciding to either stay in the merrymaking party pool or get out. In fact, sometimes it was less awkward to leave after the fact.

Calvert had known Wingate the longest, therefore it would have been the most uncomfortable if he had left as obviously as the rest. And as for

Ruffell ... well, he waited too long. Now he was trapped, a victim to his own politeness.

"Gents, g'day," Calvert greeted in an Aussie-accented reception. He made for decent small talk to break the ice. "How did you enjoy the dish the Otter organized, Colonel? We only get special treats when there are visitors, y'know. Most nights we are served dog food."

"Eh, ja, ja, das Essen war köstlich!" Baade responded with vibrant energy. His hair was certainly more down than they had seen thus far during his stay at the ski resort.

"You're speaking *the Deutsche* again, Ernie," Wingate playfully informed his friend, touching him across the back.

Much to his chagrin, Baade laughed.

He was redder in his plum cheeks than they had ever seen, as well, thought Churchill. He took a paced sip from his tumbler as he observed the foreign colonel, not quite believing he had allowed for himself to become intoxicated. If he were, it was quite unbecoming behaviour for an officer of such rank around foreign company ...

... but then again, this whole thing was high treason.

"Ze food vaz excellent! Che buono!" he finally revised, translating his previous response to Calvert and then following it up with the traditional complementary Italian phrase—which was weird hearing it with a German accent. It caused a kink to strain in each of the three onlooking Brits as they suffered the cringeworthy moment.

Forcing himself through it, Calvert followed up the conversation with a mentally coerced smile, retaining pleasantries. "And your stay, sir? Are you enjoying Switzerland?"

"Ja, very much zo. Orde haz a good team of boyz, eh?"

Calvert bobbed in agreeance. "Oh, yeah, we go alright I suppose."

Churchill exchanged a short look across at Ruffell, perceiving his ensnared state of unease.

Mad Mike was the best at brownnosing when the situation called for it. He even put Jack Churchill's talent to flatter to shame. He then caught a glimpse of their conspired expressions taunting Calvert's social limitations, and nearly tripped up on his blandishment.

"When do you leave for Germany?" he asked.

"Ve depart tomorrow."

"A shame to see you go, sir," he lied convincingly.

The men then watched as Baade finished his snifter. He and Wingate were drinking brandy cognac tonight. Wingate was also finished, and they watched as Baade called for his leutnant like a waiter to fetch a refill; like a proper gunsel.

"Duty calls, eh?" Churchill uttered with a low chin, witnessing the colonel abusing his power. His main disdain was of his duty within Nazi Germany, and the antisemitic, genocidal service he provided there.

"Es tut uns leid?"

Guilty of a social misdemeanour, Churchill's face raised at them after Baade posed a seemingly serious question reshaping the mood with an underlying severity. Wingate seemed to stop dead in his tracks of walking on eggshells all visit long, eyeing Churchill with concern.

"Zorry, Jack?" Baade asked again, this time in English.

Churchill held his ground, remaining comfortable in his tenor.

"Oh, I eh, *buono*," he over-pronounced, extending what appeared to be a conversational olive branch in light of his sly whim comment being detected by the guest. Upon the surface of their conversation, it seemed to fill the void of potential offence caused to the German, though little did Baade know it was just Churchill setting up another controversial subject for them to discuss. "It's an Italian phrase ... you seem to be a man of many *procured* customs, Colonel?"

Baade's ears heard the words and determined the cleverly blurred line between insult and compliment. Churchill clearly knew of his acuity as an erudite and intellectual fellow and knew he could perceive his discernible double-entendre as such.

Was this an act of war?

A stunned mullet, Calvert flipped Churchill a look, then at Baade and Wingate and then back again, as if this were a tennis match only he couldn't find the ball.

Wingate deliberately asserted himself, desperately trying to unruffle feathers. "I think what *Mad* Jack, here, means ...... is that Germany is a land with many neighbours ...... many acquired customs from all over Europe—"

Poised contentedly by the fireplace cradling his crystal, Churchill shrugged and then prepared to take a sip, curtly cutting him off. "Yes, yes! Something like that. Only, less *molly* and more *honourable.*"

Wingate held a watch over Churchill in that moment.

Although homosexuals were heavily frowned upon and scrutinized by the British Army and gay acts were punishable under military law, a degree of unofficial tolerance existed. This was what was to be exercised this night and whilst their effectual German visitor of questionable sexual orientation resided.

He was abiding it, and he expected Jack—and all of his Berzerkers—to do the same. What was strange was that he knew Churchill was not a homophobic man, but he seemed to be exceptionally provocative tonight towards Baade, enough to allude to his sexual tendencies.

Thankfully, smoothing the wayward path, the leutnant returned to the scene with refilled glasses of brandy for both Baade and Wingate. Indiscriminately, he distributed them to welcome hands and pleasant smiles.

"Oh, while you're at it, *cheers*," Churchill added vociferously, skålling what was left from his tumbler and holding it out to the leutnant implying his expectations for a similar refilling service as if he were a waiter. "I'll go another Glenlivet. Neat."

Both Calvert and Ruffell's eyebrows rose in astonishment.

Fuck, this was awkward.

Was Jack trying to instigate a war, here?

They both posed with their drinks, scanning around the room in search of a casual distraction or a new topic.

The adjutant gunsel held a lengthy stare at the Englishman, barely acknowledging the tumbler in his extended arm and certainly not accepting it. After a moment, he turned his head towards his CO, Baade, who nonverbally ordered him to oblige. Churchill smiled, having tested the limits and won.

Beneath his pencil-thin moustache, the cocky Churchill's cheeky smirk curled in the corner of his maw as Baade's right-hand man begrudgingly took the empty glass, snatching it, and wandered off towards the bar in the far corner of the—

"No, wait," Wingate stopped him, barely lifting his eyes from Jack. "I think Mister Churchill has had enough for tonight," he decided, speaking over his shoulder at the leutnant and causing him to halt. "I'm cutting you off."

"Me?" Churchill raised his brow, playing coy to any consequences befalling his conversational cunnilingus.

"Yes, you! You've just now been rude and ungrateful to our lovely guests ...... I'm afraid it is now bedtime. Off you go," he flicked his hand dismissively.

"Jack," said Calvert, leaning in from his seated position near Churchill by the fireplace. "You're drunk again."

"Again, eh?"

"Yes."

"Hmm."

"You're being a dickhead."

"Hmm," Jack obliged, yieldingly.

"You're lucky, Herr Churchill. Alcoholism is a severe offence where I am from ..." declared Baade in some vain attempt at extraneous reconciliation. He respected Jack Churchill, but he aimed to frighten him. "If thiz were Germany, we'd cut off your ballz for this level of conztant inebriation."

With an authoritative confidence, Churchill stood tall. "Lucky for us then, old chap, neither one of us are in Germany. See, I rather like my balls where they are. You cannot have them."

Wordlessly, they all watched as Churchill prepared to remove himself from the common room of the ski resort lounge and retire upstairs and to his room where he stewed for over an hour.

"Good evening, gentlemen."

The alcohol had gotten to him this night. More so than usual—but then again, on account of all that had transpired and all he had heard and witnessed, Jack had sunk a great many more than usual.

He blamed the late arrival of supper compared to most evenings.

Finding himself again thirsty as a camel, he lurched over his small en suite sink with a tall glass, filling it to the brim from the tap and then skålling it in a string of strong, thirsty gullets. Ever since he had arrived in the Mont de la Gouille, this mountain air constantly dehydrated the life out of him ...

Once levelling at his reflection of himself in the dark mirror and catching a breath, his focus zeroed on his own stare; his eyes weren't his own. Sure, they were a sterling, piercing blue, as always, however the detail to which he focused was his pupils. They were so small, almost a speck within the sapphire of his azure iris. Before he could analyse himself further, he realized a figure stood behind him in the room: a man in a military uniform and kilt—and it immediately startled him, mistaking him for Ernst-Günther Baade in the shadows.

It was just his friendly ghost.

Colonel MacLeòid stepped casually forth from the cold darkness with a growl. "*Hullo, laddie.*"

Churchill leaned into the mirror to greet his haunt. "Sir. You gave me a startle." He strolled past the Highland haunt and into the bedroom, flicking on the lamp on the bedside table, which resided beside an upturned clean glass and a half-loaded bottle of Glenfiddich single malt from a prior night's saturation. In the dim light, he popped the cork and loaded the tumbler two rough fingers, neat, and slung it back.

Silently, MacLeòid stood idly in the confines of the cozy resort room, observing Churchill tip one down the hatch and fill a second round to cradle comfortably.

"*Woes, laddie?*" the Glaswegian accent questioned in a soothing tone, one not frequently heard by the Angry Scotsman. He offered to console his friend and host of which he haunted.

Churchill seemed speechless.

He eventually tried to speak, but failed pronunciation.

"Supercalifrag-fragil-fragiliss ... sstic ..."

MacLeòid hunched forwards, awfully confused. "*Aye?*"

After a defeated sigh, conceding his inability to accurately articulate the fourteen-syllable word, Churchill revolved around and slanted over the small tabletop bar lining the kitchenette, clasping his fresh drink of overly potent Glenfiddich. The greasy smears of tipping alcohol on the clear crystal were evident in Jack's motions.

"Nothing. Just ... tired from training my liver, sir."

A hint of passive-aggressiveness in Churchill's tone caused his wise wank of an invisible friend to merge spaces, dawdling in close and offering a sly comfort. "*Trouble en paradise? Wanna talk 'bou et?*"

"Nothing much to say, really. The world's going mad. Turns out, you were right."

"*Aye,*" MacLeòid assented willingly, understanding Jack's grief. He had obviously heard by existential extension Wingate's conversation with Baade during their course of dinner. "*I tol' yoo I didn't trust dat queer fella.*"

Churchill shook his head with frustration, venting. "Wingate. *The Otter.* What a proper *bellend* ... It's like as if being a part of a *top-secret, black-ops-level, off-the-reservation* operation isn't enough, he's got to start climbing into bed with *Baade.*"

"*By 'climbin' ento bed', yoo don' mean ...*"

Churchill eyed him stern. "Honestly, *that* wouldn't surprise me."

MacLeòid scowled in disgust. "*Farken' yuck.*"

Although he was not directly offended by the possibility of another man's potential same-sex tendencies, the thought of such unnerved his very masculinity somehow.

Beside him, Churchill pressed off from his leaning position and began pacing the room with his drink. "I mean, I couldn't care less if he is into men's penises. It is more *whose* penis, if you catch my drift?"

"*Catch yoor driftwood, yeah, sure, laddie.*"

"This whole thing is shagged, sir. I've got to get out of here, and get back to the Second Chesters before I fall down some unscalable rabbit hole ..."

"*I think yoo're moor et risk ov 'avin' somebodeh fall inta yoor rabbit hole, but let's not go doin' anythin' hasty.*"

"*Hasty?*" Churchill boomed, halting abruptly in his march and spilling some of his dram. "A certified Nazi is down there right now trying to recruit my CO into joining some *secret intelligence society,* and what's worse, it appears that Wingate is considering the offer! What the hell is this war becoming?! Whose side am I even on?!"

MacLeòid reasoned. "*Dis es tha closest yoo've been to tha war since et was declared, laddie! Yoo've gotten yoor orders. Yoo be en tha trenches soon, fechtin' against tha Reds, nonthaless!*"

"*The Reds?!*" Churchill muttered as he swirled his beverage. "An enemy of the Führer, not England. Before we know it, it'll be a syndrome of *the friend of my friend is my enemy.*"

MacLeòid sniggered sarcastically. "*Seems we are already there, Jacky.*"

Being not the words that he wanted to hear, Churchill swigged the whole glass.

MacLeòid saw the error in his comment and stepped forth emitting a supportive tone. "*Look, Jackie, wars 'ave many fronts. Yoor jus' findin' yoorself on er diff'rent one ta what yoo expected, es awl.*"

Jack's eyes pondered the base of his almost empty tumbler. "The only front we've been on is the one we illicitly formed for ourselves."

"*Aye ... so pick yoor side,*" MacLeòid suggested with sternness in his tone. "*Stir tha pot, Jackie. Keep 'em on their toes. Chuck her en reverse.*"

Frown fading, Churchill saw the plan formulate in his mind.

He smiled his winning smile.

This was either going to be a drunken ploy ...

     ... or a historical event to turn the tide of a war.

For two whole hours, Mad Jack Churchill remained in his quarters, thinking. Sobering. *Contemplating.*

The events of the night should have been considered a series of isolated incidents occurring within the context of intoxicated behaviour. On the other hand, for those frequently under the influence, such as Mad Jack, the occurrences were seen as a significant travesty. What had been witnessed was of a grave nature. Due to his honour, the sounds heard could not be forgotten, and the knowledge acquired could not be disregarded.

It had become dead quiet throughout the Mont de la Gouille ski resort, with the last resounding noise heard by Churchill's bat-like ears stepping in the hall nearly half an hour ago; and given the trajectory of the directions, he assumed it to be Wingate and company retreating to their accommodations at the end of the hall.

In the darkness of his wood cabin room, sitting in the comfortable leather armchair by the cold glass window opposite the entrance and in a trance of deep ponderance, Churchill sat in an unbuttoned shirt, casually nursing a scotch neat, a dessert. Wide awake beyond the midnight hour, probably due to the habitual body clock set to midnight missions, he sta—

There was a sudden creak on the wooden floor.

From his meditative state, seated position in the comfy chair, his ears pricked to the sound of what he discerned to be a deliberately soft-footed step in the hall beyond his closed door. It piqued his interest. At hours after what could be considered socially acceptable, whoever it was was intentionally sneaking around like a mouse.

Narrow eyes forward, Churchill's attention concentrated.

Hunching, he softly placed his unfinished glass on the flat crafted arm of the chair, standing silently and looming over to the door where he arranged a flat ear, alas hearing nothing definitive.

Jack held his breath listening. After a moment of poise, he accessed the rattly handle and cracked the door open an inch, prying a line of sight into an eerie, stony darkness.

Stale, cold air awash his face, the grimly empty hall passage of the resort appeared ghostly and reticent, lit dimly by the warm yellow localized lime lights embedded in sconce-like decorations every twenty feet and leading to the stairwell. The air was cold, just like his lead.

The angle of the opened door showed a direct path towards Orde Wingate's room diagonally across the hall. His door was closed shut, and no light bled from beneath the horizontal slit of the entry, alluding to his timely slumber.

After a moment of reserve, Churchill opened his door fully, peeping his head out and checking both ways. There was nothing of note in the barren hall, and no further sounds followed his embedding within the environment. His socked feet trod out onto the floorboards, barely causing a noise, however, a slight deviation due to the transference of his weight was audible within the immediate presence. The floor creaked identically in the same spot that the recent spook had passed, indicating the precise floorboard of which they had strode over to be approximately three paces from Churchill's door.

Now standing unafraid in the centre of the hallway passage, Churchill cast another curious glimpse over either shoulder, in either direction. Tactically, he was dangerously exposed, though this was still an inoffensive gesture of afterhours exploration.

"*Hullo?*" he breathed in an extremely low tone.

No response.

Apparently, he was talking to the shadows.

Fearlessly, Churchill veered and meandered a step, facing the last few doors on this level before a curtain-covered double cold glass window that looked out over the east of the forest treetops. It was then that he noticed a resonation of illumination escaping from beneath the horizonal sill of an adjacent closed door.

Utilizing the silence of his woollen socks, Churchill delicately inspected further up the hall and towards the source of emitting light. Whomever the occupant within the room, they seemed to be the only ones still awake in the wing of the resort's upper storey.

He slowed as he approached, acting the shinobi in the shadows.

There were muffled sounds from within the room. It was of glasses haphazardly colliding on a stainless tray-like surface.

Jack was a naturally inquisitive man. Thus far in his impromptu reconnaissance venture, he still had complete deniability of any colluded mischief should he bump into someone and they accused him of any maleficence.

As he crept closer, he noticed that there appeared to be the slither of an article of clothing in the way, preventing the door from closing over entirely. The aperture of the door opened inwards, meaning that he had not been able to see the vertical strip of light from within the hall until he was closer.

Quietly enclosing the door at the end of the hall, Churchill cast another sly glance over his shoulder. There was nothing but a dimly lit passageway of wood and decorative tapestries before the imminence of his proximity ended. Beyond that was pitch blackness.

Churchill nearly held his breath.

Due to his persistence, he'd now be classified as spying on a Nazi ...

An instant of lingering consideration of the potential consequences hovered in the foreground of his focus before Churchill forced them into the reserves of his consciousness. Fear had no business here. He pushed past the mental barricades and silently shimmied into the path of the closed over door, taking a quiet knee and peering through the erected gap and into the warmth of humble room light from within.

Complete and utter silence.

Churchill held his breath.

The vertical strip of perpendicular golden glow shone softly on his face in the dark, and his eyes widened as obscure objects came into focus as his viewpoint scanned the angle of the room left to right.

He saw a man in an armchair ...

He saw clumps of clothing articles on the floor ...

Why there was a chair in the centre of the room before the foot of the bed was questionable enough on its own.

The man on the chair had his pants on and boots off, completely shirtless, pale, bare chested, with nipples showing. He was side on and hunched forwards. A necklace dangled from his collars, shimmering in the gas lamp light from the lantern in the opposite corner of the room.

As the man's hand fell from his tired, supported head, Jack identified that it was Ernst-Günther Baade, obviously enormously intoxicated or high on some form of recreational drug. He seemed barely cognizant, just able to hold his head straight. He had a hairy chest and a gut not unbelonging to an older gent—a soldier, perpetually sloshed on spirits, perchance haunted by a great many unquestionable demons. In that split moment, Churchill felt mourning for the fellow; he had possibly had a few, let his guard down, and was thus not in his right mind. He had sat to collect himself and his abstemiousness.

Just then, like a passing cloud shadow, another figure passed by the light source in the room, startling the spying Jack Churchill in the vertical stream of light.

It was the frame of a skinnier gentleman, just as shirtless as Baade.

This fellow was completely naked, pale, cock out and everything.

Scandalous.

Churchill had to intently track his motion in the obscure light, making sure of what he had seen. The other man was in fact bare-ass nude, shaven of pubic hair, and bearing a flaccid little twiddle that thrummed each thigh with each step like the soft beating of a skin drumkit.

It was the gunsel.

He entered the scene from offside, passing behind Baade and mounting the bed which he was sitting upon, causing him to sit upright in his rouse. From behind, the leutnant delicately embraced him, like a lover, running his fingers through his bare chest hair.

The men spoke softly in European dialect. Their conversation—call it pillow talk—caused the appalled Churchill to remain, yearning for a prospective interaction that made sense; something that may further outline the intentions of these opposing and antagonistic men.

Not that Jack was carnally concerned, erotically inclined, or even remotely interested in the happenings of this undoubtably homosexual twosome, he was serendipitously unmotivated, wanting to run for the hills ... but instead, this provided conceivably obtainable dirt he could use against this forming adversary.

He was obliged to stay—

Creak.

The sound came from Jack's direct flank in the hall—and close.

Churchill's head fast swirled, locking onto the figure in the darkness creeping in the barren, dark passage. Identity nearly fully cloaked in the shadow gloom of darkness, the unexpected man was positioned outside of Jack's room, where he had left the door open upon his exit. The light from within the room caused the outline of the character to become perceptible as *Mike Calvert.*

Attempting covertness in his sneak, the expressionless Calvert froze as Jack spotted him in the extreme gloom. He, also, had not expected to get caught.

Unexpecting of detection, and eyeing Jack's wrongdoings from a gloom proximity, he took the surprising moment to cast him a mime-like *what the hell are you doing?* gesture with open hands while he lingered in the lurch.

An impromptu engagement, Churchill brought up a quiet hand to signal him to halt and not make any further noises, which Calvert abided for both their sakes.

After a hair-raising few seconds, Churchill's deadpan attention returned to the angle of illumination into Baade's room. The two figures had now become uncannily aware of his presence outside the door—they both cast an off-putting sideways expressionless glance towards the doorway from their embracing position on the chair, attempting to make him out through the lowlight ...

The instance jarred Churchill, startling his confident composure.

The sudden realization of their attentions hit like an unexpecting minor key, sending a shiver straight up Churchill's spine. It gave him goosebumps.

Within a subsequent second, an unexpected figure suddenly strafed in front of the closed-over door of the private light loafer session. The light eclipsed.

A participant in what now appeared to be a threesome, who had been positioned the entire time and just out of Jack's view range off to the side, strode into view. His existence cast a sudden overbearing shadow, blocking the radiance of light of the room, blacking out the wide eyes of Jack Churchill as a sudden surge of shock and terror overcame him.

He was about to get caught out!

Fast as lightning, Churchill upped and bolted down the hall.

Albeit quietly as a feline in his woollen socks, he slid into the turn of his room, feeding himself graciously through the open doorway in time to send a final fleeing glimpse back into the dark passage. His door silently peeled closed as he saw the doorway to Baade's room open, and the light pour into the dark reservoir. The glow from within the room grew in its angle, signifying the wide opening of the entranceway—right as his silently closed over.

Through the intensity, Churchill exhaled through circular lips, managing to successfully seal the conjoining escutcheon plates of his door without a sound—without as much as a gust of air. Breaking a sweat, his concentrating sterling stare fixated on the handle within his white-knuckled grip. Jack gritted his teeth with focus as his tense hold on his shaky metal doorknob slowly released the wrist-twist latch.

He let go, backing away from the door silently, waiting.

His heart pounded within his chest.

He felt like an adolescent evading authority after a childish misconduct or wrongdoing. He had the sudden instinctual urge to crawl into bed, cover his head in his sheets, playing sleep in case somebody entered.

In that split moment, he wondered where the creeping Calvert had gotten to; if the half-Australian, half-British gent had good sense, he would have snuck away just after Churchill had spotted him in the darkness. At least then he would have had a head start on the incoming pursuers.

Heart stopping—there was slight pattering past his room.

It was the unmistakable sound of bare feet on the floorboards.

They seemed to linger outside his closed door for an unsettling moment before briskly moving on, searching in the darkness.

Jack's imagination saw the shirtless Baade, indignantly and irritable, sword unsheathed with wrath, trotting down the hall in search of the pervert who had just spied on his privacy ...

Ensuing, the naked leutnant, dick flapping about ...

The third man within the room, would have emerged, following suit.

It could only assume to have been none other than Orde Wingate, partially embarrassed and fuming for an eavesdropping snoop to lynch ...

Irrespectively, their posse *was* technically off the reservation.

There were no rules out here in the abyssal black(ops).

No regulations of inquest.

Reality was, for this level of treason, Jack could be killed by these men right now. They could bury his corpse in the Alps, not unlike how the Berzerker rogues had done on numerous occasions during the conquests of their nocturnal activities. Like Danny Boy: Swiss Cheese.

Chest pounding, Churchill reared into his room, eventually finding the armchair against the window opposite the door and basically unwillingly rearing into it. Comfortably, he quietly folded, weighing up the possible repercussions of being found out by the stalking hunters in the hall as he heard them quietly moving about, shuffling, whispering ... *hunting.*

This was a strange situation to find himself residing in, however Churchill erred on the side of caution and of the interest of self-preservation.

Seated in the chair, Churchill instinctively reached to his side, collecting his strung longbow and an arrow from his resting MD-1 quiver. Eyes on the door, he nocked the arrow on the slack bowstring and relaxed his guard ...

... he then reached for his scotch, taking a sip to calm his nerve.

He was ready for anything ...

... even a war if it came knocking.

In what felt like no time at all, night turned to dawn, and eventually dawn into day, circumferencing Jack Churchill's recurrent sleepless and guarded posture in the armchair with the longbow.

The sun rose on a brand new and curious day ahead ...

8   8

♠   ♠

Fire & Ice

1940, March
Winterthur Resort, Mont de la Gouille
Swiss Pennine Alps, Switzerland

These were already strange and uncertain times.

Now, they were worse, and less predictable.

Once the glow of dawn light dispersed the winter darkness saturating Switzerland, a delirious-minded, sleep-deprived, largely paranoid Mad Jack Churchill finally upped from his uncomfortable unrest in the slackened armchair. Within the same cold constraints of his cabin room, he decisively disarmed his strung longbow, releasing the tense hold on the weapon and casting it onto his kept bed doona.

Subsequent to the unending self-induced solo nightshift in which he had remained entombed in a constant state of arousal—and not the good kind— he hadn't long heard fresh footsteps out in the hall and the sound of doors opening and closing. The localized commotion was likely due to the indifferent men of the Special Z Unit awakening and convening, then feasibly heading downstairs to start breakfast, teas, and coffees.

He would have preferred to be bright-eyed and bushy-tailed, however, considering the night of suspicion and strife, Churchill hadn't slept a wink. During this severe lack of shuteye, Jack had much time to reflect, contemplate, and stew over the accounts of the previous night's happenings. Instinct and intuition running wild, he had replayed the witnessed events hundreds of times in his sobering mind. This was inclusive of the reiteration of his recent voyeurism and what he had seen in Oberstleutnant Ernst-Günther Baade's room afterhours; glimpsing his private time with his naked young leutnant and their apparent third-party goer, perceived to have been Orde Wingate.

Sure, Wingate was an opportunist. A double-dealer. A mugwump, even. But surely, he didn't take the expression of *sleeping with the enemy* as a literal term?

The entire scenario still dismayed Churchill, disjointing his professed rationale, thoroughly haunting his afterthoughts like a bad taste in his mouth—probably not as bad as the one left in Baade's leutnant's mouth the way their partying venture had seemingly unfolded.

Then, there was the Mad Mike Calvert intervention, and how his random intrusion into the events was to be understood and distinguished.

How did he fit into this equation?

What was he doing out of bed at that hour?

Was he planning on spying on them also?

Was he planning on joining them?!

Regardless of his illicit tendencies driving a force of rogues out on the town after hours, given Calvert's undying loyalties to Wingate and his wanky ways, Churchill sadly had to begrudgingly place his chips all-in on the latter.

Weighing heavily on Churchill's good conscience, something he could not excuse or forget was what happened in the events prior to the apparent threesome between the aforementioned party of exclusives. More specifically, their talks of joining forces and consolidating crusades, ultimately conjoining the efforts of a Nazi and a Kingsman, forming some sort of autonomous alliance that would somehow operate outside the climate of contemporary combatants. The fruition of such a force was almost certainly impossible, conversely these two opposing nationalists straightforwardly communicating the concept of the cause was a committable offence—even just cooperating in general was treasonous.

Disloyalty left an even worse taste in Churchill's mouth.

These lines of soldierly decorum were already blurry upon his enlistment into the aux-ops ... now they were non-existent, and that didn't sit right for a genteel and just man such as Jack Churchill. At the risk of projecting platitudes: *this wasn't what he signed up for.*

He had spent over three months within the ranks of the Otter's odd ensemble, and ever since he had met the eccentric general, he felt the man had a magnet beside his moral compass which sent it haywire, not to mention a few screws loose. Clearly, the man had a certain delinquency with authority and military governance, and some person at some point had thought it prudent to put him in a position to create his own provisionary providence with various off-books operations.

Each to their own, but still ... *Nazis?*

Churchill still had a hard time processing the possibility of a high-ranking and patriotic British officer associating with a member of fascist Germany, but that reality was now—why not the former argument as well? He felt confused and as though he didn't have the whole picture, as though this whole thing was too gloomy, too murky, and something must have been missing. Unfortunately for the adjudication of Orde Wingate hitherto, integrity didn't seem a strong suit during Churchill's critical process.

Still dressed in his loosely buttoned shirt, Churchill showed signs of a mild hesitation before following the other early risers downstairs. All bets were off as to how the consolidation of last night's incidents would unfold. Diplomacy would be key in any circumstance, but there was more than one mad hatter spiralling down this unruly rabbit hole.

Before he vacated, Churchill halted, examining his dresser drawers.

Something within them called to him in this circumstance of civil conflict, and with just as much conviction as he held for this cause, he strode over and opened the wooden doors, revealing the two heavier tartan kilts he had packed for this journey abroad. The first was the Border tartan kilt he had arrived in ... the other was the vibrant red and black crisscross of the Wallace, complete with the rabbit pelt sporran. Churchill had a preference towards channelling the Wallace in this upcoming foray.

Churchill wasted no time, stripping off first his trousers and underdrawers. He wrapped the heavier tartan kilt on, strapping it thusly whilst making eye contact with himself in the nearby mirror.

Timely, MacLeòid appeared to pay a relevant call-back compliment.

"*Lookin' smart, Maister Churchill.*"

Forming a smile, Churchill revised the old motto. "If you're going to war, you wear a uniform."

"*Aye,*" MacLeòid guffawed, inspecting him proudly. "*Ne'er stop fechtin', Jackie.*"

Churchill grabbed his sheathed sword and leather belt, strapping himself and now becoming *properly dressed*. He bowed as he spoke, now truer to himself. "*Never.*"

Cautiously leaving his room, Jack checked both ends of the empty hall, warily scanning each connecting room in passing. The common room contained a few of the Berzerker regulars, including Gentle Jerry, Scotty Wellings, and Graeme Black, and their ambient noise filled the cold halls of the resort.

The tall and slender Mick Dredge emerged from his room behind the mousey Churchill as he browsed over the mezzanine railing of the indoor balcony, inspecting the spacious lounge room. He inadvertently interrupted Jack's assessment prior to joining the crowd down for morning tea and small talk.

The two wordlessly nodded respectful salutation, then subsequently descended the stairs and joined the foray of mercenaries in the warmth of the roaring fireplace.

It was homely downstairs. The fire within the mantlepiece calmly crackled, and roasting coffee beans were an aroma to the senses. In a first order-of-the-day fashion, Dredge poured himself and Churchill a hot coffee from the pot which had likely been brewed prior to their morning attendance by the invisible ski resort concierge and caretaker.

"Cheers," Churchill remarked as he accepted the mug. His weary eyes astutely scanned the crowd as they happily conversed in the morning light shining in through the large window. Nearly all of them were utterly oblivious to the plethora of recent instances, notwithstanding their unease concerning the current company at the resort.

"Laundry day?" Dredge jousted, taking in the sight of Churchill's kilt.

Seeming a little lost, Churchill simply gawked at him. To be sure of Dredge's impartial virtue, Jack held a prolonged stare upon him as he innocuously moved from his view, finding a seat in amongst the others who appeared just as vague as he was—their carefree attitudes towards the present scenario in which they operated caused Churchill to second-guess his own levelheadedness; his own principles, ethics, and morals, but each time he was compounded back to his present heightened state of unease.

Before he could think to interrogate the circumstance further, Arthur Komrower rounded a bend in a yawning state, nursing a slight hangover. He strut through the room, coffee jug inbound. "*Morning.*"

"Arty?" Churchill asked with an askew brow. He homed in on the susceptible gent as he sleepily poured a brew and added multiple, excessive sugar cubes, seemingly uninterested in any relevant or pending predicament. With tired, red eyes, he turned in time to see Churchill lingering with his arms out.

"... what?"

"Last night?" Churchill declared, hanging on the question mark.

Komrower's hungover expression remained flat. "... what about it?"

During his heightened perplexion, the young Humphrey Ruffell entered the common room, becoming detained by Churchill's abrupt interrogative nature, pulling him into their active conversation.

"Ruffell!"

Ever well-mannered, Ruffell joined without argument or question.

"Morning. What's wrong?"

Komrower reiterated. "What's got your goolies this morning, Jack?"

After an exasperation through pursed lips, Churchill eyed them both sternly. Ruffell had at least been present last night after blackjack and thus should sympathize with Jack's appalled tone regarding the inquiry.

"What happened last night?" Scotty's Scottish brogue harmlessly inquired, slinging himself over the back of the sofa lounge, overhearing their peculiar discourse from within eavesdrop range. His loudly raised question gained the attention of Black, Dredge, and Jerry. These men were also a part of the secretive 'inner circle' within the Special Z Unit: the rogues. Typically, if something *happened* at night, it concerned them going out. As far as they were rightfully concerned, *nothing* had happened, unless they were uninvited—hence their piqued interest at this juncture.

Churchill eyed them, becoming defensive and increasingly agitated at everybody's lack of knowledge on such a prohibitive topic, and even more so their lack of apparent interest.

He addressed them in a pout. "We crossed sides last night, gentlemen! From ally to Axis! That's what happened!"

They all stared silently, a little lost.

Perhaps it was just too early for Mad Jack's eccentric shit?

"We're fighting for the Huns now!" he concluded.

With raised brows, they each formed a disordered frown.

"Eh, what?"

"What are you bloody on about, Jack?"

"Jack ..." Black directly questioned from the crowd of casual onlookers on the lounge before the fireplace. He detected a sense of seriousness within his irritated, tantruming morning aura. "Be bloody honest ... are you still a bit pickled or what?!"

"No, but apparently you all are!" Churchill stepped into the centre of their view. Continuing at a lower volume, but just as serious with his tone of voice, he took a breath, preparing to catch everybody up so that they may inhabit the same level. "Last night, I overheard Wingate speaking with Baade ... talking about a *special unit* of *special men* ... an *intelligence inner circle*, one which reported directly to *the Führer* ..."

The men listened close, some recalling the conversation from the dinner table, but none of them had apparently interpreted any dialogue exchanges such as Jack had. Maybe he happened to be situated in a prime position, able to remain attentive through the right window of inebriation by the scotch whiskeys he was chugging down in order to perceive the exchange ... then again, how could he be sure he had heard what he claimed. It was a rather serious allegation.

Black's brow elevated and his tone was sceptical. "Jack—"

"Wingate told Baade he had been priorly *excommunicated* for *treacherous indictments;* he made it sound like doing it again would be easy. That he's always *welcomed back with open arms.* That *having dirt on the right Whitehall officiaries pays off* ..."

Black scrunched his face. "He didn't say that. Not to a Hun."

A voice cut off Churchill's response—

"*In fact ...... I did.*"

The prominent echoic voice bellowed from the mezzanine balcony overlooking the common space. All those involved in the controversial conversation calmed their chops and faced upwards to see the speaker: Orde Wingate. He had risen from his slumber much earlier than usual, still dressed in his dressing gown robe, sporting messy bed hair.

The Berzerkers watched in the silence that followed as Wingate downed the metal stairs in his soft slippers, eventually descending to ground level and standing before the crowd like the accused of a courtroom plea; Jack, the prosecutor before the jury, stood foremost, and boldly opposed the Otter. The gloves were off.

Resuming a position over the elevated balcony in Wingate's absence, silent as a shadow, manifested Mike Calvert. He was dressed warm in a dark sports parka, a beanie, and laced shoes. Lingering uncharacteristically silent upstairs, he watched the proceedings unfold down below like a guardsman.

"You said all that bollocks, sir?" Black snarled, emitting the first tenor of distain within his undertone that Churchill had heard him shtick in regard to an authoritative figure such as Wingate. Black had a permanent tumultuous quality about him, but up until now, it was not a feature that would reveal itself in front of superiors.

"I did, though ...... Mad Jack is paraphrasing an ounce," Wingate smiled, acting coy. Not reading the room, it was a throwaway gesture and expression of humour not well received.

"Fuckin' *Nazis,* sir?" Black reiterated his query, upstanding from his cushiony chair and slapping the superficial reading material on the table beside his warm brew. His tone was dissatisfied and frustrated, taking Churchill's side.

Dredge whacked him. It was intended to be subtle. "Oi."

Black dismissed his friends' shooshing. "Nah, fuck that. We should be shootin' these fuckwits in their heads, not sharing dinner with them! Hate to say it, lads, but Mad Jack's bloody right!"

"You'd know about shooting Nazis, would you, Grae ......?"

Wingate's question was framed like more of an accusation.

Black's temperament holstered for now and his eye twitched.

Did Wingate know about their nocturnal activities?

"Don't bake your brain, of course I know," Wingate shook it from his attention like brushing dirt from his shoulder. Before everybody's watchful, judgemental eyes, he nonchalantly shuffled over to the coffee pot and served himself up a brew for the morning. Even took a biscuit from the arranged saucer and gave it a nibble.

Still standing centre stage, Churchill held his stare on Wingate for the entirety of this sequence, only to remove it once by seeking out Calvert up high: the would-be ringleader of their rogue nights, and Wingate's dutiful righthand man. This made him a wildcard in this heated circumstance, and his loyalties here were uncertain. Mad Mike was thought to have been keeping these forays a secret from the Otter, but he was not who he seemed, either. Even the way he stood now, positioned lurking, as though he were in a weapons envelope, about to flank his fearless leader ...

Jack's serious-toned sterling stare returned onto Wingate.

He asked, confidently. "You knew?"

Wingate's concern was casual. "About all the times you kids snuck out of the house? Daddy always knows," Wingate jested dismissively whilst he the blew the steam from the brim of his brew.

"Did your boyfriend know?" Black asked bluntly.

Wingate plonked the pot down, reassessing his pose with his neck kinked at the question of perversion. "*Boyfriend?* Oi, I only sucked his dick the once."

The men didn't know if he was serious or joking.

Churchill piped up, happy to hop over that innuendo to that *in your end o.* "So, it's true. You're a turncoat."

Wingate made more noise with the culinary items whilst everybody's eyes traced him, following his movements like he was beneath a spotlight. "Think about ...... how much ...... that information would be worth ...... to your superiors at Whitehall?" Wingate indicated his overarching loyalties. He faced the persecuting men in the lounge room, bringing his coffee mug up to his facial mug. "The Great White Shark ...... always nibbles on the bait before it bites. An apex predator ...... always assesses the worth of the prey before he commits to the meal. Of course, I knew of your nocturnal activities, gentlemen ...... and Ernie knew as well."

"*The Germans knew?!*" Komrower exclaimed from the periphery, rather perplexed that the men wouldn't act more directly upon learning of atrocities stricken against their countrymen by a foreign force. Personally, he knew he would have acted adversely.

Wingate corresponded with a nod shy of words while his mouth was temporarily full. "A bunch of men ...... found KIA by a hidden fuel depot just south of here ...... killed peculiarly by melee weaponry and arrows ...... it wouldn't exactly take *Le Chevalier C. Auguste Dupin* to determine it was you bloody lot."

Churchill frowned—specifically at the obscure and out of context reference to a fictional character created by *Edgar Allan Poe*. He then questioned with a perplexed frown, "Baade *knew* and didn't care ...?"

Wingate must have expected this turn of events.

Their unconventional ringleader presented a recent Chekov's gun:

A bodkin-tipped war arrow.

Before their very eyes, the piece of ligneous ammunition tumbled onto the table furniture, tapping with a hollow timbre.

The feather-ended projectile was most familiar to Jack Churchill. His eyes widened upon witnessing its unveiling. "It was *you?!*" he questioned, bringing his ogle back up to the professing Wingate. "*You* stole the gunsel's evidence!"

Wingate remained silent, sipping his coffee. It must have been potent, and so he carelessly twisted to return to the bench in order to help himself to a serving of sugar, stirring it in with one of a plentiful amount of wooden swizzle stick stirrers and then discarding.

Black exploded. "They killed Danny Boy for that, you sick fuck!"

Wingate erupted into uncontainable laughter, barely managing to swallow his mouthful of coffee before responding. He shook his head. "Don't worry about it. Danny Boy was a spy. We knew it, Ernie knew it."

"Where is he, then?" Dredge asked.

Wingate's focus sharpened, sure of his conclusion. "Oh, he's dead."

"Just like *that,* eh?" Black seethed.

Wingate eyed him. "Yes, Grae, *just like that.* We're all expendable ...... myself included. It's all about *worth.*"

"And what was Danny Boy worth? Surely, more than the Swiss cheese he was turned into."

With conviction in his cause, Wingate cocked his head.

"In this equation, he was worth the arrow of an archer ..."

Brief attention fell onto Churchill, of his guilt.

Komrower couldn't compute this. He shook his head, raising up from the lounge and becoming upstanding along with Black and Churchill. "This is bullshit," he said in reference to Baade and the Germans. "We killed his damned countrymen?! You expect us to believe he was happy to just *turn a blind eye* and *let us go.* Why?!"

Wingate shrugged, unbothered with the why.

Baade imaginably had his reasons for not actively—either ethically or emotionally—avenging his fallen kamerads or at least impugning their accountability for the slaughters. Either way, it had been assuaged and whitewashed in an effort by their fearless man-otter. Imaginably, in some sense, Baade could have been just as equally implicated by his actions in showing up here to his superiors in Germany as they were, theirs, to England. This whole thing needed to remain a non-event and it was plausible that Danny Boy threatened that for him. It was a trade-off.

"Unfortunately ...... you've missed your chance to ask *why?*" Wingate supplemented at Komrower and the others. "Ernie left at dawn."

His convoy would have arrived at the Winterthur Resort predawn to collect the oberstleutnant and his company—the gunsel—taking them either back to their nearest FOB or conceivably the nearest German-permitted airfield. His stay in Switzerland had concluded, and thus it was only logical that a man such as Baade would be returned to the war efforts immediately.

"They're gone?" Churchill asked despondently. He hadn't planned on *asking* Baade anything this morning ... it was more like possibly *kill.* Luckily for his greening ego, that option had seemingly been removed from the table.

Wingate faced him with his unnerving stare and elongated pauses within sentences. The man was a fucking robot. "They are ...... gone from here."

Scotty interrupted, casually leaning over the lounge arm. "Can we goe back to tha part 'bout yoo admittin' yoo wanted to werk wiv Nazis? Sorry, jus, wan er bit more clarification on that bit, b'cause that sure es Hell isn't what I signed up for ..."

Disturbed by these revelations, the others inaudibly concurred.

Wingate uttered. "I was playing an angle ..."

Churchill's brow rose at Wingate's response.

Black, Dredge, Komrower, and the others each tilted their points of view as they listened well, hearing out their berserk Berzerker ringleader. They each surveyed Orde Wingate as he circled the floor, mounting his rearend at a comfortable position on the arm edge of the long lounge, causing Gentle Jerry to desire reposition for the sake of social comfort.

Calmly, he opened with an elegy of sorts. "Some say, the world will end in fire ...... some say in ice. From what I've tasted of desire ...... I hold with those who favour fire. B—"

"'*But if it had to perish twice, I think I know enough of hate'* ..." Churchill lyricized out of tune and rhythm, completing the poem by *Robert Frost* but also calling out Wingate's capitative logic as plagiarism. "'*To say that for destruction ice is also great, and would suffice* ...'"

Caught out during the lingering silence, Wingate beamed a pleased smile. It was a digression from the resolve the men were waiting for, but Frost's poem was about the end of the world and associating the elemental force of *fire* with the emotion of desire, and *ice* with hatred. The substance was relatable from an overarching point of view, but a vantage point missed by the eager-minded.

He started on the relevant point as it was posed, "Colonel Baade is a man not unlike myself ..."

"A fruitcake?" Churchill briefly interjected, jabbing like a jestful boxer. Now that he had the endorsement of all those in the room against Wingate, he felt much more secure in his verbal criticizing of the commanding officer.

Wingate accepted the blow, choosing to continue his narrative as well as countermand Churchill's remark. "A conceiver ...... an idealist ...... a visionary ...... In times of global calamity, men like us stray from the norm of war*fighting* to breed a special type of war*fighter* for impending war*fare*. Make no mistake, gentlemen, and please take no offence, my brain is ahead of the curve from the rest ...... from all of you. The human race is on the verge of *the sixth extinction;* hence ..."

Wingate wound his wrist, wishing for the answer to his riddle.

He sat in the lurch, like some failed schoolteacher address.

"*Fire and ice,*" said Churchill.

Wingate accepted the answer of his teachings. "These are unprecedented times ...... filled with extraordinary tidings. It is impossible to stay two steps ahead of preordained annihilation, therefore ...... we need to construct *that* what is forthcoming. Fuck it. Conceive it. Thereby impregnating the future with our spawn. Our direction."

While the madman talked shit, Mad Mike Calvert traversed the metal stairs softly in the background, halting near ground level, continuing to overwatch the common room from a few rungs high on the circular staircase.

Whilst listening well, Churchill noticed his incursion, lurking in the higher ground. Strangely, he perceived some sense in Wingate's words.

In a *nanos gigantum humeris insidentes/standing on the shoulders of giants* nature of romanticism, he interpreted Wingate's encompassing insinuations. However, reading between the lines was like walking a rational tightrope or traversing a mental minefield. Perchance, his spoken words could only make sense to the type of mind pertaining a certain calibre of intellectualism, but for a moment, Churchill understood the craziness coming from between Wingate's tea-stained teeth. Maybe intelligence had nothing to do with a rational comprehension ... conceivably, one needed a certain level of madness to interpret and comprehend the notions of his ideologies ...

... *a commonsensical lost on many.*

... *but not Jack.*

Mad Mike seemed to get it. Perhaps Mad Jack did, too.

"This is filth," stated Dredge, also becoming upstanding. "Pure filth."

"*Weapons and war cannot be pure,*" cited Wingate.

"What the fuck are you even talkin' about?" Black expelled, becoming the point in case. There were far too many big words for the brute to grasp, and therefore he opted to take offence. "You daft-fuckin'-git! You're frothing at the mouth, talkin' absolute nonsense like you've got a clue! You've lost the plot somewhere in this verbal diarrhoea you're spewing, and we lads ain't buyin' it any longer!"

In the lingering atmosphere of confusion, the silence following the outburst was clamorous.

"Separatism," educated, Komrower voiced from the bedlam. "What you're talking about in all of this is becoming a separatist to our own government. That, in and of itself, is illegal, and likely considered a form of treason."

Wingate's eyeline engaged the questioner.

He had either hit the nail on the head, or Wingate was about to argue further. Either way, his runaway train was derailed—

"Sir," Churchill attempted the beginnings of a constructive counterstatement with a conservative and diplomatic tone. "We already *have* a forthcoming: we're soldiers in service of the King. Loyalists to the Crown. All clandestinity aside, we've already got a preordained direction, and that is for the greater good of Great Britain and her allies. Whether that be operating from the shadows or the light. Have you forgotten that we have received our marching orders ..."

The orders to which Churchill referred were those *'official'* unofficial mission orders to help the Finnish Army war against Russia's Soviet Red Army. Wingate had received them prior to Baade arriving at the resort and, effectively, it was what they had been training for all along.

"Those orders have been countermanded," Wingate dismissed.

"*Countermanded?*" Komrower scoffed the loudest at their unit's sudden directionlessness, as did a few of the other displeased men in the background of this unsanctioned hearing.

"Yes, countermanded," informed Wingate decisively. "It appears that, simultaneously to all our squabbling, the *Moscow Peace Treaty* has been achieved ...... and signed by our powers that be upon mount high ...... all is now *well* between Finland and Russia. They no longer require our support."

Out of frustration, Ruffell slammed his beanie down into his lap.

Open-mouthed, Black scoffed, as did Dredge.

Churchill flared his nostrils.

"Good to know ..." Scotty remarked with muttered disdain.

Dredge piped up. "And when the fuck were you going to tell us?!"

"When it became *prudent*. When we did not have German visitors staying with us at the hotel," Wingate announced with a degree of eccentricated logic. These were secretive orders issued by their current appeasers in Government, which was still Whitehall, and a team Wingate was still supposedly playing for. Wingate may have been in bed with Baade, but compartmentalization was still king.

Nonchalantly, Wingate stretched to reach within his robe pocket and Black suddenly overreacted, drawing his trusty M1911 from his personage. He may have been dressed in casual clothing, but he was always packing.

"Oi!" he shouted suddenly, cocking the hammer with his thumb and pointing it across the lounge room at the Otter: the proven untrustworthy. "I think at this point, you can keep your mitts where we can see 'em!"

The trust ...... had been broken.

What was more unsettling was that Wingate seemed unphased by the threat to his life. Without a mildest hesitation, he smiled his Cheshire cat grin down the gun barrel, then retrieved a specific totem from his pocket, holding it out for them all to see; a circular pin or pendant, stylized by a folded, curved symbol. Dangling from a thin silver chain, it appeared to be of some sort of silver serpent-like charm, with detailed engravings. The designation was lost in the current irrelevance.

"Ernie is embarking upon greatness," Wingate iterated at the sight of the sparkling serpent pendant, referring to Baade, the perpetual confidant. He held the jewellery forth as though it was some rite of passage; as though it had been ordained upon him, and they should be grateful.

From the middle of the room, Churchill mediated, turning side-on and holding a palm up to the hothead Graeme Black, gesturing to him to be calm and to lower the gun. Black barely comprehended, deescalating only slightly, still maintaining a firm hold on the weapon over the target.

Churchill returned his view back to Wingate in order to listen to the rest of his narrative, though not before noticing that Calvert up on the spiralling staircase had responded to Black's reaction at Wingate by silently brandishing a weapon of his own, positioning it angularly through the railing. The black barrel of the discreet sidearm was aimed directly at Black.

This was a Mexican stand-off, only nobody knew.

Very acknowledgement of such would cause a shootout.

Admittedly, Jack was unsure about the *wildcard* that was Mad Mike Calvert, and as to what side of the fence he would come down on having been a loyalist to Wingate for some time. Graeme Black had no idea in that moment that, if he pulled that trigger, he would be at the very least killing himself as well as Wingate.

Continuing about the justification of his collaboration with Baade, a man he seemingly now idolized the virtues of like some sort of brainwashed flog, Wingate expounded: "... Ernie is a genius. He is helping to construct a society that will operate outside of the walls of our dimensional authorities. Outside of a country. Outside of a lateral continent. Operating within the lines as they start to blur ...... precisely what I have been *striving* to create within our government but forever *failing* due to a plethora of personal vendettas and the greed of mortal man. All this time, what was needed was right in front of me ...... a sovereign state of affairs."

"You mean like the fuckin' *Vatican?*" Dredge frowned, giving a wrong answer. The comment was so stupid it didn't even receive a response.

"*The Third Reich*, though?" Churchill challenged from within his crosshairs, and Wingate's attention focused unto him, seeing through his soul. "Really?"

"Not *Nazis,* Jack. Far from it. The Third Reich will fail ... but from the ruins, the Fourth, even Fifth Reich's will prevail. By then, we shall get it right."

"Fuck this bollocks!" Black finally latched the safety on his handgun and lowered it, standing tall and affirmative. Since their orders had been revoked, they were once again directionless soldiers, well-fed but still hungry for war. "Reich or wrong, we should burn this whole fuckin' thing down. Baade's still in Switzerland ... I say we head off and cut off his convoy ... we kill 'em all."

Black watched for Churchill's reaction, almost as if to request his accord to the plan.

It was a radical direction, but the only other likely course was to let this whole thing rest and die quietly ... but that option lacked the type of closure and resolve desired by a soldier. Plus, *this way they got to shoot guns.*

"I concur. War is always a good option ..." Jack remarked assertively, undeniably onboard. This may have been the best way to undo all that had been done, and the plan wasn't entirely impossible. The roads around these massif ridges were long and windy out of the scenic Mont de la Gouille Mountain Range, and they would have to stop to uncouple the wheel chains from the tyres once off the ice. Much time was taken to travel safely in vehicles upon icy roads, such as Baade's Mercedes-Benz convoy. Men on waxed alpine skis and half a directional breadth could catch up within no time at all taking a route as the crow flies ...

There was time to ambush the cavalcade.

"What do we do with *him?*" Komrower asked, aiming his inquest at the argument-dormant Orde Wingate: the odd egg. He was still seated upon the fence of this debacle, where the mercenaries were already seeing black and white and clear as day.

Black regarded half-seriously. "The fuckin' looney bin."

Churchill confronted Wingate. "Grae is right, sir. You're in too deep, and this has gone far enough. You need to decide what side you're on ..."

After he posed the question, Churchill cast a sharpened glimpse at Calvert on the stairs almost as if to interpose the same question unto him. Watching this all unfold, Mike simply gestured to Jack a wordless wink to state what side he was on.

Naturally, he was 'hitting'.

England—definitely not Germany.

And (Maybe) not Wingate's.

Beneath clear morning skies, the squad of skiing Berzerkers sliced between trees and snow-thawing foliage, gliding effortlessly across the arctic white slopes and surfaces on their way to conquest. This was a race against the clock.

Minutes ago, they had catechized the loathed Orde Wingate into revealing the finer details of Ernst-Günther Baade's cavalcade passage, such as the disclosed route and destination. The Otter had not been as reluctant to divulge the information as Churchill had expected when they had pressed him for intelligence, revealing that the two-car convoy would be heading west along the principal backroads. Perhaps he was truly an agent of chaos.

The cars would veer through *Bourg-Saint-Pierre,* continuing along a direct route into the Aosta Valley across the Italian border; located there was an airfield diplomatically loyal to Nazi Germany, thanks to Mussolini's hesitation to enter a state of war. Until such time, Germany weren't exactly friends to Italy, but they weren't yet enemies either, hence a reluctant utilization of their airfields.

The hills on the Italian side of the border happened to be well known for this lot of Berzerkers, only it looked marginally different during the daylight. The seasons were changing; however these slopes were still snow-capped enough for them to cut off-piste, marginally shortening their travelling time due to allowing their rite of passage to be as the crow flies and practically undeviating.

If they hurried, they could catch this convoy in time!

Once Wingate had divulged the information on Baade's itinerary, Churchill, Calvert, Black, Ruffell, Komrower, Dredge, Gentle Jerry, and Scotty geared up with guns and weapons, antiglare ski goggles, jackets, boots, and aligned their ski panels. Without missing a beat, they trudged a short, lateral gradient before taking off down the southern slopes, shortcutting their route towards the border and making phenomenal time due to their extensive orienteering ability and experience traversing these lands.

Considering the German convoy would have needed to slow considerably to wind the declines of the treacherous icy westerly backroads before reaching the Bourg-Saint-Pierre route, they should have been able to get in front of them in time. In their opted off-piste direction, there was a low stretch ahead before a commune named *Saint-Oyen;* a town which the cars would need to pass in order to reach the airfield.

This was where they planned to intercept the convoy.

The area was sunken below the landmasses, therefore they could ski down with flow. From an advantageous geographical falloff, they should have been able to see from afar the two German Mercedes and their fascist red flags flapping in the breeze ...

... and lo and behold, *their target was acquired.*

The snow was starting to slicken as the climate started to warm in the month of March. Luckily for the rogues of Berzerker, today felt like a winter day, and the slopes behaved as such.

Ahead of Churchill and the others, Black cut his skis to a halt reaching a clearing yonder a high snow cornice. It was the edge of a cliff slope, and the elevation allowed for a gracious scenic view of the valley. Panting his breath, he lowered his goggles and assessed the distance through a pair of binoculars. They were nearing the depths of a basined valley within the Aosta Valley, just shy of Saint-Oyen. The small village was visible further along the lateral passage—and just beyond it to the west were two distinct black cars en route.

"I see 'em!" he stated, pointing to those pulling up around him on the cusp of the valley cornice.

Churchill cut an edge-stop behind Black, as did several other geared skiers, halting with spirited *swooshes* in the ice as they hooked their planks perpendicularly in their rapid voyages, locking their gliding treks and forming controlled brakes. This established an unrehearsed line formation and showcasing their loadout like a panoramic portrait.

They may have each swiftly carved the ice to halt their passage, but Mad Jack was the only one amidst them to do so wearing a Scottish kilt. Due to his speed, the heavy thing caught air and plumed like a parachute canopy, almost exposing his junk to the cold.

Strung longbow and quiver loaded with arrows strapped across his shoulder, and a sheathed claybeg sword on his tartan-coated, kilted hip, Churchill was properly dressed for war unlike anybody had this side of the century. He wore a plain black beret aslant upon his dome, and circular tinted alpine sunglasses on his face above his distinctive pencil-thin moustache.

Calvert was dressed in a beanie and with a trendy pair of ski sunglasses wrapped around his ears, geared with what appeared to be an a-typical Lee-Enfield SMLE, except with some sort of cylindrical cannister attachment on the end labelled aptly *'Adapter No.1'.* This was to launch the No. 68 AT rifle grenade loaded within. The tube attachment device fired a high explosive anti-tank *(HEAT)* projectile capable of penetrating two inches of tank armour via *shaped charge* technology, and was basically a portable infantry mortar issued to them by Wingate's friends at the MD-1. The device was still experimental and expected to enter service this year.

Black was kitted in all black attire, with black ski goggles and black balaclava mask protecting his face from windburn. For this fight, he went with a customized top-fed Bren light machine gun situated across his back via a strap. This particular model was complete with a forward grip, removed collapsable bipod and rear grip, and a fixed cocking handle for user simplicity and less carry weight.

Attired almost identically, Dredge was dressed in athletic gear beneath a camouflage grey smock over his parka. For this venture, he had selected to bring an American Winchester M97 pump-action trench-grade shotgun loaded with some experimental incendiary ammunition. The sixteen-gauge buckshot ammo was laced with a compound that burns rapidly once ignited, causing sizzling pyrotechnic fires to emit instead of buckshot pellets, resembling the scatter of a chandelier flare. This was not unlike that which was intended for interceptor fighters during aerial combat, known as tracers. They were banned from warfare, however, due to their prohibited status on infantry belligerents as outlined in the Geneva Convention, this lot had been issued unofficially by their mates at the Toyshop, organized for their unique operations.

The balaclava-covered buzzcut Ruffell was present with his likened silent Sten strapped firmly across his chest and fingerless gloves gripping his ski poles.

Komrower was as equally equipped. A full-length American M1928A1 Thompson submachine gun dangled across his back; this one loaded with a fifty-shot drum magazine. His ski mask was rolled up, and he currently cradled a pair of dangling field binoculars, assessing the ways ahead.

Scotty and Jerry pulled up with submachine guns of their own hanging on their backs, covered in an assortment of other pain-inflicting devices harnessed in various holsters and sheathes strapped across their military-clad physiques. Not-so-Gentle Jerry had two of the US M1918 brass knuckleduster trench knives holstered definingly upon either hip of his waist—each Berzerker had at least one tucked away. Representation. Their unit may have not stood for something ... but they did.

Standing in a file formation, the men were able to see the makeshift arena as it laid out in front of them: Baade's convoy was headed east from their right-hand side, traversing along the central strip of Saint-Oyen, and then onwards to Aosta and the airfield.

Churchill's focus zoomed, making out the airfield structures and activity. Prominently, it contained a *Junkers Ju 52* presently taxiing on the tarmac. Upon his arrival in the convoy, the Germans would waste no time in taking the bellend back to Berlin.

Their shortcut had worked, but at their current transit speed of progression, that endgame convoy could soon be out of reach ...

Beside Mad Jack, Mad Mike cycled his grasp in order to attain his rifle grenade, loading the bore chamber so that it was ready to be fired on the fly. About their stances, the men all took a moment to load their weapons and disengage respective safeties.

It seemed a warfare strategy was amidst.

"What's the plan of attack?" Calvert asked Churchill.

Churchill torqued his neck. "*Attack.*"

After an extended pause, he looked to the surrounding men.

That hadn't been much of an answer.

"Let's do this," Churchill ordered as he began their schussing, skiing like a missile towards the en route vehicles.

The moment they took to the downward slope was the point of no return ...

This was war.

Beneath the sun-kissed twilight twinkling glitter across the icy slopes, the twin glistening black Großer Mercedes-Benz 770s cruised at a comfortable speed after traversing the windy and dangerous roads leading from the mountain range ski resort.

It was a two-hour drive to the airport from where Oberstleutnant Ernst-Günther Baade would board a charted flight back to the motherland for his recirculation into the German war effort. Rumour had it, he was joining the North Africa Campaign as a part of the *Afrika Korps* ... but he had too much on his mind to be dwelling on tomorrow's troubles.

From his beady-eyed blank stare out of the window, he glanced across and to his fellow backseat passenger in the rear of the travelling automobile. Baade was dressed today in his neatly pressed officer's waffenrock attire with personalized lower garment—his red Scottish kilt. He cradled his leather officer's cap in his lap like a resting feline, caressing the eagle and cockade stamped aluminium embroidered into the leather.

In wordless expression, he reached over the middle seat and felt for his leutnant's hand—a discreet romantic gesture. His secret lover was unable to tour with him for an unspecified amount of time after today, and he would remain in service here in Switzerland. Soon, there would be an emotional farewell between the two schwule liebhabers, of which nobody but they could know, for the sake of its forbidden nature.

Inconspicuously, the adored two discreetly held hands out of the rearview sight of the two oblivious Wehrmacht soldiers occupying the front seats.

After an expressive moment, the backseat passengers locked eyes, and a small wordless smile formed in the corner of each man's mouth as they found an abundance of contentment—

Interrupting abruptly from the front, and in an off-key voice:

"*Was ist das?!*"

Words sharply disturbed the tender moment shared by the two in the back and, with composure, the pretty boy leutnant gunsel gestured rather out-of-place ...

... his hand raised and pointed past Baade, out the side window.

... he focused on something upon the downward slope of the hill.

... *something closing at a rapid speed.*

Due to the casual tone of the movements, Baade leisurely turned his head to take a gander—*and what he saw widened his stare to the size of flag-borne swastikas.*

At least half a dozen faceless armed men, incoming fast!

Clenching his teeth, Baade suddenly faced forwards and frowned, bracing himself within the tight confines against the driver's seat, alert and panicked.

"*Achtung!*"he shouted right as the might of the rushing skiers practically T-boned their vehicles like a soaring avalanche, flying in dead-stick like a collection of burst-firing bombers with no hint of deceleration.

It was an enfilade blindside assault.

Gunfire crackled to life from the inbound skiers, biting at the convoy like piranhas from the snowy scenery. Curtly intercepting and violently lashing at the vehicles, the bright starbursts and sparkling spurs from countless ricochets crackled like fireworks. Loud brunts of metallic impacts and shattering glass were all that were heard in a cacophony of drama.

From the barrel of one of the forward skiers carrying some sort of long rifle, a puff of exhuming fume followed by a finger of trailing smoke traced its way like a propelled rocket towards the first wayfaring Mercedes-Benz.

A passenger to the convoy ambush, Baade's watchful gleam tracked the traversing projectile as the rifle grenade journeyed like a speared javelin, arcing slightly before colliding into the swastika-painted side door of the front vehicle with a thundery *bang!*

Debris and fragmentation from the explosion charred and frosted their windshield, and the sudden blast caused even their own car to viciously shunt and waver as the panicked driver instinctively applied the brakes and wrangled the wheel to maintain some semblance of control.

A sudden cloud of black engulfed the road ahead following the explosion, and small arms gunfire from other faceless, balaclava-clad skiers enveloped their convoy car as they came to a jarring, screeching halt in the middle of the road strip.

Baade's scowling face raised after planting into the back of the driver's seat. His stern view scanned the roadway ahead, inspecting the damage whilst he collected his composure and returned to his senses ...

... when suddenly, the razor-sharp arrowhead of a bodkin-tip war arrow punctured through the glass window beside Baade's face, lodging itself stuck in the reinforced glass.

His angry eyes sought the projectile, immediately recognizing it.

He knew the culprit responsible for loosing such a device ...

This was, indeed, a declaration of war.

The No. 68 AT grenade squalled like a bird as it sailed accurately into the driver's side of the first black Großer Mercedes-Benz, impacting into the decorated metal door.

The result was as instantaneous as it was illimitable.

So undesirably overpowered, as it was designed to penetrate steel tank armour, the HEAT shaped charge of the propelled grenade burst through the door, shredding the metal of the vehicle as if it were mere tin foil. The expounding eruption was enough to launch both bodies lobbied within the front canopy of the cruising automobile out of the opposite passenger's side, exploding the door off its hinges in a detonation of expelled pressure.

The German passenger flung out in a ball of smoke, launched like a circus act cannon shot. What was left of the driver, now mostly in two halves severed at the torso, shot out like cooked crimson mucus from a blocked nostril behind the rag-dolling passenger in a strapped stahlhelm. The two bodies in three parts—and the steering wheel—were carried by a puff of smoke from the impact, tumbling down the opposite slope alongside the warped and dislodged car door and a sprinkle of debris.

BHOoof!

A direct result of the anti-tank weaponry on the dead-stick first car, now quavering uncontrollably, was that the second car inadvertently slammed on the brakes to create distance from the flaming wreckage.

The first Mercedes performed a shuddering death wobble as it lifelessly decelerated. Its two front tyres attached to a prolapsed axel collapsed into a spark-expelling halt on the edge of the road, flicking pinwheel sparks out either side of its carriage.

Like a chimneystack, thick black smoke exhaled from the charcoal-coated interior. The pillar of black climbed into the sky from the remnants as the vehicle coasted to a complete stop and the rear passengers rolled out from the car, barely alive: two were blackened with soot and reddened with burns, the third was on fire and died quickly.

Behind the wreck, the second vehicle—Baade's car—stopped short with its tyres locking in a high-pitched squeal. Their visibility was low as the smouldering from the first car blocked their view, and their windshield had now cracked in a spiderweb formation from the hood up as a result of the aftershock from the grenade impact, obscuring all vision.

Consistent small arms fire resonated from the hill as the deadly armed skiers glided in close, letting dangle their ski poles in order to shoot their automatic weapons in controlled bursts. They formed a crescent moon formation, tactically overarching the ambush site like a kill zone.

In loud brunts, automatic fire rebounded harshly from the metal of the cars, shattering glass windows and popping tyres, causing shrinkage as they deflated the chassis.

Their vehicle was now immobilized.

Beyond frazzled and inhaling smoke, Baade shouted in German for the soldiers in the front seats to react—for his adjutant to keep his pretty boy head down as not to lose it to a stray bullet.

With a dozen deafening impacts, deadly decals strafed the sides of the car in tracing lines of gunfire, chewing metal, glass, rubber, and even the bitumen outside without discrimination.

The gunfire assault caused bright sparks to ignite, peppering the unrelenting atmosphere, and suffocating all those left alive inside until they should finally drown in hot lead.

Outside of the ambushed convoy, the skiing Berzerkers cut into sudden halts at various points around the kill zone which they had created. They formed a semi-circle, partially encircling the vehicle.

They purposefully remained on the decline-slope side of the ambush as not to create a circular kill box around the target, risking friendly fire from offshoots. They had not the mobility or the ability to retreat in any desired direction, due to their skis on the slope. When the time came, they would have to excel forth and retreat further south and down the gulley of the tying Aosta Valley, then somehow voyage a double back to return to Switzerland.

Furthest up the hill, Jerry and Scotty pulled up behind a small rock formation midway down the slope. It would provide decent cover if they received fire, as well as be able to maintain satisfactory support from a higher position on the scene.

Ruffell and Komrower pulled up loosely after maintaining multiple extended sprays at the stalled convoy. Alongside each other, they glided to a halt, standing spaced and balanced in the open in order to accurately unload at the vehicles in the kill zone.

The same assault tactic was achieved by Black, who slid into a parallel slide with his skis to harshly absorb his speed while he unloaded at the vehicles with his automatic gunfire, including drilling one of the escaping passengers from the first vehicle with his loud Bren gun. He shot a charred man several times in the chest as he recovered from the grenade strike, killing him with bullets before he would have likely died of smoke inhalation. The soldier became flung backwards from Black's burst, flying against the crumpled Mercedes before sliding down against its exterior, coating it in crimson exit wounds.

Dredge skidded to a halt in an awkward position, blasting a bright firework of incendiary shotgun buckshot over the painted canvas of carnage. The fiery projectiles spewed across everything in a line, setting the ground around the cars ablaze. The incendiary shells blanketed everything in vibrant, frothing entrails. He rinsed and repeated, pumping and firing shell after shell into the stationary cars, roasting the dead duck and sizzling everything.

Most exposed, Calvert slid to a halt out in the open, allowing for himself to collapse onto his rear posture in order to reload the rifle grenade and eventually prepare another shot, planting the buttstock of the rifle into the earth like a mortar so it wouldn't nearly knock him over again like it had just now—the damn thing had nearly dislocated his shoulder from the punch of the recoil.

Lastly, Churchill pulled up with a *swoosh.*

He ripped the sunglasses from his face, scanning the warzone with his naked, cerulean stare as gunfire resounded all around. He prepared another arrow for his longbow, nocking the feathered end and striking an archer's pose shy of pulling the string into anchor point.

Down in the fray, there were multiple targets ...

... but he had eyes for only one ...

Suddenly, the skiers received retaliatory fire.

In the form of small calibre Schmeissers, automatic submachine gun fire crackled over the hood of the second vehicle. The front seat occupants had rapidly ejected themselves from the safe side of the convoy and sought refuge, now standing their ground. They issued avenging gunfire at the off-piste attackers, spraying mostly blindly over the cover in a defensive manner.

A Wehrmacht survivor, the last remaining from the first vehicle who was charred in soot and facial burns, stumbled through the smoke, brandishing a Karabiner rifle. He pointed it across the flaming bonnet of his vehicle and at them—Jack immediately pinged him and launched an arrow his way, marking him an active target. The arrow skimmed from the metal hood beside his stance, skimming off the steel surface and slicing the rifleman across the ear with the upward rebound, causing him to spin and withdraw, shrinking out of sight behind cover.

More incoming fire!

Churchill had to duck and weave behind the concealment of a horizontal snow-covered tree log located by his side as a volley of bullets whistled through the air about his head and audibly chomped into the ground within his proximity.

Nearby, Ruffell and Komrower lowered in their stances, adjusting themselves awkwardly on their ski panels in order to not lose balance and inadvertently glide down the slope or accidentally topple over. They exchanged sporadic automatic fire with the German defenders, resembling a type of outdated line infantry, only sliding rather than marching.

Intervals of fire chattered away in either direction as the two forces exchanged gunfire.

From his position at ground level, Churchill spotted movement in the backseat of the rear vehicle as the contained occupants made a move, exiting and using the wheel arch for cover on the opposite side.

One of them was dressed in a kilt ...

Baade.

Now outside of the stationary vehicle, the oddly dressed Ernst-Günther Baade collapsed low behind the back tyre. He escorted his leutnant, maintaining low concealment from the onslaught still raining down a hailstorm of fire and brimstone upon their location.

A stray bullet carved through the metal of the door on the opposite side and clipped Baade in the back of the shoulder blade, causing him to wince and fold down lower. Although of a slower velocity, the projectile still caused damage. His panicking gunsel with the rectal mouth came to his aide, immediately applying pressure with both his small hands and pursed lips.

Ignoring the pain, Baade's military mind focused up.

From their position on the opposite side of the ambush, they could utilize the slope of the hill leading down the valley for protection of their retreat, potentially fleeing the attackers. They would not yet be able to do this successfully unless something erratic were to happen, buying them at least sixty to ninety seconds of insurance from pursuing enemy gunfire. There was a fair distance to clear before any suitable cover to break line of sight.

... and right then, from the aloof city of Aosta and where they were headed, some sort of distant alarm sounded; an air raid horn.

During his tense scowl, Baade squinted to focus, seeing that down the winding roads away, there seemed to be some form of military activity about to respond to this attack—two whole trucks full. These were likely German reinforcements from the airstrip who had been awaiting their arrival.

They would be here in minutes.

All they had to do was hold on!

Baaaaaaaaang!

The continuous rattle of submachine gunfire was deafening.

Lying on his back in the snow powder, low behind horizontal cover, Churchill issued another arrow from his quiver and prepared it low and out of his own sight. After psyching himself up, he then tensed and used his bodily core to hoist himself vertical whilst simultaneously drawing the shot, loosing it at the enemy behind the car.

After his shot, he heard as Ruffell and Komrower utilized their army practices, preparing and tossing hand grenades at the hostile position down the slope. Although they threw them as far as they could muster, the timed explosives fell short, blasting on the open ground against their fortification in bright flashes of explosions. Fragmentation shrapnel peppered the enemy vehicles with damage, though were deemed mostly ineffective.

The enemy returned the tactic, throwing a pair of potato mashers into the sky their way—and in much better angles of trajectory.

"*Grenade!*" Black called out from his position as one landed nearby.

Churchill watched with wide eyes as Komrower and Ruffell ceased firing and upped fast, sprinted, and collapsed low behind their basically non-existent rock cover as more grenades came flying into the air ... and began to descend upon their new position.

They were going to land right on them and blow them up!

Confidently—perhaps overconfidently—Mad Jack torqued his neck for a crack and muttered to himself. "Pull ..."

Lying on his side and in a semi-tongue-tied position, Churchill quickly drew another arrow and hocked an anchored shot, tracing the dropping projectile like it was all a game of skeet shooting.

He lined the declining course of the object's curvature before gauging an adequate lead in front of it, estimating travel time and distance and speed and—

No time to calculate.

Sch-TOFF ...

His arrow launched ahead of the target, tracking to engage the falling enemy grenade as the potato masher fell upon his fellows, threatening to pull-off a perfectly accurate interception.

The arrow struck the stielhandgranate.

The falling mid-air stick grenade became suddenly collected by the kinetic force of the piercing arrow as it speared into the wooden handle, altering its flight course dramatically. It dropped just past the road, detonating away from everybody and probably confusing the shit out of the German soldier who had thrown it—let alone Ruffell and Komrower, who had expected to be blown to pieces.

Another stielhandgranate landed near Black, blowing a crater in the ground and burying him in dirt and earthly debris. His ears rang so loud he couldn't hear himself shout. Brain mildly concussed, the fearless British mercenary recovered quickly to return fire.

"*Berzerker!!!*" Calvert shouted the battle-cry as he launched his rifle grenade at the road enemy. After accomplishing the shot, he swung the Lee-Enfield across his back and upped to his feet, pulling a pistol from a pocket before skiing straight towards the remnants of the convoy in a deathly charge.

Black saw his advance and matched his energy, shouting at the top of his lungs: "*Berzerker!*" He opted to discard his machine gun rather than reload it and he, too, pushed up from the snow and built up some momentum on his skis, rushing the subdued enemy with a handgun and knife in the way that their Berzerker training had taught them.

Calvert's launched rifle grenade curved prematurely, erupting into the road beside the first Mercedes, acting as a sort of bucking at the festering, fiery wreckage. The bonnet and hood sheets flew off the car, blown away by the gust of explosive energy from the grenade blast. A barely attached rear door dislodged and flung outwards, collecting the lone German gunman with a rifle and sending him tumbling like a bowling pin.

In the chaos, Churchill felt the burst of enemy fire subside, and he upped from his snow-covered prone position parallel to the log. He holstered his longbow around his neck and shoulder, intending to tee-off, however he was abruptly overtaken by Dredge on his skis. The berserk Berzerker tore straight up the middle with his freshly loaded shotgun ablaze and his voice bellowing.

"beerZERKerrr!!!"

Churchill could have welled up in that moment.

This was the first real element of ferocious combat he had seen since his youth in Burma. This was what warfare truly felt like. This was war, and it was fucking glorious. For if he were in possession of his doodlesack right now, he'd purr and skirl a momentous melody.

A smile formed in the corner of his mouth as he observed the—*thwack!*

Like a record skipping from the pace and shattering the heartening and all-encompassing atmosphere, Michael Dredge became suddenly shot through the chest by enemy gunfire ...

A brutal burst of bullets shredded his ribcage to crimson gore.

The image shocked those who witnessed it to their core.

The young Berzerker was fired upon by one of the Germans behind the second car, who successfully produced a string of bullets into his charging warpath, ending it prematurely.

Their first real casualty.

Dredge took a bloody burst to the chest and suddenly slunk on his skis, reverting to the fold like a sliding sack of potatoes. From the force of the hit, his legs flung out from underneath, disengaging one of his ski panels and launching it flailing out the flank as he slid into an out-of-control, lifeless lump. Eyes closed and teeth bared from the brunt of the hits to his chest, Dredge fired his final pump-action shell vertically into the air.

Just as abruptly, what appeared to be mortar shells erupted on the slope above where they had traversed, exploding in the corduroy of their skis.

... *whiiiir-BOOM.*

... *whiiiir-BOOM.*

The pitch came first before the sudden eruption, blasting fifty feet behind them. The explosions echoed twenty times louder across the peaceful valley.

It was Italian artillery defences from the airfield, likely Model 35 Mortars, judging by the range versus accuracy and yield efficiency.

Another shell whistled in even closer, tracking towards the larger rock formation that Gentle Jerry and Scotty Wellings were using for cover. The two predicted the incoming blitz and bailed right as the position became directly hit and erupted, dislodging the giant boulder they had been utilizing as protection. The naturally rotary rock, roughly the dimensions of a medium-sized car, was forced forwards on the downward slope, collecting speed in an earthquaking rumble as it tumbled gracelessly down the gradient with the skiers before it toppled unchecked and off to the peripheral flank. The giant thing felt like seismic activity as it trundled through the action, picking up velocity as it skipped and bounded, tossing dirt and threatening to crush anything in its path like a let-loose juggernaut only gaining more and more power. The bass volume from its out-of-control stampede grumbled throughout the action.

"*Fall back!*" through the exponentially growing chaos, covered in soot and slate from the action, Komrower shouted. They didn't have the numbers or the ammunition for this, and it was time to cut their losses. Staggering, he retrieved the rattled Ruffell and the two decided to bail as did Jerry and Scotty. These Berzerker rogues had clearly bitten off more than they could chew with this venture, and now it was time to withdraw early and bail out. The overbearing ricochets from returned enemy fire continuously snapped and crackled at the earth about their snowy stances.

From admiring the calamity, Churchill brought forth his attention.

Black and Calvert still stormed forwards in true Berzerker fashion, and he felt inclined to support them in what could either be a valiant failure or a triumphant victory as they charged into the wide-open jaws of death. Fortune favoured the bold, but surely there was no way they would return from this onslaught.

At the last second, off in the distance, he spotted the incoming enemy trucks from Aosta about to enter Saint-Oyen from the south-east, headed their way ...

Each truck was loaded with approximately two-dozen men of some sort of German or Italian army personnel, respectively. Likely, a culmination of both from airfield postings. They appeared to be responding heavily armed and well within their jurisdiction to blow them all away, absent leniency of surrender.

The odds favoured the latter.

They needed a miracle to take on this army ...

... and just then, *one showed up.*

Quaking like turbulence tremors, the dislodged boulder from the incline rolled past the convoy location on the road, continuing ambiguously into the valley beyond the action where it faded with sight and sound. The only thing capable of stopping the force of the rolling rock would be the bottom of the Aosta Valley's low-set ravine.

In desperate anguish, the three remaining Wehrmacht soldiers, combined with Baade and his leutnant, maintained their pinned positions behind the remaining incapacitated Mercedes-Benz from the ambushed convoy.

A worse-for-wear, bloodied rifleman retired behind the first wheel arch, attempting to reload his Karabiner rifle with sticky, crimson-covered hands while the two submachine gunners recoiled below cover, exchanging intermittent fire between reloads of their MP38 maschinenpistoles. Due to desperate shooting, one of them appeared to have just one magazine left whilst the other ran dry entirely. He let drop his empty primary weapon in order to draw a sidearm from a leather hip holster.

They were running dangerously low on ammunition.

The desperate soldat made subtle eye contact with his superior, Baade, as he yanked the Walther P-38 from his leather pouch and racked the slide with his bloody-knuckled hand. The look was one absent an obvious alarm, but successfully signalled caution to his commanding officer all the same.

Baade spied about their situation; his eyes falling upon his adjutant.

"Es ist Zeit zu gehen!" he stated calmly.

< 'It's time to go!' >

The leutnant brought his worried big browns up and to his oberstleutnant where he looked longingly into his eyes. He was scared to run and fearful for his lover's life.

Baade gave him a sombrous nod, and then faced up at the others, about to relay the order of post abandonment now that the distant artillery had their ambushers on the ropes and surely on the backfoot—

"... Berzerker!!! ..."

The sound of a bass-filled, resounding battle-cry filled the vicinity.

Confused, Baade frowned ...

Surely not—

Holding his wounded shoulder firm, he rotated behind low cover in order to better peek across their vehicle concealment. He was able to spy the upper-most elevation of the slope, sighting the appearance of approximately an *additional* half-dozen skiing soldiers. Each man was armed with an assortment of machine guns, and charging in like torpedoes in surf down the snow slopes whilst bellowing at the top of their lungs: *BERZERKERRR!*

Baade's brooding beady eyes scanned across the distance, locating a centralized man who appeared to be their leader ...

... it was his ally: fucking Orde Wingate...

He bared his teeth in grimace, exploding into a hateful spite.

Quivering due to a rage overload, he rumbled at the betrayal. "*Ahh!*"

Midway down the slope, retreating Berzerker rogues each ceased their herringboning shuffle on their skis as they attempted to gain some distance before skiing away farther down the slope of the valley.

The ears of Ruffell, Komrower, Jerry, and Scotty, all pricked to the overbearing sound of a mighty battle-cry sounding from above them, and they cast a confused gleam back up the hill in time to witness the unexpected arrival of Wingate along with the rest of the Special Z Unit men. Rushworth, Bort, Batey, Bredin, even Dayan, were present amidst the numbers. This unexpected advent concerned the other Berzerkers who were not a part of the rogue-natured nocturnal activities performed in the dead of the night.

They had shown up anyhow.

Their presence flowing down the off-piste slopes between the sporadic artillery barrages caused the incoming trucks to pull up much farther away than they had originally intended, stopping to dismount their fireteams over three hundred feet east between the kill zone and the Saint-Oyen village they just sped through.

Wingate made his half-dozen men seem like an army.

Multiple Bren machine guns clapped to life by some of the men highest on the ridgeline, keeping all reinforcing enemy numbers at bay.

In the fray of the ambush site, the Wehrmacht soldier with the long-range rifle inched the edge of cover with his sights tracing the new arrivals on the slope. The hill-bound, charging enemy numbers.

Composed and cool, steadying his panicked breathing, the skilled rifleman traced the incoming skiers, marking one for the kill and squeezing the trig—*Clunk!*

Brass to bone.

From out of literally nowhere, he collected a heavy metal punch from a knuckleduster grip of a trench knife as the fierce Graeme Black rounded the Mercedes from the no man's land side of the cover.

Smashed like an unsuspecting tee-ball struck by a bat, the stahlhelm-wearing rifleman plummeted as lifeless as a corpse, lights out.

His head reacted like it weighed more than an anvil, sinking like an anchor to the abyss ahead of his flailing body and flicked feet, very likely dead from the cranial impact.

Calvert lingered at his six, knives at each knuckle and ready to throw hands. The two balaclava-drawn soldiers clicked their heels, shedding their ski boots in order to move on level, dry ground. They now wore their innersoles for speed.

"Berzerker!!!" bared tusk and wrathful, Calvert shouted through the smoke, wielding his twin M1918 trench knives up-side-down and with a boxer's posture.

A nearby submachine gunner witnessed their startling manifestation through the smoke cloud fume of the neighbouring Mercedes wreckage, especially alerted after the bludgeon of his kamerad. He reacted thusly, twisting side-on and raising his weapon.

Calvert charged in first, leaping in past Black and striking clear the German's gun as he reacted.

With metal punches, Calvert speedily dipped in low before the troop had a chance to properly bring about his aim and, in an uppercut strike combined with the single-handed recoil from the automatic rate of fire, the gunner's MP38 was sent climbing to the heavens with a loud burst. Calvert then tucked in tight, driving his other flurry of fists into the man's ribs, bicep, and then head beneath the chin, probably killing him with the force of the brass knuckleduster hilts which emitted a metallic *chink!* with every brutal contact. He proper fed the man, giving off the grotesque sound of metal meeting his jawbone, nearly dislodging his head from his shoulders.

Chunk!

With a weighty iron stamp, the Wehrmacht soldier's head snapped back like a lightweight punching bag before the transference of force hit his body, sending him over like a lifeless ragdoll figurine. He collapsed into the hollow chassis of the car with a thud that wobbled the shock absorbers in the axel before landing flash-first on the hot, glass- and debris-covered pavement.

Still amped and bellowing boisterously, Berzerkers Black and Calvert ploughed through the carnage, taking on the remaining scared soldier with the handgun.

In the closest proximity, Calvert marked him and quickly ducked a recoil behind protection of the open car door as the last soldier raised the semi-automatic handgun at him and fired, clipping the black metal paint with a *dink!*

Black then attacked at full speed from the unseen vicinity, trundling in low and even hiking up the metal bonnet of the vehicle in order to dodge his aim. The fretting gunman fired again and again, as fast as he could pull the trigger, all whilst aimlessly rearing up. Remembering well his CQC training, Black duked and jolted, sliding beneath the shooter's wild recoil as ricochets impacted against the road, each time missing him by inches.

Bam! Bam! Bam! Click ...

... the shooter's pistol slide locked back, dry and empty.

Wide-eyed, the German turned the gun side on and scanned the drawn slide of the empty firearm with absolute incredulity as, seizing the opportunity, Black quickly shot up and collided violently with the remaining stahlhelm-clad cocksucker. In a rough tackle, he brought him down as Calvert tore in from his six, wielding his dual knives through the gusting smoke haze, on approach to the final remaining high-priority targets left in the kill zone:

Ernst-Günther Baade and his *gunsel leutnant.*

At the rear of the vehicle, Baade deliberately raised from a crouched position protecting his precious adjutant, not once removing his intense stare from these two staunching attackers as they found him in the fog of war.

Even through their ski-masks, he recognized the men from a very recent acquaintance.

Smug and confident, Baade issued Calvert a coy smirk as he reached across his belt, harnessing the power of his sheathed langschwert. His hand wrapped around the hilt like a samurai, prepared for anything with the folded prowess of a praying mantis.

Feeling a sense of breathlessness as he faced the would-be boss fight of this ambush, Mike Calvert raised his brass gauntleted fists and downward daggers, unafraid, and ready to engage.

He did so.

As fast as a pant of air, Mad Mike recalled his middleweight boxing championship years in the Royal Engineers in 1933, and converted his form for use of the trench knives. He lunged in close and tight to Baade, engaging him one-on-one in what could be considered a reckless overreach of suicidal proportion.

Baade backpedalled a single long step in order to fold backwards, avoiding Calvert's heavy haymaker jabs as they whooshed through the air, even dipping on either side each once before finally taking the time to unsheathe his sword.

With a scraping *schwing!* he drew the blade, simultaneously slashing out at Calvert's posture, which the agile Berzerker managed to block by use of his twin brass knuckleduster trench knives. The short blades formed a downward cruciform when he punched his fists together, catching Baade's blade like a two-pronged fork.

Baade energetically drove a sidekick out from the canopy of his kilt, striking Calvert in the fold of his arm and casing their powerful embrace to disengage.

Rearing up a step, Calvert shook off the pain caused to his extremity, bouncing with a spring in his boxer step before preparing to reengage the deadly swordsman.

Baade swung his sword at full force, aiming to maim his opponent.

Like 'punching the mitts' in boxing sparring training, Calvert worked Baade's slashing melee with his protected fists, the brass colliding with the steel with metallic clashes.

The two engaged for a full five seconds of impressive parry-ripostes before Calvert lost a weapon from his left hand; the edge of Baade's blade gouged his knuckles deeply after it slipped from the hilt, and then a follow-through backswing lifted Calvert's remaining M1918 knife from his firm hold like a bungee. The metal from his brass knuckleduster trench knives clattered as they scattered across the road.

Almost conceding a vivisection, Calvert suddenly remembered he had a rifle strapped across his back, and he harnessed it like a military showcase exhibition drill, gun-spinning the Lee Enfield up from beneath his arm and catching it with both hands in time to block Baade's balestra-style short-step launch. The langschwert chomped through the wooden stock but ceased once it collided with the metal components housed within.

Angered by this clutch-up, Baade bared his fangs whilst bringing up his boot into Calvert's exposed sternum, punting him like a closed-door breach. The kick disengaged their fight, and the two warriors broke apart.

"Berzerkerrr!!!"

Out of the blue, the bellowing war cries of an incoming Special Z Unit duo resounded as they came in hot from hell, skiing down the slope and straight into the smoky fray, almost gaining Baade's unguarded posterior.

Unlike Calvert and Black, Jerry and Scotty opted not to remove their skis in their attack run on the dry ground after the snowy descent.

Ahead of Wingate's reinforcing army on the slopes, the duo overtook Jack Churchill by the road as he halted to remove his alpine ski panels.

They whooshed in like double-tapped bullets out of the barrel of a handgun; trench knives raised like fangs for the duelling like how they had been trained for use in Berzerker fashion.

Zooming on their glides, Jerry and Scotty arrived in unison behind Baade's position by the back end of the second car, speeding towards him comparably to jousting knights, about to properly fuck his shit up—

Swish-chunk!

Like a cornered beast, Baade quickly assumed better footing and held his longsword with an assisting hand. As they swarmed in close, he spun on his feet and performed a ballet pirouette, twirling his Scottish kilt like the petals of a dandelion in the midst.

Whilst doing so, he swished his sword with one swift motion and chopped at neck-level, separating the head of Scotty Wellings as he came in first at full-assail with his trench knife daggered in stabbing motion.

With superior reach, Baade applied severe severance.

With extreme prejudice and zero resistance, Scotty's heavy head was sliced off at the neck.

Fingers wrapped firmly through the eyelets of his trench knife knuckleduster grooves, his hand severed from his wrist in the same fluent motion of the swordsman's strike, slashing like a weighted laser wielded with fluency and precision.

After the unexpected amputations and decapitation, Scotty's inert body lost traction above his skis and his knees folded, tumbling into a violent collapse across the road before crashing somewhere off into the connecting descent of the snowy slope and into some brush.

Existing in his lost trajectory was a spill stream of red blood, streaking against the street surface like a tyre skid mark, continuing with high contrast into the snowy whites beyond.

The lopped head became airborne, sailing ahead of a gory entrail, before heavily bouncing across the road like a juicy cantaloupe, sloshing and bounding like a hunk of hollow, hairy meat.

Riposting from the same swung posture, Baade hunched inverted and then thrust forwards beneath the remnants of their allied attack, running Gentle Jerry through the core as he raised both his knives in similar stabbing motions, about to leap and wail on Baade like a savage.

Baade's sword penetrated his chest through the sternum, piercing his fabric layers and flesh, grating ribs. Blood squirted from both entry and exit puncture wounds as the five-foot doubled-edged blade skewered him, running him through.

Like an anchor, Baade was unmoving.

Jerry yanked like on a wire—his attached skis disengaged beneath him, flying outwards and discarded, just like the wind in his sail.

Eyes bulging, Gentle Jerry became promptly deprived of his life ...

Grimacing teeth stained red from blood as bile expelled up his throat like a leaky vomit, the galivanting giant sustained stern eye contact with the German who had impaled him on a pike like a spearfish. Somehow conjuring the strength to fight on, Jerry clutched at Baade's sword blade, slowly sliding himself against the suction of the wound, pulling himself all the way to the hilt in a final attempt to gain ground, swishing with his dagger. Unfortunately, Jerry's juggernauting joust subdued as he reached range of Baade, and his eyes faded of fury. He released his hold on the trench knifes, which slipped from his dead fingers with a metallic tinkle to the roadside beneath his body as the oaf collapsed to a propped position at the knees, bayoneted on the sword.

A little stunned and infuriated by what had just transpired before him, Calvert attacked Baade from the rear with a sudden surge of vigour and short run-up.

Baade's blood-spattered face emerged above the collar of his jacket, and he reacted like the closeted skilled combatant that he was.

As he charged in with quick footing, Calvert promptly received an agile sidekick from the seemingly older war veteran that propelled him over onto his tail end, winded and temporarily debilitated.

"Oi!" Churchill barked hastily, disengaging his skis and staking his poles into the muddy sleet on the side of the road. He had arrived late to the close quarters of this battle charge, witnessing his Berzerker acquaintances lose their lives in their attempts at taking down the expert swordsman. He was not unaccustomed to death but hadn't seen anybody he knew be killed for a long time—and certainly never in an execution manner such as this.

Closing distance, his gape traced the bloody remnants from fallen soldiers and onto Ernst-Günther Baade as he finally withdrew his five-foot sword from Jerry's large corpse, allowing for the lifeless lug to slump to the road now fully removed of life. Due to suction, the withdrawal of steel from meat required a great deal of strength.

In the anarchy and with a face like thunder, Baade's deathly stare met Churchill's arrival—his offer of contest.

Accepting, *he aimed his blood-red blade.*

These were curious circumstances in which these two titans had found each other, considering Baade had trained Churchill on how to swordfight and was still clearly the wunderkind.

Confidently, Churchill poised firm, reaching across and drawing his shiny basket-hilted, silver-bladed claybeg from his hip. Once retracted from the sheath, he twirled it by his side with his wrist, slicing air.

These two men had clashed blades on several occasions over the past week, but this time it was the real deal. The ante had now been upped, and this time they would be drawing blood with the intent to kill.

"Thiz zhall be interezteng ..." Baade breathed as he took a step out from the cover of the Mercedes to give himself space. The shooting from Wingate's Berzerkers up on the slope at their position had subdued now that they had men within proximity. Instead, their fire had been repurposed to the loaded transport trucks pulling up out front of Saint-Oyen, sounding off like a warzone in the background.

Churchill beheld a certain conviction taunting the German with some literary lingo. "Ever read a book? Eventually, the master always becomes bested by the student!"

Baade pursed his lips. "We zhall zee."

The amount of blood from the bullet wound to his shoulder became appropriately foremost, evidently leaking down his arm and dripping from Baade's fingertips on his left hand.

"Hardly a fair fight," Churchill said to him—this was the second time he had said this to Baade and served as a call back to their first meeting. Except, this time, a double reversal was contained within.

"No zuch thing ..." equally as wittedly, Baade responded, recalling their past usage of the phrase. It was like he was accepting the hindrance inspired by his own arrogant teachings.

Without skipping a beat, *Jack attacked.*

He dashed forwards with a recognizable lunge tactic; the intentional obviousness disguised a well-thought follow-up manoeuvre, which Baade successfully countered and riposted with a low-angled tilt aimed at Churchill's exposed calf beneath his kilt canopy. Slicing weightless air, Jack quickly tucked his limb above the slash, parrying an enthusiastic jab with his return swing, saving wounds with metallic collisions.

Successively, the two clashed steel with oscillating lunges and hunched postures, fluctuating squats with bent knees whilst attacking and blocking at full strength and full speed, chiselling the edges of their sharpened sword blades.

Chink!

Ching!

Tang!

Chink!

Tang!

Behind gritted teeth, their swords struck with wielded medieval fury.

Beneath the morning sun, their silver steel shimmered and glinted against the icy white backdrop.

During their duel, Baade controlled his langschwert with single-handed predominance. This was partly due to the bullet scathe to his shoulder, but also to belittle and provoke his opponent into reading his tactics as condescending and potentially acting rashly.

However, Churchill did not bite on the bait.

He recalled every recent teaching by the grandmaster swordsman and expert swordfighter. It was imperative to respect the art as well as the artist, utilizing his own competences and using them well, feeling he even surprised Baade on several occasions with his unpredictable style, agility, and tact.

Shuffling like Apache dancers, the two unconsciously migrated their fight away from the crashed vehicles, Bowery Waltzing out in the open in a display of fencing footwork, flexing their swordsmanship skills for all warfighters to marvel at.

Behind their inharmonious swordfight, as steel clashed violently against steel, Baade's petrified adjutant and gunsel cowered lowly behind the Mercedes. Unexpectedly, he was approached by two men appearing through the smoke, dust, and flakes of ash.

It was *Graeme Black* and *Mike Calvert.*

Black had assisted Calvert in climbing to his feet, and in doing so, the two of them noticed the unguarded Nationale Bewegung der Schweiz, Nazi diplomat hiding near the car. A damsel in distress, all on his own, he had been found minus his guardian alemán.

The German officer had long ago recovered his tiny service pistol from his belt holster and held it in his grasp as he cowered behind the wheel arch of the car, hiding.

"There you are, gunsel!" Black taunted chauvinistically as he swiftly stepped around the Swiss German, effortlessly swiping the pistol from his weak grasp as though it had been a child offering candy. "Ta!" he said, disarming the small PP handgun and tossing it across the road with a metallic declivity.

The leutnant winced, anxiously retracting as far away from the two scary men as possible, which in this circumstance, involved crawling backwards *into* the open rear door of the shot to shit Mercedes-Benz.

Lowering his head, Black followed him into the backseat, halting just in the doorway.

The leutnant had nowhere else to run or hide, and so he sat across the glass-covered leather seats, staring breathlessly at the two killers with wide eyes of dread and horror, resembling a cornered rodent.

After a moment's hiatus of execution, Black drew his M1911 in the same hand as his knuckleduster trench knife, levelling it at the scared individual and causing him to start shedding tears of fear ... but he didn't pull the trigger.

The Gerry gunsel hadn't been dismissed from this. It was just that Mad Mike had a better resolution to this poncy problem.

Ready to decree the said solution, Calvert tapped Black on the arm with something from his parka pocket, issuing him with the prepared bronze-coloured No.36M Mills bomb hand grenade.

Cracking a smile at the thought, Black graciously accepted the device and held his gun on the victim whilst he sadistically pulled the pin with his teeth, holding the device in the car with the spoon lever still clenched in his grasp.

"Auf Wiedersehen, motherfucker," Black saluted prior to casually releasing his hold on the grenade's detonator lever as well as the grenade. It fell onto the soft leather and then rolled into the abyss of the floor space.

He stepped clear and slammed shut the damaged door before dashing off into the smoke haze with Calvert, vanishing quickly away of sight—and out of dodge of the exploding grenade.

Too terrified to move, the scared stiff leutnant merely watched the weighty circular metal unit be dropped on the cushion of the seat, rolling onto the floor. He closed his eyes, tensing himself tight.

Poor cunt was barely able to process what was about to happ—
BOOM!

In the background of their swashbuckling swordfight, right as Baade swung a high-arc attack at Churchill and the two swords met in the air with a clanging *ching!* the remaining shot-to-shit Großer Mercedes-Benz 770 imploded behind them, erupting with a vivid orange fireball and hurling debris outwards.

The vehicle detonated from the internal fragmentation grenade, pelting pieces of razor-sharp shards in all directions, lifting dirt from the ground and shaking the snowflakes from the surrounding road.

The two red swastika-decorated doors launched away from the blast, bounding heavily and scraping across the surface of the road. One disappeared from sight down the ravine-side of the valley, the other skimmed like a stone across the road, taking out a set of wooden ski poles staked into the ground by Jack Churchill.

Miraculously, the debris missed them.

Chunks of hot shrapnel from the blast flung about audibly.

The thunderous explosion went off barely fifty feet from the contesting combatants, blanketing them in a sudden heatwave, and causing them both to pinch a shrug at the shoulders, momentarily distracted from their engagement.

The scorching orange fireball from the internal grenade explosion exhorted the hinged doors from the chassis, throwing them clear with a potent force as the shockwave of fire exhumed outward, gulping air to fuel to the vibrancy of the blast. The hood, bonnet, and metal roof were all removed from the metal skeletal remnants of the car as the upholstery, cushions, and lone remaining occupant were blown to kingdom come, entirely incinerated.

Two types of shockwaves hit Baade.

One physical, one emotional as he realized that his adjutant, with whom he was romantically involved, had occupied the car at the time of the detonation, and consequently the explosion had claimed his life.

Out of time's synchronization, Baade's slow-motion gaze glimmered as he witnessed the aftermath of the fiery explosion's bloom. His eyes darted yonder, noticing Graeme Black and Mike Calvert fleeing the kill zone, positively identifying them through the heat haze shimmer above the flashing fire. He immediately went from being a composed kilt-clad zen zwordfighter to an incensed monströs, monomaniacal on seeking vengeance and vile with an uncaged rage.

Relative time returned. Breathing echoic exhales which became restored to normality, Ernst-Günther Baade wandered a few steps away from his transitory stagnant engagement with Churchill, wading towards the fiery remnants. He witnessed both culprits Black and Calvert reattach their skis and fly off-piste down the connecting slope.

Recovering steadily from the shockwave, Jack Churchill next took a concussive moment to assess the developing battleground around them.

Wingate had appeared on the hills to assist the fight, stalling the German reinforcements, though it now seemed that a few of the Special Z Unit members had fallen on the slope, having taken fire from said reinforcements. He had since given the order to fall back, and the lot of them were currently slickening the slope to the west, heading away from Saint-Oyen and into the Aosta Valley, and away from the hostility.

Ruffell and Komrower had complied with said retreat order and done the same, and with Black and Calvert joining in on the mass withdrawal. This meant that Churchill was now the last man remaining at the fight ...

If one thought Churchill likely to retreat from a war then they absolutely, positively did not know Jack.

Indifferent to Baade's leutnant's unexpected demise, Churchill attempted to take the cup, spontaneously engaging Baade at his unguarded, kilted six with a cheap shot equal to a rabbit punch in a prize fight. However, he knew that even in this fleeting moment of mourning, which was about to manifest into a rage-induced flurry, that Baade still maintained the ability to counter his attack.

In this regard, swordfighting was a lot like chess, and his opponent could read the move after the move he was thinking about making. Therefore, he had to think ahead; of the next strike after the counter, and plan for the next riposte after that.

From his belt, Churchill discreetly drew his trench knife from its sheath, holding it in a downward position in his opposite hand to his claybeg. He now duel-wielded a sword and dagger simultaneously to counter Baade's longsword.

Taking a quick breath, he cavorted a two-step run-up before conducting a flèche (short running attack) at the adversary, to which Baade somehow predicted on an a questionably high precognition level, orbiting in time to parry Jack's incoming steel with a lateral slash of his own.

Upon clutching the defence to slant Mad Jack's diagonal attack away with his blade, Baade's other hand attached to his hilt, upping the power ante to his attaque au fer.

Churchill nearly lost hold of his sword from the parry, Baade deflected so fiercely. Another over-shoulder attack swept in, and Churchill blocked it using almost all his energy. It was followed by another, which Jack managed to deflect via use of his trench knife reenforcing his claybeg.

Utilizing his newfound reservoir of rage, Baade's actions swung crazily and out of control, causing Churchill to react in a backpedal whilst deflecting the heavy two-handed swings.

Churchill's boots danced about, revolving in his stance between each round of wild beat attacks and ceding parries. He slinked a few low slashes in with the dagger between Baade's eludes of the longsword, swishing air in lieu of his opponent's movements. Although a unique idea, the small blade was proving almost useless in this duel.

Jack did manage to outplay Baade at one instance where he used a sleight of hand tactic to position the M1918 trench dagger in the same hand as his claybeg. Baade hadn't noticed the juggler's switch until it was too late, and Churchill managed to riposte from a clash with a stabbing motion from beneath his hilt, staking him in the forearm through his uniform sleeve. It caused this uber-Hun to cry from the sting of pain.

Making it a double, Churchill reared an ounce, only to crane in with a savage left hook, striking Baade across his glatt rasiert clean shaven jaw. The sound of brass knuckles meeting jaw was as grotesque as expected, splitting Baade's skin before he swiped parallel in a protective fashion, keeping Churchill's nuisance at bay.

Baade finalized his sword-fighting combination with an irregular and volatile punt with his lower limb from underneath his dangling kilt canopy. His heavy boot drove into Churchill's exposed pelvic gut, sending the younger fighter flying in reverse, tumbling to a staggered heap. His steel claybeg sword and knuckleduster trench knife clattered as they became each dropped to the ground in his fumble for stability, scraping his palms on the bitumen.

Before Churchill could catch a breath and locate his lost weapons, Baade pounced upon him with a venomous sneer. He slithered in low-slung like a powerful predator, grabbing Jack's exposed throat with the big grasp from his spare hand, clutching him in a firm stranglehold.

Swooping in staunchly, Baade's grasp fully captured the dazed and defeated Churchill. By guidance of his vast double-edged langschwert blade held across his neck like a cut-throat razor, he raised Churchill to his feet with a mighty hold.

The two men locked stares.

Blade beneath Mad Jack's exposed sweaty gullet, Baade held him captive to a well slit throat or a mild decapitation.

Churchill's hands raised submissively out beside him, essentially yielding. He panted breathlessly finding himself in quite the pickle and at the mercy of his latest self-proclaimed nemesis.

It was in that moment's hesitation that Churchill was able to read the devil behind Baade's stare ...

He saw his instinctual intent to *lather in inconsequential spite* at the captive mercenary switch to *intent to kill,* and his eyes zeroed on Jack's neckline as he pressed and carved, lacerating the man's flesh clean open and gutting him like a—

Luckily, Jack read the article before it published.

With all his will, he clutched at Baade's sword hand, attempting desperately to slow the thrust of his slice whilst, with the other, locating and grasping at the exit hole of the German's shoulder bullet wound. He found the bloody socket with ease, poking his thumb in the hole as though he was plugging a bloody leak, causing the German to writhe in sudden agony ... but it wasn't enough to falter him.

Churchill's expression fractured.

He would do what he knew best.

Extracting his thumb, Jack's index and middle finger formed a firm protrusion ... the same ones used for vaginal fingering. Grimacing awkwardly from the clutch at his neck, now more from the experience of fingering a man, Churchill jabbed Baade's open wound with two fingers.

Baade roared in agony, inadvertently releasing his grip on his victim, and Jack was able to drop low and push away from his hangman executioner, performing the limbo beneath Baade's brandishing blade as he forcefully retaliated in a wild wide slice attack—*Slish!*

The action was not without its pound of flesh.

The tip of the five-foot blade nipped the edge of Churchill's left cheek as he invertedly swivelled away from the sword's swing. The cut was deep, nearly ten millimetres through soft tissue. It would scar his face forever ...

After his instinctive roll to gain clearance, Churchill dropped flat on the gravel of the road, touching and dabbing at his lacerated cheek as blood poured out of the gash in his flesh.

Baade staggered a step backwards, recovering from the surge of pain in his shoulder which almost caused him to faint. The wound was slowly sapping him of power. Whatever capacity he now endured was fuelled only by the rage of vengeance. Within two seconds, both breathless men were cognizant of their predicament and each fast reacting.

Eyes grown wide, Churchill reacted to Baade's lunge baring a ferocious axe-like chop with his sword, striking the road to gravel crumbs just inches from his athletic reverse-shoulder roll into a standing position. Jack glanced quickly and his peripherals spotted his discarded claybeg sword. He flunged himself forth, legs flailing behind his dive, in order to seize the weapon before Baade could attack again, fast grabbing at the steel piece and revolving in a fast roll—*CHING!*—he pulled up his blade and blocked the next strike with a steel scream of merging metal.

It was as if the melees melded and magnetized, binding them together behind two equal forces of power.

Beyond the locked blades, Churchill sensed the old man was tiring.

Finally, this unkillable combatant drained of power, of energy ...

With a sudden resolution, the bloody-faced Churchill shoved him in a standing, lunging advance which broke them apart. Jack fenced the arduous gent fast and deadly, tapping into a source of unknown oomph and acting faster than he had ever fought before, swinging from his left shoulder and then right, high and then low, causing Baade—for the first time—to become the one on the backpedal.

Rearing him up and gravitating their duel towards the warmth of the flames from the burning automobile, Churchill felt Baade's longsword blade intertwine with his in a particular on-and-off-manner ...

He had felt this sensation before; the sharp metal surfaces gritting and grinding together as their edges scraped in conjunction with Baade's footing tap-dancing in the revert of his own for a rhythmic instance ... and *then,* it happened ...

Before Churchill could swing another attack, Baade abruptly saw a window and lunged forwards, twirling his blade like a cyclone entangled with Churchill's, almost like he was tying a special sailor's knot.

And just like *that* ... Churchill became suddenly neutralized.

Similar to a magic trick, Baade disarmed Churchill of his sword.

With a shift of weight on his trained footing and a harness of whirling momentum impetus the opponent's blade against his own, Baade gave a twist and outward thrust of the steel entanglement with his wrist, sending Churchill's sword slackly from his loosened grasp, due to targeted vibration and centrifugal force.

The look on Churchill's baffled mug was of perplexion and displeasure. *Fool me twice,* this had been the same magic trick manoeuvre Baade had performed on him during their first-ever mock confrontation. Jack had just assumed that it was a combination of Baade showing off and him having his guard down due to it not being a real fight, however, this time it was for real— life and death. He had been striving to win this fight, and it was in that moment of realization that Churchill saw the error in his overzealousness. Baade had lulled him into a false sense of overconfidence, and then used his own energy, charge, and variating imbalance against him ...

He had appeared weak when he was strong.

Jack was exposed, unarmed, and unprotected.

The man with the blade, Baade took the moment to catch some heavy breaths. He dropped eye contact with the vulnerable Englishman in order to encircle his discarded weapon as it lied on the road a few steps yonder. Once upon it, Baade looked up and at the helpless Churchill, making sure he was watching what would happen next.

Right about now, Jack almost thought that he was about to lift it with his boot, send it flying his way or at the least, kick it his way for collection so that they might finish this duel of fates. Nevertheless, reality is often grimmer.

Baade stomped his shoe down into the metal, snapping it.

His hefty boot raised and then suddenly struck like an anvil, slamming heavily against the blade just above the hilt, shattering the steel against the road right before Churchill's disenchanted eyes.

His claybeg broke.

The blade fractured above the handle, now in two pieces.

It was during this whole process that Churchill saw past Baade and beyond the burning cars, right as a truck loaded with infantrymen with rifles arrived and immediately began dismounting. They had their sights fixed on this very altercation, and would be closing the distance with weapons raised and their fingers on the triggers.

He had seconds to finish this duel and bail ...

... the odds were greatly not on his side.

Before he had a chance to think, Churchill's chain of thought was interrupted by a familiar voice, shouting from behind the chaos.

"Oi, Jack! Ged'own!" the Aussie voice of Calvert resonated.

In a flash of peripheral scanning, Churchill whipped his view around in time to see that both Calvert and Black had circled back on their skis from their retreat, possibly once realizing that he had not withdrawn along with them and the others, and had boldly decided to return to the fight to lend a hand.

He hadn't been hard to find.

Calvert was in the process of bringing around his rifle whilst Black raised his pistol into a cup and saucer pose, squinting with one eye across the sights at Baade.

Bam ... Bam ... Bam ...

Spaced shots across the distance near-missed the low-dipping Churchill, targeting at the German with the sword. While most missed from what was left of Black's short M1911 magazine, two of the bullets struck Ernst-Günther Baade: one a graze beneath the armpit and bumping a rib, and the other in the meat of the upper thigh through his kilt.

Frown inverting, Black cast a surprised gleam upon the locked slide of his gun whilst searching for spare magazines with his free hand. He turned up empty, having lost his ammunition pouch somewhere during all the chaos. Conceding, he cursed, collapsing the slide and snapping the hammer forth prior to holstering it away, unable to intervene any further. Beside him, Calvert fumbled for his slung rifle, inspecting it for functionality.

It was still kitted with the No. 68 AT rifle grenade attachment ...

Face dripping red from blood, sweat, and tears, the boche brute winced from the bullet hits. Now grimacing his crooked, tea-stained teeth, he remained undeterred, pressing forwards after the disarmed Jack Churchill: his deemed source of his ultimate anguish.

Whoosh!

Somehow managing to duck another guillotine from the resilient unwavering, determined kilted killer kraut, Churchill reacted to Baade's staggered backswing. His huge doubled-edged longsword rushed through the air with a whistling skreich, missing Jack's turned head by an inch.

Bloody-cheeked and dripping from sweat, Churchill allowed for himself to collapse reactively from the attack. Once horizontal, he rolled evasively and quickly regained composure, upstanding and confronting his foe in a defensive fisticuff pose.

Baade was now shot a total of three times in the back and front, bleeding from a nasty laceration on his jaw, and arguably worst of all, haemorrhaging uncontrollably from a broken heart. Breathless and weary, he unsteadily loomed over Churchill like an unrelenting undead zombie; eyes bloodshot from rage, glowing brighter than hellfire.

Dragging himself forth, Baade brought the heavy longsword around for another ranged follow-through: his undying focus fixated on the scampering Mad Jack.

Like a slaughterer's wield, the heavy swing of the swordsman's blade whished through the air, trailing Churchill's well-timed nimble shoulder roll away from the slashing carve. He tucked his feet up high, managing to avoid the exhausted executioner's pivot as he stumbled on the road bitumen.

Beaten, bruised, and munted, Churchill trundled gracelessly across the debris-covered motorway, tripping up over the detached driver's side door to one of the Großer Mercedes-Benz 770s and collecting another couple of nicks and grazes. Dodging another incoming slash attack from his relentless pursuer, Churchill collapsed intentionally towards his previously placed ski panels and poles in a shuffling mess. His peepers blinked profusely across the possessions, unable to see anything he could use as a defensive or offensive weapon against his persistent aggressor who was, again, coming in fast and furious.

No time—Churchill felt him stepping in close, likely wielding his langschwert with lethal intention. He grabbed a bamboo ski pole and twisted, holding it defensivel—

Thunk!

Baade slashed, effortlessly chopping the pointed stick in half.

Observing the fatal damage dealt, Churchill brought the remaining nub in for an examination before casting it aside.

Shuffling further backwards, Churchill quickly predicted Baade's motions via his footing as he planted wide. The duellist was about to end this fight—he brought his sword upwards, arranging his hold inverted in order to yield a better stabbing motion in a downward trajectory.

He was about to impale Churchill through the heart.

Run him through like a piledriver.

Jack acted instinctively, quickly pulling himself rearward on his elbows and feet, causing the downward-thrusting blade to penetrate twelve inches lower than intended—

T'CHIS!

The blade struck the bitumen through Churchill's kilt blanket, between his legs and millimetres from his twig and two berries as he split them apart— far enough, he hoped.

With eyes wide from shock and surprise, Churchill quickly reacted, swinging his leg over in order to climb to his feet and scurry further away. As he did so, he took out his overarching foe's speared blade, which followed suite with a nimble swish through the air, nipping at his cock like a hungry croc.

The tip of the sword clipped Churchill's boot, and he fell again to his rearend, defensively facing his slow-pacing slayer. Scampering in debris and growing in exhaustion, Jack's concentration remained attentive to Baade as he slowly pursued above him like a pending doom.

Jack's hand felt a familiar device: his broken sword hilt.

In a last-ditch effort to stop him, Churchill raised the weighty handle piece, tossing it in a toppling throw at Baade, who merely swiped it from existence with his langschwert with a metallic *clang!*

The next projectile, however, he could not simply swat like a flyswatter swishing an insect ...

... for it was a No.68 anti-tank rifle grenade.

... choooOOF!

Churchill noticed his obscurely positioned comrade's contemplated tactic at the last minute, and acted just as late—or, perhaps, just in time to fool their formidable foe—by launching himself away in a lowly strafe, gliding over the top of the dislodged car door and raising it angularly as a protective shield for an impending explosion ...

Off-guard and cautioned, Baade quickly glanced around.

The last thing he saw was Jack Churchill balling up behind a swastika-painted shield.

Traced by a fast-travelling finger of smoke, the fired projectile struck the desired spot as coordinated by the rifle operator, Mike Calvert.

The 2.5-pound HEAT charge crumpled against the abrasive road surface as it detonated, striking the deep-set dirt-based bitumen like would a crashing nosecone from a fighter plane.

The earth exploded barely three-paces before Ernst-Günther Baade's boots, burying him in a cloud of black smoke, rock, and shrapnel as the pocket of road exploded in his face. Sword-wielding arms thrown up before his face to shield from the blast, kilt expanding like a parachute canopy, he became ejected from the fight like a leaf of the wind.

The unkillable kilted German was immediately removed from view by the abrupt explosion, entirely collected by the sideward impact and transferred—hopefully, finally—to the afterlife.

Behind his makeshift shield, Churchill's view became instinctually blocked from the heat of the close-proximity blast. When his squinting eyeline returned, he saw nothing but hovering smoke. Baade was gone—blown up, even.

In the absence of his adversary and the rumble of the aftermath, Jack heard familiar voices snap him back to reality.

"*Come on, Jack!*" the song of Graeme Black and Mike Calvert shouted in the distance. They viciously waved their arms and swiped their hands, calling him towards their retreat.

Navigating the flaming Mercedes-Benz convoy smokescreen caused the incoming enemy transport trucks to momentarily second-guess their advance at the scene. Within sixty seconds they would arrive, dismount, and shoot the absolute shit out of anybody still standing at this concocted kill zone.

Without wasting a second, Churchill pushed up from the road, trod into his nearby ski panels and grabbed his remaining bamboo ski pole. After the swift attiring motion, he trotted off the mark as incoming fire from the reserve army came his way.

Whizz!

Whizz, whizz!

Bullets carved through the air about his head as he leapt from the strip and onto the slope on the opposite side of the road, immediately quickening his speed with vigour as he adapted his balance accordingly. His hand found the handles of his lone pole push-off, and he pressed on even harder as more shots struck the ground around him.

Black and Calvert met him along the slope of the gulley, and eventually their rogue group caught up with the rest of the retreating Berzerker unit, and the lot of them headed back home to the resort.

Upon hearing the closing chapter of Churchill's clandestine Switzerland-era surfacing from the depths of history, Hardy's brow formed a frown amalgamated of attentiveness and disbelief.

Churchill leant back from his wireframe bunk in the bowels of the gloomy Sachsenhausen barracks in the a.m. hours of this endless stale night of encampment.

He pursed his lips and tipped his head. "True story."

Hardy shook his deep concentration, still limply cradling his pencil nub and notepad. His response was the same as every time the British dictator uttered the words to instil a sense of gravity to his far-fetched and fanciful narrative. "Sure, Jack. Sure."

The American journalist had captured much detail of Churchill's classified period, and was about to do something a nonbiased journalist keen on a juicy story should never do: give an open opinion.

"You know what," he said reading over his pages with an undertone of disdain, "your *Berzerker* pals ..."

Reading his mind, Churchill's chin raised. "What of them?"

"They were a real bunch of fuckin' assholes."

Churchill blew air out his nose with a grin.

No argument there.

I mean, let's do a summary:

Orde Wingate: fuckwit. Man had big balls, but a small cock; a cock likely to rot off from all his alleged diseases. His knob was probably as black as his heart was. By the end of this war, the man could either go down in history as one of the most questionably successful generals in British Army history, or as a complete and utter nutjob, just shy of absolute lunacy. The line was fine, but for what it was worth, Wingate ended up accomplishing much more than most mere mortals. Typically, his path was paved with good intentions, like a sort of consequentialism where the end justified the means.

Graeme Black: fuckwit. One hell of a soldier, as proven by his current stint in No.2 Commando, but a condescending gronk and an outright bellend through-and-through. At that point in time, Jack guessed he'd probably go on to win the war or die trying. That was, of course, until *Operation Musketoon* when, let's just say, Black's life changed forever ...

Michael Dredge: fuckwit. Albeit, at times, a funny bloke, he was a profound grade-A tosser who proved only in the eleventh hour to be an honourable man of conscientious moral fibre. He was heroically dead, but still a fuckwit.

Mike Calvert: brainwashed Orde Wingate flunky and a man of uncertain moral fibre, but a man not short of admirable military accolades. He would stay by Wingate's side and go on to become a founding *Chindit:* the Otter's next successful unorthodox unit. To Mad Jack, Mad Mike often found himself a sane soldier amidst an insane regime. Hopefully he would remain untainted by Wingate's dubious pastimes.

Bala Bredin and *Moshe Dayan:* actually, alright blokes.

Rushworth, Bort, and *Batey:* Fuckwits.

Scotty Wellings, Gentle Jerry: both dead, both borderline fuckwits, although they did stay loyal to the cause and honourable until the end, even if they did bite off more than they could have ever chewed trying to take on Ernst-Günther-fucking-Baade in a knife fight.

Danny Boy: one-hundred percent committable psychopath, traitor to The Crown, as well as a certified fuckwit. Promoted to Swiss cheese.

Arthur Komrower: a top bloke and trialled-by-fire hero commando. His bravery, and unstoppable, unkillable feats during the events of Operation Archery mimicked that of Jack Churchill's, and will never be forgotten by history.

Humphrey Ruffell: another top bloke, and a man of many military mischiefs shared by Mad Jack to come ...

"Jack, this whole tangent ... it's pretty wild," expanded Hardy, still absorbing what had transpired in Churchill's story. He had effectively been toe-to-toe with war crimes such as murder and disloyalty, colouring him ambivalently. "You tangoed with all sorts of high treason that fateful Christmas."

Churchill endured the silence, but did not deny.

The proximity of which he tippy-toed elements of criminal corruption, he was both aware and ashamed of. The deeds of distress were better not spoken about. Thankfully, the Special Z Unit was a classified black operation, redacted from the history books.

"Well, *you* wanted to know ..." he offered, and Hardy accepted with a pendulous gesture of gratefulness. "*Now,* you know." These secretive events were a hot item which he had craved since Jack had skipped over the details during his first biographical chapter, *Once Upon a War,* between the period of the Phoney War and the ambush at L'Épinette. "As eventful as the *non-event* was, before it was erased from history, there was one last moment aboard the Mont de la Gouille expedition worthy of mention. It happened during the weeks following the failed ambush of Baade ..."

Hardy bobbled his head, pencil at the ready. "O.K., go."

'The weeks following the botched surprise attack on Lieutenant-Colonel Ernst-Günther Baade in the Aosta Valley, along Italy's border with Switzerland, the remaining Berzerkers of Wingate's Special Z Unit retreated to the confines of the resort—forever. From there, the unit slowly disbanded, with several of the men performing an Irish exit, parting ways without so much as a farewell handshake. It was a surreal period where the remaining Berzerkers weren't sure whether to mourn their fallen comrades, stay the course of a commencing demilitarization, or run for the hills and RTU (Return To Unit), retreating back within their respective army mobilizations and forgetting that this lucid nightmare happened ...'

'Unsure whether to 'hit' ... or 'stay' ...'

1940, April
Winterthur Resort, Mont de la Gouille
Swiss Pennine Alps, Switzerland

In the days following the eventful retaliatory incident, the Berzerker numbers (and structure) exponentially decayed, inexplicably diminishing without much lasting curiosity. It had run its course; had its stint. It was time to put the old horse down.

Any man seeking their emigration was delighted to find that Wingate's admin, Mister et cetera himself, Moshe Dayan, had left the resort safe unlocked upon his own wordless departure. Upon his exodus, each man could attain their identification tags and resume their official identities upon their returns to the real world.

During these dwindling days, Churchill awoke one morning to find a near empty resort. Men had vacated overnight without so much as a sendoff. In fact, his descent to the cold lounge room was just in time to watch a hire car arrive in the rink out front. The unmarked vehicle collected Graeme Black and his two bags of luggage, and he promptly vanished without a goodbye, seemingly to never be seen or heard from again.

Deprived of all farewells, the reclusive troop's ride swiftly consumed him and subsequently vanished into the scenic Spring surroundings of Switzerland—a change of season that mimicked their own change of pace. The car likely transferred Black along the same path as the others who had recently vacated the Winterthur Resort; to a nearby airport, and on a return to the United Kingdom to be redrafted into the British Army, moving forth with his military career.

With fresh wiry stitches through his cheek to help seal his soft tissue wound, Churchill tenderly downed the stairs of the quiet hangout and entered the carpeted common room. He had never seen the place so vacant; so hollow and echoic.

He helped himself to a brew, patrolling the empty space.

View cast to his right and into the connected kitchen, he noted that the group's makeshift arsenal of gear had been completely packaged in crates and cart baggage, prepared for a pickup by a depot freight truck due for arrival at any day now.

Without notifying any of the men, Wingate had pulled the plug on this whole operation, recalling everything and incinerating truths, discarding the Berzerkers like cremation ashes to the wind. He, too, had vanished like a ghost one morning, bags packed and leaving a mere empty wire hanger in the closet.

Churchill stared vacuously through the quiet main hall of the resort; across the empty lounge room, his eyes chasing the ghosts of their respective disappearances, though no remnants were to be found. Not even a sliver.

"Everybody's gone," the comforting voice of Mike Calvert explained from his seated position up on the reception desk. Well-dressed in a wool cardigan, button up, pressed trousers, and even with his boots on, the man was probably keen to catch a cab out of this frozen hell hole at any minute. It may have even been called already, and he was enjoying a final burnt coffee from the kitchenette whist waiting his own transportation to a designated airfield; his ticket back to the real world. "Him, too."

Churchill's head tipped upon hearing his half-Australian, half-British tenor, and he strolled around the corner and into the echoic lobby.

"Pardon?" he questioned.

"The Otter," Calvert elaborated, presuming he was who Churchill may have been searching for. "He left this morning. Before dawn."

Churchill raised his chin in a big nod.

To be honest, he was surprised he had stayed so long after the falling out. He figured that, out of all of them, Orde Wingate would be the one to sneak out in silence, shimmering away into the night like the shadow that he was, like ripples upon a moonlit lake.

It was then that Jack decided this was his final day at the Mont de la Gouille ski resort. Placing his coffee down, he stepped in and leant on the bench, tucking his hands into his deep coat pockets. This whole scenario felt strange; like the last day of a school camp, all due to imminently depart. This was the unforeseeable end of a culminating venture that was always someday due to end.

"How's the cheek?" Mike asked.

"Fine-o-fine," Jack responded with a smirk that secretly caused agonizing strain. He countered in parry: "How's the hand?"

These men each had a wound that would scar due to the same enemy combatant encounter. Calvert caressed his bandaged hand, where his knuckles had been sliced deeply. "I'll live."

After an extended moment of reflective silence at this whole endeavour, Calvert shook his head and mumbled a giggle, leaping off the front desk. Once his boots hit the ground, Churchill noticed the wood crate aligned by the counter. The papers stamped across the lid weren't *outbound* like the rest, but rather read: *inbound.*

Whatever it was, it had arrived this morning for them ...

"You want the *good news*, the *very good news*, the *bad news*, or the *very bad news?"* Calvert finally established, always playing a game.

Churchill pulled his gaze from the delivery crate and focused onto Calvert, behind his eyes relaying the four options he had just read out loud.

"Okay," said Churchill, harmlessly contemplating the order of which he desired to hear these mysterious bulletins. "Bad, good, very bad, very good."

Calvert acquiesced his selection of order. "The *bad* is that the mission to fight the Ruskis is definitely off."

"Yes, I figured as much."

Tilting his head, Calvert nodded. "I'm afraid it's definitely *game-over* there. Orde left a note and a copy of the rescinded orders to *burn after reading.* Whoever was funding this aux-op finally pulled the plug ..."

"You mean *the British government?"*

"Well," Calvert shrugged, agreeing but not agreeing. "Whoever *the powers that be are*, they decided to not engage the Russians *and* the Germans at the same time. Likely in hopes of an allegiance being forged between us two akin countries later."

"*The enemy of my enemy*," Churchill gathered quoting the ancient proverb, entirely understanding the overarching tactic likely afoot from Whitehall. Calvert on the other hand, not so much. He recognized the saying but didn't fully get the reference.

"Yeah, sure. That some sort of Art of War bollocks that you're always going on about?"

Churchill snickered. "No, it's tad older than that. Predates Sun Tzu by about three centuries or so. It's an old proverb."

"Who the fuck is *Sun Tzu* when he's home?"

Wordless, Churchill eyed Calvert.

"Look, before you say anything," the mostly unintellectual defended, "I know you're an educated bastard, Jack, and I get the saying, just not who bloody said it eighty thousand years ago!"

Begrudgingly, Churchill holstered his educational lecture this time.

Instead, he moved them forwards. "Okay, so what's the *good* news?"

Happy to move on, Calvert tapped the crate with his boot and then stood aside, prompting Churchill's visitation. "The good news is that *this* finally bloody came."

Mad Jack pressed off the counter, joining him up standing and encircling the lateral dimensions of the crate coated in postage stamps and a few import declarations.

His hands retrieved from his pockets as he prepared to open the package. Stepping around the wooden crate and tilting his head down, he read the delivery instructions. It had been organized by the MD-1, probably by Wingate prior to the pear-shaping of his aux-ops.

Whilst Churchill performed a short reconnaissance of the crate, Calvert offered some relevant commentary. "'Bout two-and-a-bit months ago, we organized this through a contact of the Otter's at the Toyshop. What is it you say about soldiers without swords being not dressed or not prepared or whatever the fuck ...?"

Churchill quoted himself with utter conviction. "*Any officer who goes into action without his sword is improperly dressed.*"

"Yeah, *that*. And who said that quote?" Calvert regarded.

"I did," Churchill responded assuredly with a smile.

"Then, I guess you're about to be *overdressed*, Mad Jack."

Jack frowned at his clue.

He faced forwards, looking over the box, suddenly realizing that it could have been housing a bladed armament of some kind based on both the dimensions and that verbal hint.

"Go ahead, open it," Calvert voiced offering him his heavy-duty brass-handled service dagger from his belt beneath the flap of his cardigan, rearing up to allow him better access. "It's for you, anyhow ..."

After accepting the M1918 knuckleduster trench knife, Churchill paused. All of a sudden, a cheeky smile crept into the corner of his working cheek as he remembered just how cheeky this half-Australian, half-British bastard truly was. When he turned to face Calvert, the fact he could barely hold a poker face was enough to confirm the suspicion that a replacement claybeg had conveniently arrived.

"From the *Berzerkers* to *you*, Mad Jack Churchill. Consider it a *parting gift*, as it were ..." Calvert spliced as Churchill crouched down low and cracked the nailed lid of the crate with the blade, exposing a straw housing and a sheathed steel arm within. Rummaging the goods like an excited child at Christmas, Churchill yanked a hessian covering, for the first time presenting a new claybeg sword in a leather scabbard. Getting a better look, he wiped it clear of packing dust and hay strands.

Examining the treasure, Jack's eyes widened massively.

The shine was quite exquisite.

His hands immediately scoped into the packaging, encompassing the lateral piece. From what he could gauge after gaining a feel for the weight, the weapon consisted of the standard 38-inch length, probably double-edged due to the centralized weight bare, almost identical to the type used for official dressage for the Second Manchester Regiment, fully in-keeping with his former piece ...

... only, once his eyeline examined the hilt, something unique brightened his sterling stare.

"Is ... that ...?" at a loss for words, Churchill questioned, his engrossed stare as sheen as diamonds, taking in the beauty of the customized sword piece, especially on the weighty handle guard and hilt.

"Yep," Calvert smiled, proud of his tailored work. It was a job well designed by the Berzerkers and built by some exotic engineer or hobbyist bladesmith at the MD-1.

Churchill tilted the unit, studying the handle of the weapon ...

It was a sword with a brass knuckleduster hilt.

It was much the same as the US M1918 trench knives the Special Z Unit had made their weapon-of-choice for CQC. The Berzerkers, namely Calvert and Wingate, had the brass knuckleduster of one of the knives adapted to fit the claybeg sword, melded, and attached right below the hilt cover of the double-edged claybeg blade. It was a literal work of art; abstract, contemporary, deadly.

Extracting it from the tight, protective sheath, Churchill's sterling gaze only twinkled further examining the quality of the build concerning the blade. The sword blade's unique, traditional finish caused miniscule meandering variations in grey and silver highlight tones, hinting that a thirteenth-century-style Damascus steel was used during the forging. This style of metal was believed to be nigh indestructible as well as *idiotically* expensive. Fortunately, Orde Wingate's pockets ran deep—and his connections within the Ministry of Defence, even deeper. They had the access.

Jack gazed at the wavy infinitesimal pattern of the blade texture, even touching the coarseness with his fingertips. It was a unique texture, both rough and sleek.

Damascus steel was a blend of two dissimilar alloys of metal. Varying on which metals were chosen by the forger and how they were treated, the hardness and strength of the material varied, with the ultimate goal being performance, endurance, and longevity. A technique known as 'hybrid' Damascus was hereby incorporated at the request of the sword procurers and for the issuance of the revered Mad Jack Churchill. A blend of austenitic stainless-steel and high carbon steel was selected, obtaining an overall hardness calculated at *C47 Rockwell.*

With care, Churchill's fingers slid into the golden brass eyelet grooves with a relative and natural ease, like a hand into a tailored glove, and he handled the unit with exactitude, instinctively gaining a feel for the weight and equilibrium of the work.

"It's so heavy, but, balanced ..." he commented, admiring the weight as he waved it about, slicing the air. The thing cut like a swashbuckler's fantasy and handled even more so.

"Yep," Calvert agreed, observing. "It's a bloody work of art, mate. A dead-end prototype. Shame we never got to use it in battle, though ..."

"How ... how did you guys do this? How did you afford this?" Churchill finally managed to peel his blue eyes off the weapon in order to glance back at Calvert.

After a full three seconds, he shrugged and held it. "How'd we afford any of this pipe dream of an operation."

Still flabbergasted, Churchill was entranced on the weapon.

He hadn't stared at a woman in the way he looked at this sword.

Nodding sincerely, Churchill heeded. "Thank you."

Calvert cheered with his coffee mug. "You're welcome."

"So, what was the *very bad* news?"

Calvert's smile faded and he took a pause before opening his lips. His stare was without focus and reeked of sadness. "They're disbanding the black ops and sending us all back to our respective units ... our transfer papers will be generated en route to our return to England."

"Like rats from a sinking ship, eh?"

Mad Mike nodded in unpretentious accord.

"And the *very good* news ...?"

Calvert held up his coffee mug, proposing a toast with his reveal of the very good news for Jack Churchill. "Apparently ... the war is finally coming."

Cradling his sword like it were a new appendage and an extension of his body, Churchill's civilian beret-clad head dipped as his face dead-panned.

That was the best fucking news he had ever heard.

He reached for his coffee, raising it outwards. "I'll toast to that!"

"Chin chin."

Chink-chink.

Fitting to their departing existence, Mike Calvert's taxicab promptly pulled around the scenic rink out the front of the Winterthur Resort, Mont de la Gouille.

"Well," he gathered in valediction. "That's me ride."

Churchill had not a thing to say.

No parting wisdom to offer.

No last quim or philosophical rhyme.

He drew a blank.

"Good luck in the war, Jack," Calvert remarked, collecting his duffle bag from the lobby floor and preparing to leave their temporary home at the lodge. He cast a view at Churchill and then extended a gloved hand to shake. Jack took it firm and with the upmost respect. Mad Mike added with a degree of solace in his undertone: "And, eh, sorry for getting you involved in all of this poppycock nonsense ..."

"Are you kidding?" Churchill chortled. " *'The thief is sorry he is to be hanged, but not that he is a thief.'*"

Calvert absorbed the proverb like he always did from this literate: on the chin. Somewhere lurking within that poetic metronome was a hidden meaning about regret. It was something he was unable to decode, yet he understood the overhanging connotations enough to harmonize.

" *Thomas Fuller,*" Jack identified the quote from the famous historian on behalf of his absent academic friend, Rex King-Clark, who would usually leap at guessing the author. In this case, Mike Calvert had not a snowball's chance in hell at winning this intellectual game.

Content with the farewell, Mike headed for the door.

Something lurching in his mind, Churchill called him back last minute. Calvert stopped with one hand on the foyer door. "That was you in the hall that night ... wasn't it?"

Halting a moment, Calvert ultimately looked back in silence. His eyeline diminished whilst he contemplated an answer that avoided the truth. His answer was evident to Churchill in that delay of response.

Finally, Calvert voiced his confession. "What were *you* doing there?"

Jack grinned. Lied. "Recon."

He had to ask, still trying to find the piece for that part of the old puzzle. If he didn't ask now, he may never get another chance, thus he shot his shot.

"You?"

From a defocus over the floor, Calvert's eyes elevated to Jack, offering him the strange truth before finally saying goodbye to the wretched Winterthur Resort. "I was there to kill 'em."

Confused, Churchill's glum grin faded, and a frown formed.

Standing idle in the foyer hall, knuckles firm within the eyelets of his customized hilt of his heavy sword, he felt empowered. However, that titan-slaying statement made him feel defenceless.

Calvert was a lot of things, but he hadn't guessed that an assassin was one of them. Jack didn't judge him or discount the declaration, rather ... he believed him. He wondered who the target was—though, that should have been obvious. Out of the three men supposedly lurking within the shadows of that room that night, one of them was clearly the most evil.

"Baade?"

Calvert's eyes held true. "All of 'em."

He was going to kill Wingate as well.

The eerie silence of the echoic foyer became blown away by a gust of wind as Calvert pressed open the foyer door, bidding a final farewell to Churchill before disappearing from his life seemingly forever.

9   9

♣   ♣

A Fate Worse Than Death

1942, March
Kelburn Castle
Largs, Scotland

After very little sleep pending the big court day, Jack Churchill was up at dawn, washed, shaven, and prepared for his journey to London ahead of his session.

The early morning light illuminated his well-kept room inside of the Kelburn Castle. His quarters, like the many others at the castle, was quite spacious and homely compared to most billets around the area. This wing included an ensuite and nook before an alcove window with a view of the luscious grounds.

Naturally, Mad Jack dressed to the nines for these proceedings.

Jaw clean shaven, pencil-thin moustache trimmed, blonde hair neatly combed with a mild slick of pomade, silver buttons on his pressed khaki service dress polished, necktie straight, pinned medals buffed with a special fibred handkerchief. Churchill next took the time to shape his green beret before firmly pressing it upon his head, sure to slant the angle appropriately whilst staring at his own handsome reflection in the mirror. Content with his appearance, he nodded with approval, the aura enriching him with confidence.

Below the large interior cabinet mirror, the doily-lined dresser was decorated with his small collection of permitted effects, which included a silver-framed black and white photograph of his wife Rosamund and a second print of them both on their wedding day from last year, standing beneath the sunlight on the steps of the St. Augustine's Church in Dumbarton. Whilst already brooding, the images were a crippling reminder of how he was yet to inform Ros of the current life-altering court martial of which he was the sole respondent. This lack of candour was not out of embarrassment or a purposeful untruth and, if the time came, Jack had no quarrels about elaborating on the factual to his beloved. At this stage, even long past any preliminary instances, he was simply waiting for the moment to become prudent enough to involve his wife in his monotonous military life—especially off the back of their most recent squabble regarding talks about him stepping down from frontline roles.

Under the circumstances of war, it wasn't out of the ordinary that they would go weeks apart. It wasn't abnormal for any army family during the period, even when not stationed abroad. For all she was aware, he was between the Largs base billets and London on official vocation, which was the truth.

He heard a commotion in the hall, and it stole his attention.

Mail call.

It was early today. For the a.m. runs, letters were slipped beneath the doors for the residing officers at Commando Castle. Churchill heard and then spied the shuffle of the envelope as it slithered beneath his door, and he promptly collected it once inserting and straightening his cufflinks.

He flipped it around, examining the stamps, and script. Judging from the return address, the letter was from home, and he recognized the handwriting instantly as that of his wife, bringing a smile to his face and a change to his temperament. He slit it open with his finger and became frozen by the surprise of customary rose petals falling from the folded paper. The scarlet foliole scented the letter.

Shrub roses clipped straight from their prized front yard garden; continuation of this gimmick had become Rosamund's own calling card. It shouldn't have caught him off-guard, but with so much bearing on his heavy mind lately, she got him good. Dry red flakes rained down Jack's khaki service dress and boots, coating the carpet.

Still smiling, Churchill's beam scanned the short message.

Her sweet communiqué was slightly out of the blue, a happy coincidence especially considering she wasn't aware of the looming court martial. She mentioned missing him especially lately and desperately wanting to see him. Rosamund had been made aware of Jack's itinerary for February and March and knew of his compulsory visit to London, where he had organized to be put up at the *Union Jack Club* in *Waterloo*, located across the Thames from the conference hall where the trial was taking place. He would be there for the next three days, minimum, as advised by the court, and now it seemed he would at least have company for tonight should she come and visit. The letter alluded to such as a promise which Jack could not deny.

Churchill closed the letter with a devious grin beneath his moustache. Following court, he would plan to romance his wife, perhaps even organize to have flowers and champagne brought up to the room in advance.

Shelving those amorous plans for now, he focused on the day ahead.

Filing away the letter, he approached the chest at the foot of his bed and took a knee in order to unbuckle the latch, opening the dusty yaw wide. Inside the deep mouth of the recess, resting upon various other military paraphernalia, including several sets of different types of medieval war arrows, coiled longbow strings, and a set of deflated 1931 *Robertson of Edinburgh* African blackwood, engraved silver bagpipes housed within a green tartan bag, rested Churchill's customized knuckleduster handle claybeg sword in its brown leather scabbard. It had notably aged a little since he was issued it by Mike Calvert in Switzerland. What felt like forever ago may even seem like the turn of a few pages for some.

Churchill collected the weighty sword after a moment of poise, recollecting the topical relevance of the Berzerkers and the blade's origin in his possession since its creation in early 1940.

The brass handle had taken a beating over the years of seeing action in war. The malleable material was more susceptible to showing dents and scratches. He separated the covering, withdrawing the double-edged sword and taking the time to inspect the phenomenal patterning of the Damascus steel. As a slither of shine reflected across his face from the break of morning light sneaking in between his curtains and shining onto the metal blade, the tip of Churchill's finger roughed the sharpened boundary, finding several miniscule indentations in the blade's razor edge. The blade had sustained the damage from his swordfight with Feind during Operation Archery in December, and he was yet to appropriately consider contacting a blacksmith to attempt mending the steel. They were minute imperfections not requiring immediate attention. Wear and tear of this sort acted as mere mileage for a sword blade.

With a metallic scrape and glide, Churchill reinserted the sword back into his scabbard, spying another forgotten item within the chest which seemed prudent given the subject of the day's proceedings.

Nodding, he placed his sword down and stood. His hands attended to the dress belt currently holding up his trousers and they came down, exposing a set of hairy legs. He kicked the uniform trousers off over his polished shoes and high white socks, followed by his underdrawers, leaving his bare ass and manhood dangling free from beneath the tuck of his button-up shirt and khaki blouse as he stood with conviction over the prized item in the chest:

A Scottish kilt.

Vibrant with reds and blacks, the timeless crisscross patterns of the Wallace tartan with rabbit pelt sporran—the same one worn during his war with Baade in Switzerland, and with Feind before that, in Oslo.

A sword and kilt.

He would be wearing both these items to court today.

Today, this warfighter was fighting for his life in what could be regarded as one of the harshest battlefields known to man: the courtroom. He would not be *improperly dressed* for this war.

1942, March
Westminster Conference Grand Hall
Whitehall, London

Same as the first, the location was preserved for the second sitting of the secret trial of Churchill's court-martial, only the session was moved to one of the main 'grand' halls rather than the petite conference room they had occupied for the preliminary hearing.

Coinciding with the upgrade of assembly, the internals of this room within the mausoleum-esque building proved just as ostentatious, royal, and rich, filled with historic officialdom and pomp.

Smoothed sandstone halls with antique artworks covering walls in golden frames with trim. Bust statues of various noblemen, tassel-knitted grand tapestries, all extant beneath twenty-foot ceilings conveyed with tremendous eye-catching architectural detail on the architraves. The interior smelt of musk, red tape, and monotonous administration.

With his head held high, Jack Churchill paced down the industrious main hall of the Westminster building. At 1400-hours, he was right on time, dressed to the nines in his No.3 Commando service dress combined with his traditional tartan kilt and, naturally, atop his green beret stylishly inclined.

Having just navigated the hive of Whitehall attired traffic outside, this overconfident eccentric radiated fanatical poise and conviction. He had undoubtedly made an impression with his stand-outtish and alluring costume, his hand consistently rested on the fist-load of brass hilt attached to his holstered sidearm: his customized claybeg, further turning the heads of observant passers-by.

Unlike the preliminary hearing, he had certainly developed reservations for this big court day. He was yet to be completely quaking in his combat boots, however; if he ever did, it would be a first for Mad Jack—and he had stared death in the face numerous times in warfare.

Churchill found someone he was hoping to cross paths with before the commencement—and not for any egocentric reasons, as one might assume. Quite the contrary.

"Hullo, John," Churchill announced across the busy hall and towards a group of lawyer types dressed in fitted suits and expensive wraparound spectacles, gawking at file notes. The familiar face of Lieutenant-Colonel Durnford-Slater was standing amongst a smaller clique, dressed in his service dress and recognizable green beret, grudgingly observing the prosecution crowd. The call of his commando colleague acquired his attention—as well as the interest of other legal representatives, most which were none so accepting.

"Colonel Churchill, sir!" interrupting their reunion, the raised voice of an officiary JAG flunky quickly intervened before Durnford-Slater could so much as smile let alone denote a well-mannered response. A greaseball worm scanned across his reading glasses in order to address Jack's prohibited salutations, holding out a palm in defence. "Contact with those from the judge's bar is impermissible by both prosecution and the defence. It's forbidden."

"*Forbidden?*" Churchill frowned. What a heavy word to choose.

"Yes. You are barred any verbal contact, whatsoever."

The response was comprehensible from the court.

Discernibly, one might presume the defendant may attempt to sway the lay members who would be seating on the bench with the judge, therefore tainting their decisiveness and resolve.

Lieutenant-Colonel Lucky Laycock was present within the group of army men and, like Durnford-Slater, albeit with more surprise, scanned Churchill's Scottish garb up and down and back again. He knew the man, but had never seen him dress in a garment as such. Jack saw him rear his head amidst the crowd of lay members and legal morons. Just like Durnford-Slater, he was also unauthorized to respond in any manner.

Expression falling flat, Churchill's advance towards them in the decorated sandstone hall came to a policed halt. Although their response may have been legally appropriate, it was still a little rude and put a damper on Churchill's gentlemanly gestures.

Across the due diligent distance, Churchill's confident sterling stare held, eventually meeting Durnford-Slater's one of disappointment. Prior to the tribunal, Churchill had allured to some of what the prosecution alleged to be factual, but at least not entirely true. Now that much of this stood to reason as fact, it would be obvious Churchill wanted to clear things up with his friend rather than have him thinking the worst of him in his absence.

But rather, Jack pried ...

"*Chariot?!*" Churchill desperately asked at Durnford-Slater, referencing the codename for the operation currently underway for No.2 Commando and his alternate commanding officer, Lieutenant-Colonel Newman. What little he knew of Operation Chariot was sketchy, having not been privy to the sensitive information. He knew it was involving the majority of No.2, that it was taking place in German-occupied France, and was an imaginative amphibious attack of such. He was sincerely sore of missing out on the action of which they were embarking at any moment.

Durnford-Slater of No.3 Commando was more than aware of the operation and their timetable, and therefore privy to the operational status, as Churchill would have been, had he not been forcefully out of the loop. The operation was concurrent to these proceedings, and they were due for departure towards France inside of a few days.

Unable to articulate the details of such, Durnford-Slater merely formed a smirk in the corner of his mouth below his lampshade moustache and accompanied the smile with a solemn nod of affirmation. While Churchill was staring down the barrel of his own court martial, that information warmed his heart, for he genuinely, selflessly, cared more about Commando. He did not wish to whisper with the bench for his own benefit ... he yearned only to hear about the well-being of the men.

Churchill interpreted Durnford-Slater's gesture as operational contentment, nodding wholesomely.

Confirmation that the boys of No.2 were fine.

That the operation was fine.

That *Chariot,* the operation that he was meant to be at the helm of, was *fine-o-fine* without him. It inflated Churchill with a sense of consolation, and it may have been all he needed to get through today's bureaucratical bombardments.

Before long, the tall courtroom doors swung open and those mandatory of attendance were ushered inside of the echoic, foetid-scented space. These were appropriate legal bodies such as the relevant Jack Churchill and his legal representative with the combover, Lionel Spencer, who had arrived in time for the session.

This grand hall was indeed grand.

The ceiling was easily twenty- to twenty-five-feet high and shared the same quality of detailed architecture as the entrances and corridors linking the chamber. Wall art and wreaths were of equally magnificent décor. A monumental window lined the northern wall between the bench and the floor, allowing for a horizontal beam of natural golden light, of which in this room, the judge's stand was positioned to be elevated behind a stiff altar. This room withheld much more ceremony than the last, and therefore Churchill respected it as such as he finalized pacing across the echoic space and found his place behind his seat at the clothed table representing the defence.

Once finding his place, he audibly drew his four-foot sword from his hip. The armament act gained the attention of the armed MP in the corner who had allowed for this attendance moments ago after noting the sheathed sidearm.

Churchill pondered over the significance of this token as he laid the heavy claybeg down gently upon the tabletop; blade facing forwards and in a ceremonially accurate position. His honour was now on the line.

Spencer's brow raised. He met Churchill's grand gesture by placing his briefcase on the desk and unbuttoning his blazer.

Jack side-eyed him. "Mister Spencer."

"Colonel," Spencer responded taking a firm standing position beside his kilted counsel on the centre floor, facing the bench. He jerked his chin at Churchill's sword. "Bit of an outdated tradition, don't you think?"

"*Manners maketh man,*" Churchill quoted from somewhere that flew straight over the bureaucrat's balding little head. He deliberated an obliged elaboration, denoting a relevant brief history lesson to the lawyer. "Before the commencement of the due process of a court martial, the affected commissioned present is to make an offering: unsheathing and laying down thy sabre. It is a symbol of rank and reputation being put in abeyance."

"I know what it symbolizes!" defended Spencer. "A wether at a ram sale," he pouted whilst leaning in tight, levelling his tone. "Consider, Colonel, these penguin-garbed chuckleheads and the beak don't care if you dress pretty, talk pretty, go to Sunday School, or want only to kiss on the first date. They'll get handsy and bend you over just the same."

With a cocked brow, Churchill lofted him an earnest gleam.

Interfering with the conclusion to Churchill's compelling initial narrative and Spencer's random outburst utilizing an accurate metaphorical sexual refence to describe his forceful yielding submission to pressure, a notable commotion stirred, and the permitted members of the session entered in a single file through the side door held open by a uniformed, white-gloved MP who ceremoniously guided them to a line of seats behind a waist-high carved wooden decorative palisade parallel to the inner wall.

In the flank of the catbird seats, Churchill and Spencer watched as the convoy crowd of military dressed men and civilian suits also arrived and found their allotted chair. In keeping to the first hearing, being a secret trial, these members of the court must have directly been related to the state of affairs or at least been attorneys with some form of high clearance. Now that Wingate was apparently here for the trial, it was feasible that more spectres from the cloak-and-dagger theatre wished to oversee these glorious proceedings and had thus emerged from the nether. Some new faces present, there were slightly more attending than before, approximately eight or ten in total, who filed in behind the side railing with minimal ruckus. Dressed fancily, dutiful Constables McNaughton and Garland were again present, entering last. They remained standing against the back wall beside a uniformed MP before being directed to another row of seating within the vicinity.

Jack lately continued with sentiment. "Upon the conclusion of the tribunal, I can collect my sword along with my honour."

Spencer tipped his head dismissively at the fact Mad Jack had just put his sword out on the table during a court martial. "Well, sir ... whatever floats your boat."

"Usually buoyancy," Churchill replied rhetorically the quip.

Momentarily miffed, Spencer's austere brow sunk.

Spencer popped the lock mechanisms on his briefcase. "And what if they find you guilty? Hmm? What then?"

Churchill's focus faded briefly as he contemplated the negative course of action. It wasn't exactly pretty, although, in some ways, was at the least ceremonially fucking beautiful. "Then the tip of the sword will be inverted and turned towards me ... and I shall fall upon thee."

Awaiting a punchline that never arrived, Spencer threw him a confused sidewards glance. He hoped he was being flippant. "The whole thing's a tad extreme, is it not?"

"I am an extreme person."

"No shit, you're wearing a Scottish kilt in an English courtroom. But surely, you're joking, Colonel?"

"It's a worst-case scenario."

Spencer physically pondered, perceiving it as a question. " *Worst-case scenario* is you get dishonourably disbarred, Colonel. Kicked out of the army. End up in a special kind of prison they hide away for enemies of state and traitors to the crown. After several years of bartering, pleading a case of *superior orders* or, need be, insanity—which, let's face it, you'd qualify—and we wear them down so that they reduce your incarceration to minimum security, perhaps even local penitentiary."

Churchill exhaled, detracting from focus as dread overcame him.

He was right, that *was* worse ...

To him, incarceration was a fate worse than death.

Just then, the bailiff entered at the front of the room with resilient strides, holding the door for a row of dignitary personages and bench bigwigs.

"*All rise*," he asserted with an upheld revere.

Within the room, those who were seated promptly elevated.

Eyes trained low and facing forwards, the notables toured through the courtroom, upping the steps to the elevated bench and aligning behind the seats positioned in the limelight.

As opposed to the smaller room that held their preliminary hearing, there were four two-seater desks founded at either wing of the centralized judge's stand. In total, this set up supported eight lay members and the judge. There was a separate altar connected to the front of the room, presumably to be used as a witness stand.

Again, the bulk of these important men Jack didn't know from Adam, though guessed that again attending was a member from each sector of the respective relevant military, justice, and intelligence branch. He recognized Durnford-Slater and Laycock, and that Vice Chief of the Imperial General Staff at the War Office Henry Pownall was present once more. McNaughton's boss, Deputy Chief William Barney from the Special Investigation Branch office, was again apart of the lay members. Each wore a judgemental stare of extant predisposition upon their scowls, flinging the odd judgemental stare towards Churchill.

An MP guardsman closed the heavy single door behind a final candidate, confining them for the session, and all the unpretentious chatter from within the courtroom evaporated.

The bailiff announced above any commotions:

"*Honorary Judge MacGeagh presiding.*"

Circular reading spectacles resting on the tip of his nose, appointed Judge Advocate General Sir Henry MacGeagh entered from an alternate cloakroom-looking slip door behind the bench. He wore his official court gown and white tea cosy-looking wig piece as he entered the courtroom lastly, finding his seat directly in the middle of the bar.

"*The court is now in session. Be seated.*"

Everybody present promptly extracted their chairs and sat in a subtle orchestra of shuffling and cushioning placement.

"Ladies and gentlemen, good morning," Judge MacGeagh addressed whilst organizing the proceedings laid out before him, getting comfortable. "We are progressing case number A-8919: the *Criminal Investigation Department* on behalf of the *British War Office* versus *Lieutenant-Colonel John Malcolm Thorpe Fleming Churchill.* Are both representatives prepared and ready to commence?"

He cast an eye to his right flank where sat some men in suits on the bench: the military prosecution. Deputy Chief Barney was at the helm of this committee. In return, he cast MacGeagh a head bob signifying his preparedness for trial.

Churchill felt Spencer's stare home in on him, sidling into his peripherals and calling attention. His next sentence was in reference to their quarrels during the preliminary hearing, where Churchill had waived his right to an attorney. As a legal right, Spencer was deemed a mandatory inclusion to the due process to be at the defendant's side, yet, the lawyer wasn't about to overstep. "You want me to speak or?—"

Cutting him off, Churchill cast him a brash glint before pushing out his chair with a whoosh from his tartan kilt, becoming upstanding and formally facing forward. "Ready, your honour," Jack announced with a distinct bow and his hands behind his back.

"Very well," MacGeagh conveyed with minimal attention to Churchill's autonomous virtue or surprising attire, drawing the court martial forwards. "Colonel Churchill, the prosecution withholds the charges of you committing *high treason* and *conspiracy of conducting disloyalty to the Crown* ... To these charges I have laid before you, how do you plea?"

There was a strange pause after the question.

All attention in the air drifted and fell onto Churchill as he remained idle. He issued a delayed response to an otherwise obvious enquiry. After a furthermore extension of silence, Jack seemed to wake from his hiatus and lean forwards. "Oh, eh, still as *not guilty* as I was last week, sir," Churchill responded in kind and with a douse of humour.

"Ah, yes," Judge MacGeagh concurred as an MP messenger stepped in low before the raised bench and passed him a discreet paper note notifying him of some sort of readiness to come. "Still under the impression that famous *Mad Jack wit* is appropriate in my courtroom, I see?"

Notice seemed to fall upon Churchill's stance.

It was as if the spotlight had found him absent remark.

MacGeagh read the note he was just passed and promptly tucked it away, retaining his focus. "Since our preliminary hearing, Colonel, I've had the opportunity to read your jacket in full. Quite a page turner, I must admit."

Churchill adjusted his stance minutely, not sure if there was a compliment in that or it was merely just some form of an acknowledgement. He bowed, all the same. "Sir."

"Yes, yes," MacGeagh lowered his spectacles in order to recognize Churchill directly—perhaps even to salute him. He spoke in a measured tone. "Lieutenant-Colonel *Mad Jack* Churchill. Your military history is *impressive* to say the least," he positioned his glasses upon the tip of his nose in order to read from his papers. "*Graduated with honours from the Sandhurst Royal Military College in 1926, you served in Burma with the Second Manchester Regiment until 1936, when you honourably discharged due to a lack of excitement. During an interim of service, you mastered the stick and string, representing Great Britain in the World Archery Championship in Oslo in 1939. On September 3rd, Chamberlain's declaration of war saw your immediate return to active duty, resuming your commission as a captain, this time as a part of the British Expeditionary Force entering France, where you were positioned upon the Maginot Line ...*"

Whilst the domineering judge cultivated the court of Jack Churchill's military accolades with a tenor of praise, refreshing everybody of his commendations and plaudits, even educating others of his many celebrated victories, the man himself seemed practically apathetic. Churchill never had been one to self-indulge in his own achievements. The sense the few that knew him got from this was that somewhere there was a war waging, and he was missing out.

This all affirmed he had better places to be than here, on trial.

Turning a page, MacGeagh continued. "*... After the monotonous Phoney War period, mid-1940 finally saw you in action, ambushing a German scout team in a small French town known as L'Épinette: a rather valiant attempt at heroism. You did not receive any medals or commendations for your accomplishments this day, however, the history books shall have your use of a longbow as the last recorded confirmed kill with a medieval weapon on a modern-day battlefield. Operation Dynamo* *became enacted; you were one of the last off the shores of Dunkirk during the evacuation, where your leadership properties are cited within numerous battle diaries and mentions of dispatch. You joined the Commandos later that same year, witnessing—if not directly implementing—the Commando/LayForce schtick which saw the former prevalent. 1941 saw the events of Operations Claymore and Archery in the north, which your unit, No.3 Commando, had a prominent part of each successful mission. Operation Archery earned you a Military Cross and Bar, and a promotion worthy of leading your own battalion—*or so it should be, hitherto the unexpected ill-fated circumstance that has brought us here today ..."

Amid Judge MacGeagh's closing, the recent news hit Churchill hard.

The loss was still too soon.

"With all due respect, your honour ..." Churchill groused in a strange and unlikely turn of events, breaking Judge MacGeagh's gratuitous opening speech—which was, in turn, well-favouring of the defendant.

Interrupted, MacGeagh's focus raised from reading his stock notes. It was strange Churchill would want to inhibit or speak contrarily following the praise-laden introductory oration he had just bestowed upon the court—especially one read by the judge.

Jack continued suicidally self-effacingly. "Are we not here today for something that I am *accused* of doing? Not to listen to a register of achievements history already has documented?"

"Colonel, you're interrupting my introduction to the case; inclusive of a princely preface, of which, I coveted to mention as a complementary exposition of your successes in lieu of you failing to present a character witness for the preliminary hearing. So, by all means and with all due respect, *of course*, let's move further in step of the gallows, shall we?"

"Of course. Sir, as I already said, my accolades and accomplishments in battle against the enemy are already well acknowledged. To that extension and, *with all due respect* ... let's get *bloody* on with it, shall we?"

An absolute, deafening silence filled the court.

Audible exhales past pursed lips could be heard throughout MacGeagh's courtroom, as well as numerous rearranging of physical discomforts after encountering that severed statement and counterstatement.

Durnford-Slater could have covered his face from his friend's second-hand embarrassment. It was almost as if Jack had been given a clear stretch at a home run and all he needed to do was move ... yet, he refused, wanting instead to tee off for himself on a pitch he knew not of, and without a bat.

Beside Churchill, Spencer rolled his jaw. He slumped in his chair, dumbfounded and humiliated. Half his face was hidden beneath his hand that presently brushed his maw, discreetly hiding his abundant dismay. As far as courtroom method and argumentative strategy went, Churchill representing himself in this was an utter nightmare.

MacGeagh slouched back in his big, comfy Judge's chair.

In awe, he took the time to study Churchill.

He appeared beside himself.

"Very well," he uttered, laying down what was left of his introductory notes, along with whatever else it was he had planned to speak positively about Jack Churchill. It seemed that, in the interim, the judge may have sought a new respect for Churchill since their last trial. Guess now we'll never know since it had been blown out of the water. MacGeagh approved Churchill's stance, sustaining the show. "We shall proceed with today's trial. Deputy Chief Barney?"

"Yes, your honour?" Barney questioned.

"You have the stand."

"Yes, your honour," Barney acknowledged, affectively brought to the fore. "Of the aforementioned accolades of Colonel Churchill—the period between his commission with the Second Manchester Regiment along the Maginot Line and the ambush in L'Épinette—the accused joined a 'black operation' under the command of General Orde Wingate—"

Now a stickler for calling rank, Jack interrupted a correction.

It was important to him for a few reasons, the vainest of which was that he had now reached equal ranks to Wingate and would never let him or anybody referencing him forget it.

Churchill announced aloud, commanding attention:

"*Lieutenant-Colonel!*"

Barney paused and eyed him starkly, begrudgingly corrected. "Granted. *Lieutenant-Colonel* Orde Wingate. During the preliminary hearing, the prosecution requested the official declassification of the operation deemed 'auxiliary-ops' conducted between December 1939 and April 1940 in the neutral zone of Switzerland. To which, the defendant declared to the court that mission particulars cannot be declassified without the signing executive of the said mission's commanding officer present and obliged. That signing executive is now present, and the prosecution would like to bring forth Lieutenant-Colonel Wingate to the stand ..."

MacGeagh raised the folded note still in his possession.

It must have signified that Wingate had, indeed, arrived ...

Given the command, the courtroom door opened, and an armed MP escort brought in the wheelchair-bound lay witness, and the key to unlock the secretive and criminal events of old.

Lieutenant-Colonel Orde 'the Otter' Wingate, alive and in the flesh.

Wingate's wheelchair entrance called attention.

An adverse witness from the get-go, the discontented and seemingly lawfully detained British Army Lieutenant-Colonel—only a recent and temporary promotion since his stint with the Gideon Force—wore his tanned service dress neatly, with his dark hair sculpted in pomade in such a way that may have suggested that somebody else had cared to it on his behalf—and possibly for great reason outside of noncompliance ...

Rather obscurely, Wingate wore a white medical bandage around his neck like a scarf ...

Wheeled in against all will, he stared vacantly across the court.

Disinterested. Perhaps, even mentally absent.

Churchill's piercing blue stare locked onto the Otter as they wheeled him in, tracing onto him and absorbing every detail. It had been the first time he had seen the gent since their awkward conflict and abrupt departure in Switzerland over two years ago, though not the last time he had heard his name spoken. After the collapse of the Special Z Unit Berzerkers, Wingate had ventured on with various other questionable black-budget operations in other recessed pockets of the wide world to continue outstanding feuds with those with opposite intentions to that of the United Kingdom. His name had become commonplace due to his ongoing scandalous and odious activities, most recently with the Gideon Force in Ethiopia, which was where they had retrieved him from for this court date kicking and screaming—and seemingly not without incident.

Wingate wheeled between the bar and the bench, passing up close and before Churchill's tracing observation.

A secondary stare to rival Jack's own was that from Jethro McNaughton, who due to his own personal rivalry with the Otter and finally seeing him in person, clenched his trouser legs into the balls of his fists with contained fury at the pure sight of the chairbound fellow. Beside him, Garland detected his wrathful intent and offered a discreet reassuring gesture to her trusted offsider, silently calming him in the grandstand of this courtroom arena.

Wingate's dark and vacant thousand-yard stare seemed distant for the extent of his entrance, as well as the entirety of the courtroom appearance. The man was not just about to refuse compliance verbally, but mentally, too. He seemed a shell of himself, and as they were about to find out via his representative, for an apparent reason.

"*Lieutenant-Colonel Wingate, please take the stand,*" the bailiff requested after his wheelchair brakes had been applied and positioned by the witness stand. Two uniformed guardsmen who were tasked with escorting the seized general everywhere during his visit to England locked the wheels and assisted him in rising to the altar.

"Your honour, if I may?" a part of the Otter's lil entourage was a thin, freckled man in a dark suit. He spawned out of nowhere from Wingate's wheelchair-bound flank, speaking for him. He was permitted by MacGeagh with a formal gesture which the bailiff formally upheld.

"*State your name and credentials for the court.*"

"John Elwin Bradbury, your majesty. I am afraid that General Wing—"

"*Lieutenant-Colonel Wingate,*" Churchill interrupted again, on cue.

Judge MacGeagh rolled his eyes. "Colonel Churchill, did you graduate preschool? Are you familiar with the *talking stick* instrument to dictate democracy?"

"Eh, yes, sir, I am familiar."

"Good. Zip it. If you speak again out of turn, I will have you thrown in the brig for contempt, is that understood?" MacGeagh factored sternly.

Churchill, unaware if he should verbalize his response, inhaled briefly before sighing past his teeth. He gestured compliance, permitted a rejoining statement. "Yes, your honour. I just wish for the record to state Lieutenant-Colonel Wingate's correct rank."

"This is a secret trial, Colonel. There is no record other than the jury's final verdict."

Churchill formed a purse-lipped beam and nodded.

"As you were, Mister Bradbury," said MacGeagh, realigning the session.

"Thank you, your honour," Bradbury commenced, quickly eyeing Churchill with underlining impudence and resuming his place in his well-rehearsed monologue, doing so with an elevated brow and flicking Churchill a glare whilst he stepped past him to attempt handing a letter onto the judge's desk—it was intercepted by the bailiff, who passed it on to MacGeagh. "I'm afraid that *Lieutenant-Colonel* Wingate has suffered a rather devastating wound to the neck, and this has unfortunately incapacitated his ability to communicate verbally. As a legal representative, I am here to speak on his behalf."

There was a mild hiatus to follow as this sunk in with the court.

It was not often that a mute witness was called to the stand, especially due to extraordinary circumstances such as those surrounding Wingate's condition. Especially considering his sole purpose of being called to trial was to *verbally* sanction the results of a top-secret mission, his lack of vocal capacity led to obvious speculation.

"Well, that's awfully convenient, isn't it?" Judge MacGeagh declared aloud, none too pleased. He folded away the medical certificate Bradbury had issued, signed off by an official representative from the *Army Medical Board* of the *Royal Army Medical Corps (RAMC),* London Command. It was stamped, signed, and dated today. They must have had a busy morning getting this correspondence officiated and airtight.

Churchill remained silent, wondering what had happened to him.

Reading his mind, Spencer leant into Churchill at the bar, seeing an opportunity to quickly bring him up to speed about Wingate's situation in a whisper. The details caused Churchill's concerned brow to fade, replaced with one of astonishment, as speechless as the Otter himself.

"*Apparently he tried to kill himself en route to England ...*"

Churchill muttered under his breath. "What a pity."

"Hm?" Spencer grumbled, gleaming at the lips beneath Churchill's pencil-thin moustache, unsure that he had just correctly heard something like sympathy shown at the circumstance.

"I said *what a pity ...*" Jack articulated louder as other courtroom voices continued over theirs. "... that he wasn't successful."

Churchill's attentive stare washed over Wingate at the platform after his new convenient circumstance had now come to light and was noted. The colonel's immobile head looked like it was strapped on to his shoulders by twenty feet of white medical bandages that ran beneath his uniform jacket. The look halfway resembled the *Ndebele* people of South Africa, who wore brass neck rings known as *dzillas.*

Coinciding with his brittle physical appearance, his eyes looked dark and sunken, like he was absent within his own skull. Not many people knew it at the time, but Orde Wingate had contracted malaria (among other things) and had sought medication from a local doctor in Ethiopia instead of certified British Army medical staff, as he was afraid that the illness would give his Whitehall disparagers yet another excuse to undermine him. *Atabrine* was the drug given to Wingate by his foreign doctor, and was a treatment which can produce severe depressive side effects if taken in high dosages. Reportedly, Wingate was already depressed by the official response from Britain to his Abyssinian command and ethics in Ethiopia, and was only getting sicker from the malaria. Upon this recent charge to return back to British courts, he coincidently attempted committing suicide by slitting his own throat with a combat knife. As a result, the vote was out on if he was truly faking.

The only other person present in the courtroom who became tense upon witnessing Wingate's arrival—and potential confessions of war crimes in front of a court of law—was Henry Pownall. Currently a lay member of the bench for this trial, Pownall, a man on the shortlist of becoming the Commander-in-Chief of the British Far East Command, was a long-time liaison of Orde Wingate. In fact, the court couldn't know it yet, but his fingerprints were on Wingate's acquisition of manpower for the Special Z

Unit in question, signing over recruits for the aux-ops and feeding fresh meat into the meatgrinder. Was it getting hot in there, or was it just him?

"Your majesty, Colonel Wingate regrettably refuses to declassify the details of the black-budget operations labelled *auxiliary-ops* and the events transpiring December 1939 to April 1940 in the neutral zone of Switzerland. This is due to the sensitive nature of the events relevant to multinational confidentially agreements arranged by Great Britain and her allies—"

"Oh, poppycock!" frustratedly, Barney raised his voice from the bench, however Bradbury continued in his monotonal tone before the court. His volume overcame the prosecution's mild objection.

"—furthermore, seeing that this is not the first time my client has been pulled out of active duty to stand trial, we would also like to inform that a counter-mandate has been put forward to the War Office thereby excusing Lieutenant-Colonel Orde Wingate from any further scrutiny and eligibility of sitting trial in the future regarding anything officially sanctioned by the British Army or British government, respectively."

While this strange new destructive development unfolded on Churchill's front lawn, somehow putting his own court-martial on the backburner and confirming Wingate as being the actual hot topic for this trial, the aggressive stance with which his lawyer showcased this caused a hot flush of sorts to fluster the courtroom amidst the volume. McNaughton, specifically. The vendetta-driven man had never been so close to nailing his adversary, and just hinting at the possibility that he would be getting off on another technicality was enough to boil the investigative constable's blood.

"Your honour, this is just but another clever triviality that the ever-elusive Orde Wingate has prepared to delay the court's directive—delaying the inevitable," Barney alleged protectively to Judge MacGeagh who showed little enthusiasm towards hearing Wingate's offer, though it was dutifully obliged.

MacGeagh faced Barney, forcefully remaining nonbiased.

Wingate may have been a piece of work, and this wasn't his first legal visit, nonetheless, it was the duty of the Judge Advocate General to be willing to accept any proposals or legal propositions put forth in a court of law. Wingate may have been protected by some agenda-hungry bureaucrats at the War Office, but as protected as he might be in conjunction with some clever wording and intimidating legal stances, the validity of his statements may have only been a weak attempt to impede the process.

The defence remained silent.

As much of a dirty tactic as this was, it was in their favour.

While the courtroom drama played out, Churchill's stare fell onto Wingate at the witness stand and he held it, seething. Although the man seemed enormously disconnected, probably drugged out on a potent concoction of antidepressants and painkillers, he *did* know the man better than anybody in that courtroom, and he had not changed. He would never change. Couldn't. Not any more or less than a leopard could change his spots. Churchill had played a lot of poker during his army years, and it was in that moment that he managed to catch a chink in Wingate's armour through a notable lapse in his demeanour; a visible tell which told a thousand lies.

Noticing the slip, Churchill didn't act, rather he just retracted the acknowledgement discreetly away. Sadly, for his sake, part of him hoped nobody else in that courtroom was smart enough to see through Wingate's feeble resistance like he just had.

"*Well, this is good*," Spencer murmured softly in Churchill's ear as the two remained slouched at the bar, watching the courtroom show unfold.

Confused, Churchill puckered his brow. "*How so?*"

"*Well, here you are, trying to stay afloat with your head barely above water, and the sharks have started thrashing about and eating each other. If the magic of Wingate's lawyer works here, the whole case may become invalidated and fall through a loophole. Best-case scenario, this whole thing is overturned and we're out of here by afternoon tea.*"

"*Worst-case scenario?*"

"*Worst case, they shatter his plea into a million pieces, and we're back to square one; and you're singing about Switzerland on that very stand in ten minutes time due to a grand overruling and a court-approved affidavit.*"

The pressure restored within Churchill.

He had not forgotten that their way of ultimately getting to the Otter was *through* him, and he was not free of a crucifixion just yet. He could very well become collateral damage in their vendetta to tear down Wingate.

Visibly, Judge MacGeagh was not amused by the red tape.

Given an elongated moment of consideration, he decided to challenge Wingate's implied overture of a proposed counter-mandate. Perchance, he saw through their clever phrasing and was about to call him out. "Mister Bradbury, a mandate merely *put forward* to the British War Office intent on excusing Colonel Wingate from any further examination by the court does not make it so. *When* and *if* the War Office signs some sort of *super special* pardon for the colonel preventing him from ever sitting trial again, I shall accept it, but until then—"

"Y-your majesty, if I—"

"—until then, I expect the colonel to answer to the court in giving verbal sanction declassifying the events transpiring December 1939 to April 1940 in the neutral zone of Switzerland—"

"—y-your majesty—"

MacGeagh had been reaching for his gavel the entire time.

He snatched it up and tapped it gently, finally shutting Wingate's stonewalling lawyer up like a slap to the face.

The gavel, a small ceremonial mallet made of hardwood, was an unequivocal symbol of authority. Bashing such against the bench called for absolute attention and was typically reserved for extremities, and it seemed that Judge MacGeagh had busted it out early today, and for use concerning an unlikely speaker.

Tap!

One strike silenced it all.

He stated boldly. Officially. "Order in my court."

Bradbury silenced, puppy-eyed and shy. This shark was as brash as he was cunning, and that's probably why he had been selected to stand for Orde Wingate.

"I am not a member of the prosecution, Mister Bradbury. You do not possess the ability to talk over me in any frame or under any circumstance, so *shut! your! gob! ...*"

The whole courtroom shifted anxiously, exchanging sly leers.

Bradbury sheepishly retracted any further statement.

In the deafening silence that followed, MacGeagh sunk back in his chair an inch in order to collect his thoughts. "Now, the court appreciates Colonel Wingate's injuries and, therefore, we can recognize his inability of verbal communication. Colonel, you are excused from speaking here today."

Wingate's eyes fluttered, hinting an ounce of relief.

"However ... do your hands work?"

Silence.

MacGeagh reiterated the question to Wingate's representative.

"Mister Bradbury, do your client's hands work, yes or no?"

A deliberate smartass after his suppressing, Bradbury glanced about himself and his client after intentional delay. "Eh, yes, your majesty, to my knowledge, Colonel Wingate's hands *work*."

"Well then," MacGeagh affirmed with a signal, "due to the extenuating circumstances we find ourselves in, paired with the magnitude of the allegations held against Colonel Churchill, Colonel Wingate is hereby formally pardoned to sanction his declassification *verbally*. Instead, he may do so *cursively*. Somebody please retrieve for this man a *pen* and *parchment* for a formal declaration."

Bradbury visibly squirmed.

He eyed Wingate, who discreetly tossed him a sideways glance that undoubtedly hurt his partially severed neck.

Churchill and Spencer felt the walls resume closing in, and so they, too, also exchanged a glance and sigh.

What was unfolding, was the worst-case scenario ...

The semi-decapitated Orde Wingate sat soundlessly.

The echoic grand hall courtroom had become reticent and, at the same time, it was absolutely deafening. The childish noncompliance unfolding during such a formal setting was at the least entertaining.

"Colonel Wingate, for the second time," hiding his growing irritation well, Judge MacGeagh said again, this time raising his voice. "You are to sign the form in front of you ..."

A piece of legal paper constructed by the JAG had been placed before the witness along with a pen and the cap removed. The notion could not be made any simpler. All Wingate was required to do was sign his name, declassifying the mission, therefore enabling Jack Churchill clearance to accommodate the court with his tales from the black.

"Your majesty," the ever so nettlesome Bradbury once again opened his mouth, gaining the unwanted attention of Judge MacGeagh.

If looks could kill.

"My client would like to call a short recess—"

"Denied. The court is to remain in session," MacGeagh stated firmly, then returned his attention back onto Orde Wingate. "Colonel ... if you do not comply, I will be forced to hold you in contempt for whatever I deem to be an appropriate amount of time; time of which either your ability to use a pen returns, or your larynx heals, and you can once again speak audibly."

Wingate remained a statue.

"Colonel, in case you have not yet come to appreciate, this is an *order*."

Wingate remained mute and unmoving.

Unwilling to cooperate.

The Otter would barely make eye contact with Judge MacGeagh, opting instead to cast his dark and beady eyes across the room, staring without direction at a distant wall.

The judge tapped his gavel, signifying a ruling.

"Take him away," MacGeagh finally dismissed, displeasingly flinging his view away from the stubborn army brat and flailing his wrist and promptly his trusted bailiff. Wingate was hastily returned to his wheelchair by his MP escort and steered out of the courtroom before all sets of bleeding eyes. There was a simmer of audio as people exchanged baffled whispers and abrasive exclamations of disbelief surrounding what had just transpired.

One would assume that by Wingate not cooperating, he was in for a world of hurt ... but not Churchill. His perception of the game was too precise, too accurate, and he understood that Wingate knew how to play it better than anybody else in the room.

"Your honour, the prosecution would like to call its next witness," Barney resumed, continuing with a fresh gust of air into the proceedings and with the support of Judge MacGeagh. "We would like to call Constable Jethro McNaughton from the Special Investigation Branch."

From the row of lumber bleachers, the spotlight of attention found McNaughton. He noiselessly took centre stage with his call to fame. With immediacy and formal conduct, he cut across the courtroom floor and rounded the witness stand, finding the allocated seat. Out of his comfort zone--if Jethro McNaughton had such a thing—he seemed slightly nervous to be in front of so many people but hid it well.

"Constable McNaughton," Barney announced pompously. In this circumstance these two were from the same office, and he would be questioning his direct subordinate. "State your role for the court."

"I am the lead investigator on the case of Lieutenant-Colonel Jack Churchill committing high treason, and conducting disloyalty to the Crown," he answered truthfully.

"And during your investigation, did you find any evidence?"

"Yes, sir."

In a small gesture, Barney transferred the line of questioning onto the judge.

"What evidence have you brought forth to present to the court, Constable?" Judge MacGeagh asked after making a note on the papers on his desk. He now offered his full attention to the investigator.

"The testimony of a key witness, your honour."

After speaking, McNaughton threw Churchill a view aslant.

The two had a very recent history concerning these allegations and McNaughton's investigation. The waters were contaminated with hatred and duty, and were murky as fuck.

"Is the witness here today?"

Having just borne witness to prior stonewalling in the case, McNaughton noticeably broke a sweat following Judge MacGeagh's request. "No, your honour. The witness is an enemy combatant, incarcerated at a POW camp in Oldham. He is not permitted to testify in a British court of law nor step foot out from the prison."

Churchill found solace in McNaughton's sudden shortcoming.

Judge MacGeagh opened his palms and slouched. He was obviously extremely displeased with the constant lack of physical evidence being brought forth by his prosecution team versus Jack Churchill.

"Gentlemen, allegations remain allegations until they are proven in a court of law—*this* court. Need I remind you that these are *extreme* allegations against a well-decorated officer within his majesty's army and so far, all you have given me on Jack Churchill is jack shit ..."

Jack tried not to make his display of newfound comfort seem too obvious to the court as he wiggled in his chair.

"Your honour, if I may?" McNaughton attempted to carry the inquest. MacGeagh's lack of retort was permittance. "In your notes, there should be a copy of the transcript I printed from my interview with the prisoner, Hauptsturmführer Friedrich Feind. He is an equally as well-decorated German officer as Colonel Churchill. Let it be known to the court that since his capture during a recent Commando raid in Norway, Hauptsturmführer Feind has been exceptionally forthcoming with intelligence to the PWIS and correspondents of the Intelligence Corps. The legitimacy of every one of his prior claims is why the Criminal Investigation Department approached the accusations surrounding Colonel Churchill with a delicate sense of validity. We don't just take any *Tom, Dick, and Harry's* allegations critically about our war heroes—especially if they're originating from a prison camp."

MacGeagh accepted McNaughton's stance, and he observed the papers in his midst whilst the investigator continued.

"In our findings, Hauptsturmführer Feind mentioned knowing Colonel Churchill personally, and offered information on his extracurricular activities selling secrets to the enemy—"

"Pardon?!" Churchill scoffed, scrunching his brow and standing erect. Attention fell onto him from the bench where he suddenly remembered the official order of courtroom proceedings and how thin the ice was beneath his kilt. His lone outburst excusable, lost in a sudden onset of emotion. "Apologies," he corrected magnanimously and with a slight bow towards MacGeagh. "*Objection,* your honour. I'd like to make an *objection.*"

For some reason MacGeagh continued to humour Churchill's severe lack of formal crown court conduct. Perhaps he just wasn't bout de souffle just yet.

"Grounds?" Judge MacGeagh queried.

Churchill thought fast for the correct term. "Eh, on the grounds of ... him, that ... it's not true."

Discreetly, Spencer muttered from his low flank. "*Conjecture.*"

"Conjecture!" Churchill raised a confident fist, and then at McNaughton directly. "What I mean to say is that I doubt Constable McNaughton has any *actual* proof considering it's not true!"

"Overturned," Judge MacGeagh responded after a pinch of consideration; however, McNaughton was not off the hook. "Be seated, Colonel. Constable McNaughton, keep it concise for the court."

Whilst Churchill's kilt sunk into his seat and he tucked it back in at the edges, McNaughton conceded with a nod, correcting his statement. "Very well, then: extracurricular activities *communicating with the enemy,*" he reworded for the court. "And before the defendant chucks another sook, of *that,* I *do* have proof."

This was news to Churchill.

He took the authenticity of such a claim on the chin—for now.

"On the top of conspiracy to communicate with the enemy, Feind also alleged that Churchill was a part of a special off-books auxiliary operation funded by the British Army and commanded by Orde Wingate, wherein which the soldiers were illegally trained by multinational specialists including a high-ranking officer from Nazi Germany. An apparency which appears to have come to fruition."

The court preserved an absence of volume.

MacGeagh flung a gleam beyond Pownall, Durnford-Slater, and Laycock respectively. This was all news to him, and cast a new light on those representing the military.

During the high-strung and tense atmosphere of the courtroom following the exact accusation, Churchill locked eyes with his esteemed commando colleague, mentor, and friend, Durnford-Slater. The two had touched briefly on the topic of the validity of the indictment recently, and it was much a sore topic as ever.

Jack didn't deny it then ... and didn't now.

In light of the defendant's lack of a counterstatement to the accusation, Judge MacGeagh confronted Churchill, parting with a wise sentiment and shrewd advice for him. "Colonel, your constraint withholding of details on Wingate's special unit is admirable. Like any soldier sworn to secrecy, your loyalty is honourable. Nonetheless, you might think to reconsider your unyielding tight-lipped-ness concerning the operation. The repercussions of breaking your silence versus the consequences of being found guilty of high treason ..." MacGeagh held up both his hands, signifying them each holding an outcome and that the former was much lighter than the latter as would a set of unbalanced scales.

"Understood, your majesty," Churchill replied with a sombre bend of appreciation ... and then just when the magistrate thought he had correctly considered his options, Churchill cocked his head. "Nevertheless ... the defence requests to see that *proof* first."

"Colonel," Barney piped up from the bench, "This isn't a hand of poker. You can't just *bluff* your way out of this. There is a due process to these types of findings, and sooner or later we will get to the truth—moreover, what we perceive as the truth. Simply put, it looks a lot better if we hear it from you first."

Posing stoically, Churchill persisted, though the obvious contemplation and consideration churned behind his eyes.

"Constable?" MacGeagh turned his head to question the stand. "What evidence have you got to further support your claim?"

"A second witness' declaration, your honour."

MacGeagh inhaled air for a sigh.

Another magical witness?

"A *credible* witness, your honour," McNaughton reassured upon noticing the judge's patience growing thinner by the notion.

"Gentlemen, this *witness* better be physically here today, and be prepared to approach the stand?" MacGeagh decreed, at the end of his rope.

McNaughton exchanged a look with Barney, nodding firmly.

"He is, your honour."

"Very well. Your witness can take the stand momentarily," Judge MacGeagh affirmed with a tap of his gavel. "We will recess. Court adjourned for thirty minutes."

He tapped again, signifying the adjournment.

During the onslaught of the ruckus caused by the called recess as it surrounded them at the bar, Spencer stood, hoisting upstanding beside Churchill as he remained seated for an elongated period of deep consideration.

The lawyer looked down at him in his partially defeated state.

Churchill appeared to be wearing thin but still remained confident in his convictions.

"He's right, y'know," Spencer wholesomely regarded, referring to Barney's advice. "Imagine if this *was* poker ... what if their next witness is an ace in the hole."

"Then, old boy ... we fold. But *only* then."

Spencer held his view upon Churchill's nonchalant demeanour. He could see him now, in amongst his platoon of frogmen, rifles, and fitted bayonets, shooting the shit, being the fashionable commander that collectively gained the respect of the younger generations. He was both in awe and disrespect of the pseudo-blasé mindset.

"Colonel, you're a soldier, correct ...?"

Churchill raised his chin to the claim. "Well, I bloody well hope so, lad. Otherwise, they erroneously gave me this uniform, and I've done an awful lot of awful things—albeit, to awful people."

"Can you not see the *sacrifice play* here?" Spencer implored, leaning on his briefcase as Churchill stood, considering the collection of his decorative sword armament from the table. "It's a sentiment you should be aware of; that you can't win every battle. Same thing goes for courtroom battles. Only difference is, you can see the end coming and leastways get to pick the less devastating outcome. Soften the blow."

Churchill waggled his head, approaching his attempted wisdom fairly and with understanding whilst he stood and sheathed the weight of his claybeg at his left hip over his tartan kilt layer. "It's true, they train you in advance to have to make the sacrifice play ... to lay down over barbed wire and let the other guys crawl across you ... Agreed, sometimes it's a necessary part of warfare. But on the other hand, others instruct that alternative options exist if you know where to exact them," Churchill faced Spencer. "In that case, it could be just as easy to *cut the wire*."

Like clockwork, both Churchill and Spencer had their conversation cut short as Judge MacGeagh's trusted bailiff MP approached their bar on the open space floor in a wildly unorthodox interaction. The courtroom was almost empty now, having been relieved by the recess. In fact, they were the last two remaining now that the entire lay member bench had stepped out into the busy hallway.

"Sirs," the bailiff respectfully acknowledged. He handed Churchill a folded note. "His majesty Judge MacGeagh wishes to see you in his chambers in five minutes." Message delivered, he walked away.

"What's this?" Spencer asked with a frown, peeking over as the bailiff dismissed himself and Churchill unfolded the small note. It was a strange turn of events.

Before he even read the writing, which was a cursive invitation to meet, Churchill had a response for Spencer carrying on from their astute prior discussion: "Maybe it's the third option ... *walk around the barbed wire*."

Across the courtroom was a door leading directly to a JAG office: Judge MacGeagh's quarters. Permitted by the Judge's bailiff, who also acted as a guardsman, Churchill and his lawyer waited the appropriate five minutes before approaching for their peculiar meeting between court sessions.

Spencer had mentioned during the interim period that such a meeting was rare but not completely unconventional, especially considering that this was a secret trial. A deal could be struck outside of the courtroom, that much was legal, and a plea could be offered to the defendant privately by the prosecution. What *was* strange, was that it seemed that the prosecution already had Churchill by the short and curlies ... why would they want to waste their breath on making a deal with a stranded defence?

They entered the room through the single eight-foot door, entering Judge MacGeagh's chambers. The room was long, dim, and narrow, framed with ceiling-high bookshelves stacked with varying literature, most of it legal treatises, encyclopaedias, and casebooks. A murky stained-glass window existed at the far end behind his massive desk, illuminating the room.

The wigged and robed magistrate stood before the glowing source of daylight, tranquilly absorbing the afternoon view with his hands behind his back. Deputy Chief Barney was also present, seated in one of the two comfy leather chairs opposite the giant mahogany office furniture.

"Your honour," the beret-clad Churchill announced as he entered. After reaching the centre of the room, he remained at ease but upstanding. Spencer sidled in next to him with his briefcase, glancing around the chambers like a kid at a chocolate factory, and the bailiff closed the door for privacy.

"Colonel Churchill," MacGeagh welcomed, revolving around and extending an offering of pleasantries accessible on his desk. "Tea? Biscuits?"

Churchill's eyes swiftly bounded across the selection on the platters. Set up on a silver tray was a steaming kettle, a sugar bowl, and teacups on decorative saucers. Complimenting the tea was an array of finger foods including classic arrowroots, crumbly shortbread, and what appeared to be Dutch speculaas. Rare treasures during such harsh times of rationing, but this was how the other half lived.

"No thank you," Jack respectfully declined, maintaining his stoicism.

"Coffee, then?" MacGeagh offered further. "I can have them bring in a pot."

Churchill shook his head. "I'm fine-o-fine, sir."

"I'll ... take a biscuit," Spencer piped up awkwardly, reaching in low and grabbing an arrowroot and quickly applying some yellow butter with the provided spreading knife. There was an ungainly stillness that followed, during which Churchill realized how loud Chief Barney sipped his tea. He was the type of person who sucked his lip over the hot beverage, rather than just positioned his lips over it and tipped like a normal fucking person.

Churchill expunged the frustration with each audible slurp.

"Very well, to business," Judge MacGeagh regarded as he rotated his cushioned leather office chair and took a seat, tucking himself in. "Please take a seat."

Again, Jack declined. "I'd rather stretch my legs, sir."

With a short chortle, MacGeagh hung up on the response for an extended moment. Churchill's constant rejections of his pleasantries were starting to feel like disfavour. He bobbed his head at the final response.

"Colonel Churchill, we've read your file, back-to-back," Barney led their discreet discourse, which appeared to be framed a lot like it could be housing a proposition. "You're one hell of a soldier. A national hero. A warfighter. There is no doubt in my mind that the war effort needs you moving forwards. You are an instrumental cog in Prime Minister Churchill's war machine."

"Excuse me, is this a plea?" Spencer muttered. "Because any plea bargains offered to my client need to be put forward in writing and given well in advance of any court verdict."

"It's not a plea." MacGeagh silenced the lawyer.

"The prosecution would like to see an outcome to this where you are not reprimanded, Colonel. Not removed from Commando, or even from the army. One where you can promptly return to active duty; into a position to aspire command for your own battalion once again."

"This sounds a lot like a plea."

Barney looked to MacGeagh after being interrupted a second time by Churchill's attorney, deciding to stand and diplomatically handle the problematic lawyer. He buttoned his suit and led the way. "Perhaps you and I can step outside, Mister Spencer. Draft the terms of a potential plea bargain for your client?"

Spencer was perplexed but excited by the prospect.

This was definitely not the way the legal system worked and although it felt like a hustle, he gave in to the Deputy Chief's offer and the two stepped out of the chambers leaving alone Churchill across from MacGeagh.

Churchill watched Barney practically escort his lawyer out with force sold as an offering of biscuits. It was now just him and the judge. On his panoramic scan returning to the magistrate, Jack noticed the absolute assortment of books lining the shelves. There was a plethora of legal literature. These guys would know the ins and outs of the legal system, and there was no way this plea bargain was being offered outside of the official guidelines by accident. They knew the system so well they could manipulate it however they saw fit.

It caused Churchill to view the honorary Judge MacGeagh in a different light—one with a hue of untrustworthiness and shade of suspicion.

"You want the truth?" MacGeagh said simply, cutting to the chase.

Churchill's silence was his appropriate response.

He watched as MacGeagh levelled with him, not only in possible agenda, but in hospitality. The Judge ducked in low and opened his lower drawer, bringing up a half-tapped bottle of twelve-year single-malt Glenkinchie and two short glasses. He poured them both a dram and stepped around his desk with a raised arm, extending the olive branch to Churchill who instinctively accepted.

Drinking was the soldier's pleasure, after all, according to *Dryden*.

"This whole thing has spiralled *catastrophically* out of control," MacGeagh admitted taking up a rudimentary seat on his two-tonne mahogany furniture, facing Churchill closely. He took the time to remove his barrister wig, tossing it accurately onto the bust noggin on a nearby shelf. Sir Henry MacGeagh had thinning wavy brown hair surrounding a bald spot not uncommon of a man his age. It looked like someone had dropped a piece of devon on his head. "You've become a pawn in a much grander scheme. A grand sting, as it were."

Cradling his tumbler of whiskey neat with one arm still behind his back, Churchill's assured expression presented itself. He knew there had to be an ulterior motive to at least some of this whole scheme, and now he was about to gain a peek behind the curtain of the larger picture.

MacGeagh continued, terming his communication in a way he felt a soldier would most likely positively respond. "In a manner of speaking, you've become collateral damage ... Barney put his department onto Wingate quite some time ago, although he's been on our most-wanted board for even longer. McNaughton's got a sour history with the man, and so he was a regular bloodhound working the case, which eventually enveloped you. The blunt instrument that is Orde Wingate, consecutively colouring outside of the lines, will one day need to be reeled in and answer for the sins we permitted him to compose. Getting at you to get at him became a manoeuvre intended to flush the Otter out of hiding and gain a confession big enough to bury him in his own grave. A stake through his heart. But his eradication is, also, not entirely what we're interested in ..."

Churchill's attentive eyes were locked onto MacGeagh, tracing his every move as he pushed his posterior up from the desk and revolved around, repositioning himself before his stained-glass window and in the harsh light, taking a sip from his harsh beverage.

"Colonel, what I am about to tell you, if admitted in a court of law, I will deny ... there exists a potential for a grand conspiracy within the British government ..." MacGeagh finally elaborated. He followed up his deliberation by casting Churchill a silent gleam, underlining the severity of the claim.

Hints of distrust and suspicion had recently become the climate within which the United Kingdom existed in these trying times. Word of *spies for Germany* was commonplace during this heightened state of countrywide paranoia. Not only were the public encouraged to phone in any questionable behaviour witnessed across the countryside to the authorities for investigation, but the Government was haemorrhaging at the sides and on the verge of an aneurysm thinking of ways to combat the potential invisible forces within their own kingdom.

"... I don't have to convey how detrimental the existence of such could be to the British war effort; if there is an individual within the War Office with an agenda misaligning to ours; to the country's ..." MacGeagh leant on the backrest of his leather chair and stared into Churchill's soul. His narrative apparently struck a hiatus from continuation, or perhaps it was a calling cue for Churchill to pipe up.

The only kind of piping this lad did was the doodlesack.

During his time in the Berzerkers, Jack, in particular, had inadvertently found a front-row seat to an apparent display of high treason when he had witnessed Orde Wingate shake hands with Ernst-Günther Baade. This was only solidified further when overhearing their conversations about joining forces behind the curtain, Wingate joining Baade's idea of a secret society; a sovereign state of affairs that would exist both outside of and within existing governments and countries. When put on the spot that eventual morning, Wingate had not denied his desire of joining the secret society, albeit his actions to follow suggested that recruiter had given an official answer of declination.

It suddenly became apparent that MacGeagh recognized that Churchill knew more about what it was that he alluded to, though Jack refused to play along, acting coy. "Of course, sir."

MacGeagh maintained his stare on Churchill while he brought up his tumbler, taking another sip. Still locked on target, he placed it down and pressed his knuckles on the table.

"Let's get down to brass tacks, Colonel."

"I thought you'd never ask," Churchill said, raising his tumbler to chin to finally taste the whiskey, but he hesitated when hearing the flow of information.

"This secret society, *the Serpents,* we've been calling them ..."

"The Serpents?" Churchill cocked an eye. "Sounds slippery."

"... I know you know about them," MacGeagh collected his crystal, sauntering the office whilst reproaching Churchill, seasoning him with an introduction to this behind-the-scenes dog-eat-dog war. "The Otter knows, too. However, Wingate's unending stonewalling and lack of bloody cooperation has locked us out. Barney thought he had him with this trial."

Churchill could have shaken his head.

It was all starting to come together now, and he was finally beginning to see just how collateral he was, but he would have used a term more fittingly: *cannon fodder.* Chum thrown for a catch, who was in turn to be used as bait for an even bigger fish.

This sovereign state of affairs that Baade had been a part of before his demise must have gained traction over the years if it had been deemed a threat by the War Office ... or at least by *honorary Judge MacGeagh.*

Churchill raised his glass again to take another sip, only to refrain as his mind became snagged on something puzzling him; the conceivable circumstance that it wasn't the British government investigating this group ... but rather, an individual trying to uncover a backdoor *into* the said group ... and if so, was their reason just or *unjust.*

The heightened state of paranoia must have been contagious, and he had finally caught the bug. Churchill's stare intensified on MacGeagh with a suspicious underlining as he strangely opted not to take that sip.

"Colonel, we *know* that you're not guilty of high treason or conspiracy of conducting disloyalty to the Crown ... and I am willing to drop this whole case ..." MacGeagh offered, leaning across the table, across the trial notes, "... if you simply give me the details on aux-ops. If you give me everything you know regarding Wingate and his international contacts, and their dealings with the so-called Serpents."

Paused holding his tumbler beneath his chin, smelling the potent odour of whiskey poison, Churchill found himself deep in the realm of consideration. Logic, honour, and justice aside, he found himself bedevilled by a strange loyalty.

Regardless of the fact that he truly did not know enough about this secret society to strike a deal, Wingate hadn't folded on him or the other Berzerkers ... in fact, he seemingly accepted the fate of death by his own hand before giving up his sworn oath that incriminated Churchill of potential transgressions. Also, he had no idea what MacGeagh's true agenda was here. There was something fishy.

Finally, Churchill shotted back the whole contents of the tumbler, signifying their deed was done. Wordlessly, he placed the glass on the tabletop right in front of the unamused Judge MacGeagh.

This gesture was a symbol of his absolution to the proposition.

MacGeagh reeled back upright and stood tall.

"Very well ..." he stated disappointed. "Just so you know, the ball is rolling too fast and too heavy on this one, and I can no longer hold it back. Someone needs to be at the end of this rope, and if it isn't Wingate, it's you, Colonel. The prosecution's next witness is another nail in your coffin lid ..."

Jack craned his neck to the side. "Not the first. Won't be the last."

MacGeagh half-heartedly nodded at his unconcerned outlook.

"The reason I wanted to offer you this now is because once that court is commenced, there is no going back on certain liberties. I can't undo what gets done, is that understood? Any mention of what has transpired here in my office will be denied."

"Sir ..." Churchill opened his mouth, about to complain that even the Judge, himself, had just said that they knew he wasn't guilty ... but he abstained his own argument—however logical it may have been. Fact was, they didn't have the details on the aux-ops. Whoever their next witness was, as threatening as they seemed, it could have just been another false hand trying to call Jack's bluff. "See you in court."

Churchill turned to leave the chambers, but he stopped.

He turned, eyeing MacGeagh.

"Just out of interest," he asked at the door, facing back at Judge MacGeagh. "What *did* Wingate do to piss off McNaughton?"

Judge MacGeagh was well within his rights to deny Churchill the knowledge, especially considering he had rejected all his offers and that this meeting was done, but he chose disparagement over spiteful withholding.

"He killed his son in Palestine."

While that sunk in, MacGeagh threw Churchill a curveball.

"While we're still speaking *candidly*, as such ... the Otter is an utter piece of shit, Colonel. He's insane. A madman. Are you really going to continue to stall to protect Orde Wingate from prosecution?"

Churchill didn't have an immediate response.

And even if he wanted to change his mind, it was too late. The offer had expired the moment he had set his empty tumbler down.

Jack said nothing.

MacGeagh broached his chin. "See you in session."

Early afternoon, the court reconvened.

In much the same manner as their formal entry, all parties permitted during the court martial of Jack Churchill returned into the courtroom and to their seats. Once again, Churchill had presented his trusty sidearm onto the table, pointing his sword tip towards the bench and the JAG.

Judge MacGeagh entered, donning his white magistrate wig, and the bailiff asked the court to rise upon his entry and then become seated.

"Shall we continue?" MacGeagh announced after collecting himself and organizing the papers on his stand. He faced his right, where seated at the bench wing was Deputy Chief Barney.

Barney bobbed his head. "Your majesty, in a moment, the prosecution would like to reflect on an element of evidence provided by Constable McNaughton earlier during his testimony, where it was stated that there existed proof of Colonel Churchill illegally communicating with the enemy. Colonel Churchill, this juncture is your last opportunity to change your plea from *not guilty?*"

Focus fell on Churchill.

He stood. "The defence would like to reaffirm his plea from *still not guilty* to *very much still not guilty.*"

"Thank you, Colonel Churchill. Oh, and Colonel, we will proceed without any more attempts at humour in my courtroom, understood?" MacGeagh steadfastly stated, making eyes with Churchill. Apparently there was no love left here.

Churchill nodded singly and became seated ahead of Barney's continuation of the due process.

"During his written testimonial with Constable McNaughton, Hauptsturmführer Friedrich Feind stated that Jack Churchill reached out to him in the winter of 1941. This was during the early days of the formation of No.3 Commando by Colonel Durnford-Slater, and during a time where many soldiers not typically privy to such tactical and strategic information were obtaining and circulating sensitive intelligence."

On the right side of the lay member bench, Durnford-Slater was seated beside Laycock. The two knew the era well, as it was during the civil war of Commando versus LayForce. For the majority of the period, the two had been bureaucratic enemies.

Durnford-Slater's attention sought Churchill at the bar and the two exchanged a look. He couldn't help but mask it, but it was then that Churchill noticed what may have been a hint of underlining suspicion in his friend's eyes. That just maybe Jack Churchill wasn't all he made himself out to be ... that just maybe, these allegations held some truth.

"The prosecution would like to call upon its final witness," Barney announced. "Someone high up and reputable from British Intelligence who can corroborate Hauptsturmführer Feind's allegations that Colonel Churchill found methods outside of official channels to communicate discreetly with the overseas enemy ..."

Churchill suddenly felt sick as a realization washed over him.

The letter.

The one he sent to Feind, which he denied ever receiving.

In it, Churchill had reached out to his old foe, not only asking forgiveness for past transgressions but offering a gesture of goodwill as a symbol of eventual peace. Turning a new leaf during an interim incline of his life, Jack sent it during a transitional stage of his life, just prior to marrying Rosamund Denny.

These excuses would hold up in a court of law, regardless, it was not the context of the communiqué they were interested in ... but that Jack had sent the letter, and they could prove his communication with an enemy combatant.

"To substantiate this evidence, the prosecution would like to call a member from the *Air Ministry* analytical and intelligence sector to the stand: *Major Thomas Churchill.*"

Jack's brother.

10   10

♠   ♠

The Devil You Know

1942, March
Westminster Conference Grand Hall
Whitehall, London

Thomas Churchill entered the court.

Outfitted in his service dress, Thomas' insignia represented the rank of major, currently in the position as an intelligence officer within the Air Ministry, charged with dealing directly with the *COHQ (Combined Operations Headquarters)* liaising with statistics provided by the *PIU (Photographic Interpretation Unit)*. In fact, Thomas had been a part of the team directly responsible for the pivotal prep intel behind the scenes for Operation Archery, discerning aerial photographs and integral oblique angle pictures, marking targets and designating landing zones for the commando raid teams.

Thomas was a spitting image of his older brother Jack.

Similar height, same build, with comparable pale gleaming hair and sculpted facial hair follicles, only Thomas' was slightly blonder in shade—their father's features. When he spoke, he even vocalized in a voice of similar tenor to Jack's. Two out of three siblings, this brother duo was the more similar out of the Churchill trio, with their younger brother Robert *'Buster'* Churchill getting their mother's dark hair and features. On top of that, Jack and Thomas had a similar military career, both British Army, serving in the Second Manchester Regiment on land whereas Buster favoured the sea, serving afloat in the Royal Navy.

Jack's jaw dropped a gasp, watching his brother walk in.

His brother was testifying against *him ...?*

Whilst he strolled the space of the grand conference hall between the judge's bench and the bar where his brother was seated on trial, Thomas disconcertingly threw his older brother an equally uncertain and undesirable gleam before focusing forwards and mounting the altar.

He did appear unenthusiastic. Bound by obligation.

Perchance, he despised the fact that he was being forced to do this.

"*Witness, please state your name and credentials for the court,*" the bailiff prompted once Thomas was settled on the podium, spotlighted before a room full of inquest.

The Churchill brother hid his reluctance well, keeping things official.

He leaned in, articulating loud and clear. "*Major Thomas Bell Lindsay Churchill.* I am an intelligence officer for the Air Ministry."

Barney commenced the questionnaire. "Major Churchill, you were brought onboard to recognize the validity of an intelligence exchange from Great Britain to foreign soil in the month of January, 1941 ... is that correct?"

Again, Thomas leant in over the altar, aiming to rectify the tone of the questioning. "I was approached by Constable McNaughton from the Special Intelligence Branch three weeks ago ... at the time, he was hesitant to reveal the name of whom it was I would be assisting in the investig—"

"This isn't a confession booth, Major. Just the details, please. Thank you," Barney interrupted, conveniently obstructing any significant justification Thomas conveyed for the job, doubling as a halfway apology to his brother.

Involuntarily, Thomas realigned his posture, remaining neutral and even-handed. "I was issued postal departure dates for a physical telegraph sent through the Royal Mail from England to a subsidiary civilian company located in France."

"*Nazi-occupied* France?" Barney reiterated as a question.

Thomas paused, confused as to why there could be any misunderstanding regarding the country. "Eh, yes. *That* France." His cynicism hinted at his dislike towards this man and their enduring hostility against his brother, however it was mostly from Barney's purposeful stirring of the pot in order to provoke Thomas into appearing obtuse or even compromised; thus helping the prosecution's case by making it appear to the jury that Thomas' results were feather-weighted to aide his brother's outcome.

"*Yes* or *no* answers, please, Major."

Thomas death-stared Barney.

He was suddenly unsure if there was actually a game at play here, or if this courtroom git just got off on belittling high-ranking military men who were sworn under oath.

"Yes."

"This was a *civilian* company?" Barney asked again, well aware of the answers but wanting to steer Thomas' response to further their cause. He was selling his case, singing verses to the court, not just the chorus.

"Yes."

"What tasks do they specialize in?"

Thomas seemed to harness his brother's wit for this one.

He leant in again, torquing his neck as if they were stupid. "I'm sorry, how can I answer *yes* or *no* to that question?"

Barney blinked slowly. "*Yes* or *no* where can be, Major, thank you."

Thomas inhaled, playing it off successfully. "Sure. This independent forwarding company specializes in dispatching letters to foreign recipients non-existent on any English registrar."

"German recipients?"

Thomas' response was impartial, though he knew where this chain of questioning was leading, hence a pause of hesitation. "Sure!"

"German *soldiers?*" Barney broadened.

Reluctant to assist in furthering their objective, Thomas exhaled through his nostrils. He eyed him gravely before delivering a delayed response. "Sure!"

"*Yes* or *no,* Major."

Audibly sighing again, Thomas' eyes scanned the room as a portion of silence followed. "Yes."

"And, so ...? What happened next, Major?!"

"I was charged with reaching out to an official intelligence contact we have in France, who in turn investigated the validity of the aforementioned mail routing ..."

"And ...? Your findings, Major?! Did this independent forwarding company keep an accurate record of their forwarding addressees and senders?"

Thomas lamentably concurred. "They did."

"And what did you find through your contacts?"

"We discovered that Colonel Jack Churchill did indeed go through the extents of reaching out to a registered German officer, Friedrich Feind. At the time, Feind served Nazi Germany as a Hauptsturmführer and commanding officer for the Gebirgsjäger, 1st Mountain Division, with connections to the Einsatzgruppe-C operating out of *Lviv.*"

"*Lviv?*" Barney rhetorically questioned the intelligence which he already knew, ringing phoney as a drama student, purely doing so for obvious theatrical effect. "As in, *The Ukraine?* ..."

"Yes, sir. *That* Ukraine."

Barney should have won an Oscar for his performance this day, acting quite surprised for emphasis. Confused, he tilted his head, "From what we understand, that is to be the home of some of the most horrifically vile massacres in recent history?"

Thomas' eyeline fluttered. "Indeed."

Again, speaking out of term, and at the fact that it momentarily appeared that Barney was merely grilling Thomas for giving the answers to his questions. He did so to work the crowd; to win the crowd. Painting Jack in the corner as a conspirator with this top chap.

Barney panned his view from Thomas and onto Jack, pausing for further effect, casting a negative light on Feind; Churchill's supposed entrusted contact. He attempted to throw as much shade as possible, painting Churchill in the dark as a heinous offender. "Well, it sounds like the recipient was a, eh ... a *top chap?*"

Jack shook his head with an intentional cockeye and a chortle.

His disdain was only furthered by his horrible attempt at muttering in a low tone. "He's your witness, dickhead."

At the expense of Barney's mulligan, some sniggering occurred.

Barney's conceited expression faded fast, eyeing Churchill.

MacGeagh tapped his gavel. "Order."

With the fact still sinking in, blowing a devastatingly sized hole in Churchill's ship, now barely keeping afloat, Barney brought the hearing full circle.

"The prosecution would like to admit these confirmed findings as evidence," he held up a new manila folder loaded with everything in writing surrounding Churchill's back-traced letter to Feind. "Colonel Churchill had unsolicited contact with a registered enemy combatant within enemy-occupied territory. This *alone* is conspiracy to commit treason."

They clearly didn't have a copy of the said letter, for all they would have taken from it was the simple, regrettable act of an apology and offering Feind over for tea and bickies.

Dutifully, the bailiff walked over and collected the file from Barney, officially handing the admissible evidence to Judge MacGeagh for him to gaze over.

Nail.

Coffin.

After giving it a fast once over, MacGeagh closed the lid of the folder and raised his view across at Jack Churchill. His gaze read the verdict before he even had to deliver whatever long-winded speech the Judge had banked up to spit out.

"Colonel Churchill, please rise ..."

Hesitantly and finding it difficult to muster the strength to move under the weight of his world collapsing, Churchill hunched forward and assembled upright. His eyes dropped onto the desktop before him; about to perform the honours of following tradition: turning his sword tip upon himself.

WWHIIIIIIIRRRRRR ...

Suddenly, there was unexpected rise of discombobulating volume.

A diaphragm-rattling howling resounded, emitting from the skies, blanketing the cityscape of London. The loudness of the growing pitch flooded this internal room, wall to wall.

The lurid alarm rang out an audial, loud enough to drown out a man's own internal monologues as his brain screamed, questioning what the heck was happening.

Extreme audio flooded one's psyche; one's senses.

It was an air raid siren.

It was known as a *red warning*. This meant an attack was in progress or imminent, and the siren station at the *RAF Uxbridge* in Greater London had been engaged. The wail emitting from the base was loud enough to cover the entire city with a threat-level warning of a pending aerial attack.

Outside of bimonthly tests, the system hadn't been utilized since The Blitz. It had nearly been a year since Luftwaffe crafts had made it this far inland, dropping any bombs at designated targets across the English Channel. The situation was familiar due to this, but quite unexpected and outlandish.

Severing all proceedings like a falling cleaver—not only in the Westminster Conference Grand Hall, but across Whitehall and across the whole of London—people became possessed by the conditioning of war. Nonverbally, they upped from their respective seats and left behind all possessions, vacating immediately and without delay. As per general guidance training from instruction through mandatory seminars, propaganda, leaflet drops, and neighbourhood meetings, the crowds of the populus herded in an orderly fashion towards the nearest bomb shelter, often located beneath the ground in layers of thickened concrete. There happened to be one beneath most conference buildings in Westminster and they in the courtroom were promptly guided towards it in a systematic manner.

Ceasing all verdicts, the air raid alarm took precedence.

The JAG bench upped, escorted by trained MPs who dutifully stormed the courtroom to escort the most important members within the room; MacGeagh at the helm.

The others in the courtroom obeyed, standing and shuffling in a single file out and into the booming connecting hall, ushered towards the nearest bunker entrance which was located near the stairs in the main hall. Military Police acted as guides, waving the mass of concentrating crowds onwards, funnelling people from a multitude of rooms connecting to the corridors and towards the direction of safety from the potential bombing above the dreary clouds of England.

As out of place as it was, this event may have been commonplace ten months ago, not that anybody had forgotten the Blitz or how to act accordingly once the air raid siren sounded.

In the middle of the conference hall commotion, Thomas found Jack as they shepherded behind a crowd channelling for the doorway in a giant shambling.

During the saturating volume of the deafening siren and ensuing chaos, Churchill happened to make eye contact with McNaughton in the evacuation queue as he shuffled in behind Garland and others from the side seats. During this commotion, they had been practically forced out against all will, unable to interpose direction, nor could they verbally communicate. Durnford-Slater and Laycock filed just in front of them, queuing out into the busy hall of semi-panicking patrons, military men, and lawyers. The motley crowd was siphoning together towards exodus.

"*Jack!*" Thomas hollered through the numbing pitch, barely audible, even at a shout into his earhole. He could barely hear even himself.

"*Tom!*" Churchill retorted, grappling with his brother. Each man basically resorted to lip-reading. "*We've got to go!*"

None of it was audible or heard. Hand signals and gestures were used as they communicated, moving out and following the others towards the sanctuary within the underground shelters.

They had a lot to say right now but were unable to hear a word of it like some sick game.

"*Wait!*" Jack mouthed with a palm up, abruptly rotating in reverse from their intended direction, quickly running an errand.

Perplexed at what could be so important right now, Thomas watched his sibling return to the bar for a personal possession: a big *no-no* as trained by the authorities during a time of disciplined evacuation. All possessions were to be left behind, as nothing was as valuable as your life.

Jack had returned for his sword.

With one fell swoop, he lunged in and collected it from the table, slotting it into his floppy hip scabbard before returning to his brother's position at the rear of the queue, and the two allowed for themselves to channel through the doorway behind the others; towards the nearest bunker entrance safely below the Westminster building.

No bombs fell on London that afternoon.

Or England, for that matter.

The *all-clear* tone resonated from the same siren after approximately thirty extremely tense minutes of holding retreat in one of the bomb shelters of Whitehall, which were a bunch of interconnected tunnels resembling a claustrophobic version of the two-penny tube with several reserves for people to rest in in complete darkness.

Once the siren finished sounding, Thomas managed to sift through the crowd of packed people and find Jack in the blackness of blinking flashlights and glowing bulbs.

"Jack!"

"Tom!" Churchill hailed, taking his brother's embrace and grappling onto his sleeve in the crowd as the many zombified sheep herded towards the stairs, channelling back to the surface. It had been a while since either one of them had been present in a city during a bomb raid; protocols were very exact and very authoritatively deliberate. At present, they were exiting an alarmed state of mind, finally able to return their concentrations from concern to the court martial.

During the chaos, they had been entirely split up from anybody else who was present in the courtroom. Surely, they would all shortly reconvene, probably for an adjournment until the following day or week—Jack literally saved by the bell.

"Are you okay?" Thomas asked with an apprehensive tenor.

"Fine-o-fine," said Jack surely. "Are you?"

His question had double meaning.

"Fine," Thomas held his glance with a frown. They had a lot to talk about right now, and were fortunate enough to be in a situation where they could speak. The courts would not allow it. "Jack. Let me explain."

"There's nothing to excuse, Tom."

"No, there is! I am your brother, and I've just ..." he glanced around, ashamed. Of course, there were many people in eavesdropping range, however it seemed that due to the mild deafness of the sirens combined with everybody else's concerns lying elsewhere, busy passers-by seemed uninterested in conversation contexts happening at their flanks. Like during the unrelenting Blitz, the British spirit carried on. Thomas lowered his voice just in case. "I've just bloody *testified against you!* My own brother!" he shook his head as his vision blurred temporarily, full of brimming regret.

"Don't worry about it. You were just fulfilling your sworn oath to King and country."

"I could have refused!"

"No, you couldn't have."

"Well, I could have warned you!"

Jack tipped his beret-clad head. "Well, yes. You could have probably done that, lad."

Thomas cursed, back to feeling remorseful. "At first, I didn't know it was *you.* In hindsight, it was a rather strange request made by the Special Investigations Branch to the PIU, but I didn't think anything of it at the time. I was just eager to help the cause where I could."

"Tom, it's fine. It's done."

"Well, I guess what I am saying is that, even once I found out they were investigating *you,* I stayed on ... I figured it was better *the devil you know than the devil you don't,* right?"

Jack concurred with a head bob. "Sure."

Climbing over one-hundred stairs in the dark following the conclusion of the event, they finally reached the light of the surface, emerging from an alternate shelter entrance than the one they took during the chaos. They each looked around. Everybody topside was shaken, covered in dust and cobwebs, but okay. There didn't seem to be any damage or harm done.

In a divergence, Thomas branched out and asked a nearby helmeted topside MP through all the commotion who was directing the people traffic. "What happened?"

He shook his head and shrugged. "We don't know yet, sir. Apparently, no bombs were dropped ..."

"Were there enemy aircrafts?"

"Again, I'm not sure, sir."

Interested as well as relieved, Thomas nodded with appreciation, moving on after Jack who was headed towards the large foyer and towards the freedom of the natural light beaming in through the big open doors. Rather than immediately follow his brother, Thomas spotted some of the lay members from the trial and headed over to gain some information on what was to happen next with the proceedings ...

Jack Churchill shuffled with the crowd of others towards the bright afternoon light of the setting sun, and he squinted as he discreetly exited the building, taking to the first flight of concrete steps down onto a landing.

He searched around with his eyes in the sky, looking for smoke piles rising from the remnants of a bombing or any other evidence of an aerial attack ... but there were none.

"Jack," Thomas' voice called through the thickening crowd of evacuating bodies, catching up and carrying news for his brother. Jack turned to face him as he delivered, and the two promptly sidled to the edge of the grand staircase. Beside them was a cement barrier followed by a twenty-foot drop to street level, which was coincidently where Churchill had parked his 42WLA model Harley-Davidson motorbike this morning. "The JAG has reached a verdict, but they'll likely want to go over everything once again given this interruption, rescheduling another trial. You must have really pissed Judge MacGeagh off ..."

"Why's that?"

"Well, they haven't fully convicted you, but apparently, he wants you in confinement in the interim. He wants to keep you uncomfortable."

Jack sniggered. "Of course he does."

Thomas bobbed his head. He didn't have anything else to say, so he just observed his brother for direction.

Churchill revolved around some more, caringly observing the city of London to again check she was intact. There lingered a level of confusion in the air. "We get lucky?"

Thomas shook his head. "There was no attack. Well, not yet."

"*Yet?*" Jack eyed him with a raised brow. Being in intelligence, his brother was always in the know. In the heat of all that was happening, this discussion felt like small talk. It was a nice digression from his current situation, if only for a moment.

"The RAF is launching a new aerial offensive against targets in Germany. They have already set plans in motion to expect a tit-for-tat counterattack by the Luftwaffe directly following."

"So, they're planning on poking the bear?"

"New homeland attacks are inevitable. The Luftwaffe is going to start hitting us again sooner or later, just like they did during the Blitzkrieg. Our guys just want to get the first hit in this time is all," Thomas defended the ideals of his brains at the Air Ministry.

A moment of silence passed between the brothers as they stood on the steps of the Westminster Conference Grand Hall in the afternoon sunset, surrounded by an ocean of crisscrossing business suits and bystanders, all eager to get out after the false alarm.

"You still haven't asked me," Jack questioned focally, his strange exposition and expression of wonder falling upon his brother ...

"... Asked you what?"

"If I'm guilty."

Following his frown, Thomas turned to his brother, face to face. "The day my brother betrays the King is the day I pilot a miniscule Bristol Blenheim and fly it up *Eva Braun's* holiest of holies."

The two shared a laugh that quickly dwindled.

"Jack," Thomas shook his head, confused by an element of his brother's predicament. "These guys seemed a lot more interested in *Orde Wingate* than they are of *you,* or at least something he's involved in. Why are you going out on a limb for this wanker? Your head is massively on the chopping block. I don't know the man personally, but his name has been printed in more tabloids than *Little Orphan Annie.* He can't be that worth protecting."

"He's not," Churchill regarded firmly.

"So ... what, then? Just give him up!"

"Wingate didn't open his mouth, neither will I."

Thomas took a deep breath.

It never ceased to amaze him just how stubborn his brother could be on some of his ventures—this being a case in point. And there was something else relative that Thomas had tripped over during his acquisition of intelligence.

"Oh, also *Friedrich Feind?*" he lured. "Isn't that the chap from Oslo all those years ago?" he inquired, recollecting the period of which Jack Churchill was competing in the World Archery Championships. It was where he had first met Feind and they had shared a *dispute,* so to say ...

Jack tipped his beret. "One and the same."

Thomas muttered at the coincidence. "Hmm."

"Big story, small world."

Jack eyed Tom, noticing his intrigue.

"Don't worry, he's a permanent resident here now. We caught him in Vågsøy last year."

"Oh?"

"Yes. He should be thankful that I didn't take his head off at the shoulders."

"Perhaps you should have," reasoned Thomas, rather uncharacteristically for somebody who advocated pacifism. "You wouldn't have ended up with this bloody mess on your doorstep."

"Touché," Churchill's eyes defocused for a moment of contemplation. This was hardly the first time that somebody had said he should have ended Feind's life rather than spared it. "This is his desperate, last-ditch effort at a riposte: defamation. An attempt to discredit me during a time our good nation resides in the highest state of paranoia and suspicion."

Thomas bobbled his head. "Well, he's doing a good job!"

Churchill nodded ironically and in concurrence.

After the fleeting moment of comfort, Thomas found their figurative footing. "Look, Jack, any minute now and these MPs are going to come for you. They'll slap on a pair of tremendously uncomfortable metal handcuffs extremely tightly. You'll be hauled away."

Jack bowed, seemingly with a plan. "I am aware."

"Are you going to comply with the judge? I'm talking about jail, you realize?"

"Wouldn't be my first time in lockup, now, would it?"

"It'll be your first time sober."

"Touché, once again," Jack conceded, continually scanning the crowd that was dismounting the concrete stair slab before them; a flowing mass exodus from the Westminster Conference Grand Hall. Everywhere in Whitehall was in shambles following the presumed air raid. Some civilians were in whimpering tears and requiring consoling while others were laughing and contented, feeling blessed. It was a mixed bag of post-turmoil emotion.

His brother was right, though, and he had too much on his agenda to be stuck in the mud right now.

Although Churchill wasn't about to evade the authorities like some kind of criminal fugitive, he also wasn't about to hang around and let them take him into the custody of a police car, received like some sort of limp penis. If he acted quick, he could slip away right now during the aftermath of the air raid chaos.

"I have too many loose ends I need to tie ..."

"I thought that you may. You're not going to the hotel, are you? They'll surely search for you there ..."

Jack shook his beret-clad dome upon his brother's tactically unaware drivel. "Gosh no. I'll be heading out of town. They can reach me by telegram with the next court date via Commando Castle."

"You're heading back to base?" Thomas eyed him firm. "They'll send MPs there, too, dragging your buttocks back to London, kicking and screaming ..."

Jack downed a few concrete steps, headed towards the location he had his Harley-Davidson motorbike on the street. He had a newfound itinerary to stick to. "Perhaps it is best you *don't* know where I am going?" he responded warily towards his brother. With a hint of sarcasm, he faced him with an expansion. "Lest they put you on trial to testify against me again, under oath."

Guilty as charged, Thomas concurred.

He beamed, sensing his brother's forgiveness. "Understood."

"Listen, Tom," Jack asked with a critical tone, reaching into the pocket of his rabbit pelt sporran located at the front of his kilt. He obtained his numbered room key, issuing it foremost. "Ros was going to meet me at my hotel tonight ... she said she had something important to tell me. Whatever it is, I am sure it can wait a few days ..."

"O ... kay," Thomas played along, warily accepting the key.

"Say you do me a favour; head to my room at the Union Jack Club to intercept her? Escort her safely home to Dumbarton for me?"

"What about the *important something?!*"

"It's probably nothing. We had a disagreement a few weeks ago and we left it on an awkward note. She is probably wanting to smooth things over, as am I, just ... not now," Jack muttered remorsefully, forcefully realigning his passage for the greater good. "Promise me you'll get her home?"

Thomas' shoulders dropped. This was a tall order.

"What do you want me to tell her, Jack?"

"She doesn't know about the court martial, and thinks that I am here for work ... Just tell her something urgent has come up, and I'll see her in a few days."

Thomas reluctantly nodded, eyeing the room key in his possession.

Performing this was the least he could do.

"*Oi!*" the voice of a stern MP called from the building entrance. A pair of the uniformed guards had sighted Churchill and were homing in on his location through the crowds of dissipating civilians.

Their presence was expected, and their shouts caused a ruckus, piquing the interest of everybody out front of the courthouse.

Thomas had his back to the building, body-blocking his renegade brother. He uttered at an inhale, "... time to go."

Jack torqued his head. "Let's the games begin, eh?"

"Oh, Jack, they began long ago!" he stated as he watched his eccentric older brother first consider descending the many slap steps of the building before suddenly choosing to up the concrete barrier lining the grand exterior staircase. His dramatic action turned a lot of heads, even granting a few audible gasps of concern as they sighted him up high. Below was approximately a twelve-foot drop to street level.

Hand on his holstered sword, Churchill turned last minute to lay eyes on his official pursuers as they enclosed like sharks in the ocean before he would leap clear into a freefall. He offered a partial salute before dropping like a stone. The skirt of his kilt expanded and bloomed like a parachute canopy, emitting a weighty *whoosh* as it inflated, catching air.

If anybody had been beneath his descent, they would have had quite the show, for his gonads were shaven tidy and on-point.

Sticking the landing in the shade of the grand structure, Churchill casually stood as he sprang into a step. From beneath his aslant beret, he glanced up at the many heads of towering military police, his brother, and various rubbernecking civilians alike before sprinting off the mark like an athlete after the starting gun.

"*Oi! You!*" another MP shouted, pointing with a stiff finger. "*You are bownd by the cowrt ov lawww!*"

Hand on his downward sword, Churchill ran like a linebacker, dashing between pedestrians before launching himself onto his parked Harley like a cowboy onto his faithful steed, keying the booming engine and quickly harnessing the throttle. The decibels of the motorbike crackled like thunder, disturbing many within the street vicinity and neighbouring intersection.

Like a bullet from a gun, Churchill shot in an abrupt acceleration into the passing traffic of the street, vanishing from sight in a matter of seconds.

Behind the dramatic sequence of events, Constable McNaughton keenly observed Churchill's evasion beneath a brooding frown.

Although he was emotionally charged with concern at apprehending this man, the beam that formed on his maw was not due to the thrill of the chase ... it was because now, Jack Churchill was wanted dead or alive.

Desirably dead.

1942, March
Union Jack Club Hotel
Waterloo, London

Dusk caused a cool hue to fall upon London.

Golden streetlamps blinked on in unison, as did the headlamps of all vehicles in transit on the streets.

Struggling with the remorse of his indirect betrayal and the heavy burden of his dutiful responsibilities, combined with the gravity of his brother's dire circumstances, Thomas Churchill deemed it necessary to fulfil Jack's wishes.

He drove his dark *Ford Prefect* from the Whitehall parking garage past the Big Ben and across the Westminster Bridge into Waterloo athwart the River Thames. Tom found street parking across from the five-storey Union Jack Club Hotel and surveyed the venue.

The Union Jack Club was predominately reserved for serviceman patronage. In fact, an active service was required even just for booking an overnight stay or entering the attached associations, even the bar.

Upon flicking on the handbrake and exiting the car, Thomas wondered if Rosamund would be there already or if he would have to await her arrival. Jack had been rather scarce with the details. He preferred the first outcome, as he suspected some military police officers might come knocking for Jack to return him to lockdown at the courthouse, and at least that way he could intercept her first. He had been fast in his travels and was yet to see any uniforms patrolling the street.

Donning his khaki service dress, Thomas Churchill cruised confidently through the entrance past a saluting doorman who greeted him courteously. He approached the lifts, scanning the number upon the room key Jack had issued him: *36.* Thomas got in the called elevator gesturing to the seated operator within. "Three, please."

Reaching the third floor, Thomas exited the lift via it's scratchy wire gates and strode down the cush of the carpeted, narrow hall, breathing a stench stale of mothballs. He found 36 and rattled the key in the lock, stepping cautiously into the darkness within.

A lurch into the stillness, he was about to flip a light switch when he noticed a glow already glistening up the opposite end of the room. The radiance was warm and faint, alit from ... *candlelight?*

Thomas' tight brow loosened as he realized that he was likely about to interrupt the setting of a romantic, sensual evening. This would be awkward if she was sprawled out across the mattress covered in rose petals.

"Ros?" he bellowed, identifying himself before walking too far in and seeing something he shouldn't. "Ros, it's Tom. Are you there?"

After there was no response, he meandered in slowly ...

Unveiled to him was the amorous setting Jack had left for the two of them. A bouquet of roses on the bed, the scent of perfume, candles lit on the bedside, and a chilled bucket of champagne had arrived and was placed on the nearby dresser.

This may not have been a trap set for him ...

... but he had sprung it, all the same.

Suddenly, a figure appeared in the doorway behind Thomas.

An ominous shadow, the silhouetted appearance of a man with a fedora strafed into view, cutting the white light from the hallway. In the same instance that Thomas' awareness clued him to the presence behind him due to the shift of light, he heard the unmistakably identifiable mechanic *cli-cli-click* of a revolver hammer being cocked, now pointed at his back.

A stern command from behind followed: "*Don't move.*"

Thomas froze stiff, slowly raising his hands outwards.

He huffed instinctively. "Easy now ..."

The male figure with the gun stepped into the hotel room behind him, shutting the heavy door and sealing them within. The yet to be identified gunman moved closer, his shoes shuffling securely on the coarse carpet texture.

The snub nose revolver barrel became pushed into Thomas Churchill's lower back causing him to become more upright, and the gunman glanced beyond his stance and into the romantic setting of the bedroom. "Aw. Mad Jack, you shouldn't have."

"Listen ... I'm not Jack ... you've got the wrong Churchill," Thomas affirmed unambiguously, still holding his hands out by either side. He could only gather that whoever this gate crasher was, he was a lawful intruder and present in the pursuit of his brother. Therefore, he wouldn't shoot on sight— or continue to train the gun on him after a positive identification.

The figure leant in, peaking the profile of the military suited fellow with a portrait frame mostly indistinguishable from that of Mad Jack Churchill.

"What?!"

"I'm Thomas. Jack's brother."

"Turn around," the gunman instructed, finally gaining a positive identification in the lowlight and gloom of the room.

Thomas faced the gunman: Constable Jethro McNaughton.

Once laying eyes on his perpetrator's sibling, he lowered his snub-nosed Colt Detective revolver, a handgun popular with law enforcers requiring concealment, safely collapsing the metal claw hammer with his thumb. Judging by his body language, he was rather peeved that he had just sprung this trap on the wrong Churchill.

"Don't worry," Thomas consoled the investigator in a woollen suit beneath an overcoat whilst he lowered his spread mittens, adjusting his sleeves within his cuffs. "It's not the first time I've been confused for my sibling."

McNaughton seemed worn and tired. Exhausted, even.

His tie was loose, top button undone, and his gullet unshaven.

Thomas had met this guy once before, when Deputy Chief William Barney of the Special Investigation Branch had brought him and his female offsider into his office and recruited him into their ongoing investigation—and conveniently left out the part about the subject being his blood brother until he had already started reaching out for the mail addressee. They had met again a week ago and even then, McNaughton seemed more in control and a lot less tense than he was now.

"Where is he?" McNaughton finally interrogated, shrill of manners and short of tone. He was right royally pissed about Jack fleeing custody to the point where he nearly had the shakes, like he had consumed too much rage caffeine.

Thomas understood things may not have gone the way the Special Investigation Branch—more so, Jethro McNaughton—had planned with nailing Orde Wingate to the cross, and that it may have left him colossally hot under the collar. It appeared that he wanted to take it out on Jack, hammering him for his dishonest desertion, perhaps even unlawfully so.

After all, Major Thomas Churchill *was* in the intelligence sector. He had vetted the wayward constable after they had met to exchange findings and McNaughton fully indicated himself to be a personal threat against his brother. He found out quickly of McNaughton's vendetta against Wingate and knew about the loss of his son whilst under his command in Palestine. Details were vague from the army reports beyond that, claiming simply that his death was in the line of duty. However, through his many contacts, Thomas had dug a little deeper, discovering that the time in question was during a racially reprehensible era for Wingate's command, leading most to ascertain that McNaughton's boy was a casualty of a political involvement during a rise of Zionist movements. This suggested if not directly implicated Wingate with wrongfulness towards the British Mandate of Palestine at the time, of which for similar reasoning, he has been all but found guilty. The glove fit.

Whatever the truth, it appeared that McNaughton had grown hellbent on taking Wingate down for his sore duties of command. He directly blamed him for the death of his son; a fate that could have been different if Wingate was more for the cause than seeking his own vanity projects amidst wartime—again, all proven fact.

"I said, where is he?" McNaughton demanded again.

Momentarily infatuated with McNaughton's motives now that a darker side of him had risen to the surface, Thomas snapped out of his mental reverie and focused up.

"I don't know."

"Don't lie to me, Major!" McNaughton grumbled like an angry juvenile, gusting past Thomas and entering the perfume-fragrance of the candlelit bedroom, scanning it to be double sure with his pistol still clutched in his balled fist. McNaughton swirled in the empty space, facing him again. "You're his brother! I saw you both talking at the courthouse after the air raid. You saw him off! Now, I'll ask one last time before I arrest you for conspiracy of harbouring a fugitive: *where is Jack Churchill?!"*

"Honestly, I have no idea," Thomas implored with a level of sincerity that McNaughton detected. "He wouldn't tell me. Refused. He said it was better I didn't know."

McNaughton scoffed in a change of pace. "What's all this bollocks, then, eh? Was he planning another special night laying pipe with another one of his mistresses?"

Thomas replied with a stark frown. "It's for his *wife*. She was said to be meeting him here after the trial. It's why I came, to chauffeur her home."

"*Which wife?"* McNaughton scowled. "Just how many broads has this guy got on the line?"

"Calm down, Constable. That's a loyal husband and decorated war hero you're speaking discourteously about," Thomas advised after taking mild offence in regard to the integrity of his brother. It was unwarranted, unprofessional, and uncalled for, and he wasn't having a bar of it. McNaughton's demeanour was starting to shift from respectable lawman to loose cannon. "I suggest you show some respect and uphold professionalism."

McNaughton puffed steam, disbelieving his credit.

He sauntered closer, eyeing Thomas like he was about to deck him.

Thomas let it go, watching as the directionless constable strode over to the dresser where the chilled bucket and bottle of champagne rested, dripping condensation down onto the stainless-steel saucer. McNaughton placed his small, cylindrical .38 on the cupboard in order to pull a pillbox from his inner jacket pocket. He threw back a pill that helped with anxiety, and before there could be a subsequent response, there was a knock on the hotel door.

McNaughton fast recovered his revolver and stridently flounced forth, becoming impeded by Thomas with his hands raised in a non-threatening manner.

"Move!"

"Relax! It's going to be Ros! Jack's wife!"

McNaughton forcefully latched across Thomas' posture and flung him into the wall like a sliding door, granting himself access to the hotel entrance. Thomas grappled onto McNaughton's overcoat, and a short-lived scuffle ensued.

Walking from Waterloo Station after her train arrived in London, Rosamund Churchill had punctually found the hotel. The door opened nearly immediately after the entrant tapped, with Rosamund using the issued key Jack had left her with the concierge downstairs. Dolled up with fresh lipstick, winged eyeliner the way Jack liked it, and with a happy, playful smile on her pretty face, she was clothed in a large green overcoat and a stylish chic pillbox hat adorned with a small veil.

"Hullo, Jack?" her charming voice called softly as she peaked inside.

"Ros!" Thomas warned her—right as McNaughton tore free of his inhibiting hold, reaching out and grappling onto the door to roughly reef it open.

Having barely squeezed through the doorway with her overnight bag, Rosamund shrieked as she stowed aside of the juggernauting gunman as he brushed past her in order to scan the empty hall for her elusive husband. She fast became collected by Thomas who held her close and safe within the room, calming her heavy pants for air. The two of them faced McNaughton as he returned leaning against the closed door after slamming it, practically holding them hostage inside.

"Tom?" Rosamund asked, still breathless, shaken. She was rightfully confused and awfully befuddled as to why her brother-in-law was present rather than her husband, not to mention the dramatic scene being made by an angry unknown man with a gun. "Where's Jack?! What is going on here?!"

Thomas comforted her, letting go after a consoling embrace.

"Ros, it's okay! Everything is okay!"

Rosamund stepped rearwards, suddenly aware of the decorative nature of the room. She recognized the scent of the perfume. Jack had been here recently, dressing it up in a romantic setting for her arrival. Whatever had happened, it must have been sudden and unexpected.

"Who are you?!" she finally questioned the man with the loose tie and crooked fedora.

McNaughton composed himself, revealing a brown leather holster on his trouser belt loop under the wing of his jacket layers to promptly tuck his snub-nosed revolver away.

"Ma'am, are you aware that your husband is a wanted felon?"

Rosamund barked, displeased and offended. *"I'm sorry?!"*

"Oi, steady on," Thomas defended while Rosamund scrunched her face in utter mystification. "Jack is innocent until proven guilty."

McNaughton snorted air from his nostrils. "Yeah. Right."

Precepting from the facts that this bloke was some kind of a lawman and that Jack had been vastly distant and otherwise nondetailed regarding his recent attendance in London, Rosamund pieced some of this situation together on her own. "Tom ... what is he talking about? What is going on here?!"

Thomas faced his sister-in-law, driving her in reverse over to the end of the bed and ushering her to take a seat ahead of him delivering the news flash.

"Jack may have offered you a mistruth about why he is in the city," Thomas compiled in his head the best way to explain the story to Ros. With her big doe eyes, she watched and listened as the words stumbled out the traps of his lips. "You see, eh, Jack's, actually, eh ..."

"*On trial for treason!*" McNaughton bluntly clued her in.

Thomas exhaled a big sigh, eyeballing him past his shoulder as he knelt before Rosamund's position. Technically, he was right.

"*Trial?*" she asked in her tiny voice once Tom faced her.

He nodded sombrely. "Yes. It's for something that happened years ago, way back before Commando. Before he met you."

"Yes, dear. Sorry to say your *white knight,* ol' *Mad Jack,* appears to have been trained by *Nazis* once upon a war," McNaughton slandered, purposefully defaming Churchill. "And he may be harbouring a secret connection to the enemy as well."

Rosamund's face scrunched. "*What?!*"

"He is to be trialled for *treason!* A crime punishable by *death!*"

"Enough!" Thomas stood and faced McNaughton. "You know in your heart that isn't true! You were just using Jack to get at Wingate. And that failed, so now you're taking your pent-up frustrations out on him!"

McNaughton seemed to absorb the blow without retort.

Didn't discount it, either.

It was as if Thomas' hammer hit the nail right on the head, as much as McNaughton refused to admit or deny it. Strangely, McNaughton was well within his rights to use the full force of the law to take his aggravations out on Jack Churchill. He had a gun and an itchy trigger finger for prosecution, and he wanted to scratch that itch tonight if he could—and scot-free of consequence, due to Churchill's current status.

"It's all nonsense! The lot of it!" Thomas waved his palm in McNaughton's face, fed up. He returned to Rosamund, about to clear it up a little more for her before old mate stepped back in like a monkey wrench.

"Is it, now?!" McNaughton staunched.

Thomas held his ground, allowing for McNaughton to spit fire all over the place in hopes that he might slip up.

"A history of disobedience in the armed forces since his very cadetship ... A list of disciplinary proceedings the length of my arm, ranging from minor penalizing to disobeying direct orders from military superiors, should I continue? ... The man wore hot water bottles in his jacket lining during roll call! Defiantly took an umbrella into a drill march! This *decorated war hero* and *loyal husband* of yours has been reprimanded for some of the dumbest shenanigans this side of a circus act! Playing his bagpipes in the early hours in the officer's mess, numerous counts of intoxication whilst on duty, fornicating while on tour abroad, public indecencies whilst representing the British Army, the list goes on and on ..."

"I'm missing the part where any of that makes him a *Nazi?*"

"My husband is a hero!" Rosamund exclaimed, bouncing up from the bed and prepared to go to war for her husband. Her voice overruled theirs. "He's a good man and a brave soul! I don't care what you say he's done."

McNaughton halted in his minor pacing, staring at Thomas as he wrapped an arm around Rosamund's shoulders to calm her, whom at this stage was starting to well up and become glassy eyed as her emotions soared. She was probably tired from her journey, and now confused and scared.

McNaughton's own emotion seemed to seep through his hardened resolve then and there during their argument. In order to stop his own chin from shivering, he tensed his jaw and bared his teeth as he delivered the next lines, "My *son* was a brave soul. My *son* never disobeyed orders. Never kicked up a stink in the service. He respected his superiors, his regiment. My *son* didn't deserve to *die* at the hands of some *madman* that your *hero husband* is now lying to protect!"

His sincerity seemed to strike a chord with them both.

His conviction was overbearing. Scary.

"Okay," collecting himself, McNaughton muttered. He reached into his jacket pocket and acquired his official notepad. He rifled through the pages, tearing out a specific slip and offering it out to the two related Churchills. They stared at it, puzzled. "Take it. Go see for yourselves."

Reluctant, Thomas reached out and took the notepad page.

It had an address written on it. Somewhere in Sheffield.

"You want to see how much of a *hero* your husband and brother truly is, go to this address tonight."

"What's there?"

McNaughton nodded, certain. "He is."

"How are you suddenly so sure where Jack is?"

"Because! If he's not *here*, and he's not returning to *base*, then ... I can't think of anywhere else he would go," McNaughton determined with all his investigative prowess and advanced character perception combined. As far as he could discern, the only other place Jack Churchill may visit during his hot hour away from the courts may have been the Glenn Mill inmate, Feind.

However, given the hour and with a kingdom-wide bulletin out against his name, attempting access of a military establishment was an extremely unlikely occurrence.

"Nether Edge?" utterly perplexed, Thomas' reading eyes wandered.

Heeding exhaustion, McNaughton levelled with them. "Although it's true, Jack Churchill may not be a Nazi, he sure as hell isn't the man you both think he is. Brace yourselves for what is coming next, for this isn't going to end well. I'll soon see you on the other side of his conviction."

Speechless, they watched as McNaughton left the hotel room, disappearing into the hall and towards the lifts.

After he vacated the room, another figure in the doorway to room 36 became focal. Her presence had been as a ghost, overseeing her partner's point. Slim, slender, and clad in a female business suit complete with a cloche hat, Viviane Garland offered both Thomas and Rosamund an expressionless green and gold gleam before she followed her offsider.

She and Rosamund Churchill exchanged an elongated stare with one another. It was an instinctual square-up, fuelled by Rosamund's flaring emotion and Garland's brute mentality to charge a worthy opponent, especially in the rarity of a same-sex fatale.

At her steadfast resolution over her husband in where there existed an undercurrent of physical dominance, Garland gave a slight smirk before peeling off after McNaughton. It was a last minute undermine to entice Rosamund into siding further with her husband; against them.

Following the confrontation in room 36, Thomas escorted Rosamund downstairs and through the foyer belonging to the Union Jack Club. They exchanged no words at this juncture, both sensing an essence of mourning regarding the circumstances and lurching indication that neither one of them may have known Jack.

There were no signs of Constable McNaughton or his phantom female cohort, Garland, but he had undoubtedly called a unit to the Sheffield location to apprehend Churchill, if he was not travelling there his hellbent self.

Wasting no time, they climbed into Thomas' Ford and headed north. It would be a long drive back to Dumbarton, and they would be fortunate to make it before midnight.

"You're taking me to Sheffield?" Ros sternly questioned once they hopped on the motorway out of London and towards Birmingham.

Hands firmly on the wheel and with his focus on the road, Thomas bowed into the wheel. Onus unyielding, even now they were faced with this new information, his voice crackled with unfavourable purpose and stern obligation. "No, Ros. I am taking you home."

"Sheffield is on the way. Let's stop in. I need to see Jack."

"It's a detour. Ros, it's a long drive. I need to focus ..."

"I really do need to see him, Tom. It's important."

"Is it about the argument?" Thomas asked, trying not to be dismissive of a seemingly unimportant issue in comparison. Opening up to somebody was not his strong suit. He took her lack of response as confirmation. "Don't worry. Jack told me."

"Told you what?" she expounded in the form of a vent, changing lanes from what her private topic actually was to address this direction. "That he would rather continue to actively seek out a war to fight overseas than get a safe desk job at home and be with his family. I love the man, but he's a thrill-seeking daredevil."

Thomas remained stoical, but there was no argument.

He opted to change the subject, pointing his focus forwards.

"Ros, this really is going to be a long drive ..."

Frustrated, Rosamund glared out the passenger's window and folded her arms, remarking cheekily to her driver. "You don't need to tell me. I was just on the train here all bloody day."

Thomas threw her a sidewards glance with a slight smirk.

He had always thought Rosamund's raw humour and frequent use of curt witticisms boldly humorous. Women of the era were usually shy to be so brash. She was a daring broad, and from a breed more nonchalant than the character of his own wife, Gwendoline; her behaviour was much more decorous and proper, so to speak. There was nothing wrong with her attitude or her personality, he just never imagined hearing his wife backchat with something to say the way Ros did at times. She was younger than Gwen, and her characteristics were probably born from a different upbringing.

Thomas didn't mind or take offence. It was just different to what he typically encountered. Detecting her disappointment, he eyed the road as the yellow headlamps illuminated the consuming asphalt. "Sorry, dear. Jack's wishes, and I owe him one. He said to tell you that he would see you in a few days."

"Is he going to call me from jail?" she jousted, disjointed.

"He's not going to jail."

Deep in the passenger's seat, Rosamund tensed her folded arms.

After a minute, Thomas was found to be fuming over the course of Jack's predicament. He saw no harm in speaking his mind, his frustrations, and elaborating for her sake.

He shook his head, fuming internally. "All he had to do was give this corrupt general up, you know ... he's just too damn proud for his own damn good. His pride is his own worst enemy, always has been. It'll get him killed some day."

Rosamund faced him, listening as it was his turn to vent.

"Yeah, if a bloody bullet doesn't," she furthered satirically.

"He knows what they want—what they really want—but he just won't give it to them, because it requires breaching orders. He's too damn stubborn around breaking rules."

Ros gasped with a sarcastic look. "Um, have you *met* my husband?"

Thomas bobbed his head with a grin. "I mean *certain* rules."

Silence crept in around them. For a spell, there was just the gentle hum and vibration of their travelling car on the road at night.

Rosamund tried again. "So, let's go ask him."

Thomas shook his head at her convincing tone, then cast Ros a quick glance and a raised brow.

"We *can't*," Thomas responded, steadfast on his objective here, and that was to take the next exit towards *Birmingham* and not *Nottingham*, the direction of Sheffield.

He may have been good at hiding it, but deep down, he was afraid of what it was he might find out about his brother if they ventured to the address McNaughton provided them with ...

"Tom ..." her tiny voice uttered a confession. "I'm pregnant."

In the quiet seconds to follow, Thomas Churchill felt goosebumps appear on his arms and the back of his neck at the reveal. His eyes widened. His tense brow subsided. There was a perplexed moment of breathlessness followed by a sudden unveiling of happiness for her, and for Jack, but he withheld his celebration in wait of her follow up.

He exhaled congratulatorily. "Ros, that's incredible, wonderful news! Congratulations! I ... I don't know what to say, really ..." Thomas' crest flinched. "Is Jack aware of this?"

"He doesn't know yet."

"Why are you telling me?"

"So that you'll do the right thing and help me get to Jack!" Rosamund pleaded with a sulk. It suddenly made so much sense as to why she was in such a hurry to get to London to talk to Jack. It had nothing to do with their argument, nor was it a romantic R&R or a fondling foray. It was something far more wonderful—and game changing, as far as Mad Jack was concerned. This was huge, and it just might reel him in.

Whilst watching the blur of the road in the headlights, Thomas stewed on how his brother may take this news. Subconsciously, he had his reservations about Jack Churchill stepping into fatherhood, but then again, nobody is a dad until they are. As far as Rosamund was concerned, it may have just been the key to solving everything; the sedative to his recklessness, the catalyst of his settling down, stepping him off the frontlines and from the crosshair of war. Notwithstanding, as far as the present was concerned, it may have also been enough to convince Churchill to give up Wingate—if it wasn't too late.

Rosamund continued selling her motive. "I need to tell Jack! Maybe then he will cease this foolish, stubborn endeavour, and get out of this court martial. And come home to me."

She held a good case.

Her agenda here aligned with Thomas', in what was best for Jack.

This wasn't unfamiliar territory for Thomas Churchill regarding starting a family. He and Gwendoline had their child in May 1940. At the time, he had been an instructor at the RAF school of aerial photography and had been since 1934, where prior he had served in Burma as a part of the Second Manchesters. Thomas had been optimistic about rejoining frontline fighting, but with the option of homeland service available, it proved a healthier option to stay and assist in raising a newborn baby. Jack may have been the older sibling, but his interpersonal growth had apparently finally blossomed. This was his turn to get in the backseat and let others take the wheel for a change.

Thomas took the Nottingham exit.

Rosamund noticed the variation in direction and, at first, said not a word. Instead, a smile developed across her face.

She eventually turned to face the driver, exchanging a look with Thomas that said thank you.

1942, March
Rundle Road
Nether Edge, Sheffield

Nether Edge was a quaint suburbia within the city of Sheffield, and it was a ghost town upon the hour of their arrival.

Their dark Ford Prefect was almost the only car on the road this late, nearing the address of McNaughton's issued destination a little after 9 p.m., eyes pitched like a pair of wide-eyed orienteers searching for treasure with a map.

"This is it ..." Thomas advised after turning their slow coasting vehicle onto *Rundle Road,* deep in the foreign civilian neighbourhood. This was the address written on the page McNaughton had supplied them with, along with a name of a resident which Thomas was about to doublecheck.

Whilst they cruised, Rosamund sat upright in the passenger's seat. Their anxious arrival was especially nerve-racking for her, as she feared seeing her husband in another perspective, and they had no idea what they were getting into. All they had to go off was McNaughton's ominous and biased word of warning.

Thomas didn't want to jinx it just yet, but other than a recruitment office in the business district and a signal squadron and signal regiment south of town, there were no military facilities in Sheffield. Whatever this location was, it was a residential, informal visit conducted by Jack. Although he refused to believe it, given the *Don John* womanizing ways of the *Casanova Churchill* days of old, Thomas' rational mind could not fully rule out infidelity.

Browsing out the windows whilst their vehicle cruised along the quiet suburban street, the twirling red light from a police lamp cycled through the windshield as they loomed upon ground zero. The strobing lights gained both of their attentions in the dark of the Ford cabin, and Thomas brought them to a roll just shy of the scene of a parked army Tilly, probably from the local base, as well as a local police vehicle.

Without a word spoken through their agape, dropped jaws, Thomas and Rosamund observed speechlessly as the spectacle unfolded in an almost slow-motion scape of experience as harsh details flooded their minds.

From the house across the street, army men with MP painted on their helmets chaperoned from the front door a handcuffed Jack Churchill. He was still in his beret, his military suit, and his kilt, but had been disarmed of his claybeg sword. A troop at the rear followed their escorting of the arrested prisoner towards the parked tilly truck, carrying the weapon at arm's length with a strange look upon his face.

Behind them all, the local police officers stayed at the house, speaking with who appeared to be the resident: a woman in a dressing gown.

An attractive type ...

Jack's type.

Rosamund's gaze was indeed fixated on her husband as she saw him be escorted by the military police and fed into the rear tray of the truck to be taken away, nevertheless, her attention drifted back towards the unknown blonde bombshell on the front porch of the house. There was a jealous hatred fuming there in that wordless moment.

Thomas observed his brother get caught and taken away in cuffs. To be honest, he was expecting to eventually see that sight—and it hadn't been the first time he had seen Jack apprehended by the authorities, therefore the image didn't shock him in the way it may have affected Rosamund. However, like her, his view returned to the female directly held in relation to Jack's happenstance here in Sheffield ...

... and then his eyes widened.

He recognized her ...

Thomas blinked profusely, focusing deeply on her.

It was Scarlet Kristina, from Oslo.

J ♣

A Farewell to Arms

1942, April
Combined Operations Headquarters
Whitehall, London

A great convolution transpired in Great Britain between Churchill's apprehension and the scheduling of the final court martial. Many incidents caused unfortunate delays.

What was meant to be a week's break until the final court date where the verdict would be issued for case A-8919: the *Criminal Investigation Department* on behalf of the *British War Office* versus *Lieutenant-Colonel John Malcolm Thorpe Fleming Churchill*, on the grounds of committing *high treason* and *conspiracy of conducting disloyalty to the Crown,* progressed into approximately a month of postponements and interruptions.

Jack was in lockdown for the entirety of the prolonged proceedings, and understandably the desolation was driving him crazy, for some animals are not meant to be encaged.

During the first two weeks of delay, the JAG opted to relocate Churchill from the objectionable in-house cells and to a more upper-class solitary custody. Under escort, Churchill was moved to the COHQ in Whitehall, where there were several predominantly unused lodgings for visiting nationalists and dignitaries. These secured premises were of much higher standards than the local law enforcement enclosures typically used for courtroom custodies. Ultimately, the intention of such five-star treatment was in case of the off chance that the detainee was deemed innocent, it proved much harder to sue for discomfort damages.

Throughout the magnitude of delays and hardships on the outside world during what could only be explained as the world war stepping it up a gear and reaching the coast west of the English Channel, Churchill was permitted phone calls and cursive communication delivered by Royal Mail where he was able to communicate with his wife, Rosamund, informing her of the complicated situation albeit via a simplified version of the proceedings. Rosamund was understanding of his situation and his containment in London for the court martial and reciprocated to him her love—seemingly unknowingly of any other details involving her husband beyond that. His brother, Thomas, acted as an intermediary for any further communication with the outside world, also informing his command at No.3 Commando of his abrupt interruption from service. Respectively, executives convincingly concurred, explaining Colonel Churchill's absence from base as nothing but official business.

Attorney Lionel Spencer issued Churchill with a copy of the court transcripts. Being a secret trial, these were not easily obtainable and existed only for JAG reflection and probably wouldn't once the case was closed. This was permitted for the defendant's own reference to the proceedings thus far. Spencer had also managed to slip in a little extra curricular reading material; the latest pinups, as well as all the information he could obtain on McNaughton's deceased son from Wingate's operations in Palestine, as requested by Churchill. This was a stray tangent which was to bear fruit ...

While the world continued to spin outside of Churchill's predicament, the war found its way home. This was the main reasoning for such a delay for a verdict. Becoming known as the *Baedeker Blitz*, a series of localized bombing attacks by the German Luftwaffe on English cities ensued upon the United Kingdom, beginning a period much reminiscent of the Blitzkrieg. The bombings were retaliatory in nature, striking back against the Royal Air Force's airstrike offensives, starting with the bombing of *Lübeck* in March.

A point of interest; the title given to the aerial raids derives from *Baedeker:* a chain of German tourist guidebooks, inclusive of detailed maps, which were used to generate the targets for the bombings. Hitler was enraged after the decimation of Lübeck, and he demanded his air force retaliate. He ordered: *'That the air war against England be given a more aggressive stamp. Accordingly, when targets are being selected, preference is to be given to those where attacks are likely to have the greatest possible effect on civilian life. Besides raids on ports and industry, terror attacks of a retaliatory nature are to be carried out on towns other than London'.* Both a warning and a threat, the War Office issued Londoners with the knowledge that this could have been a feint, knowing full well London would likely be again targeted by air raids.

Since then, the scourge was simmering. Both *Exeter* and *Bath* were punctually bombed over two consecutive nights, causing widespread damage and nearly five-hundred casualties combined. The Luftwaffe next attacked *Norwich*, dropping more than ninety tonnes of explosives and causing almost seventy deaths. This raid was followed by the bombing of *York* causing limited damage, however killing eighty English civilians.

The gloves were off again, and Britain had received a harsh reminder that they were still well and truly at war with Germany.

Nobody needed a reminder of that fact more than the world's greatest warfighter: *Mad Jack Churchill.*

Before long, Jack Churchill's court date was finally in attendance.

This was the end.

Prior to its commencement, Churchill had been brought a clean uniform garb, which he combined with his existing tartan kilt to uphold his ceremonial value, along with his breast of glossy medals and polished silver buttons, as well as various other exceptional effects. Like in war, if the man was going down, he was going down swinging and looking damn fine in the process. He was permitted further shoe polish and allowed to make himself presentable, and at his furthermost request, the requisition of his custom claybeg sword imperiously at his hip and in good fashion.

In much the same course of proceedings as his court appearance in late February, the whirlwind of due processing soon found Churchill being escorted to the Westminster Conference Grand Hall and then situated at the bar in the centre of the grand hall. It felt so familiar, it was like it was yesterday he once stood in these boots.

Lawyer Lionel Spencer promptly appeared at his side to see through the court martial, appearing to have not aged a day over the weeks since Jack had last seen him.

Permissible courtroom attendees entered once the moment became appropriate, becoming procedurally seated crosswise. During their quiet ingress, Churchill spotted McNaughton and his femme offsider, Garland, dutifully situate amongst a bunch of suits and ties. Also, amongst those attending guests, appeared his brother Thomas Churchill, attired in his military suit with representing symbology. Jury-esque, they poured in to see this long-awaited grand verdict of the defendant.

Spencer hoisted his briefcase onto the desk beside Churchill, blocking a rather large portion of his rubbernecking glance at the notable presences.

"Colonel," the balding lawyer greeted. Within his monotonal linger, Churchill sensed a tone worse than ennui—it was defeat. Nonetheless, Spencer had still shown up here to take the beating, and that showed a precise quantity of veracity that was a rarity amongst his breed of men. He was willing to take the pounding, no matter the odds. That said something.

"Mister Spencer," Churchill politely nodded, absorbing the fulfilment of his arrival. There was an overdose of giddiness in the tenor of Jack's voice that tripped up his lawyer's pacing, causing him to frown and analyse his etiquette. Churchill had always been as he had known him, a *manners maketh man* type (his words), however Spencer found it hard to understand the *why* in upholding the grandeur whilst staring down the barrel of a gun of a guilty verdict. Now was the time for moping, misery, and the settling in of an imminent crippling depression ... not any type of solace, for there was none to be had. No pending relief. No hope. The time for that was long gone.

Perhaps he should have pursued an insanity plea?

"You're doing ... *well,* I see?"

The twitch of a smirk enlightened Jack's mood. "Fine-o-fine. This whole nightmare is finally about to be over."

"This case?"

"This war," Churchill articulated strangely, causing himself to frown. As though the realization was a new sensation for even him. He had been contemplating it to the world's end, but never spoken it aloud until just now. It sounded foreign, maybe a tad dramatic, but right for *him.* "For me, anyhow."

The level of theatrics nearly caused the attorney to cringe; though, Spencer watched with curious attentiveness as Colonel Churchill drew his hip-holstered claybeg with decency and pride, presenting it out before them above the bar to place the weapon down—only this time, with the blade pre-emptively facing inwards.

Churchill had already conceded defeat ...

... and he was content with it.

The bench entourage next entered under MP and bailiff guard, including Chief Barney from the Special Investigation Branch office ... and that was it. This session, Barney was the *only* familiar face Churchill recognized from the lay members, with both No.3 Commando Lieutenant-Colonel Durnford-Slater and SAS Lieutenant-Colonel Laycock absent for these final proceedings.

Perhaps they had more pressing matters ...?

... or perhaps they couldn't bear to see Jack ~~persecuted~~*. Crucified.*

Breaking his odd, gladdened mood, a depressive sensation overcame Jack upon realizing their absence. He was okay with losing the case, with losing the war, even ... but he was not okay with his brethren being elsewhere for his send-off ...

Logically, there could just have been more important stuff requiring the attendance of two of the highest-ranking Commanding Officers within Commando, especially in these times of growing cataclysm, resulting in sound logic for their absenteeism from court today. That said, Churchill felt that they had lost faith in him, that they had both rather not hear his verdict. It silently pained him.

"Oh, by the way," Spencer leant in, last minute. "I thought you'd want to hear it from me; your dear friend Orde Wingate *slipped away ...*"

Churchill's attention broke away from the bench. "He's dead?"

"Oh," Spencer reiterated with a follow-up chuckle, "no. I meant, he *slipped away*, not from life, from England. He's abroad, back in rotation, no doubt running amuck on some foreign soil, stirring the pot as he does."

The Otter had been recalled to combat, leaving for *Rangoon* sometime in mid-March, thereby escaping whatever custody Judge MacGeagh had used in an attempt to withhold him. Getting away scot-free again was a likely scenario regarding Wingate's conviction. The man was a regular *Harry Houdini* when it came to answering to Whitehall politics or formal prosecution.

Learning this news, Churchill was not surprised.

He uttered, "The perks of having many friends in high places."

Before long, the guards closed the doors behind the bench members' grand entrance, confining them for the commencement of session. The mild courtroom chatter within the room dissolved.

"*Honorary Judge MacGeagh presiding.*"

The announcement coincided with MacGeagh's appearance from his chambers. As per usual, he was dressed in his black robe, displaying his white magistrate's wig.

"*The court is now in session. Be seated.*"

All those present promptly hauled their chairs and sat.

"Good morning, ladies and gents," Judge MacGeagh addressed while organizing the proceedings set before him. "We are here today concluding case A-8919: the *Criminal Investigation Department* on behalf of the *British War Office* versus *Lieutenant-Colonel John Malcolm Thorpe Fleming Churchill.*"

The calm sterling stare of Churchill rested upon MacGeagh, imagining the magistrate holding a singular palm card reading one word and one word only ahead of today's belated proceeding:

Guil–

A historical cameo.

All of a sudden, with an abundance of dramatic effect strong enough to blow air into the lungs of all those present within the stale environment requiring resuscitation, the closed courtroom doors burst open with the force of the biggest cock and balls in the British War Office ...

A man standing over six-foot tall in a slender suit and with oblong-sculpted features, narrow nose, and short, jet-black hair waltzed the limelight, literally crashing the gates. While the figure strolled with a sense of overbearing confidence, his eyes panned across the lawful surroundings with a buoyant yet assertive gaze, as though he owned everything in the courtroom.

Recently promoted from the rank of *Commodore,* an already phenomenally high position within the British armed forces, his naval dressage now showed his even more befitting classification of *Vice-Admiral.*

This uncanny intruder was none other than *Louis Mountbatten:*

Cousin to the King.
First World War veteran.
Chief of the entire COHQ.

Whispers filled the echoic courtroom as they observed his intrusive saunter. Nobody stopped his entrance—couldn't if they tried.

Respecting his history of stalwart warfighting and resonating valour confined within an astounding naval career off the back of the First World War, Mountbatten had always been a favourited candidate for the paramount position holding the reigns of the COHQ by Prime Minister Winston Churchill. He had actually been the first choice to helm the department, though, at the time of the department's founding, bounded by duty, Mountbatten had been unwilling to leave his navy crew aboard the *HMS Illustrious.* Prior to the Illustrious, Mountbatten saw harsh combat as captain of the *HMS Kelly,* which was sunk by German dive bombers in May of 1941 during *the Battle of Crete*—a battle that served as the basis of the *Noël Coward* film *In Which We Serve* recently published by *British Lion Films* and popularized in the western world. This was to a large portion attributing to Mountbatten's recent household name assertion. The film promised to be a faithful retelling of the battle, with Coward, himself, directing as well as portraying a fictional version of Mountbatten. The two were friends, and Coward copied some of his favourable speeches, word-for-word, into the movie for accuracy.

Mountbatten had been mentioned in dispatches in August 1940 and again in March 1941, where he was awarded the Distinguished Service Order and eventually promoted to commodore. One month ago, he was upgraded to *vice-admiral* during the tidal wave of ascribable fame carrying him to the would-be heavens. The man was infallible and infamous.

From the beginning, Mountbatten's leadership remit was more extensive than that of his predecessor, Admiral Keyes—with all due respect to the honorary man. Prior to his promotion to COHQ office, Mountbatten had served as an adviser to Keyes and the Combined Operations and, from the external viewpoint, his experience seemed sparser, therefore more sufficient than what Keyes had ever been in office. Nevertheless, in the few months of having him in command, Mountbatten had made better use of the instruments at his disposal and appreciated that organizing small-scale raids were to be only the first step in a campaign of combined operations that would eventually bring him greater authority to help win the war.

A moment of celebrity serviceman differentiation overcame Judge MacGeagh like a hot flush, and the audience within the courtroom grew instantly agitated by the interruption that could only be described as a guest appearance.

"Admiral Mountbatten ...?!" Judge MacGeagh acknowledged off-key as his bailiff and MPs half-heartedly intercepted the admiral and his two

uniformed guardsmen entourage—a supportive body inclusive of Colonel John Durnford-Slater—as they pressed through the sealed doors and entered the floor like sacrilege on holy grounds (or was it the other way around?) They halted once realizing their inept jurisdiction to discontinue the intruders' just passage, helplessly peering to their JAG officiaries for any hints of guidance, to which there was none.

MacGeagh's bailiff took a sole stride in lawful obtrusion of Mountbatten, halting only once overwhelmed with how far out of his jurisdiction he was in even attempting to stop the admiral in his tracks, holding up a palm whilst helplessly, powerlessly, scanning back at the judge stand.

Mountbatten finally halted; his focus falling to this pesky bailiff.

"Son, don't."

The staunch bailiff's ears folded. His shoulders drooped and his defensive palm faltered, eyeing the floor in disgrace. Mountbatten's aura was just too formidable.

"Go over there, and sit down."

Sad-faced, the bailiff obeyed, taking his leave and sitting himself down in the corner of the courtroom, facing the wall with his head down at the floor. It may have been belittling, but it was also fucking hilarious.

Unamused, MacGeagh removed his spectacles.

"To what do we owe the incursion?"

"*Incursion?*" Mountbatten questioned with an acute brow, confidently striding further into the centre of the courtroom floor and stealing the spotlight. It had been years since he had stepped foot within the grand hall, briefly intaking the vast anal-retentive décor and blocking the stench of staleness from his nostrils like the steam of hot piss in a urinal. "With all due respect, your honour, it appears that *you* are the one who has intruded."

The heat was definitely on in this courtroom. Full blast.

Churchill made direct eye contact with his friend Durnford-Slater, and all of a sudden, seemed vindicated. There was a precipitous wave of comfort that washed over Churchill, and all seemed fine-o-fine again.

Still seated, Judge MacGeagh raised his palms. His confusion of the accusation was understandable, considering *he* was a judge, and they were in a court of law. His court.

A degree of silence persisted, however Mountbatten held his ground.

"I *beg* your pardon?!" MacGeagh delegated with a level of respective diplomacy reserved for members of such hierarchy. "This is my courtroom, Admiral. We are in session."

"I beg *your* pardon, sir. I must protest."

The volume of the courtroom mumbling increased.

Judge MacGeagh boiled tomato red in the face.

"Excuse me?!"

"Your honour!" Mountbatten then nodded towards Churchill, attaching him directly to the basis of his intrusion. His intentions were clear. "It has come to my attention that Colonel Jack Churchill of my Commando force has been called to order, and thus away from crucial active duties. I am afraid I am going to veto this hearing due to extenuating circumstances."

MacGeagh shook his head. Wobbled his cheeks. "Impossible."

"With respect, I assure you that it is not."

"What *extenuating circumstances* could be more important than upholding the law and due process, Admiral?"

"Lil' thing called *the Second World War!* Perhaps you've heard of it?" Mountbatten held direct eye contact with MacGeagh.

A deafening silence followed and lingered.

"Your honour," Mountbatten levelled with MacGeagh, "tomorrow morning I am to be seated in the war room with key members of the Allied Forces against Nazi Germany. For the first time, this will include the Americans, where we will be engaging in what could be the most important meeting thus far in the campaign against the enemy. I need all my battalion members present and represented. With Colonel Newman down and out, that means 2 Commando needs a new commanding officer ... and that man *must* be Jack Churchill."

Mountbatten glanced across at Churchill. The two locked eyes.

After an elongated moment, Mountbatten's view panned back around to the honorary Judge MacGeagh, who was remaining mute.

"I will accept no substitutes. And I assure you, neither will *Winnie the Bulldog*, understood?"

As the courtroom chatter continued to flutter, slowly drowning MacGeagh in second-hand embarrassment, Mountbatten held his own, knowing what needed to happen and attaining the most diplomatic cause of action he knew to make it so.

He approached the judge, speaking softer. "With all due respect, I regret having to barge in here, bursting the doors like a morning turd after the first sip from a cup of jo, but I needed to rush in order to save *you* the humiliation of tapping that wee hammer thinking it haute couture and then *me* the unpleasantries of undoing your knots afterwards. I've got a war to win, I have no time for poppycock or monkey business," he turned and faced the courtroom, making a heard declaration. "With the power invested in me by the entirety of the British War Office, I am hereby excusing Colonel Churchill from any further courtroom persecution unless directly discussed with me and with my approval, and I can already guarantee you now, I don't have time for borderline hearsay accusations sidelining my men for weeks on end."

"With all due respect, Admiral," MacGeagh stood his ground and his JAG jurisdiction. Mountbatten allowed for him to speak. "The verdict's already been made by the court ..."

"That's good. And I just told you mine. And guess what?" so confident in his convictions, Mountbatten turned to walk away with a mic drop before even delivering his punchline. "My 'dict's bigger."

He threw a sly gleam at Churchill at the bar.

"Colonel ..."

Churchill's chin raised, listening so intently his ears bled.

"War room. Tomorrow. Oh-nine-hundred. Check?"

Clad in the kilt, Churchill raised from his seat as the orders bounced within his earholes. He issued Admiral Mountbatten a singular nod.

"Sir!" and he saluted.

Mountbatten casually returned the gesture and promptly faced forwards, casting the salute as he vanished through the open door, vacating the courtroom battlefield as quickly as he had appeared and leaving it in ruins.

This court martial had been derailed.

It was a rare sight to see, but Judge MacGeagh was beside himself.

Frustrated and irate, he was left processing the colossal undermining that had just befallen his courtroom whilst it was in session, and he were presiding. MacGeagh hid his embarrassment well, saving face by promptly rising from his seat and collecting his scattered papers. Next, he sought an exodus, concealing an undeniable ineptitude. Mountbatten wouldn't get away with impunity from that inappropriate use of his power, alas, there was nothing the JAG could do to overrule his verdict at this present juncture. It would be an uphill battle to even see the admiral to a hearing foreclosing what had transpired, let alone organize a rescheduling of Churchill's case in the distant future. The exertion for the prosecution simply wasn't worth it for him.

For a moment, MacGeagh took it out on his bailiff, shouting at him over the volume of the dismissed courtroom to *get up off his arse.*

Confused by their sudden defeat, Chief Barney watched with disillusioned eyes as MacGeagh vacated with his whimpering bailiff without so much as a *court dismissal* or a strike of his gavel. Barney hastily arose and scurried behind MacGeagh, attempting to follow his slithering passage into his chambers, however, the cold door closed in his face, stopping him awkwardly in his tracks. Directionless and humiliated, he knew not where to go next, and so he filed towards the normal exit ahead of everybody else.

The courtroom adjournment fell into shambles.

Members from the bench raised and collected their briefcases, slung jackets, and eventuated towards the gaping doorway, onwards to their following trials and business and commitments.

The world spun around Churchill in the centre space, and he felt an almost overwhelming rush of relief breeze around him, rejuvenating his temperament, his outlook, and even his faith in the armed forces. It was like a gigantic doorstop wedge had been driven beneath the swinging gate, suddenly halting all progress indefinitely. A full stop of monumental connotation. Perhaps he was right where he belonged?

The war worked in mysterious ways.

While the flurry of permitted visitors filed towards the exit, McNaughton blindsided Churchill out on the floor, pulling in fast beside him and stopping short.

"Congratulations!" he squabbled with haste but with some underlining appreciation in his tone which Churchill immediately detected. Imaginably, he had just cracked some happy-calm pills and couldn't pop a nitrous oxide fuelled stiffy like usual.

Churchill twisted to face him, about to cop the brunt of his defeated and departing dialogue.

"You've finally been promoted to the same corrupted untouchable leagues as Wingate!" he accused with an imperious sense of bitterness and impending self-deprivation concerning the topic. It would not have been hard to imagine Wingate being relieved from condemned custody in much the same manner as Mountbatten had just rescued Churchill, albeit without the theatrics. With utter disgust, McNaughton shook his head whilst delivering his updated interpretation of Jack Churchill; in the shade of venality and dishonesty. "An accrual of behind-the-scenes friends in high places. You've breached the ranks of those 'beyond reproach' ... you've obtained complete and utter immunity ... you're invincible, sir, and once again I congratulate you. I hope that you are proud ..."

Over his shoulder appeared Constable Garland.

She appeared prepared to save her offsider from embarrassment.

She had his back, even in this frustrated eruption. It was a plausible outburst of exasperation, for never had McNaughton been so close to closing the case on those responsible for his son's death—in this personal case by six degrees of separation and a mild association, Jack Churchill—and he had fallen short, just like all the other times. Wingate had escaped scot-free, and now it seemed Churchill was about to follow in his footsteps, free as a bird.

Hereby, Churchill took on the role of the bigger man, holding his ground but allowing for McNaughton to vent and spit his fuming verbal acid. Although the tables had properly turned and there was no need to further recoil, Jack retained an ace up his sleeve.

McNaughton allowed for his emotionally projecting self to become towed away by Garland, but before he stepped too far, Churchill caught his attention.

"Constable ..."

Still seething, McNaughton froze.

"Your son's name was *Wallace James Wellings* ..."

Hearing the name of his son struck a harsh chord, and a sensitive one at that. In his already sensitive state, McNaughton could easily be pushed from tipping to boiling point if referencing his son's name was misappropriated or used in any sort of vain by a man he saw as his rival.

In the foreground of the dismissing courtroom, McNaughton slowly revolved around. His stare locked back onto Churchill, eagerly hearing him out; hoping he'd misstep or disrespect his son, in order to justly knock his head off with a balled fist carrying the might of a charging rhino.

"*Wellings,*" Churchill repeated, adopting a respective angle intent on presenting his education on the back story rather than his mild name dropping. "His mother's maiden name. You separated in 1929, when he was a teenager. His mother gained custody and returned to Scotland, where she died six years later from pneumonia."

McNaughton took slow strides towards Churchill. There was an unpredictable amount of a pent-up something within his closed fists, cocked like loaded guns. Garland remained barely a step away, carefully observing his expressions and preparing to react in restraint if he did, yet so far, he was holding it together.

"Colonel ..." McNaughton exhaled while he collected his mental state and emotions regarding discussing this topic out loud. He gave what was undoubtedly his only warning. "Be very careful about where you steer this conversation, for it may be your last."

McNaughton was balling his knuckles.

Churchill broke eye contact in a conceding demeanour, hinting that his intentions were not hostile. His sterling beads finally returned unto McNaughton's eyeline as he stayed the course.

"I knew him as *Scotty.*"

McNaughton's tense brow loosened.

It was a nickname issued to his boy during childhood.

... what?

"Sir, your son did not die in Palestine. And, for whatever it's worth, Wingate didn't get him killed either—not directly, at least," Churchill revealed the newfound knowledge he had collected whilst in lockup by connecting very difficult to find puzzle pieces. Spencer had successfully acquired classified recruitment files concerning McNaughton's son and, during his spell in solitary, Jack had joined the dots between his service career after recognizing Wallace Wellings from his service headshot—minus the nonregulation mohawk he had donned throughout the Berzerker era. Contrary to what official British Military records state, he was never KIA in Palestine. Rather, he had become drafted into Wingate's clandestine Special Z Unit, which was the reasoning for the category particulars on his death certificate.

Engaging in proud service, Scotty was a Berzerker, like Jack, and although the confidentiality of his ill-conceived doom may have remained the same, the specifics as this mourning father knew them were incorrect. Win or lose today, Churchill had planned to offer the information to McNaughton at some stage because he firmly believed he deserved to know the truth about his son.

"I am proud to say I knew your son. I served in Switzerland by his side, and I was with him at the end where he fell in warfare against Germany with the greatest of honours any demise on the battlefield could bear fortune."

Stunned, McNaughton was motionless. Paralyzed.

He didn't believe it at first, but at the same time, knew it to be true.

His eyes welled up, becoming glassy and sheen.

With an inversion of her own frown line, Garland inched forwards, clutching at his sleeve and supporting her colleague as the truth hit him harder than an emotional tsunami.

His voice crackled. "Why are you telling me this?" stopping his chin from quivering, McNaughton questioned after the extended moment of silence where Churchill turned and collected his effects from the table: singly, his 38-inch claybeg—his honour, reinstated. He holstered the weapon at his hip, restoring it much alike his confidence.

"Because you deserve to know," Churchill remarked truthfully as he started to leave the courtroom. Upon his absence, Jack paused alongside the stationary fellow. In the short time he had known him, McNaughton had always been a force to be reckoned with, armed to the teeth with vengeance and fury. It was rare to see him vulnerable. Jack confessed further to reason his divulgence. "I have enough enemies already, Constable. Enough wars to fight. I don't need another ... and I surmise that neither do you."

"*Enemies?*" McNaughton deliberated the term and then turned his head side on to look to Churchill. "Colonel, if not Orde Wingate, do ... do you know who took the life of my son?"

Churchill regarded with certainty.

"General Ernst-Günther Baade killed your son."

"*Baade?*" McNaughton's breath simmered, envisioning the adversary. It wasn't the first time he had heard of this fable. His stare drew focus over a thousand yards as he suddenly visualized the faceless culprit, focusing his energy on him—and then it clicked. "Was he not the Hun brought in to train you?!"

Churchill scoffed, admitting a further sincerity.

"All he did was train me how best to kill him. He's dead."

The density of McNaughton's glower prematurely diminished.

He cast Churchill a look as his suddenly newfound resentment collapsed in on itself before it was ever fully constructed. It was probably a difficult truth to learn after the delivery of an already impossible revelation, and it expressively caned McNaughton.

Churchill bore a tense look upon him after delivering the outcome of Ernst-Günther Baade. After their brief altercation with blades, he had seen the eccentric kilt-clad German be blown to pieces. Granted he had never been offered the chance to pay any respects (or disrespects) to his corpse, Jack had always been sure of that closure.

Churchill gently hoisted a hand up and onto McNaughton's shoulder, showing a display of compassion towards a man who, up until very recently, had been a sworn enemy and vice versa. The physical contact with the gent offered a furthermore degree of solace. "The one lifeline I had here today, was war. And it came calling, reeling me back into a position where I can one day reengage evildoers like Baade on the battlefield. The undying, recurring enemy."

McNaughton's teary stare and attention returned onto Churchill.

He still couldn't bring himself to liking Jack, but he now respected him. There was finally a mutual respect between the two men.

Right as McNaughton left with the notable lack of a departing remark under the wing of his consoling constable, they passed Thomas Churchill. He had lingered after the stand had filed for the exit, awaiting his brother's availability for comment.

"How many lives do you have left, Jack?" Thomas asked off the cuff as he took his brother's protruding palm in thorough handshake, bringing it in close for a chest-to-chest embrace. Having missed each other, the two shared a prolonged moment of brotherly love before striking each other across the shoulder blades and breaking apart.

Jack shook his head at the remark comparing him to a cat with his apparent nine lives. "I think now, I am all out."

His loyal government-appointed defence attorney, Lionel Spencer, briefly interrupted with a clearing of the throat. He had packed up his case and opted for a farewell with Churchill. "Colonel."

"Mister Spencer," Jack turned to face him. "Thanks for everything. I couldn't have done it without you."

Spencer held an odd expression of doubt followed by a wink whilst he shook Churchill's hand. "Yeah, you could have."

Jack smiled. "Perhaps."

Spencer gladly conceded. "Stay out of trouble, Colonel."

Churchill simpered, silently waving him off as the lawyer disembarked the bar, respectfully gesturing a farewell to Thomas upon his push off. He vacated the grand hall behind the others.

The Westminster Conference Grand Hall was near empty now following the exodus of the dismissal, leaving just the two Churchill brothers standing focal.

"*Stay out of trouble?*" Thomas quoted with squinting eyes. "He clearly doesn't know Jack."

"Indeed."

"So, out of the frying pan and into the fire?"

Jack eyed his brother. "Not until oh-nine-hundred-hours tomorrow, at least. I was contemplating a night off."

"Haven't you just had a bloody holiday?" Thomas jested before catching Jack's attention with his touch, ceasing their gravitation towards the exit of the courtroom and stopping them still and serious. "And no, I mean with Ros. Jack ... she knows about Sheffield. We happened to see you there—with *her*."

The news hit Churchill like a ton of bricks.

He went pale. Flabbergasted.

"W-what do you mean *you happened to see me?*"

"Ros and I ..." Thomas admitted. "I haven't had a chance to give you the head's up since the last court date, but McNaughton got inside Ros' head ... admittedly, he got inside my head, too. We followed you that night. On his instruction, we went to Dumbarton via Sheffield, just in time to see you be arrested ... in time to see you with another questionable and *familiar* woman ..."

With the weight of a slow rolling wave, Churchill's eyes crashed inside his head. All this time exchanging letters and phone calls with his wife while he was in lock-up, Rosamund was aware of the existence of Scarlet Kristina and she had said nothing. Left in the dark and seething, she quite possibly feared and thought the worst about her husband.

"Sorry, but ..." Thomas apologized, though he didn't seem all too remorseful, alluding to the following: "Are you out of your goddamned mind, Jack? Another woman? Really?"

Churchill defended sternly. "It's not like that!"

"It isn't? I am no fool, Jack. Are you telling me that *that* was not the same blonde bimbo from Norway all those years ago? The one you were unhealthily infatuated with? Whatshername?"

"Scarlet Kristina."

"*Scarlet!* That's it. *The Queen of Sweden* they called her, eh?" Thomas shook his head, mildly bedazzled as he recalled the person and the events partook as though they were yesterday. "I had forgotten all about her," he cocked his brow, "clearly you hadn't. What are the odds she ended up in England upon the commencement of war, eh?"

"It's a *long* story," Jack leaned his head. "Like I already told you, Tom ... it's not like that."

"Alright, what's it like, then, Jack?"

Churchill paused for a moment, considering his options at this juncture. The obvious one was to come fully clean to Rosamund about who Scarlet was, and about his strictly platonic relationship with her. Although alike typical males, a susceptibility to infidelity existed, there was one thing Jack Churchill was irrefutably more devoted to than the British Army and the King of England: and that was his wife. In fact, Jack's reasoning for the visitation that night was directly relating to the court case—an avenue he was playing close to the chest.

"Did you tell Ros who she was?" Churchill enquired.

"It's not my place to tell, but ..." Thomas shook his head softly. "Her heart was already broken, Jack ..."

The damage was done.

"Jesus Christ," Jack clenched his eyes and held them closed. The news of his love's heart experiencing such a degree of pain reflected onto his own. It made him feel sick to his core.

He slowly nodded, about to be reaping the whirlwind of his envisioned sin and conceding. "She suspects the worst, then? That she's a mistress of mine?"

"Made for a really quiet ride home, I'll tell you that much," Thomas informed as he watched his brother pace out on the open floor, staring up at the grand hall ceiling. "There were many inconsolable tears."

Churchill exhaled a long sigh, depressurizing his head.

McNaughton. Fucking McNaughton. That bloke played his cards a little too well, going in not just for the kill, but to raze the landscape. It was a surprise he didn't have Jack doubting himself the way he had turned everybody against him during this silent war.

"Suggest you head home and see her right away ..."

"I can't," trounced, Churchill waved his arms emotionally. He insinuated that he had to stay in London. "I have that meeting tomorrow morning."

Thomas tilted his head. "Then, sir, you are in a spot of bother."

Churchill eyed him, holding a hopeless shrug.

It was then his brother realized the hardship. As important as resolving this privation was, and how detrimental allowing for the distance to stew would be, Jack Churchill was due in Whitehall tomorrow to continue his inescapable warpath. Of this, he had little choice.

"What are you going to do?"

Jack pursed his lips.

Reared into a corner against his will, he knew only of one more avenue to take. He had spent his life wanting something from the war and subsequently giving in to its demand of sacrifice, time and time again ... however, this time, he wasn't wanting anything from it. Not anymore. The tables had turned and turned again, and it appeared that this time the war wanted something from him. This was the war's turn for sacrifice, and not the other way around.

Churchill's focus finally climbed from the floor and to his brother.

The stare he held said a thousand words; a tale of his own verdict ... of resignation. Their long drive home became a breeding ground of discussion concerning Mad Jack's mad decision.

A farewell to arms.

Dusk dawned upon the horizon of yet another closing to what felt like a definitive page-turning chapter of Mad Jack's immediate narrative.

Chaperoning him upon his brave voyage back home, Thomas' dark Ford Prefect pulled into the gravel driveway of the quaint Churchill residence in Dumbarton, delivering the fallen knight as night fell.

Surprised by her husband's unexpected evening arrival after being gone for so long, Rosamund Churchill addressed the advent, emerging abruptly from inside. Dressed down in a plain beige house dress and with her tidy hair in a bun, she stripped off a pair of wet rubber washing gloves as she pushed open the loose screen door to their cottage home, beholding a yearning look of concern.

The car door opened, presenting her husband Jack Churchill.

For his return home, Jack remained in his service dress and Wallace kilt applying his beret firmly aslant. Absent to his attire, he had removed his claybeg sword across Thomas' backseat along with his few bags of luggage. After all, for this battlefield, he wouldn't be needing a weapon.

From his place in his driver's seat, Thomas minded through the windshield with a smile on his maw and a twinkle in his eye as the two reunited out the front.

As agreed ahead of time, he would venture off to refuel and then patiently wait with the car in order to get Jack back to London if this whole thing struck out. They had no idea how Rosamund would take the news of Scarlet Kristina—or Jack the news of her pregnancy for that matter, which was still unbeknownst to him.

Before slipping the car into reverse, Thomas cast his sister-in-law a simple comforting wave through the glass. He and Mrs Churchill had had the opportunity to become better acquainted recently. Even under the harsh circumstances and bleak revelations, it had been a positive development for the two of them, striking a stronger bond.

Beneath the windshield, his eyeline briefly returned to a piece of paper constructed by his brother on their drive home. It was a formal letter of resignation from Commando and from the British Army.

Jack had hinted to his brother in the past that he was interested in stepping off the frontline. Now that marriage and the prospect of starting a family had consumed his life, the decision had been on the cards long before the army had questioned his loyalty; berated him for service duty.

After another once-over, Thomas folded and rested it in the console. Admiral Mountbatten would not be taking this resignation lightly. In fact, he hadn't mentioned this to Jack yet, but he wouldn't be entirely surprised if he rejected the offer completely.

Thomas would pay good money to be a fly on the wall at 0900-hours tomorrow morning, when Jack tactically flakes the meeting after Mountbatten's monumentous liberation of him from court ...

It was a trainwreck waiting to happen, hence their prompt return to London for Jack to hand in the letter in person at Whitehall.

Beneath the twilight setting, Jack progressed towards the front step that existed between two beautiful rose gardens that were still in full bloom. It was the first time ever he had seen their wonderful colours, however the only true beauty Churchill recognized upon taking to those two steps was that of his wife.

Rosamund's eyes glassed with happy tears. It was as though, in that moment of reconciliation, no matter the possible lingering transgressions or untruths, all was momentarily forgotten.

Love flourished, just like the roses.

The sentiment mimicked Jack returning from war ...

... and in many ways, he was.

There wasn't a word shared between them at first. Overwrought with emotion, the two beloveds embraced first with a wholesome cuddle and then an avid kiss at the lips. Their mouths pressed, and tears finally fell down Rosamund's cheeks, wiped away by Jack's soft touch as the two gazed intently into one another's cerulean stares.

"Hullo, dear," with a smile, Jack finally spoke softly between their pressed hips and soft hold. He noted Rosamund's lack of usual greeting concerning his arrival, hoping it not a sign of unfavoured change. "I made it."

"For how long?" she asked fulsomely, evidently already bracing herself in preparation for the onset of unbearable heartbreak and distraught.

Jack held his longing stare into her glassy sky-blues. Along with the sustained eye contact was a certainty that would otherwise be lacking.

"Forever."

The term caused Rosamund's brow to lower. She doubled back after a pause in where Jack did not resend the phrase. He seemed authentic. Serious. Wholesome.

"Ros, I'm done with this life," Jack admitted with a thrown glance at his uniform, signifying the army service. He cast his view aside, feeling it necessary to dramatize this quote as it expelled from the lips beneath his pencil moustache. He removed his beret, touching the emblem sewn into the band. "*'When Alexander saw the breadth of his domain he wept, for there were no more worlds to conquer.'*"

Rosamund physically pushed a step away from beneath Jack's own breadth, and he saw that her frown had returned. Her critique was that from an old playful bant between them about Jack's habits to quote from his classical education.

It broke the mood, but only a little.

"You're not about to start quoting aimless literature to me again, are you? You know I don't care for it—unless it's *Baum,*" she jested.

Jack smiled greatly as he looked to her face. He was half-serious in the delivery of his quote from *Plutarch* to her, knowing it would ruffle her feathers, nevertheless denoting the context of which, he was at his most sincere. He now spoke from his own script. "I have no more enemies to conquer. No more wars to wage. For eternal service, they want me ... but they can't have me, for I am yours."

Rosamund read the sincerity in his eyes while she heard his words. Absorbed his truth.

"All yours."

Rather than explain further, Jack's hand collected the soft skin of her cheek and leant in for another idealistic kiss, taking advantage of the sentimental tone that left her contemplatively vulnerable. However, with a surprise twist, Rosamund mustered the strength to tow away an inch to pose a question. A rather serious one.

"*Just* mine?"

Jack's sealing eyes reopened, observing and identifying the reservations residing within hers. He remembered suddenly that she knew that he knew that she knew about Scarlet Kristina. This was accurate, gathering that Thomas would have spilled the beans to Jack on the way here about their detour to Sheffield. Although she was ecstatic for this news and his ultimate decision to remain at home with her and live a simple life, understandably she couldn't help but wonder if what caused the ruling to be made was due to her knowing about the other woman.

"Scarlet Kristina," Jack uttered. The very verbalization of her name seemed to physically harm Rosamund, causing her to wince. "That's her real name, anyway. Her legal name is now *Joan Witherby,*" Jack began, looking down at her hands as he held them gently between their porchlight embrace. "It's a long story that goes way back. As you would imagine, it has a lot of *swordfights, bagpipes, boche bellends,* and *beneath-blimp battlefields* ... and I plan to share every detail, if you want to hear it."

Although Rosamund could not hide her discontentment in the moment, she deflected a little with humour; a trait both her and her husband shared. In fact, it showed she still had faith in her man. That he was still the good guy in all of this and that she was willing to hear him out to improve her comprehension.

"Well," she uttered, "I'd be disappointed if there weren't at least *one* beneath-blimp battle."

Although finding Jack's revelation funny, as intended, Rosamund held her hesitant ambivalence. There was only one part of the story she needed to know, and it cut through the charades of humour like a knife through warm tension.

"Do you love her ...?"

Forming a straight face, Jack brought his eyeline to hers, staring deep and heartfelt. Of this, he was one-hundred percent sincere.

His head shook to accompany the candour of his confirmation.

"I love *you* ... nobody else," he stated with firm gravitas.

The words sunk in, and Rosamund believed his truthfulness.

"There isn't anything romantic between Scarlet and I ..." and Jack smirked at an ironic truth as he told the tale with inside anecdote. "Truth is, there never really was."

Rosamund let fall another happy tear, and she laughed her situation off. Jack held her more closely, gently, fully understanding of her emotions given the circumstances.

Brightening the mood, she glanced out into the drive, spotting Thomas' Ford still in the drive with him in it. "Is he supposed to be your getaway driver in case I didn't believe you?" she teased.

Churchill cuddled her at the side, peering out over the front yard and drive. He yearned to come up with something comical to further dissolve the mood, but nothing relative leapt out at him to release off the cuff and before long, too long had passed for it to be funny.

... but like always, his humour found a way.

"No, no, not at all ..."

They stared at Thomas through the windshield, who in his solitude, had no idea that he had become the butt of a joke. His head tipped as he realized that he was being spoken about, his expression was that of a clueless onlooker.

"Actually, it's possible that Tom's forgotten where he lives again."

Rosamund burst out in laughter, still sniffling from the emotion.

Churchill enveloped his wife beneath his arm and gave Thomas a wave— it was a signal for him to return in a timely manner, let him not be sitting in the driveway unnecessarily for the time Jack was going to take for unwinding and mending bridges—perhaps even finally taking a shower and having a proper shave.

The car audibly disengaged the brakes, and the headlamps blinked on as Thomas slowly reversed out, peeling away for a hiatus.

"Come on, let's head in," Jack stated as he accompanied her towards the front door under the shade of the awning. As much as he needed it, they didn't have all night to smooth things over, and he would have to delicately orchestrate that as such.

"Jack, wait," Ros called, breaking his gentle guide. She sobered from sniffling, but her mind was now one of seriousness. "You can't just ... *quit the war*, can you?"

"Sure I can," Churchill remarked nearly as a throwaway. "I wrote it in a letter and everything," and then with a cynical slur to himself. "Hopefully *this one* doesn't land me in a court-martial."

"No, that's not what I mean ..." Rosamund expressed as she stepped past him and into the lounge room of their cozy cottage house, and Jack followed wordlessly attentive. The front door closed behind them. The air was warm inside, and it smelt like home. Rosamund had a gramophone on softly in the background, a *Bluebird* label record playing *'I'll Be Seeing You'* by *Dick Todd*, a baritone with orchestra. "The army is all you've ever known, and I know how much it means to you. I don't want you to give that up for me, that's not what I meant when this whole argument started back in February."

"I know," Churchill caught her with gentle hands. "I didn't want to back then. But a lot has changed." His brow twinged: a self-realization. "I've changed."

In that moment, his all-seeing, all-knowing wife slanted her view of her husband, as though she had caught him at a lie somewhere in amongst all these truths.

Churchill asked through a happy gleam. "What is it?"

"Tom told you, didn't he?" she cross-examined with a playful squint, instinctively placing a hand over her stomach as what resided within became a focal topic. Churchill saw her instinctual gesture and prepared appropriately before she said it.

"That, I'm—"

"You're pregnant?!" Jack surmised from barely a clue.

Regardless of how the knowledge had come about, whether his brother had spilt the news on the car ride home or Jack had discovered the information via tells here and now, it was inconsequential to the fact. Rosamund teared up again with overwhelming emotion, and she leant into her husband: the surprised and astounded Jack Churchill.

"*You're pregnant?!*" he said again with a quavering in his voice. They hugged in embrace, and he continually stroked her brunette hair. His eyelids pinched shut, and the burning sensation of waterworks moistened his own stinging eyes, leaking down the sides. This was amazing, life-changing news.

The fact of the matter was that Jack Churchill had made the aforementioned decision prior to learning this information. Whether or not

Rosamund knew that right now didn't matter. The end result would remain the same.

"I love you, Jack Churchill," she whimpered during the tenderness, and Jack pulled them apart in order to look her in the face: the redness of her heated eyes caused her crystal blue eye colour to sparkle brighter than the midday sky, and she had never looked more enchanting or picturesque, even on their wedding day. In this moment—in every moment—this woman was a worshipful goddess to him.

She was the cure to his madness.

"And I love you," he replied, stroking her hair. He revised their wedding vows. "Till death us do part; whatever happens moving forth, I vow to be at your side."

"Are you going to be at my side, or am I going to be at yours?"

"I'll let you take point from time to time," Churchill jeered at a grin.

After their playful exchange, his attention hardened, drifting downwards and to where Jack held his lowered hand over her non-showing stomach, caressing it ever so gently and welcoming the life that grew within with such a beautiful gesture of love.

Ruining the moment to begin another, Rosamund remarked in a whisper: "How's about you start by following me upstairs?"

The two ascended, holding hands like a pair of giddy lovers.

"It's why I wore the kilt, you know?" Jack quipped. "Easy access."

Rosamund chuckled with her big grin beaming, leading the charge to the bedroom with energy, vitality, and happiness.

1944, September
Sachsenhausen Concentration Camp
Oranienburg, Germany

"You expect *me—nay—*you expect *the readers* to believe at one stage in your triumphant, well-decorated, star-spangled career, that you *quit* the army?"

Motionless in his composing tracks, Hardy appeared unconvinced.

Having been momentarily interrupted in his conduct of meticulous storytelling, Churchill froze still, almost offended, and looked at him through the gloom. He would offer an article of irrefutable knowledge.

"Well, hardly the first time, is it?"

The period of which he referred, between Burma and France during his service with the Manchester Regiment, may have been cause for a holiday under differing circumstances, but were grounds for his statement, nonetheless.

"Yeah, but this time's different," Hardy further doubted. "You quit back then because there was a lack of action. Now, it's in abundance. At this point in history, the entire *world* was at war. You said it yourself, this was when even the Americans climbed onboard. They were finally in talks of operational collaboration with your nation's War Office, hence Mountbatten's *oh-nine-hundred-hours super special meeting.*"

"Indeed," Churchill concurred chummily. "Unbeknownst at that moment, that meeting was quite possibly one of the most important meetings for the Allied Forces during the war. It was one of the first proceedings to encompass *Supreme Commander of the Allied Expeditionary Force Dwight Eisenhower.* Eisenhower accompanied the commanding general of *the Army Air Forces, Lieutenant-General Arnold,* to London to assess the effectiveness of the theatre commander in England, *Major-General Chaney.* It was there, the *powers that be* spoke about the future of allied combined operations. Sessions touched briefly on *Operation Jubilee, Operation Musketoon,* foreboded *Operation Husky,* and even the classified op that would end up becoming *Operation Mincemeat.*"

"*Mincemeat?*" Hardy glared, unfamiliar. "Never heard of it."

"Exactly."

Hardy shook his head quickly, realigning their discussion. "I still don't buy it. How'd you end up here then, at the meeting, and not safe behind some desk teaching cadets which way to point a rifle?"

"All in due time, my lad," Churchill modestly remarked. "Hiatus from war notwithstanding, you're correct in saying the period was short-lived. Maybe we should categorise it more as a momentary lapse in motive; that perhaps I had forgotten that peace was not a right bestowed upon thee. It had to be earned via a debt paid through sacrifice. A wise man once told me: *'if you want something from this war, you've got to be prepared to give it something in return' ..."*

"*It?*"Hardy glowered, hung up on Churchill's connotation, inferring the Second World War to be some sort of sentient being capable of commerce or trade.

"The war," Churchill emphasized, detecting his injudicious American friend's mild confusion as if he was stupid. It became apparent that, somewhere, the mentality of Jack Churchill considered the war to be a conscious phenomenon, like a god, and any rite of passage through thus life had to be bartered. It seemed deep-seated within his psychosis, relative as religion.

Cruising yond the eccentric war-cultist quip by Churchill, Hardy continued stridently. "And Rosamund, she dropped the Scarlet Kristina thing just like *that*, huh? She didn't keep you out in the doghouse for a few weeks or anything?" Hardy attempted to further qualify Jack's story.

"Not at all. We made love then and there, actually."

Hardy sniggered as Churchill finally ceased the digression, putting them back on track.

"Much like Tom withholding the news of Ros' pregnancy from me, Scarlet's story was a complicated one ... the entirety of her tale's particulars were not mine to tell, not even in my own biography. Not that it stayed much of a secret for long, somehow staying relevant ..."

1942, April
Churchill Residence
Dumbarton, Scotland

On his side of the bed, Churchill sat upright after having just hunched over to lace his boots, subsequent to slipping on a pair of pressed khaki trousers. They more appropriately matched his battledress uniform attire than the kilt did.

He checked his wristwatch in the warm lamp light as Rosamund reached out from the mess of bedsheet and blankets with her naked arm in order to caress his hand. Her hair was out and fell upon her shoulders. Jack allowed for himself to be drawn in by the sight of his pregnant wife, his lips finding hers.

Comfortable and satisfied by the intimacy just shared, Rosamund allowed for Jack to lift away from her and round the bed, putting on his button up shirt from a hanger. It was now after 7, such an odd time of night to see him getting dressed for work.

"I'm sorry I have to leave you again—but only briefly," he stated fixing his collar. Among other things, he had explained to Rosamund the importance of his immediate return to London to hand in his resignation from Commando.

"Can't you just send the letter in the post?"

"*The post?*" Churchill exhaled with a comical smile. The last time he had used the Royal Mail he had nearly ended up before a firing squad. There was logic supporting his preference against her suggestion. He sat on her side of the bed, comforting her. "The post will take days, dear. My meeting is at nine a.m. tomorrow morning. And be prepared, I may even need to see it through until they can find another replacement to run No.2. Nevertheless, this will set things in motion ..."

She nodded understanding.

In that moment, they heard a car arrive down in the driveway outside. The awareness coincided with a slither of passing light from the headlights through the curtains.

"My *chaperone* awaits."

After another compassionate moment in which he used to ease Rosamund, the untucked Churchill upped and found the rest of his service dress attire in order to formally appear at Whitehall. On the spare armchair they had in the far corner, he discovered slung his discarded necktie. They were on top of a sealed package and two envelopes; mail intended for him received at home for him during his absence.

With an interested gaze beneath his frown—specifically at the package—Jack ceased dressing and collected the shoebox-sized carton, studying the multitude of over-lapping external shipping labels and discerning the stamp headers. It was an old, reused box from addressee: '*J. Witherby*', aka *Scarlet Kristina*. Due to his extended leave, the parcel had been forwarded from the Largs base to Jack's residential address.

"What's this ...?"

"I didn't know whether or not to open it ..." Ros admitted after inspecting her husband's pause, leaning over his shoulder. Mildly exposing herself, she inclined from the bedsheets, having noticed him discover the package from his then-suspected mistress. "It came a week ago."

Churchill's gaze drifted from the parcel, realizing what it could be ...

In his own time tonight, after their long-awaited making of passionate love, mending bridges, he had further explained the backstory of Scarlet Kristina to his wife. This included the admittance of his childish infatuation with her when he had first met her in 1939 and also featured his aforementioned enmity with Friedrich Feind. He did not lie or refrain, referring to her as the infamous *one that got away* that everybody has during their life, but grateful for. With her disappearing from sight and mind, Jack became able to find his true north with Rosamund Denny. He had gone into detail about his recent findings through Feind's admission, that Scarlet had defected from Germany to Britain and was living under a false name in Sheffield. Jack acknowledged that he went out of his way to find her and when Ros and Tom had seen him that night, it was strictly to begin an unofficial debrief of Feind, and conduct a search for potential counter-defamation. Jack admitted that he felt handling her debrief outside of army intelligence or MI5 to be a smarter choice considering she was still technically married to a high-ranking Nazi officer, rather than dob her into the authorities, who would undoubtedly have arrived to slap handcuffs on her wrists and put her in solitary for a shakedown. She would have been treated like a spy—like a Nazi—and he wouldn't in good conscience have that.

Jack had discovered her home address and knocked on the front door and, after some heart-heavy chitchat, asked her to supply and bring forward any potential intelligence she may have kept from her husband; any old theoretical inconsequentials such as notepads, possessions, clothing that may contain pockets. Anything. Scarlet had told Jack that she did not keep much during her defection from Germany, however there were some things in a long-standing storage chest that may have been mixed in with her possessions; clothes, peripherals, and such. Once they had reached the United Kingdom, she discarded them at one of her relatives' new residences, of which she was unsure of the address or contact information considering their newly issued identities. She was forthcoming; though, it would take some digging. Reality was, anything they had kept of Feind's had likely been tossed with the trash.

Before Churchill's arrest soon after, she had vowed to attempt reaching out to her relative for any of Feind's possessions and would have whatever items found posted out to Jack at the base.

It seemed she had come through.

Churchill made an unappeased grunt and put the package back.

"Open it," Rosamund told him after noticing his reluctance. If any of the reasoning behind him not wanting to continue was to protect her feelings, she wanted to make clear that she was fine with it.

Churchill paused, lingering.

"Jack," Rosamund's head craned. "Stop being dramatic."

Exercising obstinance, he leered back at her. "It can wait."

"What if she found something important?"

Either him giving in or maybe it was just to humour his wife, Churchill second-guessed the decision of abstinence and picked up the parcel. Carrying it over, he sunk onto the end of the bed.

Wrapped in the messy bedsheet, Rosamund shuffled nearer and cuddled herself around him to co-observe the findings.

Jack unravelled the twine bindings and pulled the staples, shifting the box in order to view the contents in the lamp light. First and foremost, there was a letter handwritten by Scarlet. With nothing to hide, Churchill opened it for them both to read.

Short and sweet:

'You should have killed him.' - S.K.

Jack audibly cussed, casting Rosamund a bashful glint.

"Yes. Everyone keeps reminding of me that."

The remainder of the contents gave off a rather ominous appeal. Foreign and portentous, they smelt of leather, mothballs, and fascism, for they were once the belongings of a Nazi war criminal.

Unfortunately, tangibility was still nil next to zilch.

There were various old papers, text and cursive all in German.

Inconsequential transfer orders, monthly dispatches, outdated orders of the day. What appeared to be a weather guide of various locations across Eastern Europe was contained within, as well as a *German Infantry Pocket Handbook* dated 1937—basically an outdated SOP manual. A set of silver cufflinks rattled around the box, some foreign reichsmark coinage, some insignificant merit pins, a ring, a loose metal necklace, the chain of which was tangled amongst, and lastly in the bottom: an officer's cap bearing the *Totenkopf*, trademark of the *Schutzstaffel*, complete with Gebirgsjäger unit insignia: an edelweiss flower—something Jack had become familiarized with since the unexpected events of their cathartic though awfully coincidental military incursion during Operation Archery.

Although this intelligence was engrossing ...

... it was unfortunately exceptionally outdated.

Jack reached in and pulled out the hat, carefully tipping off everything else into the bottom recess of the hollow carton. He examined it crest and under, failing to shrug free the irritant necklace that was tangled upon the buttoned silver SS insignia. Suspended from the thin chain, an irrelevant, annoying lone emblem dangled beneath the cap ...

Churchill's stare sought it out in the lamp light, forming a frown.

As useless to him as the denominations of foreign currency, at first, he thought it nothing more than a sig rune of some type, popular with many German badges with many different connotations and meanings, however, as the curved piece shimmered in the lamp light, he recognized the resemblance to a snake.

A serpent.

Churchill's scowl suddenly released, and his eyes grew wide—

Wider than ever!

His fingers quickly captured the dangling necklace charm and snapped it free, holding it poised, discarding the hat paraphernalia and showing the piece to Rosamund nurturing at his shoulder.

"Say, does that look like a snake to you?"

She looked carefully and agreed. "Yes."

Jack's eyes snapped forwards and into a thousand-yard stare.

In a flood, many thoughts convoluted his attention, festering his brain, poisoning his mind, whilst simultaneously churning his stomach. It was all due to a sudden awareness which stimulated his every thought, and like a regular jack-in-the-box, he then sprung up from the mattress, tipping the contents of the box onto the floor.

He held the necklace in his extended grasp, staring at it as though it contained a treasure, the key to human existence, the holy grail ...

Balled jewellery in his fist, clenched tight with flexing frustration—so tight that it dug into his skin, causing a harm which the pain only steadied his drive—Churchill was on the cusp of yet another climax.

"What is it, Jack?" concerned, Rosamund questioned from the bed, pinning the sheet to cover her nakedness.

Churchill slowly shook his head as he bit his lip.

It was the same kind of motion one made when the realization that they had just been outplayed overcame them; when they recognize they were defeated some time ago, and only just now realized.

He had seen this symbol before—long ago.

Due to the chaos of the period, he had just forgotten it with time.

Breathing in and sliding into a deep reminiscence, Churchill found himself back at the Mont de la Gouille ski resort in Switzerland, in the March of 1940. It was the night before he and the Berzerkers decided to take on Ernst-Günther Baade, ambushing him along a route in the Aosta Valley ...

An awkward event, one which Churchill had not breathed a word about since it had happened; where he had snuck out of his lodgings and discovered Baade, his young gunsel, and Wingate sharing what appeared to be some queer sexy-time undressing themselves—or at least Baade was being undressed by his skinny leutnant whilst Wingate watched. Whatever kinky shenanigans were happening that fateful night, Jack did not want to know, and even after all these years, shuddered at the thought, however, a minor detail observed that night: something dangling from Baade's neck along with his dog-tags, was *identical* to that now in Churchill's hand.

It was a symbol.

They were in the same surreptitious separatist group together.

Feind was the key to everything!

Much alike Feind's estranged wife, he had existed directly beneath their noses, hidden in plain sight.

Q ♥

The One That Got Away

1942, April
Churchill Residence
Dumbarton, Scotland

Like a charging stampede, a heavy set of feet came thumping down the carpeted steps of the thin cottage staircase. Churchill descended them at hasty pace in his polished boots, rounding the wooden bellend, and catapulting himself towards the neighbouring wall where their home phone landline was situated upon a cabinet.

Barely dressed due to this intervening rush, his necktie dangled undone around his popped collar, and his uniform shirt was untucked. This incomplete attire on a stature of man such as Jack Churchill was evidence of just how dire the situation was.

Churchill ripped the hand pieces from the brass candlestick telephone, eagerly twirling the circular dial with his fingertip in order to reach the Hollywood Hotel switch operator. He knew the Largs base had someone stationed there for emergencies twenty-four hours a day since the new air raid attacks.

"Hullo, operator?!" puffing, Jack spoke the second the audible connection became established in his ear. "This is Colonel Churchill, service number *34657*. I must speak with the commanding officer in charge or the warden on duty for Camp 2 in Oldham. This is an emergency and requires the upmost priority. Are you able to patch me through via tie-line or– ... yes, yes, give me their number– ... yes, fine-o-fine, I'll hold ..."

While Churchill spoke rapidly on the phone with the base, Rosamund ventured down the padded staircase in a pair of crocheted red slippers and her dressing gown over her silk night-dress. They were the first pair of footwear she could find to put on. She quietly finished down the descent, holding onto the timber railing at the base behind Jack, who threw her a fast glance and acknowledged her presence.

Although a verbal response stopping Jack's newfound warpath was on the tip of her tongue, a certain angle of advantageousness prevented her from stating the obvious. She was a smart girl. Churchill had just mentioned how he had no more enemies left to conquer and, therefore, had become susceptible to settling down and moving away from the frontline. If this man, an enemy—and not just any enemy, but Jack's self-proclaimed archenemy, Friedrich Feind—was let loose, then she would lose her husband in the whirlwind of his pursuit. She knew this and therefore would need to slacken the reigns upon her man here, letting him chase the prize, otherwise she risked losing grip altogether. It was a strange paradox.

Before he could say a word to her, the operator came through for him on the other end of the wire, finding the requested telephone number for the dispatch of the POW camp at the old Glenn Mill—the camp housing the diabolical, fiendish Feind: an apparent established member of the *serpent* secret society.

"Ye— ... Yes, thank you," Churchill regarded as he hung up the mouthpiece, freeing up his hand from the creased page of a rustled notepad and pencil on the nightstand. He immediately prodded his finger into the ring dial, cranking the number for the prison camp.

At first, there appeared to be no answer.

"Blast!" Churchill fumed, hanging up with a loud *clang.* He immediately tried again. After a minute, the same result. It became apparent that their dispatch may have been unmanned after hours ...

With frustration, he again plonked down the earpiece cup and microphone incorrectly off the hook while he struck a strident pose, contemplating how to proceed next.

"I'm going to have to go there ..." with a shake of the head, he pondered verbally and to himself. His gaze met Rosamund's as she lowered her rear onto the step. "Unless ..."

Her heavy eyelids said it all.

"Jack, it's late. Can it not wait until the morning ...?"

"It cannot!" Churchill remarked sharply before searching his pocketbook for contact information for a certain someone. Upon retrieving it, he wound the number dial and coupled the ear and mouthpieces accordingly, listening to the phoneline as it clicked and established through the wire.

The line connected and started ringing ...

And ringing ...

Then finally, the line connected, and a grumpy, half-asleep, coarse voice of a familiar character was on the line.

"*Yes?*"

"H-hullo?" Churchill asked, concentrating hard. He had not expected anybody to answer this late. The line had established, and he could hear what sounded like resonating ambience on the other end of the wire, but nobody had greeted with an appropriate welcoming salutation.

"... yes, what do you want? Who is this?"
Churchill asked delicately. "Constable?"
Behind him, Rosamund's attention honed.
She knew that man. The times must have been desperate if Jack had resorted to calling one of his new antagonists.
"Who is this?!" the voice asked—an all too familiar voice. *"Are you aware of the hour?!"*
"Constable Jethro McNaughton!" Churchill ensued, identifying the caller sternly. "This is Colonel Jack Churchill."
McNaughton's subsequent curse word was inaudible as Churchill excitedly continued, speaking over him.
"Pardon the hour, I'm terribly sorry to call you so late, but it's rather fortunate that you are still—"
"What do you want, Colonel?!" McNaughton barked, prematurely ending Churchill's sentence. The two may have buried the hatchet, but obviously in an exceptionally shallow grave.
Churchill's eyes blinked profusely.
He was in a hurry to get this out anyhow, so for McNaughton to be limiting the niceties was a godsend.
"It's Feind!" Jack stated simply. "It has *always* been Feind!"
"... what are you talking about?"
"He's in on it!" Churchill exclaimed, suddenly concerned that in his fluster, he may have not been making complete sense. He figured McNaughton had known about Wingate and his rumoured secret society, but he may have needed a memory jog. *"The damn slippery snakes!*—or whatever you lot call them!" and then once again for those misinterpreting their secret enemy's affiliation. "I believe you lot may refer to them as by a moniker known as the *Serpents.*"
The phoneline went eerily quiet.
"... go on ..." McNaughton's tone bartered, his appetite for investigative source material suddenly whet by Churchill's alluded findings. Churchill was clearly not privy to the information the Special Investigation Branch had on the secret group known to them as the Serpents, but the fact he knew their working prefix was enough to rope in McNaughton.
In a roundabout way, Churchill cut to the chase. "I know that your office knows of their existence, and are investigating. I've just come across new intel that proves that the prisoner Friedrich Feind not only knows active members of the group but is an established member himself! He's been right beneath your nose this entire time, playing you like a damn fiddle!"

Surrounded by darkness in the afterhours of his office at the Criminal Investigation Department building in London, illuminated by a single lamp light on his desk, sat apathetically one Jethro McNaughton. The constable looked worse for wear after a long day off the back of a long couple of weeks, however this day had been especially tough on an already drained psyche.

The revelation of his son's true fate had caused him to spiral.

The news Churchill had offered him may have been counterproductive and borderline self-defeating for the already self-destructive Jethro McNaughton. Evident by the half-empty bottle of *Johnnie Walker* on his desk atop of mounds of paperwork, it became apparent that the pursuit of vengeance may have been what was holding him together all these years. His quest for justice, his thirst for Orde Wingate hanging at the end of a rope, it was all he got up for in the morning. He had just now realized that without it, he was lost ...

McNaughton propped forward, placing down his tumbler containing neat scotch and he leant into the lamp light on his paper-cladded desk, honing in with focus.

"Colonel ..." he exhaled, shaking his head. "What evidence could you have possibly come across since I saw you last? You're a free man, just ... let it go. Move on. Leave this investigative bungle to the professionals. I respect you ... for telling me about my son ... but, I don't ever want to see your face again. You go off, now, 'n march into battle, 'n try not to catch a bullet to the jugular, you hear?"

Jack's voice shouted down the phone. *"McNaughton! For god's sake, you stubborn bugger, listen to what I am telling you!"*

McNaughton pursed his lips, squinting to force soberness.

While he allowed for Churchill to continue, pinching the once-piece telephone to his ear with his shoulder, he reached to his side and collected his pillbox. He slid it open and subtracted a tablet, feeding it down his gullet and chasing it down with a big swig of scotch.

"On a silver bloody platter, I am giving you a member of the elusive Serpent group! ... It's Feind! He's your man! Think about it!—"

"—He always knew about everything! Information he shouldn't have! Operational details, like Switzerland! Not only that ..." whilst Churchill spoke, he observed the dangling silver snake-charm necklace that was still currently wrapped around his fingers, "... I found a necklace in amongst his possessions—"

"How did you obtain his possessions?" his investigative mindset taking charge, McNaughton interrupted and spat down the phoneline. *"What possessions, Colonel?"*

Churchill rolled his eyes. "It's a long story. Listen, Constable, I believe that these necklaces are only worn by members recruited into the group. I've seen them before ..."

The line was silent.

"... you willing to testify to that?"

"No!" Churchill faced forward and barked. "This is off the record! Look, I'm heading to Oldham now to see Feind—"

"—*I implore that you meet me there!*" Churchill established his direction— the same as his moral compass: towards the enemy.

"Wait, Colonel!" McNaughton exclaimed, pushing out his chair to stand. "The prisoner, Friedrich Feind, you'll ... you'll find him long gone from Camp 2."

"*Pardon?!*"

"His name got picked on a bargain a few weeks ago ... a *prisoner exchange* ..." McNaughton regrettably informed. He leant across his desk, rifling for particulars hidden somewhere amidst his thick stacks of papers on his unorganized filing system. Finally, he found the particular memorandum concerning the closure of any further communication with a witness regarding one of his cases. That was how he knew about Feind's selection for the prisoner exchange.

"*Constable, you better be pulling my leg ...*"

McNaughton gestured a bow. "No, I'm being dead serious, Colonel. We were done with him. I'm sorry. Here it is, here ..." on his desk, he rotated the page so that he could read. It was a single printed page, nearly automated in the wording of its communiqué. McNaughton's attentive peepers grazed over it.

"*What does it say?!*"

"Hang on."

Leaving Churchill in the lurch, McNaughton placed down the phone entirely to collect his spectacles from somewhere on the desk and applying them to his face in order to be able to read the fine print.

He resumed his hold of the phone call.

"Yes, it says here he was selected for a prisoner swap along with three other German officers held at the *Toft Hall* camp in *Cheshire.* This is dated from almost two weeks ago."

The news came down on Churchill like an anvil.

"*Two weeks ago?!* When do they ship out?" he asked with brimming angst. He exchanged a look with Rosamund, who was still by his side on the stairs, sharing his anxiety via the one-sided conversation.

"*It says by the conclusion of April.*"

"It's April now!" Churchill shouted. "What date?!"

"*It ... it doesn't say! It just says April,*" McNaughton's line went quiet. "*I'm sorry, Colonel. You're too late to get him. He's in the wind ...*"

Churchill's face fell flat.

That sudden wave of defeat flooded over him, pressing the air from his lungs and the hope from his heart.

"If it's any consolation, I happen to know a good way to deal with having your hopes and dreams pulled out from beneath you," McNaughton narrated on the other end, followed by what sounded like another sip from a whiskey glass.

Churchill's frown focused, staying the course. "It's still April for two more days, Constable ... they may have relocated him to an airbase for transport. This whole thing could still be in-transit. Quickly find out whatever else you can and meet me at the Glenn Mill. I'm—"

Suddenly, the ambience of audio all around them flooded with a wailing tone from somewhere in the centre of town. It started off nothing more than an annoying pitch before quickly climbing to that of a siren's volume within the winding seconds, drowning out all other noise, loud enough to wake the dead at the local cemetery.

Churchill bared his teeth as he blocked his other ear.

The noise was so loud it scratched his brain.

In a pirouette, he spun to see Rosamund on the stairs as she, too, clenched at her ears with both hands and squabbled from the overbearing pitch.

It was the local air raid siren!

What timing!

"McNAUGHTON?!" Churchill shouted into the microphone cone piece. *"CAN YOU STILL HEAR ME?!"*

"Colonel?! What is that dreaded noise?!"

"AIR RAID! MEET ME AT THE CAMP!" he articulated in a shout, about to slam down the handset and launch off the mark like an athletic sprinter. *"WE'VE GOT TO STOP HIM FROM LEAVING THE COUNTRY!"*

"Colonel?! W-what?!"

"THE CAMP! MEET! ME! THERE!"

Without an audible sound through the wail, Churchill hung up the telephone, folded his shirt collar down, and immediately grabbed his chevron-sleeved khaki military blazer from the coatrack, slipping it over. Next, his green beret, taking the time to position it firmly aslant. In the flurry, the suited Churchill convened by Rosamund at their closed front door.

He moved beyond her and towards the doorway, piercing through whilst he shielded his ears from the cacophony of merciless sound that saturated all vocal airspace.

Once pushed out and into the open space of the outdoors, it became evident that the local air raid siren was almost just as loud outside as it was inside. The nearest base with a siren was located at Inveraray to the west—the old stomping grounds for No.3 Commando. It was no guarantee that they were about to be bombed, but the transmitters had obviously picked up something in the airspace headed this way from across the English Channel.

Thomas was standing outside of his car amongst the audial flood, just as confused and scanning into the night sky in search of any clarity. His head panned around and onto the house once the porch light became flicked on by Jack, and he saw his moderately dressed brother leaving the house. Rosamund was present in her nightgown and slippers, shouting after him.

"*Jack!*" Rosamund bellowed with a vein in her neck. Her tiny voice was barely audible through the siren that saturated everything. "*Jack!*" she called again, this time grabbing his attention by accelerating quick enough to harness a hold of his sleeve.

Jack gestured at Thomas, shouting at him to get in and start the car.

He did so, immediately keying the engine.

The vehicle turned over without so much as an audible sound.

Churchill faced his wife. "*I have to go!*" he shouted loud and firm so that she could hear his enunciations.

"*I know!*" she responded with an oddly placed understanding that was in accord with his aspiration and yearning here. Churchill was almost surprised. He was expecting her to try and stop him—and in reference to her previous state of mind, she knew she had to let him go in order to keep him—*but it got better ...*

"*I'm coming with you!*" she yelled through the audio, reaching back in to close their cottage front door as Jack downed the steps and started walking across the driveway towards the car. He halted and spun, stopping her with a palm.

His frown inverted, bewildered. "*Pardon?!*"

Noticing her husband's perplexion, Rosamund threw a gesture back at the house. "*You prefer I stay here, with this going on?!*" she argued with undeniable validity at the air raid alarm.

Churchill's tense brow faded, and his head tilted.

She had a good point.

Rosamund affirmed her plea further, making for a good argument.

"*Remember ... we aren't leaving each other's sides!*"

Churchill read the certainty and the devotion within her big blue eyes. She meant every word of her statement, and there would be no arguing—and there was no time for it.

Thomas shouted over the purr of the car engine and the chaos of the air raid siren. "*Jack?! What's going on?! We need to find a shelter!*"

On the driveway, through the overbearing chaos, Churchill beamed a smile at the love of his life. He affirmed to her: "I vow to be at your side."

And with that, he offered her his hand, which she boldly accepted, and they both turned and continued towards the car—together, husband and wife in tandem.

"*Go on! Get in, then!*" he directed, and they all climbed into the car.

Jack entered the passenger's side and Rosamund straddled across the whole backseat, shoving over Jack's existing luggage and stowed possessions from earlier in the day. Once piled in, they closed the open doors, blocking out a portion of the air raid noise, at least enough to not have to shout.

"Hello."

"Hi," Thomas regarded sideways, glancing at Rosamund who had just now jumped into his back seat. He then looked towards his passenger, Jack, prompting an explanation.

Churchill nodded, eyes forwards. "Change of plans ..."

Thomas gathered. "Yes, I assume we are seeking shelter?!"

"No!" Jack shook his head firm. "We head for Feind!"

1942, April
Glenn Mill (Camp 2)
Oldham, Lancashire

They spent the first half of the drive to Lancashire switching between radio stations. The *BBC Forces Programme* had the best reports on what targets the latest Luftwaffe air raids had struck with their lightning war. Or as it had become known this time around, the Baedeker Blitz.

The dark Ford Prefect had sped along the empty roads all the way from Dumbarton, reaching Oldham in record time, just under two hours, however, the way their attentions were glued to the engrossing radio broadcast particulars, listening for news on city casualties to follow *Exeter, Bath, Norwich,* and *York* that were each hit in previous weeks, the drive had felt like mere minutes.

"So, this *Feind* twat, he's in on it, is he?" Thomas Churchill recapped after persevering with the sporadicity of his brother's storytelling between the volume knob on his radio being dialled up to curtail whenever further blitz details were revealed.

"Always has been, apparently ..." the green beret-clad Churchill regarded whilst riding shotgun, having just filled his chauffeuring brother in on why they were headed towards Camp 2. Naturally, Thomas had shown an interest in the knowledge of the intelligence quality; intelligence being his professional field, albeit of a different calibre.

Suddenly, another relevant report came through the radio waves, and Jack reached for the volume knob to turn it up momentarily.

"... *'a series of bombs were dropped in Cumberland, missing the city limits but destroying a portion of the Grizedale base said to be home to almost one-thousand German Prisoners of War. The Midlothian County was not without incident with reports, claiming that the army base located near Milton Bridge was also targeted by the German Luftwaffe this evening'* ..."

"*Milton Bridge* ..." Jack repeated undulating the volume. "The *Woodhouselee Camp* is there, is it not? Why are the Huns bombing so close to their own POWs? Surely, they're aware that they are *prison camps* and not *army bases?*"

So far, during the aftermath of these latest aerial sightings, they comprehended that no major cities had been bombed, rather, several small, specific towns had been targeted. Oddly, two of them held known POW camps belonging to the enemy. What Jack referenced was that it seemed ludicrous that the enemy was bombing their own people, where Thomas' intelligence-minded approach would elaborate with a strategic mindset.

Thomas explained to the best of his intelligence scope. "If any of the inmates in those camps were discovered to be haemorrhaging information harmful to the German war machine and they found out about it, then ... *bombs away.*"

Jack oversimplified. "Cutting out cancers with hand grenades ...?"

Thomas held a shrug.

"Can't say it's not effective, I suppose ..." Jack responded cynically and with a narrow shake of the head.

They were ten minutes out of Camp 2, about to turn onto *Wellyhole* which ran most the way through Oldham. As they did, their fore-view across the bonnet of the headlamp-lit road corrected from the curve of travel, and they noticed the unmistakable warm glow of fire-lit smoke clouds wafting thick on the nightscape horizon ahead in the distance ...

It was a bomb site.

Something ahead had been bombed, something yet to be reported over the radio, and something that caught the attention of both military men.

With her blue eyes spying through the windshield at the giant glowing brown plume, Rosamund leant forwards. Her mouth falling agape as the radiance from the bombing site illuminated her pretty face in the shadow of the backseat.

Their black Ford turned onto Constantine, where the start of the prison camp fences became visible. There was a lot of activity up ahead before what appeared to be the primary source of the blaze and pluming smoke. The back end of the Glenn Mill had been bombed.

The fences were fucked and there were cautioned bodies standing idly everywhere; authorities, swarming like ants in uniforms, from firefighters to local law enforcement and army personnel. There were flashing lamps and flashlight beams shimmering ubiquitously. People shouting, pointing fingers, all in a fuss.

" *Whaaaat* in the *blazes* ...?!" Thomas murmured as he pulled their car over short of the chaos by the entrance. The nearest he could park was along the street still a hundred feet from the main building, flagged down by a perspiring policeman with white gloves and a whistle.

Directly ahead, just off the road, was a flipped prisoner transporter truck. It was emitting thick smoke from its cranked, sideways bonnet.

Against its turned-over elongated side was a lineup of worse-for-wear German POWs who had been unfortunate enough to be aboard when their bombing brethren had dropped their payloads, either blowing the truck over or at least causing the driver to tip them during the scamper. They appeared to have been promptly detained, contained under gunpoint, seemingly unwilling to break any rules of restraint, and were fully complying to the men with rifles.

"What happened here?" dropping down his window, Thomas asked the policeman maintaining the cordon. He took a break from directing traffic and approached the driver's side door, having noticed the military uniforms of the men within the civilian vehicle. Henceforth, he offered them a different set of information to what he would offer the public, a show of professional courtesy.

"The camp got hit!" stating the obvious, he exclaimed over the ambient volume of the aftermath. "The whole back fence got destroyed and apparently this truck blew a tyre trying to take a shortcut like a bat out of hell!"

Jack ducked low and questioned out the same window. "Do you know if all the prisoners are accounted for?"

"I'm not sure, sir! I heard quite a few got killed in the bombing!" the cop spluttered through a gust of smoke that still wafted through the night air like fog.

Thomas faced Jack. "Maybe your man got roasted?"

Jack eyed him, feebly. "We're not that lucky."

"It's started a fire behind the east barracks and in one of the office wings! Not sure why Gerry wants to incinerate his own folk ... Better them than us, eh, chaps?!"

"You mind if we head in?" Thomas queried soon after, inferring that they had some semblance of official business being here.

The policeman was hesitant, but he wordlessly waved them on through considering they were uniformed and of authority.

As they passed the overturned army truck, Churchill wound down his passenger's side window in order to better survey the site—namely the faces of the prisoners that were present. He instructed Thomas to drive slower. Once they passed, and he was convinced Feind was not a part of their load, Jack sat back down with his eyes focused on the bright orange back-lit prison camp.

Home to two-thousand prisoners, the muddy-faced, smoke-spluttering populace of the Glenn Mill had been rounded up into the main yard beneath the warm glows of overlapping searchlights and the heavy barrels of countless Lee-Enfield rifles from the watchtowers. All hands were on deck to retain order and limit collateral.

The falling ash in the smoke gusts grew thicker in the beams of their headlights as they arrived in the allocated parking zone before the main building. Civilian operators and military police from the prison staff roster had evacuated to the parking area, amassing before them and causing Thomas to slow. Numerous fires had broken out throughout the buildings and although all the staff present had made it out alive, some were injured and burnt, and nearly all of them were suffering from probable smoke inhalation.

Unable to search a parking space amidst the anarchy and confusion of stopped vehicles, tank trucks from the firefighters, and army tillies, Thomas brought them to a halt staring straight at the front double doors. His headlights illuminated the crowds of people as they carried more barely conscious bodies from the smoke-filled interior, and Thomas left them on purposefully to help illuminate the exterior.

Jack and Rosamund opened their doors simultaneously, followed by Thomas who seemed a little hesitant concerning becoming lost amongst all this fresh confusion, not wanting to get in the way of the rescue duties.

"Stay in the car, dear," Jack directed as he and Thomas advanced into the madness. They closed their doors one after the other.

"Are *you* staying in the car?" Ros countered in reference to their pact about staying together, and Jack shot her a glance. He then sighted a gesture at her slipper footwear as she trod on the edge of a muddy puddle.

Like a spectator at a tennis match, Thomas looked from one Churchill to the other and back again. He once detested Rosamund's ability to backchat, but when it was with Jack, he found it rather humorous.

He cocked his head. "I'm *not*, but ... your call, dear."

Not risking the minefield of muddy puddles, Rosamund retracted back into the door, staying with the car as the Churchill brothers strode forth, passing between running bodies and motion. Shortly after he saw the familiar face of Jethro McNaughton in an overcoat and fedora—he had met them there. Toothpick twigging between his teeth, the constable either had a bad case of dandruff or that was ash on his shoulders.

He had brought with him his faithful accomplice, Viviane Garland, who was in a slim-fitting overcoat that shaped around her waist and cut-off just above the knee, exposing some leg that Jack nor his brother could go without noticing, even during the surrounding chaos. She stood beneath an umbrella which protected her not only from the snowing slag, but the water from the misty rainfall that had started to fall over Lancashire.

"Constables."

"Colonel, Major," McNaughton greeted with his hands in his pockets and his offsider at his flank. Beneath the brim of her canopy, Garland cast both Jack and Thomas a miniscule yet respectful nod. "What were the odds that *this* POW camp would get hit right after your supposed findings, eh?"

"Knowing Jack's luck, I'd say pretty high odds," Thomas imposed.

"*Supposed findings?*" Jack sneered at McNaughton's critical inquest.

Before their eyes, he raised a hand encompassing an item of jewellery. After releasing a held breath, McNaughton reached out and appropriated himself with the piece belonging to the incarcerated Feind. The silver necklace; the quintessential portion being the snake symbol.

"*This* is it?!" McNaughton said in an unentertained gasp.

Churchill took it back from his undesired paw, defending his convictions. "During my time in Switzerland, I encountered other men who wore charms such as these."

"And you're sure it's not just a coincidence?"

"I wouldn't have thought that a man like you would believe in coincidences?"

"I don't!" McNaughton quarrelled. "Not in my religion."

"Gentlemen!" Thomas intervened, dishing some sound logic. "We each drove all the damned way here ... why don't we just find the wanker and ask him."

His cue reset the pace.

"What did you find out?" Jack asked McNaughton in reference to his request that he do so on their short-lived telephone conversation prior to their rendezvous.

"Feind is bound for a prisoner exchange in three days, on May 1st. He and three other German captives are to be transferred to the RAF base at *Attlebridge* tomorrow and flown to an undisclosed location east of Normandy. The following day, he will be exchanged for a high-priority British officer currently being held by the Germans."

"One British officer?" Thomas quantified. "Four for one? Who the bloody hell struck that deal?"

Toying with the pick between his teeth, McNaughton shrugged, for he didn't make the rules.

"That means he's likely still here then, correct?!" Jack applied rationale. It was the only thing he took from McNaughton's reveal of gathered intel.

"Feasibly," McNaughton bobbed, glancing around at the mayhem.

Churchill took a few short steps in flank of their conversation, glancing out into the big spotlight-lit yard where nearly two-thousand residents of the prisoner camp had been rounded up and situated under armed guard in the wet grass for what was presumably a headcount of sorts. The thickening rainfall was visible in the beams of the powerful lamps.

Feind was likely out there in amongst the congregation.

"Good, good. So, he's still here somewhere, does that mean we go home now? Come back tomorrow when the world is not on fire?!" Thomas remarked half seriously. His sullen query was not met with a response from his brother.

"Good luck getting him out of there anytime soon," McNaughton commented as he sidled beside Churchill facing the yard view beyond the fence, standing shoulder to shoulder with the ally he once hunted.

Jack shook his head slightly.

Something didn't feel right.

"If he was due for processing he wouldn't be in the general population," he looked back at the main administrative building. There were a few German inmates in their rundown attires amongst the medical crews and prison personnel who had been evacuated from within the building and not the yard. They had been lined up against the outer wall and put on their knees, well-behaving under the lines of several MPs with pistols at the hip. Gravel crunching beneath his footsteps, Jack approached them, getting a good look of their faces in an attempt to identify Feind camouflaged amidst all this mayhem. None of the men fit his description ... except for the last one on the end, looking downwards like a sorry sod.

Double-taking, Churchill stepped closer.

He was locked on target. "Oi, you there!"

He approached the kneeling soldier on the end who had his face down, looking at the mud.

"I said *oi!*"

The non-English-speaking solider finally looked up after hearing Churchill's aggressive tone as it homed in on his mark. It was a younger gent with dark features, and who somewhat resembled Feind, but was not him.

Jack suddenly experienced déjà vu from a time prior to discovering his archenemy in the wild war, where he would mistakenly see his face in any crowd.

Met by another dead end, Churchill exhaled.

Although the news of Feind still being present in the camp was positive to their proactive manhunt, the fact he couldn't easily be found would keep him up all night, especially given his findings and even more the recent bombing bringing down half the back fence. From what they understood, the preliminary headcounts tallied that all prisoners were accounted for within the confines of the Glenn Mill and that there had been no escapees, however, Churchill remained unconvinced and would stay that way until proven otherwise.

"*Lieutenant-Colonel Jack?!*" a tiny female voice called out through the livewire pandemonium. Her petite tone pierced the racket of the chaos, catching his ears and the attention of those around him. The tiny voice belonged to Miss Mabel Blagbrough, the head secretary hand, admin, and overall caretaker of the Glenn Mill. Her voice was as colloquially playful as the first time she had pronounced Jack's name.

Churchill and the other members of their motley group panned to see her emerge from the double doors of the main admin office and checkpoint, covered in soot and grime from the black burning indoors of the building. She assisted a burnt, breathless prisoner over her shoulder, escorting him out of the blaze like the angelic heroine she was speculated to be.

It quickly became apparent that the life Mabel had just saved from inside was that belonging to another of the many prisoners of war.

Her hair was wet from steam, sweat, and soot, and her cheeks were redder than intended from the morning makeup ritual. She was looking at Churchill and smiled her pearly whites through the darkened grime. This young girl was a fan of this handsome war hero and was happy to see him there to lend a helping hand not unlike a light in the darkness.

"*Oi! Get away!*" a voice from offside abruptly shouted at her direction, creating a scene out of her apparent rescue. The sudden intensity startled her.

They all watched as an on-edge prison guard straddled in and shoved the seared-sleeved, red-cheeked casualty out from Mabel's care, discarding the wounded man to the ground in a fresh coughing fit in order to better cast the sights of his pistol. He was backed up by another tempestuous-mannered guard.

"He's fine! Oi! Settle down, you big oath, he needs help!" Mabel exclaimed from the sideline, shouting over the brutes as they encircled the spluttering prisoner, apprehending the already clearly incapacitated man. She cared for everybody's well-being, not just the ones on the outside of the fence, but inside too. And they seemingly respected her for that. Her generosity was a testament to her tenacity around these parts, and her solicitous fosterage would go down in history as such.

Wearing a concerned frown beneath his rain-wet beret, Jack marched forth to get a better look at the chap to make sure it wasn't Feind. It wasn't. As well as the assessment, Churchill then found himself abruptly embraced by the breathless Miss Blagbrough. He caught her before she could fall and assisted her a few steps away from the building near the first row of cars where Thomas helped carry her back to his nearby parked Ford. Holding the canopy of her brolly above her escort, Garland and McNaughton shadowed their path. Once they neared, Rosamund opened the door so that they could place her in the comfortable and sheltered passenger's seat. There she could take a load off and gain some fresh, clean air.

Rosamund quickly moved around the vehicle after opening the door, prudently observing Constables McNaughton and Garland as they encircled Tom's car. The last time she had met the two investigators they had been less than sociable, and so she kept a cocked eye on the two of them like an irate chihuahua. Those first impressions weren't ones she would be forgiving any time soon.

"Are you off your head going back into a burning building, ma'am?" McNaughton removed the toothpick from his maw in order to stridently question now that she was outside in the cool night air and spitting rainfall, away from the heat of the smoke. Once the adrenaline started wearing off, she could catch a nasty chill in this cold manner. "That's a job for these gents, not a young lass such as yourself."

Soot on her brow, Mabel shot McNaughton a look that could kill.

She was clearly one of the new-age types of broad, ripe with independence and no longer of the stereotypical victim to sexist quips of the chauvinist and chivalrous macho male men.

"Sorry, I didn't know I needed a penis to save lives?"

A silence flooded the vicinity.

Everybody's lips pressed tight and stared at McNaughton as he suddenly became a burn victim.

"E-excuse me?" McNaughton frowned, confused and caught off-guard by that quip. He cast a glance about himself, seeing only females surrounding him in that moment. "Ma'am, I meant the authorities."

"Uh-huh. I know what you meant! *This* damsel is not of distress, sir."

Garland heard her tone of voice and a rascal smirk curled the corner of her mouth. She subdued it in the nick of time as McNaughton cast her a leer before strolling a few steps away to cool down.

"Mabel," Jack beckoned, gaining her attention. He squatted down in the open door before her. "Are you okay?"

"Here," Thomas interjected only to offer an army cantina from a supply stash he had in the trunk. He unscrewed the cap for her. It was old water but fresh.

"Thank you, mister," Mabel accepted the metal container, taking a big swig. She took a few extra moments to gain her breath and slow her heart. The poor thing was exhausted, coughing, and covered in charcoal. She had bravely risked her life to save the lives of those few locked up in the back rooms of the main building as it filled with smoke ahead of flames. The act was heroic to say the very, absolute least.

Now that she had recovered an ounce, Churchill questioned Miss Blagbrough. "My dear, do you know a prisoner by the name of Friedrich Feind? He is about my height and build, with duelling scars across his cheeks and a crooked nose. He would have been brought to the Glenn Mill in January."

Mabel bobbed her head, recalling the man. "Of course! *Friedy.* Yes."

"*Friedy?*" flabbergasted, Churchill pronounced her pet nickname for Feind. The sobriquet was obviously derived from Friedrich and was phonetically pronounced *Friday* like the day of the week, only with a Welsh accent.

"He's the man that you visited—the man you *both* visited," she referenced furthermore, inferring McNaughton's past visitations at the Glenn Mill also. McNaughton recognized her positive identification of the one inmate out of two-thousand, and it sincerely surprised him. Mabel shook her head at Jack and gave him a cheeky smile. "He was none too happy after you left him that bottle of liqueur ..."

Churchill beamed, dismissing it quickly. "It's an inside joke."

McNaughton overshadowed him, talking from above.

He reinserted his toothpick between his gritting teeth in order to appear more brute. "Supplying prisoners of war with contraband is a criminal offence, Colonel."

"Well, perhaps you can put me before a court martial?" Churchill arced up, casting the constable a challenging gleam for an extended moment until McNaughton seemed to drop it. Jack brought his attention back to Mabel through the open car door. "Mabel, do you know where *Friedy* might be located right now?"

Mabel frowned her smeared brow with confusion, unsure why they would not already be apprised of his recent transfer. "Friedy is gone, Jack," she informed. "He was on one of the transports that moved out earlier tonight ..."

Churchill's tense brow loosened ...

"Just *tonight,* you say?"

She nodded. "It was going to be tomorrow, but they moved forward the schedule. I don't think it got very far. A truck rolling out of here apparently crashed when the bombing started—just up the road away ..."

As her words fell upon their ears, Churchill raised from his kneeling position, becoming upright and rigid. Like a robot, his eyeline scanned northeast. From their location in the car park, he was able to again spot that turned-over transport truck through the thin veil of falling drizzle. The event was raw, and there was still activity around it, with a group of prisoners lined up against the vehicle under armed sentry, likely still being processed.

"We drove past that on the way in!" McNaughton stated making the same realization right as Churchill did.

"Us too!" Thomas corresponded. What was odd was that Jack had paid great attention to the cast of sad faces as they had passed by the overturned vehicle. Feind had not been amongst their ranks.

"Feind wasn't with them ... unless ..."

Churchill's expression faded.

Like a bolt of lightning, he took off the mark in an all-out sprint out of the car park and onto Constantine Street, pelting through the curtain of growing rainfall. Alone, he ran through the consistent cascade with an athlete's pace a length away from the warmth of the prison camp conundrum, eventually reaching the group of prisoners by the overturned vehicle, about to be escorted back to the Glenn Mill under guard.

"Hold!" he shouted, incoming and with his hand raised.

The guards became alerted to see him running towards them through the rain. He was in uniform, unarmed, and of high rank, therefore they did not perceive him as a threat to them or their prisoners.

Jack slackened the speed of his sprint as he came near, lining the row of the prisoners up on a parallel pass, examining them all with precision and concentration. He again noted that Feind was not a part of their rollcall as he was supposedly according to Mabel Blagbrough, and he trusted her intelligence.

In a panicked bark, Churchill targeted one of the four armed MPs guarding the POWs. "How many prisoners were onboard?!"

A full two seconds of confusion passed in which Jack grew impatient. "Huh?!"

"Your prisoners! Were they all accounted for?!"

The MP guard watched with a frown as the drenched Churchill passed them all by, stepping into the overturned truck in order to examine the inside carriage for himself, seemingly searching for a missing person.

"Sir, the driver said eight passengers in total," he replied as the huffed Churchill returned into frame. "The *driver*, an *armed guard*, and *six prisoners*. And we got eight, total."

"Are you sure of this?!" Jack queried with alacrity. His tone of voice seemed to pester the MP, offending him. "*Eight, total?!* Was that including *him* and *his colleague* or just *him?!* He wasn't counting himself, was he?!"

The guard squinted. "Ask him yourself, he's back at the building in one of the ambulances—"

"I don't have time for that!" Churchill exclaimed in a fluster. He faced the guard, laying hands on his sleeves in order to exact certainty from the fellow. "I need to know exactly what he said to you! Now!"

"That!" the guard shoved Jack's hold clear, and he pointed at the floor onerously. "He said that!"

"*Eight?!*" Churchill repeated after a breath.

"Yes!"

Another moment of consideration passed.

The result here was obvious, but something seemed amiss.

The maths was right, but the answer was still wrong.

Rather outlandishly in their standstill, Jack squinted and started scanning the dark surroundings of their perimeter. There was a field across the road followed by a distant, foggy tree line leading into a paddock, and a trainline on the opposite side. If Feind had escaped the crash and ran on foot, in the dark of night and the low visibility of rainfall, he had a big head start and could be anywhere by now ...

The peeved MP guard ogled at Jack as the sprinkle of rain fell upon them, slowly saturating everything through the layers. Churchill's face revolved around to face him, hinting a solum sign of desperation.

"Look, are you *sure* there is not one missing?!—"

"I'm sure, sir!" he concluded with a sternness in his tone, now projecting frustration. He cast a look across his shoulder to the horde of droopy prisoners and wet armed guards. "C'mon you lot! Let's move out!"

After his order, they marched on, returning them to the masses of the Glenn Mill camp, leaving Churchill standing idly before the turned-over truck and appearing as dire as his situation, and the weather complimented his mood.

From the car park, the others from their motley posse could see Churchill standing out in the rain, alone and aimless.

Whatever he had found out there had him stumped, chin just about touching his chest. Not even the damper downpour could wash away the misery of his onset melancholy.

From his position a few feet away from the car, McNaughton stood out in the open, unafraid of the wet beneath the brim of his fedora cap. His eyes focused on Churchill in the distance by the vehicle wreck. Like him right now, similar heavy thoughts began to weigh a load.

An inspective contagion, he followed Jack's eyeline as he scanned the wide-open nightfall. There was nothing but more darkness through veils of sprinkling rain and slag.

One thing was certain, and that was that he had not found Feind where he was supposed to be.

McNaughton cussed in a breath as the realization suddenly set in; regardless of Friedrich Feind's affiliations with the serpents—a secret group, the existence of which had barely been proven, however a part of an active investigative lead either in his office at the Special Investigation Branch of the more authoritative Criminal Investigation Department—he was a convicted POW now technically unaccounted for: a fugitive. He was an extremely dangerous enemy combatant, and he was on the loose. This was an even bigger problem in and of itself.

Thomas Churchill appeared behind him, leaving the women to the dry space of the car. Enough time had passed that he was wondering what results his brother had found. "Good or bad?"

McNaughton shook his head with little optimism. "Not good."

Inside the black Ford, light rain resonated on the tin roof of the stationary car. The three female occupants resided within and around silently.

This was partly due to them being unfamiliar with one another, but even those who were had incredibly little to talk about.

While Garland body blocked the cold at the open door, Mabel's observant eyes noticed the twinkle of the wedding ring on the woman in the back seat's appropriate hand. She put two and two together after also noticing that Lieutenant-Colonel Jack had a wedding band. Up until now, she admitted a crush on the handsome high-ranking army man, and that infatuation had only increased once she read up on his accolades, turning pages like it were an obsession. There was a decent article published by *The Battlefront Gazette* in 1940 entitled *Dunkirk Jack!* which referenced Churchill's adventures first-hand. The man was a stud, a hero soldier, and respected warfighter, and it undoubtedly raised her heart rate.

... but now, that adoration was at an end.

"You're Lieutenant-Colonel Jack's wife, aren't you?" Mabel piped up and asked gently. Garland was at the open door, beneath her umbrella. The vixen would eavesdrop every word of their conversational exchange.

Slightly hesitant to respond, Rosamund looked to Mabel.

A natural distaste towards the cute young girl had blossomed upon first laying eyes on her, based on the way she looked at and interacted with her husband. She could tell she had a thing for him, and she knew her man too well. Jack wasn't shy to the affection of good-looking gals and, although harmless, would likely indulge the opportunity.

"I am."

"I'm Mabel. What's your name?" she asked in a petite voice that matched her frame and features.

"*Mrs Churchill*," she delivered sternly and to prove a point.

What was said next caused visible strain for Mabel to admit—it would have been hard for any person capable of humility and humbleness. She struggled with the delivery for only a moment before contentiously surrendering to her respectable virtues.

"Well ... you're a very lucky woman, Mrs Churchill ..."

The phrase landed on Rosamund's ears, and she received the compliment well, regardless of her unreasonable stand-offish response. But it was more than just a compliment. It was a primal denouncing of Mabel's affection towards her husband. To whatever extent, she appreciated the submission. That was even disregarding her prior reticent response.

"Rosamund," feeling remorseful, she extended an olive branch. "Call me Ros," she replied in full, not holding any grudges. Directly following what she had said, something caused Rosamund's brow to crinkle.

Mabel nodded with a grin. "Ros."

Rosamund glowered, adjusting her seat as she considered something out loud. "You know, that's the second time someone has said that to me in as many weeks ..."

To what she referred was Viviane Garland's phrasing of the sentence with what appeared to be dissimilar in context, or what she perceived as dissimilar. Mabel's use didn't have a follow up about it being a shame insinuating that Jack was a war criminal or a disloyal husband.

With that profession, Rosamund veered her view around to Garland as she poised outside of the car in the rain, purposefully catching her attentive expression. Garland was a strong and independent femme fatale, and she needed to be to carry her weight in a profession typically dominated by strong male stereotypes. She needed not hide her opinions, and very much did not, even upon an uncovering.

She maintained a mild smirk overhearing Mabel's admission before calmly looking away into the night.

Rosamund observed her body language.

After a short while, Churchill returned to the others.

Beyond troubled, he wore a brow chock-full of disconsolation.

At the foreground of the activity of the Luftwaffe bombing aftermath, McNaughton and Thomas anticipated his return, waiting by the car.

They didn't even have to ask.

Jack's mad look said it all.

"He's gone ..." the soaked colonel informed, stating the obvious and what they feared as the worst.

On the other side of the black Ford Prefect and beneath an umbrella, Garland loomed. Her attention raised. Along with her attentiveness, was that of Rosamund and Mabel, who emerged on the other side of Thomas' car.

Nobody had anything to offer in the way of a physical solution or even verbal support; however, McNaughton arose to the challenge.

The next logical course of action here was to go home, for there was nothing more they could do other than report a supposed man-on-the-run, declaring Friedrich Feind a fugitive status. First thing tomorrow, he had the authority to propose this new information about Feind's affiliation with the secret society to his superiors at the Criminal Investigation Department. From there, they could launch a fuller inquest into the so-called *Serpents* and investigate this new evidence lodging to the bone and picking it clean. As for the search for Feind, the appropriate channels could be contacted regarding his truancy, most likely through the prison sector or local police. It was the army via the Royal Military Police or the Provost Marshal's problem now, and they would likely initiate a manhunt for Feind.

Before opening his mouth, there was one irrefutable trait that both McNaughton and Churchill shared, and it was an obvious invariable present in the mood: persistence.

McNaughton questioned before an imaginative crime board of evidence and profiler notes on the subject. "Say he is on the run, where would he go?"

Feeling as though he should know the answer, Jack eyed him keenly.

Thomas played devil's advocate. "Why *would* he run?"

They each looked to him as if to ask if he was serious.

"Well, he's a prisoner of war who has just escaped confinement," suggested McNaughton. "Of course, he's going to fucking run."

Once again with that logical brain of his, Thomas suggested the simplest of answers, deeming it the most rational. "No, I mean, think about it from his prospective: as far as he knows, he's home-free to Germany as of the 1st of May, right? It's in his best interest to stay shackled until they deport him for the exchange ... Running is, well, dumb."

During his brother's brainstorming, Churchill made eye contact with the veteran investigator. He was a man bound by obsessive complications, not too much unlike himself, and the two gents knew how similar they each were.

"The exchange was never a sure thing," McNaughton replied, theorizing the rationality from another point of view. As he did, it became apparent his inquest was merely buying time for Jack to shuffle the deck, coming out aces with the endgame; a ploy known only to him.

Jack declared as it became apparent. "The one that got away ..."

Churchill's attention raised, pinpointing McNaughton across from him. He had two cents. "He's not gone yet, Colonel."

In a flutter, Churchill shook his lost expression into a concentrated frown, drawing an elaboration. "No, not him! Nether Edge ..." he stated surely. "It's where he's headed. Trust me. For him, *she* is the one that got away ..."

McNaughton grunted, implying something unspoken.

He knew there was a lot existing within that history, perhaps even a love triangle, but he needed not pry. The evidence spoke for itself. Given that, he bowed a single, granting nod towards Churchill.

A regular Sherlock and Watson—they were on the same page.

The realization hit Thomas then after and his pose collapsed in on itself. It suddenly all made sense that Feind would go after his ex-wife (technically *wife* as they never became unbetrothed after her flight from fascism), especially now that he had been made aware of her existence in Sheffield, no thanks to Mad Jack's own ego.

"Let's mount up!" McNaughton declared, immediately jumping to action and searching his pockets for the car keys of his parked vehicle.

"Wait," Thomas composed with his hands out and brow raised. "This is all conjecture, is it not? We don't even know if that was his transport ... for all we know, he left earlier and is halfway across the country! Or he's still in that big crowd of Gerrys in the yard!"

Churchill and McNaughton weren't interested in those options.

They knew Feind. Knew the game. He was on the run—he had to be.

"You could be chasing shadows, gentlemen!" Thomas hollered after their unrestrained presumptions.

"I'm riding with you," Churchill said at McNaughton with certainty, ignoring his brother's esteemed logic. There was something sound about their theory about Nether Edge and it was binding.

"I'll get the car," McNaughton said without protest as he disappeared into the lot, moving quicker than Churchill had ever seen before. The scent of blood was in the water and this shark was on the hunt.

Jack kindly commanded to the group. "Mabel. Is there a telephone inside one of the offices that aren't ablaze? A landline of which we can call out?"

Mabel thought about it for a moment, eager to help. "Yes, I believe maybe the guardhouse on the other side. That whole wing should be fine."

"Good," Jack nodded at his brother. "Tom, go with Mabel. You know half the British Military—see if you can get a hold of anybody who knows somebody stationed at Attlebridge."

Thomas disputed. "Oi, hang on. You don't think we should get the warden to do another headcount first—before we go ahead and ignite a full-scale manhunt for this bloke in the middle of the night?!"

"And waste an hour or three playing duck, duck, goose?" Churchill scrunched his face. "There is no goose. The goose has already fled the coop. Time is against us. Every minute we waste, the closer he gets to crossing the Channel, and we can't have that!"

Thomas shook his head, wordlessly conceding.

"Get the RAF on the line. Tell them to ground any flights out in the next two days that Feind may have been scheduled for. Use whatever excuses you need. Find out who is in charge here from the local law enforcement, get them to put up a perimeter, and give them Feind's description. We want him caught dead or alive, but preferably the latter."

"*Dead or alive?* Okay, whatever you say, *John Wayne,*" he mocked as he rounded the car and met the delightful Mabel Blagbrough as she stood up beneath Garland's umbrella canopy, offering her his arm which she took with a grin.

"Hello," she greeted.

"Ma'am, grateful for your assistance. Please, lead the way."

Lastly ... *Rosamund.*

Right then, as Churchill addressed her remaining presence, McNaughton pulled up in his staff car, a hard top dark green *Minx tourer.* Garland collapsed her wet umbrella before climbing into the back seat behind the driver's side, wasting not a second.

McNaughton's window was down and the engine running, eager to become a comet along the quiet night backroads.

"Coming or staying?" Churchill offered with an open hand.

In the interim of Rosamund's response, Churchill watched Garland climb in and close the door before turning his face back to his displaced wife, joining McNaughton in mild exasperation.

Rosamund was even dressed the part for someone extremely out-of-place; a civilian in her dressing gown and slippers, she couldn't look any more of an émigré if she tried.

Standing behind it, she slammed shut the back door of Thomas' car, symbolically giving her answer. In case it wasn't enough, she added verbally: "Till death us do part, remember?"

A smile slowly crept into the corners of Churchill's mouth.

McNaughton tapped the horn to hurry them along, and Rosamund quickly and delicately trotted across the mud, dodging larger puddles and slosh before taking her husband's outstretched hand that guided her to the car—*but, she abruptly stopped ...*

In the sudden hiatus of her movement, Jack's smile faded and concern crept into his frown.

"What is it?" he asked, losing his happy sneer upon seeing Ros' expression alter into one of deep momentary thought. Whatever the concept was, it was one big enough to prompt her briefly returning to Thomas' car and risk stepping back in the puddles.

A moment later, she closed the door and reembarked after retrieving something that, quite frankly, she was surprised that her husband had forgotten about during all the fuss.

His claybeg sword.

Rosamund showed the belt-strapped device to Jack as she returned, feeding the four-foot sheathed weapon into the backseat of McNaughton's ride as she climbed in beneath Churchill's wing.

He shut the back door and entered the passenger's side front.

After they had both climbed in, the vehicle shot off the mark in the pursuit of justice ...

... into the nether.

Into the Nether

1942, April
Rundle Road
Nether Edge, Sheffield

It was midnight by the time their car reached the city limits of Nether Edge, nethertheless, the immediacy of the chase was yet to grow stale for those riding within McNaughton's hard top dark green Minx tourer.

Following the country-wide air raid, the small town was still awake with activity. This was not outlandish considering most of England had just persevered through yet another recent air raid threat. The threat of aerial attacks was becoming the new norm around the United Kingdom, as were many late nights with eyes peeled to the skies.

Although the shrill sensation of panic still resonated in the cool night air, from what they could tell, Sheffield had come out unscathed from any bombings. Needless to say, many of the shaken townsfolk were wide awake following the alarm. This community undoubtedly housed an air raid siren sounding off at the same time that Jack and Rosamund had heard the one in Dumbarton, disturbing everyone's peace.

Their hour-long car ride with the two Special Investigation Branch constables had been without verbal dispute. It had been without much of anything, in fact.

In the backseat, the women sat quietly.

Nothing exchanged but the occasional glance bartered between them, where upon one of the ladettes would catch the other's drawn gaze, capturing the fascinated eye set they each secretly had for one another. They were each a woman from another world and, due to a wild course of events and happenstance, were now seated side-by-side. Respectively, they found each other's domains interesting from a *grass-is-always-greener* point-of-view.

In the front, McNaughton finally spoke.

The entire trip, Churchill had surmised that there was something the old man investigator wanted to get off his chest. Something on the tip of his tongue. On several occasions during the quiet car travel, McNaughton had opened his mouth to speak, only to lose the words. A mere medically diagnosed hyperventilation, a digestion issue, or some sort of defence mechanism deep-seated within his mind prevented him from expelling any communications comprising of human sentiments. Upon a final attempt, McNaughton seemed to scale those walls ...

"My son ..." he finally started, taking the toothpick from his teeth and tossing it to the floormat. The slight pauses between his breaths exhibited indications of difficultly conveying his dialogue—and for obvious emotional reason. "How did he, eh ..."

Seated casually, Churchill panned his range around and faced the driver. He recognized this type of disclosure. It didn't need to be awkward or shy, granted, it was hard.

McNaughton's brow-flinching focus remained on the road, though he did manage to cast his commando passenger a gleam. His eyeline called for as much assistance in asking the question as they did the denial of an answer, for he did not want to hear.

Jack identified the internal struggle.

He surely did not owe McNaughton any favours, and thus he let him labour before assisting mercifully.

Churchill inhaled. Opened his mouth. Moved his lips to respond, only to have the words restrained by his brain, and he sighed. There was a sudden realization of the severity of description he knew of Scotty's death at the hands of Baade, and those details would hurt to be heard by someone who cared for the deceased.

Churchill censored. "Bravely."

McNaughton shot him an incensed look, then eyed the road.

"I'm not a sissy, Colonel," he responded strongly. Use of the phrase *sissy* caught Jack's attention ten-fold, albeit for alternate, personal reasons that typically resounded in a Glaswegian brogue. "Nor am I a weeping war widow, a tormented child, or ale of any such fragility you should feel the need to suppress detail. Tell me what you know and spare no detail."

Contemplating this, Churchill held his stare at McNaughton.

"Okay, then. He was *beheaded*. Decapitated by a Nazi with a sword," he informed, much to McNaughton's surprise. He may have thought he was ready to hear any graphic detail of his son's slaying, however he was not expecting that outcome.

In the silence, McNaughton deduced the visualization to himself.

It would have been disheartening and suppressed him thusly.

"It was quick," Jack consoled, though unfortunately he knew a little bit about decapitation, no thanks to (ironically) Orde Wingate's teachings. He remembered Wingate advising that the human head remains conscious for up to twenty seconds after severing at the stem of the neck. So, in all inaccuracies regarding decapitation meaning instant death, the head does remain briefly alive once severed from the body. It was entirely likely that Scotty stayed alive for a short while after his beheading, and it was unlikely that it was actually '*quick*'.

Although his attention to the road persisted, McNaughton's stare seemed clouded over after hearing the information. He readjusted his seating during the deafening silence between sentences.

"And this man, Baade ... you said he was dead, right?" whilst driving, he threw Churchill a sincere ogle, hungering for details to fill a void. "Tell me how he died."

This one, Jack had no reservations about conveying.

"During an ambush, Baade was *bludgeoned, shot, sliced,* and then eventually *blown up* by a rifle grenade which I saw be detonated at his feet."

"You're sure he's dead?"

Churchill cocked his head to cast him a certain gleam. "He's dead."

That last bit seemed like a forced reinforcement of fact.

It was the first time Jack Churchill had subliminally revealed to himself that he may not have believed Ernst-Günther Baade to be deceased and departed from this world ...

McNaughton was a remarkable detective.

Overqualified in perception, he possessed a natural knack for detecting deception, no matter how minute.

The tone of Jack's delivery and the silence that followed caused him to flick him a look, hinting of Churchill's unconscious uncertainty to the perceived truth.

Personally, the thought of Baade still surviving out there, existing to be castigated, somewhat excited McNaughton. This entire revelation was news to him, so he was indifferent to entertaining the fact Baade wasn't as deceased as Churchill had believed all these years.

Possessing the natural instinct to pry, McNaughton probed with his eyes upon the road. "You encountered Baade in Switzerland in early 1940 after first having an initial run-in with Feind in Oslo in 1939. That's, what, a period of six months ...?"

Churchill's stare intensified out the window. "About that, yes."

He felt McNaughton cast him a few looks between watching the road. There was a pause of suspense between his follow-up question that Churchill could not help but feel intimidated by, almost as if he was challenging his truths.

Jack finally faced him. "Just what are you probing at?"

"Nothing. *Small world,* perhaps," McNaughton faced the windshield while Churchill took a turn studying the investigator's expression. "You ever wondered how much of a coincidence it is; that Feind knew Baade? How, in that interim, he happened to tell his mentor of the English geezer who tried to swordfight him in Oslo, and that Baade remembered that detail? Enough to remember it and place it as you ...?"

"I've been told I have a memorable persona," Jack deflected.

"No. Really."

"Small world," Jack shrugged, agreeing with his prior statement.

Unconvinced, McNaughton murmured. "Mm-hmm."

Churchill faced the passenger's side window.

McNaughton was right.

Something did not add up in the timeline between Feind and Baade crossing paths and the opportunities of their shared communiqué. It was far more likely that Baade did not perish that day in 1940 and that he lived on to see and converse with Feind somewhere in-between, hence they would have *both* known Mad Jack Churchill mutually.

Up until very recently, the thought of Baade still existing in this world had never crossed his mind. Churchill remarked rationally out the window before turning to face McNaughton. "Well, I guess we can ask the fiend in a minute, eh? When we catch the bastard."

McNaughton bobbed his head, hopeful, though it took a lot to get this seasoned veteran excited for a bust. This whole thing was a long shot, not to mention, a stretch.

"Whole lot of nothing out here," he remarked topically. "Good place for somebody to disappear, huh ...?"

Churchill's eyeline defocused, detecting a topical segue by the master detective.

"How is it that you came about Feind's wife?"

"He told me. You're not the only expert interrogator around these parts, Constable," Churchill admitted to McNaughton's surprise, and he chortled at the response.

Again, Jack's view wandered out of the passenger's side window, viewing the passing nightscape. McNaughton was right—Nether Edge truly was out in the middle of nowhere.

"An accidental slip up, no doubt."

"No, actually," Churchill's brow cocked. "He thought he'd lost her forever ... he pursued her family's defection for a while before giving up. Searched for years, spared no expense. Even sent an expert hunter-killer known as a bloodhound after her."

"A *Bluthund?*" McNaughton questioned, familiar with the term for such an operative. Bluthunds were expert investigators, usually trained assassins, commissioned by and at the disposal of Nazi Germany, usually under the sphere of the Abwehr. They were embedded English-speaking sleeper operatives. If Feind had sent an asset after his estranged wife and her family's prevarication into England, and he had turned up empty-handed, then her scent had truly vanished.

Churchill nodded at the fact; unknowing just how lucky Scarlet was to have disappeared so cleanly—and survived.

McNaughton torqued his neck with certainty. "She's fortunate, then. Bluthunds usually find the scent and see it through."

"She was right beneath his nose all along," Churchill remarked solemnly, and his brow tightened. "As he was, ours."

On tight approach of the Nether Edge address, Churchill rode high in the passenger's seat. His tiring yet observant sterling stare scanned the moonlit darkened outskirts of town in nearly the same manner he had the entire trip from Lancashire, searching for any scampering persons. He was driven by a dedicated retribution, and it was keeping him wide awake and roused, fuelling him like caffeine.

His gaze examined the foggy haze floating above every empty gloomy paddock, every connecting roadway, every nook and cranny, searching for a lone interloper to possibly identify as one Friedrich Feind, but instead, only finding the flurry of scampering stray cats and scattering rodents. The whole circumstance reminded Churchill of the years prior to Operation Archery, such as his forays through France, L'Épinette, Dunkirk, and eventually Vågsøy—where his path finally *did* cross with Feind—and how he would subconsciously search for his face in every battlefield ...

Only now it was different.

Now, he knew for sure he was out there.

"Well, this is disconcerting ..." stated McNaughton upon their eventual arrival out front of the residence of Joan Witherby, aka Scarlet Kristina. Of all the houses they had passed, almost all of them had their lights on; the occupants, awake, some even standing on their front lawns, talking with neighbours, all with their eyes trained to the skies ... the Witherby address, however ...

... not a single light on.

... not a curtain undrawn.

T'was ominous as fuck.

Snipping the lights on their decidedly silent approach, McNaughton soon killed the engine, gliding them into a soft brake and perpendicular park across the driveway entrance along Rundle Road. Once stopped, he quietly popped open his door, as did Garland and Churchill with their tactical awareness dialled in. Rosamund was a step behind, way out of her league now that this eerie circumstance had suddenly developed ...

They kept their voices down and their actions soft, beholding deadly intent.

"Stay here, darling," Churchill directed as he prepared to climb out. Like the two law enforcers within their company, his grave frown was fixated on the house up the sloped driveway and front lawn. His brow retained a certain seriousness, preparing for action, for apprehension of the suspect at large.

From beneath his jacket layer, McNaughton drew his trusty Colt Detective snub-nosed revolver from a concealed hip holster. He turned to Garland, who had presented a small Beretta pistol from her clutch handbag.

As it got serious, Constable McNaughton instructed: "Stay here. Get the Mod 11 from the boot and watch our backs."

Garland nodded obediently, rearing up and preparing to lean against the concealment of the vehicle beside Rosamund, keeping the civilian army wife safe in the process.

"*Mod 11?*" Rosamund questioned in a whisper.

Garland said not a word, weaving around her and accessing the trunk of the Minx tourer. Within were the usual peripherals one would expect to see in a Government car, the foremost being a Remington Model 11-48 semi-automatic twelve-gauge shotgun slung in a canvas sheath harnessed to the underside of the boot lid.

Garland huffed, tucking away her pistol in order to retrieve the heavy, clunky piece. She wasn't overly a fan of the big gun, but such was protocol in circumstances such as these.

She brought it around, softly closing the trunk door and resting it in her arms across the bonnet of the car. Her only response to Rosamund's question was a cast gleam from her sentry posting; a deathly stare soon to be across the iron sights of the weapon, awaiting a target.

On the lawn, McNaughton maintained his gun at hip level, preparing to trot towards the house. He fired a question back at Churchill as he sidled beside him on the grass turf. "You got my six or what?"

After a lack of response, he paused in his preparedness, looking back over his shoulder for Churchill who was apparently taking his time. He realized this was due to him retrieving something from the backseat of the car ...

His claybeg sword.

Churchill attached the peripheral to his hip via a complicated drop-leg leather holster strap, feeding an eyelet with his finger and drawing it tight, eventually upping the curb and positioning himself alongside McNaughton.

"Are you having a laugh?" McNaughton asked with his hands out, holding the revolver casually on his palm for a moment.

Rather than reply, Churchill merely drew his four-foot sword, reaffirming his fingers through the eyelets with a deadly grip. He made eye contact with McNaughton but offered no verbal response, only nodding, singly that he was ready to fight.

McNaughton shook his head.

The two wasted not another second.

They took to the sloped driveway in the dark of night, approaching the potentially hostile house: McNaughton with his pistol at the ready, Churchill with his sword out by his side.

Utilizing the newly established *cup-and-saucer* tactic of supporting the shooting hand with a spare hand, the fedora-clad McNaughton moved forwards behind the defence of his gun that scanned the environment in front of him like a searchlight beam.

Beneath his signature green beret, Churchill supported his sword grip, holding it up and before his right shoulder and forming a defensive '*roof guard*' posture which came in over the top of his comrade. The stance was outside of typical fencing posture, in which the swordsman used both hands, but at least this way, he was ready for anything in a high stance.

As they reached the front steps, still in complete darkness and disconcerting, suspenseful silence, McNaughton cast back to Churchill a look. The rain had long since passed, which meant the glistening on the old man's forehead was from him breaking a sweat from the pressure.

"Take the back," he whispered with a sling of his head. Where they were right now, the concrete driveway continued alongside the neighbour's fence and presumably to the backyard where there was a shelter and what appeared to be a clothesline. Again, minimal light.

Churchill frowned and looked him up and down.

There was no way that he was taking the reserve role on this one.

"*You* take the back. I'm taking the front."

"I'm the one with the firearm, Colonel. I'll take the front," McNaughton argued in a hiss.

Churchill was unmoving.

He did not know how to lead from the back.

After encountering stiff opposition, McNaughton rolled his eyes.

Breaking their operational stalemate, they heard an audible creak from within the residence: evidence of somebody not only lurking within the intentionally dark premises, but probably aware of their presence.

Chilled to the core, the two bartered a glance. The noise had not been either one of them, and the lights remained off inside. It hailed as suspicious.

"Both take the front, then?" Churchill compromised.

The two were quick to respond to the noise, both leaping up and onto the front porch beneath the awning and into dense dimness, taking a tactical knee. McNaughton did so with his shoes tapping the step up and Churchill scaled the garden, leaping the two-foot gap. Both men hugged the walls between windows on either side of the front door.

Churchill glared across at McNaughton with wide eyes.

This was a situation he had not expected to find himself in four hours ago when he was balls-deep in his wife.

Each man, respectively, was not unfamiliar with how to breach a boarded-up hole, however both men were trained to do so marginally differently to reflect different situations. Given these were domestic circumstances and not a battlefield in a warzone, Churchill appeared to let McNaughton take point in this urban instance. He cast him a bowing gesture, implying to take charge ...

"This is the authorities!" McNaughton shouted. "We are armed!"

Whilst he announced their presence, Churchill lowered his blade and inched diagonally along the porch, attempting to peak through the edge of a glass window, nearly able to see into the home between the wall and the curtain. There was a warm glow resonating from inside, possibly from a gas lantern or a small lamp within a connecting ro—

There was abrupt motion inside!

Footsteps. Running.

Something clothed in pale clothes crossed his view and the movement was accompanied by soft treads on floorboards which both he and McNaughton heard and distinguished.

"I got movement ..." Jack reported in accord, adjusting his view and standing alongside the window beside the door.

McNaughton's hand reached beneath the creaky flyscreen entry and felt the wooden doorknob, giving it a jiggle. It appeared to be locked internally. He repeated a similar announcement from before.

"This is the authorities! We're coming in!" he shouted sternly. His voice was loud in the quiet of night, setting off a neighbour's dog nearby who barked repetitively.

He stood tall, opening the screen door fully as Churchill pushed off the wall and crossed paths, leaping back down onto the lawn. He took up a position directly aligned with the door.

"Allow me!" he declared with good manners. McNaughton obliged and watched Jack launch up the front steps and fly kick his boot into the flat of the door beside the twist handle, driving with weighted force.

With a boisterous burst and fracture of splintering wood from around the locking mechanism, the door flung wide open from the vigour of Churchill's boot, smashing into a piece of situated furniture on the opposite side, noisily breaking something decorative. The action made a disturbance followed by deafening silence that incited suspense.

Gloved sword at guard, Jack took three steps in as quietness resonated following their forced entry. He raised his bladed weapon with a metallic *swing*, striking an offensive pose with nobody to stab. There was nobody present. No welcoming or unwelcoming party.

Behind him, McNaughton brought up the rear, scanning past him with the sights of his revolver. They were between the space of a tight, dim hallway and connecting carpeted living room. Other than the glow from a lamp located on a timber side table in the room, the place was cloaked in an eerie darkness. Down a hallway stretch, there appeared to be another light on in a kitchen area.

The two men held their position at the entrance for an extended moment of surveillance, listening for any response to their access. So far, there had been nothing. With vigilance, they advanced to secure the area.

They separated.

McNaughton moved in and right, letting close the screen door as he stepped onto the soft carpeted living room with his handgun cupped before him. The living room was decorated with a luxurious lounge piece with fluffy pillows and an extinguished stone fireplace built into the exterior wall. It seemed to loop around into a dining room that was alit with residual light from the kitchen at the back of the house.

Instances of pareidolia constantly stimulated the men as in the dim and darkened indoors, perceptions of various ornaments and curtains occasionally mimicked people.

"Miss Witherby?!" McNaughton announced, proceeding through the room with caution, sweeping from behind his gun. "Joan Witherby, are you here?!"

In an alternate direction, Churchill took an extra step in the direction of the narrow, opaque hallway, decisively branching from McNaughton's advance.

"*Scarlet?!*" he asked in a friendlier tone, utilizing her real name with hopes of gaining a more trusted response. A lack of any reply by her was concerning. He tried again: "*Hullo?! It's me, Jack!*"

He stepped into a carpeted room on the opposite side of the hall, believed to be the master bedroom. The space felt vacant; however, Jack could not help but travel back through time at the redolent scent of Scarlet's perfume that lingered in the aroma of the air. He had flashes of his younger and less experienced self, of the Norwegian sunrays, the excitement of the Oslo games, and the dangerous enticement of the Queen of Sweden. She had a hold of him then—perhaps she always will. Whilst his nostrils breathed the scent in again, Jack's eyelids closed over like he had become inhibited; possessed by a memory. As though it were the first time he saw Scarlet's serene hazel stare, spliced by traces of emerald-green. Entranced in smell memory, his glare traced over her plump yet sharp lips, professionally outlined by geranium red lipstick. Tall, her golden blonde hair danced beneath a stylish wide brimmed hat that feinted a pseudo-halo of shade, which only added to her angelic appearance. An hourglass physique was incredibly bound in a Fontainebleau-like summer gown, draped over an inescapable high-chest cleavage that eclipsed all other vision.

He was momentarily mesmerized.

It was fortunate that there had not been an armed assailant waiting to spring an attack from within the shades of that bedroom, for he would have fallen prey as an easy target.

After a few seconds, he fought the overpowering sensation, tearing himself back to reality and surveying the scene strategically, searching the environment for threats and hostiles.

In the living room, McNaughton inched his way towards the glow of the connecting kitchen space. Slowly creeping towards the light, his fedora-attired head scanned low left and open right, aware of any places between furniture in the dark where somebody could be lying in wait or hiding.

Revolver now up by his head with both hands, finger wrapped around the trigger, he finally rounded the wall and into the growing source of light. Carpet met tile flooring. The illumination from the kitchen lit up his face as he entered in a strafe behind his gun's righteous aim as he allowed for it to once again lead the way. Across the kitchen space, there appeared to be laundry and backdoor access to his side as he quietly coasted. Just the wind, but a tap of a hinged door followed by a whistle caught his attention at his flank and he panned his guns arms just to be sure ...

Right as McNaughton scanned offside, a nimble bodied individual appeared to rise up from hiding below the kitchen counter ahead of his progression and launched off the mark like a sprinter, vanishing into the dark hallway and headed straight towards where Jack had ventured.

"*Freeze!*" he shouted, whipping his aim back around but too slow to train his sights, let alone even identify who he had just heard and seen in a slither of motion. McNaughton lifted his gun arms skywards and jogged quickly in pursuit ...

In the bedroom, the daydream-free Jack Churchill heard McNaughton's shout, and he immediately stepped back into the hall in time to see the same silhouette of a hunched, short figure duck into another connecting room between them. McNaughton appeared in the light of the kitchen in the absence of the person, and the two men converged on either end of the doorway like two arms of a tightening vice grip.

Hearts pounding, they each hugged the wall beside the doorframe, respective blade and bullet weaponry at the ready ...

Outside in the moonlight and in the quiet suspense, the overcoated Viviane Garland and dressing gown-clad Rosamund Churchill remained safe on the opposite side of the parked staff car.

Garland had her arms poised across the roof of the government vehicle, leaning gracefully whilst cradling the large Remington shotgun, keeping a trained aim while continually surveying the quiet house.

With an equally focused stare, Rosamund shared her duty.

It had been over two minutes since their respective partners had entered the premises, vanishing into the void of potential hazard, into the nether, and officially into harm's way. The anticipation was overbearing to say the least, especially for Rosamund.

She stood alongside Garland with an expression of eagerness, toying mindlessly with the wedding ring on her left hand while her focus remained glued to the Nether Edge property. Much weighed on her mind right now, taking a lot away from the suspense of the current situation. Friedrich Feind was a bad guy and needed to be stopped, yes, but there was more to her yearning of his capture ...

... his apprehension would free her man, reasserting his mindset to calm. They could go back to normal and peacefully progress.

... his evasion would condemn Jack, putting him back on the same unstoppable warpath hitherto the recent life-altering decisions.

But not only that. There was no discounting from whose house it was they had ventured: *the one that got away.* She was likely about to come face-to-face with Scarlet Kristina.

"You want the gun once we get in there?" Garland asked out of the blue, breaking the ice as well as Rosamund's deep chain of thought. Contextually, she must have been playing even though her tone of voice was serious.

Rosamund frowned, confused. "Sorry?"

"Once we get inside, I mean?" Garland cryptically elaborated, momentarily taking her eyes off the prize to seemingly mess with the innocent Mrs. Churchill. "You know where we are, eh? That's your husband's mistress in there ... *the other woman,*" she tempted further, doing well to hide her mischievous, shit-stirring grin. Garland curtsied her neck as she returned her view forwards. "I know how I would react if I ever found out my husband was cheating on me—if I had time for a man, that is."

Garland felt Rosamund's retorting stare, and so she finished her rhetorical *what-if* with a rather large and impactful exclamation mark and use of indecorous profanity and savagery.

"I'd cut his bloody pecker off ... and punt her in the cunt."

Rosamund's brow dissolved into a firm scowl at the horrible statement and foul language. Even *she* was no lady, but that was extremely unladylike. Surely even sailors didn't swear so vulgarly.

Silence ensued.

Across the gun, Garland ogled her shocked expression. "What?!"

Rosamund recovered from her recoil. "Bit crude, was it not? Besides, it's not like that with my Jack," she defended her man with the truth, finding both physical and emotional comfort stability.

"If he's got a penis, then I've got a spoiler warning for you, darl."

"No, really," Rosamund expounded, more assured than anything in the world. "Jack told me all about her and their history. It's complicated, but noth—"

"*Nothing happened?*" Garland finished her sentence but as a question. "Yeah, right, darl. Trust me, your husband's a male and men are liars and cheats. They're all the same. I can guarantee you, he fucked that broad in there. Smashed her more times than you have your little toe on the coffee table. Probably harder, too."

Frown forming further, Rosamund studied the outrageous specimen with a shotgun for a moon-lit minute. Viviane Garland spoke her mind. She was truly either a force to be reckoned with, or a cold-hearted bitch. Maybe both, somewhat admirably.

She was a woman with some respectable qualities; a strong, independent, and powerful female in a commendable position of power. A pretty little thing on the outside, she said it how it was, with no filter. She was hardly the first female law enforcer; however, her existence was still a massive minority in the field. Given all of that, her astuteness and offer of wisdom should have been an easy pill to swallow for any susceptible woman in her right mind. Although her tone was convincing and she did have a certain experienceable and relatable charisma about her, Rosamund was not as persuaded as most vulnerable women would have been given the circumstances. She knew her Jack and trusted him.

In turn, she stated with a certain solidarity and, this time, a double entendre. "You *clearly* don't know Jack."

Thinking her unpersuasively naïve and too stubborn to yield, Garland simply grew a smirk over her face. "Why don't you just wait in the car, darl. Let the professionals handle this scene, yeah?" she issued condescendingly.

Not far from seeing red, Rosamund scoffed. "Do you know *if* and *when* a professional shall be arriving? Right now, it's looking pretty scarce, *darl.*"

Garland bit her lip to hide a smile. It wasn't often somebody—let alone, a female—bit back the way Rosamund did. She whipped her a partially defeated expression, alluring to her subverted expectations. "You sure there isn't a dastardly dame hidin' somewhere inside you, *miss Denny?*"

"It's *Churchill!*"

Garland shrugged. "We'll see."

Stare intensifying, Rosamund grimaced with repulsion; at both the swear words and the notion. Offence not taken lightly, she shook her head wordlessly.

Offering her nothing short of a smug smirk, Garland focused up, watching the house across the sights of the big fucking shotgun. It was then she realized that there was a figure in gumboots casually trotting across the lawn from the neighbouring property, now upping the front step and lingering just outside the kicked open door.

It was a blonde woman in a white dressing gown.

"*Oh, shit!*" Garland cussed, leaving her guard post and running after the motion they had apparently let slip by. Swinging the shotgun in her strides, she commanded to her unarmed sidekick: "Come on, darl!"

Inside the dubious Witherby residence, Churchill and McNaughton were perched on either side of a doorway. Silently, the two men counted down from three to tactically breach the room in which their elusive intruder had evaded them moments ago.

Mutely, McNaughton counted with his fingers.

Three ...

Two ...

One!

Rolling around the doorframe on his shoulder, McNaughton stabbed his hands into the room, cupping his revolver, whilst Churchill simultaneously entered with an en garde fencing stance, blade tip first. Both egos barely fit through the doorway in uniformed unison.

Locked on target, the armed duo froze rigid ...

A single, lone figure standing idle in the room, partially hiding behind a small bed—a child's bed—stooped lower behind cover, trembling in fear and whimpering beneath wheezing breaths.

The young fella was scared out of his wits, shivering.

He was around three-feet tall, dressed in striped terrycloth pyjamas, with a sock half off one foot.

The two scary men shouted instructions from their offensive stances.

"*Freeze!*"

"*Don't move!*"

Both their sets of eyes grew wide, their faces flat.

Before any reveal could be made ...

Before any explanation could be mustered ...

... an unexpected, unknown woman came running up the front steps outside the home, jingling house keys. With a confused way about her, she boldly reefed the screen whilst taking in the broken wooden doorway and the splintery mess in the hall. All the debris carnage could not have amassed to the fear she was experiencing regarding the safety of her son. She had left him in the house to sleep while she had traversed next door to have a chat with her friendly neighbour ensuing the conundrum of the false air raid alarm, and their subsequent reemergence from the shared bomb shelter in his backyard.

With half of her blonde locks still wrapped in curlers and nightgown swathed in an almond-brown dressing gown, the panicked face of Scarlet Kristina burst through the doorway, eyes wide and panting in panic.

"*Brutus?!*" she cried in a puzzled whine whilst concurrently realizing who was in her house as Churchill and his cohort stepped back into the hall, observing her untimely entry.

Swiftly, all the falling puzzle pieces landed into place.

"*Jack?!*" Scarlet questioned as their stares locked in the gloom of the low light—her green eyes were glassy with shock. She clutched at her chest, covering her pounding heart.

"Scarlet!" Churchill responded in a reassuring tone, lowering his heavy sword and swapping hands, disengaging his fingers from the intimidating knuckleduster eyelets. "Are you okay?! Where were you?!"

"What do you mean! What are you doing here?!"

Jack stepped over to calm her with his touch.

"Scarlet, it's not safe—"

With a confused frown upon her scrunched face as emotion overcame her, Scarlet's gaze lit up as her son, Brutus, suddenly exploded out from between the two men, running towards her at a force stronger than gravity.

Scarlet dropped to her knees in order to collect the tearful young boy in pyjamas as he collapsed into her open arms. She embraced him tenderly, cradling his collapse, sheltering him from the frightful scenario they had found themselves in this night.

Whilst McNaughton and Churchill watched the warm hug from the hallway, they saw Garland and Rosamund come trotting up the driveway and onto the front porch. Although they had had one job, Scarlet had seemingly slipped by their sentry, luckily without incident—and clearly not under any duress from Feind.

... he wasn't here ...

For both the women, it was a comforting and heartening sight to see a mother reunited with her child during a moment of panic and despair, however succinct.

For the men, the sight raised more questions than answers.

It meant their man was not here ...

... and that this was yet another dead end.

The minutes that passed following the bitterly disappointing conclusion seemed more like hours. The reticence insulated the pace to the point of complete cessation void of composition.

Their long strides of pursuit had decelerated.

In due process, Scarlet Kristina calmed and tucked her son back in bed, and whatever of the bedtime routine was kept as natural as possible. Once finished, she emerged in the lounge room where Churchill and his wife, and McNaughton and his partner were each seated with fresh brews of steaming tea—a consensus that saw each beverage mostly untouched. This wasn't out of incivility or discourtesy, simply put there was too much at stake to enjoy a drink.

Brimming exposition was due to follow.

Both Churchill and McNaughton took turns informing Scarlet that her estranged Nazi husband, Friedrich Feind, had escaped from a local prison and was on the loose, and that he may have become aware of her existence during his internment. She was advised to close and bolt all doors and windows following their visit here tonight and to remain alert, yet it did seem that Feind had not ventured here following his escape from Oldham.

After the discussion, Churchill followed Scarlet into the bright light of the tiled kitchen. She had withdrawn to tip out the contents of her midnight-hour visitors' beverages and wash up. He poised on the opposite side of the wooden counter, chatting to her as casually as could be, although the whole circumstance was unnatural.

"I've been meaning to say thank you for the parcel."

"It's fine. I'm glad you got it," she replied at a bashful beam, running water from the sink faucet. She still appeared rather emotional.

Jack furthered, wishing to achieve comfort through consolation. She had to know that it was instrumental to the war effort. "The contents within were instrumental in us discovering something integral about your husband ..."

Holding her hand under the running stream, Scarlet's cheek crinkled as she scrunched her expression. Something about what Churchill had just said provoked repulsion and she immediately riposted, addressing it. "Can you *not* refer to him as that?"

"Your husband?" Jack catechized whilst self-reflecting. He realized why, answering his own question, and nodded understandably. "Of course." He changed the topic to something less official. "I, eh ... wasn't aware that you had a son ...?"

Scarlet gleamed. It was a tainted solacement to her former predicament, however, she did not appear to want to elaborate.

"Is he his ...?"

She nodded, causing a tear to drop from her closed eyes.

"A final parting gift before my defection."

"Does he know ...?"

Scarlet shook her head.

In that moment Constable McNaughton entered the kitchen via the hall, partially intruding. He had been talking something over with Garland in the other room and had even removed his fresh toothpick in order to appear more professional.

"Sorry for the interruption. Colonel, a word?"

"Fine-o-fine," Churchill remarked, casting Miss Kristina a comfortable smirk before removing himself from her eavesdropping range, following McNaughton back into the lamp-lit living room.

After the men left the kitchen, Rosamund Churchill appeared from the shadows of the dark connecting hallway, appearing in the peripheries of the sniffling Scarlet Kristina cleaning at the sink. She clogged the drainage hole with a plug, preparing to wash up the cups piled on the bench.

They were alone.

Rosamund froze for a moment upon laying eyes on Scarlet.

This discreet interaction was most outlandish and unnatural, but she decided to break through the barriers of the typical resentment marginalization. She was better than that.

She continued into the light of the kitchen and Scarlet became aware of her presence with a mild startle, throwing her a look past her shoulder.

Rosamund halted, unsure if she was welcome ...

Scarlet noticed her hesitation and gave an awkward smile followed by a nod of approval for Jack's wife to converse with her.

There was a hanging tea towel on the handle to the oven, and Rosamund collected it whilst moving beside Scarlet who remained facing forwards, rummaging porcelain cups below the surface of the sink water. She clearly knew that Rosamund was Jack's wife and felt both embarrassed and probably threatened by her to some extent.

"Here," Rosamund presented a hand, reaching out for a clean cup with the towel, offering to help dry up.

Extenuated by the redness from her cried eyes, Scarlet's exquisite emerald-greens flickered to her with an obvious uncertainty and discomfort. "Thanks."

Without another word exchanged for a full twenty seconds, they toiled over the basin, washing and drying, side-by-side.

On the last clean cup Scarlet passed to Ros before draining the sink and drying her hands, she noticed the sparkling wedding ring on her finger, bringing the elephant in the room to addressment.

"How long have you been married?" Scarlet asked.

Rosamund paid note to her ring and it being the catalyst of the personal questionnaire by her husband's *one that got away*. It was a surreal circumstance, the contemplation of which meant there was an unnaturally long pause between question and answer which led to Scarlet feeling that she may have overstepped.

Embarrassed, she shut herself down. "Sorry, I—"

"No, not at all," Rosamund brushed it off, taking her time drying this last teacup. She looked Scarlet in the eye, noticing her anxiety on the topic and coming to realize that she had nothing to fear about this goldilocks gal, and it was about time Scarlet Kristina knew that too. "A year."

Her honest response broke a little bit more of the ice.

"That's nice," Scarlet responded. "I am happy for you ..."

Rosamund observed Scarlet as she cast a gleam from the kitchen to Jack in the living room. There was an underlining longing behind her gaze. Rosamund detected it all in a heartbeat: if things had been vastly different regarding their first impressions, they may have even ended up together. It pained her to envision it, even involuntarily, but they were a good match and there was an obvious chemistry existing in the afterglow. Though, she clearly had a type for sword-wielding soldiers. Rosamund had never met or even seen Friedrich Feind, but she remembered Jack had referenced how similar of a man he was to him, born of another nation. Believably, this was why they fleshed so well as mortal enemies, and was the reason for whatever attraction to have existed here with them both and Scarlet Kristina.

"For you both," Scarlet added, returning to Ros. "You're very—"

"*Lucky?*" Rosamund accidentally snapped and it caused Scarlet to again consider ceasing in her dialogue. She was very much on the edge of complete reluctancy to further anymore of this conversation, the discomfort was overwhelming.

"Eh, I was going to say *beautiful* ..." she replied hesitantly.

The compliment came as a surprise to Rosamund, as she was standing there, again basking in the natural bombshell beauty that Scarlet possessed, writhe with jealousy.

Scarlet instead paid a commendation followed by a twist of phrase that won her over indefinitely. "*Jack* is the lucky one," she offered with a beam that instigated Ros' own expression of contentment. The two shared a sensible, sisterhood chuckle.

Meanwhile, Churchill had followed McNaughton into the carpeted living room, where their conversation became conducted secluded from certain ears.

"Constable?"

McNaughton faced Jack, reinserting his pick between his teeth, speaking with it gyrating like an ore from the starboard side. He already knew this wouldn't be what the overly protective army colonel wanted to hear. "We're going to have to bring her in for a debrief."

Churchill tilted his head at that absurdity. "Pardon?"

"Colonel, she's profoundly implemented in all of this," McNaughton rationalized, removing his toothpick when it got serious. After all, there were protocols which he was sworn to uphold. "She's entangled in the roots, deeper than she even realizes. She could be guilty of knowing certain things."

Jack was stern, being sure to keep his voice down. "The only thing that poor girl in there is guilty of is successfully escaping the Third Reich and the fascist Nazi regime!"

"She's the spouse of a Nazi! Collaboration is collaboration."

"She defected for a reason, *Jethro!*"

"Doesn't change the facts, *Jack!*"

"And what about her son, huh?! He a Nazi collaborator, too?"

"What did you think was going to happen, here, Colonel? You'd keep some secret muse of the suburbs to *debrief* on your own accord?"

"That's not how it is, and you know it!" Churchill balled a fist and pointed. They were revisiting a familiar territory with that insinuation of infidelity.

"I'm sorry, but that's just the way it must go. It's procedure."

"*You're sorry?*" Churchill outburst. He had always feared this outcome coming to fruition regarding how the wings of British Intelligence got things done. She could be mistreated by his government if she was brought in, hence why he wanted to debrief her privately. Safely.

The telephone bell resounded in the background of their argument before it could get any more heated. It was a call to this extension which they had been greatly anticipating.

"I'm just following protocol, here ..." McNaughton explained as Garland entered the lounge room in the backdrop of their discordance. The commandeered home phone abruptly stopped ringing once she answered it, putting the caller on hold.

"Excuse me, sirs," she interrupted, jerking her chin at Churchill; her green-eyed stare with golden flecks blinking profusely. "It's for Colonel Churchill."

Churchill swapped one last look with McNaughton before vacating their stand-off, tending to Scarlet's private telephone on the edge of the hall of which they had requisitioned for official use this evening.

"This isn't over," he stated prior to disengaging. Churchill collected the microphone and earpiece thusly from Garland, who left to converse discreetly with McNaughton about their predicament of due diligence. "Tom? What have you got for me?"

"*Jack, it's Thomas.*"

Churchill's eyes blinked in a flutter. His brother's telephone etiquette left a lot to be desired.

Who else could it have been?

"Yes, I realize that."

"*I finally heard from my friend in the RAF...*"

"Go on ..."

"Well, he didn't know anything about any prisoner exchanges," Thomas Churchill informed, still present at the Glenn Mill guardhouse office, utilizing their landline. The fires were mostly out and order had been restored. "However, after some digging around and calls being made—thankfully everyone is still up after the air raid—I managed to find out that your man, Friedrich Feind, is already long gone, Jack."

"... p-pardon me? What do you mean long gone?"

"Yes, I'm afraid that it wasn't just the prisoner transfer that was brought ahead ... they moved the whole darned thing forwards; discharge, departure, everything. His flight left yesterday morning at dawn ..."

"*... he's long gone, Jack.*"

Back at the Nether Edge residence, the news fell upon Churchill like a planetary weight. He collapsed beneath it.

He had an audience comprised of men and women nearly as eager as he was in finding out news on the capture of Feind. From differing points of origin, they had each stopped what they were doing to observe Churchill on the telephone.

Whatever the news, it was not good.

They watched as the beret-clad character revolved around into the gloom of Scarlet's hallway, hiding his faltering expression. Pressing his back against the wallpaper, Churchill nearly slid down the sheer surface upon receiving the bad news from his informative brother and his PIU and RAF connections. His body language said it all.

"*Jack?*" Thomas' voice could be heard questioning on the other end of the phone line. "*Jack ...? Hello ...? Jack, does that mean I can go home now?*"

Churchill let the earpiece drop from his head as he fell victim to a momentary lapse in conviction. He recovered fast, raising the piece back to his head and speaking into the mic.

"Thank you, Tom. That will be all," he managed to communicate—rather impassively—before abruptly hanging up the telephone, left in a pool of silence to process the intelligence he just had dropped upon him.

In the blurry background of his collapsing stance, Rosamund Churchill was the only one who strode nearer from the anxious living room crowd. She waited a moment, observing her husband's noticeable demise in the seclusion of the dark hallway after receiving what could only be the worst news.

"Jack?" she questioned before lowering herself to the same height as her husband's dramatic stance. She collected the telephone pieces and gently interlocked them properly, then placed a hand on his shoulder.

"He's gone ..." let alone to everybody else, Churchill remarked unto himself. The realization caused him to contemplate reality for an extended moment, almost oblivious to his wife's presence. In the meantime, McNaughton and Garland respectfully entered the vicinity, overseeing Churchill's broken stance. Scarlet Kristina did the same from the kitchen via the connecting hallway, still holding a damp tea towel in her midst.

Jack explained for all their benefits, finally becoming more aware of his enclosing surroundings. "They moved the prisoner exchange forwards. Feind left the United Kingdom yesterday morning ... he's already returned to Germany, and will soon return to circulation ..."

Stunned, Scarlet Kristina wasn't sure how to feel.

On the one side, she was relieved that he was no longer in the country, therefore no longer a proximity threat to either her or her son, but on the other hand, she had a soul after all ... She realized that having such an evil soldier of his calibre back in service for the opposing force of a world war was not a good thing.

In the lamp-lit living room, Garland exchanged a sly look with McNaughton. This news was also a rather big hiccup for their investigation's jurisdiction, not to mention for those at the Criminal Investigation Department tracing the serpent syndicate contingency. Capturing and questioning Feind would have been their first real bit of evidence supporting the validity of the group—maybe their only, ever.

In the deafening silence, Rosamund caressed Churchill's sleeve, consoling him in this prolonged trice of burdensome disappointment. She felt for her husband and what he must have been feeling knowing that his most confidently captured, hated enemy was suddenly gone with the wind.

That *other* thing weighed even heavier on her mind now ...

Rosamund could see it in Jack's thousand-yard stoical stare ...

He had alluded to quitting the army ...

... but he would chase this villain to the ends of the earth.

No matter what blessings were bestowed upon their home, nothing could keep Jack Churchill from returning to battle. She could already tell that no matter how one framed this picture, it was of war.

"Flights in and out of England have been delayed a lot as of late, due to the bombings," although McNaughton was accepting of the news, the contrarian in him had an opinion to voice. He reinserted his toothpick. His unintentional positivity seemed to prop up Churchill, breathing air into his lungs like a dose of oxygen to an asphyxiating victim.

"What are you saying?"

"Well, it's entirely possible he's still stationed on-base. In England."

The resuscitation returned Mad Jack's soul behind his piercing blue eyes, and they fluttered, processing the validation.

The thought, as well, had crossed Churchill's mind ...

Right when they thought it was over!

Jack blinked about himself, waking up from this sudden onset of melancholy. He pressed up to a standing posture and returned the gesture of soft touch to his wife as he looked from her and to McNaughton, his eyes still on the prize for whatever little worth was left. Fact was, if they earmarked rationality for a moment of optimism, and suggested that Feind was at RAF Attlebridge due for a dawn departure yesterday, even something as insignificant as a twenty-four-hour delay meant they had a new deadline of dawn this coming morning.

The clock was ticking ...

The sun was rising ...

"If that is the case, Jack, and your brother can't get through to anyone in the air force to ground the flight in time, he's going to be gone in less than five—no ..." McNaughton deliberated, causing his own sentence to ellipsis in order to quickly check his wristwatch, correcting himself once realizing the time he had stated to be rather generous. "*Four* hours."

Sheffield to Norwich was a three-hour drive ...

Not to mention it was dark, there was likely post air-raid traffic around London due to checkpoints, and Jack would need special clearance to get into the Attlebridge base, let alone find where the hell Feind may have been detained. And that was *IF* his flight was even delayed, and he was still on this side of the Channel.

"It's too late," Garland suddenly spoke out. Relatable to the majority of those present in the hallway and connected living room, she was only stating the obvious. "It's a fool's errand. You're chasing a shadow," she added, and to McNaughton modestly: "Again."

She honed right in on his drive.

Like Churchill, the characteristic of devoted obsession was as much a gift as it were a curse for Jethro McNaughton.

His offsider in the Special Investigation Branch, Garland, typically turned a blind eye to his obsessive tendencies as it usually helped drive a case. Conversely, in this circumstance, and especially since his recent discovery of Wingate's innocence in relation to the death of his son, his fascination with Feind had come hard and fast to fill the void. It was fast becoming immensely unhealthy.

"He's gone," she instilled further, seeing McNaughton eye-to-eye so that he would listen to her wise words and not just hear them.

In the silence that followed, McNaughton's conceit became evident. He wasn't a dupe, hellbent on justification every time. As firm as religion, he didn't believe in coincidence, therefore allowed for this dangerous mindset to become defused. Churchill, however ... not so much.

Unlike his respective partner, Mad Jack believed in stranger things happening.

Churchill noticed Garland cup the car keys in her palm, signifying that their vehicle was off limits. If McNaughton couldn't chase this shadow, neither could he.

"As much as I hate to admit it, she's right, Jack ..." Rosamund voiced her opinion on the subject, and her words called Churchill's attention, partially placating his yearning to chase the wind all the way to the coast. "Let's just ... *go back home.*"

In that moment, as Jack looked into Ros' crystal-clear gaze, a strange sensation overcame his attentiveness. His sterling stare raised from his wife and to Scarlet Kristina as she lingered in the hall.

Her stare was already on him and what resonated behind her eyes spoke a googolplex of poetries; fables of fear from her past foreboding her future, an unescapable and indescribable dread knowing of his existence, and possibly even a hint of desire for the hero the longer he returned her longing gaze. Above all, the look in her emerald eyes echoed a cry for help like a siren song, harking Churchill back to Oslo; to the last time he had viewed her as the damsel in destress.

He failed her back then ... he wouldn't fail her again now.

"My bike?" Jack asked.

"It's in the garage," Scarlet responded before he could explain any further. She quickly reached into the slide drawer of the wooden cabinet beside her, fast finding a tiny key amidst the papers, odds, and ends within the rummage and tossing it his way with a metallic twinkle.

Churchill caught the key, and an adventurous smile broke the mood.

Within seconds, he took off out of the front door and down the step, rounding the house, and strolling along the moon-lit driveway before raising the collapsible garage door.

Inside Scarlet Kristina's garage rested a military green Harley-Davidson 42WLA motorcycle. It was the same one Churchill had borrowed from the base back in late February to ride to and from London for his court martial. During all the chaos and moving about, Jack had used the bike to get to Sheffield just prior to his arrest, where it had remained. Scarlet had kept his vehicle safe until his return.

This was it!

This was how he made it to the coast in time.

He had to be quick ...

There was no time to spare ...

There was a version of this where Mad Jack mounted the motorbike, sending sonic reverberations for miles as he scolded the countryside with the thunderous aftershocks from his raucous military green three-speed twenty-five-horsepower engine.

He would physically race the sunrise, making it to RAF Attlebridge in Norwich in the nick of time, maybe even crashing the gates of the airfield, chasing down a taxiing Douglas C47 as it encircled the tarmac of a runway, cleared for take-off, reaching her before her landing wheels could retract and getting his man—his archenemy ...

... that being said, real life is not without a sense of irony.

Friedrich Feind was a lot like Jack Churchill in many ways; in this instance, instead of chasing a woman, he chased a war like a fleeting sunset beyond a distant horizon ...

Aberrantly, real life was also not without its idiosyncrasies.

Jack Churchill was no longer like Friedrich Feind.

Residing idly in the gloom of the dusty garage shed space, Churchill sat upon his stationary motorbike. His face drooped, despairingly looking upon himself; his uniform, unable to shake the weight of an overbearing sense of disappointment as it fell upon his shoulders. He had failed to become the leader of No.2 Commando for Operation Chariot due to this impeding endeavour—he'd be damned if he would fail to see its timely demise.

Committed, he inserted the key ...

Facing the direction of the street and the source of light, Rosamund appeared in the beam and in his path on the driveway, eclipsing the radiance like a metaphoric angel with a halo.

With his head downwards and arms stretched across the handlebars, the beret-clad rider throttled the motorbike to life, in-turn illuminating her dressing gown in the glow of the lamp light once it flicked on, and he noticed her ...

... noticed the heartbreak on her face as her welling eyes finally burst with tears.

Sure as a solid brick wall—or a water buffalo—it was enough to prematurely end the rampage of his ride. Churchill leant up, eventually killing the noisy engine, enveloping them in an eerie calm reflective of his tale in this moment.

He chose the woman over the war.

In the quietness of the moment that followed and in a staggered advance, Rosamund approached Jack on the bike as he sat in a seeming dismay, requiring some sort of commiseration to function in the absence of chasing war.

Emerging alongside him on the bike, her tiny voice vocalized: "You made it, soldier?" Euphonious to the ear, Churchill seemed to break from his solitary mindset, hung-up on the situation. Right now, she was all he could see ... and from this moment on, *she was all he would see.*

This wasn't the end of his war ... but it was the end of this pursuit.

Subdued, he chortled at the call back, one that both was long since overdue and relevant to his restoration of humility. He acknowledged her fully, and never before had she shone so brightly beneath the paleness of moonlight. "Yes, ma'am."

Eyes welling with emotion, he cuddled his face into her bosom, wrapping his arms around her as she lastly approached. Rosamund held him in gentle enfoldment, resting her head on his. For them both, this hectic hurrah was finally *over.*

Till death they do part.

Within the Witherby residence, proceduralism reigned supreme.

Now that Churchill had vacated, the two constables from the devised section of the Special Investigation Branch within the Criminal Investigation Department appeared to prey upon the vulnerable and exposed Scarlet Kristina like bureaucratic hyenas upon an undefended, unprotected gazelle.

"Misses *Kristina* ... or is it, Miss *Witherby?*" said Constable McNaughton as he enclosed upon her with a splinter between his gritting teeth, backing her into a corner within her own home.

Intimidated and defeated, Scarlet Kristina took a seat in her lounge room alit by warm lamp light. Enveloping her position, the tall McNaughton became flanked by his fearless offsider, Constable Garland.

"Although I can appreciate the importance of preserving your past and keeping it a secret, Miss Witherby, considering the level of the exposure of your former life, the attention of the Criminal Investigation Department is rather acute. It is procedure to bring you in for debriefing. Not to mention, you're an illegal immigrant, so, there is an element of due processing requiring acknowledgement there also ..."

Upon the falling of his hefty, arduous words, Scarlet closed her eyes shut. She had been dreading this outcome since day dot. She wasn't mad at Jack; at McNaughton, per se, this was merely deliverance.

"*Debriefing* ... or *interrogation?*" she questioned rather unpretentiously, gazing wholly upon her arresting officer and his petite partner, apparently able to see beneath the veil of interpretation semantics. She may have been a former popstar, but she was not injudicious or stupid.

"Well," McNaughton huffed, continually playing coy—but Garland stepped in, bitchiness at the ready.

"Oh, darl," she said rather compassionately, though evidently pulling a whopper of a punch. "You should have thought of that before you married a Nazi ..."

As a teardrop fell from her face, Scarlet's view panned onto her.

Due to her sex, she had assumed that Garland would have been much more sympathetic in nature towards her than McNaughton, but apparently this duo was *bad cop, worst cop.*

Conceding, Scarlet's face lowered, and her eyes narrowed, accepting of her fate here tonight. She had a good run, but her journey had ended.

McNaughton's head tipped, gnawing his toothpick like it were a nervous twitch. He was confounded by her willingness to cooperate—the last time he had experienced this from a foreigner, it had been Feind. "You're not more worried by this, ma'am? What about your son?"

"Your nation has rules. Standards. My son will be cared for—in fact, he may be the reason you can't throw me into a pit for the cockroaches to ravage. He'll be cared for until this is done with, perhaps until the war is over, besides, what choice do I have?" Scarlet asked, standing up. "All I ask is that you do not view me as my husband."

"Thought you didn't want us to call him that anymore?" Garland barked provocatively, hinting that eavesdropping private conversations was her speciality. "Or is that just Jack?"

Garland stepped forth with a pair of handcuffs intended for her ...

Disgruntled, Scarlet shook her head. "I thought narcissism was mostly a male trait," she said, offering her hands in fists. "I guess I was wrong."

The bitch didn't bite the bait. "Wouldn't be the first time, eh?"

"Freddy used to say '*Alles hat ein Ende*' ..."

Whilst McNaughton observed his partner cuff their newest prize for the brass, intrigue of the foreign tongue got the better of him. "And what's that mean?"

"*Everything has an end.*"

"Ah," McNaughton inhaled, underwhelmed. "Can't agree more," he said confidently after Garland applied the bulky metal handcuffs at her front. "Write that down, eh?" he instructed his offsider, who procedurally complied once her hands were free of duty, recording the newest quote into their journal with all the others that tickled his fancy.

"*Alles hat ein Ende, nur die Wurst hat zwei,*" Scarlet furthered, exhibiting the full quote, followed by its English translation. "*Everything has an end, only the sausage has two.* Are *you* the sausage, Constable?"

McNaughton held up a hand, gesturing for his scribe to stop scribbling the quote in the records. He no longer liked it.

Quickly irate, he eyed Scarlet Kristina exasperatedly.

"You moved from this obsession of a man, *Wingate*, onto *Jack*, then to *Freddy*, and now that he is in the wind, you're onto me," explained Scarlet in her defence against McNaughton's seemingly relentless chain of persecution. "You're a dog with a bone, Constable. In Sweden, we have a saying you can write down in your little book: '*den som gapar efter mycket mister ofta hela*'. Means: '*he who grabs for too much loses all*'. This is *you*. You will end up with *nothing*."

Not bothering to put pencil to paper, Garland scoffed audibly, nauseated by the prospect. She did not notice that her esteemed collaborator had frozen upon absorbing the sentiment, almost paralytically heeding to her word.

She led the way towards the front door of the Witherby residence, uttering: "Enough of this foreign gibberish." Incensed more than a gremlin after midnight, Garland had had enough, wanting to restore to their procedural normality. "Let's head back and get her processed. At least we're not empty-handed—"

"*Joan?*" the new voice of a stranger questioned rather obliquely. The appearance of a complete unknown given the circumstances startled them all, causing Garland to flinch and feel for her pistol, sidestepping for both cover and line-of-sight for her partner.

"Who is that?!" the frowning McNaughton asked after what erroneously felt like an extended moment, harnessing Scarlet firmly whilst whipping his jacket flap back in order to expose the holstered revolver at his hip and lay his palm across the wooden butt.

Garland leaned out from partial cover, observing the civilian foreigner in the shadows of the night through the open front door. He was located on the front lawn of the Witherby residence, dressed warm in a coat, hand gloves, and a stitched flat cap which ominously shaded his bearded features.

"Jesus," she uttered to her tired self, scoping the newcomer to their scenario, and relieved that it appeared to be a resident nobody. "Some *Good Samaritan* fellow ..."

Scarlet piped up after recognizing the voice. She spoke softly into McNaughton's cautioned earhole. "It's Ludwig. My neighbour."

The Sherrington resident next door was a widowed gentleman by the name of *Ludwig*. A good neighbour, *Ludwig* often looked out for fellow (supposed) widow Joan Witherby and even allowed her and her son access with him in the bomb bunker in his backyard whenever the air raid siren would sound across the skies of Britain.

"Relax, Constable," Scarlet barked whilst McNaughton processed, albeit at a delayed response time. "It's not Friedrich Feind, *remember*, he's long gone. Just like it wasn't Friedrich Feind when you chased my son down and gave him the fright of his life!"

McNaughton snarled in retort. "I am aware, Miss!"

"*I say, just what is going on 'ere?!*" Ludwig questioned as he precariously upped the front step, viewing the scenario with wide and confused eyes. His voice had a hint of a Cornish accent. "*Do I need ta call tha coppers?!*"

"Constable, please kindly advise Mister Ludwig that we *are* the coppers. Inform him of his new babysitting duties regarding Miss Witherby's son and kindly ask him to *fuck off* for the time being. I am tired, and any acts of do-gooder, good neighbour, humanitarianism-grade stonewalling or resistance to our cause will be responded to with aggression."

"Yes, sir," Garland obeyed with a content grin, approaching the front doorway and granting Witherby's nice neighbour with a flash of her credentials and a polite conversation absent detail, although, anybody with eyes could see that she was being taken into custody.

"Sir, please stay where you are!" regarded Garland, acting professional in her defensiveness as she advanced upon Ludwig, meeting him beneath the porch light. It became evident that he had concerned eyes for Joan Witherby, attempting consistently to retain sight of her over Garland's shoulder.

"Please be gentle with him ..." said Scarlet in handcuffs, under the guidance of Constable McNaughton. He obviously knew nothing of her secret identity or past and knew her only as the single mother Joan Witherby from Nether's Edge, Sheffield. "He is a gentle soul—always looking out for me and my son. Even lets us stay in his bunker whenever the air raid's wail fills the night ..."

McNaughton's eyes fluttered, insinuating her good looks. "Yes, I'm sure he's got no other intentions than keeping you safe and sound, Miss."

At the door, Garland almost had to physically halt Ludwig's stalwart advance towards keeping his beloved neighbour safe.

Witherby's good neighbour wore a well-kept short beard, and it appeared to be covering some evident scarring upon his face. In a fleeting observation beneath the illumination of the porch light glow, Garland's observant eyes caught sight of his features, assuming there lied some sort of violent history ...

"Sir, I asked you to please stay where you are!" she repeated more sternly, stopping him from entering the home. Ludwig complied, halting at the door. His eyes irrevocably bled for Witherby, concerned for her well-being.

"*But, of course!*" he bellowed compliantly, looking towards Garland and respecting her authority to uphold the law. Whatever business they had arresting Witherby, it must have been merited?

Whilst Ludwig bowed his flat capped dome, peering further inside, Garland further observed several of his features. If not for her astute perception, she wouldn't have noticed the threat lurking within ...

Ludwig's very appearance here was strange.

His temperament, flaring from concern to calm, appeared phoney.

He wore gloves. This concealed his fingers.

He wore a hat, baggy coat, and stubble to conceal his expressions.

As Garland further observed his persona, she observed that his distant hand seemed to hover between layers, and that those layers concealed something deadly ... on such a nonthreatening fellow, his body language read as hostile.

Inside, McNaughton had similar concerns regarding the perception of his character, although his were shrouded by an overbearing sense of recognition—he had seen this fellow previously but was struggling to place where.

Then, it hit him.

"Oi, hang on. I know you. You're the bloke from backstage of the show, aren't you?" he stated at a growing frown, realizing where he had seen Ludwig before: lurking behind the scenes of the concert which happened to star Scarlet Kristina as the primary act. At the time, he had taken him as some sort of deaf and mute caretaker for the horses.

The identification appeared to take Ludwig by surprise.

The moment of processing was all that was needed for Garland to better study his character further, detecting an anomaly afoot, even tilting her head past his third person standing in order to gain a better insight of what it was he held within a concealed grasp ...

"*Oi!*" she suddenly shouted, engaged, reacting as her hackles went up, standing on end. "*Hands where I can see 'em!*"

She drew her gun—

Ludwig was faster.

Unexpectedly fast.

Too fast.

As Viviane Garland went for her pocketed Beretta, Ludwig's confounded good neighbour-guise diminished in an instant. His expression aborted and into one of the vacant-eyed killer.

With the speed, strength, and skill of an automaton, he blindly grappled with her wrist as she went for her weapon with one hand whilst with the other, discreetly presenting his own elongated, tailored piece from between his layers, pointing it towards her at his lower flank.

T'Ch! T'Ch! ...

Two shots from a suppressed handgun, muffled by point-blank range, emitted as gusts of compressed air between the two figures.

Garland flinched both times as she became shot through the core.

Her eyes widened and face fell flat, mouth agape, caught completely off-guard by the sudden and surprising betrayal. Even to her, her death was most unexpected.

Robbed of life, the stance of the shocked vixen immediately drained of ability and faltered, relinquishing the partial hold of her weapon as she collapsed to the floor in a dead-weighted heap.

Before anybody could mentally react, including McNaughton in the living room, Ludwig's eyes switched targets. In a subsequent heartbeat, he exposed, raised, and extended his suppressed, tubular weapon, catching it with steady hands whilst evolving into the forward lean of a shooter's pose. Pointing his killer weapon directly at his next mark, a dead-aim eye became immediately trained.

T'Ch!

The cylindrical silencer at the end of the small pistol fired one last time, shooting a subsonic, small calibre bullet into McNaughton's head as he grappled with Witherby's cuffed wrists whilst attempting to scrounge for his own hip-mounted sidearm.

Mouth murmuring an unintelligible sob, his head violently snapped out to the side, eyebrow bursting with a bright red drip. Scalp tearing, skull appearing to fracture, he fell to the carpet with a heavy *thwump!* Unresponsive and lifeless after the brutal headshot.

Scarlet Kristina shuddered and then shrieked.

"Joan!" Ludwig shushed her scream, communicating unnaturally calmly after committing the double murder homicide of two law enforcement officers, killing them where they juridically stood. Indoors, he approached her with an open palm and his weapon down-guard, attempting to earn her trust in the sudden chaos.

"Please be calm, luv!" he whispered, keeping her quiet, for the first time showing a side of his secret-self that she, her secret-self had never seen. "We must leave. It's no longer safe to remain in this 'ere life."

Bearing an angled frown, the perplexed and petrified Scarlet Kristina watched as her now unmasked friendly neighbour advanced upon her, softly touching her hands and feeling the metal handcuffs confounding her wrists together. He acted her unwanted knight in shining armour.

"W-w-who are you?!" she muttered through a string of discomposure, eyes welling whilst he encircled her, still partially training the sights of his weapon upon the downed Criminal Investigation Department constable as he laid with his firearm drawn in his cold fingers.

Ludwig obtained the snub-nosed revolver from McNaughton's grasp.

Now armed with two weapons; one in each hand, he trained the iron sights of both simultaneously and within extremely close range at his face in case the victim proved unexpectedly alive. Luckily for McNaughton's unresponsive corpse, there was no reaction. And so, he got to keep what was left of his face ...

"Come now. It's time to go ..." Ludwig commanded, taking charge.

He stood up tall, tucking the additional firearm into the rear of his belt whilst commanding the situation, attempting to ferry her via her handcuffed mittens away from harm's way.

Although the gunshots were suppressed, the vicinity-wise Churchills had heard them from outside, alongside the Witherby residence. The sharp noises had collected their combined attentions, piquing their interest—and caution.

Unknown to Rosamund, Jack had heard those types of silenced gunshots before in his military career. Whatever the weapon, it was suppressed and likely of small, subsonic calibre, given the echoic nature of the cracks almost breaking the sound barrier.

Concerned, Rosamund drew a scowl following their strange resonance. "What was that?!"

Jack ceased his embrace with her, holding her at an arm's length whilst standing tall and inspecting the direction of the action: within the house.

Something had gone awry.

"Get to the car," he directed, suddenly slipping back into combat mode. "Wait there until I have secured the area and it once again becomes safe and secure."

"Jack, what was that?!" Rosamund questioned, growing anxious.

"A gunshot, dear," he remarked, surely and making stern eye contact with his wife. She barely believed it, given what she knew about gunshots and how loud they were, and so he added: "A *special* gunshot. Whoever has pulled the trigger means business. Go! Now!"

And with that, Rosamund shuffled in her slippers.

She took to the driveway, headed towards the glow of the nearest streetlamp which coincidently illuminated Constable McNaughton's car, where she would seek refuge for her husband's antics.

The shuffling footsteps across the coarse driveway asphalt called the acute attention of the silent killer known only as Ludwig, and he immediately gravitated towards the front doorway in order to lay eyes on—and gain sights upon—the running target.

Without so much of a word, he enacted his evasive protocols, opting to eliminate all means of his findings.

He released hold of Joan Witherby—aka Scarlet Kristina—in order to cup his pistol hand through the doorway, tracking the running woman with the sights of his American High Standard pistol. The model had an elongated, thin barrel where the silencer prevailed for suppression. It was chambered in a low calibre, .22LR rimfire cartridge ...

Lining the target ... *he pulled the trigge—*

WHOOSH—Chink!

Out of nowhere, the blade of a sword swept the weapon from the killer's gloved hands—a cut-throat-sharp sweep intended to dismember the limbs from his body, however, fell short in the motion and collected the metal from the pistol instead.

The silent gun went off as the sword collected the piece, sending a bullet into the driveway behind Rosamund's feet with a spark flash and loud *pinggg!* that resounded in the quiet night.

Disarmed of his weapon by an unexpected doorframe aggressor, Ludwig instinctually reared through the gateway portal as a follow-up sweep from the swordsman came carving, striking the wood of the doorframe by his posture as he recoiled indoors forming a guarded expression—simultaneous to which, his body language suggested a willingness to protect Scarlet Kristina who remained begrudgingly by his flank.

The green beret-clad Churchill rounded the door, armed with his customized claybeg sword in a mid-guard posture and ready to pursue justice. Within his peripherals, he noticed Garland maimed inside the doorway—she was breathing short and shallow, hinting at some sort of respiratory distress due to internal puncturing, likely of the lungs. She was pale and profusely bleeding. McNaughton was also down, located further in and behind the disarmed gunman.

Churchill identified the hostile as having recently posed as a civilian, given his appearance and flat cap. Whoever he was pretending to be— neighbour, friend, fellow Sheffield resident—he clearly wasn't who he seemed. He was who Scarlet had recently shared the bunker with, some sort of sleeper operative who had remained secret in her new life until this very moment; a sequence of recent events threatening to unveil and expose her— the *trigger* to a *trigger* man.

Suddenly, Churchill's appropriation towards this hostile caused a change in his body language. His brow inverted upon perceiving the realization. "*Danny Boy?!* Thought you were dead, old chap!"

The same thing happened for the killer disguised beneath the flat cap. "*Mad Jack?!*" he questioned, suddenly relaxing into an upright stance. He squinted, forming an expression on his poker-faced, vacant-eyed face, "Jack Churchill, is that really yer? Fancy meeting yer again?!"

Churchill let drop guard of his heavy sword for the moment. If it hadn't been for the recent reminiscing of past Berzerker events, Churchill may not have put the pieces together in that moment—furthermore, he did the maths surrounding Danny Boy's post-Berzerker history.

"It's you. You were the Bluthund Feind sent, aren't you?"

"Not sure what yer mean?"

"Tell me, were you a German spy all along?!"

Danny Boy blinked. The expression upon his scarred mug may have been hidden by his beard, but it was the same recognizable one he had possessed that morning Churchill had seen it from beneath his ski mask— when he had been exposed performing a double-cross at the Mont de la Gouille Winterthur Resort.

Jack was now beginning to question if it had been an act all along; had Danny Boy been working for Germany, infiltrating Wingate's operation, or had he defected and been recruited afterwards in exchange for survival. Either one fit his killer of killers persona.

Danny Boy did not elaborate. Perhaps he had forgotten.

Perhaps he had been reprogramed to forget.

"Baade loaned you to find Feind's runaway wife, eh?"

"Not just me ..." Danny Boy evaluated past Churchill's initial question about initial integrities, shaking his head with a degree of concealed exertion for the latter. His continual existence across the pond was a proud labour. "He sent others over the years. I have had to quietly eliminate them all an' bury all trace of their conclusions ... of their dead ends ..." he looked to Scarlet fleetingly. "... all to keep yer safe, me love."

The admission was enough to cause Scarlet's concerned brow to falter. "*Love?*"

Thankfully, Churchill interjected in a *speaking of former lives* manner which egged him on further. "You always had an unhealthy thing for Scarlet Kristina, didn't you?! A restless obsession born of untimely context," he computed, putting all the missing puzzle pieces into place one after the other, on an absolute roll. His deliberation retained the view of the defendant on trial. "An unprecedented coincidence, life interjected you into her proximity. It only makes sense you'd sacrifice it all for a chance to stay in her life!"

He recalled in that moment his fascination with The Queen of Sweden, dating way back from when he had known him in the Special Z Unit, when they were both Berzerkers—before he had betrayed the group and been outed as a result. During this outcome, Ernst-Günther Baade had clearly made him a proposition to join Nazi Germany and work as a spy in Great Britain. A sleeper agent. A *Bluthund.*

Jack cast an extremely fast gleam to the discarded pistol as it lay on the porch. Danny Boy's American High Standard gun still had the same acrylic sweetheart grips featuring a faded monochrome image of Scarlet Kristina which he had obtained from a magazine in 1940.

The whole thing suddenly made perfect sense.

Danny Boy had not been able to complete his mission for Feind in either killing or reporting back his findings of Scarlet Kristina in England. Instead, he had likely feigned his death and leaned into his own disappearance as far as Nazi Germany was concerned, taking up a new life as friendly neighbour *Ludwig*, where he could watch over her indefinitely.

In that moment of deliberation, Danny Boy's beard-covered scarred mug flinched a disgusted expression. "Jus like tha old days, Jack, yer limitless ornate prose n' convol'ted flow'ry deliv'ry 'as come ad nauseam. I 'ave decided that I still I dun like yer, an' that it is time for yer ta die."

And with that, Danny Boy whipped around from the rear of his belt a concealed second handgun: the late McNaughton's revolver.

The bulkier piece handled unlike that which he habitually wielded; heavy, lug, albeit unbalanced, and the trigger pull was heavy, too.

Jerked forth, the gun went off loudly at Jack, brunting at Danny Boy's shoulder with more recoil than he was used to. The delayed hammer collapse along with the overall weight caused him to miss the target as Churchill withdrew in a counterclockwise revolution through the gaping doorway and out of sight.

Short-lived clumsiness aside, Danny Boy was no amateur when it came to conducting ballistics. Evenly spaced, a second, third, and fourth shot from the revolver traced Jack's tight evasion through the house wall, blindly pursuing his cowering movements with prediction.

The result came to quick fruition.

With an audible *thud!* the body of Jack Churchill collapsed just outside of view on the wooden porch deck, evident to the assailant through the rising gun smoke and wafting debris.

The visual drop of the claybeg sword in the doorway was confirmation of his successful kill—dropped from Mad Jack's cold, dead fingertips ...

With a heavy metallic clatter, the medieval weapon had fallen to the ligneous decking with a discarded acoustic clanking, shuffling before resting silently ... dead, like Churchill was, just out of view, given the sound of that bodily collapse.

The stress of his sweaty brow faded, and Danny Boy beamed as he became upstanding. Proudly, he brought the smoking revolver up by his head as he perused confidently towards the doorway in order to inspect the kill. "Not so *unkillable* after all," he confidently muttered ...

With an utter disregard for his own safety during this instance, Danny Boy meandered through his own warpath, about to trace the remnants of Churchill with his remaining bullets once in view only to find ... nothing—

Rather, Churchill had faked it all along.

Taking him by surprise whilst the killer stepped over his downed claybeg sword, thrown as a distraction to sell the act, Danny Boy became a victim to his own overconfidence.

Hugging the wall frame tight and with the speed of a striking cobra snake, Churchill reached over with a death grip, grappling with Danny Boy's pistol hand with one hand, whilst with the other, driving a well-placed fist into his cheekbone.

Like lightning striking, the ultimate hit landed.

Collected concussively in a flash of white, Danny Boy faltered massively, even dropping hold of the weapon that fired once again into the ceiling during the disarmament, raining down fibrous debris like snowflakes or ash.

Like an extremely poorly choreographed dance, Churchill retained his latching on his person, anchored to his weight, moving in with an off-balanced scuffle of boots on decking. His subsequent actions acted a one-sided boxer in an imaginary ring, driving fist after fist into each side of the unexpecting assailant's maw as he recoiled, rearing into the walls of the front porch and rebounding from each vertical surface.

Between punches, Churchill clenched and cocked Danny Boy's wrist grotesquely to the right, causing him to painfully disarm of the revolver.

Viciously, Mad Jack threw another few wallops into his dipping head as he folded over, one time even sandwiching Danny Boy's dome between one of his thrown fists and the hardwood wall as it made contact, surely causing a comatose combination—somehow just falling short, or being overcome by Danny's Boy raw tenacity to win a fight.

Incoherently possessed by some sort of vengeful devil, the bloody-faced Danny Boy conjured the energy to spring up and fight back, spritely parrying Churchill's next incoming fists and then somehow finding a way to trip and flip the avid commando onto the stairs of the Witherby front porch, dismantling his whimsical assail and leaving him a daze.

Landing on the gloomy grass of the front lawn, Churchill fast rolled and recovered, gazing intently up at Danny Boy whilst he prepared his balled hands for the next free-for-all brawl to end a life.

Gawk fixated upon Churchill, Danny Boy chortled through a blood bubble in his nostril.

He glanced down and to his flank: his discarded pistol lay within arm's reach. He was quick enough to grab it and shoot Jack, and his cockiness in knowing this avenue added to his shit-eating, gore-stained grin. This was about to become an obscenely easy score to settle.

"Yer had yer shot, Jack ..." he prepared his stance adjacent to the weapon, about to snatch it into possession and kill Churchill. "Now it's time fer m—"

Boom!

An unexpected gunshot originating from the street severed his lethal contemplation.

Danny Boy was instantly incapacitated, collected by a spread of what appeared to be buckshot from an unknown, streetways assailant. The buckshot blast caught him across the chest and upper left side, causing him to flinch violently as though on a fishing line reefed by the haul. His clothes popped to threads like a burst pillow.

Boom!

A subsequent shot from the same surprise gunner fired away, again striking the sleeper operative across the already peppered chest, this time blowing the already recoiling Danny Boy from his feet and into a bloody submission against the front porch wall of the Witherby residence with an almighty, meaty-sounding, wet *thwack!* that collected wooden debris from the surrounding wooden walls, painting them with cherry mush.

Churchill ducked his beret-clad head and hunched from the loud shots. He tossed a sharp look back, seeing his wife, Rosamund Churchill, standing by McNaughton's car, utilizing their police-issue Remington Model 11 semi-automatic shotgun—as inadvertently taught by Viviane Garland tonight, prior to her assumed demise.

What a sight to behold.

A third, delayed shot from the unexpected warrior woman's shotgun struck the stiff-standing Danny Boy with one-hundred percent accuracy across the chest, finishing his stagnated partial collapse like a meat tenderizer up against the porch wall, quaking the timbre, and draining him of his diminishing life source.

He finally slumped, wearing the vacant dead stare of a proper victim, face strayed with droplets of his own chesty gore, with elements of smoking partial ribcage bone exposed through his perforated layers. His final lung breath was practically visible.

Finally, Churchill became upstanding, analysing his wife's resolve as she finally recognized the destruction she had caused with the shotgun, killing a man in hot blood. She felt no remorse beyond her empowered expression, through the smoke gust, nodding to her husband as though she already knew she had done good.

Catching his breath, Jack finally bowed with an approving grin, still momentarily paralyzed by her surprise. Numb from the action-packed astonishment, he straightened his messy beret.

Most unexpectedly, his wife had just won this war for him.

With the death of Danny Boy, Churchill realized Garland, who was laying nearby, appeared to still be breathing. He tended to her immediately, as did Rosamund to the fullest of her nursing abilities—applying immediate pressure.

Garland came to fully, her reddened green eyes flickering, responding to Rosamund's compression to her wounds, for it caused severe, agonizing pain.

Scarlet Kristina wasn't far behind, willing to aid her assistance in whatever way she could to this aftermath of chaos. Through glazed eyes, she caught a glimpse of what was left of Ludwig—aka: Danny Boy—her uncanny neighbour. His life had diminished, blank open eyes staring off into an aimless nothingness.

"Hang in there, *darl!*" Rosamund said stridently, applying pressure to the bullet wounds to her abdomen with both hands, getting them bloody.

Scarlet appeared and assisted quickly. With her handcuffed mittens, she found and tore off nearby material with which to better clog her bleeding wounds, then immediately charging for the nearby telephone to call emergency—however, at that very moment, the red flashing bulbs of lights became noticed as police and ambulance arrived on the scene. Other fellow Rundle Road neighbours were amassing on the lawn and street, rubbernecking the hive of late-night activity.

While Rosamund hovered over Garland, and the two made eye contact. "You're not dead yet, you *dastardly dame!*" she declared, admitting a cheeky sneer which caused her to wince. The declaration was received positively by the pale-faced Garland, who beamed with bloodstained teeth. As the called ambulance doctors arrived, she appeared prepared to fight on.

Deeper inside, the curious Churchill investigated further, prior to conversing with and debriefing the Sheffield local law enforcers when they arrived.

It soon after became known that McNaughton had also survived his thought-fatal wounds. The .22LR small calibre bullet which had struck his head had bounced from the exterior of his skull, causing him to fall temporarily unconscious from the headshot. He was promptly whisked away to the nearest hospital.

Irony:

Danny Boy, who had the drop on all his engaged adversaries at this juncture, was the only one pronounced dead at the scene.

Unkillable

'Thereafter, the trial of Jack Churchill simmered down. All relevance to Orde Wingate, the Berzerkers, even the Serpents vanished into the ether, just from whence they came. Although Operation Chariot was a huge success, the small amount of negative fallout caused things at the War Office discomfort. They thrived to be better. To move faster. That although this mission was deemed a victory, they needed to aim higher.

'From Chariot, the finer totalities were 169 men killed in action (105 Royal Navy and 64 Commandos) and 215 becoming prisoners of war (106 Royal Navy and 109 Commandos). Intelligence confirmed the Allied prisoners were first transported to La Baule and then transferred to Stalag 133 at Rennes. Lieutenant-Colonel Charlie Newman was among those captured, hence Colonel Jack Churchill's immediate and resolute promotion into the command of No.2 Commando.

'Vice-Admiral Mountbatten's meeting went ahead and Churchill attended—a small handwritten letter of resignation remained in his pocket, never seeing the light of day. As Jack aforesaid, this meeting was possibly one of the most important hitherto the Casablanca Conference the following January, wherein the rousing grandiloquence by Winston Churchill about

Italy being the soft underbelly of the impregnable enemy cocoon that enveloped Europe. This discourse eventually persuaded the Americans to consider his proposal, and thus the abominable Operation Husky became set upon.'

'Their focus may have been upon the heat of North Africa, but the target over this new horizon was not a mirage ... it was to become one of the largest-scale Allied amphibious landings on the continent of Italy. It was to be the first of its magnitude, and the first conducted with the combined efforts of the armies of Great Britain and the United States of America.'

1942, April
Orcombe Point
Exmouth, Exeter

Following the objectives set in motion by their most recent Whitehall meeting, the cathedral city of *Exeter* in the greater city of *Devon* had become the halfway point between the newfangled bases of operations for both No.3 Commando in *Weymouth* and No.2's fresh Special Training Centre (STC) established in *Paignton.*

Due to the independent growth of No.2 Commando, the battalion needed a stomping ground of its own for training; and to further step out from beneath the shadow of the wing of No.3. Both locations were an intrepid march south of England compared to where their previous bases had been located in Scotland; Inveraray, and Largs respectively.

During this mammoth period of transition, Churchill said his sweet goodbyes to No.3 Commando. It was a long goodbye, inclusive of such brethren within: Colonel John Durnford-Slater, Captain Peter Young, Lieutenant Bruce Giles, Corporal Ernest *Knocker* White, Sergeants Joe Mills and the one-eyed Scot, George *MacWilly* MacWilliam. The family of No.3 was gone for now, but never too far away.

In his fresh absence, No.3 would continue training ahead of an exploratory raid said to be taking place in *Dieppe,* France, in conjunction with the Canadians before eventually doing their part for the upcoming grand invasion of Italy.

Like the attention of No.3 was on the Dieppe raid, codenamed *Operation Jubilee,* Churchill's No.2 had an upcoming focus on *Glomfjord,*

Norway. Again, Commando would be operating in the north and with the Norwegians, this mission designated *Operation Musketoon.*

Green beret upon his dome, the wind glazed his pencil-thin moustache as Jack Churchill cruised along the coastal close in *Exmouth* upon his motorbike. Motoring beneath a warm morning sun, his freshly washed and minted 42WLA model Harley-Davidson motorbike thundered along the seaside skirt, leading him to the coastline feature and lookout known as *Orcombe Point.*

Although he was excited to meet an old friend for lunch, Musketoon didn't stray far from his mind. This was the first dangerous mission since Archery to which he had been attached. The only difference was, this time, he was calling *all* the shots. In effect, the stakes had never been higher, nor the terrain more treacherous.

The finer details of Musketoon remained a secret to most, however Jack knew them all. The objective was the destruction of a German-held powerplant in Glomfjord. Uniquely, rather than a full-scale raid assault, this operation would be an infiltration stealth mission, consisting of a small handful of ten commando troopers and two Norwegian fighters from the 'Norwegian Armed Forces in exile'. Survived by his legacy, this force was a similar army to that the late *Martin Linge* had created with the *NOR.I.C.1.,* only more organized. A scalpel manoeuvrer, the goal was to have this unit delivered covertly from across the North Sea via submarine and surgically inserted into harm's way. By the time the fireworks lit up the sky, they would have faded back into the same shadows from which they originated and just as silently.

Stealth, shadows, knives and silent takedowns ...

Mad Jack had just the weapon for such covertness!

The operational elements to the mission excited Churchill.

So much so, he had posed a request to the War Office to personally oversee the ground force for the operation. Due to the high risk of the operation and unlikely odds of the soldiers returning without capture, Mountbatten's office had politely advised Churchill of his superior (sheltered) role within the battalion-sized unit; an appointment at the top. Such a position came with luxuries, such as conservatism, and to select a proficient (expendable) subordinate to head the landing party.

Being the boss came with many perks, but it meant he could no longer be his usual mad self. He could still lead from the front, but ... from behind. From far behind.

Unhappy with this conclusion, Jack searched for loopholes in command. During their last communiqué on the topic, the War Office had informed Colonel Churchill that in the event of his electives becoming incapable of completing the mission, he may choose a successor ...

Mountbatten didn't know it yet, but that successor was about to arrive in the eleventh hour, and for all intents and purposes, it was to be *him*. There was no way he was missing out on a war after what had happened with the Saint-Nazaire Raid, especially one so intimate and private. It was a few against many—odds the way he liked it.

Churchill's bike reached the lookout.

It was blustery, with an easterly ocean breeze caressing the long grass on the hills that overlooked the rocky beach below. The sun was out on this fine afternoon, establishing a rather pleasant temperature.

Beret-clad and khaki uniformed upon his American motorcycle, Churchill promptly recognized his lunch date ahead of the physical curve in the closing distance as he coasted, eventually pulling up.

Old and best friend *Rex King-Clark* waved from his location upon a homely public bench overlooking the picturesque cliffside view. Beneath the familiar maroon beret, King-Clark came dressed in his battledress and insignia belonging to the good ol' Second Manchester Regiment, of which he had always been and would always be a conscript of. His golden hair blew about from beneath his beret in the coastal salt air, that scoundrel cowlick always returning to place.

"Hullo, Clark!" Churchill greeted in a shout against the wind current after flipping his kickstand and dismounting his motorcycle. The parking spot was still far from the bench and the wind barely carried his voice.

For a gleeful moment, King-Clark watched him stroll nearer beneath the golden sun before becoming upstanding, offering his welcoming handshake gesture. The two shook hands and then seated on either side of an item wrapped in greasy newspaper.

"Hullo, Jack. How are you?"

"Hungry, lad," Churchill remarked, nodding. He had barely seen his friend since his wedding a year ago, when King-Clark had been solely responsible for getting him there on time. He was his best man—and always would be. "You?"

"Thirsty."

King-Clark watched as Churchill raised a leather cooler bag containing glass bottles. He had transported the cooler into the heavy-duty luggage rack on the motorbike, a space typically utilized in on the army service bike for radios.

Jack placed the cooler down on the bench.

The whole thing looked like some sort of dodgy exchange.

"... Ready?"

"... Indeed," King-Clark remarked as both parties prepared to unveil their goods simultaneously.

The newspaper wrapper reveal: hot chips and battered fish ...

The leather pouch reveal: two chilled Gold Star longnecks ...

Lunch was served.

"Cheers to us," Churchill announced most informally, grabbing the bottles and handing one to King-Clark. He also pinched a salty chip from the pile. King-Clark used his thumb to unhinge the lightning-type swing closure lid. They chinked glasses and took a generous swig each whilst they became seated on either flank of their lunch; each man taking in the view whilst eating the finger food. They slouched and relaxed in each other's company. An unspoken contentment existed in that moment.

The rocks of Orcombe Point hold a unique dip, causing a rare type of erosion from east to west which is what makes the site so special. Due to the corrosion of layers, the oldest rock cores become exposed and are found amongst progressively younger rocks forming the sheer cliffs. These coastal exposures along the seashore provide an incessant series of *Triassic, Jurassic,* and *Cretaceous* rock formations traversing approximately 185-million years of the Earth's antiquity. It was quite a visual spectacle to observe.

"How's the new command?" King-Clark asked, starting the first of their conversational topics.

Churchill bobbed his head, still gorging on hot chips, eventually able to articulate a response. "Not without its drawbacks."

King-Clark scanned his micro expressions for tells.

He knew exactly what it was Churchill was sour about giving that regard. "You can't have your cake and eat it too, old boy," he remarked unbiasedly towards his friend. After all these years, he could read Mad Jack like a book, and that idiomatic proverb summed old mate up to a T and his lack of comeback showed that Churchill knew it.

"There's a mission coming up," he started his lopsided tale between fries as they enjoyed the feast and the beers, staring at the sun as she showed the first signs of setting. "A daring one, at that."

"Is there any other type for you lot at Commando?" commented King-Clark, wordlessly referencing the recent Operation Chariot and Newman's one-way journey. "Case in point: the *HMS Campbeltown.*"

Churchill bowed modestly, catching the reference to the now famous navy ship that was exploded after ramming the dock gates in Saint-Nazaire harbour as a pivotal part of Operation Chariot, rendering the German-occupied port useless for the foreseeable future. On that topic, Jack digressed truthfully:

"They're giving Newman the *Victoria Cross* for that one."

Indifferent to his point, King-Clark bent his neckline. "VC or no VC, what happened to Newman would have happened to *you* had your promotion not been delayed by the court fiasco. That would be you sitting in a German POW camp, missing the war, not him. This whole thing played out like a bizarre twist of fates if you ask me."

"When your number's up, your number's up," Churchill rationalized, today feeling rather passive with regards to the lifecycle of the soldier. He had already shed enough mental tears of sympathy towards Charles Newman's unappealing conclusion. "Newman knew the risks going in, as do I now. Only difference is, they shan't be taking me alive."

King-Clark flinched a grimace. "Really?"

Jack shot King-Clark a sideways glance that demanded expansion upon such a question of his self-sacrificial leitmotif.

Need he quote his favourite Meagher quote again to this fellow?

"I just figured things would be different now ..." suggested King-Clark, referring to Churchill's family circumstances and Rosamund's pregnancy; all information disclosed over the same telephone call during the week that had prompted their meet up. He added on a short but appropriate foray from topic, for he had not had the chance to say so in person. "Congratulations by the way ..."

They took the time to tap bottle necks with a glass tap.

"Cheers."

As their glass bottles tinked, Churchill absorbed the sentiment which his long-time best friend served. A fresh sense of emotionalism overcame him when he glimpsed upon a world with him absent now that his wife and son existed. It was a strange and foreign feeling, and Jack was unsure if he liked the look of it on him.

"So, you'll be taking a backseat for a while?" assuming logic, King-Clark gandered a guess, reshaping this conversation for what he hoped to be the better of his friend. "Let someone else with a lot less to lose take the wheel for the next journey or two, eh?"

"That's ... *the plan*," Jack said, unconvincingly.

King-Clark raised his bottleneck to his lips only to become snagged, eyeing his friend's obvious irritation with that instance of agreeable candour. "Jack, this *daring mission* that you speak of ... this isn't going to be a repeat of *the Lofoten Islands* debacle again, is it?"

The events to which King-Clark referred were Churchill's *Mad Jack* exploit to sneak aboard the ships of the *6th Destroyer Flotilla* as they departed the *Faroe Islands* a week out from his pre-planned wedding. Churchill had become uninvited from the mission, nevertheless, he formulated some half-witted plan to sneak aboard and help complete the mission that he had been unjustly exiled from and return with enough time to be wed at St. Augustine's in Dumbarton. Rex King-Clark had been a key member of that foolish endeavour, being the one responsible for air-lifting Churchill out of the Lofoten Islands and flying him back home in a seaplane he had 'borrowed' from the *RAF Calshot* airbase where he had been attaining lessons to fly.

Churchill eyed him with a dismissing leer.

"Never."

A few seconds passed where even Jack, himself, remained unconvinced of his answer.

"Well ... nothing planned as yet."

King-Clark pursed his lips and scanned away at the coastal horizon for a moment before responding. "Well, Jack, I'll have you know that you're on your own next time you want to pull a stunt like that."

"At least there won't be a wedding to be late for."

"No, there'll likely be a *divorce* on the other end this time!"

"Yes, well, naturally, Ros wants me to follow in my brother's footsteps and mount a desk somewhere in England," Churchill stated an obviousness given their family circumstances and Churchill's position within the army.

King-Clark concurred with Jack's wife. "Well, of course, she does. You're a tad less likely to cop a bullet there, Jack. One might argue that you've earned your tenure."

Churchill nodded along with his sarcasm. Truth was, he saw the situation from all perspectives, as well as his own. "It creates quite the blunder for the coming mission. For this next one, Clark, I fear I may have been born for ..."

Hitting a cue, King-Clark faced forwards and then toyed with the remainder swirling in the bottom of his beer. "Speaking of *missions* ... they're transferring me to India. Effective immediately."

Jack's brow flinched, surprised. "Oh?"

"Yes. A permanent position."

"Right. *India?*" Churchill's crest raised. He had heard a lot of rumours about fresh commonwealth transfers to India ahead of war in the Pacific against the Japanese. They were gearing up for a whole other war over there, and it would likely be just as gritty if not worse than that of the European or Mediterranean theatres of operations.

There was the sudden sense of forlornity in knowing that he might not see his friend for a long time, if ever again, once the conflicts kicked off. It was no secret that the war against *Tojo's* formidable armies would be a brutal one. "For how long, do you reckon?"

King-Clark shrugged, unknown. "Until the war is over?"

They didn't know it then, but right here, this moment would be the last time that Jack and Rex spoke for a very long time. They would each embark upon their own great individual crusades, warring against their respective archenemies. They each had so many differences, Commando for Second Manchester Regiment—Green for Maroon beret—Hitler for Tojo, it was hard not to recognize the similarities between the two … they both fought for honour and freedom.'

Both men watched the waves crash upon Orcombe Point for a moment.

It felt strange. Sombre. Not a word was exchanged.

They ate. Drank. Ate some more. Drank some more.

Small talk was exchanged—all nonchalant, as always, before eventually they parted ways. Each man was so similar in the sense that they refused to acknowledge that this was potentially the end; the last time they would see one another, shake one another's hand in embrace.

Even until the end …

… they parted ways.

1942, May
Special Training Centre
Paignton, Devon

"All right, gents. On *three,* say *'commandooo'.*"

The hired photographer was a good sport. His jovial voice resonated from behind his photographic gear, jesting as he attended to the focus pull of the tripod-mounted camera lens. Prepared to press the button, the picture camera facing three rows of organized gents in battledress uniforms, green berets aslant.

The group of fresh No.2 Commando Officers either seated on the bench, floor below, or standing behind all smiled for the photograph as the camera flash blinked, freeze-framing their cross-armed poses in film.

Click!

The photograph was taken, an image forever frozen on this date and time, May 1, 1942. Surrounded by the likes of his new Merry Men, Jack Churchill was poised mid-centre.

An unshakable sensation of awkwardness overcame Jack on his first day as an official No.2 Commando member, let alone their commanding officer. He contained his rampant consciousness, not letting any gracelessness defeat him.

Churchill shook hands with and made the acquaintance of a lot of new faces, nonetheless, the tides of war couldn't impact the calendar 'photo day' for the battalion.

Coinciding with the new undertaking of command, much of the unit's dramatis personae changed after Operation Chariot. There were a lot of new men situated within the ranks of No.2, some older than others, many greeting today for the first time. However, the biggest newbie of all being their new leader, Colonel Mad Jack Churchill.

Naturally, it was a weird sensation when Churchill met this group of already established commandos, an atmosphere akin to a first day at a new school. No.2 had always been a distant cousin to No.3 of which he adored. Whilst in service within No.3 as second-in-command, he had aided Durnford-Slater to reestablish the unit and even helped raise the flock of frogmen fighters. Thence and consequently, a certain birthright had been recognized commandeering leadership of the battalion. An unstoppable warpath which spoke for itself, following the succumbing of Colonel Newman, Jack Churchill was an ostensive replacement.

Once the yearly photographs had been collected by the government-hired photographers, Churchill had a chance to properly handclasp with the well-decorated officers existent within No.2. Each one of these distinguished and honourable men was in command of a section within the Troops comprising No.2 Commando; this battalion-sized unit of which he was now in overall authority. An organic growth, he saw himself ascending into Durnford-Slater's shoes this day.

Rollcall time.

No.2 Commando officers:

Within his embodiment of command was Churchill's new second-in-command, a former captain from within the No.4 Independent Company, *Captain Harold Blissett*. As exclusive adjutant, Blissett was a well-spoken individual with a mid-part of short brown hair slicked with pomade and a chevron moustache which mimicked the off-centre hair part a dome. He had puffy ham cheeks which hinted to an internal battle of hereditary overweightness, but from what Churchill could tell on this, their first meet, all the power to him for keeping the chub at bay. He seemed steadfast, intelligent, and reliable enough for Jack to entrust orders and duties for a positive start to any leadership role. For what it was worth, Blissett was best friends with celebrity *the Duke of Wellington*, who coincidentally happened to be a member of No.2 Commando and the CO of Two Troop. More on him shortly.

Major Godfrey Franks was next. Franks may have ranked over Blissett and would prove a loyal advisor in Jack's wars to come, though he retained the role of chief advisor to the officer's core conduct, which placed him, hierarchically speaking, behind Blissett. He was tall, capable, and presented this day with an even thicker chevron moustache. Franks was the previous commander of Three Troop and had lost his best service friends *Lieutenant Morgan Jenkins* and *Lieutenant Tom Peyton* recently in the infamous Saint-Nazaire Raid. The hurt was still real, the seeking of vengeance even more so.

Next in command was Intelligence Officer *Lieutenant Michael Stilwell.* He was a clean shaven, neatly groomed, extremely well-educated individual who was a former member of the *Coldstream Guards.* Stilwell would typically be attached to One Troop.

In the descending order of the commanding officers was *Captain Samuel Jenkins,* CO of One Troop. Jenkins was a former *South Wales Borderers* member, smooth-shaven, squat, and disgustingly religious. Also within One was *Lieutenant Richard 'Dick' Wake,* former *Buffs.*

Two Troop was led by the popular *Captain Henry Wellesley,* aka *Lord Mornington,* better known to nobleman England as *'The Duke of Wellington'.* Lord Mornington, *the 6th Duke of Wellington,* was, in-person, a short, stout bloke with a particularly globular head, parted dark hair and a neat moustache to match. To be fair, characteristically, he was humble and humorous, and very favoured among the men for such a nobleman situated amongst the 'fodder'. This celeb wasn't playing soldier—he was one. Mornington's Two Troop was backed by such section leaders as *Lieutenant John Douglas Rosling,* a blonde man with a spotty moustache of former *Welsh Regiment* fame, and *Lieutenant John Jeffreys,* former *King's Own Scottish Borderers,* a tall loyalist with bulging eyes.

Numerically, the next was Three Troop.

A familiar face helmed the Troop, that of *Captain* Graeme Black, former commando of the original No.2 Commando, pre-SAS appropriation by Robert Laycock. When the original No.2 Commando was drafted into the 11th SAS Battalion at the start of the year, Black had managed to remain a green-blooded commando. He was one of the original members to repudiate section migration. Following his recent promotion, Black had also received command of Three Troop. Three was backed by the boyish charm of *Lieutenant Joe Houghton,* former Queens Own Cameron Highlanders, with his chestnut pyramid moustache. *Lieutenant David Peters* was a section chief, tall bloke, wingnut ears.

In command of Four Troop was *Captain Laurence MacCallum.* A former Second Manchester Regiment recruit, much respected by Churchill who was also a Second Chester at heart. MacCallum had a round face with a lampshade moustache much in the style of John Durnford-Slater. *Lieutenant*

Bavister handled the main section within Four, renowned for ever-chugging on his baccy pipe, reeking of rich tobacco. Filthy habit, top bloke.

Five Troop were entirely new faces to Churchill.

Commanded by *Captain Richard F. Broome*, an experienced gent of curly dark hair and a stache to match, backed by section chief *Lieutenant Guy Faulkner Whitfield;* a handsome gent constantly beaming his youthful smile.

Six Troop was where the cameos from Jack's past were plentiful.

Headed up by *Captain Richard Hooper*, of Operation Archery fame and now known better by fresh moniker *'Dickie'*. Hooper was formerly Graeme Black's commanding officer present during the Måløy Raid and, like Black, Hooper was another original No.2 Commando member who refused Lucky Laycock's requisitioning into the SAS. All respects to the Special Air Service, rejecting their uniform status showed Hooper's loyalty to Commando and Churchill immediately respected that. During their Combined Operations mission on Vågsøy Island last year, No.3 and No.2 had not always gotten along, but they were brothers bound by loyalty here.

Six Troop was also sectioned within by none other than *Second Lieutenant Jos Nicholl*, formerly of the Second Manchester Regiment and No.3 Commando. The young, spectacle-wearing, pointy-nosed Military Chaplain was well known by Colonel Jack Churchill, and it was utter fate that the two men were crossing paths here again after a degree of absence. The two went way back. Furthermore, of the soldiers from Churchill's past was the one-eyed Scotsman *Sergeant George 'MacWilly' MacWilliam*, transferred from No.3. Another ghost from Jack's past, an unemployed corporal by the name of *Humphrey Ruffell* had also recently been drafted, beefing the sovereignty and familiarity of Six Troop for Churchill ten-fold.

A legacy Troop.

"Leftenant Stilwell," Churchill called as the group of officers strolled from the outer grounds field after the photographs had been taken, headed back towards the main area of the Paignton STC where an assembly had been called for the official inauguration for their new No.2 commander. Chief of the entire Combined Operations, Vice-Admiral Louis Mountbatten, would be present this morning as an important guest speaker to the men. He would be addressing the unit and officially presenting Churchill as their commander, as well as offering some considerate words for the fallen of the Saint-Nazaire Raid, taking the time to announce all commendations appropriately.

Intelligence Officer Lieutenant Michael Stilwell halted amidst the crew of battledress gents gravitating towards the assembly, and slowed to match Churchill's pace. He responded enthusiastically. "Yes, Colonel?"

"That latest letter from mount high?"

Stilwell cocked his brow upon hearing the informal designation.

He was yet to fully encounter the nonchalant composure of Mad Jack Churchill, and thusly, he corrected with a diplomatic tone. "Do you mean, *the War Office,* sir?"

"Yes, that one," Churchill confirmed as adjutant Blissett appeared in-step, walking by their flank across the grass field and listening in. "They again rejected my application to personally head Musketoon. I would like to know how soon we could draft a follow-up letter?"

A confuddled expression formed over Stilwell's face.

Why did he desire to personally attend this operation?!

And so persistently?!

They were clearly yet to know Jack.

Blissett affirmed to his CO. "Sir, they rejected your request due to the high-risk nature of the operation," he added with an accurate Chess allusion. "You don't risk your *knight* when there are *pawns* to play."

"We're all knights on this battlefield, Captain," Churchill declared sternly, glancing across at him past Stilwell, welcoming his constructive input but shooting it down just the same.

"Contrarily, sir: to Whitehall, we're *all* pawns," Blissett countered, then thoroughly gestured Churchill. "Except for *you,* that is. I think they've learned a lesson from Chariot when we lost Newman. They could've had an adjutant leading that charge and obtained the same result."

All the while, Churchill shook his head.

"Incorrect," he stated simply, respectfully. "Newman was incapable of leading from behind. It was not in his blood, as it is not in mine ..."

In their march, Blissett and Stilwell exchanged a glance.

His stimulating rouse was as inspirational as it was disconcerting.

This was either an extremely honourable sentiment or an exposé to just how eccentric (and possibly suicidal) Churchill was commanding a battlefront. Right now, on his first day, the chips fell somewhere in the middle. It was at least an admirable attitude for them to rally behind considering they wouldn't have a choice but to follow this mad man's orders once in the fray.

"Major Franks," Churchill furthered in-step, gaining Godfrey Franks' attention from the forward strings of strolling officers sprawled out across the green grounds.

In the surrounding crowd, Lord Mornington also slowed in his march in order to join in on this impending conversation, as did Captains Jenkins, Hooper, Black, MacCallum, and Broome, and then eventually Lieutenants Nicholl, Rosling, Houghton, and Bavister. Nearly the whole officer squad drifted closer in their joint march across the open plane.

"Sir?" replied Franks.

"We spoke the other day about how you lost two of your closest friends in Saint-Nazaire—and again, my condolences ..."

Put beneath an emotional spotlight before everyone, Franks wondered where their new colonel was going by bringing up such an ill-fated and painful reminder, seemingly applying it to prove a point—not only to him, but for a cluster of officers.

Pressure on, Franks gestured respectfully, and Churchill continued.

"If you had the chance right now, today, at this very second, knowing of their ill-fates, and the fates of all those brave lads who have striven ... would you go with them on Operation Chariot ...?"

Heat fell on Franks.

After barely a moment's contemplation, he bowed in simple concurrence. "In a heartbeat, sir," Franks replied, altruism in his tone.

Churchill accepted his response, knowing it to be true.

"There's your answer, gentlemen," Churchill dared venture, instilling his virtues early among these men. It was at this point in their promenade march that Churchill halted, causing them all to do the same, snagging on his words of wisdom. The many faces of the No.2 officers encompassed him, ears glued and listening well. "I have zero intentions of ever leading this battalion from the rear. I plan to be at the helm, both off and on the battlefield. I'll be the first *on* and last *off* any war front, every time. And if I shall fall in our commando crusade, I would hope Franks steps in. And Blissett after him, then so-forth."

Silence befell the men.

Where they stood now was a stone's throw from the assemblage area.

In the silence of Churchill's short speech, they could even hear the crowd of three-hundred commandos as they gathered in the main area ahead of the muster where Jack was about to be up on stage in front of the whole battalion to make an address.

"Bloody-hell, Jack," Captain Graeme Black, one of the only men brave enough to take a stab at their commander due to his comfort in knowing Churchill for many years prior to his new posting, stated off-the-cuff. "You're supposed to save that lecture for the lads."

The momentarily kaput officers shared a laugh following Black's jeer both with and at their colonel's expense. Soon after they heard the toned skirl of Scottish bagpipes playing from the assembly, and it drew them in.

Jack recognized the tune: *Black Bear.* It was an odd choice since Black Bear was typically a marching-off song, not to mention fast paced. In hindsight, it set a happy mood for the morning, and the men must have been enjoying it.

The positive energy they each exhumed was a response enough to absolve Churchill of the cheese in his grand sentiment that was clearly well received.

Finalizing their march and filing into their places within the organized crowd, the officers each dismissed and attended to their many sections forming the embodiment of the No.2 Commando assembly.

Soon, Jack Churchill would address them all from centre stage.

One-by-one they passed by Churchill, some taking his hand in gentlemanly embrace, others respectfully patting him across the shoulder as they personally offered their compliments to his command.

Lagging behind, Lord Mornington was one of the last men to pass by Churchill right as Jack lifted his cue cards from his breast pocket, about to read over the notes of his prepared speech one last time.

His lingering gesture caught the colonel off-guard.

"Captain?" Churchill offered him a parting recognition, to which Mornington was slow to receive. It became apparent that this was because the Duke of Wellington may have still been hung-up on Churchill's impactful words.

Finally, he took Jack's hand, grabbing him firmly on the shoulder. He locked stares with Churchill, affirming what was either about to be an awkward dispute or uplifting acknowledgement of appreciation.

"Colonel ... please call me *Morny*," he said simply. "The lads all do."

Releasing the tense breath he didn't realise he had been holding, Churchill smiled at the honour, clambering well his hand within his.

In-kind, he remarked: "Call me *Jack*."

The STC assembly area was massive.

Recently refreshed, there were numerous design similarities between the old Inveraray CTC and this big STC in Paignton. The biggest addition was just that—size.

With a far open clearing of flat, freshly clipped grass, there was enough space for several cricket pitches on these grounds. The troop barracks aligned the right side of the acreage, each on a diagonal angle like new-age parking spots along a side street, and beyond them was the admin building access, fencing, and the entrance to the trainline that connected to Exeter. The place had its own train station.

On the opposite side was the vast array of obstacle courses, gymnasiums, and pits. An armoury block, distantly placed munitions bunkers, and garages housing various army vehicles. Beyond all of that, some dunes and barbed wire followed by the beaches of the *Tor Bay.*

For the assembly this morning, centre stage was a simple raised platform and mounted podium stand used to oversee the many formations within No.2 Commando. At present, a young band trooper with a doodlesack and rosy cheeks performed Black Bear for the masses. Eventually, the belting pitch of the bagpipes ceased and, after ceremoniously saluting the adjacent officers, he marched away.

"*A-ttennnnnn-tion!*" the voice of a drill sergeant boomed through the silence that followed, causing all three-hundred men of No.2 Commando to form a rigid pose in complete unison. The bass-filled strike of their combat boot shuffle resembled thunder boom as they each poised straight and with their arms by their side.

After another loud exclaim, the assembled sea of green berets raised a salute in harmony as Vice-Admiral Mountbatten stepped out from the crowd of high-ranking officers on the periphery of the stage, taking to the centralized podium with that same sense of overbearing confidence he consistently exhumed. Mountbatten was six-foot-tall and slender, towering most men at the best of times, let alone at a raised height on the stage. He returned the salute to all the soldiers before him, who then became at-ease with their hands behind the small of their back.

"*Gentlemen ...*" Mountbatten began, scanning out over the massive crowd with an assertive sense of contagious conviction. In formal ceremony, Churchill observed him from the sidelines of the stage along with some others within the higher ranks of No.2.

Their aspiring eyes admired Mountbatten with a dialled focus.

This man was a god to army men.

His speech went on to recognize the achievement of No.2 Commando during Operation Chariot. He awarded 89 decorations for the raid, including Victoria Crosses (VC) to officers *Lieutenant Commander Beattie, Lieutenant-Colonel Newman*, and *Commander Ryder,* and posthumously to *Sergeant Durrant* and *Able Seaman Savage* respectively. These were men Churchill had never had the pleasure of making an acquaintance, however now that he was a part of the No.2 family, their names seemed to immortalize more profoundly. Distinguished Service Orders (DSO) were awarded to a *Major Copland, Captain Roy, Lieutenant Boyd,* and *Lieutenant Platt.* Other decorations awarded were *four* Conspicuous Gallantry Medals (CGM), *five* Distinguished Conduct Medals (DCM), *eleven* Military Crosses (MC), *seventeen* Distinguished Service Crosses (DSC), *fifteen* Military Medals (MM), and *twenty-four* Distinguished Service Medals (DSM). Furthermore, four men were awarded the *Croix de guerre* by France and another *fifty-one* brave souls were mentioned in dispatches.

Mountbatten physically brought the medals from Whitehall.

They were on show beside the podium, laid out on a table. The awards would find their accepters once they were returned to Britain, as many of them were POWs. Of those fallen, they would be received by their next of kin.

The Vice-Admiral's speech was both heartfelt and concise. No.2 Commando applauded his conduct ahead of him passing the mantle onto Churchill. Before he did, though, he ended his address with a battalion-famous crowd-pleaser:

He clapped his hands, and almost immediately the men all knew the verses to the hymn, and chimed in.

It was the impromptu elegy of Charles Newman.

It was bittersweet in his absence. An owed ode.

Clap-clap-clap!

"*Here comes Charlie!*"

Clap-clap-clap!

"*Good ol' Charlie!*"

Clap-clap-clap!

"*Here's our Charlie, now!*"

In his absence and as the round of applause for Mountbatten's piece diminished, Churchill stepped stridently onto the stage. He could see men within the crowd smiling, laughing, even wiping away a couple of leaking tears for the losses of their fellow servicemen.

They missed their old CO, and Newman was undoubtedly a matchless man for the most part. These were some impossibly big shoes to fill.

"I am a man of few words ..." Churchill began his speech with laconism. To the surprise of everybody in the audience, they watched as after a resonation of silence that followed his one-liner, Colonel Jack Churchill simply nodded across the crowd before turning to walk away.

In the fleeting seconds, over half of the population in the crowd cracked a smile and turned to their neighbour in the crowd, audibly questioning if that was really all their new commanding officer was going to say—

Before much of the chatter grew in volume, Churchill himself revolved back around to the podium now donning a cheesy leer of his own, shaking his head at how bad his own humour was. The fact the joke was so terrible was why it worked so well with the military men.

Down in the chortling crowd of monkeys, Graeme Black wasn't smiling.

Although he respected Jack Churchill, his tolerance to his funnyman antics had grown sour years ago. His show-ponying ways were wasted on him. Somebody standing next to him who was applauding nudged Black's arm, gesturing for him to lighten up.

Deadpan, Black offered Churchill a mere burst of short applause.

On the stage right, the slender Vice-Admiral Mountbatten exchanged a look with some of the other officers from Commando. His rectangular-shaped features and Greek nose gazed upon them none too amused.

His stare softened, leaning across to speak with one of his aides.

It was done so in such a tone that they could overhear ...

... *this wasn't his type of humour.*

"*Remind me to approve Colonel Churchill's next suicidal request to helm Operation Musketoon.*"

Allowing a moment for the chatter to die down, the acting master of ceremonies Jack Churchill placed both hands upon the wooden podium.

"It is of a popular opinion that I share, that Colonel Newman is irreplaceable. And that's something coming from his replacement," started Churchill with an ounce of satirical humour to further break the ice. "Nevertheless, I vow to do my best for No.2 Commando ..."

His words became wholesome, uplifting, and humble. To the many officers who knew Jack Churchill and what he was capable of through leadership were already crestfallen upon thee. The many men of each their Troop would undoubtedly follow suit once they got to know their new lieutenant-colonel and commanding officer.

"I would like to muse over Colonel Newman's tremendous work in recruitment, instruction, and efforts in forging a fighting unit that he could lead into battle anytime and at any place, and against any army. *Charlie* ... he managed to keep his troops at a razor-sharp level of efficiency. Under a lesser leader, morale would have surely gone tits-up after Chariot, but by his clever use of innovative training programs, managed by sheer force of positive temperament, he succeeded in improving the ailment of the *readiness* of the commando ... that is a legacy I strive to maintain going forth. Let's cut the ceremonies for a minute; for those who do not know who I am, I am not here today to pull on my own bollocks and make you want to go to war for me .... it is *I* who wants to go to war *with you*. I've been a part of your distant cousins situated up the coast in Weymouth since they were restored by Colonel Durnford-Slater after the Dunkirk Evacuation. If there is one thing I have come to learn about the commando, it is that we are an *unkillable* creature ... even in *death,* we are unkillable ... so join me in pledge, my friends—my brethren—to never stop fighting ..."

While Churchill's speech boomed on, we are transported across the country to alternating locations and interchanging characters of curiosity, both of the present and near future:

1942, May
Churchill Residence
Dumbarton, Scotland

Late afternoon, and during a sequence out of time, the sun set over Dumbarton as Jack Churchill arrived home on his motorcycle, presumably after a long stretch at the new Paignton base down south.

Battledress khakis worn neat, with new No.2 Commando designation sewn ensigns, green commando beret pressed proudly upon his dome, his olive Harley-Davidson coasted along the streets.

He was coming home.

Jack cruised straight into the driveway of his residence, slackening speed to halt. A stabilizing boot trod onto gravel right before the well-attended rose garden afore his quaint cottage home.

Beloved wife Rosamund Churchill awaited his arrival.

Curly bangs of her brunette hair swathed her face as she leaned against a porch beam, red lips, pink cheeks, soaking in the warmth of the evening sunset which caused her cerulean eyes to radiate like vibrant blue fire. Naturally show-stopping, she became draped in the late afternoon glow of the outdoors, wearing a loose, comfortable pallid gown. It was undone at the front lest bursting at the seams, presenting the growth of a baby bump.

Beaming, Churchill forked out the kickstand and dismounted his steel steed, wasting not a second to sink into the wide-open arms of his beautiful wife. Without a word exchanged, their two gleaming smiles conjoined in a kiss, and Jack humbly descended to be at level with her navel. Playfully embarrassed as he made sounds and spoke with their in-utero child, the end of days couldn't have wiped the radiating beam from Ros' face whilst she adored her husband and their happy life ...

1942, May
Special Training Centre
Weymouth, Dorset

Further along the southern shoreline on this very morning and in a Special Training Centre just like the one in Paignton past Exeter and the coast, the brown eyes of John Durnford-Slater climbed into the clear skies, his lampshade moustache leering towards the southern horizon ...

Somewhere in that direction was his good and loyal friend Jack Churchill, a fresh Lieutenant-Colonel and now a commanding officer of his own battalion—*who'd a thunk it?* As a once mentor and superior to the one still known to many as Mad Jack, Durnford-Slater was both surprised and proud of his colleague's aspiration and accomplishments, and he took solace in the knowledge that this event was the right course of history.

The continually ascetic Jack Churchill may have not been the most ambitious of men, but anybody who served within his presence would tell you unequivocally that he was born to lead. That much had always been true, and now his destiny was coming to fruition.

Churchill's departure from No.3 Commando may have been gloomy, but necessary for the growth of the British Army and the Allied Forces—*for the victory of the war,* for that matter ...

1942, May
Manchester Regiment Garrison, Ashton-under-Lyne
Greater Manchester, England

Exiting the administration office on the grounds of the regimental headquarters in Greater Manchester, Captain Rex King-Clark paused a moment in order to mount his maroon beret upon his dome. Suited up and neat in his brown battledress and polished boots, the meticulous act of perfectly balancing his beret slant was reminiscent of Mad Jack's constant pretence of maintaining immaculate attire.

He took a palliative observation towards the dreary skies high above England. There was something in his stare that exhumed both contentment and discomfort.

A passionate unease, it was as if to say *goodbye* to his home.

King-Clark next grabbed a luggage bag from his side and continued to a parked Greyhound bus in the garrison parking lot. The large vehicle was loaded with the last batch of Second Manchester Regiment officers and inbound for an airfield where a plane waited to transport them to South Asia for their next entry into the war.

He mounted the metal steps of the bus and found his seat against a window, greeting fellow Second Chester soldiers.

Through the reflective glass, his gaze glowered over the view of the Second Manchester Regiment Garrison buildings, establishments he had adored and called home for decades, for what may very well be the very last time ...

1942, June
Dhana
Madhya Pradesh, India

Upon arrival in the Far East, Orde Wingate had been appointed CO once more by *General Archibald Wavell,* British Army Commander-in-Chief for India. Utilizing his gift for assembling off-the-grid troop elements, Wingate was requested (off-the-books, naturally) to organize guerrilla groups; long-range penetration units to fight behind Japanese lines in the jungle. They'd fight dirty. Deadly.

Issued command of the Indian 77th Infantry Brigade, Colonel Wingate created India's first special forces, designated simply as the *77,* but more known by the sobriquet: the *Chindits.* The name was fitting since it was based on a corrupted version of a mythical Burmese lion called the *Chinthe.*

The 77 were made up of British soldiers as well as Indian infantrymen, typically the former teaching the latter at this newly established training centre in *Dhana* near the *Saugor* district in *Madhya Pradesh.* It was here that, the enigmatic Otter would toughen up a specially recruited group of like-minded eccentrics by having them camp in the Indian jungle during swamp season, all whilst training them for tactical warfare.

Not his first rodeo with the infamous madman, Mad Mike Calvert was onboard for another bout of questionable warfighting.

The perversion of warfare typically experienced when fighting alongside Orde Wingate consumed one's soul and felt like a drug. Forever tainted, Calvert was an irrefutable addict to the decrepities of his destructive detestations.

He equal parts hated being there ... but also secretly loved it.

Even at nine in the morning, the jungle was sticky and hot.

Within their wee camp, a nowadays version of Calvert donned a freshly shaved head with permanent five o'clock shadow. Regulation standards typically went out the window when part of one of Wingate's units.

In this humidity, he was constantly sweating bullets ...

His clothes were soaked through and smelly ...

Balls constantly stuck to a leg ...

Resting in a lean over an oiled-up Owen gun whilst he waited for the rest of the immediate unit to get ready within the desert camp, his stare fell upon the bearded Wingate across the crowd wearing an Indian sun helmet. He was outside of his swamp tent but still under the flap hanging overhead. He was in the process of tucking in a protective headscarf that hid his neck scar before throwing his peculiar homemade necklace of raw onions around his head. He joked it was to keep away the vampire bats—which scarily existed in these jungles of India, along with a hundred different poisonous creepy crawlies, venomous slithering reptiles, and razor-toothed hunting beasts that prowled up trees and in deep gully bushes. And that was all before the rifle-wielding nips of the *Imperial Japanese Army* that were undoubtedly lurking, waiting to banzai charge with astounding numbers and boundless boldness.

This place was literal Hell.

This place was literally Hell, and Mike Calvert was at home.

1942, June
Institut Saint-Joseph
Ciney, Belgium

A month ago, the *Tante Ju* responsible for transporting a string of prisoners from England to Germany was inadvertently shot down by an instance of friendly fire.

Friedrich Feind was onboard the Junkers Ju 52 aircraft when the silver trimotor transport received a salvo of antiair fire over occupied France—the emplacement likely confusing the friendly Junkers with a Flying Fortress given the hour of the incident.

The Junkers made a crash landing in a Flanders field in Belgium, where they were met by locals. Survivors were transported immediately to the nearby *Kriegslazarett (Military Hospital)* in *Ciney*, located in the province of *Namur* known as *the Institut Saint-Joseph*. The German-seized civilian hospital was run by the Catholic community of the *Frères des Ecoles Chrétiennes*.

Woken in the dead of night by the murmurs of his injured bed mate, of which in this wing he had almost a dozen neighbours, half of which were mummy-wrapped due to severe burns, Feind sighed. Luckily uninjured for the most part, he was sleep deprived more than anything. His wounds were minimal and mostly isolated to a severe jarring of his left leg from the crash. Scratches and burns on his hands and face were minimal, barely requiring thin dressings.

Restless, he glanced to his flank, gazing upon the unlucky soul who had survived the plane crash when it would have been a mercy to have perished. The man was wrapped from head-to-toe in bandages from second and third-degree burns, and all his fingers on both hands had been amputated due to trauma.

Of the few times he had been conscious and coherent thanks to pain medication, Feind had spoken to him briefly. His name was *Arno* and he was from *Buxtehude*, a town on the *Este River* in Northern Germany.

All things considered in the aftermath of these eventful endeavours, Feind was exceptionally fortunate. Not to only have luckily endured a plane crash, but to have escaped imprisonment by the Allies after surviving losing a battle in the north.

A rare sensation to see on the face of a man bearing such burdens, a smile of comfort formed upon Friedrich Feind's relieved mug. And it held for an extended moment.

What tore his fleeting happiness down was the significance on his mind concerning his selection for the prisoner transfer, as somebody high-up in Oberkommando der Wehrmacht or Schutzstaffel saw value in his specific return to duty ...

Albeit with a master plan in progress intended to bring an enemy of Germany down, given his competence with the English during his time spent incarcerated in order to make plays, he was nervously starting to realise that his specific liberation may have been due to his disclosure. His meditated extraction could have solely occurred to shut him up ...

His freedom could come at the price of a dreadful dissolution.

1942, June
McNaughton's Billet
Hounslow, London

From one Hell to another ...

In a West London lodging established above a street-level convenience store that was shut more often than it was open, teetering on the edge of foreclosure, Jethro McNaughton was slumped on the lounge in his cheaply rented apartment. Late at night, he was still dressed in his overcoat in his own home following another shitty shift at the office for the Special Investigation

Branch. He had been back at work for a week after a leave of absence, recovering from a head trauma which had left him with a pink scar.

Ever since that fateful night, nothing had felt the same ...

Tonight, he had retired home with a fresh bottle of bronzed poison that he consumed straight from the bottle.

Drowning his sorrows, dowsing his demons, McNaughton stared at the blank wallpaper whilst he listened to the radio.

His apartment was a dark mess. As a testament to his laziness, the thrown apartment keys even skidded from a tabletop and disappeared into the abyss of mess. Moving boxes still lined the walls from twelve months ago, when he had moved into the city. A lamp had even been set up upon a mountain of them, establishing them as a permanent fixture of the décor.

The floor was littered in scattered newspapers and work cartons filled with pages wrapped in manila folders. Much of it associated to the eternal hunt for the elusive Orde Wingate: the man he thought had killed his son, and now a trail recently terminated. The life transition from pursuing shadows coincidently seemed to have happened the same day he was shot in the head, and he was just now putting two and two together.

While the 1932 model General Electric radio played the BBC broadcast as background noise, all McNaughton could hear was the demons in his head. They spoke about his dead son and reminded him of his incapability of ever seeking revenge on those responsible for his demise, for the man responsible, a German villain by the name of Ernst-Günther Baade, had supposedly already perished, and the closest thing to an accomplice, Friedrich Feind, had now fled the country and far from his reach ...

There was an overwhelming sense of hopelessness that McNaughton doubted he could defeat like he had once before. Dealing with the illness of depression was not a new mental adversity for him, for he did it on the daily, however without a possible light in the darkness to drive that said quotidian, all lights were slowly diminishing.

The demons were a lot louder than usual. He tipped back the bottle, another big swig. The grogginess of alcohol intoxication began setting in, numbing the pain, dampening the voices, and hopefully bound to knock him out again; put him out of his misery for another day.

With a groan, McNaughton arched forward on his seat, planting down the bottle on the ligneous table surface with a forceful impact. His other hand reached in and retrieved his uncomfortable revolver housed in a leather holster from his belt, about to place it down on the same table ... but his mind caught him wandering.

His eyes glazed over the weapon in deep contemplation.

Alcohol was a good way to drown the voices. Most nights it worked wonders, though it was becoming harder to keep them down for as long nowadays ... but *this* ... *this* may have been the answer to keeping them down for good.

One hand resting on a bottle of booze, loaded pistol in the other, his tired and strained stare lost focus between the two items, searching desperately, fleetly for meaning. He discarded both items loudly to the table, becoming dizzily upstanding, and wandering wobbly out and across the room to where his eyes fixated upon a stack of book spines.

McNaughton staggered a few steps across the messy floor, knocking over old booze bottles from nights prior, where he eventually collapsed before a book pile. He managed to pull an album out from the stack, finding a dated photo featuring his family ...

Young Wallace was being embraced by his mother; McNaughton's estranged wife, who had sadly perished from pneumonia of the lung due to exacerbated health issues such as malnutrition and poor living conditions attributable to The Depression.

There wasn't anybody responsible to hunt for her death.

His eyes welled up, red and stinging.

The sentiment was too much to bear whilst under the influence of alcohol, overstimulating his emotions, and McNaughton embraced his arms around the photograph, holding it close to his chest before collapsing fully on the rug, eventually crying himself to sleep ...

1942, June
Churchill Residence
Deddington, England

Dinner at the Churchill family home in *Deddington, Oxfordshire,* was a warm reception. Belated due to busy scheduling, the family had gathered to celebrate the second birthday of Thomas and Gwendoline's daughter, Rosemary.

This was the first time since their belated Christmas festivities—of which Jack was late, due to the operation in Norway. He joked he was helping Santa Claus at the north pole.

This time around, they were missing the youngest of the Churchill trio, Buster, although his wife Olive and their seven-year-old son, Mark, had travelled from their new cottage in *Borehamwood,* a town in southern *Hertfordshire,* to see the family.

Excitedly, this was the first time Alec and Elinor *Nellie* Churchill had seen their daughter-in-law Rosamund since before the announcement of her pregnancy—a new *Churchill* grandchild was on the way.

Glad times were shared over dinner with cake as well as happy tears from mother Churchill, who was over the moon expecting another grandchild.

With plans to put up the entire family in the spare bedrooms, the kids and elderly Alec Churchill went to bed just after supper, leaving the 'big kids' up and childless. Jack foolhardily suggested they go to the circus as it was in town along with some tech expo and get a few drinks. Have 'the night off from the kids' while their mother looked after them.

Half-serious in his suggestion, Nellie considered it a great idea and was more than happy to watch her slumbering grandchildren for a few hours. Thus, Jack and Ros, Tom and Gwen, and Olive piled into Thomas' Ford and hit the road to the outskirts of town. The nightlife in Deddington shone brightly upon their faces through the windshield as they spied not only the bright pinwheel lights of the circus rides and dome, but also a tech and gadget exhibition across the strip.

To their trained eyes, Jack and Thomas noticed an influx of Yanks troops out on shore leave present throughout the festivities, which coincided with the ongoing arrivals of more and more Americans into the United Kingdom, dating from January. For over two years, the British had been single-handedly holding off Nazi Germany. Events such as this festival were a subtle way of siphoning US dollars into the British economy.

"About damn time," was Jack's only remark to his brother.

The families enjoyed a night out on the town, kid-less, whilst being able to act like kids themselves.

They picked fairy floss off wooden sticks and ate peanuts from kraft paper bags. They threw balls at tin cans and shot cork guns at bullseyes for prizes. They laughed at circus clowns, and at numerous attractions aimed to entertain the masses. The girls had fun hanging out like sisters, and Jack and Thomas managed to share a moment or two to discuss Bob Laycock's latest stunt: attempting again to recruit Thomas into Commando. It wasn't the first time, as he had subtly been trying to get Tom enlisted since the early LayForce years. However, what *was* new was Thomas' consideration of joining the armed forces again and leaving the intelligence sector ...

Much to Jack's chagrin—and after naturally assuming Thomas had said no—they put a pin in that unfinished conversation, preferring to live in the moment with their significant others and Buster's wife, having all the fun as it was such a rarity during this era.

Across the road, they were one of the last crowds through the tech expo, feasting their eyes on futuristic prototypes of upcoming cars, planes, and even found a new-age automated photobooth, like what they had in *Times Square* in *New York City*.

It was six pence a column row: four pictures per column.

The three Churchill wives got in and took some cute stacks, followed by another which Jack and Thomas photobombed considering the booth only comfortably sat two—three max.

Brothers Jack and Thomas sat in for a session with Olive in the middle, kissing her on either side of the cheek, joking that they would send the photo to their younger brother aboard the Victorious to make him playfully jealous.

They did.

1942, July
HMS Victorious
North Atlantic Ocean

Afloat about the Atlantic Ocean, the icy air searing the ship exterior was blistering.

Pulling in from an outer deck passage, the rugged-up *Robert 'Buster' Churchill* retired to his cabin quarters after a noisy night in the mess with the lads, following another long day between operations for the *Fleet Air Arm* aboard the aircraft carrier the *HMS Victorious.*

The youngest Churchill brother only loosely resembled his brothers. He had Tom's height but was what would have existed if Jack were balding from the edges, like some savage widow's peak through his darker hair—a balding that was odd considering he was the youngest of the siblings. No moustache, either, for he was inefficient at growing facial hair.

Unravelling his many layers such as a scarf and gloves and long deck jacket, he saw the mail call delivery on his bed. It had been a tiresome day of take-off drills for the aircrew of the *884 Squadron,* of which he had been stationed amongst after graduating as a pilot.

Training with outdated *Fairey Fulmars* fighters, the 884 was practising for a string of upcoming missions taking place in the Mediterranean Sea, one of which where they would be tasked with protecting the *Santa Maria Convoy* carrying supplies to *Malta* in the future *Operation Pedestal.*

Buster hadn't seen his family for an age. Hadn't seen his brothers for even longer, and he was beginning to feel homesick.

He collected the letter, studying the addressee's handwriting once more. It was from his wife, Olive.

Buster flipped on his sconce lamp and unlatched his folding desk in his claustrophobic seaman quarters, pulling up a collapsable wooden stool. Using a letter-opener, he ripped the envelope seal, unfolding the page from within before his wide, enthusiastic eyes, when a black and white glossy photo column unexpectedly dropped from the fold.

He arranged it in his view, studying the photobooth row of four slightly different photographs of the same three people taken a few seconds apart.

All smiles were his two sister in-laws, Rosamund and Gwendoline, playfully sandwiching his wife—who appeared happy, and it warmed his heart to see her face—along with his two older brothers, Thomas and Jack. They were out somewhere back home, having a good time, and it only fuelled his homesickness more.

His smile was stagnant, and it only grew once he studied the images.

The fun they would have been having whatever night that was that they were out together was contagious.

The photos had writing on it, inscribed in ink by his wife:

'*Missing you*'.

Buster held it and beamed a delighted beam.

After reading the two-page letter from Olive that updated Buster on how little Marky was going being educated in a small preschool in the shire, how their Borehamwood cottage had a leaky sink and an uneven benchtop that was driving the lady of the house insane, Buster prepared a blank page beneath the warm glow of his lamp in order to construct a reply ...

The next letter he would write would be a serious one for his superiors; a formal request to visit home after Operation Pedestal.

One month later, the Churchill elders and respective family received an important telegram from the War Office:

Their son; brother; husband, Buster Churchill, was dead.

Killed in action on August 12, 1942, the escort operation he had been preparing so viciously for along with the 884 was a success. The convoy reached Malta ... but at an immeasurably high cost—especially to the Churchill family.

1942, May
Special Training Centre
Paignton, Devon

Still standing at the pedestal stage, Colonel Jack Churchill concluded his inaugural speech to the assembly, addressing the hundreds of commandos present at the Paignton STC ...

The new Merry Men.

His men.

In closing, his own words seemed to strike a chord within him; resonating within his soul unbeknownst at this moment that his brother would soon fall in battle. They hit home even then, firmly believing these words as he spoke them to No.2 Commando.

"Even in *death,* we are unkillable ..."

The weathered version of Mad Jack Churchill, all battered and scarred, reminisced none too comfortably. "... I was at the Paignton base at the time of receiving the news of Buster's death. I was in-step of drafting another letter for the War Office, one final time demanding for them to reconsider me heading Operation Musketoon ... needless-to-say, I ... well, I dropped the whole thing in a heartbeat. Instead, Graeme Black headed it up."

In the sorrowful silence, Jack shook his head mournfully.

It wasn't so much for the reminiscence of his brother's passing as it was with regards to Musketoon; as though *that* had been the reasoning for the operation's pitfall.

Not fate or history would have had it any other way ...

In a segue of topic, Churchill had a realization. "... I think that's why Tom eventually took up Laycock's offer and joined Commando ..."

"I forgot you had another brother ..." reflected Hardy, recalling that he had only ever really seen Thomas. "Sorry for your loss."

Churchill bowed melancholically, appreciative of Hardy's condolence. The genuine commiseration was only surpassed by his investigative compulsion.

"How did it happen, if you don't mind me asking ...?"

"At sea ..." Jack obliged, none too burdened of the particulars.

Hardy bobbed along considerably, allowing for Churchill to elaborate.

"It happened only a month or two after I was commissioned CO of No.2 Commando. Buster had taken part in the ill-starred Operation Pedestal; the most dangerous of all the Malta convoy ventures. The mission objective was to successfully transfer supplies—and, above all, *oil*—to the struggling garrison there. They were in grave danger of having to surrender to Italy and, by extension, Nazi Germany. Apparently, the 884 squadron was still flying obsolete Fulmars, which had long-since been superseded by Hurricanes and Spitfires which the RAF had been flying for months. Their convoy sailed well into the North Atlantic, reducing the risk of any air attacks by the enemy, before curving acutely to the south and passaging through the *Strait of Gibraltar*. The fleet spread out in the Mediterranean, creating a formation composed of stowing the carriers in the posterior of the convoy, behind the freighters, so they could see clearly ahead. Buster's ship, the *Victorious*, was in company with her sister-ship, the *Indomitable* and the *Eagle*. The first action was on the afternoon of the 11th, when the convoy ran into a nest of German U-boats. The Eagle was hit and sunk. Her aircraft, which were all airborne at the time, instead landed aboard the Indomitable. The next day was one of continual and unrelenting attacks, where the Indomitable became hit by large bombers, irreparably damaging the forward and aft flight decks. This buckled all lifting gear, and any further take-offs were inaccessible. Subsequently, a bomb penetrated through more than four decks and then exploded outwards, killing fifty sailors in one hit ..."

Hardy scoffed painfully. Those numbers were high, even for somebody who was barely in the know of casualty rates. Fifty sailors dead in a second was tragic.

Churchill continued with the best of his knowledge on the history of the events. "This incident occurred at the height of the onslaught, and all airborne aircraft belonging to the Indomitable were rerouted to the Victorious—Buster's ship. Consequently, the flight deck became crowded with planes, and to permit any airborne aircraft to land, any partially damaged planes were physically 'tipped off' the deck into the sea. Desperate times, desperate measures. Thusly, Buster and a few other brave souls cleared some space. They took to the skies ... he took part in two brave sorties, successfully shooting down a large Italian four-engine bomber called a *Kingfisher* on his initial attack run. There was a live broadcast system upon the Victorious, and the names of winning pilots were announced whenever they downed an enemy aircraft. It was almost as if their battle had a live audience, and Buster was a star player. They cheered him on boisterously."

Hardy maintained a smug beam, listening to the tale of Jack's brave brother: his final chapter. It was heartwarming to hear his heroic tale ... heartbreaking to already know the ending.

"On Buster's second sortie, he defied all odds and engaged a larger Italian aircraft at extremely close range ..."

"Bold," stated Hardy, breaking the mood for an instant, though, it was only to pay compliment in a roundabout way. "Wonder where he gets that from, eh?"

Churchill chortled a grin before his eyes defocused, recalling what happened next to his brother. His smile faded. "He was either wounded by the enemy's rear-facing machine guns, or his aircraft sustained serious damage, as it was seen by witnesses to have tilted over mid-flight, and slowly plunge into the sea ... this sequence of events was the last anybody ever saw of Lieutenant Robert 'Buster' Churchill ..."

"May he rest in peace," Hardy closed, and Churchill nodded respectfully for his deceased brother. "Sorry to hear it, Jack."

Churchill shook his head, burying the emotions as they crept up to try and blindside him in his weak state. "Don't be. He knew what he had signed up for—just like I have. A body was never recovered ... Buster perished at sea. Alone. Within the coming weeks, we gave him a respectable funeral at *the Parish Church of Saints Peter and Paul* in Deddington. It's always a strange feeling: attending the funeral service of a man whose body was not present to be buried ..."

Hardy nodded politely, unable to relate.

"In October, Olive was sent a certificate from the King and a copy of official mention in dispatches awarded to Buster—*Lieutenant, Robert Alec Farquhar Churchill, R.N., H.M.S. Victorious.*" Jack had it memorized, "It read: '*For outstanding service in the action in which he lost his life.*'"

After a moment of cold reflection, Jack overshared further:

"Y'know, I lost two brothers in one month," he stated cryptically, alluding to more death to come. "One blood, one ... well, one I didn't realize was my brother until it was too late."

♠ ♠

Operation Musketoon

1942, September
Special Training Centre
Paignton, Devon

Another night of restless slumber saw Churchill rising from his officer's quarters at half the midnight hour. He slipped on his battledress, mounted his beret, adjusting it quietly, dutifully in the mirror of the dim lamp light within his lodging at the Paignton base.

Conscious of the hour, Churchill was mindful to make as minimal noise as possible as he closed the door to his room in the officer's barracks, marching softly along the padded hall, down the stairs, and out the front into the quiet calm of night.

The autumn weather provided for a rather clear sky.

The threadlike clouds in the atmosphere above appeared backlit by the glow of a full moon, the cast light of which illuminated the landscape of the planet with a turquoise hue, making for effortless navigation.

Marching across the ghostly STC, Jack took in the nightscape whilst breathing in the calm, fresh air. He pondered again the same topic responsible for keeping him up at these odd hours of the night:

Operation Musketoon.

Churchill found his way to the operations centre.

Located just across the other side of the base, he arrived within minutes. Other than guardhouses and checkpoints, it was the only active building on the entire Paignton campus.

On the third floor of the main administration office, left wing, was a carpet-lined, sound-proofed floor guarded by an MP with a pistol in his leather flap hip holster. The centre was typically reserved for operation briefs where the exchanging of top-secret information may be securely divulged. Most army bases had a room designated for such activities.

Jack's rank would clear him entry.

Tonight, and for the previous seven nights, the dimly lit room had been occupied by at least one man with his head glued to a *Hallicrafters S-27* army intelligence-grade encoded radio receiver, sitting over a table littered in maps, transcript papers, and old pencil shavings. The wall was decorated in hanging maps of the world, busy with corkboards peppered with pin drops and spider-web string formations correlating relevancies, positively besieged in a tabloid jungle of virtual information.

Tonight was an especially important night. The room was manned by three men, all wired on caffeine and cigarettes, dressed down with their ties loose, sleeves rolled, and battledress blazers hanging on the backs of chairs.

The knock on the door caught them by surprise, and one of the confused men put down his cigarette on the edge of an ashtray to stand and answer it. It was Intelligence Officer Lieutenant Michael Stilwell. He removed the large, wired headset from his balding dome and fixed his slicked hair part, leaning precariously in to crack it open an inch.

On the other side of the thick door, standing beside the armed guard, was the mild-mannered and sleepless Colonel Jack Churchill.

"Hullo, Mike. Room for one more?"

"Colonel ...?" Stilwell greeted, astonished to see him. "Of course."

Churchill entered the clandestine, unventilated space. The haze of cigarette smoke beneath the radiance of warm lights clouded like overcast weather, floating above a centralized desk. The men seated at the tabletop extremities, combined with the thickened stench of tension, caused the environment to appear much like a poker tournament room—only the stakes in this game were truly life and death.

Stilwell's surprise wasn't just due to the hour of Churchill's intrusion, but because of something else monumental which had just happened tonight. The coincidence of Churchill showing up right now had the intelligence officer slightly bewildered. "How did you know, sir ...?"

"Know what?" Churchill's brow raised whilst sauntering into the room and partially addressing the intelligence strung up about the place. Occupying the room were two other dweebs from army intelligence who Jack barely knew but had seen around the operations sector in-passing. One was in a white dress shirt and black trousers, a civilian intelligence analyst possibly even on loan from *Bletchley Park*, and the other was an aspiring military intelligence officer, geared in familiar khaki.

Both devoted officers seemed indifferent to Churchill's entrance into the room, overshadowing their intelligence gathering and deciphering work. Their heads were locked between the earmuffs of headsets plugged into radios, basically on another planet. One man had a pencil tip scratching away at a transcript and on maps, an index finger on the page of an open codebook. The other was seated behind a typewriter, clacking away and forcefully smashing the metal lever to move the carriage, adjusting the line spacing. His concentrating stare squinted through the smoke from the cigarette butt burning between his lips.

"We just got news!" Stilwell elaborated excitedly. After closing the door, he reassumed the position above his chair, browsing over the tabletop of scattered intelligences, preparing to update Churchill. They had been anticipating an update from Musketoon for days. "The powerplant is *gone.*"

The positive vibe of the good news fell upon Churchill.

He may now be able to finally sleep.

No amount of stress could refrain him from his quips, though.

"Gone where? Who moved it?"

Stilwell's eyes rolled. "Gone! As in ... *boom!*" his gullet grumbled.

Conceding to his lack of sense of humour, Churchill bobbled along, gesturing understanding.

Their last transmission was three days ago, when they had been made aware of the undetected arrival of Black's team to Glomfjord. Operations had received an update from the commander of the *Junon (a French Minerve-class submarine)* that the twelve men had successfully made land via a dinghy which they hid amongst the coast rocks. The team then proceeded inland to establish an outpost in the hills surrounding the outskirts of the objective zone. They would remain in the hideout until such time that Black determined it appropriate to launch their attack on the powerplant.

Their mission objectives were simple:

Stealthily infiltrate the Glomfjord hydroelectric power station, quietly eliminating any German guards they encountered along the way to prevent their detection. They would do this via specialized equipment, such as silenced submachine guns and the use of knives.

Once in, their mission was to break off into two groups.

Group A was comprised of *Sergeant O'Brien, Privates Trigg* and *Fairclough,* and the two Norwegian *Corporals Djupdraet* and *Granlund.* They would strike the two high-pressure water pipes on a decline from the top of the mountain into the plant, located on a plateau which dropped straight down into the freezing plane of *lake Storglomvatnet.* Upon reaching their objective, O'Brien's group were to plant plastique explosives in an effective circular configuration to blow a three-foot hole in the steel pipes. They would attach a thirty-minute delayed fuse to said charges, awaiting the cue of other explosives going off inside the actual powerplant from Black's group, which was the signal to activate their fuse.

Group B encompassed the other seven commandos: *Captains Black and Houghton, Lance Bombardier Chudley,* and *Privates Smith, Curtis, Abram, Makeham.* This primary group were to infiltrate the rear of the powerplant's main building, eliminating any enemy resistance. Whilst some of the men planted explosives amongst the machinery with ten-minute delay fuses, the other commandos would locate the area within the station where the Norwegian civilian workforce slept with the goal of extracting them from harm's way. The workers would be rudely awoken, gathered, and ordered to abandon the powerplant via an access tunnel that ranged over one-and-a-half kilometres long, which was the only land route between the station and the villages in the surrounding fjord.

This tunnel would also become the escape route for Black's group, whilst taking the northerly mountains would be O'Brien's. They would not rendezvous at any preorganized destination. Rather, each respective group intended to march the neighbouring terrain towards the border, eventually shedding any military paraphernalia to blend in with the civilian populace with the goal of reaching Sweden and await an extraction at a later date.

The first phases of the raid were due to be conducted between the 15th to the 19th of September, thereupon Captain Black's best field judgement ... it was now midnight of the 21st, hence their sweating foreheads in operations.

Churchill questioned Stilwell with a firm glower.

"Any further elaboration?"

Stilwell had enthusiastic peepers while he searched for the right transcript amongst the desk mess of paper transcripts and situation reports. He immediately offered it to Jack whilst he summarized. "We heard from our friends in the SIS who received an update from the French Navy a few hours ago: there's been explosions reported in Glomfjord. Two of them! Big ones!"

The news was music to Jack's ears as his eyes skimmed the uninspiring printed writings of the transcript version. The two big explosions would have been the detonation of both objectives, of that much he was as sure as that of Stilwell and his intelligence community.

"Any word of the men?" Churchill asked. "Did they make it out?"

Stilwell gestured towards the radioman's current efforts.

"We're about to find that out ..."

Churchill eagerly watched as Stilwell approached his man, collecting some of the hanging transcribed transcript whilst the attentive analyst diligently dissected the audio transmitting from his earpiece and typed it into text. Overshadowing the active typewriter, Stilwell waited appropriately for his clacking fingers to cease and palm to strike the carriage return, allowing release of the paper.

Stilwell took a moment to observe the notes, stepping closer to the lamp-lit table of which, on the other side of, Jack Churchill's cerulean stare scanned his face for tells of what news might come. Judging by the drop in Stilwell's facial expressions, the news may have been a contrite type of good.

Churchill was unable to wait any longer. "Well?!"

Blinking to retain focus, Stilwell lowered the page onto the desk, leaning almost breathlessly into the lamp light. His face processed the events, about to convey them to Jack.

"Well, by the looks, O'Brien's group has made it out ..."

"And what of Black's group?"

Stilwell's agape mouth closed. He shook his head in sorrow.

There was an undertone of dread whilst he briefed from the communiqué. "The enemy have captured Black and his men ..."

The news hit Churchill like a punch to the guts—and it showed.

Piercing his emotional shield, his face dropped as he turned away from the hovering poker light, pacing the outskirts of the room for a moment of silent contemplation, of brooding. The risk of capture had always been high for the men on this mission. Nevertheless, that was before they had learned of Hitler's latest imperative to his armies ...

The Commando Order.

Capture effectively *meant* death.

This foul order had been issued by the *Oberkommando der Wehrmacht (OKW)*, the high command of the German armed forces, and stated that any and all Allied commandos encountered in *Europe* and *Africa* shall be killed immediately without trial. The order specified that even if identified and uniformed soldiers surrendered as prisoners of war, they were to be met by swift volatility and extreme prejudice. Any commando or small group of commandos or a similar unit, operators, agents, or saboteurs not in proper uniforms who were to fall into the hands of the German forces by some means other than direct combat—by apprehension by local police in occupied territories—were to be directly handed over to the jurisdiction of the *Sicherheitsdienst* intelligence agency for their immediate execution.

This meant that if Black and the six men in his group were captured here on this mission—a mission they went into under the premise that surrender was still an option—they were likely not going to be taken away to a POW camp to wait out the rest of the war to come home like the troops captured during the Saint-Nazaire Raid ...

The rules of the game had changed, mid-play.

This time around ... *they would be executed.*

Churchill cupped his pencil-thin moustached maw with his hand whilst he digested the news. Without a word to say, he closed and massaged his tired eyes into his skull, attempting to squash out the stress.

This was heavy news. Sad news.

Another successful mission ... but at what cost?

In the coming days, the official story given to *The Red Cross* by Germany was that the seven men captured, identified to be Black, Houghton, Smith,

Chudley, Curtis, Abram, and Makeham, had escaped from their custody and never been recaptured.

This news should have been met by glad tidings and popped champagne, as it carried connotations of hope that these soldiers would one day return to England ... however, Jack Churchill and the men of No.2 Commando knew the truth.

That was a tall tale by Germany to cover their deletion.

A constitutional smokescreen.

A face-saving cock-and-bull fairytale told and maintained by the Huns to prevent receiving any immediate flak from the treaties established during the Geneva Convention, to which Germany damn-well knew they had signed in regard to their unlawful executions of signed prisoners of war ...

Prisoners being out in the yard at night-time was a rarity.

This appeared to be a *besonderen anlass* (special occasion).

Blisteringly bright spotlights shone over the outdoor open location as a group of seven ruggedly kept Englishmen with their hands on their heads, draped in torn clothes, darkened bruises, and dried blood, were forcefully led out into the open of the prison camp's barbed wire courtyard. Their boots sploshed in the mud, slipping as they were shoved by aggressive German soldiers strapped with MP40 submachine guns and itchy fingers on the trigger.

These men were going through hell.

During the past few weeks, the British POWs had been sent to *The Colditz Castle (Oflag IV-C)* for intense interrogation and kept in solitary confinement. They were next transferred to the *SS-Reichssicherheitshauptamt (RHSA)* headquarters in Berlin, where they were probed further and with more scrutiny, one by one, including being interviewed by the renowned interrogator *Gestapo Müller.* They remained in Berlin until the 22nd of October, when they were then transported to this new concentration camp. They arrived yesterday and had received a less than generous reception.

Exposed in beacon-lit situ, the seven surrendered prisoners marched on and into the open ground, anticipating what may lay next for them ...

A uniformed *Schutzhaftlagerführer*—the head of the detention camp—and his adjutant appeared, accompanied by guards, and a flock of visiting men. These visitors were dressed in dark leather trench coats, gloves, and caps sporting the *Totenkopf*—German for *death's head.*

Out in the scrutinous eyes of the yard, the British prisoner's line formation finally came to a halt. The men faced forwards to where a prominent higher-ranking German officer tolerantly awaited their arrival and, one after the other, their knees were forcefully concaved in the sludge, compelled to bow.

Privates Reginald Makeham, Cyril Abram, Eric Curtis.

Lance Sergeant William Chudley, Sergeant Miller Smith.

And lastly, *Captains Joseph Houghton* and *Graeme Black.*

With a grimace or scowl each, clothed in shredded and stained uniforms, sunken-eyed, bruised and bloody-faced, these tired, drained and *confused* men knelt before their apparent firing squad.

Out in the open of the muddy prison grounds, they were blinded by the plethora of searchlight illumination beams. The intense glow was overbearing, causing each man to squint and look askance, unable to visibly see any of the surrounding gunmen—of which, there were many.

"You okay?" hands on his head, Black hissed to his side at Houghton, who had taken a bullet to the arm during their death-defying escape from the Glomfjord powerplant. It had been a few weeks, and the wound had festered badly due to a lack of attention from their captors. His arm had gone yellow and ached profusely.

Pale-faced and clammy, Houghton barely responded. He only coughed and spluttered before mildly straightening his posture as the dutiful soldier. Due to his overly British attitude, he had also earned himself a blackeye and a split brow from his unfriendly defeaters.

In a row, the brave commandos each knelt patiently.

This was due to them being at gunpoint, yes, but their undying, unwavering professionalism as soldiers was also their only way of saying *fuck you* to their aggressors whilst they accepted whatever fate awaited them here, this dreaded night ...

Taking a break from recording the biography of the titular man himself, ghostwriter Felix Hardy followed Churchill's off kilter daytime stroll out into the midst of the prison yard.

This fresh morning, the brisk, muddy yard was open season for inmates permitted to trot about freely within the fences of the Sachsenhausen Concentration Camp, however, the weather was particularly overcast and pre-tempest. As a result, the yard was mostly vacant of other POWs, and the two were secluded.

Beneath numerous watching riflemen in the multitude of guard towers surrounding the POW camp, the ruggedly bearded Jack Churchill led his equally weathered and unkempt American friend into the dead centre flat of the concentration camp courtyard, where their muddy march stopped ...

"Jack, why are we out in the yard?" Hardy questioned with his hands in his overcoat pockets, his brow inverted, and a heavy suspicion of immediate rainfall. The precipitation in the air was thick, and it was about to storm any second.

Within the deep reservoirs of Hardy's coat pocket rested his invaluable notepad, with pages filled of *The Unstoppable Warpath of the Unkillable Jack Churchill:* an ongoing saga. This volume of which Jack hadn't yet titled, but it would be something about kings and queens, Jack and of course, the war.

Out in the open of the muddy prison grounds, Churchill stopped his leading march and pivoted to face Hardy as though he was a pupil, and this, an excursion. It was a special outing for today's storytelling chronicle.

Churchill pulled his ratty woollen-gloved hands from his coat and pointed at the sludge between their mud-lacquered, tatty boots. Patrolling in his mind, he nodded to himself as he searched the barbed wire boundaries, sure in himself that he had found the right place; the correct location—as though an X marked the spot between the lining fences and the surrounding guard towers.

Jack stated with conviction. "It would have happened out here ..."

Hardy eyed the wet, trudged earth. "What did?"

"The first instance of *The Commando Order* ..." Churchill accumulated saliva within his mouth and could have spat with disgust. He shook his head with revulsion. "The official *Laws of War* state: *'it is especially forbidden to declare that no quarter will be given'.*"

Hardy's eyes squinted, not following. "*No quarter?*"

"Yes. This was established under Article 23d of *The Hague Convention.* The Geneva Conventions, which Germany attended and somehow omitted their complied consent and conformity, states something similar. You see, funnily enough, in war, there are various guidelines which each respective belligerent is required to follow. One such, defines who should be considered a prisoner of war upon capture. This specified enemy soldiers in proper uniforms, as well as entails the conditions of their treatment post surrender ..."

"They're war criminals ..." Hardy stated with a profound sense of declaration. He scanned the boundaries and the domes of the Stahlhelms perched atop the edges. "Every dog has his day, though. Eventually."

Churchill hiked the sides of his long overcoat before squatting down low on the mud, reaching down with his fingerless gloves in order to curiously touch the sticky earth surface, digging them into the filthy grunge an inch. There was a meaning behind his intentional griminess.

He bobbed his head with certainty. "This is where it happened ..."

With a saddened stare that now cared little for the impending thunderstorm above the Sachsenhausen and the falling droplets, Hardy watched observantly, listened intently, and felt empathetically as Churchill told the rest of the story regarding the doomed fates of the Operation Musketoon members. Their tragic ends were met on October 23, 1942 ... and they were met *here.*

The heat from the spotlight beams shone hot upon their trembling bodies, though temperature wasn't a factor of their shivering. Although they hid their fear paralysis behind butch demeanours, the men were so terrified that they could barely feel anything at all.

All in a line, the seven commando prisoners had been positioned before a firing squad of guards and staunch Schutzstaffel overseers. Beyond the blinding of the many torch lights, the stahlhelm silhouettes of the German guards surrounded their stance. Armed soldiers were prepared to drill them full of holes if they attempted to run or even contemplated putting up a fight. If only these few brave souls knew the actual truth; that it was, in fact, these enemy combatants—even the SS—who were secretly scared of them: the infamous unkillable British Commandos.

"Gentlemen!" through a scowl, Graeme Black announced with a stern tenor in his voice. He wasn't addressing the enemy—he was addressing his men. He had detected something potent in the air; something fateful, something wicked. His chest filled with courage, for it felt like this may have been for the last time. The Commando Order was a label of terminology still unheard of to these soldiers; however, their astute minds could read between the lines of this degree of punishment.

Hands still on his head as he knelt in the mud beside his commando compatriots, Black continued firm and proud: "It has been both an *honour* and a *privilege* to have served by your sides!"

Although his words were intended to comfort his commandos, they were a cause for concern amongst some—especially those of lesser ranks, who immediately began to panic upon perceiving an obvious sense of culmination. Their elevated heartrates and increased breathing became evident; their bodily reactions came too late to prompt a *fight or flight* intervention—

From behind, a pistol suddenly sounded in the night.

Causing them all to flinch, the lethal weapon emitted stridently from behind their kneeling formation. The wielder: a faceless leather-clad Schutzstaffel executioner.

Blam!

A bullet struck the back of Makeham's lower cranium.

Lifeless, he collapsed forward, face-first into the mud.

Kneeling beside him and casting quick, panicked gleams, Abram's respiration rapidly increased. Unable to even think, his eyelids pinched closed and his—

Blam!

A muzzle flash of light and his life was taken.

The PP pistol in the outstretched leather gloved hand belonging to a ruthless SS officer cycled another harsh round, striking Abram in the back of the head and flipping off his lights like a switch. His body limped, sagging into the sludge face-first with no need to gasp for air.

These ducks in a row were shot like fish in a barrel.

Curtis was next to fall, shot in the back of the neck, his lifeless corpse doubled over, followed by Chudley, who let out an all-mighty and echoic: "*Fuck you, you German cunts!*" right as the pistol sounded with another deafening gunshot in the yard, striking him in the back of the head. He planted facedown, twitching grotesquely in the mud.

Drained of all ability to react, Smith was teary eyed with shock and depleted. The next bullet slapped the back of his head acting as a mercy, ending the torment of his looming execution. May he rest in peace and continue to serve in the afterlife with the fallen commando before him.

Second last was Houghton.

Borderline paralytic and shuddering, clenching his teeth, he was shrugging his shoulders in prep—

Blam!

The bullet struck above his exposed neck, ending Houghton's life right beside Graeme Black as he knelt helplessly at the end of the row of his fallen friends, involuntarily gasping for air as if he were suffocating.

In this, what was certainly his final moment, he dared to cast a glower to his flank. With wide eyes, he viewed the line of bodies as they lay lifeless and face down in the blood-soaked sludge. Shadows cast by the many beams of the overarching spotlights illuminated their corpses ominously, accentuating the red blood as it mixed with the brown mud.

Black felt the scorching heat of the gun barrel as it panned laterally, now aimed at the back of his head. He had a second of life left, and it flashed before his eyes as he pinched them closed, accepting defeat.

Click ...

Trigger pulled and the circular hammer of the PP fell, striking steel.

Instead of a gunshot, the metallic *clack* of an empty pistol caused the kneeling Black to flinch at the shoulders in what had inadvertently become a torturous tease.

The Germans spoke nonsense behind him.

Inhaling as though he had just submerged from the deep, finding himself breathless, Black dropped his dutiful stance. He lurched forwards onto his hands in the wet mud, barely able to prop himself up. Somehow, he mustered the strength to hold himself from collapsing, almost succumbing to gravity and passing out from the stress entirely.

In the glowing hum of the multitude of spotlight glows, the SS officer presenting the executions remained behind the last remaining commando. Most unprofessionally, he cursed and muttered, delaying only to reload his Walther PP—a sidearm with a magazine capacity of only six—which had somehow caught the executioner by surprise, due to the mechanical slide failing to lock on the final round. Another soulless, shark-toothed SS officer barked insults at his flank, and another had the audacity to chuckle at his expense.

His thick, leather-gloved fingers wriggled tight into the pistol's handle cap, pulling the empty clip before searching another from somewhere in his array of leather pouches. Eventually, his endless fiddling bore fruit. He inserted a fresh clip into the handle and slapped it in tight, needing to hit it again with more strength to lock it in place. Racking the slide up high, his lack of weapons-handling experience could not have been more obvious. Smirking at his peers who sniffled chuckles at his ineptitude, he extended the pistol forth to deliver the final bullet of the execution row ...

... his finger wriggled, squeezing into the small trigger guard ...

Hunched over, Black took deep breaths—his last breaths.

He closed his eyes and waited for the end ...

In that moment, he found a surreal sense of serenity.

Of peace, of tranquillity.

... a moment he was then heinously robbed of.

"*Haaaalt!*"

A strident voice of an observer resounded across the night-time prison yard, emanating from somewhere beyond the powerful white burn of the forward spotlights that hid the identities of all those standing before the mass execution.

The SS executioner presently aiming the gun at the back of Black's neck disengaged his trigger pull at the last second, gently resting the gun by his side as his view watched on.

In the seconds that followed, a tall, mysterious figure emerged from between the most prominent light beams.

He was towering, solid, and wearing what appeared to be a skirt—nay, a *kilt*. He even appeared to be carrying an armament that protruded diagonally from his middle belts, resembling a sword.

Eyes bloodshot and vision blurry from prolonged shock of which he was no doubt overdosing dangerously, Graeme Black blinked profusely about himself whilst he panted open-mouthed to retain air in his lungs.

The figure he witnessed was still only a silhouette, but he could have sworn blind that the outline of the kilt-wearing, neatly uniformed, soldier-type was *Mad Jack Churchill ...*

His wide-eyed stare focused through the burning pain of the blinding lights, making out more identifiable detail of this newly arrived figure ... and unfortunately, Black recognized the man he was staring at, only ...

... he refused to believe it.

He shook his head in utter disbelief.

Barely able to raise his voice, he muttered: "But, you're ... you're *dead?!*"

A chortle emitted from the nose of the one and only Ernst-Günther Baade as his plump, pockmarked mug became more identifiable due to light beams and cast shadows. He wore a smug smile upon hearing Black's comment.

Just like the first time Black had laid eyes on him in Switzerland, in 1940, Baade held the same permanent discerning frown upon his forehead, a resting judgemental stare.

Baade's strides finally ended now that he was in full frame out before the kneeling commando prisoner, and he rested one hand upon the hilt of his holstered sword—another common feature he unanimously shared with Jack Churchill, other than the Scottish kilt with battledress attire.

Whatever unit Baade was attached to nowadays, he was apparently in charge of issuing Hitler's Commando Order.

Baade spoke to the pistol-packing executioner, and he dispersed.

Without much of a hiatus to follow, Baade drew his weighty langschwert from his decorative hip scabbard, arresting it in both his hands as he circled the kneeling Black, an event that was ironically full circle.

He would now be his executioner.

Graeme Black waited benevolently for the old German man to sidle his location ... and then raise the heavy sword with an audible brush of clothing and heave ...

The double-edged blade dropped like a guillotine into his kneeling neckline, and Black closed his—

Chunk!

Jack Churchill's fingerless woollen gloves collected the sample of the mud from the earth located in the dead centre of the Sachsenhausen Concentration Camp.

The notion was that in theory, this would be the same soil Graeme Black and his men touched in the moments of their executions. This earth absorbed their blood, and Churchill had been made precipitously aware of this uneasy fact.

He stared at the grime on his fingertips, distinguishing it ...

Jack's focus finally rested forwards, staring off into the distance through barbed wire and cheval de frise barricades as his mind recognized the sacrifice made by those brave commandos on this specific spot, two years ago.

Rain fell.

It coated them, soaking them whilst they paid due respects ...

His mouth uttered a phrase from his inaugural speech, when he had joined No.2 Commando as the commanding officer.

"Even in death, we are unkillable ..."

EPILOGUE
No Quarter

1942, June
Institut Saint-Joseph
Ciney, Belgium

Upon a bright Saturday morning, a young nurse at the lower-level clerical station of the Institut Saint-Joseph recovery wing welcomed a visiting German officer with a bright smile. Bright morning light shone in through the propped doorway and many windows lining the walls of the hospital building.

"*Guten Tag!*"

"Guten Tag, Fräulein!" responded the jovial German man as he stepped inwards with a briefcase by his side, clenched firm. The delight in his tone captured the attention of another nurse who was managing some folders in trays, and she cast him a gleeful twinkle, happy to offer help.

The Feldgrau Kleiner Dienstanzug that he wore was less elaborate than the full dress uniform, but was still considered as a formal option for certain occasions or duties—such as the hospital call he made today at a Kriegslazarett in Belgium.

His uniform insignia was that of a unit they saw rarely during their occupation by Nazi Germany. Typically, at the hospital, all they encountered were generalized Wehrmacht units and occasional Luftwaffe personnel from the closest airbase located in *Florennes* to the west. This man, however, exhibited the rarer service symbols of the Schutzstaffel, and he wore the black-collared uniform and cap to match.

His attitude did not match the intimidating reputation of the SS.

He was all smiles and happy frown lines.

Behind a set of circular spectacles, his enlarged hazel eyes appeared kind and sympathetic. Gentle, even.

"Hallo ..." he took the time to extend a pleasant greeting to the additional nurses nearby, seated behind the station. He was not short of pleasantries or smiles and offered them out like candy. Finally, his attention returned to the lady in the centre, to whom he now offered his complete attention. "Vor etwa einem Monat stürzte eine Junkers Ju 52 auf einem Feld in Flandern unweit von hier ab. Die Überlebenden wurden zur Genesung in dieses Krankenhaus gebracht."

< *"Approximately one month ago, a Junkers Ju 52 airplane crash landed in a Flanders field not far from here. The survivors were brought to this hospital for recovery."* >

The nurse, who was listening intently, indicated acknowledgement.

She knew the whereabouts of the plane crash survivors, but she also knew that it was not the protocol to release the information or identities of any patients checked into the hospital without appropriate clearance.

"Ich bin hier, um meinen Freund zu sehen."

< *"I am here to see my friend."* >

The friendly SS officer was convincing with his inquiry.

And the smile sold it all, wrapped in a pomp, silk bow.

Before long, the jovial German was brought upstairs and wordlessly shown the wing in which the Junkers plane crash survivors were stationed. Second from the end of the hall, it was a laterally shaped, shared room, housing approximately eight beds with a walkway down the centre aisle.

He bid the nurse farewell with a bow, gesturing that he wished to find his friend alone. She complied, offering him a pleasant smile before parting.

In her absence, the SS officer faced the room.

His holding smile ... *faded.*

It was a transformation. From chill to kill(er).

Gradual in pace, he illustrated an unwavering conviction.

Although his march forward was slow, it was unstoppable in momentum. With calm glances at either flank, he read the names on the hanging charts located on the hood of every bed. Most of the injured, bandage-wrapped, bed-ridden occupants were unresponsive or asleep. Those who were awake, watched his saunter with minute acknowledgement, not that his frightening rank permitted so much as a salute as did a cause for full-grown men to hide beneath their bedsheets.

His hovering attentiveness gravitated onto a bed, second last on the window-side. There was a tree directly outside the mostly frosted window, the canopy of which obscured the light and cast unique, jagged shadows. Birds were active, dwipping excitedly, loud enough to hear through the glass.

"Ah," the jovial German uttered, seeing the small birds and identifying them as though ornithology may have been his pastime. "Der Waldkleiber," he softly informed the sleeping occupant whilst he stood at the foot of the bed. "Interessante Tatsache: Kleiber besitzen kräftige Zehen mit drei nach vorne gerichteten Krallen. Zusammen mit einem kurzen Schwanz ermöglicht ihnen dies, sich mühelos von Bäumen herunterzubewegen."

< *"The Wood Nuthatch. Fun fact: Nuthatches possess powerful toes with three forward-facing claws. Along with a short tail, this allows them to move down trees with ease.'* >

He gently placed his leather satchel on the bed beside the sleeper's leg whilst spectating the long-billed, short-tailed, blue-grey and black birds flutter about between the branches.

"Schön," his lips whispered ... his eyes then drifted down and into his unlatched bag, where his gloved hands presented a traditional rigid tube, piston syringe, and glass vile partially filled with a liquidambar.

He filled the syringe and carefully cleared any air from the tube with a concentrating gaze before his stare defocused from the needle and acquired the sleeping patient.

"Zeit, dir dein 'Vitaminstoß' zu geben, Herr Feind."

< *"Time to give you your 'vitamin boost', Mister Feind."* >

He silently prodded the needle into the bandaged leg of the sleeping patient, Friedrich Feind, causing him to react very minimally. He barely stirred enough to wake, and the jovial German merely beamed a happy smile.

His soft voice whispered. "*Schlafen.*"

< "Sleep." >

The price of his freedom had become known ...
    His *dreadful dissolution.*
    Friedrich Feind would drift away in his sleep ...
    ... and he did.

The unstoppable warpath of the unkillable **Jack Churchill**

will continue in ...

I Came, I War, I Conquered

About the Author.

Benjamin Blackie was born in Camden, New South Wales in 1987. Growing up, he often found more comfort outside of everyday life in watching shows and movies, reading books and graphic novels, playing games, and generally exploring the vast variety of creations and art forms made by others, as well as developing and practicing his own imagination. Still does.

He currently resides in Sydney with his wife, son, and daughter, and remains close with friends and family who enrich his life with love, inspiration, and encouragement every day.

www.ingramcontent.com/pod-product-compliance
Lightning Source LLC
Chambersburg PA
CBHW020244030726
47499CB00001B/44